Dear Reader:

Welcome to the thirteenth century, one of my very favorite eras, when men tilted and jousted, roaring out orders and commands, and expected women to wear their wimples, scrub their backs in the bath, feed them well, and keep to their place—somewhere right at the level of their favorite hound. That is male myth, and charming though it may be to some, we all know it was the women who kept everything together, the women who brought the men to reason whenever necessary, the women who even managed to flavor the medieval times with a dash of civilization. What a spawning ground for stories of how men and women courted and married and dealt with each other!

The first of these stories, *Fire Song*, came out in 1985. At that time I hadn't thought of a trilogy, just of Graelam de Moreton, who had appeared in *Chandra*, my very first medieval novel written way back in 1982. He was the original "extremely bad boy," and I fell in love with him, thus he had to have his own book, *Fire Song*. Graelam is tough. He's a warrior who is harder than they usually come; ruthless, a man who takes what he wants and the devil take the hindmost. He meets his match, however, in the gentle Kassia of Belleterre, a lady as innocent and guileless as the rainwater that flows through Graelam's calloused fingers. The more implacable he becomes, the more he ends up giving, the more he yields.

In *Earth Song*, the second novel of the trilogy, you'll see how well Philippa de Beauchamp deals with Dienwald de Fortenberry, whom we first met in *Fire Song*, when he got on the wrong side of Graelam de Moreton. Fortenberry is a charming rogue whose sheep all went over a cliff during a storm, leaving him with no money to buy wool to clothe his people. Philippa and Dienwald will have you in stitches wondering what each will try to do next to the other.

In *Secret Song*, the final novel of the trilogy, you'll meet Roland de Tourney again. He's a handsome devil with a subtle wit and quick tongue, who knows he's in big trouble when he meets Daria of Fortesque, a woman as daring, as clever, as fascinating as he is himself. Ah, but he fights to the bitter end. And as a special bonus, all the characters from the first two stories appear in *Secret Song*.

I hope you'll enjoy all three of the novels; and, please, read them in order—it's more fun that way.

Catherine Coulter

The Song Trilogy

The Song Trilogy

~

Fire Song

Earth Song

Secret Song

CATHERINE COULTER

SEAFARER

SEAFARER BOOKS
a division of Penguin Books USA Inc.
375 Hudson Street, New York, New York 10014

First published by Seafarer Books, a division of Penguin Books USA Inc.

First Seafarer Printing, May 1994

Fire Song, Earth Song, and *Secret Song* were originally published by Onyx,
an imprint of Dutton/Signet, a division of Penguin Books USA Inc.

ISBN 0-8289-0851-6
Printed in U.S.A.
10 9 8 7 6 5 4 3 2 1

PUBLISHER'S NOTE:
These stories are works of fiction. Names, characters, places, and
incidents either are the product of the author's imagination or are used
fictitiously, and any resemblance to actual persons, living or dead,
events, or locales is entirely coincidental.

The Song Trilogy

To best friends,
Randi and Bob

1

"By all the fires in hell, Guy!" Graelam shouted, pointing between Demon's flattened ears. "A dozen whoreson villains against a merchant and six men!" He wheeled around in his saddle and yelled back to his men, "Let's show these damned French bastards what the English are made of!" Even as he spoke, he dug his heels into his destrier's sides and smoothly unsheathed his gleaming sword. Demon thundered down the grassy rolling hill into the small valley below, his silver-studded bridle glittering in the bright sun.

"A *Moreton! A Moreton!*" Graelam shouted. He clapped his visor down and swung his huge sword in a wide vicious arc. His two knights and dozen men-at-arms closed behind him, their cries echoing his own. Graelam coolly studied the band of brigands thinking they had chosen an ideal spot for a coward's attack. And one of the men under attack was no merchant, he realized, as Demon crashed into a horse, tossing the rider high into the air. The man was richly garbed in wine velvet over his chain mail, and sat astride a magnificent bay stallion. He obviously had a knight's training, for his sword was flashing like silver as at least six of the brigands circled him, four of them on horseback. But despite his prowess as a warrior, unaided he would soon be cut to pieces by his six attackers.

Graelam yelled again, "*A Moreton! A Moreton!*", and half of the brigands, no fools, dashed toward the forest, while six others continued their furious attack on the lone man.

He fights well, Graelam thought, and in the next moment he rode into the fray, a grim smile on his face as his sword sank into a man's throat. Blood spurted upward, splattering Graelam's mail, but he ignored it, riding Demon straight into another brigand's horse. Demon rose to his hind legs, slashing with his forelegs at the horse's neck. At the same moment, Graelam sliced his sword through the man's chest, sending him spinning to the ground, a thin, surprised croak tearing from his throat. He closed beside the warrior, protecting his flank, and laughed aloud as the remaining rogues, screaming from wounds and fear, fled after their fellows into the forest.

The fighting had lasted five minutes, no more. Save for the groans of the wounded men, all was peacefully silent again. Graelam calmly handed his bloody sword to one of his men-at-arms, then dismounted and turned to Sir Guy de Blasis, one of his knights.

"Only Hugh is wounded, my lord," Guy said, panting a little, "and not badly. The vermin were cowards."

Graelam nodded and approached the richly clothed man. "Are you hurt?"

"Nay, but I would be fodder for the crops were it not for you. My thanks." He pulled off his helmet and shoved back the chain mail covering his head. "My name is Maurice de Lorris, of Belleterre." He smiled widely at Graelam, his eyes twinkling.

He fights like a much younger man, Graelam thought, taking in the close-cropped graying hair and the deep lines radiating from his dark green eyes. He was still a well-looking man who had not grown soft in the manner of many older warriors. He had not an ounce of fat on his wiry body and Graelam could see the play of firm muscles in his shoulders and arms. "You are breathing hard, my lord," Graelam said. "Come, rest awhile and tell me why a party of brigands would attack you."

Maurice nodded and dismounted, aware that his heart was pounding painfully in his chest and his breathing was coming in short, jerking gasps. But Christ's bones, he thought, it had been a good fight!

"You are wounded."

Maurice looked stupidly at the bloody rent in his velvet surcoat, and cursed softly. Kassia would have difficulty repairing the jagged tear. "'Tis nothing," he said, shrugging it off.

"Guy," Graelam called. "Have one of the men bring me some water and cloths."

He smiled down at Maurice. "I am Lord Graelam de Moreton, an Englishman, returning from the Holy Land. I was beginning to believe that I was traveling through an Eden," he continued, looking around at the gently rolling hills of Aquitaine. "Bloody boring it was becoming. I thank you, my lord, for the sport."

"Your timing bespeaks divine intervention," Maurice said, wincing as one of Graelam's men ripped the velvet surcoat beyond repair to clean and bind the wound in his arm. "You say you were in the Holy Land?" he asked, looking more closely at the large English warrior

who had saved his life. At Graelam's nod, he continued
in a saddened voice, "Word reached me about Louis.
The poor king dying like a piece of filth in that godfor-
saken land. A saint among men, but now what does it
matter? Your valiant Prince Edward, did he survive?"

"He did indeed. But enough talk for you until you
are stronger, my lord."

Maurice found himself leaning gratefully against
Graelam's massive chest. Graelam eased him down beneath an oak tree, then rose to survey the damage
wreaked by the brigands. He pulled back his mail and
ran his hands through his matted black hair. "Guy," he
called, pointing toward a mortally wounded man who
was groaning on the ground, "dispatch that brigand to
hell."

It was odd, Graelam thought, but none of the wagons
had been touched. He pictured the battle in his mind,
recalling the six men who had attacked Maurice de Lorris.
If contraband had not been their goal, then . . . He
shook his head and continued his inspection. Three of
Lord Maurice's men were dead and two wounded. He
gave his men further instructions and walked back to
Maurice, whose arm now rested in a sling.

Maurice studied the dark, powerful man who had
saved his life. English or no, he was a splendid specimen, and a fierce fighter. And, Maurice thought, his
eyes squinting against the afternoon sun, he was young
and healthy, his mighty chest firm and solid as an oak
tree's. He was a man well used to command, a man one
could trust. He saw the frown furrowing Graelam's
brow and said, "I know your thoughts, my lord, for
they echo my own. There are thieves aplenty in this
world, but a force such as attacked me is unusual.
Aquitaine is well-governed, and it stretches the imagi-

nation to believe I was attacked by such a collection of men for a mere three wagons of wine."

"You have enemies," Graelam said matter-of-factly.

"It would appear so." Maurice shrugged and looked directly into Graelam's dark eyes. "What man does not?"

"An enemy who also is too cowardly to do the work himself.

"So it would appear." He looked thoughtful for a moment. "I have no proof," he said finally. "There is but one man who would go to such lengths to have me removed from this earth."

With the excitement of battle receding, Graelam felt weary, more from the weeks trekking from Sicily than from wielding his sword. He rubbed his hand over the muscles knotted in his neck.

"I had forgot," Maurice said. "Your Prince Edward is now king. Does he return soon to claim his crown?"

"Nay. He has the wanderlust. And there is no need. England is at peace and his uncle, the Duke of Cornwall, will protect what is Edward's."

"But you, Graelam de Moreton, I hear in your voice that you wish to be home."

"Aye. Fighting the heathen in the Holy Land was an exercise in bloodletting and disease and frustration. The treaty Edward negotiated with the Saracens will keep the Christians safe for some time, at least."

Maurice looked thoughtfully at the English knight. "We are but three days from my home, Lord Graelam," he said. "Will you accompany me to Belleterre?"

"It will be my pleasure," Graelam said.

"Good," Maurice said, his thoughts turning to Kassia. He would have three days to determine if this Englishman would prove a worthy husband for his only daughter. Belatedly he asked, not meeting Graelam's eyes, "I suppose you have a family eagerly awaiting your return?"

"Nay, but my castle, Wolffeton, is likely falling to ruin. A year is a long time to be gone."

"Ah," Maurice said, and sat back against the oak tree, closing his eyes.

2

Kassia shrugged out of her ermine-lined cloak, folded it carefully, and laid it across the saddle in front of her. It was much too beautiful to wear, she thought with a smile, remembering her father's sly looks when he presented it to her on her last birthday. She had teased him that it was a gift for a princess and not a simple maid living in the wilds of Brittany. As for her nurse and maid, Etta, she had tisked behind her hand, claiming the master was spoiling her baby, but Maurice had only laughed.

Kassia raised her face to the brilliant sun. It was a beautiful spring day, with soft puffy white clouds dotting the blue sky, and air so pure and clean and warm that she couldn't seem to breathe deeply enough. She turned slightly in her saddle and looked back toward Belleterre. Her eyes glistened with pride at the sight of the four round towers that rose proudly to formidable heights, guarding the surrounding countryside like massive sentinels. Thick gray stone walls, aged to mute grace over the last hundred years, connected the huge towers, forming a large square atop the rocky hillock. Belleterre was not only her home but also a strategic fortress, commanding the River Morlaix. No enemy could sail from the sea up the river without the soldiers of Belleterre knowing of it. And no enemy could escape detection landward, no matter how stealthfully they tried, for the castle commanded the highest hill in the area. As Kassia gazed beyond the thriving town of Morlaix, toward the sea, she remembered the stories her father had told her of the violent past when powerful men had fought to gain control of Brittany. Belleterre had survived, for even the stoutest war machines had faltered and failed before they could draw close enough to harm Belleterre with their flaming balls of fire. Siege was their only fear and her father would remind them of it every year when the crops were safely stored. Kassia, every bit as fine a housekeeper as her grandmother had been, would ensure that the outbuildings were well-stocked with wheat and fodder, the meat cured, and enough flour and salt purchased to withstand the forces of the King of France himself.

Thomas, one of her father's squires, reined in beside Bluebell, drawing Kassia from her thoughts. "My lady," he said, pointing to the east, "a group of men is approaching. We should return to Belleterre."

She nodded, remembering her promise to her father, and urged Bluebell into a canter back to Belleterre. She smiled, thankful that he would be home within the week. Home with enough wine from Aquitaine to last him a decade! How she had teased him, chiding him about the red lines on his nose from too much drinking. He had believed her until he had stared closely into a silver mirror and come after her, bellowing. She had felt so guilty that she had allowed him to trounce her in chess.

Pierre, the porter, raised the portcullis, and their small troop rode into the inner bailey. As always, Kassia felt a sense of accomplishment when she viewed the cleanliness of the outbuildings and the well-swept cobbled ground that slanted gently downward to the outer bailey so that rain could not collect and stagnate. There was no filth, no untidiness in her home, and all who lived within the keep were well-fed, and clothed in stout wool. A group of children were playing near the large well, and Kassia waved gaily to them. They also were a part of her huge family, and she knew each of them by name. "We live in a rabbit warren," her father would complain with a smile. "Sometimes I cannot even relieve my bowels without someone about."

"Thomas," she said after he had helped her to dismount, "have Pierre close the gates until we know who our visitors are."

"Yes, my lady," Thomas said, unable to entirely keep the worship from his voice. He was Kassia's age, and his father held sizable lands to the east, but he knew, sadly, that Kassia regarded him as a brother. It was just as well, he thought, turning to speak to Pierre, that he would win his spurs within the year. He did not think he could bear to be around when her father gave her in marriage to another man.

"Damned whoreson!" Pierre spat, watching the dozen riders approaching Belleterre. "'Tis that miserable Geoffrey de Lacy. I recognize his standard. It should be a weasel and not a proud eagle. How I'd like to tell the lout to keep his hide away from Belleterre and my lady!"

"I will see what Kassia wishes," Thomas said.

But Kassia had heard, and she called to him to open the gates. Geoffrey was her cousin, son of her father's sister, Felice. Evidently his strident, altogether disagreeable mother had not accompanied him this time. Thank the saints for one small favor, she thought. If only her father were here! She climbed the wooden stairs to the outer wall and watched Geoffrey draw his small troop to a halt at the base of the hill. He was richly attired, as usual, in dark blue velvet, and she imagined that his pale blue eyes were assessing the worth of Belleterre. She chewed on her lower lip, wishing she could refuse him entry. But, of course, she could not.

"Kassia, 'tis I, Geoffrey," he called up to her. "May I take my rest for a while?" She did not even bother to call back to him, Geoffrey noted, his lips thinning with annoyance. Proud little bitch! Once he was wed to her, he would teach her manners. He could not prevent his eyes wandering lovingly over every inch of Belleterre as he and his troop of men rode slowly upward toward the massive gates. It would be his soon. He would be lord of Belleterre and away from his mother's infernal harping and sharp tongue.

He straightened his shoulders, pasted a smile upon his face, and rode his destrier into the inner bailey to where Kassia now stood awaiting him. He had not seen her for nearly six months, and he felt a tingling of pleased surprise as he noted the soft curve of her breasts, more fully rounded now, more womanly. He admired her magnificent chestnut hair that caught the sunlight in its thick silken strands, falling in lazy waves to her waist. But he did not like her eyes, though they were a brilliant hazel, wide, and framed with dark thick lashes. They gazed at him too straightly, directly into his face,

into his mind. She was forward for a woman; his damned
uncle had coddled her, not teaching her her place. But
on this visit Geoffrey had no trouble smiling as he
viewed his future home and his future wife.

"Kassia," he said, dismounting to stand beside her.
"You become more beautiful with the passing months."

"Geoffrey," Kassia said shortly in acknowledgment,
disregarding the caressing tone of his voice. "My father
has not yet returned from Aquitaine."

"Ah, it is not just your father's company that draws
me."

"What does draw you, Geoffrey?"

His lashes lowered over his eyes, hiding their annoyed expression. "The lovely day, and you, my cousin.
May I spend an hour with you? Unfortunately, I must
return to Beaumanoir by evening."

Kassia nodded, picked up her skirts, and led him up
the winding stairs into the great hall. "I trust your
mother is well," she said.

Geoffrey laughed. "My mother is always in good
health. She is particularly in fine fettle when I am
about, a likely candidate upon which to vent her spleen."

"Well," Kassia said, bending a bit, "she treats you
better than she treats me! Imagine her telling my father
that I am far too young to manage Belleterre! As if I
were some silly twit raised in a convent!"

Geoffrey relaxed at the honest laughter in her voice,
and her eyes were twinkling in the most beguiling way.
It was wise of him, he thought, to come here today. He
would be the one she would wish to see when she
heard about her father. He would have her, willing or
unwilling, but he preferred her to want him, to accept
him. The thought of forcing a lady was distasteful to
him. She motioned him to a chair and he again noticed,

with pleasure, the soft roundness of her breasts as she
gestured with her hand.

"You have not grown taller," he said.

"No, I fear it is my fate to forever be at the level of
my father's Adam's apple. Would you care for some ale,
Geoffrey?"

He nodded and sat back comfortably in the high-
backed chair. It felt like home already. It was not her
father's chair, but nonetheless it was solid and intri-
cately carved, and lasting, like Belleterre itself. He
watched Kassia give orders to a serving girl, her voice
gentle and pleasingly soft. "Kassia is like her mother,
Lady Anne," his mother would snort upon occasion.
"Soft and spineless and without spirit." But Geoffrey
knew she was wrong. Kassia was gentle because she
had been raised gently. She appeared soft because her
father treated her with unrelenting affection. He doubted
if anyone had ever spoken roughly to her in her life,
except of course, his mother. But she had spirit, perhaps too much for a girl. His eyes drifted down to her
hips. So slender she was. He wondered if she would
bear him sons without dying in childbirth as her mother
had. His own mother had informed him that Kassia was
late in developing into a woman, and he winced, remembering her crude discussion of Kassia's monthly
flow of woman's blood, not begun until she had passed
her fifteenth year.

Kassia handed him a goblet of ale and a slab of cheese
and freshly baked bread. "I am certain that Thomas will
provide your men with refreshment." She sat down
across from him in an armless chair and looked at him
with her direct gaze. "Why are you here, Geoffrey?"

"To see you, cousin," he said, breaking off a piece of
bread.

"My father would not approve."

"Your father is wrong not to approve. I have never done him ill and he is my uncle, and I am his heir."

"Nay, Geoffrey," she said steadily. "I am his heir."

Geoffrey shrugged. "Let us say that your husband will be his heir."

She knew well what he was thinking and it angered her. She said, gazing straight at him, " 'Tis so sad that my brother did not live. Then no man would look at me and at Belleterre as one and the same."

Geoffrey shifted uncomfortably, but managed a dismissing laugh. "You do not hold yourself in sufficient esteem, cousin. Believe me, I value you for yourself alone."

She wanted to laugh in his face for his blatant lie, but she felt a tingling of fear and rising gooseflesh at his words. Geoffrey was smooth as oil, but today his meaning was all too clear. He was eight years her senior and she remembered him clearly as a boy, tall and gangly and mean, particularly to her brother, Jean. She knew that her father had blamed Geoffrey for her brother's drowning, and because her father believed him responsible, so did Kassia. Maurice had forbidden Geoffrey to come to Belleterre for five long, very peaceful years, until his sister's merciless harping made him relent. But every time Geoffrey came to Belleterre, her father would mutter about vipers and bad blood.

Kassia wondered now at Geoffrey's motives, and decided to push him. "Yes," she said agreeably. "I suspect that one day I will have to wed. But of course, my father will select my husband."

"Or perhaps the Duke of Brittany will."

"That could only happen if my father were dead."

"We live in uncertain times," Geoffrey said smoothly.

"Just last week one of my men, a strong fellow and young, fell ill of a fever that wasted him within a week. Yes, life is quite uncertain."

"Surely such a philosophy is not at all comforting," Kassia said. "Do not you believe that God protects those who are good?"

"You speak like a child, Kassia. God has little to do with the affairs of men. But enough of grim subjects. Tell me how you are amusing yourself during your father's absence."

Although Kassia knew that Geoffrey wasn't at all interested in her activities, it was, nonetheless, a way of passing the time until he left. She told him of her herb garden, of the medicinal properties of certain substances her nurse, Etta, had taught her about, and the construction of a new outbuilding for their temperamental cook, Raymond. She gazed at Geoffrey beneath her lashes. He was beginning to drowse in his chair. Kassia took pity on him and halted her monologue.

"When Father returns," she finished, her eyes lowered to hide the laughter bubbling within, "I am certain that we will all become drunk as jongleurs with the wine he is bringing."

She did not see the penetrating look Geoffrey shot her, a look that softened briefly with regret. "A pity that I will not be here to join in your festivities," he said only.

"Yes, isn't it? Oh my, the hour has flown by with amazing speed! You must, I suppose, be on your way."

She rose expectantly, and Geoffrey, seeing no way of delaying, also got to his feet. He looked down at her lovely face, remembering clearly how he had thought her as plain and unappetizing as monk pudding but two years before.

"You will send a messenger to Beaumanoir if ever you wish to see me?"

Kassia cocked her head to one side, thinking it an odd question, and a most unlikely circumstance, but replied easily enough, "Indeed, Geoffrey. I bid you Godspeed."

She watched him mount, returned his jaunty wave, and walked to the top of the east tower, not leaving until he and his men were specks in the distance.

She ate her evening meal with Thomas, chided a serving maid for an unmended rent in her kirtle, and went to bed, a headache beginning to throb at her temple.

The next morning Kassia felt oddly weak, but she ignored it and prepared to ride Bluebell, as was her habit. The morning sun was bright overhead, yet she felt cold, and her throat was feeling scratchy. "You are being silly, Kassia," she told herself aloud, for she could count on her fingers the number of days she had been ill during her life. When Thomas prepared to help her into the saddle, she could not seem to grasp Bluebell's reins. With a small cry she fainted, falling backward into his arms.

3

Maurice cursed loudly and fluently as one of the wagons mired itself deeper into the muck. And still the rain poured down upon them, in thick, cold sheets. They were circling the Noires mountains, more like barren sawtoothed crests than mountains, Graelam thought, and the rain had turned the narrow winding trail into a quagmire.

Graelam, weary and drenched to the skin, dismounted and added his strength to the back wheel. He wished he were home. But as he pushed with all his might, he thought philosophically that he would have been sodden with or without Maurice's company. The thick mud made a sucking sound and he heaved again with the men. The wheel, once freed, jumped into the air, and three casks of wine tumbled to the ground.

"Tonight, by God," Maurice said as the casks of wine were loaded again into the wagon, "we will be dry. 'Tis near to Beaumanoir we are, and I plan to ignore my witch of a sister and drink away my damp bones! And you, my lord, are my guest!"

"Where is your sister's keep?" Graelam asked.

"Near to Huelgoat. I pray the damned lake hasn't flooded the countryside."

Graelam, who had never heard of Huelgoat or its lake, merely grunted. During the past three days, he had learned a great deal about Maurice de Lorris, and even more about the long-lived antipathy between him and his nephew and his sister, Lady Felice de Lacy. "She had the nerve to insult my Kassia's housekeeping," Maurice had told him. "My Kassia, who could manage your king's Windsor Palace!"

Graelam thought cynically that *his* precious Kassia was assuming saintlike stature with every word from her sire's mouth. He was regretting his agreement to stay at Belleterre, even for a few days. This Kassia was likely a rabbit-toothed, carpy female, so unattractive that Maurice was courting him, Graelam de Moreton, an Englishman and a virtual stranger, as a possible husband for his daughter.

But he liked Maurice. He enjoyed his wit and the outrageous tales he spun. He hadn't even lost his sense of humor when the skies opened up and made the entire troop feel like drowned rats. And, Graelam knew, under Maurice's skillful probing he had likely told him all Maurice wished to know. He wondered, smiling to himself, if Maurice would like to know that his first wife had had a wart on her left buttock.

"As for that nephew of mine," Maurice had grunted in disdain the afternoon before, "he's naught but a worthless fool."

"Mayhap a dangerous one," Graelam had said calmly.

"Aye, 'tis possible," Maurice had agreed. "Slimy bastard!" He had told Graelam about his son, Jean, a fine lad, who, he had long suspected, had been left to drown by the jealous Geoffrey. "He lusts after Belleterre, and his mother has encouraged him. She had the effrontery to tell me to my face that her son was my heir! My heir, all the while looking at Kassia as if she were naught but a fly on the ceiling! Aye, I know what is in both of their minds. Kassia wed to that malignant wretch and my sister lording it over everyone at Belleterre!"

"Why," Graelam had asked Maurice, "did you not remarry after the death of your son?"

The veil of pain that had fallen into Maurice's eyes had shaken Graelam, and he needed no words to answer his question.

And now he would meet Maurice's sister, Lady Felice, and perhaps the nephew, Geoffrey.

Beaumanoir was a small castle, of little strategic importance, Graelam saw, set near the edge of a narrow lake. The water was dirty brown and churning, but had not yet flowed over its bounds. Nor did Beaumanoir appear to be a rich keep. The surrounding countryside was dotted with hilly forests of beech, oak, and pine, and the rain-drenched soil looked poor. He was aware of ragged serfs, shivering and miserably clothed in the inner bailey. He followed Maurice up the stairs into the hall, Guy at his heels.

"Brother dear," a tall woman said. "What a pleasant surprise. My, how very wet you are, Maurice. I hope that you will not die of a chill," she added, her smile ruthlessly insincere.

Maurice grunted. "Felice, this is Lord Graelam de Moreton. We are both in need of a hot bath and dry clothes."

She was a tall, slender woman, Graelam saw, and not unhandsome, even though she must be over forty. Her hair was hidden beneath a large white wimple.

"Certainly, Maurice." Felice glanced more closely at Graelam de Moreton and felt a quickening of blood in her veins. Lord, but he was a man, and handsome! Felice gave sharp instructions for her brother's bath to a serving wench and walked toward Graelam, her hips swaying gracefully. "You, my lord," she said softly, "I will see to personally."

This is all I need, Graelam thought, to be seduced by Maurice's lustful sister in my bath. He was tired, and all he wanted was to drop in his tracks. Aloud he said, "You are all kindness, my lady."

He left Guy in front of the open fire in the hall, a shy serving wench hovering over him, and followed Lady Felice to the upper chambers.

"Your son is not here, my lady?"

"Nay," Felice said. "He will be sorry to have missed his uncle."

If Geoffrey were behind the ambush in Aquitaine, Graelam thought, it did not appear that his mother knew about it.

"I am certain," Graelam said, "that Maurice is of the same mind."

Felice did not notice the sarcasm in his voice, her attention on lighting the candles in her chamber. "Ah, my lord, 'tis not elegant, for I am but a poor widow." Her voice rose sharply toward a cowering serving girl: "Betta, see that Lord Graelam's bath is prepared, immediately! Now, my lord, let us ease your . . . discomfort."

She is very efficient, Graelam thought, as she deftly assisted him out of his sodden surcoat. She unlaced his mail, clucking at its heaviness, and gently laid it in a corner. To his chagrin, she knelt before him and unfast-

ened his chaussures. It was common practice for a lady
to assist a visitor in his bath, but her caressing hands
were anything but matter-of-fact, and made him aware
that he hadn't had a woman in several long weeks.

When he was naked, he felt her eyes upon him,
studying him and his burgeoning manhood, he thought
sourly, as if he were a stud for her stable. Belatedly she
handed him a thick wool cloth to wrap about his loins.

"I see that you have known much battle, my lord,"
she said, her voice low and throaty. She reached out
and touched the long scar that ran along his left side
and disappeared beneath the cloth.

"Aye," Graelam said, wishing only for the serving
wenches to return with the hot water.

Felice did not move away from him. She breathed in
the male scent of him, the fresh rain smell mixing with
his sweat, so potent that she felt her senses reel.

She stepped away from him when three serving
wenches hauled buckets of steaming water into her
chamber and heaved them into the wooden tub. She
herself added cold water and tested the temperature of
the bath. Satisfied, she rose and beckoned Graelam
with a smile.

"Come, my lord, 'twill revive you."

Graelam pulled off the cloth, relieved to see his
manhood lying soft against him, and stepped into the
tub. The feel of the hot water made him draw in his
breath with sheer pleasure. He leaned his head back
against the edge of the tub and closed his eyes.

"I did not know that my brother called an Englishman
friend," Felice said, her voice soft and close.

"We have traveled together from Aquitaine," Graelam
said, wishing that the woman would leave him in peace.

He felt a soft soapy sponge drift slowly over his shoulder and forced himself to keep his eyes closed.

"I see," Felice said, moving the sponge over his massive chest. Her finger tingled at the touch of him. "Lean forward, my lord, and I will wash your back."

Graelam did as she bid. "Aye," he continued, "I will journey with Maurice to Belleterre. He wishes me to spend some time there."

Did he imagine her sucking in her breath? He said with great untruth, "I wish to see his daughter, Kassia. I have been told that she is a beautiful girl."

The sponge halted a moment on his back. "Kassia," Felice said, "is a sweet child, though my brother spoils her shamefully. Once she is wed to Geoffrey, I fear I will have to teach her many things. As for her looks"—he could feel her shrugging—"she resembles her mother, so of course my poor Maurice is somewhat prejudiced. Only passable, one would say. Now, my lord, lean back and I will wash your hair."

Graelam knew he should mind his own business, but her confident assumption that Maurice's daughter was to wed her son aroused his curiosity. He had gotten the distinct impression that Maurice would send his daughter to a convent before he would allow such a thing. But then, his thoughts continued, had Maurice died, Kassia would be at the mercy of her aunt.

He leaned his head back and reveled in her fingers rubbing soap into his scalp. Though it was none of his business, he said nonetheless, "I did not realize that Geoffrey was a suitor for Kassia's hand."

"Oh," Felice said, "Maurice will come about. He has this odd dislike for his own nephew, but 'twill pass. After all, Geoffrey is his heir."

She rinsed his hair and bade him to rise.

"Heir?" Graelam asked, aware of the sponge descending slowly over his belly. "I would have thought that his daughter is his heir."

Her hand paused, and he felt her fingers softly tangling in the thick black hair of his groin. His manhood swelled.

"How magnificent you are, my lord," Felice said, and to Graelam's surprise, she giggled like a young girl.

"The air is cool, my lady," he said, gritting his teeth. "I would wish to be done."

"Certainly, my lord," Felice agreed, but she continued her assault on his body, touching and exploring every inch of him.

"Should you not see to your brother's comfort?" Graelam asked, an edge of desperation to his voice. He was not made of stone, but the thought of bedding this woman left all but his eager manhood cold.

"My brother," Felice said dryly, "is likely enjoying the . . . services of Glenna. I will fetch you one of my son's bedrobes, my lord."

Graelam took the cloth from her and dried himself, relieved that finally she had left him in peace. It was in his mind to relieve himself to prevent further unwanted reactions from his body, but she returned too quickly, a rich burgundy velvet robe in her hands.

"I fear, my lord," she said in a clipped, almost angry voice, "that my brother is demanding that you come to him." She ran her tongue over her lips, hoping to entice him, but his attention was on the robe.

Graelam smiled at her, a slow, seductive smile that made her knees tremble. "Perhaps," he said softly, "if Maurice is not with this Glenna, I could enjoy her services."

It was cruel and he knew it, but he refused to spend the night half-awake, waiting for her to crawl into bed beside him.

Two spots of color rose to prominence on her cheeks and she wheeled about and left the chamber.

Graelam walked quickly down the stairs into the hall, still wearing Geoffrey's bedrobe. He heard Maurice's mocking voice: "You did not tell me, dear sister, where my nephew is. Does he take no interest in his home?"

"I do not know where Geoffrey is!" Felice snapped, watching him tear the chicken meat off a bone with his strong teeth. Damn him, she thought enviously. Just last week she had lost another tooth, this one dangerously close to the front of her mouth.

She saw Graelam approach and felt fury course through her. She had offered herself to him, and he had refused her. She touched her fingers unconsciously to her jaw, feeling the slack flesh, and winced. Soon he would be comparing her to Kassia.

Maurice smiled, his mouth full of chicken meat, and motioned Graelam to join him.

"Did my lord Graelam tell you, Felice, that he would be spending some days with Kassia and me at Belleterre?"

She heard the malicious tone, but forced herself to smile, albeit frigidly.

"Aye," she said. "Geoffrey rode to Belleterre but a few days past. It seems that Kassia was most pleased to see him."

Maurice howled with laughter, a piece of bread flying from his mouth. "Kassia," he said, "is her father's daughter. Her pleasure in her cousin's company can only reflect her sire's pleasure in his nephew's company, and that, my dear sister, is nil!"

"You, Maurice, are merely jealous that you have a

worthless girl! Geoffrey is a warrior and is rising in
favor with the duke."

"I am not surprised, if he has his father's oily tongue
and your cunning, sister."

Graelam chewed thoughtfully on his meat, watching
the two of them spar. At least, he thought, it appeared
that Lady Felice had all but forgotten him. He cast an
eye about for the wench Glenna as he drank his ale.

"If only," he heard Felice say angrily, "I had not
been born a female, Belleterre would be mine! And
you, Maurice, you would sell your homely daughter's
hand to the devil to keep Belleterre from its rightful
heir!"

"You are never satisfied, sister. 'Twas you who insisted
upon wedding Gilbert de Lacy. His was the bed you
wanted, so now you may lie in it."

"Where is Guy?" Graelam asked Maurice in a brief
moment of silence.

Maurice said absently, "The little slut Glenna found
the fair Englishman much to her taste. She is likely
teaching your knight a thing or two."

So much for that, Graelam thought, and downed the
remainder of his ale. He rose and laid his hand on
Maurice's shoulder. "We've a long ride tomorrow, and
I, for one, am ready to take my rest."

Maurice shot a snide look toward his sister. "If you
don't mind, dear sister, my lord Graelam and I will
sleep in Geoffrey's chamber. As an Englishman, he is
too polite to protect himself!"

Felice gave Maurice a venomous look and Graelam a
small, disappointed smile.

"I thank you, my lady," Graelam said, "for your
hospitality. The bath was most refreshing and the meal
sits well in my belly."

"And he wants nothing else sitting on his belly, sister!"

Felice hissed a retort, but Graelam could not make out her words. He found himself wondering if the two of them had argued and baited each other all their lives. He was mildly disappointed that Geoffrey had not been present. He would have liked to take the man's measure himself.

The rain, thankfully, had stopped during the night, and the sun was fast drying the muddy road by the time they left Beaumanoir.

"'Tis a relief to be away from that viper's nest," Maurice said.

Graelam cocked a thick black brow. "You gave as good as you got, Maurice. Indeed, I fancied that you were much enjoying yourself."

"Aye," Maurice said. "Felice has never bored me. I gave her two casks of wine for her hospitality and her . . . disappointment."

"She is a most insistent woman," Graelam said only.

As for Guy, Graelam found the young knight heavy-eyed, but he forbore to mock him.

They passed through hilly forests of oak and beech, cut through by gorges, ravines, and tumbled rocks. Untilled moors dotted with yellow gorse and purple heather stretched to barren summits, giving views of tilled green valleys beyond. Maurice grew more excited as they drew closer to Belleterre. "We are near the Morlaix River," Maurice said. "You can nearly smell the sea. The soil is rich here, fortunately, and our wheat crops are plentiful in most years. We also have cattle and sheep aplenty, and their noxious smell and loud baas fill the air in the spring."

Graelam nodded. "'Tis much like Cornwall," he said.
"The beggers also abound there. It is a difficult task to
keep them out of the crops. God be praised that we
grow most of our wheat and barley in a valley, protected from the salty air and the sea winds."

Twilight was falling when they crossed the final rocky
rise. "There"—Maurice pointed proudly—"is Belleterre."

Belleterre was not a sprawling pile of stone, as was
Wolffeton. Nor did its aura of strength lessen its beauty.
Graelam's military eyes took in its battlements and its
prominence in the countryside and the river. Belleterre
was a fortress of no mean value.

As Graelam turned to tell Maurice some of his
thoughts, Maurice shouted, dug his heels in his destrier's sides, and rode like a wild-eyed Saracen up the
steep path to Belleterre. The rest of his men, save
those driving the wagons, fell into line behind him, all
of them shouting and waving.

Graelam said to Guy, "When you are within the
walls, I want you to examine the fortifications. Wolffeton
is in need of repairs. Perhaps you will learn something
useful. As for me, I fear that I will be drinking a lot of
wine and smiling at Maurice's precious daughter until
my mouth aches."

"The girl Glenna told me that Kassia de Lorris is a
gentle girl and possessed of considerable beauty."

Graelam grunted. "I care not if she be as winsome as
Queen Eleanor or a crone with no teeth," he said.

As he rode under the iron portcullis into the inner
bailey, he noted the winching mechanisms and the
thickness of the inner walls with approval. The inner
bailey itself surprised him. It was flawlessly clean and
orderly. Even the cobblestones were set into the earth

on a slight incline so that rainwater would not collect.
He was examining the outbuildings and the stables
when he heard Maurice shouting at the top of his lungs,
"Kassia! Kassia!"

There was something wrong. The many people who
were in the inner bailey were strangely quiet, staring
toward Maurice or talking in whispers to each other
behind their hands. They had the look, Graelam thought
suddenly, of sheep who had lost their shepherd. He
dismounted from Demon and handed the reins to one
of his men.

He looked upward at the huge keep, and the winding
thick oak stairs that led to the great hall. Suddenly he
heard an anguished cry. "Kassia!"

Graelam galloped up the stairs and found himself in a
huge, high-vaulted chamber. He was vaguely aware of
the smell of lemon, and sweet rosemary from the thick
rushes that covered the stone floor. There were exquisite tapestries covering the walls next to a cavernous
fireplace. He saw Maurice stride toward an old woman
and begin to shake her shoulders.

"My lord," Graelam said, closing his hand over Maurice's arm. "What is the matter?"

Maurice made an odd keening sound and released
the old woman. "'Tis Kassia," he whispered. "I am told
she has a fever and is dying."

He rushed like a madman toward the stairs that led
to the upper chambers, Graelam at his heels.

Graelam drew back when Maurice flung open the
door to a chamber at the top of the stairs. The room was
filled with a sickening sweet scent of incense, and the
myriad candles cast long shadows on the walls. There
were four women surrounding a raised bed. The silence
was shattering. Two coal braziers burned next to the

bed, and the heat was stifling. Graelam found himself walking forward toward the bed.

Maurice was bowing over a figure, his rasping sobs soft and painful to hear.

"My dear child, no . . . no," he heard Maurice say over and over. "You cannot leave me. No!"

Graelam moved closer and stared down at Kassia de Lorris. He felt a knot of pity in his belly. The pitiful creature was a parody of life. Her hair had been cut close, and the flesh of her face was a sickening gray. He saw Maurice clutching at her hand. It looked like a claw. He could hear her pained breathing. Suddenly Maurice jerked back the cover, and Graelam stared in horror at several leeches that were sucking at the wasted flesh of her breasts.

"Get them off her!" Maurice yelled. He clutched at the blood-engorged leeches, ripped them from his daughter's flesh, and hurled them across the room.

The old woman, Etta, touched his shoulder, but he threw off her hand. "You are killing her, you old crone! God's bones, you are killing her!"

The girl could be fifteen years old or a hundred, Graelam thought. He could even see the blue veins standing out on her eyelids. He wondered briefly what Kassia de Lorris had looked like before she had been struck down. Poor child, he thought, his eyes narrowing in pity on her face. He wanted to do something, but knew there was nothing he could say, nothing he could do. He turned slowly and left the chamber, the sound of Maurice's curses and sobs filling his ears.

Guy was speaking in a soft voice to a serving wench. When he saw Graelam, he quickly walked over to him and said in a hushed voice, "The girl is dying, my lord.

She came down with the fever some four days ago. She is not expected to last through the night."

Graelam nodded. Indeed, he was surprised that she still clung to life.

"The serving wench thinks that the priest should be fetched."

"That is Maurice's decision." Graelam ran his hand through his hair, realizing that Maurice's thoughts were all on his daughter. "Have the priest brought here."

He and Guy ate a silent meal, attended by quietly crying servants. Graelam wondered where all Maurice's men were, but forbore to ask the servants.

"'Tis a rich keep," Guy said, looking around the great hall. The trestle table shone with polish and there were cushions on the benches. "I am most sorry for Lord Maurice."

"Aye," Graelam said, his eyes resting a moment upon the two beautifully carved high-backed chairs that stood opposite each other not far from the warm fire. Between the chairs was an ivory chessboard, the pieces in place. He tried to picture Maurice and Kassia seated opposite each other, laughing and playing chess. His belly tightened. Damn, he thought, he didn't want to be touched by the girl's death. He felt suddenly as though he were trespassing. He was, after all, a stranger.

He found himself drawn to the chairs, and he eased himself down, a goblet of ale resting on his knee. He found his eyes going every few minutes toward the stairs. The priest arrived, a bald, watery-eyed old man whose robe was tied loosely about his fat stomach.

The time passed with agonizing slowness. Graelam dismissed Guy and found himself alone in the great hall. It was near to midnight when he saw Maurice walk like a bent old man down the stairs. His face was haggard and his eyes swollen.

"She is dying," Maurice said in a strangely calm voice. He sat down in the chair opposite Graelam and stared into the fire. "I found myself wishing that you, my lord, had not saved me. Perhaps if I had died, God would spare Kassia."

Graelam clutched Maurice's hand. "You will not say that, Maurice. A man cannot question God's will." His words sounded glib and empty, even to his own ears.

"Why not?" Maurice said harshly. "She is good and pure, and gentle. It is not right or just that she be cheated of life! God's blood, do you understand? I wanted you, the man who saved my life, a strong warrior who knows no fear, to take her to wife! To protect her, and Belleterre, to give me grandchildren! God be cursed! 'Tis an evil that takes her from me!"

Graelam watched helplessly as Maurice dropped his face into his hands and sobbed softly. He pictured the small girl in the chamber above and felt pity choking in his throat. He had seen horrors unimagined in the Holy Land, but it had been the utter waste that had disgusted him, not the actual misery of the people. He did not want to be affected by the death of one girl. By the saints in heaven, he did not even know her!

"Maurice," he said urgently, "what will happen you cannot change. Belleterre is yours. If you wish it to remain yours, you must remarry and breed more children of your own. You must not give up!"

Maurice laughed, a humorless, bitter sound that made Graelam wince. "I cannot," he said finally, very quietly. "I contracted a disease some ten years ago. It left my seed lifeless."

There was nothing to say. Graelam closed his eyes,

leaning back in the chair, only the sounds of Maurice's ragged breathing breaking the silence of the hall. He felt the older man's hand upon his arm and opened his eyes to see Maurice looking at his face with feverish intensity.

"Listen to me, my lord," Maurice said, his fingers tightening on Graelam's arm. "I will repay my debt to you. Belleterre is near to the coast and thus not far from your lands in Cornwall. Even if my Kassia's blood cannot flow in the veins of Belleterre's descendants, yours will. 'Tis noble blood you carry, my lord Graelam, and I would call you my son and heir."

"That is not possible, Maurice," Graelam said. "I am an Englishman, and your liege lord would never grant me your lands. Nor do I deserve to have them. Maurice, I would have saved your life had you been a merchant! You must make peace with yourself, and perhaps with your nephew. There is no choice."

Maurice's eyes glistened with purpose. "Nay, my lord, attend me. If you wed my Kassia this night, you will be her husband and entitled to Belleterre upon my death."

Graelam drew back, appalled. "No! By God's teeth, Maurice, your mind is rattled! Your daughter is dying. Leave her in peace!"

"You would not be burdened with a wife unknown to you. You will have only the responsibility of Belleterre. What matters it to Kassia if she is wed before she dies? What matters it to you?"

Graelam hissed out his breath, his body hard and coiled with tension. "I will not marry the child! I buried one wife, I will not wed another only to bury her within hours! See you, Maurice, 'tis madness, 'tis your grief!"

Maurice drew back in his chair, but his eyes never wavered from Graelam's face. "Hear me, my lord. If Kassia dies unwed, my own death warrant is signed. Geoffrey will not wait for my body to rot with age. He will take what he believes is his. But with you as Kassia's husband—"

"Widower!"

"—widower, Geoffrey will find himself helpless against a powerful English nobleman! I cannot save my daughter, but I can save Belleterre! Marry her, Graelam, then you will go to the Duke of Brittany and swear your fealty to him. I ask nothing more of you. You can return to England with naught but honor, and the promise of rich lands for your sons!"

Graelam rose swiftly from his chair and paced to and fro in front of the older man. "You do not even know me!" he said, striving for cool reason as he came to an abrupt halt in front of Maurice, his arms folded over his powerful chest. "I was a stranger to you until less than a week ago! How can you trust your lands to a man who could, for all you know, be the biggest scoundrel in all of Christendom?"

"I would rather trust my fortunes to an unknown scoundrel than to a known one. Be you a scoundrel, my lord?"

Graelam gritted his teeth. "Leave be, Maurice. If you fear your nephew, I will kill him for you before I leave Brittany. Does that ease your mind?"

"Nay," Maurice said quietly. "Belleterre must have its lord, and he must be strong, ruthless, and a fearless warrior. You must be the future Lord of Belleterre."

Graelam stared at him in stunned silence.

"Even now," Maurice continued, "Kassia could be drawing her last breath. If you do not wed her, my lord, I will lose everything I hold dear in this wretched world. By all that's holy, man, do I ask so much of you? I take nothing from you, only give! You do not lose your vaunted honor! You suffer no shame!"

It was not Maurice de Lorris' passionate words that decided Graelam at that moment. It was the unashamed tears that streaked down his cheeks.

"Let us get it over with," Graelam said.

Graelam held Kassia's hand in his as the priest said his marriage lines in the early hours of the night. He felt the delicate bones and knew a moment of utter pain. Maurice's scribe had hastily penned the marriage contract, and in the bleak silence of the stifling hot chamber, Graelam de Moreton signed his name and titles. He watched silently as Maurice guided Kassia's hand over the parchment.

"My daughter writes," Maurice said, his voice quavering. "I taught her."

It was done. Graelam heard the soft rattling deep in her chest and knew that the end was near. Slowly he drew off his ring, thick pounded gold inset with onyx, the deep imprint of a wolf raised on its surface, and slid it onto Kassia's middle finger. He closed her fingers into a fist to keep the ring from sliding off, and gently laid her hand over her chest.

"Come, my lord," Maurice said. "There is much to do before I grieve."

Graelam took one last look at his wife, then followed Maurice from the chamber.

"It will be morning soon, my lord. You must journey immediately to St. Pol-de-Leon, 'tis on the northern coast. The Duke of Brittany is at his castle there. You will only tell him that you have wed Kassia de Lorris and present to him the marriage contract."

"I am known to the duke," Graelam said. He remembered the powerful Charles de Marcey, a proud man, but a man Edward approved. Graelam had bested the duke in a joust. He wondered if de Marcey would remember.

Maurice's eyes glittered and he rubbed his hands together. "Excellent! You must swear fealty to him. Kassia's death will be kept a secret for as long as possible."

"Very well, Maurice. I will return—"

"Nay! There is no need, my lord. I will bury my daughter and you will continue on your way." He paused a moment, his eyes lowered to his gnarled hands. "I wish to grieve alone. I will be safe from Geoffrey, for your marriage will be proclaimed far and wide. I thank you, Graelam de Moreton."

Graelam saw a tear fall on the back of Maurice's hands. He felt a portion of his grief, but he knew no words to ease it.

"I wish you well, Maurice," he said. He took the older man in his arms and pressed him tightly. "I will share some of your pain, my friend."

"I thank you," Maurice said again, and drew back, his shoulders straightening. "You must leave now. Godspeed, my son."

Graelam halted his small troop to gaze back at Belleterre bathed in the crimson streaks of dawn. It was a magnificent castle, and he could not prevent the surge of pleasure that one day Belleterre would belong to one of his sons.

"Guy," he said to the silent young knight beside him.

"You know what has passed. I wish you to keep all to yourself. Ensure that the men keep silent also."

"Aye, my lord," Guy said. "I . . . I am sorry, my lord."

"Yes," Graelam said in a harsh voice. "So am I."

He wheeled Demon about and dug in his heels. The powerful destrier bounded forward, and soon Belleterre was lost to view in a cloud of dust.

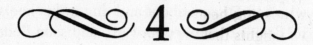

4

Charles de Marcey, Duke of Brittany, slouched in his chair, his thoughts not on the two knights squabbling before him, but on his wife, Alice, and her petulant demands. Always another jewel, or a new gown, always something! Damn her for a bitch, he thought irritably, shifting in his chair. She dared to berate him for taking a willing girl to his bed, when she, frigid witch that she was, refused him her favors. His sudden movement momentarily silenced the two knights, and they looked at him expectantly.

He waved his hand, frowning. "Continue," he said shortly. And to his scribe he said, "You, Simon, are recording the . . . essence of this problem?"

"Aye, my lord," Simon said, crouching again over the small table in front of him.

Poor Simon, Charles thought, he grows hunchbacked in my service. He sighed, wishing he were hunting, for it was a beautiful spring day, the air fresh and crisp. Anything but listening to squabbles about a keep small

42

enough to fit in his hauberk! The two young men needed
bloodletting and he wondered idly if he shouldn't let
them go at each other. He was aware that Simon was
giving him one of his looks, damn the old man, and
pulled his wandering attention back to the two men.

The morning hearings droned on. Charles informed
the two knights that he would consider their respective
claims and waved his hand in dismissal.

"My lord," Robert de Gros, his closest friend and
chamberlain said, approaching him. "An Englishman is
here, claiming to know you. He says it is a matter of
some urgency."

Charles raised a thick auburn eyebrow and looked
from Robert toward the doorway to the chamber.

"Graelam de Moreton! By all that's holy!" Charles
roared, leaping up from his chair. "I had thought we
would be lucky and your hide would be skinned in the
Holy Land!"

Graelam proffered a mock bow and strode forward,
relieved that Charles remembered him and appeared
glad to see him. "The Saracens cannot fell an Englishman,
my lord," he said.

Charles grasped him by the shoulders. "Do you never
learn to show respect to your betters, Graelam?"

"Edward," Graelam said smoothly, his voice mocking, "never had any reason to complain. How the devil
did you know I was in the Holy Land?"

Charles laughed, buffeting Graelam on the shoulder.
"Your King Edward has scribes to write letters, my
lord, unlike the rest of his illiterate followers. I hear
that you, Graelam, are one of the few to return with
riches from the Holy Land."

"Aye," Graelam said, "perhaps even a jewel to ornament your wife's lovely throat."

"That," Charles said, "is the best news I have heard today. Come, my lord, let us speak in private and I will hear this urgent business of yours."

Graelam followed Charles from the suffocatingly ornate hall filled with chattering lords and ladies into a small chamber that held but two chairs and a single table. The court life Charles led was making him soft, Graelam thought, studying the Frenchman. Although he was but five years Graelam's senior, lines of dissipation marred his handsome face, and a paunch was beginning to thicken his belly. But his thick auburn hair was unmarked by gray and his dark eyes were sharp with intelligence, his boredom of a few moments before replaced with interest. He certainly looked prosperous enough, Graelam thought, eyeing his rich crimson robe with its full ermine-lined sleeves.

Without pause, Graelam handed Charles the marriage contract. "I am wed to Kassia de Lorris of Belleterre. I am here to swear fealty to you as my liege lord and gain your official sanction."

To Graelam's surprise, Charles threw back his head and roared with laughter. "That sly old fox," he gasped, tapping his finger against the parchment. "Ah, I cannot wait to see the fury on poor Geoffrey's face!"

"Geoffrey de Lacy is here?" Graelam asked, feeling a tingling of anticipation.

"Sit down, Lord Graelam, and I will tell you about the nest of hornets you have stirred."

Charles bellowed for wine, then eased back in his chair, his hands folded over his belly. "How timely your announcement, my lord," he said blandly. "My coffers don't yield enough."

"They never did," Graelam said dryly. "Unfortunately, the riches I gained in the Holy Land must be spent in reparation of Wolffeton. What I offer you in return for recognizing my marriage is a strong sword arm and fighting men to protect your lands. I am at your disposal, say, two months of the year. And, of course, a ruby perhaps for your wife."

"Well, that is something, I suppose," Charles said, sipping at his wine. From the corner of his eye he saw the serving wench hovering near the doorway, doubtless, he thought irritably, one of his wife's spies. He turned a narrowed eye on the wench and she quickly disappeared.

"My wife," he muttered, "likes to be informed of everything. I should not wonder if she knows when my bowels move!"

Graelam cocked a disbelieving brow. "You, my lord, under a woman's thumb? You tell me that age will shrivel my manhood?"

"'Tis my manhood I protect!" He gave a doleful sigh. "I once believed her so lovely, so innocently sweet. And her body still tempts me mightily."

"Your lady's body is yours," Graelam said, waving a dismissing hand. "Saint Peter's bones, Charles, beat her! A man cannot allow a woman to rule him, else he is no man."

"Ah," Charles said, not offended, "thus speaks a man who has never known a tender emotion. Though," Charles added, frowning into his wine, "the saints know that emotion lasts not long. The troubadours have done men a great disservice. Their verses make the ladies dream of softness and love, and a man, witless creature, plays the part to get what he wants."

"In England men are not such fools."

"Still so harsh," Charles said blandly. "Let us say,

Graelam, that one must suffer a wife's inquisitiveness if she is to suffer his dalliances."

"A woman should have no say in a man's affairs," Graelam said, impatience clear in his voice. "If I remember aright, you were surrounded in England by ladies who wanted naught but to share your bed."

"Aye," Charles said, his eyes growing soft with memory. He sighed deeply. "Alas, a man grows older, and must take a wife."

"I would beat any woman who dared infringe on my wishes, wife or no. A woman is to be soft and yielding, her duty to see to her master's pleasure and bear him sons."

"And your dear young wife, my friend? Is she gentle and submissive enough to suit you?"

Graelam was silent for a moment, seeing the gray death pallor of Kassia's face. "She is what she is," he said shortly.

"I can almost pity the girl," Charles said, feigning a deep sigh. "There is no chivalry in Englishmen. I hope you did not rip her apart on your wedding night with that huge rod of yours."

"Maurice de Lorris sends his greetings," Graelam said abruptly. "And his continued pledge of fealty."

"As does his beloved nephew, Geoffrey de Lacy," Charles said softly. "Geoffrey, until your arrival, Graelam, had convinced me that he should have Kassia de Lorris' hand. He also pledged fealty and . . . other things."

"Then he lies," Graelam said calmly. "I have visited his keep, Beaumanoir. His serfs are ragged wretches, what men I saw appeared swaggering louts, and his mother—"

"The less spoken about Lady Felice, the better," Charles interrupted.

"—and I would willingly dispatch Geoffrey de Lacy to hell as meet him."

"I imagine Geoffrey will feel the same way—until he sees you, that is. He is brave enough, but not stupid. 'Tis odd what you say about Beaumanoir, for Geoffrey possesses wealth. Lord knows he is lining my pockets. Very well, Graelam de Moreton, what's done is done. You have my official sanction and I accept your pledge of fealty. Breed many sons, Graelam, for the line of Belleterre is a noble one, old and proud."

Graelam bowed his head, and if Charles chose to think it silent agreement, it was his right. The only way he could hold Belleterre after Maurice's death, Graelam knew, would be to kill Geoffrey. The thought gave him no pause of regret.

"Now, my lord Englishman, tell me about your adventures and how you gained your riches. Mayhap I can still relieve you of some of them."

Graelam obliged him, recalling the long, desperate months in the Holy Land, and the outcome, the Treaty of Caesarea. "The Holy Land is replete with fools, Charles, greedy fools who care naught for anything save filling their coffers. They ignore the misery and death that surround them. The treaty"—he gave an ironic laugh—"will protect the fools for another ten years. As for my riches, my lord duke, I gained those in a raid on a Saracen camp."

He looked into the swirling red wine in his goblet and shook his head, not wanting to share that particular adventure with Charles.

He said abruptly, "And you, how many sons now carry your proud name?"

"I am cursed with three daughters and but one son. Ah, Graelam, the adventures we shared! Do you remember that merchant's daughter in London, the one with the witch's black hair?"

"Aye, the little tart nearly exhausted me!"

"You! Ha, 'twas I who shared her pallet and her favors!"

"You rearrange the past to suit yourself, my lord duke." Graelam rose from his chair and proffered Charles a mock bow. "But since you are my liege lord, I will not trifle with your fanciful memories."

"You are a dog, Graelam," Charles said. He lowered his thick auburn brows and said in a sly voice, "Do I take it as the new bridegroom you will remain chaste during your visit here?"

Graelam refused to be baited, and gave Charles a crooked grin. "I have no taste for the pox, my lord duke. My carnal needs can wait."

The duke roared with laughter. "Ah, Graelam, I cannot wait until the evening dinner to see how you avoid the amorous advances of all the ladies! Alas, I am weak of flesh. I will have my chamberlain show you a chamber."

"I must leave on the morrow, Charles, but I gladly accept your hospitality this night."

"Back to your blushing bride, huh?"

Graelam paused but an instant. "Aye," he said. "I must get back."

Graelam was markedly silent the following morning when he and his men left St. Pol-de-Leon. The coast was barren, battered ceaselessly by the merciless sea winds. Jagged cliffs rose to savage splendor about the rock-strewn beaches. There were no bushes or flowers to soften the bitter landscape. Graelam was impervious to his surroundings, his thoughts on his encounter the previous evening with Geoffrey de Lacy. The great chamber with its huge trestle tables held enough food to supply Edward's army in the Holy Land for at least a week, Graelam had thought. The duke had taken great delight in introducing Graelam to Geoffrey de Lacy, enjoying the other man's rage, for enraged he was, Graelam saw.

"You must welcome Lord Graelam de Moreton to the family," Charles said jovially, his eyes alight with deviltry on Geoffrey's pale face.

Geoffrey felt such fury that for a moment he could do nothing but think of the dagger in his belt. His long fingers unconsciously stroked the fine-boned handle.

"I have heard much about you," Graelam said, studying Geoffrey as he would any enemy. Geoffrey de Lacy was about five years his junior, Graelam guessed, a tall, slender young man blessed with broad shoulders and a pleasing face. His hair was dark brown, but it was his eyes that held Graelam's attention. They were a pale blue and shone from his face like slivers of blue ice. He wondered cynically, remembering Lady Felice's randy disposition and dark coloring, if Geoffrey had inherited his features from his father or another.

He watched Geoffrey run his tongue over his lower lip. "I did not know," Geoffrey said, his voice as icy as his eyes, "that my esteemed uncle knew any Englishmen."

"Ah," Graelam said easily, knowing that the duke was enjoying himself immensely, "I did not meet him until very recently. Indeed, I saved him from being murdered by a band of ruffians in Aquitaine." Maurice's conjectures were right, he thought, catching the flicker of guilt in Geoffrey's eyes. And dismay and frustration.

Geoffrey realized that he must get a hold on himself,

for the duke was standing near, all attention. He stared at the harshly handsome man who was regarding him with something close to contempt. How he would like to slit the English bastard's throat!

"His gift to me," Graelam continued coolly, "was Kassia's fair hand and Belleterre. I shall . . . cherish my possessions."

"Kassia is too young," Geoffrey said, pain and fury breaking his voice. "She is innocent and trusting—"

"No longer," the duke said, laughing, a leering gleam in his dark eyes. "Innocent at least. Lord Graelam is a man of strong passions, as I'm certain his young bride realizes now."

Geoffrey pictured Graelam naked, his powerful body covering Kassia's, pictured him thrusting between her slender legs. "Kassia was to have been mine," he growled, unable to contain his rage.

"I suggest that you forget both Kassia and Belleterre," Graelam said. "Your own keep, Beaumanoir, is much in need of your attentions. Of course, I did not see many of your men. Perhaps they were off elsewhere, following your orders."

"You make insinuations, my lord," Geoffrey spat, his hand going to his dagger.

Before he knew it his arm was caught in a grip of iron. "You, my puppy, had best forget your plans and disappointments, else I will break your neck. If ever Belleterre tempts you again, you will find yourself with your face in the dirt."

Geoffrey tasted fear like flaky ashes in his mouth. Hatred boiled inside him, making him tremble. "You will regret what you have done, my lord," he said. He ripped his arm from Graelam's hold and strode from the chamber.

A fine drizzle began to fall and Graelam pulled his cloak more closely about him. He cursed, unable to keep the image of Kassia de Lorris' ravaged face from his mind. He could still hear the soft rattle rising over her labored breathing. She was dead and buried now, poor child, beyond Geoffrey's twisted desires. He found himself worrying about Maurice, and wondered if he shouldn't return to Belleterre. But no, Maurice had been adamant. He had wished to grieve alone, and Graelam knew he must respect his wishes. He wondered how long Kassia's death could be kept a secret. He imagined that within the year he would be returning to Belleterre to defend it from Geoffrey's greed. He smiled grimly at the thought of running Geoffrey cleanly through with his sword.

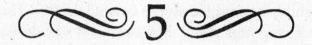

5

Kassia was trapped in darkness. She realized that her eyes were closed, but she hadn't the strength within her to open them. She heard a hoarse, whimpering sound.

"Hush, my baby." She heard a soft, crooning voice, Etta's voice, and she quieted.

She felt a wooden object pressing against her lips.

"Open your mouth, Kassia. 'Tis beef broth." She did as she was bid. The delicious liquid coursed down her throat.

"Papa," she whispered.

"Yes, *ma chère*. I am here. A bit more broth and you can sleep again."

Maurice gently wiped the trickle of broth from her slack mouth and raised worried eyes to Etta.

"Time, my lord, 'twill take time. The child will live. She's a de Lorris."

"Aye," Maurice said, his voice sounding as tired as he felt, "a de Lorris." But Jean, his son, had been a de

Lorris, and he had died. So young he was, so innocent
and helpless.

He sat back in his chair, his eyes upon his daughter's
ravaged face. He wondered idly if the final absolution
the priest had granted would serve her when the time
came for her to really leave this earth.

"Fool," he muttered to himself. "Your brain is becoming fodder for the cows." He thought of Graelam de
Moreton, and felt a shudder go through his body. He
would not think of Graelam now, nor what that proud
warrior would think or do when he discovered his wife
lived.

"Papa?"

"Aye, poppin."

"It is raining. 'Tis a marvelous sound."

Maurice gave her a gentle kiss. There was a sparkle
in her eyes again, and her face had lost the grayness
and hollowness.

"You look tired," Kassia said, her eyes narrowing on
her father's face.

"You worry about yourself, Kassia, and let this old
man be. By the saints, child, I have prayed until my
knees are knobby and stiff." He clasped her slender
fingers, gently stroking them. He felt such happiness
that he could burst with it. Her fingers, of course, were
bare. He had tucked Graelam's ring into a leather pouch
in his chamber.

"I have had such dreams, Papa," Kassia said. "I remember your voice, of course, but there was another as
well. A voice I did not recognize, speaking in a soft
way."

"'Twas likely one of the women you heard," Maurice
said.

"Nay, 'twas a man's voice. His voice was deep and slow."

"A dream," Maurice said. She was still too weak, he told himself, to know the truth of the matter. He could not believe that she remembered Graelam.

"Aye," Kassia said, her lashes sweeping over her eyes. " 'twas a dream."

The days flowed into nights. Kassia slept, spoke briefly to Etta and her father, and ate. At the end of a week she had strength enough to raise her hand and scratch her head. Her fingers slid beneath the simple cotton wimple and touched short tufts of spiky hair.

Maurice entered her chamber to see tears streaking down her face.

He rushed to her bed, guessing their cause when he saw the wimple lying beside her. "Fie, Kassia," he said. "'Tis but a head of hair, naught of anything. I had not believed you so vain."

Her tears stopped, and she sniffed.

"Within a month you will have soft curls and look like a sweet choir boy."

Suddenly she smiled. "Perhaps you should invite Geoffrey to Belleterre. Were he to see me like this, he would soon lose his desire to wed me."

"There, you see," Maurice said uncomfortably, "there is always a bright side to things. As for Geoffrey, that whoreson dare not show his face here. Now, Kassia, I've brought you another goblet of sweet wine from Aquitaine."

"I think I've already drunk a cask, Papa! If I continue swilling I will have a veined red nose!"

She sipped the wine, enjoying its smoothness and warmth. "Papa," she said. "I want a bath. I cannot continue to lie here and wallow in my own filth. Then I want to lie in the garden and feel the sun upon my face."

Maurice beamed at her, feeling his heart swell. "You shall have whatever you desire, poppin." He wrinkled his nose. "You are right about the bath. That must be first."

It was a golden day in Cornwall. The sun shone hot and bright overhead and the stiff sea breeze smelled as sweet as the clumps of wildflowers that grew on the surrounding hills.

Graelam felt utter contentment as he drew Demon to a halt at the edge of the sloping cliff and stared down at the white-crested waves that crashed against the rocks below. From St. Agnes Point, a sharp jutting finger of land, he had a view of at least thirty miles of northward coastline. The rugged cliffs gave onto land so savage and desolate that even the trees were stunted and twisted from the westerly gales that pounded them. Beyond St. Agnes Point lay the small fishing village of St. Agnes, as desolate and rugged and timeless as the craggy cliffs it hugged.

Graelam remembered his hikes along the winding footpath below St. Agnes Point when he was a boy, exploring the caves and calmer coves that indented the coastline, and felt the savage beauty of Cornwall burn into his very soul. He turned in his saddle. Inland, beyond the ragged cliffs, were rolling hills where sheep and cattle grazed, and between the hills, in narrow valleys, farmers tilled the land. His land. His home. His people.

Rising behind him like a rough-hewn monolith stood Wolffeton, fortress of the de Moretons since Duke William had deeded the lands to Albert de Moreton after the Battle of Hastings over two hundred years ago. Albert had torn down the wooden fortress of the Saxons and had erected a stone castle that would defend the northern coast of Cornwall from any assaulting forces, be they marauding Danes or the greedy French. On stormy nights lamps were lit in the two seaward towers, warning off ships from the deadly rock-strewn waters.

In the distance he could make out the stonemasons repairing the seaward wall, eroded over the two centuries by the ferocious sea storms. The jewels he had brought with him from the Holy Land had brought a respectacle price, enough to repair the walls of Wolffeton, the outbuildings, his men's barracks, and to purchase sheep, cattle, and a half-dozen horses. As for the great hall and the upper chambers, they had not changed much since Albert's days. That had never mattered to Graelam before, but upon his return a month before he had found Wolffeton lacking. The long walls beneath the soot-covered beams in the great hall looked primitive and bare. The rough-carved trestles and benches, even his ornately carved chair, were equally bare, with no thick velvet cushions to soften their lines. The rushes strewn across the stone floor had not the sweet smell of those at Belleterre, and there was not one carpet to deaden the heavy sound of booted feet. There were, he thought ruefully, no comforts, even in his huge bed-chamber. His long-dead first wife, Marie, had not seemed to care, nor did her half-sister, Blanche de Cormont. He was but growing soft, he grunted to himself, wanting the exotic luxuries he had grown used to in the east.

Rolfe, his trusted master-at-arms, had certainly maintained the discipline of Wolffeton during Graelam's year away in the Holy Land. But there had been problems awaiting his return, problems that an overlord's ab-

sence engendered. There were judgments to be rendered, feuds to be settled, laxness among the castle
servants to be halted. Blount, his steward, had kept his
records well, but even he could not force a greater
production of cloth or discipline the wenches whose job
it was to keep the castle in good order. But it gave
Graelam a good feeling to be thrown back into the
management of his keep and lands. The vast number of
people who spent their lives at Wolffeton were his
responsibility and his alone.

He thought again of Blanche de Cormont. He had
returned to Cornwall a month before to find her wringing her hands when she saw him, tears shining in her
eyes. He had not recognized her until she had reminded him that she was half-sister to his first wife.
Soft-spoken, shy Blanche, a widow now and with no kin
to take her in, none save him. She had come to Wolffeton
some three months before his return home. Blount
hadn't known what to do with her, so she had remained, awaiting Graelam's return. She was not old,
perhaps twenty-eight, but there were faint lines of sadness etched about her mouth, and her brown eyes,
when they rested upon him, were liquid with gratitude.
Her two children, a boy and a girl, she had told him,
her soft mouth trembling, were being raised by her
cousin Robert, in Normandy. She, their mother, had
not been welcome, particularly, she had added sadly,
touching her hand to her rich raven hair, by Robert's
young wife, Elise, a woman jealous of her husband's
affections.

Well, Graelam had thought then as well as now,
there was no harm in her residing at Wolffeton. She
waited on him, served his dinner herself, and mended
his clothing. It was odd, though, he thought, that the

castle servants did not seem to like her. Why, he could
not guess. She seemed unobtrusive enough to him.

Graelam's thoughts turned to the Duke of Cornwall's
impending visit. King Edward's uncle had always seemed
like a second father to Graelam, indeed, more of a
father than his own had been. Though the bond between them was deep and affectionate, Graelam devoutly
prayed that the duke was not coming as his overlord to
request his services. A year of his life spent in the Holy
Land fighting the heathen Saracens was enough for any
man.

With these thoughts, he turned Demon away from
the cliff and rode northward back toward Wolffeton.

At the sound of approaching hoofbeats, Blanche de
Cormont pulled the leather hide from the window opening in her small chamber and watched Graelam gallop
into the inner bailey of Wolffeton, his powerful body
gracefully at ease in the saddle. She felt a surge of
excitement at the sight of him, and her fingers twisted
at the thought of running them through his thick black
hair. How alike and yet different he was from her
husband, Raoul, curse that bastard's black heart. She
hoped he was rotting in hell. Like Raoul, Graelam
expected her to serve him as unquestioningly as any
servant, but unlike Raoul, he was a virile, handsome
devil whose bed every young serving wench at Wolffeton
had shared willingly. And, of course, Graelam hadn't
once raised his hand against her. But then, she thought
cynically, she was not yet his wife. A wife, she knew
from painful experience, was like any other of a man's
possessions. As long as she kept to her place and was
exacting in pleasing her husband, she was treated as
well as his hunting dogs or his destrier.

Blanche gnawed on her lower lip, wondering how

much longer she should pretend the shy, self-effacing widow's role she had instinctively assumed when Graelam returned to Wolffeton. Her first husband, Raoul, had painfully taught her that her high spirits, her occasionally stinging tongue, and her pride were not acceptable in a wife. And her stubbornness. She supposed she was being stubborn where Graelam was concerned, but she wanted him and fully intended to have him. A widow and a poor relation had no real place, her children no real home or future. Perhaps, she thought, it was time to give Graelam some encouragement, perhaps even slip into his bed, if she could find it empty one night!

She would wed Graelam and then bring her children to Cornwall. She missed them, particularly her son, Evian, a bright lad of eight years, but her decision to come to Cornwall was all for his sake. He would become Graelam's heir, for Blanche intended to bear no more children. The pain of her daughter's birth still made her grit her teeth. At least childbirthing hadn't killed her as it had Marie, her long-dead half-sister. Blanche shook off old memories and turned away from the window. She would meet Graelam in the great hall, send the sullen serving wenches out of the way, and serve him some ale herself. She gazed one last time in her polished silver mirror, and curled an errant strand of black hair around her finger. I must please him, she thought, I must.

To her disappointment, Guy de Blasis accompanied Graelam. She was wary of Guy, despite his good looks and polite manners, for she sensed that he guessed her plans and disapproved. Still, she pasted a welcoming smile on her face and walked gracefully forward, her soft wool gown swishing over the reed-covered floor.

"Good day to you, my lord," she said, smiling shyly up at Graelam.

Graelam pulled his attention from Guy and nodded. "I have news for you, Blanche. The Duke of Cornwall is paying us a visit next week. I do not know the extent of his retinue, but doubtless he will bring half an army with him, 'tis his way. At least," he continued, now to Guy, "the barracks will be finished, so his men will not have to sleep in the keep. We will go hunting again before he arrives. Let us pray we bag more than a rabbit."

"A deer at least, my lord," Guy said, "if we divide the men into three separate hunting parties."

"Some ale, my lord?" Blanche asked softly.

Graelam nodded, his thoughts elsewhere. "Ah, and some for Guy too, Blanche."

Blance saw Guy grinning at her, and she frowned at him, but she nonetheless left the hall, her discomfiture kept to herself.

Guy waited until Blanche was out of hearing. "Have you heard anything from France, my lord? From Maurice de Lorris?"

"Nay, but then, what would I hear? If there is a message ever from him, it will doubtless be to inform me that Geoffrey is trying to steal Belleterre from him. I pray that de Lacy will keep his treacherous sword sheathed until Wolffeton is fully restored."

"I doubt he would try an outright attack," Guy said dryly. " 'Tis more his way to sneak about and hire men to do his dirty work." He fell silent a moment, then sighed deeply. "That poor girl," he said at last. "I, of course, did not ever see her, as did you, my lord, but the servants talked to me of her, as did her father's men. They all believed her a sweet child and kind and full of laughter. Aye, 'tis a pity to die so young."

Graelam pictured Kassia's lifeless fingers held in his hands as the priest droned out the marriage words. He had only time to nod when Blanche reappeared carrying a tray with two goblets filled with frothy ale.

"Thank you, Blanche," Graelam said, his tone holding dismissal. Blanche saw Guy quirk a fair eyebrow at her and for a moment she glared back at him. Damn him, he guesses my very thoughts!

"Certainly, my lord," she said sweetly. "Perhaps, Graelam, when you have finished speaking with Guy, you can spare me a few moments? To speak of the entertainment for the duke."

Graelam. She had used his name but the week before and he had not seemed even to notice her familiarity. Perhaps she was making headway with him.

"Perhaps this evening, Blanche," Graelam said as he wiped the white foam of the ale from his upper lip. "I have a new mare to inspect."

Guy laughed aloud, his eyes on Blanche's face. "Do you mean, my lord, that lovely little Arabian, or that equally enticing little two-legged filly named Nan?"

"Both, I fancy," Graelam said, and rose from his chair. "Nan you say her name is, Guy?"

"Aye. No virgin, but again, lovely as a rose whose petals sparkle with the morning mist. And quite young, my lord," Guy continued, knowing that Blanche was listening to their conversation. It was not that he disliked Blanche, he thought, following Graelam from the great hall down the thick, well-worn oak stairs. She was indeed lovely, his body recognized that, but she felt she must needs playact with Graelam. Guy knew she wasn't the meek, gentle creature she showed to Graelam when he had come upon one of the serving wenches in tears, a livid bruise on her cheek from the slap Lady Blanche had given her. He had told Graelam of the incident, but his master, after speaking to Blanche, had told him that the wench had deserved the slap for insulting his sister-in-law.

It was odd, Guy thought as he walked beside Graelam into the inner bailey, how his master enjoyed women in his bed, pleasuring them until they squealed with delight, but had little understanding of them outside his bedchamber. To Lord Graelam, women were soft bodies and little else, save for the one, Chandra de Avenell, Graelam had tried to steal and wed nearly two years before. But even that beautiful creature, though she had doubtless intrigued Graelam with her warrior ways, had been only a challenge to him, like an untamed mare to be covered and broken by a stallion. He suspected that Graelam's black fury following his failure had resulted more from wounded pride than injured feelings. But now Chandra de Avenell was Chandra de Vernon, and Graelam had made peace with both her and her husband in the Holy Land. She was nothing more to him now, Guy knew, than a vague shadow of memory.

The wench Nan appeared none too clean, Graelam thought as he watched her, her arms pressed against her breasts to better entice him, as she drew the bucket of water from the well. Her thick long dark brown hair would be lovely were it not lank and stringy from lack of washing. Her face was a perfect oval and she smiled at him pertly.

"If she were bathed," Graelam said to Guy, "I wouldn't kick her out of my bed."

"Nor would I," Guy said, laughing.

"How many men have enjoyed her favors?"

"Not many, my lord. She was married quite young, when she was fourteen, to a young man who worked with the armorer. He died some two months ago from the wasting disease. According to my knowledge, she has kept her legs together, awaiting your return."

Graelam gave the girl a long, slow smile, then turned away toward the newly repaired stables. "Now, Guy," he said, " 'tis time to see the four-legged mare."

A gale blew in that evening, and the shutters banged loudly in Graelam's bedchamber. He had spent the past two hours trouncing Guy in a game of chess and drinking more ale than was his habit. He was not overly surprised to find Nan lying in his bed.

Indeed, he thought, she did have lovely hair. It was now clean and shining and he wondered idly how long she had spent in a bathing tub to prepare herself for him. He strode to the edge of the bed and smiled at her as he stripped off his clothes. He watched her eyes widen when they fell to his swollen manhood.

"Ye are huge, my lord," she gasped.

"Aye," Graelam laughed, "and you'll know every inch of me."

He drew back the cover and studied her plump white body. "Aye," he said, his dark eyes caressing her, "every inch."

He fondled her and kissed her, pleased that her breath tasted fresh. Her soft flesh was silky and giving beneath his fingers and his mouth. When she was throbbing and hot, he pressed himself between her open legs. She sheathed him to his hilt, wrapping her legs about him, drawing him even deeper, and he realized vaguely, not particularly displeased, that she was as experienced as any whore. He reared back, thrusting deep, and felt his body explode. He rolled off her onto his back. He wondered if her soft cries of pleasure had been real or feigned.

"My lord?"

"Aye?" he said, not turning to her.

"May I rest with ye the night? 'Tis cold and the storm frightens me."

"Aye, you may stay."

He felt her fingers running through the thick tufts of hair on his chest. "But expect, my pet, to be awakened during the night. My appetite for you is but momentarily sated."

Nan giggled and stretched her length against his side, hugging herself to him. She had pleased him, she thought. Now life would be better for her. Aye, much better. She smiled into the darkness at the thought of the sour looks Lady Blanche would cast her. The old bitch wouldn't dare to touch her now.

"Well, Graelam," the Duke of Cornwall said as he tilted his goblet to his mouth, "I have seen several wenches' bellies swollen with child."

"And you're wondering if it is my seed that grows in their bellies?"

The duke shrugged. "It matters not. What does matter is that you have legitimate heirs for your lands, not bastards."

"Ah," Graelam said with a crooked grin, "I was wondering when you would tell me the reason for your visit to Wolffeton. Not, of course, that I am not delighted to greet you."

The duke was silent for a moment. He and Graelam were alone in the great hall, sitting opposite each other next to the dying fire. The trestle tables were cleared of the mountains of food from dinner. The jongleurs Graelam had hired were long in bed, as were all of Graelam's men and the duke's.

"I have heard from Edward," the duke said. "He and Eleanor are still in Sicily. I carry the responsibility for his children whilst he must travel. And England's coffers pay for his adventuring."

"I have certainly paid my share!"

"That you have, my boy."

"It is because of your strength and honor, my lord duke, that Edward need not come running back to England to fight for his throne. The barons are content. England is at peace. He knew great disappointment in the Holy Land, and if he chooses to travel to mend his weary spirit, so be it."

The duke sighed, raising an age-spotted hand. "Aye, 'tis true. Edward has grown into a fine man. Men follow him and trust him. Once I feared that he would be weak and vacillating, much like his poor father."

Graelam said quietly, "As much as you hated Simon de Montfort, my lord duke, 'twas from him that Edward learned his administrative ability. It held us in good stead in the Holy Land. There is no doubt in any man's mind that Edward the king can be trusted and obeyed. He is also a valiant warrior."

"Aye, I know." The duke shook his white head. "I become an old man, Graelam, and I am weary of my responsibilities."

"And I weary you with this late night. Perhaps, my lord," Graelam continued, a glint in his dark eyes, "before you retire, you would care to tell me the reason for your visit."

"I have found you a wife," the duke said baldly.

Graelam was not surprised by his words. Indeed,

during the past five years, the Duke of Cornwall had upon several occasions presented him with likely heir-esses. Graelam cocked his head at the duke, saying nothing.

"Her name is Joanna de Moreley, daughter of the Earl of Leichester. She is young, comely, rich, and above all, appears to be a good breeder. 'Tis time you wed, Graelam, and produced heirs for Wolffeton."

Graelam remained silent, staring into the graying embers in the fire.

"You still do not hold Lord Richard de Avenell's daughter dear, do you?"

"Nay," Graelam said. "Do you forget, my lord, the Lady Chandra wed Sir Jerval de Vernon? He, not I, managed to tame her. To my ultimate relief, we all parted friends."

"So I hear," the duke said dryly, "which brings me back to the Lady Joanna. Do you deny that you have need of heirs, Graelam?"

"Nay," Graelam said slowly, his thoughts upon his second wife, dead within hours of their marriage.

"Is there another lady who has caught your fancy?"

Graelam smiled at the impatience in the duke's voice. "Nay," he said again, and shrugged. "A wife is a bur-den, my lord duke, a burden that chills my guts."

"You are nearing thirty years old, Graelam! Do you wish to be an old man like me before you see your sons become men?"

And there must be an heir for Belleterre, Graelam thought suddenly.

"You begin to convince me, my lord," he said, "with your terrifying logic."

"Forget not," the duke continued, more tolerantly now, for he scented victory, "that even the wealth you

brought from the Holy Land does not go far enough to
provide you comforts within your keep." He looked
pointedly at the bare stone walls and the reed-covered
floors, and doubted not that there were lice mixed with
the refuse and bones. The furniture was scant and
roughly hewn, with no soft cushions for a man's weary
buttocks. The beamed ceiling was black from years of
neglect, and the wall sconces were as black as the
mutton-fat rushes they held. "A wife who brought a fat
dowry and housewifely skills would make Wolffeton a
truly noble keep."

"But a wife," Graelam said wearily, leaning his head
back against the high-backed chair. "'Tis something
that haunts a man all his days."

"As I said," the duke interrupted, "the Lady Joanna
is comely. Perhaps you would learn to care for her."

"Care for a woman?" Graelam arched a thick black
brow up a good inch. "If she were a good breeder,
'twould have to be enough. Why does Leichester choose
me?"

"As one of the king's closest friends," the duke said
with weary patience, "as well as being my vassal,
Leichester need look no higher. Any of his neighbors
would think twice before encroaching on Leichester's
lands with such a powerful son-in-law."

"You have yourself seen this Lady Joanna?"

"Aye, once about six months ago. As I said, she is
comely, and built just like her mother. And, I might
add, that woman has borne with ease five sons, four of
whom have survived."

"I suppose she would expect to be wooed and have
songs written about her eyebrows."

"You are a hard man, Graelam. I offer you a rich
plum and you complain about playing the suitor."

"And if I beat the wench for disobedience, I suppose I can expect tears and reproaches and her father upon my neck!"

"Just keep her belly filled with children, and she'll have no time for disobedience. As to wenches you take to bed, it would be wise to be somewhat more discreet once you have a wife."

Graelam thought of Nan, who was now likely to be sleeping peacefully in his bed. "I must think on it, my lord," Graelam said, rising and stretching.

The Duke of Cornwall rose also and faced the young man he loved more than his own worthless son. He gave him a wide smile. "Think quickly, my lord, for the Lady Joanna will arrive next week . . . for a visit. She will be accompanied by some of her father's men as well as her ladies. If you suit, the wedding will be attended by her parents and me, of course."

"You wicked old man," Graelam said, a dull flush of anger rising over his face. "You woo me with reason, then clamp down your chains!"

"Plow the wench in your bed well, Graelam, for it would be wise to forgo your appetites once the Lady Joanna has arrived." He clapped his hand to Graelam's shoulder. "Don't be angry with me, my boy. 'Tis for the best."

"Christ's bones," Graelam growled. "Best for whom?"

But the Duke of Cornwall only laughed. "You'll make a lusty husband for the girl, Graelam. Be content."

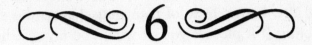

6

"The Duke of Cornwall has arranged a marriage for me," Graelam said to Blanche. "Lady Joanna and her retinue will arrive next week. Can you make preparations for her comfort?"

Blanche stared at him, unable to take in his words. Married! She wanted to scream and cry at the same time, and strike Graelam until he bled like she was bleeding inside. She lowered her head, running her tongue over her suddenly parched lips, and listened to him continue, his voice as indifferent as if he were discussing the weather.

"If the girl is pleasing enough, I will wed her."

Blanche clutched at his words like a lifeline. "You do not know her, Graelam? You have never seen her?"

"Nay. I know nothing about her, save she is an heiress." Graelam shrugged. "If she can breed me sons, I suppose it is enough to ask. Her father is interested in gaining me as a son-in-law because of my friendship with the king and the Duke of Cornwall."

Blanche's thoughts raced. Surely all was not lost! Graelam cared naught for this Joanna, had never even seen the wench. She still had time. "My lord," she said finally, her head lowered modestly, her voice softly shy, "it is likely that the Lady Joanna, being such a young girl, knows little of managing a keep the size of Wolffeton. If it pleases you, it would be my . . . honor" —she nearly choked on the word—"to assist her in gaining the necessary knowledge."

Graelam gave her a perfunctory smile, thinking absently that she was a gentle, accommodating woman. "Thank you, Blanche." He wondered briefly if she knew herself how to manage a keep, for Wolffeton had certainly not changed since she had come here, and he had given her free rein within the keep. Perhaps, he thought, not wishing to be unfair, the food had improved somewhat.

Blanche retired to her small chamber, gently closed the door, and smashed her fists against the wall. How could he, she raged, be drawn into a marriage, and it not be to her! She had been too shy, too modest, she realized when she was calmer. She had not given him enough encouragement, and thus he saw her as a mere adjunct to his household and not as a desirable woman. Damn him! Her lineage was every bit as respectable as this Joanna de Moreley's! The fact that she was not an heiress as was Joanna did not hold long in her mind. Graelam must be made to realize that she, Blanche, would be the right wife, the only wife for him. But Graelam had mentioned breeding sons off his wife, and that stilled her a moment.

She walked to the small window, pulled back the wooden shutter, and stared down toward the practice field. She saw Graelam, stripped to the waist, wrestling

with one of his men. She could see the sweat glistening
off his back, the twisting of his powerful muscles. Ah
yes, she thought, she would teach this Joanna a thing or
two! Her fingers clutched unconsciously on the edge of
the window, as if they were touching Graelam. "Damn
you, my lord," she cursed him in a hoarse whisper.

Much later, when Blanche lay in her narrow bed,
alone, she considered her son. She would write a message to her cousin and have him send Evian to Wolffeton.
Once Graelam had met her son, perhaps he would
forget his desire for his own son. After all, the boy was
also his half-nephew. She realized that she was assuming she could still gain him as her husband. I will be his
wife, she vowed softly, and if he still demands I bear
him a child, I will do it. She hated the thought of the
inevitable birthing pain and the bulk of a child in her
body. For a moment she rebelled against her woman's
lot, against the sheer helplessness of it. Stop it, Blanche,
she scolded herself silently. You have not won yet. But
she would win, she had to. Her son's future and her
own lay in the balance. She fell asleep somewhat calmer.

The next morning Blanche had to contend with the
servants, the pert Nan in particular. They had supposed, Blanche guessed, that she would become the
future mistress of Wolffeton and had thus given her
grudging obedience. She trembled with rage when Nan,
the wretched little slut, said in a snide voice, "If ye
want a new gown, mistress, ye'd best ask his lordship.
Likely he'll buy his new young bride anything, but his
old sister-in-law, who will be but his poor relation . . . ?"
Her voice fell away like sharp droplets of rain dripping
off stone.

"You little bitch!" Blanche said, her voice trembling,
hating both Nan and herself for the truth of the wench's

words. She reached for Nan's long braid, now clean from weekly baths, but Nan was faster. She scurried out of the chamber, laughing aloud.

"I'll have you flogged!" Blanche yelled after her, knowing full well that it was an empty threat.

"The master won't allow that," Nan taunted her from a safe distance. "He likes me smooth and soft. He'll not let ye beat me!"

"Slut! Just wait until your belly swells with child! You'll see then how much the master cares about you and your soft hide!"

"He'll give me a fine cottage and mayhap a servant of my own," Nan retorted.

The other servants snickered behind her back, Blanche knew, but at least they obeyed her orders, albeit with the slowness of mules trekking up a cliff. She ground her teeth and bided her time until Lady Joanna de Moreley came, and Evian. Graelam had seemed reluctant to have her son come to Wolffeton, but Blanche had managed to cry pitifully, an altogether honest reaction, and he had finally agreed.

Graelam grunted and heaved as he helped the masons fit a huge slab of stone into place on the outer eastern wall of Wolffeton. He stepped back and dashed the sweat from his forehead with the back of his hand. He felt exhilarated from the physical labor, for it had kept his mind off Joanna de Moreley's impending visit, which he dreaded. He thought of the message he had sent to Maurice de Lorris several days before, and felt a spurt of unwanted pain for what had happened. He heard nothing from Maurice, and assumed that Geoffrey had made no move on Belleterre. Surely it could not be long now before Geoffrey found out about Kassia's death. Belleterre was not that isolated, and over two months had passed.

Graelam stretched, enjoying the pull of his tired muscles, and headed toward the cliff path that led to the narrow beach below. The surf pounded against the naked rocks, splashing spray into wide arcs in the air. He stripped off his clothes and waded into the tumbling water. Feeling the powerful tug of the tide against his legs, he let himself be dragged forward with the outgoing waves. The water was cold, raising gooseflesh on his body, but he ignored it and plunged facedown into a high-crested wave.

Some minutes later he heard a yell from the cliff above him and turned to see Guy waving toward him. He started to answer, but a huge wave smashed against his back and sent him sprawling onto his face. When he fought his way out of the sea, his face smarting from the coarse rocks and sand, he heard Guy's laughter. He strode onto the narrow beach and shook himself, much in the manner of a huge mongrel dog.

"My lord! Dress yourself before your bride sees you in your natural wonder!"

Graelam cursed softly. The girl was two days early. He did not doubt that his days of peace were over. He dressed himself quickly and strode up the cliff path.

"My lord," Guy said, a wide grin splitting his well-formed mouth. "I fear the Lady Joanna will see us side by side and send you about your business." Guy preened in his green velvet and patted his hand to his golden hair, his laughter ringing above the raucous sound of the seabirds.

Graelam didn't rise to the bait. Instead he asked, "Is all in readiness for the lady?"

"Do you mean has Blanche swallowed the prune in her mouth and managed a welcoming smile?"

"If you had something to offer her, you larking, conceited buffoon, 'tis that lady you could take off my hands!"

"'Tis not my bed Blanche seeks, my lord!" Guy straightened suddenly, a slight worried frown puckering his brow. "'Twas a mistake allowing her to send for her son."

Graelam felt thoroughly irritated. "For God's sake, Guy, leave be. Blanche is comely and endowed with the proper shyness and modesty a lady should have. If I wed Lady Joanna, I shall find Blanche a husband. With her son in tow, it proves she is a good breeder."

Many of the servants would applaud that decision, Guy thought. Blanche had not been overly patient with any of them, so awash was she in her disappointment. He felt a tug of pity for her, as well as something else he was loath to examine. He shrugged. It was none of his affair. He said aloud, "Nay, my lord, do not waste your ill-humor on me." He paused a moment, then added, "there is but one thing that bothers me."

"I suppose I must ask you what it is, else you'll taunt me with your useless guile."

Guy gave him his sunny smile. Their relationship was more in the manner of an indulgent older brother toward a younger sibling, not liege lord to one of his knights. "Why did you agree to this match when it so obviously displeases you?"

Graelam had asked himself the same question many times during the past weeks. "A man must have sons," he said finally. "Now, let me meet my sons' mother."

*   *   *

Kassia walked slowly through the apple orchard, her face lifted to the bright sun overhead. She smelled the sweet scent of the camellias, hydrangeas, and rhododendrons she herself had planted, and heard the comforting drone of the bees in the hives just beyond the orchard. Hugging her arms around her body, feeling the sun warming her bones, she knew the joy of simply being alive.

Her favorite gown of yellow silk still hung loose, but it didn't bother her. She smiled fondly at the thought of her father, ever watching her with worried eyes, encouraging her to do naught but rest and eat. She looked up to see her nurse, Etta, whose ample figure was now walking purposefully toward her, a bowl of something doubtless very nourishing and equally distasteful held in her hands.

"You should be resting, mistress," Etta said without preamble. "Here, drink this."

"Another of your concoctions," Kassia said, but obligingly downed the thick beef broth. "I need to prune my fig trees," she said thoughtfully, handing the bowl back to Etta.

"Fig trees!" Etta said on a mighty sigh.

Kassia cocked her head in question. "I am well enough to do just as I please now. Come, Etta, you know you enjoy my delicious figs."

"Aye, my baby. 'Tis not your figs that are on my mind at the moment."

"What is on your mind?" she asked.

"Your father. Another messenger arrived a while ago."

"Another messenger? I did not know there was even a first, much less a second!"

"Aye," Etta said. "He does not look happy."

"Then I shall go to him and see what is wrong."

"But you should rest!"

"Etta, you and Father are treating me like a downy chick with no sense. I am feeling much stronger, and if I keep eating all the food you stuff in my mouth, I shall be fat as my favorite goose."

"Hurrumph," Etta said, and followed her mistress back to the keep.

Maurice had dismissed the messenger and sat staring blindly in front of him. He didn't realize he was wringing his hands until he felt his daughter's fingers lightly touch his shoulder.

"Father," Kassia said softly. "What troubles you?"

He managed to wipe the worry from his face and smiled at her, drawing her into his lap. She was still so slight, weighing no more than a child. But her vivid hazel eyes were bright again with glowing health, and her beautiful hair now capped her small face in soft, loose curls. He thought of the message and pulled her tightly against him. Time had run out.

He felt her small, firm breasts pressing against him, reminding him yet again that she was no longer a little girl. She was a woman and a wife. He drew in a deep breath and pulled back from her so he could see her face.

"You are feeling well, *ma chère*?" he asked, avoiding the issue.

"Quite well, Father. Much better, I gather, than you are. Now, what about this messenger? Etta also let slip that this was the second one. Is it Geoffrey?"

Kassia could see the beginnings of deception in her father's eyes and said hurriedly, "Nay, Father. I am no longer at death's door. You must tell me what troubles you. Please, I feel useless when you treat me like a witless child who must be protected and cosseted."

He knew there was no help for it. None at all. Slowly he said, not meeting her eyes, "Do you remember telling me that you dreamed of a man's voice? A man you did not know?"

"Aye, I remember."

"You did not dream him. There was such a man. He is an Englishman, Lord Graelam de Moreton. He accompanied me to Belleterre. You see, I was attacked in Aquitaine by brigands, and Lord Graelam saved my life, he and his men. He is an honorable man, Kassia, and a fine man, a warrior who was just returning from the Holy Land. I found myself telling him about that whoreson Geoffrey, and indeed, we stopped at Beaumanoir one evening. He met your aunt, and managed politely enough to avoid her bed. I will not deny that by the time we reached Belleterre, I was thinking of him as the perfect husband for you. I told him much about you. When we arrived, I was told that you were dying. Indeed, there was no doubt in my mind that you would not survive that night."

Kassia was gazing at him with such innocent incomprehension that for a moment Maurice couldn't continue. He coughed, raked his fingers through his hair, and mumbled something under his breath.

"Father," Kassia said, "I do not understand. What of this man, this Graelam de Moreton?"

"He is your husband," he said baldly.

Kassia was very still, her eyes wide and disbelieving on her father's face. "My husband," she repeated blankly.

"Aye." He pulled her tightly against him again and breathed in the sweet scent of her flesh. "Aye," he said again. "Let me explain what happened, my love. I was convinced that you were going to die. And I also knew that Belleterre would be lost to Geoffrey. I convinced

Graelam to wed you before you died. It would be he, then, who would have Belleterre, and not that bastard Geoffrey. He argued with me, Kassia, but I wore him down, with guilt. He finally agreed. The next morning he left with the marriage contracts to go to the Duke of Brittany. The duke approved the marriage, and Graelam, according to my wishes, returned to Cornwall. I did not write to tell him that you had lived. I saw no reason for it until you regained your strength."

Kassia was gazing at her father, utterly dazed. Married! She was married to a man she had never even seen! She heard herself say numbly, "But why did you not tell me, Father?"

Maurice shifted uncomfortably in his chair. "I did not want you to become upset, not when you continued so weak."

"But you are telling me now. What has happened?"

"The messenger who arrived today was from Lord Graelam, informing me that his master is to wed an English heiress."

"I see," Kassia said. She felt weak with shock. Married, she thought again, and to an English lord! She stared at her father, trying to understand.

"There is more, Kassia. The first messenger was sent by the Duke of Brittany. Evidently Geoffrey found out that you were still living at Belleterre, that you had not accompanied your husband to England. He has tried to convince the duke that your marriage was all a sham, a plot by me to keep you and Belleterre out of his hands. The duke demands an explanation. If the explanation pleases him not, he threatens to have the marriage annulled and wed you to Geoffrey."

"Is this English lord, this Graelam de Moreton, strong enough to protect Belleterre from Geoffrey?"

"Aye," Maurice said, eyeing his daughter carefully.

It was odd, Kassia thought, sifting through her father's words, but she felt the stronger of the two now. He looked ill with worry, and, she realized, he was dreading her anger at what he had done. Perhaps, she thought, she would have done the same thing were she her father. She loved her father more than anyone else in the world, more than herself. And she loved Belleterre. She thought of Geoffrey, sly, greedy Geoffrey, and felt a rippling of a shudder at the thought of him as her husband. She said, very firmly, "I understand, Father. I do not blame you for what you did. Do not distress yourself further."

She slid from his lap and forced a calm smile to her lips. "I must prepare myself, Father. I will return with this messenger to England, to my . . . husband. It would not do at all for him to take another wife."

Maurice gaped at her, wondering why she was not in tears, remembering her mother's tears, shed so quickly and with such devastating effect.

"I think also," Kassia continued thoughtfully, "that you should pay a visit to the Duke of Brittany. You could tell him, I suppose, that I fell ill and was unable to accompany my husband back to England. There is some truth to that! And, Father, you must not worry about me. I had to marry someone, and if you believe this Lord Graelam to be a fine man, then I am satisfied. I only wish he were French and lived near. I shall miss Belleterre."

"Cornwall is not so far away," Maurice said helplessly. He suddenly realized that he did not know Graelam all that well. He was a man's man, a brave warrior, strong and proud. How would he deal with a wife he had believed dead within hours of his marriage? Kassia was so innocent, so very young. He had protected her, guarded her, shown her only gentleness and kindness. My God, he thought, what had he done! He rose with sudden decision. "I will accompany you, Kassia, to Cornwall."

"Nay, Father. You must protect Belleterre from Geoffrey's grasping hands. 'Tis the Duke of Brittany you must see."

Maurice continued to argue, but Kassia knew that he had no choice in the matter. She knew she had no choice either. She felt tears sting her eyes, and resolutely blinked them back. She pictured this Lord Graelam and imagined him to be no different from her father. "Is he old?" she asked, dreading his answer.

"Graelam? Nay, daughter, he is young and well-formed."

"A kind man, Father? Gentle?"

"I trust so, Kassia."

She smiled. Young and well-formed and gentle, like her father. All would be well.

"Graelam gave you a ring upon your marriage. I have kept it safe for you."

"I suppose it would be wise to have it. I imagine that I look a bit different than I did on my wedding night."

Kassia left her father and hurried to her chamber, calling Etta. "Imagine," she said as she shook out a yellow wool gown, "I am married, and I didn't even know it! Etta, did you see this Lord Graelam?"

"Aye, my baby. He was most gentle when the priest said the vows. He held your hand through it all."

"And he is young and handsome?"

"Aye," Etta said. He was also formidable-looking, a huge man who could crush her gentle mistress like a fly. "Aye," she said again, "he is as your father described him." Likely, Etta thought, Lord Maurice was quite flattering in his description of his son-in-law. After all, Lord Maurice was a man, just as was the powerful English nobleman. And did he have any choice? "Now, my baby, I will send some servants to assist you. I must pack my own belongings."

Kassia smiled widely and threw her arms about her old nurse. "We shall conquer England again, Etta, just as did Duke William two hundred years ago!"

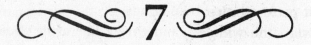

7

Joanna de Moreley held the hooded peregrine falcon gracefully on her wrist and eyed the wretched Blanche from beneath her lowered lashes. Miserable bitch! Her mare suddenly sidestepped and the falcon shrieked, digging his claws into her thick leather glove. Joanna would have liked to fling the falcon into the nearest pile of dung, but Lord Graelam was watching her. She smiled prettily, but jerked the mare's reins, hurting her tender mouth.

Graelam turned away, a frown gathering on his brow. Although the mare belonged to Joanna, it angered him that she would so mistreat the animal. He sighed, wishing he were miles away from Wolffeton, in the heat of battle, breaking heads with his ax, feeling sweat trickle down his face and back with exertion. Anything but playing the gallant to this ridiculous vain girl! She was not ill-looking, he admitted to himself, and he supposed that her arrogance, bred by an overly doting father and mother, he could control soon enough, once

she was his wife. Her hair was fair, so blond in fact that
when the sun shone down upon her head, it appeared
nearly white. He had always been partial to fair-haired
women, until now. Her best feature, now covered with
a wimple that appeared like stiff flapping wings, left
him little to admire. He had eyed her body carefully
and noted the wide hips, well-suited for childbearing,
and her abundant breasts. Perhaps, he thought doubt-
fully, her proud opinion of herself would turn to passion
once he had her in his bed.

He heard Blanche question Joanna in her soft-spoken
way, and winced at Joanna's patronizing tone when she
answered. It hadn't taken long for Graelam to realize he
would have no peace in his own castle until Blanche
was gone. Unfortunately, he had had two weeks to
compare the two women, and to his mind, Blanche,
already gentle and submissive, would make his life less
troublesome. At least Blanche was no budding shrew.
He hardened his jaw. If Joanna proved difficult, he
would beat her. The thought of her dowry had not
swayed him; indeed, the jewels he had brought back
from the Holy Land had provided him enough to finish
the work on Wolffeton, enough to buy sheep and more
cattle for his freehold farmers and two villages, and
finally enough to bring at least another dozen men-at-
arms into his service. No, it was the Duke of Cornwall
who had pressed him into this alliance. With Edward
still out of England, it would not be wise to anger the
king's uncle.

"My lord," he heard Joanna lisp in that affected way
of hers, "I grow overheated. My mother does not like
me to spend too much time in the sun."

Graelam grunted and turned his destrier back toward
Wolffeton. Damn the Duke of Cornwall anyway! He

had chosen to accompany Joanna's parents and their impressive retinue to Wolffeton for the wedding. The duke was no fool.

Joanna gazed ahead at Graelam's back. He was rather boorish, she thought—no honeyed compliments coming easily to his lips, unlike some of the young knights at the king's court—but he was handsome and strong. She would mold him to her liking once he was her husband. As for that witch Blanche, she would see her soon gone! She stared toward his castle, Wolffeton, and shuddered. It was a monstrosity, a graceless heap of gray stone in the middle of nowhere that boasted no comforts for a gently reared lady. Joanna smiled. Where her husband would be stupid and boorish, she would be witty and cunning. She would rule him as easily as she ruled her father. She would not suffer by spending her years immured in Wolffeton. Perhaps a few months of the year, but that was more than enough!

The smile on her lips began to hurt, but she did not know when or if Lord Graelam would swing about in his saddle to say something to her. Her eyes bored into his back. She had grown up with five brothers and she knew well what power a woman could wield with her body. She had seen Graelam once without his shirt and had felt a gentle tingling in her belly at the sight of his massive chest and arms, tanned by the harsh wind and sun. Her eyes had roved downward and she had shuddered slightly in anticipation. She was not a virgin, having lost that commodity some four years before in the eager arms of one of her father's knights. She doubted that Graelam would know the difference in any case, and if he suspected that her cries of pain were feigned, she would have a small vial of chicken blood ready to blotch her thighs.

Blanche rode beside Sir Guy, wishing she could grasp his knife and hurl it into Joanna's back. And he knew what was in her mind, damn his impudence! She realized quite clearly that her ploys during the past two weeks had failed miserably, even though her gentle manner had shown in clear opposition to Joanna's snideness, winning her approving looks from Graelam. It was clear to the meanest intelligence that Lord Graelam spent less and less time with his betrothed as the days went by. But it did not matter. There was but one recourse open to her now. She raised her chin, and her eyes gleamed with decision.

"Dare I ask what you are planning . . . now?" Sir Guy said, drawing his palfrey closer to her mare.

Blanche gave him a dazzling smile and quirked a beautifully arched brow at him. "For a . . . boy, you show great interest in things that do not concern you."

"And for an older woman," Guy said, unabashed, "you show too much interest in my lord. I tell you, Blanche, you have lost. Accept your defeat. Graelam will find you a husband." He felt himself frown slightly, disliking that thought.

"You are a fool," Blanche said, her smile never slipping.

"It is you who are the fool, my lady," Guy said, his voice gentling, for he knew well her distress. Why, he wondered, would she not accept the truth? "Lord Graelam is honorable. He has agreed to the marriage. He will not break his word."

Aye, Blanche thought. It was Graelam's honor that would play to her advantage.

I wish that stupid old man would keep his bony hands to himself, Blanche thought angrily as she eyed

Joanna's father, Lord Thomas, from beneath her low-ered lashes. She would have dearly liked to slap his hand away and tell him what an old fool he was, but she kept still, slewing her eyes toward the acrobats per-forming in the great hall. She found no amusement in them. She felt a knot form in her throat as she gazed at Graelam, and a renewal of her determination. At least, she thought, he did naught but drink wine and speak to the Duke of Cornwall, paying no attention to his be-trothed. Joanna's lips were drawn in a tight line, show-ing her displeasure at being ignored, and that made Blanche's mood somewhat better. Damn her, Blanche thought. She knows Graelam does not want her. She signaled to a serving wench to refill Graelam's goblet. She felt Lord Thomas' bony hand once again trail up her thigh and she shifted away from him. His wife, Lady Eleanor, seemed oblivious of her husband's vagar-ies, content to speak softly with Sir Guy and gaze about the great hall of Wolffeton with a satisfied and propri-etary eye.

Finally, Blanche thought, finally, she could excuse herself. She curtsied gracefully and left the hall. She heard Sir Guy laugh and tossed her head.

It seemed that she waited in the darkness of her small chamber for hours. She had begun to sweat and quickly rose from her bed to pat a damp cloth beneath her arms. She paused a moment and stared at herself in the polished silver mirror. Her body was lush and large-breasted, with full, rounded hips. There were faint lines from childbearing on her belly, but in the candlelight he would not see them. She began to hum softly to herself as she slipped a sheer silk shift over her head. She patted her soft hair into place and walked quietly to the door and opened it. All was quiet at last.

She carried the candle, protecting its thready flame with a cupped hand, and sped toward Graelam's chamber. She unlatched the door quietly and slipped inside. She paused a moment, then smiled at the sound of his snoring. He had drunk a lot of wine. He would likely not come to his senses until it was too late. And as Sir Guy had told her, Graelam was an honorable man. If he took an unmarried lady in his bed, he would also take her hand in marriage. Why, she wondered, had she not thought of it before? She stifled her guilt and her sudden apprehension, and raised her chin. I will not be a coward! I will do what I must!

She walked quietly to his huge bed and stared down at him a moment, the candle held high. He lay naked on top of the covers, for the night was warm. She was not immune to his male beauty and let her gaze rove the length of his body. Even in relaxed sleep, she could see the ridges of muscle that banded his belly. Lower, she saw a long jagged scar, running from the top of his thigh to near his groin, showing white through the black hair. His manhood lay soft and flaccid in the thick matting of hair and she felt the urge to touch him, to caress him, to bring him to life. She set the candle down on the small table beside his bed. Slowly, ever so quietly, she slipped the shift over her head. She prepared to crawl into bed beside him, when a sudden gust of wind came through the small window. The candle flickered and died. She cursed softly to herself, but quickly realized that the moonlight would be ample for her purposes.

She lay down beside him, pressing her body along his side. Slowly she leaned over him and ran her fingers lightly down his chest. He sighed in his sleep but did not awaken. Blanche sent her searching fingers lower until they curled around him. With gentle insistence she began to stroke and caress him.

"Nan," she heard him mutter, still half-asleep, "I told you that we would bed together no more. Leave off."

Her fingers tightened about his burgeoning member, and she smiled as he groaned. Suddenly his arms were around her, drawing her on top of him. She felt his mouth, hard and demanding, close over hers. She quickly parted her lips to his thrusting tongue. She felt his hands stroking down her back to her buttocks, kneading them fiercely, pressing her against his swollen manhood.

Soon, she thought triumphantly, soon she would cry out, but not until Graelam's seed had burst into her belly. She could not wait to see the look on the Duke of Cornwall's face!

"God's bones!" Graelam shook his head, clearing away the dregs of wine that clouded his mind. "Blanche!"

She had no time to say anything. His hand clamped over her mouth and he threw her onto her back, one massive leg thrown over hers. She knew a moment of fear; then she relaxed and smiled up at him.

"What the devil are you doing here?" he demanded harshly.

Blanche moved seductively against him, changing her plans abruptly. "I love you, my lord," she said almost in a whimper. "Do not marry that—"

Her interrupted her, appalled. "Shut up, woman! Have you no sense, no pride! Jesus, Blanche, I very nearly took you!"

"You may take me, my lord, if you will but marry me," she whispered, rubbing her breast against his arm.

Graelam cursed long and softly, surprising even Blanche with his coarse fluency. "I cannot marry you. I will not marry you," he managed finally. "For God's sake, woman, get out of here before someone discovers you!" As if he knew she would not obey him, Graelam rose off the bed, jerking her with him. He leaned down and picked up her shift. "Put it on," he said tersely. "And go quietly. I will tell no one, and neither will you."

"Do you not want me, my lord?" Blanche said rather desperately, thrusting her breasts out so that her nipples brushed his naked chest.

Graelam felt his outrage and his anger dissolve. Blanche was such a gentle creature and he saw tears glistening in her eyes. He said quietly, more calmly, "It is not meant to be, Blanche. I am sorry, but I am promised. You cannot be my mistress. You are a lady. 'Tis a husband only who can know you."

I would never be your mistress, she wanted to yell at him, but her body was still shuddering from her brief moment of pleasure. She felt tears of disappointment and despair streak down her cheeks.

Graelam pulled the flimsy shift over her head, for in truth, his body was reacting to hers and he had no intention of shaming either himself or her. "Come," he said softly, "you must return to your chamber. We will both forget this, Blanche."

She wanted to scream, to bring Joanna or her ferret-faced mother running, but she knew she could not. He would strangle her if she did, particularly since he was full-witted again. It wasn't fair, none of it. What would become of her now? What would become of her poor son? At least show a bit of pride, she scolded herself. She squared her shoulders.

Graelam watched her silently slip from his chamber. He walked back to his bed and threw himself down on his back, his arms pillowing his head. Jesus, he thought, women! But that wasn't fair. Blanche was so sweet and shy. He mustn't blame her overly for her actions. She only thought she loved him. He would find her a husband, and quickly. He remembered the feel of her body against him, the touch of her fingers caressing him. Her body was full and round, the way he liked his women. He realized with a start that if he had indeed taken her, the consequences could have been enough to make the bravest man shrivel. He thought idly that perhaps it would have been just as well, if he could have survived the pandemonium that would doubtless result. He would, he decided, prefer Blanche to wive, rather than Joanna. He flipped over onto his stomach and willed himself back to sleep. It was over and done with and his fate was decided.

Kassia felt dazed from weariness, but she forced herself to sit straight on Bluebell and gaze ahead at Wolffeton. It was a huge fortress, as solid and lasting as the rugged countryside surrounding it. When their vessel had arrived four days before on the southern coast of Cornwall, she had eyed the odd foliage and trees—palm trees, she had been told—and the calm, warm countryside, so different from Brittany. The closer they had drawn to Wolffeton, the more at home she had felt. It was unforgiving, demanding country, and if she were not so dreadfully weary, she would have delighted in every coarse-haired sheep and fat-bellied cow they had seen. They were riding close to the rocky cliffs and she could hear the battering rush of the waves against the rocks. Wolffeton, the home of Graelam de Moreton, her husband . . . now her home. She felt a surge of fear so strong she wavered in the saddle. She was in a foreign country, going to a man she had never seen before. It was lunacy, sheer lunacy. Her courage had left her slowly, seeping away just as her strength over the past week and a half. Now all she wanted to do was turn tail and hide.

"My lady!"

"Nay, nay," she managed, getting hold on herself. "I am fine, Stephen." She smiled at one of her father's oldest and most trusted retainers. "Just tired, that is all. It has been a long journey."

Too long for his slight mistress, Stephen thought, gazing at her with worried eyes. And what would her reception be like? His jaw hardened. No one would insult his young mistress, no one! His gloved hand dropped unconsciously to his sword.

He saw the uncertainty in her wide eyes, and the fear. She was only a young girl, he thought. How could Lord Maurice have allowed her to journey here without him? But of course, Stephen knew the answer to that. That whoreson Geoffrey!

"Rest a moment, my lady," he said to Kassia. "I will see that the men look fit to greet Lord Graelam."

Kassia nodded, nearly beyond words now. She gazed back toward the small litter and wondered what Etta was thinking now. She watched Stephen ride among their twenty-odd men, doubtless cursing some, praising others. Their journey had been thankfully uneventful. No brigands would dare to attack such a large force. But she was so tired; she wanted to do naught but fall from her saddle and sleep. But she could not. She could not shame her father or her men. Kassia forced her back to stiffen. She felt dirty and travel-worn. She was afraid to ask Stephen how she looked.

She waited patiently for Stephen to join her at the

head of their troop. She lightly tapped her heels into
Bluebell's fat sides and her mare broke into a rocking
canter.

They rode through the small fishing village of St.
Agnes, so like the villages along the coast of Brittany
that Kassia felt no ill-ease at the dour glances of the
villagers. The only difference, Kassia thought, smiling
to herself, was that at home the villagers would pull
their forelocks at her presence. The rutted road continued eastward from the village, up a winding incline
toward Wolffeton. Kassia became more impressed and
awed the closer they drew to the thick, massive outer
walls. No one, she thought, could take this castle. She
felt a moment of pride, then laughed at herself. This
great keep was not hers. She felt her blood curdle at
the thought that had not been far from the surface
during her journey. What if Lord Graelam de Moreton
had already married?

Stephen raised his arm for the men to halt. Kassia
watched him ride toward the man who was leaning
from one of the great towers. She did not hear their
conversation. The man disappeared and Stephen rode
back to her.

"The fellow thinks me mad," Stephen said, a half-
grin splitting his wide mouth. "I told him that his
master's bride was below."

Kassia gave him a dry smile. "Mad indeed," she said.
She turned back at the sound of the thick oak drawbridge being lowered. It came down over the dry ditch
with a heavy thud. She urged Bluebell forward, but
Stephen's hand came out to clutch at the reins.

"No, my lady, not yet."

They watched in silence as the iron portcullis was
slowly winched upward.

Stephen eyed her for a minute. "Remove your cloak from your head, my lady. No man would attack when a woman was present."

Kassia obligingly lowered the rabbit-lined hood from her dusty curls.

Stephen nodded slowly, but motioned her to ride behind him. They rode over the drawbridge, the horses' hooves pounding with a deafening roar on the thick wood planks. It was a warrior's keep, Kassia realized vaguely as they slowed their horses to a walk. The outer courtyard was not precisely filthy with its dry mud ground, it was simply that there was no sign of care. They continued through another, narrower arch into the inner bailey. There were at least fifty men, women, and children staring at them silently. Loudly squawking chickens strutted about and several cows mooed impatiently, doubtless wanting to be led to the grassy field outside the castle walls. A dog barked loudly at a black cat. There were several old outbuildings, for cooking, laundry, and storage, Kassia thought, and a new barracks sat next to a low thatched-roof stable. She became aware of the soldiers, standing stiffly all around them, eyeing them as possible enemies.

Kassia had no more opportunity to examine her surroundings. Her eyes went to a tall blond man, quite handsome, who stood on the lower steps of the keep, waiting for them to come to him. She felt a tired smile come to her lips. Her father had told her that Lord Graelam was comely. He was indeed. And he looked gentle and kind.

He came down the steps when they halted and she had a moment to admire his graceful carriage. He was younger than she had expected. He walked directly to her and raised his arms to help her down from Bluebell.

He stared at her for a long moment, as if trying to remember her, Kassia thought.

"Lady Kassia," he said, more a question than a statement.

"Aye, my lord." She saw he had deep blue eyes, kind eyes that laughed, she thought, and relaxed even further.

"You are something of a . . . surprise, my lady. We had believed you—"

"Dead? Nay, my lord, I survived." Kassia looked down at the chipped cobblestones beneath her feet. "I am pleased that you are not angry, my lord. But I could not allow you to wed, not when you had a wife who still lived."

"You mistake the matter, my lady."

Kassia raised huge eyes to his face.

"I am not your husband. I am Sir Guy de Blasis, one of Lord Graelam's knights. At your service, my lady."

Guy bowed to the slender young girl before him. It had not occurred to him that she would mistake him for Lord Graelam. But then again, she had never even seen his master.

Kassia swayed where she stood and Guy quickly caught her arm to steady her. "There is no reason for you to be afraid, my lady," Guy said gently. "Lord Graelam is within and he is not yet wed. Your timing, in fact, is exquisite. The wedding is tomorrow." As he spoke, the enormity of the situation broke over him. Poor Joanna! Poor Blanche! He wanted to laugh, but he saw the pain of utter weariness in Kassia's eyes, and gently cupped her elbow, pulling her forward. He spoke to one of Lord Graelam's men and motioned him toward Stephen.

"Your men will be taken care of, my lady. Now it is time for you to meet your husband."

Kassia felt the warmth of his hand through her cloak.

But still she felt cold, icy to her very bones. Pride, my girl, she wanted to shout. Her feet obeyed, yet each step upward was a terrible obstacle to overcome. She stepped into the massive hall. It was darker and cooler within, and for a moment she could see nothing for the dim light. She shook her head, allowing Guy to lead her toward the end of the hall. She saw a man seated in an ornately carved high-backed chair. Next to him, seated in a smaller chair, sat a young woman with blond hair so light that it looked nearly white. There were at least fifty men and women standing about, some richly garbed. She became aware suddenly that all the voices were dying away. Closer and closer they came to the man. She could see him clearly now. He was as dark as Guy was fair. He appeared huge, even seated, and his face looked stern and forbidding. Oh no, no! she thought frantically. Not this man!

"My lord," Guy said in a loud voice, "may I present your wife, Lady Kassia de . . . Moreton, to your guests."

The young woman seated beside Graelam let out a shriek and jumped to her feet. Lord Graelam merely gazed at her, his face telling her nothing.

There was a suddenly furious babble of voices, all of them raised, all of them outraged. Kassia was vaguely aware of an older man, richly garbed, stepping toward her.

It took a moment for Guy's words to sink in. Graelam looked at the slight girl, covered from throat to toe in a dusty cloak. He saw the short curls capping her small head. He ignored the strident, angry voices about him, ignored the cries from Joanna and the guttural moans from Joanna's mother, Lady Eleanor. Slowly he rose from his chair, his eyes never leaving her face. It was the short, curling chestnut hair that made him believe it was Kassia de Lorris, for he could not place this girl into the wraith's body he had seen at Belleterre.

Suddenly he could not help himself. He threw back his head and roared with laughter. Laughter at himself, laughter at the uproar this girl had caused, laughter at the sudden inevitable turn his life had taken.

Kassia gaped at the huge man whose whole body was convulsed with laughter. She felt the hostility and the blatant disbelief of the people around her.

"I carry your ring, my lord," she said in a loud, clear voice.

She slid it off her finger and thrust it out toward him.

Graelam stopped laughing. He stared down at his ring, banded with thick horsehair to keep it on her slender finger.

He heard Lord Thomas shrieking like an idiot woman, demanding to know the meaning of this outrage. He heard Joanna or perhaps Blanche, he couldn't tell which, yelling insults at the girl. Another woman, likely Joanna's mother, was wailing with piercing loudness.

"Graelam," the Duke of Cornwall said in a voice of awful calm, striding forward, "perhaps you will tell me the meaning of this? Who is this girl?"

Graelam ignored him. He stepped closer to Kassia and gently cupped her chin in his hand, drawing her face upward.

Kassia felt his dark eyes searching her face. She could not bring herself to look up at him. Why did he not say something?

"My lord," Joanna cried, "I will not allow you to have your whore here! How dare you!"

Blanche was laughing, her eyes alight with malicious joy on Joanna's contorted face. "Well, my *lady*," she said softly to Joanna, "it appears your wedding must be to another."

"You bitch," Joanna said furiously, turning on Blanche, "she is but a whore! She will be gone soon, and forever! My father will not allow her to remain!"

Kassia was not deaf. *A whore!* She turned angry eyes toward the women, but no words came to mind. Her husband still had said nothing. She felt herself again begin to tremble. What was going to happen to her? The light seemed to grow dimmer. The terrible women seemed to weave before her eyes.

"I . . . I am sorry," she gasped, her frantic eyes going to her husband's face. For the first time in her life, she welcomed the blessed darkness that was welling up within her, letting her escape from this nightmare. For the second time in her life, Kassia collapsed where she stood.

Kassia felt great weariness, but the blackness that had engulfed her was receding, forcing her back to consciousness. Slowly, fearfully, she opened her eyes. For many moments everything was a blur. Then she saw a man—her husband—beside her, his dark eyes expressionless on her face. She made a small gasping sound and tried to pull herself up. She felt covered with shame that she had fainted like a silly sheep in front of all those people.

"Nay," Graelam said, "lie still."

She obeyed, heeding more his tone than his words. His voice was gentle, unlike his roaring, mocking laughter.

"Where am I?" she asked, hating herself for her pitifully wavering voice.

"In my chamber, or rather I should say, our chamber. Are you still ill?"

His voice was still gentle and she managed to meet his eyes. She could read nothing. His face was impassive, giving her no clue.

"I am sorry. I am not given to fainting. The journey was long."

She felt his fingers lightly touch her arm and she tensed. He released her, a slight frown marring his forehead. "There is much we have to say to each other, my lady. Your arrival was . . . unexpected. But first, I will leave you to rest and regain your strength."

"I am sorry," Kassia said again. "There was no time to give you warning. Please do not blame my father. He sought only to protect me."

"Doubtless he did," Graelam said dryly. He picked up her hand and gently slid his ring back on her third finger. "Your nurse, Etta, is squawking loudly outside for her baby. Shall I bring her to you?"

Kassia's head throbbed, and she blinked rapidly to keep his face in focus. "What will you do?" she asked.

"That, my lady," Graelam said, standing to stare down at her, "will be most interesting to see. I but hope that you will not become a widow just as I believed myself a widower."

He turned with those words and strode across the chamber to the thick oak door. He did not look back at her.

Kassia was aware of Etta bending over her, gently soothing her brow with a damp cloth. "Rest, my baby," she heard her nurse croon softly, and she willingly obliged.

Graelam left his chamber thoughtfully. Lord, what an ungodly mess! Never, he thought, for as long as he breathed, would he forget his first sight of Kassia, standing beside Guy, holding herself so straight, fear dilating her huge eyes. Yet she had come, bravely. Nor would he ever forget the sight of her quietly crumbling, all life gone from her. Nor the feel of her slight body in his arms as he carried her to his chamber. His wife, he thought, shaking his head. A scrawny girl, no larger than a child, and now she was his responsibility. He gave another spurt of laughter. He had, after all, succumbed to Maurice's arguments, and done himself in! He pictured her face again, so quiet in repose, for he had studied her carefully before she had regained consciousness. He had wanted to feel anger, to rage at her, but when she had finally awakened and he saw the deep uncertainty in her eyes, he had felt compelled to treat her gently. He was a fool. What in God's name was he to do? He had ignored his gloating sister-in-law and the moaning Joanna, and carried Kassia out of the hall. He supposed, as he took the final step into the hall, that he would rather face an army of infidels than this group.

8

The thread of flame from a single candle broke the darkness. Kassia blinked, stared a moment into the flame, remembering quite clearly everything that had passed since her arrival at Wolffeton.

"How do you feel, my baby?"

Kassia smiled wanly at the sound of her old nurse's soft voice. "Alive, Etta," she said, "alive. Is it very late?"

"Nearly ten o'clock in the evening. You slept for six hours. I have food and mulled wine for you."

Kassia slowly pulled herself up and Etta quickly came to place pillows behind her head. "What I really want," she said, staring at her dirty fingernails, "is a bath."

"First you eat," Etta said firmly, "then I will have those lazy sluts bring you hot water."

"Lord Graelam," Kassia said, hearing the thin thread of nervousness in her voice, "where is he?"

To her surprise, Etta laughed. "Ah, your lord! What a man that one is!"

"What do you mean?"

"I will tell you while you eat. I kept the victuals warm over a small brazier. This great keep will vastly improve with you as mistress, my baby. The food is barely edible, and the servants do naught unless Lord Graelam is about."

"You are too stern, Etta," Kassia said, but the pork was clearly stringy and overcooked.

Etta regarded her young mistress with a worried eye. She had been raised in the midst of people who loved her and obeyed her because they loved her. But Wolffeton was vastly different from Belleterre. "Tell me now, Etta," she heard Kassia say. "What happened whilst I slept?"

Etta eased her bulky frame into the one chair in the large chamber. "Well, after I was certain that you were all right, my baby, I slipped into the hall below. I have never heard so many people arguing at once in all my life! And the screeching from Lord Graelam's betrothed!"

Kassia felt a surge of guilt, but it was tempered with the anger she had felt at the insults that lady had hurled at her. She sipped at the warm wine. "I hope her heart is not broken."

"Ha, that one! Lord Graelam should kiss your feet, for you saved him from a wretched existence. As to the other one, well, we shall have to see."

"What other one?"

"Lady Blanche, Lord Graelam's sister-in-law."

Kassia frowned, wondering if her wits had gone begging.

"Lord Graelam, I discovered from one of the servants, was married before, a long time ago. His wife's half-sister came to Wolffeton some three or four months ago to live. Why, I don't know." Etta shrugged. "She

did seem quiet enough and quite the lady during all the
shrieking and arguing. Eat the potatoes, my lady," Etta
added, her eyes upon Kassia's trencher.

The potatoes were half-cooked, Kassia found, but she
would not give Etta the pleasure of admitting it.

"Now, where was I? Aye, your husband is quite the
man. He had to roar for quiet but once, and all obeyed
him, even the Duke of Cornwall. Aye, you stare, my
baby. The king's own uncle! 'Twas he, according to
what I heard, who arranged the marriage with the
heiress. His face, I tell you, was a bright crimson! As
for Lord Thomas, Lady Joanna's father, he looked for all
the world like a boiled turnip. But Lord Graelam soon
put all of them to rout. Told them, he did, all that
happened at Belleterre. He even produced the marriage contract so there could be no doubts as to your
status as his lady wife. At that, Lady Joanna was forced
to close her mouth, but her mother kept wailing in the
most ridiculous way. Lord Thomas finally slapped her.
That shut the old harridan up, you may be certain! He
announced to the Duke of Cornwall that he would not
remain at Wolffeton another day. Then he took his wife
on one arm and his daughter on the other and marched
them out of the hall. I know Lord Graelam was smiling,
though he tried to hide it. Praise be to Saint Anne that
you'll nay have to see any of them again."

Kassia did not admit her overwhelming relief at Etta's
words. She still shuddered at the thought of standing
before them in her travel-stained clothes. It appeared
that her husband had protected her.

"Etta," Kassia said abruptly. "Where is Lord Graelam?
Is this not his chamber?"

"He is in the hall, speaking, I believe, to the Duke of
Cornwall. All the others have retired, thank the Lord!"

Kassia shoved the trencher off her lap. "My bath, Etta. I will not face him again looking like a dirty urchin. Nay, do not argue with me! I am not ill!"

Graelam sat in his ornately carved chair across from the Duke of Cornwall, a goblet of wine in his hand. The hall was quiet at last, with but the two of them.

"St. Peter's bones, Graelam, this has been a fine day!" the duke said acidly, his thick gray brows drawn ominously together.

"Aye, it has certainly been a day I shall not quickly forget."

"This girl, Kassia de Lorris—"

"Lady Kassia de Moreton," Graelam said quietly.

"Aye, 'tis true you only saw her once?"

Graelam nodded. He felt oddly exhilarated, as if he had just fought in a battle. "She was near death. I would not have recognized her save for my ring and her short hair. Her hair had been shorn, you see, from her fever."

"She is quite young, Graelam," the duke said thoughtfully. "Aye, quite young. You never bedded her."

Graelam arched a thick black brow. "Indeed, my lord."

"Then you can still be rescued from this mess," the duke said. "Annulment. The marriage was never consummated. 'Twill be an easy matter, and the girl will soon be on her way back to Brittany."

Graelam looked thoughtful, then said slowly, "Belleterre is an impressive holding, my lord duke. The keep is magnificent, the lands rich. Upon Lord Maurice de Lorris' death, it will come to me. If you will, the girl is as much an heiress as Joanna de Moreley."

"But she is French!"

Graelam merely cocked an incredulous brow at the duke.

"You will not have this travesty of a marriage annulled?"

Graelam stroked his fingers across his jaw. "I will speak to the Lady Kassia again tonight. Tomorrow, my lord duke, I will tell you my decision."

But the Duke of Cornwall was not finished. His incredulous fury had calmed, but he still felt the fool, a feeling he did not appreciate. "I do not know why you couldn't have told me of the damned girl," he growled, "and your ridiculous midnight marriage."

"As I said, my lord duke," Graelam said patiently, "I believed her dead. What reason was there to tell you?"

"I cannot believe you prefer her to Lady Joanna," the duke continued, ignoring Graelam's question. "She has not half Joanna's beauty. Indeed, she looked like a skinny boy, and a dirty one at that."

"She has been quite ill," Graelam said mildly. "Some food will fill her out and a bath will take care of the dirt."

The duke knew he was losing, and it galled him. Abruptly he said, "What if her illness rendered her barren? Ah, I see you had not thought of that!"

Graelam did not immediately reply. He was seeing Joanna's distorted features, hearing her venomous words. Even a barren wife would be preferable to that shrew. "Nay," he said finally, "I have not given that any thought as yet."

"You must," the duke snapped, rising from his chair. "Give it much thought, Graelam, before you make your decision. You told me yourself that your only reason for marrying was to breed sons."

"Aye," Graelam said. "That is what I told you."

Graelam saw the duke to his chamber, then drew up

suddenly outside his own. By God, he thought, his wife was within. His *wife*. He quietly opened the door and stepped inside. He blinked rapidly at the sight of Kassia in his wooden bathing tub. He could see naught but her thin white shoulders. Slowly he backed out and firmly closed the door. At least the girl didn't appear ill.

He returned after some fifteen minutes. "My lady," he said softly, not wishing to frighten her.

Kassia jumped, dropping her tortoise shell comb to the floor. She tried to rise, but Graelam waved her back into the chair. He glanced at her old nurse and curtly nodded toward the door. "I wish to speak to your mistress," he said.

The duke, Graelam thought, would perforce change his opinions if he were to see her now. She looked like a small impish child, with her great eyes staring at him, unblinking, and her short damp curls framing her pixie face.

"How old are you?"

Kassia stared at his abrupt, harsh tone. "Seventeen, my lord," she managed at last. He continued to regard her, and Kassia touched her fingertips to a thick curl that fell over her forehead. " 'Tis my hair." She raised her chin. "Father told me I must not be vain. My hair will grow, my lord."

He wanted to laugh aloud at her pitiful show of defiance. Instead, he only nodded and walked to the bed. He saw her wary look, but ignored it, and sat down. "I saw your nurse below during the discussions. I imagine she told you what happened?"

"Aye," she said, nodding.

Graelam saw her clutch her bedrobe across her breasts, her great eyes never leaving his face.

"Are you cold?"

"Nay, my lord," but she pulled the protecting cover over her legs.

"I am nearly twenty-nine, Kassia," Graelam said. "A great, venerable age to one so young."

"My father is forty-two," Kassia said. He saw the barest trace of a dimple near her mouth when she added, "'Tis Etta who is the venerable age, my lord. She is near to fifty."

Graelam was silent for a moment. "The Duke of Cornwall wishes to have this marriage annulled."

Kassia cocked her head to one side, and he saw her incomprehension. "I do not understand, my lord. My father told me that our priest wed us."

"Aye, but our marriage was not consummated." Still she gazed at him with those great innocent eyes.

"That means, Kassia, that I did not take you to my bed."

He watched a flush creep over her pale cheeks.

"It means that we are not truly man and wife until I do."

He saw her pink tongue trail over her lower lip and her eyes flew to his face in consternation.

"Are you a virgin?"

"No man has touched me, my lord."

He was tempted to smile at the display of defiant pride in her wavering voice. He had never doubted she was a virgin, yet he had purposefully embarrassed her. He was not certain why he had done it.

"Enough of that for the moment," he said. "Now, you will tell me why your father did not send me a message that you lived."

"My father loves me, my lord. He feared that such news, until I was completely well again, would harm me. I did not even know you existed—save for my dream . . ."

"What dream?"

A slight flush warmed her cheeks. "I told my father that I had dreamed that another man had been near me. A . . . a man with a gentle voice."

Graelam had been called many things in his life, but never gentle. "Continue," he said.

"It was nearly two weeks ago that he told me of your message. But that was not all, my lord. My cousin, Geoffrey de Lacy, had somehow discovered that I was still at Belleterre and had not accompanied my . . . husband to England. He evidently convinced the Duke of Brittany that our marriage was a sham. My father feared that the duke would set the marriage aside and wed me to Geoffrey."

Graelam heard the tremor of fear and distaste in her voice. "Aye," he said. "I know about Geoffrey."

Kassia sat forward, her voice earnest. "You must understand, my lord, it was never my father's intent to harm you in any way. He much admires you. There was simply no time when your messenger arrived. He wanted to accompany me, but of course it was not possible. Whilst I traveled here to Cornwall, my father went to see the duke."

"Geoffrey is dangerous, albeit a coward. He will not give in so easily."

"I know that, my lord. But my father told me you were a valiant warrior, that you would protect Belleterre if Geoffrey tried treachery."

"Do you wish to remain here at Wolffeton as my wife?"

"Why, of course," she said, her young voice strong and sure. She cocked her head at him. "If my father chose you for my husband, my lord, I would never gainsay his wishes. And," she added, clinching the matter, "Geoffrey must never have Belleterre."

Aye, he thought, the girl would follow the devil if her
father asked it of her. It disturbed him that she saw him
through the eyes of her father. "You have ridden through
my country, Kassia. It is not gentle, but savage and
rugged."

"It reminds me greatly of Brittany, my lord. 'Twas
the southern coast I found unlikely."

Graelam nodded and rose from his bed. "You will
rest and not leave this chamber. I am informed by my
betrothed's father that they will leave on the morrow."
He paused a moment, his eyes sweeping over her.
"And you will eat. You are still very thin; a strong wind
could blow you away."

She nodded. As he turned and strode away from her,
she felt a wave of guilt that she had taken his bedchamber. He opened the chest at the foot of the bed and
drew out a blanket. Without looking at her again, he
left the chamber. For the first time he was real to her,
the man who was her husband, the man who now
controlled her life and her destiny. She felt no fear, for
after all, her father had picked this man for her. She
slid down under the warm covers and quickly fell into
an exhausted sleep.

Graelam wrapped the blanket closer about him and
pressed his back against the stone wall. He had dismissed all the men and servants from the great hall to
ensure privacy for his conversation with the duke. But
now they were back, and he had had to step carefully
over the snoring men. The lord of Wolffeton, he thought
with a crooked smile, sleeping on the floor! And all for
the scrawny child who slept in his bed and was his wife.

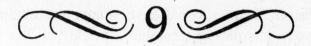

9

Graelam leaned against the northern stone tower and watched Thomas de Moreley's retinue disappear in whirls of dust over the rocky hill toward St. Agnes. He found, somewhat to his surprise, that Joanna's departure had lifted almost a physical weight from his spirit. She had eyed him glacially as she sat her palfrey in the inner bailey, her gloved hands clutching spasmodically at her riding whip.

"I bid you Godspeed, Joanna," he said calmly.

Joanna quivered with humiliation and rage; he could see it clearly in her face as she had spat at him, "And I wish you to hell, Lord Graelam, you and that skinny little slut you claim as your wife!"

Graelam shook away the image of Joanna, clapped Arnolf, the porter, on his stooped shoulder, and quickly made his way back to the great hall. It was early and he found he was ravenous. He bellowed for food.

"A blessed escape," Guy said blandly as he seated himself across from Graelam at the trestle table.

Graelam swallowed the crunchy heel of bread and downed the remainder of his ale. "Perhaps," he said, wiping the back of his hand across his mouth. "One woman is much the same as another," he added on a shrug, disregarding the relief he had felt upon her departure. "Joanna would have suited me, eventually. Her body was pleasant enough. Should you like me to talk to the Duke of Cornwall for you, Guy? Mayhap you would make Lady Joanna a suitable husband."

"I would take to my heels," Guy retorted, laughing. "You speak of a wife like one of your destriers, my lord. Surely a woman is not an animal to be broken."

"Mastered, Guy."

Guy said quietly, "What if the lady is already as gentle as a soft summer rain?"

"Without guile you mean? I have known but one woman who was as true as a man, and she, Guy, was about as gentle as a viper!"

"Ah, Lady Chandra de Vernon."

"Aye, a prince among women."

"Your . . . wife, my lord," Guy said suddenly, his eyes gazing beyond Graelam's left shoulder. He rose quickly. "I bid you good morning, my lady."

Graelam swiveled about to see Kassia standing at the foot of the stairs. In truth, he had forgotten about her. She was looking toward him hesitantly.

"Come," he called to her. "We will start fattening you up this instant."

He could not be certain, but at his hearty words, he thought a blush stained her pale cheeks. She is graceful, he thought, watching her walk toward him. She was wearing a gown of soft blue wool, belted at her narrow waist. Her short chestnut curls glistened in the morning light and for a moment he wondered how soft they would feel in his hands. He frowned at the thought, for as she drew closer, he saw that she appeared very fragile, her delicate bones too prominent. He felt an unwanted surge of guilt, for he saw her suddenly as she was at Belleterre.

Kassia saw her husband's frown and her steps slowed. She saw a sympathetic smile curl up the corners of Sir Guy's comely lips, then, unwillingly, she turned her eyes back to her husband's harsh countenance.

"My lord," she said shyly, and proffered him a deep curtsy.

"You are well, my lady?" Graelam asked, his eyes on the curls that caressed her small ears.

"Aye, my lord, quite well." She nodded to Sir Guy and to the dozen men-at-arms who sat at another trestle table, staring at her with open curiosity. She did not see Stephen or any of her father's men.

"Stephen, my lord?"

"He has already broken his fast, my lady," Sir Guy said, "and is seeing to the supplies for his return to Brittany."

"He . . . he plans to leave soon?" She turned wide, questioning eyes upon her husband.

"I will tell him when he is to leave," Graelam said. He rose and it took all of Kassia's resolution not to cower. Which was foolish, she scolded herself silently. He had been naught but kind to her, but he was so large, so forbidding, her skittering thoughts continued. "You will eat now, Kassia," he said to her. "I must see to the Duke of Cornwall. He also wishes to depart today. Guy, take the men to the training field. With all the festivities, they have grown fat and lazy."

He strode out of the hall without a backward glance, leaving her to the mercy of utter strangers. Guy did not want to leave the shy girl, but he had no choice. He motioned to the men, smiled once again at Kassia, and left the hall.

Kassia slipped into the smaller chair next to her husband's. She glanced at the crusts of bread and the pale unripened cheese and shuddered.

" 'Tis not suited to ye, my lady?"

Kassia tensed at the barely veiled insolence in the serving girl's voice. For a moment she was totally bereft of speech. The girl was young, as young as she, and quite pretty, as rounded and plump as Kassia was thin. And, Kassia thought on a silent sigh, her hair was thick and long, flowing down her back.

"What is your name?" she asked quietly.

"Nan, my lady."

Kassia suddenly remembered a serving wench who had remained but three days at Belleterre. She had insulted Kassia, thinking the twelve-year-old girl too young to retaliate. Kassia now smiled at the memory. "Nan," she said, "I would like a glass of fresh milk and three slices of freshly baked bread. As for this cheese, you may eat it yourself, or feed it to the pigs."

Nan stared at the little upstart. She was smiling sweetly, but there had been a tone of command in her voice that made Nan start.

"There are cows to be milked, are there not?"

"Aye," Nan said, her eyes narrowing. "But there's no more bread, not until this afternoon."

"Fetch me the milk and I will see to the baking of bread myself." Kassia nodded dismissal to the girl, praying silently to herself that she would obey her. To her relief, the girl, after shooting her a venomous look, flounced away. Kassia forced herself to eat the cold bread left by her husband. She was aware of at least a dozen servants skulking about the hall, all wanting a glimpse of her, she supposed. Her housekeeper's eyes took in the reeds scattered haphazardly over the stone floor. They were not filthy, at least they didn't offend her nose, and that was probably because of the wedding guests at Wolffeton. But they were dull, and there were no sweet-smelling herbs. She ran her hand over the table. It was badly gouged, old and battered, and this was the master's table! She shook her head, shocked at the lack of care. The wood beams overhead were black with years of smoke and soot, making the hall even darker than necessary, and there was a feeling of damp and cold. Two old-fashioned lavers stood near her table. They had seen no polish in years, she thought. She wanted to set the servants to work immediately, but it was her husband's face that stilled her tongue. He was the master here. Until he gave her permission to attend to his keep, she would be wise to keep her mouth shut. She closed her eyes a moment, wondering if her husband would indeed keep her. Annulment. He could set her aside, he had told her that himself, unless the marriage was consummated. She could not prevent the shudder at the thought. She was ignorant, but not stupid or blind. She had seen animals mate and knew that somehow men did much the same thing to women. But she had never seen a naked man, and thus was uncertain just how they accomplished the sex act. If mares could tolerate it, she thought, so could she. And, she realized, she must tolerate it to save Belleterre from Geoffrey. She became aware of the serving wench, Nan, standing at her elbow, and she flushed, wondering if the girl could see the terrifying thoughts in her eyes.

"Yer milk, my lady," Nan said. She set the goblet in

front of Kassia, none too gently, and some of the warm milk sloshed onto the table.

Kassia felt a spurt of raw anger, and she wanted to slap the insolent girl, or, she thought, personally plunge her smirking face into a pile of dung. There was probably a lot of that around! She was saved from a decision by the appearance of her husband, accompanied by an older, fierce-looking man, the Duke of Cornwall, she supposed. She turned to dismiss Nan, when she saw the girl's eyes resting possessively and intimately upon Lord Graelam. Ah, she thought with no particular emotion, so that was why the girl was surly and insolent. She smiled and rose, curtsying deeply to the older man.

Graelam said calmly, "My lord duke, this is Lady Kassia, my wife."

The Duke of Cornwall felt a tug of surprise. The slight little creature standing so resolutely before him, her large eyes fastened upon his face, bore little resemblance to the dirty urchin who had so insolently forced her way into the hall the day before. She was a lovely girl, and had an air of great sweetness about her. And uncertainty.

He felt a tug of protectiveness that surprised him. He was too old to be such a fool. But nonetheless he said in a very gentle voice, "Lord Graelam is blessed in his bride, my lady. Allow me to welcome you to England."

"Thank you, my lord duke," Kassia said. "Even in Brittany, your name is much revered. My father used to tell me that you should have been the King of England, for you are brave and decisive, and fair to all your people."

The duke laughed. "It is God who decides these matters, my lady," but nonetheless, Graelam saw him preening at her praise. He wasn't certain whether to be annoyed at her flattery or pleased.

"My father also says that our own king, the sainted Louis, was too much in God's service. That God should have released him to rule his people."

"And what do you believe, my lady?"

"I, my lord duke? It is my belief that there is quite enough misery and injustice at home to keep the most sainted of men well-occupied."

"Well, my lord," the duke said to Graelam. "Perhaps it is your wife who can convince Edward to return to take his throne. I will remember your words, my lady, when next I write my nephew."

Kassia flushed at his kind words, and said quickly, "There is but bread and cheese to offer you, and fresh milk."

Graelam frowned. It was a miserable offering to the king's uncle! "Nan," he roared. "Bring food for the duke!"

"Fresh milk," the duke mused aloud. "It has been a long time, my lady. Yea, a very long time."

"It is very beneficial to your health, I am told, my lord duke. Please, will you not be seated?"

Graelam eyed his wife. She was acting every bit the lady of the castle, and for some reason, that angered him. Perhaps her pleasing hesitancy before him was all an act. Perhaps she was just as much the shrew as Joanna.

"I will see to your milk, my lord," he said to the duke. "This glass is for my wife." He thought perversely that she was more in need of it than the duke.

Kassia looked quickly up at her husband. He was kind, she thought, and she had no reason to fear him.

He could not, after all, help his harsh looks and huge body.

The Duke of Cornwall chuckled at Graelam's retreating back and obligingly settled his old bones into Graelam's chair. "Tell me of Brittany, my lady," he said, drinking the milk she handed him.

"It reminds me much of Cornwall, my lord," she said, sitting on the edge of a bench, all the world like a precocious child eager to please. "Perhaps a bit colder." She shivered, her eyes upon the damp stone walls of the hall.

"Wolffeton has long been without a mistress, my lady," the duke said kindly. "Lord Graelam is a warrior and thus pays heed only to his fortifications. And his sojourn in the Holy Land left Wolffeton in my nominal care. The serfs have grown lazy, I fear."

"I know nothing of fortifications, my lord," Kassia said firmly, "but I will endeavor to make Wolffeton more pleasing for you on your next visit."

The duke shifted slightly in his chair. He had thought Kassia a pleasing child, but without spine. Now he saw differently and he felt a surge of concern for her. Graelam was no gentle man to be ruled by a woman.

The duke's silence made Kassia shiver with dread. "Has my husband . . . accepted me, my lord duke?" she asked quietly, unaware that her fingers were clutching the wool of her gown.

The duke frowned. "So he spoke to you of an annulment," he said.

Kassia nodded. "Aye, last evening." She raised her head and gazed at the duke directly, her eyes proud and intense. "He must accept me, my lord duke. My father chose him to be my husband and the protector of

Belleterre. Perhaps he prefers the Lady Joanna, but I will bring him wealth and much valuable land."

"Aye, he told me as much." The duke set down the empty goblet and hunched forward in Graelam's chair, his bony fingers tapping together. "My lady," he began, "your husband is a powerful man. The alliance with the de Moreleys would have added to his power and his wealth. He is a close friend of my nephew, the King of England. You offer him land, 'tis true, but to hold it, he will have to fight, undoubtedly. And that, my lady, requires fighting men."

"You are telling me, my lord duke, that my father asked too much of Lord Graelam?"

The duke chuckled. "Nay, dear child, Graelam is not a man to be led by the nose. He is more comfortable bashing heads than sitting in his castle. He is a man bred to war. 'Tis just that I would prefer he fight in England, if need be, or in the service of the king. I tell you this so you may understand. A marriage is an alliance between two houses, each bringing value to the other. You have brought Lord Graelam value, but to keep it, he will tempt his unscrupulous neighbors to take advantage of his absence."

"You believe," Kassia said slowly, "that I should allow my marriage to be annulled?"

"Nay, child. You are being too fair. You cannot protect both your father's interests and Lord Graelam's. I suspect that your loyalties still lie with your father. After all, you do not know your husband. Allow Lord Graelam to decide, and do not interfere." The duke sat back a moment, watching Kassia think about what he had said. She is intelligent, he thought, not particularly discomfited by his observation, even though she was but a woman.

"I believe," Kassia said finally, "that Lord Graelam has already decided. He presented me to you as his wife."

"Aye, he has decided, my lady. But your problems are not yet solved. There is still Charles de Marcey, the Duke of Brittany, to placate. This cousin of yours appears to have some part of the duke's ear. You must bear a son within the year, my lady, else Charles may still believe your cousin's charges that this marriage is a sham."

A child! Kassia gulped, her hands moving unconsciously to her belly.

"Ah, Graelam, I was just giving your bride an old man's advice."

Graelam set another goblet of milk before Kassia. He cocked a black brow at the duke, saying nothing.

"It would perhaps be worth your trouble to take Kassia for a visit to Belleterre and to the Duke of Brittany when she is carrying your child. Her swollen belly would do much to still her cousin, I believe."

Graelam slanted a look toward Kassia at the duke's blunt words. She was sipping her milk, her eyes downcast. "You are right," he said calmly. "But first my lady must regain her health and her strength."

"I am strong and healthy now, my lord," Kassia said, her chin thrusting upward.

The Duke of Cornwall threw back his head and laughed heartily. Graelam saw Kassia's face drain of color. He grinned, knowing she had not realized the import of her words. "It is wise, is it not, Kassia," he said, "to think carefully before you speak?"

He was teasing her, Graelam thought, somewhat surprised at himself. Rarely had he jested with a woman. He turned to the duke and assisted him out of his chair.

"I will take my leave of you, Graelam," the duke said. "I have but one word of advice to you, my lord," he added, his eyes resting for a moment on Kassia. "Wolffeton now has a mistress—"

Aye, Kassia thought, likely several mistresses, given the look on the serving wench's face.

"—a lady to add comfort to your keep." The duke paused, seeing Graelam frown. It was true, he thought, he was meddling. It was none of his affair. "Aye," he said, "a lovely mistress. Perhaps I will see you both in London," he added, "if I can but convince my nephew to return to England. I plan myself to oversee his coronation."

"Edward loves splendor and ceremony," Graelam said. "Make your letters to him reek of this and perhaps you'll seduce him home."

"Aye, mayhap I will." The duke rubbed his hands together. "Mayhap I will hint to him of rebellion. Edward is like you, Graelam. He prefers nothing more than fighting. I must take my leave. My lady, I came to Wolffeton expecting to be bored with ceremony. You provided a charming diversion."

10

Kassia carefully held up her skirts, not wanting to dirty them in the muck from the rain that had fallen earlier in the afternoon. It was disgraceful, she thought, filth so close to the cooking outbuilding. Her husband obviously had no interest in the place where his meals were prepared, but Kassia kept her thoughts to herself, for the moment.

"You are not overtiring yourself?"

"Oh no, my lord," Kassia said quickly. "Your keep is surely vast, but I wish to see all of it."

"Even the armorer's?"

There was a touch of amusement in his deep voice, and Kassia, emboldened by it, smiled impishly up at him. "Aye," she said, "even the armorer's. Perhaps I can give him some suggestions to improve your gear."

They toured the falconery after the armory, and Graelam, seeing Kassia's excitement, gave her a peregrine falcon for a gift.

"He is mine?" she asked, gazing at the beautiful bird, who was in turn regarding her with an unblinking stare.

"Aye, he is yours."

"Oh, thank you, my lord!" Without thought, Kassia clasped his arms in her delight at his generosity.

"Do you hunt?" he asked, smiling down at her.

She nodded happily and turned quickly away from him to croon soft words to her falcon. "What is he called, my lord?"

"Strangely enough, his name is Hawk."

Her tinkling laughter rang out. "Ah, you are much too noble to carry such an insulting name," she said to her falcon.

"When you are stronger, we will hunt," Graelam said. "Hawk can bring down a heron without breaking his speed."

Kassia wanted to tell him that she was strong as a mule, but indeed she was tiring. The long journey had weakened her. That, and coming face to face with a man who was her husband, and a stranger.

"I thank you, my lord," she said. "You are very kind."

Her voice rang with sincerity and Graelam felt inordinately uncomfortable for a moment. "Your father, my lady," he said harshly, "was perhaps overly generous in his view of me."

"My father," Kassia said firmly, "is never wrong about a person's character."

"Thus I am kind because Maurice tells you so?"

"Aye, and of course, you did give me Hawk."

"I did, did I not?" Graelam said. "Come, Kassia, it is beginning to rain again. I do not wish you to become ill."

Graelam strode toward the keep, Kassia hiking up her skirts to keep up with him. He turned at a sharp

cry and saw her stumble on a slick cobblestone. He
caught her easily and lifted her in his arms.

"I am clumsy," she said in a breathless voice.

"And you weigh no more than a child."

Kassia turned her body against him and he felt her
soft breasts against his chest. His body reacted immediately. She was his wife and he could take her now, if he
wished. His breathing quickened.

Unaware of his thoughts, Kassia laughed softly. "When
I was recovering from the fever, my father was forever
pouring his Aquitaine wine down me. I feared I would
become a drunkard with a red nose. I promise that I
will be plump as a spring goose before long, my lord."

He did not reply and Kassia smiled contentedly. He
was kind and strong and he appeared to at least like
her. She felt his arm tighten beneath her thighs and
sudden rosy color washed over her cheeks. She ducked
her head down against his shoulder. They had entered
the hall, yet her husband still held her close.

"Good afternoon, my lord."

Graelam's hold on her eased and he let her down.
"Blanche," he said. "Have you yet met Kassia?"

"I bid you welcome," Blanche said sweetly. She stared
at the girl standing so close to Graelam. She looked for
the world like a boy with her tumbled curls, and skinny.
Blanche smiled. She knew Graelam preferred women
with more ample proportions. He could not be pleased
with this sorry excuse for a wife. During the long preceding night and the equally long day she had finally
accepted the fact that she would never be mistress of
Wolffeton, and Graelam's wife. It was, she supposed,
her fervent dislike of Joanna that had kept her from
seeing the futility of her wishes, that and the growing
dislike she saw Graelam evince toward his betrothed.

But Joanna was gone and Kassia was here, already wed to Graelam. But what of my son? she wondered.

Her smile didn't reach her eyes, but Kassia, still flushed at her reaction to her husband's arms, did not notice. "Thank you," she said quietly.

"I am Lord Graelam's sister-in-law," Blanche said. "Blanche de Cormont. Would you like a cup of ale, my lord?"

"Aye, Blanche," Graelam said. He looked down for a moment at Kassia. "And a cup of wine for Kassia."

Kassia watched Blanche give instructions to one of the serving wenches. The girl appeared sullen, her eyes darting toward Kassia before she took herself off.

Blanche walked gracefully to Graelam's chair and carefully pulled it away from the trestle table.

"I understand," she said to Kassia, "that you have been quite ill."

Kassia nodded, pleased that Graelam motioned for her to sit beside him. "Aye," she said. "But I am well now."

"Perhaps not entirely, yet," Graelam said.

Blanche took the goblet of ale from the serving girl and handed it herself to Graelam. She nodded to the girl to give the wine to Kassia.

"You still look rather pale and . . . thin," she said, sitting herself near to Graelam. "Perhaps, my lord," she continued in a soft voice, "you wish me to continue in my present duties until she is stronger?" *Why am I doing this to myself when there is no hope?*

Kassia stiffened. She shot a look toward her husband, waiting for him to tell his sister-in-law that she needn't bother. To her chagrin, Graelam smiled warmly at Blanche. "Aye, thank you, Blanche." He downed his ale, wiped his hand across his mouth, and asked, "Where is Guy?"

"I do not know," Blanche said, her lips thinning. How he must be laughing at her now!

Graelam rose from his chair. "Kassia," he said, "I must meet with my steward, Blount. Why do you not rest for a couple of hours?"

Kassia didn't know what to say. She was too uncertain of her husband to tell him plainly that she wished to direct the servants, but without his permission, she could accomplish nothing. She knew Blanche was watching her. She nodded, saying nothing, and watched her husband stride from the hall.

"We have the evening meal in two hours," Blanche said. "Would you like me to have one of the serving wenches show you to your chamber?"

Perhaps she is his mistress, Kassia thought, and thus her power with him. But no, that made no sense. Lord Graelam would not take his own sister-in-law, and a lady, to his bed. She looked about the hall, seeing at least a dozen servants watching them. Did they expect her and Blanche to pull each other's hair out?

"Not as yet," Kassia said.

"You are scarce more than a girl," Blanche continued after a moment. "Your marriage to Lord Graelam came as a shock to everyone. I shall try to shield you from the . . . unkindness of the servants and Lord Graelam's men."

For a long moment Kassia gave Blanche a puzzled stare. "Why should anyone be unkind to me, Blanche? I do not understand your concern."

"Wolffeton is a very large keep. There are many servants to direct. I doubt that you have the experience to make them do your bidding."

Kassia laughed warmly. "My home in Brittany— Belleterre—is as vast as Wolffeton. My mother died when I was quite young and I have kept my father's castle for a number of years. Indeed, I read and write and keep accounts. My husband did not ally himself to an orphan waif, Blanche." She was tempted to ask what experience Blanche had had, for the keep did not show a woman's caring attention.

"I am pleased," Blanche said. She dropped her eyes to her lap to cover her sharp disappointment and frustration.

"My lord Graelam," Kassia said after a moment, "did he care mightily for Lady Joanna?"

"Lady Joanna is very beautiful," Blanche said honestly. "Her hair is long, to her hips, and nearly silver, it is so light. Aye, he has—had—very strong feelings for her."

Kassia unconsciously touched her fingers to her own short curls. "I see," she said, feeling suddenly miserable.

"Lady Joanna also has . . . strong passions," Blanche continued. "In that, she was well-suited to Lord Graelam. He is a very demanding man, so I have heard. I hear the serving wenches gossip—only the comely ones, of course. He is evidently so large a man that he has hurt some of them. And, of course, he never tires."

Blanche saw that Kassia was staring at her, uncomprehending. So it was true, just as she had heard. Graelam had not taken his young wife as yet. The thought of Graelam coupling with Kassia made her continue. "You are very small," she said in a pitying voice, leaning close to Kassia. "I hope that you will be brave enough to bear the pain."

"My lord is kind," Kassia said.

Blanche heard the uncertainty and fear in her voice.

Graelam deserved a shrinking wife in his bed, damn
him. "Of course," she said lightly, and rose. "Now that
he is wed," she added gently, "perhaps his other women
will be relieved of their duties, for a while at least." She
knew she was being cruel, utterly mean, in fact, but
she stifled her guilt at her lie, for her own disappointment was too fresh to bear in silent submission. She left
Kassia, now parchment pale at her words, sitting rigidly
in her chair, her hands twisting in her lap. At the very
least, Graelam would regret not taking Blanche to his
bed when she had offered herself to him. Perhaps, she
thought, his innocent little wife would quickly come to
despise him. It would be her revenge. She had nothing
else, at least for the moment.

Graelam frowned toward Kassia's bent head. She was
pushing her food about on her trencher, paying no
attention to her food, to him, or to anything else in the
noisy hall.

"Why are you not eating?" he asked. "Are you feeling
ill?"

Kassia looked at his huge hand lying lightly on her
arm. He had introduced her formally as Lady Kassia de
Moreton to all his men-at-arms, and all the servants.
His wife. His possession. He would hurt her. She forced
herself to look at him. She saw concern in his dark
eyes, and blinked. Blanche had to be wrong. He was
kind. He would not harm her.

"I . . . I am a bit tired, my lord, that is all."

"You may retire in a few minutes. I will join you
later."

No! Her tongue touched her lower lips in her
nervousness.

It was an unconsciously sensuous gesture and Graelam

turned quickly away from her. He called out to Rolfe, his master-at-arms, "What have you heard of de Fortenberry? Has he kept to his own lands?"

"Aye, my lord," Rolfe shouted back, above the din of voices. "The man is many things, but he is no fool. He knows you would burn his keep down about his ears if he dared to attack any of our demesne farms."

"I have heard," Guy said, "that Dienwald de Fortenberry buried his wife some months ago. Perhaps he would be interested in the Duke of Cornwall's assistance in finding him another."

Graelam merely grinned and said, "I wish another twelve or so men, Rolfe. Many men lost their masters in the Holy Land and have become no more than vagabonds."

Kassia listened to their talk. She wished she could ask Graelam to direct some of his wealth toward the keep. She became aware that Blount, the steward, a cadaverous man of middle years who was once, she had heard, a priest, was speaking to her and turned politely to attend him.

Blanche slipped from the hall and made her way to her chamber. So de Fortenberry had no wife, she thought, hope beginning to stir through her. Nor did Graelam, not really, not yet. Despite what she had told Kassia, she doubted Graelam would take his young wife until he believed her strong again. She sat on her narrow bed picturing Kassia's pale face at her words. If he were tempted, perhaps the girl's fear would stop him, at least for a while. Unwanted tears spilled onto her cheeks. I am a wretched witch, she thought, yet I cannot seem to help myself.

Kassia's fear had quieted. Her husband was still below in the hall discussing various matters with his men.

He had gently patted her hand when she had excused herself, but he had appeared distracted. Surely he would not harm her. She tightened the sash of her bedrobe more tightly about her waist and snuggled down under the covers. She was nearly asleep when she heard the bedchamber door open. She sat up, drawing the blanket to her chin. Graelam entered, holding a candle in his hand. His dark eyes locked on hers from across the room.

"I had hoped you would be asleep," he said.

She wanted to ask him where he was going to sleep, but the words lay leaden in her mouth. She said only, "Nay."

"Do you miss Belleterre and your father?"

She nodded, praying he would not see her nervousness.

He set the candle down atop a chess table and began to take off his clothes. He had stripped to the waist when he heard her gasp. He turned to see her staring at him.

"Did you never attend your father or his guests in their bath?" he asked gently.

She shook her head.

"You have never seen a naked man?"

A chestnut curl fell over her forehead as she again shook her head.

Graelam was silent for a moment, watching her. He knew fear when he saw it. An unwonted stirring of pity went through him. He slowly walked to the bed and sat down beside her. He could feel her tensing, though she did not move away from him.

"Listen to me, Kassia," he said quietly. "You are young and innocent. Your husband is a stranger, and you are living amongst strangers. You have also been very ill." He paused. "Must you stare at my chest?"

Her eyes flew upward to his face. "I am sorry, my lord," she whispered.

He felt a surge of impatience at her for acting like a whipped puppy. "You have nothing to be sorry about," he said harshly. "I fully intend to sleep in my own bed, with you. I will not take you. But you will become used to me. When you are well again and have added flesh, you will become my wife."

He rose and pulled off the rest of his clothes. "Look at me, Kassia," he said.

Kassia raised her eyes. He was standing by the bed, sublimely indifferent in his nakedness. He felt her eyes roving over his body, and despite himself, his member swelled. He quickly eased into bed beside her. He heard her erratic breathing.

"The scar, my lord," she said hesitantly.

"Which one?"

"The one on your leg that goes to your—"

"My groin?"

"Aye. How did you get it?"

"In a tournament in France, some ten years ago. I was careless and my opponent was quick to take advantage of it."

"And the scar on your shoulder?"

He was silent for many moments. "That," he said slowly, "was a gift from a lady."

"I do not understand."

"'Tis a very long story. Perhaps someday I will tell you about it. Now go to sleep, Kassia. Tomorrow, if you are feeling strong, we will go riding."

"Yes, my lord."

But she did not close her eyes until she heard his deep even breathing. She pictured his body, so different from hers, and felt her face grow hot. She had been taught modesty. Evidently men were not. Blanche was right, she thought, huddling near the edge of the bed, her knees drawn to her chest. He would hurt her. She tried to imagine him covering her as a stallion would a mare, and penetrating her body. She quivered with dread. How would she bear the pain?

11

Graelam turned in his saddle at the sound of Kassia's bright laughter. A sea gull was swooping down, nearly touching her shoulder, and she tossed another bit of bread high into the air. The gull squawked loudly, and dived to catch it.

She guided Bluebell forward to escape the half-dozen gulls now gathering behind her, and reined in beside him, her eyes crinkling with pleasure.

Graelam gazed at her, remembering again how she had looked early that morning, her legs drawn to her chest, her pillow hugged in her arms. He had reached out his hand and gently touched the soft curl over her temple. A sudden fierce protectiveness had flooded him and he had quickly drawn back his hand, angry at himself for his weakness. His abruptness with her when she had come into the great hall to break her fast had made her draw back and gaze at him uncertainly. He had left the hall quickly, aware of the silent condemnation from Drake, his master armorer, and Blount, his steward.

Damn them for not minding their own business, he thought now, but he smiled back at her, unable to help himself.

"Oh! Look, my lord!"

He followed Kassia's pointing finger to the sea lion who was diving in the waves. They had ridden to the southern boundaries of Graelam's land, then turned downward along the coastline.

"Would you care to rest awhile?" he asked her.

She nodded happily, still watching the sea lion.

He swung off Demon and tied him to a wind-bowed cedar, then clasped his hands around Kassia's waist and lifted her down.

She walked quickly to the edge of the cliff while he secured Bluebell's reins. It was a bright, windy day and Kassia lifted her face to the sun, feeling it warm her. She turned to see Graelam unfasten his cloak and spread it on the ground.

She sat down as would a child, her legs crossed in front of her. Graelam joined her, stretching out on his back, resting on his elbows.

"The man who was hurt this morning," she said. "Is he all right now?"

"Aye," Graelam said shortly, disliking to be reminded of his own stupidity. He had pushed his men too hard after he had left the hall, until one of them, careless from fatigue, had been hurt.

Kassia lowered her eyes to the rocky cliff edge but a few feet away. "I . . . I am sorry if I offended you, my lord."

"You did not offend me," he said roughly. "I had much on my mind this morning." It was a half-truth and as much of an apology Graelam had ever offered to a woman. After a moment he asked abruptly, "Do you believe Geoffrey was responsible for your brother's death?"

Her eyes clouded for a moment, in painful memory. "If he was," she said slowly, "it would mean that he is evil. I remember the day very clearly. My brother, Geoffrey, and I had a small boat and we would take turns rowing it to the mouth of the cove and fishing. On that day, Geoffrey and Jean ran ahead. My father and I were nearly to the cove when we heard Jean scream. Geoffrey was standing at the edge of the water, and he started yelling and pointing when he saw us. My father watched his son drown and there was naught he could do.

"He ordered the boat brought to shore after my brother had been buried. There was a jagged hole in the bottom."

"Surely that is not proof enough," Graelam said.

Kassia shook her head sadly. "But you see, I had taken the boat out the day before. It did not even leak. And there is more. Evidently Geoffrey could swim. Yet he had stood on the shore watching my brother drown. He could have saved him. When my father found out, he went into a rage and ordered Geoffrey from Belleterre. That was eight years ago. My father's sister, Felice, kept after him to allow her to visit Belleterre occasionally. She and Geoffrey have been allowed to visit three times in the past three years."

"How old was your brother?"

"He was but eight years old when he died. I was nearly ten years old. I am not certain that Geoffrey did kill my brother. Perhaps he did not rip the hole in the boat. Perhaps his only fault was that he was a coward, and was afraid to try to save him. I do not know."

"Geoffrey is still a coward," Graelam said. "I am glad you are safe from him now."

There was warmth in his voice and Kassia turned to face him, her eyes glowing with pleasure. "You sound like my father," she said.

"I am not your father!" Graelam said harshly. "His eyes fell to her breasts, the wool of her gown outlining their small roundness by the wind. "Tell me about your mother."

Kassia cocked her head at him, wondering at his constantly shifting moods. "She was very loving and gentle. I do not remember her very well, but my father has told me often of her goodness. And what of your mother, my lord?"

"Her name was Dagne, and unlike your mother, she was not particularly loving and gentle. My father had oft to chastise her for her disobedience and ill humor."

Kassia stared at him. "You mean he *struck* her?"

"Only when she had earned his wrath."

"And when your father earned her wrath, did she strike him?"

"She was a woman. Of course she did not strike him. But I recall her tongue was very sharp on occasion." That was half-truth if ever there was one, he thought. His mother had been about as soft-spoken and gentle as a snake. Not, of course, that his father had ever done anything to call forth more gentle emotions from her. He shrugged that thought aside as Kassia said sharply, "That, my lord, is hardly the same thing! My father would never harm someone smaller and weaker than he. Surely a man could not love a woman and still wish to hurt her."

"Kassia, you do not understand," Graelam said patiently. "It is a man's responsibility to discipline his wife. It is her duty to obey, to serve him, and to bear his children."

"Being a wife does not sound very pleasant," Kassia said. "I think," she continued with alarming candor, "that I should prefer being a dog. At least he is petted and allowed to run free."

"There are benefits to being a wife rather than a dog," Graelam said dryly.

"Oh?" Kassia asked in a tone of disbelief.

He raised his hand and lightly stroked his fingertips over her jaw. "When you are ready, I will show you the benefits of being a wife."

Her eyes widened as she remembered Blanche's words. She blurted out, without thinking, "Oh no! That is not a benefit! That is worse than a beating!"

Graelam dropped his hand and stared at her. "Kassia, it is natural for you to be nervous, perhaps even afraid, of what you do not understand. But lovemaking is not a punishment, I promise you."

"Why do you call it lovemaking?" she asked rather wildly. "It is like animals, and it hurts, and there is no love."

Graelam could not believe his ears. Nor could he believe his patience. "What did your father tell you?"

She shook her head, refusing to look at him. "Nothing. He said nothing."

"Then why do you believe it will hurt?"

Kassia bowed her head. "Please," she whispered. "I . . . I will do my duty when I must. I know that you want sons."

"Who told you it would hurt?"

"A . . . lady," she said in a taut voice. "She told me that you . . . that men were demanding and cared not about a woman's pain. She told me I must bear it."

Graelam cursed long and fluently, the more foul of his curses thankfully whipped away by the wind. "This lady," he said finally in a very calm voice, "was wrong to say such a thing to you, and she lied." He sighed, knowing he had not been truthful. "There are some men who are not interested in a woman's feelings, but not all men are like that."

Kassia turned wide, innocent eyes to his face. "Are you like these men, my lord?"

"I will not hurt you," he said.

She remembered his huge naked body, his swollen member thrusting toward her. She remembered his strange abruptness with her that morning. She said nothing.

"Perhaps you misunderstood this lady," he said. "There is a bit of pain the first time when your maidenhead is rent. But if the man is gentle, pleasure quickly follows and the pain is forgotten."

She was gazing at him, disbelief written clearly in her eyes.

"There is no reason for you to disbelieve me. I am your husband."

"You are . . . different from me," she whispered.

"Aye, God willed it so." His voice was clipped, for his patience was near an end. Still, it bothered him that she should fear coupling. "Kassia, you have seen animals mate." She continued staring at him, mute. "You have seen me naked. My rod will enter you. Do you understand?"

"I have seen a stallion cover a mare. Will it be like that?"

He wanted to laugh. "Sometimes," he said. "But usually you will be on your back, beneath me."

"Oh," she gasped, her cheeks flushed.

"The proof will be in the doing," he said, and rose.

She stared up at him. He blocked out the sun, and she shuddered.

"Kassia," he said, "you cannot remain a child. Come, it is time to return." He stretched out his hand to her. She hesitated a moment, then thrust her hand into his. "Your hand is cold," he said as he drew her to her feet. He pulled her against him. She was stiff as a board. Slowly he began to stroke his hands down her back. "A wife is her husband's responsibility," he said. "I will take care of you." He felt her ease against him and lay her cheek trustingly against his chest. "Tonight you will become a wife. No, don't stiffen." He smiled over the top of her head. "Did you not tell me that your father trusted me to be kind to you?"

He felt her hesitation, then felt her nose nodding up and down against him. "It is not your monthly flux, is it?"

He heard a small gasp; then she shook her head, burrowing her face into his tunic.

"Look at me, Kassia." When she hesitated, he gently cupped her chin and raised her face upward. "Now, hold still and relax." He touched his fingertips to her lips, then slowly lowered his head.

Kassia jumped when his mouth touched hers. It was not unpleasant. His lips were warm and firm. She felt his tongue glide over her lower lip, and she frowned, wondering at the sudden spurt of warmth low in her belly. She felt his fingers tangling in her hair; then he released her. "That was not so bad, was it?"

"Nay," she admitted, her head cocked to one side, her eyes studying his face intently. "My stomach feels warm. It is very odd. I've never felt that before."

He grinned, a boyish grin that made him look very young. "Come," he said. He lifted her onto her mare's back and swung into his own saddle. During their ride back to Wolffeton, he wondered at himself. Never had he had such a discussion with a woman. But there was something so vulnerable about Kassia, and it made him furious at himself, yet still protective of her. He supposed it was simply her candid innocence that made him babble on like a chivalrous fool, or, he thought, his lips twisting in a rueful smile, a besotted father. Oddly, he did not want her to fear coupling with him. He would arouse passion in her, he had the skill and he would force himself to patience. She was young, malleable, and he did not doubt that she would be easily molded into an obedient, gentle wife. The future stretched out pleasantly before him in his mind.

Graelam wooed his young wife that evening. He gave her all of his attention at dinner, ensuring that she drank two goblets of sweet wine and ate most of the spicy stew that he shared with her. And he touched her, light caresses that brought color to her cheeks.

"You have eaten almost enough," he said, and sopped a bit of bread in the remainder of the stew and fed it to her himself. She smiled at him and he felt an unusual warmth pervade him. He drew a deep breath, and it was her sweet scent that filled his nostrils. Her chestnut curls glowed with reddish glints in the rushlight.

"My hair will grow," Kassia said, aware that he was staring at her.

He wrapped a loose curl around his fingers. "Your hair is so soft," he said. "As fine as a babe's."

A dimple he had not noticed before deepened beside her mouth. "But, my lord," she said impishly, "you do not want a babe for your wife."

He chuckled and ruffled her curls. "You are right, my lady, particularly tonight."

Her eyes widened, but she did not draw away from him. He was pleased. He turned and nodded to a minstrel, Louis, a Frenchman he had invited to stay at his castle in Cornwall for several days. The small dark-eyed man, sun-baked from his travels, had been playing softly throughout the meal, and now moved forward to sit on a stool in front of Graelam's daised table. He smiled toward Kassia and played several haunting cords on his lute. "To your lovely bride from Brittany, my lord," he said, and bowed his head, strumming the strings lightly. "I have christened it *Fire Song*."

> *'Tis a fire in the blood that draws me*
> *to thee, my maid of Brittany.*
> *A softness in your eyes that makes me*
> *dream of nights in your gentle arms.*

His voice, gentle as spring rain, filled the silent hall. At his words, Kassia smiled shyly at her husband.

> *Your woman's beauty meets my hungry eyes*
> *calling me, my maid of Brittany.*
> *'Tis a fire in the blood that makes me*
> *yearn to hold thee close.*

Graelam pressed his shoulder against hers and gently squeezed her hand. "A fire, my lady?" he teased her softly. "Soon we will know if he speaks true."

> *The sweetness in your smile draws me*
> *to thee, my maid of Brittany.*
> *'Tis a fire I long to give thee*
> *the fire of my song and my heart.*

Louis kept his head down as he softly played a cre-

scendo of minor chords. At the finish, he raised his eyes
and bowed his head to Kassia.

"'Twas well done, Louis," Graelam called out over
the enthusiastic clamor of the men. "I am pleased as is
my lovely bride."

"It is my pleasure, my lord," Louis said. He began
again, this time a song of the great Roland and his death
fighting the Saracens at Roncesvalles.

Graelem said quietly to Kassia, "Go to our chamber,
Kassia. I will come to you soon."

Kassia rose and nodded to Blanche, who was sitting
quietly beside Blount, the steward.

"God give you sweet sleep, my lady," Guy said,
smiling at her. He watched her wave a slender hand at
him, then turn and walk from the hall. His eyes went
back to Graelam. He had never before seen his master
treat a woman so gently. It boded well, he thought.

Graelam lifted his goblet to his lips and sipped slowly
at the sweet wine, his eyes thoughtful. A woman should
want a man. He would make Kassia respond to him,
make her moan softly, and make her forget her maid-
en's fear. The fire in his body would warm her. He
downed the rest of his wine and rose from his chair
when Louis finished his song. He saw a speculative look
on Blount's craggy face, an open smile on Guy's, and
knew that all his men were in no doubt about how he
would spend his night.

"Please continue, Louis," he said to the minstrel. "As
to the rest of you louts," he called out to his men,
"listen well and learn." He strode from the hall, feeling
something of a fool, for everyone knew he was going to
his wife. He took the stone steps two at a time. He
opened his chamber door and saw Kassia seated on the
bed, wrapped in her blue wool bedrobe.

"Come here, Kassia," he said.

She slipped off the bed, clutched her robe closely to her, and padded to him on bare feet. He held out his arms and she moved against him, wrapping her arms about his waist. He closed his arms about her back, and began to gently stroke away the tension he felt in her shoulders.

"You smell so sweet," he said, inhaling the lavender scent of her. He stroked his long fingers through her hair, massaging her scalp and tangling the soft curls about her ears. He drew her more tightly against him, lifting her against his hardening manhood.

Kassia raised her head from his shoulder and gazed into his dark eyes for a long moment. Slowly, without instruction from him, she closed her eyes and pressed her mouth against his. She felt his exquisite hardness against her belly and felt again that strange tremor of warmth flow through her.

Graelam swung her up in his arms and carried her to the bed. He laid her on her back and sat beside her. Slowly, he untied the sash about her waist. She gave a soft distressed gasp, and he stopped.

"Did I tell you about my destrier, Demon?" he asked.

She stared up at him, blinking in surprise. "Nay, my lord."

"He was bred near York," Graelam said softly. "His sire was called Satan and his dam, Witch." He lowered his head and gently kissed her closed lips. He caressed her lower lip with his tongue, all the while talking quietly about his stallion. "He saved my life in the Holy Land when a Saracen would have carved me. He reared up and stomped the fellow." He realized belatedly that though he spoke softly, his words were anything but seductive and soothing. Why the devil was he talking to her about his damned horse? He shook his head at his own foolishness. "I want to see you, Kassia," he said, and drew her robe apart.

Her hands fluttered up, but he stilled them, clasping them lightly above her head. "You have beautiful breasts," he said.

"I—I am small," Kassia said, "but I will be larger when I gain flesh."

"You are perfectly shaped," he said, surprising himself. He did not like slight women, but somehow, Kassia's delicately rounded breasts appealed to him. And the soft pink nipples, so smooth now, not yet tautened with passion.

"You are staring at me," Kassia said.

"Aye." He grimaced at the memory of Maurice tearing the leech from her breast and flinging it across the chamber.

"I do not please you, my lord?"

"You please me well," he said. "I feel well the minstrel's words." He lowered his head and kissed the column of her throat. Slowly he touched his lips to her soft flesh until he lightly flicked her nipple with his tongue. She gasped and he raised his head to see her staring at him, a stunned look on her face. He smiled and lowered his head to suckle her gently. He could feel the pounding of her heart against his cheek.

"Someday," he said, lifting his face to look at her, "our babe will suck at your breast thusly."

He felt her hands stroking in his hair, pulling him closer to her breast.

"Oh!"

A look of pain flashed across her face.

"What is the matter?"

"I—I don't know," she gasped. A cramp twisted in her belly and she cried out.

Graelam sat up and laid his hand to her cheek.

She suddenly lurched up, her face ashen. "I am not well," she cried.

He handed her the chamber pot just in time. She retched until there was naught left in her belly.

"I am sorry, my lord," she whispered, and moaned, drawing her knees up against the vicious cramps.

"Hush," he said. What had she eaten that he had not, he wondered, worry gnawing at him. Had he forced her to eat too much? Had her fear of him made her ill? He dampened a cloth and gently wiped her sweating face. "Lie still. I will get your nurse."

He watched helplessly as Etta crooned over Kassia, feeling her belly with gentle hands.

"What is wrong with her?" he demanded.

Etta shook her head. "She ate something that was bad, I think." She rose. "I will make her a potion, my lord."

At that moment, Graelam felt a cramp in his belly, and doubled over. "Christ," he muttered, and strode quickly out of his bedchamber.

At least, he thought a few minutes later, his belly empty, it wasn't her fear of him that had made her vomit. He checked with his men in the hall. None were ill. The cramps continued and he gladly drank the potion Etta handed him.

" 'Twas the stew," he said. "Only Kassia and I shared it, and she ate the most of it."

She was moaning pitiably, her arms wrapped around her stomach. His cramps were lessening, yet he knew what she felt and it frightened him. She was so slight, and had not half his strength. He sat beside her and pulled her into his arms, rocking her.

"She will sleep soon, my lord," Etta said, hovering protectively close to her young mistress. "And she has nothing foul left in her belly."

Kassia's head lolled back against his arm. She said vaguely, "I shall hang the cook up by his heels with his head in the stew."

Graelam was thinking of a more ferocious punishment for the hapless cook.

"You will be all right tomorrow, my baby," Etta said, gently wiping the damp cloth over Kassia's forehead.

"I am so ashamed," Kassia whispered, and burrowed her face against Graelam's arm.

"Don't be a fool," he said sharply. "Can you sleep now, Kassia?"

"Aye," she muttered.

He laid her on her back and drew the covers over her. "I will call you if she worsens," Graelam said to Etta.

The night was a long one. Kassia awoke every several hours, her belly convulsed with cramps. Graelam forced her to drink, but she could keep nothing down. Finally, toward dawn, she fell into a deep sleep, and he allowed himself to relax.

It was near to noon the next day when Graelam entered to find Kassia awake. The chamber reeked of sickness and he felt nausea rise in his belly at the stench.

"She has drunk some broth, my lord," Etta said proudly at Kassia's accomplishment.

"She will not keep it down if she must remain in here," Graelam said. He strode over to his wife and wrapped her up in blankets. "I am taking her outside.

Clean the chamber and open the windows. Burn incense, whatever, just get rid of the stench."

Graelam carried his wife out of the keep. He ordered Demon saddled.

"What are you going to do with me?" Kassia asked, clutching at Graelam's sleeve. Now that the cramps were gone, she felt mortified. He had held her whilst she had retched. All night he had cared for her. She wanted to bury her face in his shoulder and never look him in the face again.

"Perhaps I shall toss you over the cliff," Graelam said, hugging her tightly against his chest.

"I would not blame you," she sighed. "I have not been a very good wife to you."

Graelam laughed deeply. "You have not been a wife at all. Now keep your tongue quiet in your mouth."

He held her in his arms as he guided Demon over the lowered drawbridge. "Breathe deeply, Kassia," he said.

He rode to the cliff and dismounted, tying Demon to a low juniper bush. He eased himself down against a bowed pine tree and settled Kassia in his lap. "Now," he said, "you will think about being well again."

"I am so ashamed," she said.

"I was also ill. We have both survived. Now, I want you to be quiet and breathe the clean air."

He felt her burrow trustingly against him, her fist closing about his tunic. He dropped a light kiss on her forehead and leaned back against the tree trunk and closed his eyes.

"My lord."

Graelam opened his eyes and looked up at Guy. He shook away the remnants of sleep.

"It grows late," Guy said quietly, for Kassia still slumbered.

"I will come soon, Guy."

"Is she all right?"

"Aye, thank God. Did you speak to the cook? What is that varlet's name?"

"I gave him—Dayken is his name—the flat of my sword against his fat buttocks! He swears the meat was fresh. I do not understand it. It's almost as if—" He broke off, shaking his head.

"As if what?"

"Nothing, my lord."

"If you have something to say, Guy, say it!"

Guy scratched his ear. "I like not that only the two of you fell ill."

"I like it not either," Graelam said softly. "The only question is who, Guy?"

"A woman's jealousy can lead her to do vicious things, my lord."

Graelam grunted. "So who is this woman, Guy?" he asked.

"Not Blanche, I am certain of that." Indeed, he had spoken to her, watching her beautiful eyes for signs of deception. He did not want to admit to his profound relief when he realized she was innocent. Guy shook his head, perplexed. "All knew you were to bed your lady last night." He flushed as his master's eyes narrowed on his face.

"It need not have been a woman, Guy," was all he said.

Kassia stirred in his lap and raised her head from Graelam's shoulder. "My lord?" she whispered, her voice foggy with sleep.

"'Tis naught, Kassia," Graelam said. "How do you feel?"

She smiled, and the dimple deepened beside her mouth. "Hungry," she said.

"Excellent. I am certain that your nurse has a pot of broth awaiting you. Your belly isn't cramping anymore?"

She flushed, seeing Guy, and shook her head.

Graelam rose easily, and shifted Kassia in his arms. The blankets fell away and Guy glimpsed the white curve of her breast.

"I'll get Demon, my lord," he said quickly, and strode to his master's destrier.

12

The afternoon was overcast and a chill wind blew from the sea. Kassia stood watching Graelam, his powerful chest bared, wrestling with one of his men, a huge fellow who had the look of a mighty oak tree. The men formed a half-circle, calling out explicit and coarse advice.

Kassia moved closer. She saw the concentration on her husband's face as he circled the other man. He lunged so suddenly that she blinked in surprise. He gave a fierce yell as he hooked his leg behind his opponent's and toppled him to the ground. He slammed down on top of him, pinning his shoulders.

The men cheered and Graelam stood up, offering his hand to his man. He met Kassia's eyes at that moment, and smiled.

She waved to him shyly and called, "We have a visitor, my lord."

Graelam spoke to his men, then strode to his wife, flexing his shoulder muscles. He looked at her closely, studying her face for any signs of lingering illness, and satisfied, asked, "Who comes, Kassia?"

"Blanche's son, my lord."

Graelam frowned a moment, having forgotten the boy.

"Blanche is smiling. I am pleased her son is here." *Her son will give her something to think about other than you!*

One of Graelam's men tossed him his shirt and tunic. "Wash me down first, Kassia," he said, and walked beside her to the well in the inner bailey.

Kassia filled the bucket and poured it over her husband's head and back as he leaned over. He shook himself and donned his shirt.

"My tunic, Kassia," he said.

"Oh!" She had been staring at his chest, wondering why it made her heart pound to think of tangling her fingers in the dark curling hair, or suckling at his nipples as he had hers.

Graelam wondered at the sudden delicate flush on her cheeks as he pulled his tunic over his shirt.

They walked into the hall. Blanche was talking to three men, all travel-stained and weary-looking. A slender boy, some eight years old, clung to the side of one of the men.

"My lord," Blanche called out. "My son is arrived. Evian, this is Lord Graelam de Moreton, your uncle by marriage."

The boy peeped from behind the man. The man gave him an indulgent smile and shoved him forward. "'Tis a bit shy he is, my lord. I am Louis, from my lord Robert's household in Normandy."

"I bid you welcome, and thank you for delivering the boy safely," Graelam said, then squatted down to the

boy's eye level. He had his mother's dark eyes and dark
hair, but was saved from being pretty by a square jaw
and a broad forehead. "You will be my page," Graelam
said. "If you are competent at your duties, you will one
day be my squire. Does that please you, boy?"

"Aye, my lord," Evian said. He studied Lord Graelam
with intelligent eyes and became his slave at that moment. Graelam dropped his hand on the boy's shoulder, patted him, then rose. "You have already met my
wife, Lady Kassia?" he asked.

Evian nodded, his eyes turning toward Kassia. She
was giving him a welcoming, open smile, and he gave
her a tentative one in return.

"You are most welcome, Evian," Kassia said.

"I am nearly as tall as you, my lady," Evian ventured.

"Aye, in another year or so, 'tis I who will be gazing
up at you."

Blanche grabbed her son's hand. "He can sleep in my
chamber, Graelam."

"Nay, Blanche. Guy, come and meet my new page.
The boy will sleep outside my chamber, on a pallet,
and take his meals with the men."

He is not like his mother, Kassia thought, and immediately chided herself.

"I have been living with my mother's cousin," Evian
said confidentially to Guy, "in Normandy."

"Evian, I would like to speak to you!"

The boy turned large reluctant eyes back to his mother,
wishing she would not treat him like a little boy.

"Nay, let him go, Blanche," Graelam said, to Evian's
immense relief. "You can cosset him later." He turned
to Louis. "Come have some ale, your men also. Nan,
bring drink!"

*   *   *

"He is a fine lad," Graelam said to Blanche that evening. "Your cousin has raised him well, but 'tis men's company he needs."

Blanche forced a bright smile to her lips. Graelam was pleased with her son, just as she had hoped he would be. But it was too late. "You are most kind, Graelam," she said softly. Such a pity that Nan had not mixed more of the vile herbs in the stew. Blanche knew the wench had done it, for Nan was unable to keep the smug, triumphant grin off her face when she believed no one was looking at her. Blanche frowned, lowering her eyes. Jealousy was a terrible thing, and it made her writhe in self-reproach, hating herself for her feelings, even as she searched for ways to undermine Kassia. Life has not been fair to me, she would tell herself over and over, the litany her excuse.

Kassia watched Graelam and Blanche speaking together, and felt a strange burst of anger. Unlike her, Blanche was endowed with a full and rounded woman's body and her long dark hair glistened in the rushlight.

"Your thoughts are not pleasant?"

Kassia turned to Guy "Blanche is very beautiful," she said honestly, bewilderment at her jealousy sounding in her voice.

"That is true," Guy said honestly. "But she need never concern you, truly. Lord Graelam could have wed her had he wished to."

Kassia gave him a sad little smile. "It appears that my lord could have wed any lady he wished. 'Tis his misfortune that he came upon my father in Aquitaine, and that I didn't die."

"Lord Graelam saw much misery in the Holy Land," Guy said pensively, "disease, starvation, butchery that seemed to know no end, but never did it really touch him. Yet I tell you truthfully that after he came from your chamber, believing that you were dying, his face was drawn in anguish. You touched him as no other ever has—man or woman. Even now he treats you gently, carefully, and my lord is not a particularly gentle man. When you fell ill from the food, he was distraught. He told me that it was not fair that you should regain your health, only to come to Wolffeton and lose it again." Guy paused a moment, watching Kassia's brow furrow deeply in thought at his words. "Lord Graelam is also a man of strong appetites," he continued carefully after a moment. "Yet he is more concerned with your well-being than his own needs."

"But I am well now," Kassia exclaimed, then turned scarlet at her loose tongue.

Guy grinned merrily at her and raised his goblet in a silent toast. "Your noble husband approaches, my lady."

Kassia raised her face to her husband. She looked like such a naughty child that Graelam laughed.

"I have been telling her of your . . . prowess, my lord," Guy said blandly.

Kassia choked at his double meaning, and Graelam arched a thick black brow. His eyes fell to Kassia's trencher and he frowned. "What have you eaten?"

Kassia, who had consumed chicken, fish, and fruit, merely shook her head at him. "I have been a glutton, my lord. May I serve you now?"

He nodded and sat himself beside her. "The boy, Evian," he said to Guy, "we must begin to toughen him up."

Kassia looked down the trestle table at Evian, who was leaning sleepily against Drake's massive shoulder.

"The lad seems willing," Guy said, "though his mother would like to turn him into a lapdog."

Graelam merely grunted, and talk turned to de Fortenberry and his ever-nearing raids. It seemed to Kassia that Graelam was looking forward to crossing swords with the man; indeed, he hoped that de Fortenberry would attack some of Wolffeton's outlying demesne farms. She watched her husband, and saw that he was not eating as much as he needed. 'Twas the wretched cooking, she knew. She must see to her responsibilities as chatelaine soon. If only Graelam would cease treating her like an invalid! He still looked to Blanche, and Kassia found that she did not like that at all. She had noted during the day that the servants heeded Blanche's orders, but slowly and sullenly. Her housewifely hackles rose. They would obey her, and promptly, or she would know the reason why.

She leaned over to pick up an apple from the plate in front of Graelam. Her breast accidentally brushed against his arm. She felt him stiffen and he paused perceptibly in his speech. She hung her head, embarrassed, and was unaware that he gazed at her speculatively for a long moment.

Graelam was surprised at the surge of desire he felt, thinking again that Kassia had scarcely enough womanly curves for his taste. Yet, thinking of her lying soft and yielding in his arms, her trusting eyes upon him, made him anxious, as he had never been before. Tonight, he thought, tonight, he would take her. He must take her.

"Your hand, Kassia," he said, laying his own palm-up on the table beside her.

She tentatively laid her hand in his and watched as his fingers closed around hers. A frown crossed his brow and she held herself very still, not knowing what he was thinking.

She is so slight, he mused, curling his fingers around

her slender wrist. He had promised her there was no pain in coupling, and hoped he was right—that his size wouldn't hurt her. He must go easily with her. He felt a renewed tightening in his loins at the thought of her naked beneath him. He said abruptly, releasing her hand, "Go to our bedchamber now, and ready yourself for me."

Kassia knew that her cheeks were flushed. She remembered quite clearly the odd sensations she had felt before she had fallen ill, and she knew that Graelam wanted to make her his wife this night. She walked from the hall, imagining that all the men knew exactly what was in her mind and in her husband's.

Etta awaited her in her bedchamber.

"Ah, my baby," the older woman scolded her fondly, "'tis tired you are. You should have stayed abed as your husband wished you to."

"Nay," Kassia said on a nervous laugh, "I am not tired, but I would like a bath."

Etta shooed Nan and another girl, Erna, pointed-chinned and scraggle-toothed, from the chamber after they had filled the wooden tub, then scented the hot water liberally with lavender, Kassia's favorite scent.

As Kassia disrobed, her eyes kept flying toward the chamber door. She did not luxuriate in her bath as was her wont, but scrubbed herself quickly. She turned to ask Etta for her towel and became mute at the sight of her husband standing in the doorway, his arms crossed over his chest, gazing at her.

"Is the water still warm?" Graelam asked.

She nodded, sinking down in the wooden tub until only her head showed above.

"Will you scrub my back?"

He had moved out of her range, and Kassia eased up

a bit to see him again. "Aye," she said, "I will." He was tugging at the ties on his tunic. As he pulled it over his head, she scurried out of the tub and grabbed at the linen towel.

"Kassia, help me."

The tie on his chaussures was knotted. She wrapped the towel securely around her and dropped to her feet before him, her nimble fingers on the knot. She could feel the heat from his body; had she the courage, she could touch the growing bulge in his groin. She stilled suddenly at the touch of his fingers in her hair.

"Soft as a babe's," he said quietly. The knot untied, Kassia lowered her arms, resting her cheek against his thigh.

"Come," he said, and lifted her to her feet. He drew off his chaussures and strode naked to the tub. Kassia giggled at the sight of him, his knees thrust upward, as he settled himself into the tub.

"I amuse you, wench?"

"You are so large, my lord!" She smiled contentedly as she soaped a sponge and began to stroke it down his back. She soaped his thick hair, careful to keep the lather from his eyes. "I used to shave my father," she said as she rinsed his hair.

"Did you now?" he said, swiping the water from his eyes. His eyes crinkled as he looked up at her. She had time only to gasp in surprise. He jerked the towel from her, grabbed her about her waist, and swung her into the tub onto his lap.

Kassia fell forward, her arms looping about his neck to steady herself. "Oh," she said helplessly, her mouth but a breath away from his.

"Aye," he agreed softly, and pressed his hand against the back of her head, bringing her to him. He lightly pressed his mouth against hers, undemanding, exploring her soft contours. He dropped his hands down her back, drawing her closer until her breasts were pressed against his chest.

"A small wife is not such a bad thing," he said, gently nibbling on her earlobe. He lifted her carefully so her hips were resting on his belly. "Give me your mouth, Kassia."

"I . . . I don't know what to do," she said, feeling like a stupid fool.

"I will teach you," he said. "Part your lips."

She did as he bid her and drew back startled at the touch of his tongue against hers. "That feels . . . strange," she whispered, her hand stroking through his wet hair without instruction from him.

"Strange good or strange bad?" he teased her.

"I don't know," she said honestly. "Can you do it again, my lord?"

"A willing pupil," he murmured against her parted lips. He wrapped his arms around her back and pressed her tightly against him, deepening the pressure with his lips. He eased instantly when he felt her stiffen, and was rewarded soon with a quiver that ran the length of her slender body. Slowly, he thought to himself, go very slowly. He felt gooseflesh rise on her arms and laughed. "How the devil do I get you out of this thing?"

He lifted her above him, only to have her slip in a welter of arms and legs. She landed flat against him, her belly against his swollen manhood. Her eyes flew to his face and she knew a moment of fear when his hands pressed against her buttocks, molding her against his hard flesh, and he moaned roughly deep in his throat.

"The water grows cold," she said in a thin, high voice.

Graelam closed his eyes tightly for a moment, getting a hold on himself. The last place he wanted to take his virgin bride was in a tub of cool water. And she was frightened, he heard it in her voice. He kissed her lightly on the tip of her nose and thrust her away from him. Kassia grabbed the towel and quickly twisted it around her. But she didn't avert her eyes when he stood in the tub, magnificent in his nakedness.

"I wish that I looked as beautiful as you," she said wistfully.

He stared at her a moment. No woman had ever before told him he was beautiful. He said lightly as he stepped from the tub, "A scarred, hairy warrior?"

"Aye," she said, "and endowed with great power and strength." She handed him a towel. "My father told me once that the more valiant the knight, the more gentle he was in his physical strength. I think he must have been thinking of you, my lord."

"Your father did not know me, Kassia," he said sharply. It made him uncomfortable to be cast in a chivalrous hero's mold. "I am as I am. Do not grant me virtues I own not."

"No, my lord," she said docilely, but he saw the impish dimple deepening beside her mouth.

He drew on his bedrobe and strode to the chamber door, yelling for the servants to empty the tub.

"Get into bed," he called over his shoulder to Kassia. "I do not want you to take cold."

Because she was nervous, it seemed but a moment of time before they were alone, the door firmly closed, her husband walking toward the bed.

"I play chess quite well," she blurted out.

He merely grunted, knowing there was nothing he could say to ease her wariness of him. "How does your belly feel?" he asked, drawing off his bedrobe and sitting down beside her.

Kassia's tongue darted over her lower lip, an unconscious, very sensuous gesture. He gently laid his hand on her belly and probed lightly. "I am truly all right," she said.

"You are so small," he said on a frown, his eyes on his splayed hand. He could touch her pelvic bones with the tips of his stretched fingers.

To Kassia's surprise, she felt a bolt of heat sear through her stomach and her eyes flew to his face. "Oh," she gasped.

He lifted his hand and she knew a moment of disappointment. He saw it in her eyes, and was pleased. She was innocent of a woman's pleasure, but not cold-natured.

He stretched out above her and gently stroked his fingers along the column of her throat.

"Should I not douse the candle?"

He shook his head, leaning down to kiss the pulse in her throat. "Nay, I wish to see all of you, wife, even to the soft white flesh between your thighs." She quivered at his words, and he continued in a soft, tantalizing voice, "I want you to watch me looking at you. I will know your body better than you will know yourself. You have such softness and beauty for me." He cupped his hand slightly over her woman's mound and rested it there.

"Open your mouth for me, Kassia."

He touched her even teeth with his tongue, gliding slowly, then gently plundered the depths of her warm mouth. He clasped her in his arms and pulled her onto her side against the length of him.

"Be at your ease, dearling, I will not hurt you."

She believed him and melted against him, slipping
her arm around his ribs to stroke over his smooth back.

"I . . . I want to feel you against me," she said when
he released her mouth for a moment.

He quickly loosed the sash of her bedrobe and flung
it open. He pushed the robe from her shoulders, pausing a moment to gaze down at her breasts. "You are so
delicate," he said, more to himself than to her. "So soft,
like the Genoese velvet I bought in Acre." Slowly, his
eyes on her breast, he stroked his fingertips over her
smooth flesh, drawing closer and closer to her silken
nipple. He felt her tremble slightly and leaned his head
down to take the smooth tip into his mouth. He felt her
nipple tauten in his mouth, and gently drew on it,
savoring the texture as he suckled. He cupped his hand
around her breast and pushed it upward to better possess her. He felt her arch her back and slipped one arm
beneath her. He sought out her mouth again. To his
delight, he felt her hand glide down over his hip,
gently kneading his muscles, exploring his body as he
was hers. As her searching fingers neared his groin, he
felt himself stiffen in a nearly painful need.

"Touch me, Kassia," he groaned softly.

Unerringly she touched her fingers to his throbbing
manhood, and he heard her sharp intake of breath as
she tried to take him in her hand. "Don't be afraid,
sweetheart," he whispered between nipping kisses on
her throat. "You will be soft and wet and ready for me.
Let me show you."

She grew utterly still as his hand roved over her ribs
to her belly. He kneaded the soft flesh a moment, then
laid his hand over the curling hair of her woman's
mound. "You are holding now a man's desire," he teased
her softly. "I am an obvious being with no hidden

treasures. Unlike you." Gently he probed until he found her yielding flesh. "Here is your woman's place of pleasure. A small treasure, of infinite beauty and enchantment." He heard her gasp in surprise and captured her mouth as his fingers continued to caress her rhythmically. "Does that please you?" he asked into her mouth.

Kassia could think of no words. Her hips were pressing up against his beguiling fingers and the only sound from her throat was a ragged groan.

"I feel so odd," she gasped. She tightened her hold on his member, making him grimace. He prized her fingers loose, aware of her disappointment that his fingers had left her. "I would look at you now, sweeting."

He reared up, parting her thighs. "Open your eyes and look at me, Kassia. There is no shame between husband and wife."

He touched his fingertip to her and watched her hips twist. He slowly parted her, and was startled at the provocative sensuousness of her. She was all delicate soft pink, her woman's flesh lush and moist with her growing desire. Slowly he lowered his head and touched his lips to her. Kassia nearly leapt off the bed, a cry of utter surprise tearing from her mouth. "Oh no!" she cried. "My lord, you must not—please!" She pressed her hands impotently against his shoulders.

"Hush, Kassia, do not interfere with a man's pleasure."

"But you should not . . . surely!"

He laughed, his warm breath making her tingle. He continued to nuzzle her, explore her, learn what pleased her, but she would not ease, her embarrassment too great. He sighed, knowing he should not expect her to fall like a ripe plum into his mouth. He left her and lay beside her, drawing her into his arms. He began to kiss her deeply, even as his fingers caressed her, and he felt her slowly ease, tentatively returning his kisses.

"Kassia. Look at me."

She clutched at his hand that rested on her belly.

"Feel how soft and ready you are for me." She felt his finger slip inside her. She gasped at his assault, and tried to pull away from him.

"Nay, little one." She was very small, stretching to hold his finger. He pushed deeper inside her until he felt her maidenhead. He probed gently against it, but it held fast. He cursed silently. She was stiff and afraid, and there was nothing he could do about it, save get it over with. Slowly he drew up, parted her thighs, and guided himself into her.

Kassia's eyes flew to his face. She tried to hold herself still, but she felt a pressure building inside her, felt herself stretching painfully. She gasped and tried to twist away from the pain. Graelam held himself still within her and brought his weight down over her. "Kassia," he said softly, gently kissing her. "Hold still."

She blinked. "It hurts," she whispered.

He could not help himself, and moved deeper, pressing against her maidenhead. He felt her stiff and tense beneath him, and gritted his teeth against the overwhelming urge to drive forward and plunge into the sweet depths of her. He held perfectly still, hoping she would become accustomed to the feel of him. He pressed harder against her maidenhead, but the barrier was as taut and strong as an Amazon's shield. "Sweeting, I must cause you but a moment of pain. Hold onto me, Kassia." He looked down at her as he spoke and saw that her eyes were firmly closed, her face drawn in pain. What stopped him cold was the tears slowly trickling down her cheeks.

He could not explain his action to himself, for never before had he forgone his own need. He pulled out of her, feeling her flinch as he withdrew, and clasped her tightly against him.

She clasped her hands around his back and sobbed softly against his shoulder. He stroked her, calming her, until she eased.

"'Twas not so bad," she whispered, pulling away from him slightly to see his face. "I am sorry I am such a coward. You did not hurt me greatly, truly, my lord."

He wanted to laugh and to curse vilely at the same time. Instead, he kissed her until she was breathless. At least, he thought, he had stretched her somewhat.

When she lay snuggled against his side, her breathing even in sleep, he stared into the darkness, cursing himself for seven kinds of a fool. He should have gotten it over with. A woman's tears had never before touched him with such devastating result. A wife's maidenhead was a man's pride, yet he would have gladly forgone that small barrier to save her pain. That realization made him frown. She was, after all, but a woman, his possession, a creature whose only purpose was to give him pleasure and provide him with sons, and see to the management of his keep. But rant as he would at himself for his display of weakness, he could not dismiss the pain he had caused her. Ignorant little wench, he thought. She did not even realize she was yet a virgin!

13

She seems so proud of herself, Graelam thought, both amused and puzzled, as he watched Kassia chew on a piece of warm bread the next morning. With sudden insight he realized that she believed herself a woman now, a wife, and was pleased with her accomplishment. She was more confident, teasing his steward, Blount, as if she had known him all her life. And the old fool was grinning back at her as if she were bestowing upon him the greatest gems of wisdom imaginable.

Damn, he swore silently. How was he supposed to inform her that her maidenhead was still firmly in place? He sighed. He didn't want to tell her, but neither did he have any intention of letting this state of affairs continue. It had been his fault, of course, all because he had not wanted to cause her more pain. Abruptly he said to her, "Kassia, I wish to ride. You will accompany me, in an hour."

She met his eyes shyly, but with a knowledgeable gleam in hers that made him want to laugh and berate her at the same time for her ridiculous ignorance. "'Twould be my pleasure, my lord," she said sweetly, but he saw the impish dimple peeping out.

Exactly an hour later, Kassia, a triumphant smile on her lips, walked to the stables to meet Graelam. So much for Blanche and her attempts to frighten me, she thought, unconsciously squaring her shoulders. She had not meant to say anything to Blanche, but the sight of her giving the servants orders had ruffled her feathers. Now, Kassia had thought, she was the mistress of Wolffeton, and its management was her responsibility.

She had said calmly to Alice, a woman of middle years who seemed to have common sense and the respect of the other servants, "I wish to inspect the looms after I return from my ride with my lord. I think all of us need new garments."

"I doubt," Blanche said sharply, before Alice could speak, wondering at this show of spine from the skinny twit, "that your . . . husband will approve. He little appreciates unnecessary expense."

"It is the Wolffeton sheep and their wool that are of concern," she said. "I doubt my lord cares a whit, and I would trust that he would not concern himself with household matters."

"The old woman who did all the weaving died some months ago. There is no one else to assume her job."

Kassia gaped at her in astonishment. "That is ridiculous!"

"I fear 'tis true, my lady," Alice said.

"Aye," Blanche said, a pleased smile on her lips. "I, of course, asked Graelam for funds to hire a weaver to come to Wolffeton, but he refused."

"Well, I should think so," Kassia said. "I will, of course, teach the servants to weave and sew properly.

If you please, Alice, see that all is in readiness for me when I return." She knew she should keep her mouth shut, but her resentment at Blanche overflowed once Alice was out of earshot. "I wonder that you do not possess such skill, Blanche."

"I am not a servant!"

"A wife's responsibilities number many things, amongst them the knowledge to train servants. Just as a wife also enjoys many benefits, such as pleasure in her husband's company!"

Blanche paled. So Graelam had taken the girl, and evidently he had not hurt her. "Perhaps," she said nastily, her disappointment coming to the fore, "when your belly swells with child, you will not so much enjoy your husband's randy company! Whilst you retch and grow fat, you can rest assured that he will not be so concerned. Perhaps he will even provide you with another chamber, so he can continue to enjoy himself with his other women."

"You speak as if you know," Kassia said calmly, but her heart was pounding furiously.

"I?" Blanche gave a dry laugh. "I am simply not a silly little girl who believes her husband is a gallant lord. I doubt Lord Graelam was faithful to my half-sister for above a month!"

"Graelam," Kassia said quietly, "is an honorable man. I cannot, of course, say anything about your half-sister, but I know he would never break faith with me." She was beginning to feel the nibblings of guilt, for she was not blind, and she knew that Blanche had wanted to wed Graelam. "Blanche, let us not disagree. You should not have lied to me about coupling."

Blanche shrugged. "So you are larger than you look.

I did not lie to you, I merely did not want you to go blindly like a sheep to slaughter."

"Thank you for your consideration," Kassia said dryly. "Now I must go."

Kassia felt pleased with herself. As to Blanche's terrible accusations, she knew it the result of jealousy. Coupling wasn't the terrible ordeal Kassia had believed it would be; his part of it had hurt a bit, but nonetheless, she had felt some pleasurable sensations at her husband's touch.

"You are looking thoughtful."

Kassia's face flooded with embarrassed color at her husband's voice. "Oh! I was just . . . that is, you were . . . It is a lovely morning, is it not?"

A thick black brow winged upward. Graelam reached out his hand and cupped her chin. "If I threaten to beat you, will you tell me what your thoughts were?"

She smiled, rubbing her cheek against his palm. "'Twas wool, my lord! Pure and simple wool!"

He leaned down and lightly touched his lips to hers. "My thoughts, also, were pure and simple."

She gave a saucy giggle. "I do not believe you. Mayhap you have simple thoughts, but never pure ones!"

"Perhaps I should beat you," Graelam said thoughtfully. "A man does not want an impertinent wife."

"Behold, a docile creature," Kassia said. She dropped him a deep curtsy.

She no longer fears me, he realized. He supposed it pleased him—at least, that she did not fear him sexually. And she made him smile.

He said nothing as they rode from the keep southward along the coast road. The day was deliciously warm, for which he was greatly relieved. He shook his head at himself. Never before had he approached coupling with less passion and more planning. He gave Kassia a sideways look, but she seemed entirely possessed by the scenery. The road roughened downhill, then flattened out, swinging toward the cliff edge. To Kassia's surprise, Graelam left the road, slowing Demon to a walk, and disappeared for a moment over the edge. She followed him without question and saw that there was a well-worn path down the cliff to the beach below.

"It is not steep," Graelam called over his shoulder, "but go easy!"

When they reached the pebbly beach, Kassia drew in her breath in pleased surprise. "Oh, how lovely!" she exclaimed, slipping off Bluebell's back.

The beach formed a deep half-circle, its arc protected by the overhanging cliff. Scraggly bushes and a few bowed trees provided more protection. As Graelam tethered Bluebell and Demon on long leads, Kassia walked around the beach.

"This was my own private place when I was a boy," Graelam said, coming up behind her.

Kassia raised her face to the bright sun overhead and closed her eyes. The only sounds were the crashing waves and the squawking of the seabirds. "It is so peaceful," she said, turning to face him.

"I am pleased you like it."

"We should have brought some wine and bread."

"Kassia," he said suddenly, "how do you feel?"

"My lord," she scolded him lightly, "I am as healthy as my fat Bluebell. You needn't concern yourself further!"

"Are you sore?"

"Sore?" She cocked her head to the side, a habit she had that he found charming.

"From last night," he said.

"Oh!" She pressed her hands against her cheeks and shook her head.

"As I said," Graelam continued calmly, "this is a very private place. No one will disturb us here."

She looked utterly taken aback. "You wish to . . . couple with me now?"

"Aye," he said baldly.

"But it is daylight! You can see . . . Surely you cannot—!"

"Hush, Kassia," he said. "Come here."

She had not considered that her husband would wish to take her again so soon. She supposed that one coupled occasionally, when the man wished it, but . . . "I feel so stupid," she said, and stepped against him, her head lowered against his chest.

She felt his arms go around her, pulling her more closely against him. "Why do you say that?" he said, lightly kissing the soft curls over her temple.

"You will laugh at me, I know it," she muttered. She raised her face and felt an odd longing course through her as she stared up into her husband's dark eyes. "I did not believe that one coupled frequently. Perhaps just once, to create a babe."

He looked startled; then he squeezed her tightly until she squeaked. "Creating a babe, Kassia, usually takes a lot of effort. It is a task that most men willingly seek. And, dearling, it will be up to me to make you want to couple too, quite often."

She looked doubtful, but did not further question him, particularly when he lowered his mouth to hers. She stood passively against him, embarrassingly aware of his large hands stroking down her back to cup beneath her buttocks. Now that she knew about a man's desire, she knew from his hardness against her belly that he wanted her. She remembered Blanche's taunts about Graelam sleeping with other women. If a man was always so eager to couple, was a woman, any woman, merely a convenience?

Graelam released her and gently set her aside. She watched him silently as he spread two thick blankets on the ground and smoothed them out.

Never, Graelam thought again, had he approached coupling with less enthusiasm. He was well aware that Kassia had not responded to him and it made him grind his teeth. Damn her, she could have at least pretended! On the heels of that thought, he quickly retrenched. No, he wanted no acting from her. Indeed, he was pleased that she was too ignorant to feign pleasure. It meant that when he brought her to pleasure, he would know it. Patience, he reminded himself.

He sat down on the blanket and patted the place beside him, then leaned back on his elbows and watched her approach warily and slowly.

When she eased down beside him, he did not touch her. He was surprised when she said hesitantly, "Have you known many women, my lord?"

"There is one more that I would know," he said. He turned on his side to face her and gently drew her down onto her back. "This morning, you were not afraid of me. You were, if I am not mistaken, quite pleased with yourself over sharing my bed, over becoming a wife to me."

"Aye, 'tis true," she admitted, frowning at his ease in reading her thoughts. "And I do not believe that I have ever really feared you, my lord."

"When all I wish to do is give you pleasure, it is foolish for you to do so." He was lightly stroking her hand as he spoke. Very slowly he eased his fingers over her belly and began to gently knead her.

Kassia had closed her eyes and she knew the moment he leaned his head over hers, for he blotted out the sun. Unconsciously she ran her tongue over her lips to moisten them. She heard him suck in his breath, then felt his lips, gentle and undemanding, explore hers. He did not have to tell her to part her lips. She felt an unaccountable urge to do so. He did not ravish her mouth, merely teased her with his tongue, lightly foraging, taunting her gently.

Kassia wanted to feel more. Without thought, she raised her arm and pressed her hand along the back of his neck and pressed down. He deepened the pressure and the odd, tingly sensations she had felt briefly the night before coursed through her.

"Oh," she whispered into his mouth. He lifted his head and smiled down at her. "Please, my lord, do not stop."

His fingers were pressed together, lightly resting in a wedge between her thighs. "What do you want me to do, Kassia?"

Her hips jerked upward against his hand, and she blushed at what her body had done. "Everything!" she gasped.

Graelam laughed, a pure, deep sound, and hugged her against him. "You are too warm," he said, and began to unfasten her tunic. She squirmed against him, unable to help herself. His movements were smooth and fast, and soon she was lying beneath him in naught but her thin linen shift.

For a long moment he merely stared down at her, his eyes roving from her face downward until they came to rest at her belly. Slowly he lifted her shift until she was naked to her waist. He did not mean to think her beautiful, but oddly enough, he found her so. Her legs were long and straight; he touched his hand to her white flesh and gently stroked downward. It was rare that he spent so much time seducing a woman, but he realized vaguely that somehow his own pleasure was tied to hers. Slowly, gently, he continued exploring her, then parted her thighs with his fingers. Her warm moistness made him smile triumphantly. Kassia trembled as his fingers neared the soft, hidden seat of her pleasure. But instead of giving her what she wanted, he rose suddenly and jerked off his clothes. Nearby he laid down a small jar of cream, not letting her see it.

"Sit up," he said.

She did as he bid. He slipped her shift over her head, then pressed her again onto her back. He lay beside her, the heat of his body making her quiver, and let his fingers rove again over her belly. He kissed her, letting her deepen the pressure. He felt her hands frantically clutching at his back.

"Kassia," he said softly, "I would love you now, and you will not say me nay, nor will you feel embarrassment or guilt."

She stared up at him vaguely, not understanding, only knowing that her body was somehow an instrument she didn't control. He watched her carefully as his fingers caressed her. When he dipped his fingers into the cream and slowly entered her, she gasped, her eyes flying to his face. She grasped his arm, but he merely eased more deeply into her, soothing her, easing his way.

His fingers pressed against her maidenhead, but not hard enough to hurt her. Her muscles tensed around his fingers, and he groaned at the thought of her doing that to his manhood. Damn, he thought vaguely, he had not felt such lust since he was an untried boy. He lowered himself over her, careful not to hurt her with his weight, and slowly eased down her body until he was on his knees between her parted thighs. She tried to jerk away from him when he nuzzled his face against her, but he merely tightened his hold, drawing her hips upward.

Despite what he had said, she felt consumed with embarrassment, her rising passion crushed. Surely he should not be doing that to her, not with his mouth! She tried to wriggle away from him, but he held her firm.

"Give in, Kassia," he said, his warm breath touching her intimately. "Relax."

Graelam teased her soft woman's flesh, willing her to respond to him, but she did not. Time, he thought, it would take time to make her at ease with him. His lips left her reluctantly, and he felt desire roaring in his head. The softness of her, the sweet taste of her, her woman's scent made him wild to bury himself deep within her. Slowly he parted her thighs and eased into her. The cream soothed his way.

He kept his eyes on her face. "Kassia," he said, holding himself perfectly still.

Kassia felt the pressure of him inside her, but there was no pain, only a fullness that was not at all unpleasant. She opened her eyes and smiled up at him.

"Sweeting, I must cause you bit of . . . discomfort. Hold onto me. It will be over quickly."

She clasped her hands around his back obediently not understanding. He tore through her taut maidenhead, seating himself to his hilt within her. He took her cry of pain into his mouth. Her body was quivering, but he knew he could not leave her, not again. He kissed away her tears, trying to concentrate on her, to keep himself in check. But it was no use. He moved slightly, feeling the tight sheath squeezing him, and that brought him over the edge. He possessed her, driving deep, rasping groans coming from his mouth.

It was many minutes before Graelam raised himself on his elbows and gazed down into her pale face. "You are mine now," he said, and generations of possessiveness sounded in his deep, hoarse voice.

"Why did you hurt me?"

He kissed her lightly on her mouth, a slight smile curving his lips. "You were still a virgin, sweetheart."

She blinked at him. "But last night . . . you came inside me, you . . ."

He carefully eased out of her and lay on his side beside her. "Last night," he said slowly, "I did not finish what I started. I could not, for I was hurting you too much. That is why I brought you here today. I wanted to get the damned business over with. Kassia, did you feel any pleasure?"

She nodded.

"When next we couple, there will be only pleasure, I promise you. Will you trust me?"

"How can there be pleasure?" she managed, her eyes fastened on his chest. "You are large and will remain so."

"'Twas the rending of your maidenhead that caused most of the pain, and now I promise you it is no longer there. That small barrier did not wish to allow a man within."

"Even my husband?"

He smiled, relieved. "We will use cream until you are well used to me."

He was stroking her tumbled hair and she turned her face to nuzzle her cheek against his palm. "Did I please you? I am so ignorant. I do not know what to do."

"You pleased me. You will respond to me, Kassia, once you forget your embarrassment."

"Do I not need skill, my lord?"

He thought of her killing hold on his manhood the night before, and grinned ruefully. "Aye," he said, "I will teach you."

"When?"

"Greedy wench!" He squeezed her tightly until she yelped for breath. "When you are no longer sore from this plowing, sweetheart."

14

Graelam led his fatigued men into the inner bailey, a
smile leaping to his eyes at the sight of Kassia, clutching her gown above her ankles so she would not trip,
hurtling down the steps of the great hall toward him.
He quickly dismounted, tossed Demon's reins to the
stable hand, and caught her up in his arms. He held
her above his head for a moment, feeling her warm
laughter flow over him like soothing balm.

"Welcome home, my lord! Did all go well at Crandall? Who is the new castellan? There was no fighting,
was there? You were not hurt?"

He gave her a quick kiss and set her down, aware
that every eye in the castle was enjoying their reunion.
"So many questions," he teased her softly. "Everything
is fine, Kassia," he added quickly, seeing her pale at
the dried blood on his sleeve.

"But your arm," she said in a shaking voice.

"I took a fall when Demon slipped, 'tis naught. Such
a welcome, and I was away but four days."

She laughed and hugged him. "When I was told you were approaching, I ordered water taken to our bedchamber for your bath. Or would you prefer some ale first? Come, my lord, and I will attend you."

He smiled at her tumbling excitement. "I will follow in a moment. First I must see to Demon. I fear his hock is bruised."

"May I help you, my lord?"

Graelam turned to Evian. "Well, boy, you are looking fit. Aye, come with me. My lady, soon." He added, dropping his voice. "'Tis more than a bath that I desire."

He grinned at the rush of color to her cheeks, patted her shoulder, and strode toward the stables, Evian trying valiantly to keep pace with him.

"You are looking well, my lady," Guy said, drawing her attention from her husband's retreating figure.

"What? Oh, Guy!"

He mocked her gently. "You are not concerned about my health, my lady?"

"You, sir," she said with a scolding frown, "are but a worthless knave! It is your responsibility to see that my lord comes to no harm."

"True," Guy sighed. "I fear Graelam's thoughts were on other things, thus his clumsiness. He is the only one of us who has shucked off his fatigue like an old cloak, and all at the sight of you, my lady."

Kassia laughed disclaimingly but turned pink with pleasure at his words.

"I see Blanche hovering about like a disapproving abbess," Guy observed.

Kassia's smile faded somewhat.

"Has she been a trial to you, my lady?"

"Nay, truly, 'tis just that she . . . well, she is unhappy, Guy."

"I imagine she tries to treat you like an unwanted guest," he said shrewdly. "Graelam should find her a husband, and soon." But something deep within him hated that thought. Damn her, he thought, irritated at both himself and her. Why couldn't she let go? But he knew the answer to that. Blanche was strong-willed and determined. She could see no other course open to her.

"She spends much of her time in the chapel," Kassia said. "I fear she is praying not for a husband, but for ways of doing me in. But enough of my woes, Guy! What happened at Crandall?"

"All went just as Graelam thought, and I will leave your husband to tell you about it."

"No fighting? No attempt at treachery?"

"Nay, 'twas revoltingly tame."

"You may be disappointed because there were no heads to knock together, but I am relieved! Just you wait for supper. 'Tis my major accomplishment in the four days you have been absent."

"Strung that varlet Dayken up by his worthless heels?"

"Nay, but I did discover that one of his assistants, a poor fellow who spent most of his time being kicked about and cursed, is really quite accomplished. 'Tis he who now does the cursing!"

The roast pork was tender, well-seasoned, and altogether delicious. Graelam saw that Kassia was regarding him for all the world like a child waiting for her parent's approval, her own food untouched. He sampled the other fare with negligent thoroughness whilst he talked with Blount.

"The merchant Drieux would settle at Wolffeton, my lord," Blount said. "He of course brings some dozen or so men with him."

"And their families?"

"Aye, my lord. As you know, we need no more labor in the fields or in the mill. Our wheat production already exceeds our needs."

"I know it well, Blount. What we do need is money and the ability to trade our excess wool. Prepare a charter. I will meet with Drieux when it is done to settle on terms."

"If it is successful, my lord, it is likely other craftsmen will make their way here."

Graelam nodded, then turned to Kassia. "Did you procure some new wine, my lady? I believe I find something of an improvement."

Her lips tightened until she saw his dark eyes were alight with laughter.

"The merchant Drieux, you know, my lord," she said demurely. "He wished to be in your good graces. The wine is from Bordeaux."

"You lie as fluently as do I," Graelam said, smiling at her.

"But imagine how fluent I shall be when I have gained your years, my lord!"

Blount, trying to hide his gasp, said quickly, "Nay, my lord, 'tis not the wine that is different. My lady but jests."

Graelam turned a surprised look toward his steward. "'Tis the pork, my lord!" Blount continued feebly.

Graelam felt something of a shock when he realized that Blount was trying to protect Kassia from his wrath, that he had, indeed, expected Graelam to be furious at his wife's gentle teasing. But Graelam wasn't angry. He had, in fact, been on the point of continuing the jest with his wife when Blount interrupted.

"And the bread and vegetables and pheasant pie,"

Kassia added on a laugh, wondering why the well-spoken, polished steward was fumbling about for his words.

"I imagine," Graelam said coolly, "that there is even an improvement in the apples. Do they taste redder, Kassia?"

"Actually," Kassia confided, leaning toward her husband, "I did polish yours on my sleeve."

Graelam claimed her hand and slowly raised it to his lips. "I doubt," he said softly, "that this excellent meal—aye, I did notice, you may be certain—could taste as tempting as do you."

"Oh," Kassia said helplessly as his tongue lightly brushed over her palm. She was thrown into confusion, but Graelam merely sat back in his chair and grinned shamelessly at her. He was relieved that his robe was full cut, for his body was reacting just as shamelessly to her.

"He is bewitched," Blanche muttered just loud enough for Guy to hear her.

Guy turned thoughtful eyes to her flushed face. "You must cease this, Blanche," he said finally. Christ, if only he had something to offer her! "Listen to me," he continued in an urgent voice. "Kassia is his wife. That is an end to it. And," he added, seeing that she would say more, "he appears quite pleased with her. How oft must I remind you?"

"Things change," Blanche said. "Aye, he will soon grow bored with her."

"'Twould make no difference in any case."

"Mayhap he would send her back to her father, or she would leave."

"I doubt, Blanche, that you will still be at Wolffeton should such a thing occur."

"You take her part too! Can it be, Sir Guy, that you are also bewitched with the skinny little—"

"Blanche," he said, now thoroughly irritated with her folly, "I would that your thoughts matched your outward beauty. Stop being such a bloody shrew!" Guy turned abruptly away from her, his eyes upon his master and mistress.

Graelam bid an abrupt good night to his men, and rose, grasping Kassia's hand. "At last," he said, drawing her arm through his.

"Does your arm pain you, my lord?" Kassia asked as she skipped up the stairs to keep up with him.

"Nay, 'tis other parts of me that are in dire pain."

Concern washed over her face. "Pray tell me. If I cannot ease you, surely Etta will know of a suitable remedy."

"Presently," he said.

Once inside their bedchamber, he firmly closed the door and leaned against it, watching her. "I have missed you," he said.

"And I you, my lord." She smiled up at him, but he saw that her hands were twisting nervously in the folds of her gown.

"Four days and you fear me again?"

She shook her head. "Nay, I do not fear you, my lord."

"I am relieved. You do know, do you not, how you will ease me?"

Her eyes flew to his face. "Your arm!" she blurted out. "You will hurt your wound."

"There are few stitches to rend, and the bandage is secure. I would ask that you help me out of my clothes."

She did as she was bid, saying nothing until he stood in front of her naked. His desire for her was obvious and she backed away. "Chess!" she exclaimed. "I am really quite good, my lord. Would you like to—"

He cut her off, his brow knot in a frown. "Kassia, I do not want to play chess. I want you naked and in my bed."

She was a fool, she thought, to have wished him home so quickly. "My lord," she said as calmly as she could manage, "I do not wish . . . that is, I cannot be naked!"

His frown deepened. "You cannot still be sore from our last coupling. 'Twas nearly five days ago."

"Nay, I am not sore."

"Kassia, look at me!"

She wanted nothing more than to sink into the fresh reeds beneath her feet and disappear through the floor. Slowly she raised her face, so embarrassed that she was trembling.

"I told you that our coupling would not hurt you again." He heard himself speak the words gently, reassuringly. It bothered him that she did not want him.

"I know," she said quietly. "I would willingly come to you, my lord, but I cannot. Please, I—"

He burst out laughing, and grabbed her, pulling her tightly against him. "You are silly, Kassia," he said. He cupped her face between his hands and lowered his face to kiss her. He felt her start, as if in surprise, and for a moment she responded to him. Then she stiffened, a small cry of distress muffled in his mouth.

"Sweetheart," he said, smiling down at her, "it is your monthly flux, is it not?"

She nodded, mute with embarrassment.

"That is no problem, you will see. Come now, I will help you undress."

She stood still as a stone.

Graelam slowly loosed his hold on her. He guessed
that her embarrassment could not be easily overcome.
He felt his desire fading. Oddly enough, he did not
want to force her, did not want to ease himself in her
body without her feeling equal need for him. "Do you
feel discomfort in your belly?" he asked her gently.

"Nay," she whispered, "'tis not that, my lord."

"I know." He sighed and stepped away from her.
"How much longer, Kassia?"

"Another day or so."

"Come to bed when it pleases you," he said. He sank
down into the soft feather-and-straw mattress and forced
himself to turn on his side away from her. When she
finally slipped into bed beside him, she was wearing
her bedrobe.

He turned and pulled her against him. She was rigid
as a board. He kissed her gently on her forehead.

"I am sorry," she whispered against his chest. "'Tis
just that I have never spoken of such things, save with
Etta."

"I am your husband," he said. "You must learn to
speak to me of everything."

"That is what my father said."

"Your father," Graelam repeated blankly.

She did not reply and Graelam continued to stroke
her back. "You see," she said finally, propping herself
up on her elbow, "I did not become a woman for a very
long time. There was a count from Flanders who saw
me at Charles de Marcey's court when I was fifteen,
and asked my father about marriage. 'Twas Etta who
told my father that I must have more time. He was
upset with me for not telling him myself. But I was so
ashamed." She burrowed her face into the hollow of his
neck.

"What happened to the count?" Graelam asked.

"Once Father and I returned to Belleterre, I worked very hard to convince him that I was indispensable to his comfort. He forgot the count."

"And will you prove yourself just as indispensable to me?"

"Of course," she said, and he could picture the impish smile on her face. "Did not your wine already taste better?"

Graelam grinned into the darkness until his mind finally convinced his body, still vividly hungering of her, that he must wait another day . . . or so. "Perhaps we will play chess tomorrow night," he said.

Graelam stepped into his bedchamber, a frown on his face, for he was worried about Demon's still swollen hock. Also Nan had purposefully brushed her body against him, an invitation clear in her eyes. It had angered him that his body had leapt in response. And there was Blanche, sobbing her heart out against his tunic. He sighed, drawing up at the sight of Kassia, so immersed in her sewing that she did not hear him. He drew closer, a reluctant smile appearing on his lips at her look of intense concentration. His eyes fell to the garment in her lap, and his smile faltered, then disappeared entirely. It was a singularly beautiful piece of burgundy velvet that he had brought back from Genoa.

"What are you doing?"

Kassia jumped, jabbing the needle point into her thumb. "Oh!" she cried, and quickly licked away the drop of blood before it fell to the velvet.

"I repeat," Graelam said, pointing to the velvet on her lap, "what are you doing with that?"

"I wish you had not come in so stealthily, my lord!

Now I am found out!" She smiled winsomely up at him, and felt her smile crack at his continued scowl.

"I do not recall having given you permission to rifle my trunk and make yourself free with my belongings."

She cocked her head as was her unconscious habit, but he felt no tug of amusement, not this time. "Well?" he demanded.

"It did not occur to me, my lord, that you would be . . . upset at my taking the velvet. It is a lovely piece and I thought—"

"What is mine is mine," he said coldly. "If you wished to make yourself a new gown, you should have asked me."

"I thought," she began again, raising her chin just a trifle, "that I shared in your possessions, just as you share in mine."

"Your father," Graelam said, his voice becoming even colder, "did me a great disservice. What is yours is mine, my lady, and what is mine remains mine."

"But that is hardly fair!" she blurted out before she could stop herself.

"God's bones!" Graelam muttered. "Just because I have allowed you to play at being mistress of Wolffeton—"

"Play!" Kassia bounded to her feet, the precious velvet falling to the floor.

"You will not interrupt me again, madam. Pick up the cloth. I do not wish it to become soiled. And remove your stitches."

She stared at him, so indignant that she could find no words. His kindness to her since his return was forgotten. "And what, my lord," she said at last, her voice trembling, "did you intend the velvet for?"

It was Graelam's turn to stare at his wife. He had likely been a fool, he realized, to treat her so indulgently. And poor Blanche. Had Kassia treated her as unkindly as Blanche had sobbed to him? He gritted his teeth. "Pick up the velvet," he repeated, "and let me hear no more of your ill-humored tongue."

Etta, standing still as a tombstone outside the bed-chamber door, listened with mounting fear. Seldom had her gentle mistress ever spoken in anger to anyone. She launched through the open door just as Kassia, too angry to be afraid, shouted, "No!"

"My baby!" Etta exclaimed, rushing toward her mis-tress. "Have you nearly finished with your lord's tunic? He will be so pleased. Oh, forgive me, my lord! I did not know . . . my eyes . . . I did not see you."

Graelam was stopped cold. His eyes narrowed on the old nurse's guileless face, then slewed back to his wife. Slowly he leaned over and picked up the velvet, spread-ing it out over his arm. He looked at the exquisite stitching, traced his fingers over the width of material, and felt a fool. Without raising his head, he said in Etta's direction, "Get out."

Etta, clutching her rosary, fled the bedchamber, praying that she had saved her mistress.

"It is a tunic for me," Graelam said.

"Aye. You are so large, and your shirts and tunics so worn and ill-fitting. I wanted you to be garbed as you should be."

He looked at her for several moments, trying to still his guilt. "You will ask me in the future," he said, and tossed the velvet to her. "And, my lady, you will an-swer me honestly when I ask you a question."

With those emotionless cold words, Graelam turned on his heel and strode from the bedchamber, leaving Kassia to grind her teeth and jab her needle into the velvet. Upon reflection, she knew she should have told him immediately that it was not a gown for herself she was making. But how dare he treat her so! Ill-humored tongue! Looking down, she realized she had set several very crooked stitches and jerked them out of the velvet, venting all her fury on the hapless thread.

15

Graelam stood on the ramparts, looking east toward rolling green hills. He had tried to concentrate on the administrative problems Blount had brought him: two peasants who wanted the same girl for wife; a dispute over the ownership of a pig; and a crusty old man who had wanted to sell Graelam his daughter. But it was no use.

He turned westward and watched the sun make its downward descent. A slight breeze ruffled his hair, and he impatiently smoothed it out of his eyes.

"My lord."

It was as if he had willed her to appear. Slowly Graelam turned to Kassia, standing some distance away from him, her head bowed.

"My lady," he greeted her, his voice clipped.

"The baker has made some pastries I thought you would like—almond and honey, your favorite."

Graelam cursed under his breath. "Can you not come closer?"

She obeyed him, but her step was hesitant. He watched the sunlight create glints of copper and gold in her hair. He felt a pang of guilt and it angered him.

"I don't want the pastries," he said when she came to a pained halt in front of him.

"I did not really come for that reason," Kassia said, raising her head.

She was pale and he saw the strain in her eyes. Damn, he had but chastised her for taking the cloth! "Why did you come?" he asked.

"To tell you I am sorry. I should not have taken the velvet without your permission."

"Then why did you do it?"

"I wanted to surprise you." She looked at him searchingly, hopeful of some bending, but his face was impassive. "I meant no harm."

He saw her blink rapidly and lower her head. Kassia quickly turned away from him, not wanting him to see her tears. Her anger at him was gone, and she had hoped that he would smile at her again and dismiss the entire incident. But he looked all the more grim.

Graelam cursed, and grabbed her arm. "I did not give you permission to go," he said harshly. He closed his hand more tightly about her arm, feeling her delicate and fragile bones that would snap like a twig under his strength. "Why do you not eat the pastries? By all the saints, you are so slight that a breeze could sweep you away."

Kassia did not understand him. He sounded furious, yet his hand had eased on her arm, and his fingers were gently massaging where he had clasped her so harshly.

"Truly, my lord," she said at last, "I did not mean to anger you. I did not think—"

"No, 'tis obvious," he interrupted her, hating the pleading in her voice. He dropped her arm and turned slightly away from her. "You gave orders to have the outbuildings whitewashed."

"Aye," she admitted in a small voice, cursing herself at the same time for her cowardice. Were she at Belleterre, she wanted to shout at him, not only would she have given orders to whitewash the sheds, but she would have also overseen, with her father, the drawing of the charter with the merchant Drieux. Would he give her authority to act as mistress of Wolffeton one minute, and withdraw it the next?

Silence stretched between them. "Have I your permission to go now, my lord?"

"Why, my lady?" he asked, turning to face her again. "Do you not find my company to your liking?"

"I must tell the servants not to whitewash the outbuildings."

"I want it done. Leave be."

Her eyes flew to his face. He smiled at the spark of anger he saw there. But it immediately recalled another matter to mind. "What did you do to Blanche in my absence? She was very upset."

She cocked her head to one side, clearly puzzled. "I . . . I do not understand."

"She was crying earlier." Indeed, she had wet his tunic through. "You are not to give her orders, Kassia, or make her life unpleasant. She is a gentle lady, and deserving of kind treatment."

Surely, Kassia thought, he could not be talking about his sister-in-law, Blanche! Before she could stop herself, she blurted out, "Which Blanche do you mean, my lord? One of the serving maids?"

"Perhaps," he said coldly, "Blanche could teach you submissiveness and the proper respect for your husband."

She felt such a surge of anger that she feared what she would say if she remained with him. She gasped her rage, turned on her heel, and ran as fast as she could back along the narrow walkway.

"Kassia! Come back here!"

She tripped on her long gown at his furious voice, and swayed for an instant, the cobblestones of the inner bailey rising upward toward her.

"Hellfire, you stupid wench!" Graelam roared, his gut wrenching at the sight of her weaving toward the edge of the rampart. He lurched forward, grabbed her arm, and jerked her back. "Have you no sense?" he yelled at her, shaking her so hard her neck snapped back.

She cried out, a soft, broken sound that froze him. He stared down at her white face, cursed savagely, and pulled her against him. He enveloped her in his arms, unconsciously rocking her. She leaned pliantly against him, her cheek pressed against his chest. He could feel her small breasts heaving against him as she tried to stop her gasping breaths. He felt a bolt of lust so powerful that he was momentarily stunned. He realized vaguely that it was born of fear for her, and anger, but it did not matter. She was his wife, dammit, and he had not possessed her for six days!

In one swift motion he lifted her over his shoulder and strode toward the steep wooden stairs that led down to the inner bailey. He paid no attention to the scores of gaping servants or to his men who watched his progress. He was breathing hard when he finally reached their bedchamber, but not from exertion. He kicked the door closed behind him and strode to the bed. He eased her off his shoulder and laid her on her back. He pulled his trousers open, his hands shaking, then turned back to her. He jerked off her leather slippers, pulled up her clothes, baring her to her waist, and flung himself down over her.

"Damn you," he growled harshly, and kissed her brutally.

Kassia felt suspended, as if time had stopped, and she was another, gazing down upon the furious man savaging a girl who was no longer she. She felt his hands upon her, roughly jerking her legs apart. When he reared over her, she realized starkly that he was going to force her. Still, her mind held her utterly still, like a stick puppet with no will of her own. She felt his fingers parting her, felt his rigid manhood thrust inward. A tearing pain seared her, plummeting her mind back into her body. She screamed, a high, thin wailing sound that melded with his harsh breathing, and her body fought the pain. She began to fight him, striking his shoulders and back with all her strength, but she was impaled, helpless.

Graelam felt himself tearing into her small, unwilling body. Thrusting his full length, he seated himself to his hilt. Her pounding fists made no impression on him as he sought to subdue her, to force her to utter submission. He flung himself onto her, grasped her face between his hands, and thrust his tongue into her mouth. At the taste of her salty tears, his mind balked, but his body, intent upon release, rammed into her until his senses blurred and his seed burst from his body, filling her. He was insensate for several moments. It was her helpless moan that jerked him to awareness. He raised himself over her and stared down at her face. Her eyes were pressed tightly closed, her thick lashes wet spikes against her cheeks. There was a spot of blood on her lower lip, bitten in pain.

He closed his own eyes for a moment, wishing he could close out the enormity of what he had done.

"Kassia." Her name was a growl of pain on his lips. He withdrew from her, feeling her quiver, and drew her into his arms. She lay utterly still, unresponsive even as he smoothed the curls back from her forehead.

"Look at me, damn you! Kassia, open your eyes." He clasped her jaw and shook her head until her lashes fluttered and she looked up at him.

What he saw chilled him. She was staring up at him, and he knew that the wide, unseeing look in her eyes reflected her thoughts.

"Stop it!" he shouted at her, shaking her shoulders. She did not respond. For the first time in his life, he felt himself to be despicable, a brute who had hurt someone who had not half his strength. He knew a churning fear that made him tremble. "Kassia," he whispered, and buried his face in her hair.

"You hurt me."

Her small, stricken voice made him jerk his head up. The blind look was gone from her eyes and she was regarding him like a child who does not understand why the parent has struck him.

"You promised you would never hurt me again. You lied to me."

He wanted to beg her forgiveness, but the words stuck in his throat. Never in his life had he uttered such words to a woman. Images of his father telling him that a wife was her husband's possession, to do with as he pleased, careened through his mind. A woman had no will; she existed only through her husband and through her children. He was struggling with himself when she spoke again, softly, her voice holding no anger, no reproach.

"You told me that being a wife was better than being a dog. You told me that there were benefits to being a wife."

"Aye," he said helplessly, "I told you that."

"I think," she said very clearly, "that I should prefer being a dog."

"You have no choice in the matter!" he said sharply. "You are as God fashioned you."

"Must I also blame God?" She moved away from him and he let her go. She pulled her clothing down and stood a moment by the bed. She looked remote, yet utterly calm. "Have I your permission to leave now, my lord? There is the meal to see to. I would not want you displeased."

He stared at her, frustrated, sunk in his own guilt. "Go," he said harshly. She turned away without another word. He saw her weave a moment, then stiffen and walk slowly toward the door.

Graelam closed his eyes a moment. He pictured the Earl of Drexel in his mind, the man whose page and squire he had been, the man who had knighted the very young Graelam for saving his life at the Battle of Evesham. He had attended him after the battle, as was his wont, and watched his blood lust become sexual lust. It did not surprise him, for he had seen his lord take both willing and unwilling women. But the peasant wench had screamed and fought. The earl had merely laughed, cuffing her senseless. "What else are women good for, lad, if not for a man's pleasure? The stupid wench wasn't even a virgin." He had shaken his head, perplexed. The fat priest with them had said nothing. It was a point of debate among Church prelates whether or not women possessed a soul. Then why, Graelam thought, did he feel so despicable, like a mindless, rutting animal? Kassia was his possession. There would be no one to say him nay or even look at him askance if he beat her within an inch of her life, with or without just cause.

Why then did he feel as if he had destroyed something precious, as if he had wantonly crushed a rare flower underfoot before its petals had unfurled?

He rose slowly, like an old man, and straightened his clothes. He paused, seeing blood on his member. He cursed softly to the silent chamber.

Blanche smiled and said gaily to the stone-faced Sir Guy, "Such a shame, is it not, Sir Guy?"

"I do not know what you are talking about," he said coldly, not looking at her.

She laughed. "Ah, such a pity! But I do not suppose you heard her screams? And look at her now. No longer the proud, preening little fool she was!"

Guy had been looking at Kassia. She looked dazed, her face so pale as to be waxen. He saw Graelam lean toward her, and felt himself stiffen as she jerked away. Everyone in the castle knew that Graelam had abused his wife. To Guy's surprise, only a very few of the men had appeared untouched by his actions. Most of them had been tensely silent. Even Blount, Graelam's crusty steward, had tightened his thin lips in anger. Of course Blanche was delighted. He turned to her, and felt his own anger near the boiling point at the smug smile on her lips. He wanted to shake her until her teeth rattled and kiss her until she was breathless.

"To anger Graelam so quickly," she said, shaking her head in mock sorrow. As to her own stirring performance, she firmly repressed her guilt, saying over and over in her mind that she must see to herself and her children, for there was no one else to. She didn't understand why she acted such a witch in front of Guy. *It is because he champions Kassia.* It angered her that he did, but she refused to examine why this was so. After all, he was merely a landless knight. She saw him gazing toward Kassia, and the words flowed angrily from her mouth. "I heard that she had stolen some precious cloth from his trunk. Perhaps he will send her back to her home, where she belongs. Surely, Guy, you do not defend her?"

She supposed that she achieved what she wanted. Guy's lips were drawn in a thin line and his fine eyes glittered at her. His calmly spoken words took her off guard. "Do you know, Blanche, I am tempted to marry you myself. Were you my wife, I would beat you senseless."

"If the girl were not such a fool," Blanche said finally, wishing his words did not dig so deeply, and hating the shuddering response they aroused in her, "Graelam would not have struck her. She thinks herself above all of us. My lord would not long tolerate such airs."

Guy closed his eyes a moment against the temptation to haul Blanche over his shoulder that very instant and carry her from the hall. What he would do with her once he had done this, he didn't know. He forced his attention back to Graelam. He could not understand the lord of Wolffeton. Until today, Graelam had been so gentle toward his lady. There was no doubt in Guy's mind that he had missed Kassia during their absence from Wolffeton. His greeting of her upon their return was proof enough. What, he wondered, was in his lord's mind?

Graelam speared a bit of tender fish on his knife, and thrust it into his mouth. He could feel the tension radiating from Kassia. The fish tasted of fear, her fear, of him.

Damn her! He didn't want her to be afraid of him. He wanted to hear her laugh again, to see the dimples deepen in her cheeks.

I have no choice, Kassia was thinking. No choice at all. I do not understand him, yet I must bear whatever he metes out to me. The events of the day had effectively destroyed all the budding happiness she had known since she had come to Wolffeton as his wife. Why had he been so gentle with her at first, if it was his intention to become a ravening beast? She closed her eyes, knowing that soon she would have to share his bed. Would he force her again? She picked up her goblet of wine, but her hand was shaking so badly, she quickly lowered it back to the table. Where is your pride, you spineless wench? Will you spend the rest of your days cowering, wondering if he will turn on you again if you serve him a meal not to his liking or speak to Blanche in a voice that pleases him not?

Her chin went up, and she sat straight in her chair. Slowly she turned to face her husband.

"My lord," she said quietly, drawing his attention from his baked heron.

He looked at her intently, and she had to call upon a strength she had not known she possessed not to cower. "Aye?" he asked, his expression impassive.

"I would like to . . . understand my role at Wolffeton."

He saw the firmness in her eyes, and felt a moment

of pleasure at her defiance. But she is but a woman, his mind told him. A woman, especially a wife, must never dictate to her husband. "Your role," he said calmly, "is to see to my pleasure."

Her eyes remained steady on his face. "You told me that you had allowed me to play at being mistress at Wolffeton. I know that I am young, my lord, but I managed Belleterre since my mother's death, a holding just as vast as this keep. Is it your pleasure that I indeed be the mistress of Wolffeton?"

She saw his eyes go briefly toward Blanche, and felt a surge of fury wash through her. She spoke without thought. "Why did you not wed her, my lord? Why did you not allow our marriage to be annulled?"

It was odd, Graelam thought, but he did not have an answer to her question. Indeed, his thinking continued, how dare she even question him?

"You are the mistress of Wolffeton," he said coldly. "But you will not harm those less fortunate than you. Do you understand me?"

Again she blurted out her thoughts, sarcasm thick in her voice. "I, fortunate, my lord?"

"Enough, Kassia!" His voice, a low hiss, washed over her. He clutched her arm, and her courage, illusory at best, faltered. She knew she could not try to jerk away from him, not in front of fifty people! Not in front of Blanche or the serving wench, Nan.

"As you wish, my lord," she said, bowing her head. "As mistress of Wolffeton, I will need funds to see to improvements within the keep."

"There are none," he said shortly.

"Soon you will sign the charter with the merchant Drieux. In my experience, the charter will bring you immediate access to goods."

He stared at her a moment. "In your experience? A woman should not understand those things," he said slowly. He saw the mounting frustration in her eyes, and shrugged. "Very well, you have my permission to speak with Blount. But, my lady, you will not instruct him."

"Aye, I understand," she said, her head still bowed. "He is a man, and thus far superior to me. I am not to annoy him with my silly questions and demands."

"You understand well," he said sharply. "See that that sarcastic tongue of yours stays quiet in your mouth."

Her hand balled into a fist in her lap.

"Aye," he added softly, "and watch Blanche. I find her . . . attitude and demeanor much to my liking."

"As you wish, my lord. It will be just as you say, my lord. May I now be excused now, my lord? I wish to retire."

Even though her words reeked with meekness, Graelam knew that she was mocking him. Her submissiveness was feigned. It both pleased him and angered him. She was unlike any woman in his experience. She was gently bred, and yet he had treated her cruelly. He sighed. "You may go."

Kassia endured Etta's worried frowns and clucking advice all during her bath.

"Please, leave off, Etta," she said finally, wrapping her bedrobe securely about her.

"But, my baby, you cannot continue to challenge your lord!"

"I did not say that I had," Kassia said sharply.

Etta shook her head sadly. "There is no need. I know you."

"Would you prefer that I lie down upon the floor and let him tread over me like a rug?"

"He is not your father, my baby. He is a man who is used to command, a man who—"

"Odd," Kassia said in a low voice, cutting Etta off, "until this day I had begun to believe him as kind and gentle as my father. I was a fool."

"He owns you!"

"Aye, what a joy to be owned by a man who hates me!"

Graelam paused a moment, her words searing through his mind, then pushed the bedchamber door open. "Go," he said to Etta, his eyes upon Kassia.

Etta cast her mistress a pleading look, and took herself off.

Kassia could not look at him. She felt utterly vulnerable, clothed only in the flimsy bedrobe, and alone with him. He took a step toward her, and she flinched, stepping back.

"Get into bed," he said, standing motionless before her. "And take off that robe. You will wear nothing unless it is your monthly flux."

She did not move. She saw herself as she had been today, lying helplessly beneath him. She winced anew at the memory of the pain.

"Is that order so difficult for you to understand?"

Even as the words flew from her mouth, she knew that she was a fool to try to bargain with him. "Only if you swear to me that you will not force me again."

"Damn!" he swore. "I will take you whenever it pleases me to do so!"

"No!"

The small defiant word held him frozen for an instant. He took another step toward her, only to halt again when he saw tears swimming in her eyes.

"Go to bed, Kassia," he said shortly, and turned away from her.

He heard no sound or movement. "Do as I tell you," he said over his shoulder.

"I . . . I am afraid of you."

The whispered words made him close his eyes over an elusive pain that he did not understand.

"I swear I will not force you," he said finally. Perversely, the moment the words were out of his mouth, he felt that he had given in to her, and saw himself as one of those weak men he despised. He added, knowing well the cruelty of his words, "You are a child, and as unresponsive as a nun. It would give me no pleasure to take you again. You do not have a woman's grace, a woman's yielding, or a woman's softness."

She wanted to scream at him: *Like your slut Nan?* But she said nothing. She walked slowly to the bed, slipped between the covers, and pulled them to her chin.

She listened to him splash in the tub. Slowly, without wishing to, she stroked her hand over her body. I have the body of a child, she thought. Would he have been more pleased with her if she were full-fleshed like Blanche? Her hand paused a moment in the valley of her belly. Her pelvic bones were still prominent when she lay upon her back. She tensed and quickly whipped her hand away when her fingers lightly touched the nest of curls. She did not want to touch herself where he had. When she saw him step from the tub, she tightly closed her eyes.

She heard his firm footsteps toward the bed. She held herself rigid, terrified that he would not keep his word.

But he did nothing. He lay on top of the covers on his back, motionless for many minutes. Suddenly he turned toward her. Startled, she whimpered softly, and rolled to the side of the bed.

He cursed softly, but made no move to touch her. Kassia did not ease until she heard his breathing become slow and regular in sleep.

16

"What lovely stitches," Blanche said. "I can scarce see them. You sew them much more proficiently than I."

Kassia's fingers froze over the material. She looked up warily at Blanche. "Thank you," she said finally, her voice clipped. The last thing she wanted to endure was more baiting and insults from that lady! But Blanche was smiling at her.

"Do you mind if I sit with you for a while? I have a rent to mend in my tunic. Perhaps I can improve my stitches if I watch you closely."

"What do you want, Blanche?" Kassia asked without preamble.

Blanche lowered her head a moment. She said softly, "I want us to be friends, Kassia. I know that I have not been kind to you."

Kind! You have treated me like a blight!

Blanche persevered, her voice liquid with shame. "'Twas jealousy that made me act as I did. I wanted Graelam, but he chose first Joanna, then you. It was not well done of me. I wish there to be peace between us."

Kassia did not think herself a gullible fool, but she was lonely, and terribly unhappy. The past week and a half had dragged past even though Blount had enthusiastically approved everything she wished to do within Wolffeton, and work had begun. It was not that she was bored or felt useless. No never that. She was the mistress of Wolffeton. She felt herself go tense remembering how Graelam had watched the great hall scrubbed clean of years of filth, sniffed at the fresh reeds that were scattered with a special mixture of sweet rosemary, lavender, and other herbs and flowers handed down from Kassia's grandmother. She had waited for him to say something, anything, but he had merely grunted, ignoring her.

Blanche saw Kasaia looking wistfully toward the far whitewashed wall and guessed the direction of her thoughts. She said with gentle praise, "You have performed wonders. I had not believed Wolffeton could be so beautiful." She forced herself to sigh softly. "And the servants respect you and obey you. I wanted to make changes, you know, but they would not heed me. And the cushions you are making! How often I have wished to be more at ease in my chair!"

That brought a reluctant smile to Kassia's lips. "Aye," she said with a bit more enthuaiasm, "I have felt the same way."

"Will you let me help you?" Blanche asked humbly. "I do have some skill with a needle."

"Aye," Kassia said again slowly, still wary of the incredible change in Blanche. "If you would like, 'twould make us all more comfortable that much sooner."

The two women sewed together companionably until

the light faded. "Just a few more minutes," Kassia said, "and I shall be through with this cushion."

"It is for your lord?" Blanche asked, her voice sympathetic.

"It is," Kassia said shortly, wondering what Graelam would say, wondering if Graelam would even notice.

She started when Blanche reached over and gently patted her hand. "All will be well between you, Kassia. You will see. Graelam is a man unused to gently bred ladies, but your care of him will soon change his thinking."

Kassia felt tears cloud her vision. "Perhaps you are right, Blanche."

"Of course I am right," Blanche said stoutly. "Whilst you finish your lord's cushion, is there something you would like me to do?"

Kassia sniffed back her tears. "Nay," she said, managing a wan smile. "The servants have things well in hand. I do thank you, Blanche. I really do."

Graelam noticed the rich red velvet cushion immediately. It was thick and soft, stuffed with goose down, and beautifully made. He ran his hand over its smooth surface.

"I have begun another cushion for the back of your chair," Kassia said.

He heard the wariness in her voice but ignored it. "Will you make more cushions? For your chair as well?"

"Aye, but 'twill take me several weeks."

"The material appears very valuable. Did Blount approve its purchase?"

Kassia wanted to throw the cushion in his face. She fought down anger at his barely veiled accusation, but was saved from answering him by Blount himself.

"Aye, my lord," he said proudly. "I agreed with your lady that Wolffeton should boast only the best. With her skill, it is achieved."

Graelam grunted and sat down. "It is an improvement," he said, and reached for his wine goblet.

Blount gave his master an incredulous look. He caught Lady Kassia's eye, and bit back his words. He did not understand Lord Graelam. He had been in a black, savage mood for so long now that the household was afraid to come near him. His bellows of anger made their blood run cold. But to treat his gentle lady as he would his servants! Blount shook his grizzled head and walked slowly down the trestle table and seated himself down on the bench beside Sir Guy.

Kassia waited until Graelam had drunk two goblets of wine and eaten heartily of his dinner. "My lord," she said carefully.

"Aye?"

He can't even bring himself to look at me! She gritted her teeth and continued. "The merchant Drieux assures me that we can barter wool for carpets from Flanders. The carpets at Belleterre come from Spain, but he tells me that Flanders weaves beautiful ones as well. I thought crimson, to complement the chair cushions."

"Carpets, my lady?" Graelam asked, turning slightly in his chair to face her, his dark brows raised. "Is it your desire to turn this keep into a palace? Do you find Wolffeton so much to your distaste?"

Damn you, my lord! she thought. She knew well that Graelam had been to the Holy Land and admired the comfort and luxury of the furnishings there. Her father had told her so.

"Aye," she said baldly. "If you do not wish to barter wool, I will send a message to my father. Surely he will be most willing to fill Wolffeton with beauty."

"You will send no message to your father!" He hit his fist against the trestle table, making his trencher tremble.

"Very well," Kassia said calmly, forcing herself to hold firm in the face of his ill-humor. "What is your wish then, my lord?"

I am spiting myself, Graelam realized suddenly, and the little witch knows it well. God's bones, he wanted to break her! How dare she criticize his home? She had held her little chin high and ignored him during the past days, knowing that she was safe from him at night, for, fool that he was, he had sworn he wouldn't force her. The power he had given her unthinkingly!

He was saved from a reply by Guy's laughing voice reaching him over the din. "My lord! You have the look of a man whose buttocks are well content! Will you grant your lesser men such comforts?"

"All you deserve, Sir Guy," Graelam shouted back, "is the flat of my sword against your buttocks!"

There were hoots of laughter from the men, and Drake, the armorer, slapped Guy on the back. "I'd say," he chortled, "that yer young butt needs nothing more than a good strapping."

Graelam turned back to his wife. She was laughing, and there was a gentle smile in her eyes. He followed the direction of her gaze and felt himself stiffen. Guy! She was smiling at the handsome younger man openly. A knot of anger burned in his gut.

"Kassia!"

She flinched at his harshness, her smile at the men's jests dying on her lips. She forced her eyes to his, and waited for him to continue.

"Fetch your cloak. I wish to speak to you."

She hesitated, cursing herself for her cowardice, but still afraid of his intentions.

He lowered his voice to a soft, menacing snarl. "Would you prefer the privacy of our chamber?"

She jumped up from her chair. Nan stood closest to her, and she called to the serving girl, her voice abrupt in her fear. "My cloak, Nan. 'Tis in my chamber."

Nan gave her a venomous look before leaving the hall.

Kassia downed the remainder of her wine, willing herself to be calm.

"Are you always so sharp with the servants, my lady?"

She gave him a wide, uncomprehending look.

"*My* servants?" he added with stark emphasis.

"You mean your slut," she muttered under her breath, bur she shook her head, her eyes lowered.

Kassia felt Guy's sympathetic gaze upon her as Graelam led her from the hall, his hand cupping her elbow. She looked at him, giving him a tentative smile.

Graelam jerked at her arm. She walked hurriedly beside him down the deep-set stairs and into the inner bailey. The moon was nearly full and cast a silvery light over the keep.

She drew a deep breath. "Where do you wish to go, my lord?"

"To the ramparts."

Would he throw her over? She pictured her body flailing through the empty air, hurtling toward the ground, and shivered.

When they reached the east tower, Graelam halted, clasped both her arms, and turned her face to him.

Slowly he eased his hands down her arms, his dark,

brooding eyes never leaving her face. She felt his fingers circle her throat and tighten slightly.

"You will not escape me in another man's arms," he said softly, his fingertips lightly stroking her slender neck.

"I . . . I do not know what you mean, my lord," she whispered.

"Do you not, my lady?" He stared down at her pale face, and his lips twisted. "A woman is born with lies already forming in her mouth. Most women, I fancy, have the wit to hide their coy looks in their husbands' presence. But you, Kassia, you were blessed with a father who could not believe ill of you. Listen well, lady wife. I will not tolerate being made the fool, the cuckold."

Kassia could only stare at him. He believed she wished one of his men as her lover? The only one of his men she spent any time with at all was his steward. It was so ridiculous as to be laughable. She said sharply, forgetting her fear of him, "Am I no longer to smile, my lord? Am I no longer to speak to Blount? By all the saints, he is old enough to be my father!"

"'Twas not Blount who won your winsome smile, my lady. You will cease your woman's deception. You will never lie with another man, and if it is your woman's wish to have your belly plowed, 'tis I who will do it."

"No!" she gasped. "You promised me!"

"Think you I will allow Guy to enjoy your favors when my back is turned?"

"Guy," she repeated blankly.

"Aye, even his name sounds soft on your lips."

"You are ridiculous," she hissed at him, drawing out each word.

Graelam gave a growl of anger and jerked her against

him. She struck her fists against his chest, but he only tightened his hold and her arms fell uselessly to her sides. He lowered his head, and she twisted back, feeling his kiss land on her throat. His hand wound in her hair, holding her still, and she sobbed softly when his mouth crushed against hers. His tongue was stabbing against her lips to gain entrance. She pictured herself when last he had taken her: docile as a stick, passive, enduring the pain without fight. Let him beat me, she thought. She parted her lips slightly, and when he thrust his tongue into her mouth, she bit down on it, hard.

He drew back from her in fury. "You little bitch," he panted, touching his mouth. Grabbing her shoulders, he shook her until her head lolled back on her neck. Suddenly he dropped his hands and took a step back from her.

Frantic words burst from her mouth. "And will you force me again? Rape me? I want no man to touch me, do you hear? No man! You are all brutes, selfish animals! You spoke once to me of pleasure. Ha! There is none for the woman. She must lie still and endure your cruel rutting! You have done naught but lie to me, Graelam! I hate you!"

He raised his hand, wanting to cover her mouth, to shut out her torrent of words, to bring her against him again. She jerked away, shrieking at him. "Kill me then! I care not!"

His eyes narrowed on her face, dark as the night. Without a word, he turned away from her and strode down the wooden walkway to the inner bailey. He paused but a moment, her soft sobs reaching him, and cursed under his breath.

She is but a woman, my possession, damn her! Her

worth is only what I choose to grant her. Still, he could not shut out her broken sobs, after he was too far away to hear them.

Kassia rose slowly, aware suddenly that she was shivering from cold. She pulled her cloak more closely about her shoulders and walked back toward the keep. Graelam's men-at-arms were in the inner bailey, and she forced herself to square her shoulders and walk up the deep stairs into the great hall, ignoring their glances. Servants were clearing off the trestle tables. She saw Blanche from the corner of her eye, but did not stop. She reached the bedchamber, but her hand froze on the huge brass handle. No, she thought frantically. He is within. I cannot bear to face him now. She turned away and walked slowly toward the spinning room. Moonlight streamed through the unshuttered windows as she stepped quietly into the darkened room. She heard strange grunting sounds coming from the corner where bolts of material were stacked.

She saw them clearly. Graelam was astride Nan, his powerful naked body thrusting between her white legs. Nan was groaning, her hands stroking frantically over his back, her legs wrapped around his flanks.

Kassia felt bile rise in her throat. She was not aware that a soft keening sound came from her mouth. She jerked around and ran from the room.

Graelam's lust drove him blindly. He was intent upon exorcising Kassia's pale, distraught face from his mind. He heard the odd wailing sound, and turned quickly to see Kassia flee from the room. His lust disappeared as if it had never existed. He jerked out of Nan's body, and rolled over, staring toward the door.

"My lord," Nan whispered urgently. "Please . . ."

He wanted to vomit, to curse, to rail at himself for

being such a bloody fool. He said nothing, merely rose and began to pull on his clothes.

He heard Nan call out to him, but he ignored her. He strode to his bedchamber and flung open the door. Kassia was not there. He called out her name, hating the fear in his voice. She was not in the keep. He ran toward the stables, knowing well that she could not simply ride away from Wolffeton, for the porter would never raise the portcullis or lower the drawbridge for her. The postern in the eastern wall! His blood froze in his veins as he remembered how he himself had shown Kassia the hidden entrance into Wolffeton. Her mare, Bluebell, was gone. He drew a deep steadying breath, knowing that she had only minutes on him, and quickly drew on Demon's bridle. He swung himself onto his destrier's broad back.

He saw her quickly enough, riding along the cliffs, her mare's pace frantic. He yelled her name, but she did not slow.

He leaned down close to Demon's neck and urged him forward. The mare was no match for the powerful destrier.

Kassia heard the pounding hooves behind her. She didn't look back, for she knew it was Graelam. She dug her heels into Bluebell's sides, her sobs echoing with her mare's labored breathing in the still night.

Graelam tried to grab the mare's reins, but Kassia pulled her sharply, jerking her so close to the edge of the cliff that Graelam felt his blood turn cold. He dared not crowd her. He kept pace until the ground evened out, then turned Demon sharply toward the mare and grabbed Kassia about her waist and lifted her off Bluebell's back. She fought him, struggling wildly, hitting at

his chest with her fists. He pulled Demon to a halt,
pressed Kassia tightly against him, and jumped to the
ground.

"You little fool," he muttered, tightening his hold
about her slender ribs. "God's bones, you could have
killed yourself!"

"I don't care."

He eased her back to look into her face. He expected
tears, waited for her to plead with him. To his utter
surprise, she drew back her foot and kicked him in the
shin. He grunted with the sharp pain.

"You test the fates," he said, his voice low and calm.

She said nothing, merely stared up at him.

"Did you really think to escape me? By yourself?
Have you no wits at all?"

"What could have happened to me, my lord?" He felt
her stiffen, felt her draw herself up. "Mayhap brigands
would have caught me. What could they have done to
me? Beat me? Rape me? Cut my throat?" She shrugged,
looking away from him, out over the white-capped sea.

"You saw me in the weaving room."

She cocked her head, her eyes wintry. "Aye, I saw
you." She heard him draw in his breath, but continued
in a deadly calm voice, "Forgive me for interrupting
your . . . pleasures." She shrugged again. "At least it
keeps you away from me."

"You . . . angered me," he said.

She looked at him searchingly. "Will you send me
home, my lord? Back to Belleterre? 'Twill still be yours.
My father would not renege on your agreement."

"No!"

"Why not? You care nothing for me."

"You are mine," he said very softly, "and what is

mine I keep. Never again try to escape me, Kassia, else I will lock you away."

Unbidden, the image of Graelam thrusting into Nan rose into her mind, and she felt such fury that she felt she would choke on it. She drew back her hand and slapped him as hard as she could.

"Now you will either kill me or let me go," she hissed, her voice breaking with little gasps.

No woman had ever struck him. One man had, once, long ago, and he had died very quickly. She was so small, so fragile. He could kill her with one blow. He did not move. "You will bend to me," he said finally, very quietly. "Aye, you will bend to me, for I am your master and your husband."

She stood stiff as a stone before him, her silence defiance.

"Come, Kassia," he said, taking her arm quite gently. "We are returning to Wolffeton before my men mount a search."

She knew she had no choice. If she struggled with him, he could simply subdue her with one arm.

As she rode beside him back to Wolffeton, she felt the maze of anger and shock recede from her mind. Dear God, what had she done? She did not want to be a prisoner; she did not want him to beat her. She ran her tongue over her dry lips.

"What will you do?"

He heard the thread of fear in her voice. She will bend to me, he thought. But he hated her fear.

He said nothing. When they rode into the inner bailey, Guy rushed toward them, his face drawn with worry. Graelam saw him gaze toward his wife, and felt a renewed surge of anger at the tenderness in Guy's eyes.

"My wife wished for a midnight ride," he said curtly. "See to our horses," he continued to the stable boy. He pulled Kassia off Bluebell's back and led her into the keep.

Blanche watched Graelam draw Kassia toward the stairs. She stayed in the shadows of the hall, a small smile lifting the corners of her mouth. Soon, she thought. Very soon.

17

Graelam stood against the door of his bedchamber, his arms crossed over his chest, watching Kassia walk slowly toward his chair and ease down on its edge.

"Why did you run from me?" he asked abruptly.

She did not look up. He saw her hands twisting frantically in her lap.

"Why?" he repeated.

"I . . . I don't know," she said finally.

His dark eyes gleamed. "Could it be, my lady wife," he drawled softly, "that you were jealous? Nan is a comely wench, and enjoys a man well."

Her head shot up, and he felt a stab of anger at the incredulous look on her face. Was she so impervious to him then?

"Aye, jealous," he repeated, even more softly this time.

The words tumbled out before she could halt them. "Jealous because my husband takes another woman? Nay, my lord. If you do not choose to honor our marriage vows, who am I to gainsay you?"

"Then why did you run from me?"

"I . . . I did not wish to stay," she said, knowing he could see the lie in her eyes. She could not answer his question, even to herself. She had felt fury and such unhappiness that she had not thought clearly. She had thought only to escape.

"Ah, Kassia," he said, striding toward her. "You begin to try my patience." He saw her eyes darken as he approached her, and her slender body stiffen. He stopped. "You are such a curious little thing," he said, stroking his chin thoughtfully. "You strike me, revile me, and tremble with fear before me. And you lie to me. Come here, Kassia."

She heard the steel in his voice, even though he had spoken softly, almost meditatively. Slowly, hating herself for her cowardice, she rose and walked to him. She stiffened when he closed his hands over her arms.

"Look at me," he said.

She obeyed him.

"Listen well, wife, for I will not tell you again. You will keep your winsome smiles to yourself, and away from Sir Guy, or any other of my men for that matter. And, Kassia, if ever you do something so stupid as attempt to flee from me, I will treat you like an ill-broken mare." His hands tightened on her arms. "Do you understand me, wife?"

"I understand you," she whispered.

"Do you? Do you really? I wonder. Your father was like soft rain flowing through your small fingers, wasn't he? He suffered your woman's demands, your woman's wiles, without complaint. Indeed, he was so besotted with you that he did not see the power you wielded over him. I am not your father. To assist you to understand me, I will be more specific, my lady. If ever again you attempt to flee from me, I will tie you to my bed. I will spread your legs wide, and I will use you until I am tired of your skinny body. Now do you understand?"

"I understand," she whispered again.

"Good." He released her and calmly began removing his clothing. He paused a moment, then strode naked to the door and opened it.

"Evian!" he bellowed.

The small boy scampered up from his pallet. "Aye, my lord?"

"Fetch me a goblet of wine, boy."

Graelam turned and stood indolently by the open door, as if daring her to gaze upon him. "You do not wish to look upon your husband?"

Kassia felt a frisson of alarm. She moistened her lips and forced herself to gaze at him. "I am looking," she said.

"Do you feel no quickening between your slender thighs my lady? No desire to share your husband's bed?"

His mocking voice made her forget her fear of him, just as he guessed it would. "Shall I get Nan for you, my lord?" she asked coldly. "Perhaps," she continued, "the wine will help you, for I do not believe you are ready for her."

He drew in his breath, his eyes glittering with amusement. "Wine my lady wife, has not that effect. A drunken husband is an impotent one. But that is what you would prefer, is it not?"

"Allow me, my lord, to have a cask sent from Belleterre for you."

He threw back his head and laughed deeply. "You do not break, do you? Particularly if you are more than ten feet away from me. My distance gives you courage. Ah, my wine. Thank you, boy. Go back to your bed now."

He shut the door with the heel of his foot, downed the wine, and walked to his bed, knowing that her eyes followed him. He stretched upon his back and turned his dark eyes toward her. "Let us test the power of the wine. Remove your clothes, and then we shall see."

She shook her head, mute.

"You fear me again?"

She nodded, hating herself, hating him.

"Very well. Blow out the candles to preserve your modesty. I will not tell you again, Kassia."

She scampered to douse the candles. She looked warily toward the unshuttered windows. Moonlight flowed unhampered into the room. She picked up her bedrobe and fled to the far corner of the chamber. Her fingers worked clumsily at the fastenings of her gown. She did not understand him. There had been no ladies in her life to guide her in dealing with a man such as he. But how to deal with a man who mocked and laughed at her, a man who seemed at one moment to despise her and the next to threaten her when she had tried to escape him?

She drew a shaky breath, and drew her bedrobe tightly around her.

"Kassia, I await you."

She shivered at the words he had spoken. He knew that she feared him, knew that she was helpless against him. She slipped between the covers and lay perfectly still.

"Come here."

His voice was soft, even beguiling. It was the same voice he had used when she had first come to Wolffeton. That time seemed so long ago now. He had been gentle, drawing her trust to him. She remembered teasing him, smiling at him, enjoying his touch.

"Please," she whispered, even as she forced her body to turn toward him.

His arms closed around her, drawing her against him. He felt the tension in her, could hear her short, gasping breaths as she tried to still her fear of him. One of her hands was drawn into a fist and lay against his chest.

Graelam frowned at himself as his hand gently began to knead the nape of her neck. If he wanted to take her, he should simply rip aside her clothing and possess her. A promise to a woman meant nothing. A promise, he reminded himself, gave a woman power. He felt the delicate bones of her shoulders as his hand gently continued its slow kneading. As the minutes passed, he felt the tension ease from her body. Her tight muscles relaxed under his probing fingers. His promise to her. He smiled into the darkness. No, he would not force her again. He would make her beg for him.

He continued stroking her until he felt her heart slow and her breathing even into sleep.

He turned on his side, facing her. He gathered her against him, and felt himself grow hard at the feel of her soft belly. He smiled, harshly, and willed himself to sleep.

When he awoke early the next morning, Kassia was wrapped in his arms, one of her slender thighs between his legs, her cheek burrowed into the hollow of his neck. Slowly he eased his hand inside her bedrobe and began to caress her buttocks. She feels like soft satin, he thought, and his body leapt in response. Her legs were slightly parted, easing his way, and he rested his fingers against her warm softness, savoring the feel of her, the delicate womanness.

As his fingers rhythmically stroked her and caressed
her, she sighed softly in her sleep and drew closer to
him, her arm tightening over his chest.

Kassia moaned, and the sound from her own throat,
deep and aching, brought her to consciousness. Her
lashes fluttered in the dim early-morning light. She was
first aware of encompassing warmth, then a tingling
sensation low in her belly. She lay very still, not understanding, her mind still befuddled with sleep and the
gentle, aching dream that had made her want to burrow
and move sensuously within it. She felt a raspy breath
against her temple. Graelam. She stiffened, aware of
his body, his fingers tormenting her.

"Hush," she heard him say softly, his lips feathering
lightly against her ear.

She felt the sensation burn deep within her, and her
body, without her permission, moved against his questing fingers. She felt the thick hair on his chest against
her breasts, and she pressed herself more closely against
him.

"That pleases you, doesn't it, Kassia?"

She moaned, her hands clutching at him.

Suddenly his fingers were gone, and he had left her.
She watched him stupidly as he rose from the bed and
gazed down at her. She stared up at him, her body
bereft, not understanding. She trembled with need,
and suddenly awareness flooded over her, and she knew
what he had done to her.

"Aye," he said, his dark eyes alight on her face. "Will
you beg me to take you now, my lady wife? You must
beg me, you know."

She quivered with fury at herself, quivered with her
own weakness. "I hate you," she whispered, the words
coming from her mouth in a hoarse croak.

He threw back his head and laughed deeply.

She felt so humiliated, so light-headed with rage at what he had done, she could not control herself. She jumped from the bed, oblivious of her nakedness, and flung herself at him, pounding her fists at his chest, yelling her fury at him.

He clasped her hands easily. "Remind me, Kassia," he said in a taunting whisper, "to tell you how to hurt a man." Carelessly he picked her up in his arms and tossed her back onto the bed.

"I hate you!" she shrieked at him. "You are cruel, an animal! I will hurt you!"

"Oh no, wife," he said, his eyes narrowing on her pale face. "A possession does not harm its master."

She closed her eyes against the utter hopelessness his words brought her.

"I wish to break my fast," he said coldly, his voice matter-of-fact. "Dress yourself and see to it."

Kassia chattered with desperate gaiety as she rode beside Blanche. She saw the look of pity on the other woman's face, and grew silent. Whatever had happened to change Blanche was a blessing, Kassia thought. She had been naught but sympathetic and kind during the past several days. Kassia was grateful to her when she suggested that they ride this morning. She wanted nothing more than to escape Wolffeton, for even a brief period of time. Escape her husband and that knowing, mocking look in his eyes.

"Evian is a kind boy," she said, breaking the silence. "The men have taken him under their wings."

"He worships Graelam," Blanche said. She saw the pain in Kassia's eyes and quickly said, "Forgive me. It is a lovely morning, is it not? And the sea is so calm, like polished glass."

"Aye," Kassia said shortly. "Let us ride to the east, Blanche."

"I do not know if we should." Blanche appeared to hesitate, a frown appearing between her brows.

"'Twas you who disdained an escort, Blanche. We are well on Wolffeton land. There are none to harm us."

"I suppose you are right," Blanche said. "I worry because your husband did not give us permission to ride out. I do not wish to anger him."

He is angered no matter what I do, Kassia thought bleakly.

Dienwald de Fortenberry sat easily on his destrier, calmly eyeing the two riders coming toward him. He recognized Blanche readily enough, but it was the other woman who held his attention. She wore a voluminous cloak and a hood covered her hair. The lady Blanche was undoubtedly correct, he thought. No man who cared for his wife would allow her to ride unprotected, even on his own lands. She was a shrew, Blanche had told him. Spoiled and sullen, and Lord Graelam would be glad to see the last of her. He had been tricked into taking her to wive, forced to recognize her.

The two men who had accompanied him were growing restive. He glanced back and frowned them to silence. He would play the game according to Blanche's rules, he thought. Some minutes later, he waved his men forward. They rode out from the cover of the trees toward the two women.

Kassia saw the men coming and felt a moment of alarm. The man at their head was richly dressed. When he raised his hand and waved at them, she drew up Bluebell.

When the man drew close enough for her to make out his face, she knew she had been wrong. He was looking intently at her, and his eyes were narrowed and cruel. For a moment she could not draw a breath. "Blanche!" she cried, her voice a croak. "Flee!"

She wheeled Bluebell about and dug her heels into her mare's sides. The wind tore the hood back from her hair. She felt her heart pound frantically against her breast. How could she have been so stupid as to ride out without men to accompany them?

She saw the shadow of the man as he closed beside her. She tried to jerk Bluebell away, but Blanche was riding close on her other side, hemming her in. She screamed as the man leaned over and grabbed her around her waist and lifted her easily. She fought him, kicking wildly, her hands flailing at his face. He drew to a halt. "Hold, my lady," he said, and shook her.

Kassia was beyond reason, and she continued to kick at him.

"If you do not stop your struggling, I will throw you facedown over the saddle."

Kassia went limp. He gathered her against him, sheltering her in the crook of his arm. She saw the two other men surround Blanche.

The man wheeled his horse about, shouting at the other two men to bring Blanche.

You are such a fool, Kassia. Such a fool. She heard herself ask in a small, thready voice. "Who are you? What do you want?"

Dienwald said nothing, merely spurred his destrier to a faster pace. They rode east for some twenty more

minutes. When he waved his men to a halt, Kassia was
rigid with fear.

He leapt from the saddle, carrying her as if she were
naught but a feather. He eased her to her feet. "You
will stay here, my lady," he said in a clipped, cold
voice. "If you try to leave, I will beat you senseless."

Dienwald watched her carefully, to judge if she would
obey him. Her face drained of color. She would obey
him, he had no doubt about it. "What is that woman's
name?"

"Blanche de Cormont. Please do not harm her."

His brows lowered a moment. "Lady Blanche," he
called out. He motioned the two men to stay with
Kassia, then strode toward Blanche.

"Please," Kassia called after him, "do not harm her!"

"Come," Dienwald said to Blanche.

He took her arm roughly and led her into a copse of
thick oaks.

"You have done well, my lord," Blanche said crisply,
shaking off his hand.

"Of course," he said. "The jewels."

"Ah, certainly." Blanche pulled a leather pouch from
the pocket in her cloak. She opened it slowly and
spread out a heavy barbaric necklace of thick pounded
gold. Diamonds and rubies glittered from their set-
tings, huge stones that made his eyes glitter as bright as
the jewels.

"It is beautiful, is it not? Certainly valuable enough
to take her to Brittany."

"Lord Graelam brought it from the Holy Land?"
Dienwald asked, fingering a large ruby.

"Aye. But neither you nor I, my lord, have anything
to fear. Lord Graelam will think his wife stole it to
escape him."

Dienwald raised his eyes from the beautiful necklace. "If it is so valuable," he said slowly, "will he not try to find her, just for its return? I would, were I he."

Blanche smiled easily. "I doubt that he will realize it is missing for at least a few days. And when he does, it will be too late. He will likely believe her dead at the hands of her . . . cohorts." She shrugged. "That, or he will believe her returned to her father in Brittany, in which case he would assume that she had long rid herself of the necklace." She cocked a taunting brow at him. "There is nothing for you to fear, my lord."

"You have planned this well, my lady." He gently wrapped the necklace back into its leather pouch and thrust it into his tunic.

"Aye. I have had naught but time to do so."

"'Tis odd," he continued, looking back at Kassia. "The little chick was afraid for you."

Blanche laughed, but it was a grating mirthless sound. Still your ridiculous guilt, you fool, she chided herself. The girl would certainly be better off back with her father. Graelam had made her life a misery. Blanche was but doing her a favor. Her eyes did not quite meet Dienwald's as she said, "Kassia believes me her friend. You will find her something of a fool. But you will not harm her."

"Oh, but that is the rub, is it not? Whatever am I to do with her?"

"Return her to her doting father," Blanche said sharply. "The necklace is worth your trouble to send her to Brittany. There is no reason to kill her or harm her in any way."

Dienwald smiled. "Do you not fear that Graelam will go to Brittany to fetch her? Perhaps he will believe her story that she was kidnapped."

"Nay. I know him. His pride will not allow him to go after her. In the unlikely case her father demands that she return to Wolffeton, he will never believe her foolish story. Never, I promise you. And you, of course, my lord, would not be so . . . careless as to tell her who you are."

"Nay, I would not be so careless, Blanche. But what if her father forces her to return? Will that not spoil your plans, my lady?"

Blanche smoothed the sleeve of her tunic. "I am not certain her father will force her back. But in any case, it will be a long time before Graelam learns that she is in Brittany. He cannot stand the sight of her. He treats her like a servant. She is nothing to him. He will have the marriage set aside quickly enough when he learns that she lives. The Duke of Cornwall will help him."

"And you will wed him?"

"Of course."

"When you return to Wolffeton, my lady, what will you tell Lord Graelam?"

"Why so much interest in my plans, my lord?"

Dienwald shrugged. "I have no desire to have the powerful Graelam de Moreton breathing down my neck, all through the carelessness of a woman."

"I will tell him that his wife hired two men to help her escape from him. She feared killing me, and thus I was bound and left."

"And, of course, managed to free yourself before you came to harm. It would seem that there is nothing more to discuss. I suggest, my lady, that you scream a bit, for the benefit of the little chick."

Blanche glared at him, then shrugged. "Perhaps you are right, though I do not see that it matters much."

Dienwald was quiet a moment, as if in deep thought. "Scream, my lady. One never knows."

Kassia heard Blanche's frantic screams. "No!" she cried, and would have run toward the copse, but one of the men grabbed her arms and held her still.

Some minutes later, she saw the man come striding toward her, straightening his clothes. She paled, realizing what had happened, and moaned softly in her throat.

He stopped in front of her.

"You . . . filthy animal! How could you harm a helpless woman!" She tried to struggle free of the man's hold.

"Perhaps," Dienwald said softly, frowning even as he spoke at her heartfelt cries, "you should think of yourself for a moment."

Kassia looked up at him. She had remembered his face set in lines of cruelty. But he didn't look cruel now. His hair, brows, even his eyes, were the color of the coarse-grained brownish-gray sand on the beach. There was even a line of freckles over his high-bridged nose. He was not a large man, she realized, not overpoweringly large like Graelam, but he was built solidly, and she knew she would be no match against him.

"What did you do to Blanche?" she whispered.

"I raped her," he said quite calmly, "and let her go."

He watched her eyes grow large with fear; then she lowered her lashes and stiffened her shoulders. "What will you do with me?"

"We shall see, little chick," he said. Dienwald felt an unwonted surge of guilt at the miserable show of defiance from this pitiful little scrap. "Come, we ride now . . . No, you will not ride your mare, you will sit before me."

He would rape her, she thought. But what did it matter? Nothing mattered.

She allowed him to lift her in front of him. His destrier pranced to the side, disliking the extra weight, but Dienwald spoke softly to him, and he quieted.

They rode in silence for an hour or more.

"Who are you?" Kassia asked at last.

"You may call me Edmund," he said lightly. "And I will call you Kassia. That is your name, is it not?"

She nodded, and he felt her soft curls graze his chin.

He frowned over her head, his eyes between his destrier's ears. She had not once mentioned her powerful husband. It was as Blanche said. Graelam despised his wife, and she knew it well.

"Your husband, why was he not with you?" he asked abruptly. "It is not wise for two women to ride unescorted."

She laughed. The man who had raped Blanche and stolen her was lecturing her! "My husband," she said, not hearing the helpless bitterness in her voice, "did not know we would be riding. 'Twas my fault. We are still on my husband's land. I thought no one would dare. . ."

"You were wrong," Dienwald said shortly. "And you are something of a child in your reasoning, are you not?"

"'Twould appear so," Kassia said.

"And also a shrew?"

He looked into her face as he spoke, and saw the incomprehension widen her expressive eyes. "A shrew," she repeated blankly. She sighed deeply. "Mayhap I am. My lord makes me so angry sometimes. I fear that I am sometimes unable to moderate my feelings or my words."

Why was she speaking to him as she would a person she had known all her life, and trusted? It was idiocy. She was an idiot.

She did not realize that two tears had welled up in her eyes and were trailing down her cheeks.

"Stop it!" Dienwald growled at her. "I have given you no reason to cry."

She blinked, and knuckled her eyes with her fists, as would a child. "I am sorry," she said. "I am afraid."

He cursed softly and fluently, some of his words more coarse and descriptive than Graelam's.

"Will you not tell me where you are taking me?"

"Nay. Keep your tongue behind your teeth, my lady. We have some distance to go before we rest for the night." His actions did not match his harsh words. His arm curved more protectively around her slender waist. "You are tired. Sleep now."

To her befuddled surprise, she did, nestled against Dienwald's chest. He heard her soft, even breathing, and realized that she was stirring feelings in him that he had thought well dormant for years now. He was a fool, he thought, to be drawn to this pitiful little female.

She awoke with a small cry on her lips, and struggled briefly against him until he said, almost unwillingly, "I will not hurt you, little chick. We will stop for the night."

"Why do you call me 'little chick'?"

He gave her a twisted smile, lifted his hand, and lightly ruffled her curls. "Because your hair is soft and downy and you are small and warm."

For an evil man, Kassia thought, growing more bewildered, he was not behaving as he should.

Dienwald called a halt some minutes later. He dispatched his men to hunt their dinner, and motioned Kassia to sit quietly beneath a tree. He watched her fidget a moment, then said curtly, "The ride was long.

Go relieve yourself." His eyes narrowed cruelly. "Do not attempt to flee me, or it will be the worse for you."

She believed him, just as she believed Graelam.

It was not long before she was helping Ned, a short, wiry man who looked as fearsome as her childhood images of the devil, pluck and prepare the rabbits. She stared at him when he said in a kind voice, "Nay, lass, ye cannot skewer the beast like that. Watch."

She sat back on her heels, blinking at his seeming kindness. The smell of the roasting rabbits filled her nostrils, and her stomach growled loudly. She knew that she should likely be fainting or at least wailing in fear, but oddly enough, it did not occur to her to do so. Whatever they wished to do with her would be done. It was not in her power to stop them.

"Eat, little chick," Dienwald said, handing her a well-cooked morsel. He ate silently beside her, saying nothing. Afterward, he left her a moment, his eyes a silent threat, and spoke to his men. They moved away, to protective positions, Kassia supposed, about their small camp. The evening was warm and the sky clear. The skimpy meal sat well in her stomach. She waited.

Dienwald stood over her, his hands on his lean hips. "Well, little chick, do you think it time I raped you?"

18

She stared up at him, her eyes wide and helpless upon his face. "I wish you would not," she said.

"Then what should I do with you?" he asked irritably.

She moistened her lips with her tongue. "I do not know."

He eased down beside her, and sat cross-legged, staring into the dying fire. "Nor do I," he said more to himself than to her.

He turned to face her. "How came you to wed Graelam de Moreton?"

She gazed at him uncertainly a moment, then shrugged inwardly. There was no reason not to tell him. "He did not wish to wed me," she said. "'Twas my father who . . . convinced him to do so."

Dienwald stiffened. At least about that Blanche had told him the truth. "A man like Graelam is not easily convinced," he said.

"You sound as if you know my husband."

"Let us say," Dienwald said dryly, "that I have a healthy respect for de Moreton. But continue."

"You are right, now that I know him better, I wonder how my father accomplished it. You see, I was dying, and have no memory at all of wedding him."

"I think," Dienwald said slowly, his eyes never leaving her face, "that you will tell me the whole of it."

She repeated to him all that her father had told her. She paused a moment, then said calmly, unaware of the thread of bitterness in her voice, "Then I thought perhaps he cared for me, just a little, you understand. But 'twas not true. I do not understand him. It is likely that I am too stupid to understand his motives."

"You are not stupid," Dienwald said sharply, even as he mulled over what she had told him.

"Then unfit to be a wife."

He ignored her words. "You tell me he refused to annul the marriage in the face of the Duke of Cornwall's wishes?"

"Aye. I have come to believe that he bears with me only because he cares for my father, and, of course, for Belleterre. He is now my father's heir, and Belleterre is a very rich holding."

"If he put you aside, Belleterre would still be his. At least he could battle your father and your greedy cousin for ownership."

"You are likely right," Kassia said thoughtfully. She turned suddenly to face him. "Edmund," she said, unaware that she had used his name, "are you holding me for ransom?"

"And if I were?" he asked evenly.

She shrugged, a helpless smile curving up her mouth. "I only wondered. I do not know what Graelam would do."

Saint Peter's teeth, he cursed silently. She was naught but a little chick, as innocent and trusting as a child. He had thought to rape her—what man would not? He had thought even to keep her until he tired of her, mayhap even kill her to save the expense of sending her to Brittany. The surge of protectiveness he felt for her alarmed him. He jumped to his feet.

"You weary me with your chatter."

She flinched at the harshness of his voice, and he felt like a man who has just kicked a small animal.

"Kassia, sleep now. We will speak further in the morning."

He tossed her a blanket and walked to the other side of the fire.

She wrapped herself in the blanket and curled up in a tight ball. Why had he not raped her as he had Blanche? She shivered. Perhaps he still would rape her. Perhaps his seeming kindness was all a sham. She shook her head, wondering if she would ever understand any man. Her last thought before she slept was of a bloody battle between her father and Graelam for possession of Belleterre.

Dienwald handed her a hunk of bread. "Eat," he said, and turned to speak to his men.

She chewed the dry bread slowly, wishing she had a goblet of milk. Her fear, in abeyance the night before, had returned full measure when he had awakened her at dawn. She swallowed the bread and waited for him to return.

"What will you do with me?" she asked, looking up at him.

"I will tell you whilst we ride," he said.

Ned tossed her up into Dienwald's arms. She settled herself, and waited for him to speak.

"Why do you not let me ride my mare?" she asked at last.

"I don't know," he said.

"I cannot escape you."

"I know."

"Edmund, please tell me what you intend. I am very afraid."

She felt his arm tighten around her and winced.

"Kassia, if I gave you the choice, would you prefer to return to your father in Brittany or to Wolffeton, to your husband?"

"If you are asking me who is more likely to pay you a ransom, I do not know."

"I am not asking you that. Answer me."

She sighed. "I cannot allow my husband to claim Belleterre and fight my father. If you gave me the choice, I would return to Wolffeton. It is where I belong."

"Do you care for your husband?"

Dienwald expected a vehement denial. For many moments she said nothing.

He slowed his destrier to a walk, and Kassia found herself staring unseeing at the sharp-fanged boulders in a near hillside. She swallowed convulsively, remembering yet again Graelam's kindness to her when she had first come to Wolffeton. His gentleness when he had taken her to his bed. His concern at her pain. What had she done to make him despise her? The stupid material she had taken to sew him a new tunic? She wasn't aware that tears were slipping down her cheeks.

"I am stupid," she said in a choked voice.

"Ah," he said.

Suddenly Kassia stiffened in his arms. "Edmund, you are going in the wrong direction! We are on Wolffeton land!"

"I know, little chick."

She tried to twist around to look at him, but he held her firm. "We are still several hours from Lord Graelam's keep. Sleep. I believe you will need your strength."

"I will never understand men," she said.

He smiled over her head. "Mayhap not," he said gently, "but you will not change. You must not change."

"I would not know where to begin," she said on a helpless sigh. She leaned back against him, trusting him as she did her father, and fell into a light sleep.

"Little chick. Wake up."

Kassia straightened, looking around her as she shook the dregs of sleep from her mind.

"Wolffeton lies just beyond the next rise. I can take you no farther." He laughed softly. "I have no wish to face your husband. I fear he would peel off my hide."

He pulled his destrier to a halt and nimbly jumped to the ground, Kassia held firmly in his arms. He set her down gently.

There were so many questions in her eyes that he began to shake his head in answer. "Listen to me, Kassia," he said, lightly stroking his hands over her arms. "You will take care when you return to Wolffeton. Do you understand me?"

He knew that she did not. He ground his teeth, but self-interest kept him quiet.

I will try to do as you say, Edmund," she said, her head cocked to one side, her great eyes wide upon his face.

"Go now, little chick." He leaned down and lightly kissed her mouth, then quickly released her. "Ned, bring her mare!"

He tossed her onto Bluebell's back. "Remember what I told you," he said, then thwacked the mare's rump.

He stood quietly, watching her ride toward Wolffeton.

"My lord," Ned said, coming up to stand beside him.

"Aye?"

"The lass rides into hell, methinks. Ye did not tell her of the woman's plot."

"No, I did not." Dienwald turned and grinned rakishly at his man. "As I told the wench, Ned, I have no wish to have Lord Graelam after my hide! If she knew who I was, the chances are that sooner or later her husband would find out, and not be content until he had me roasting in hell's fires!"

"But that other lady. She knows ye, my lord."

"Aye, but to harm me, my friend, she would be doing herself in. And I have the feeling that Lady Blanche cares as much about her pretty hide as I do about mine."

Ned spat onto the rocky ground.

Guy ran a weary hand through his hair. His eyes blurred with fatigue, yet he knew he would ride again within the hour to continue the search, this time north-ward. He walked down the steps from the keep into the inner bailey, pausing when he heard men shouting. Had Graelam found her? He galloped down the steps, and came to an abrupt halt at the sight of Kassia, alone, riding her mare into the inner bailey.

"Guy!" she called, waving to him wildly even as she slipped off her mare's back. "Guy!"

She ran toward him, her hands outstretched. Guy wanted nothing more than to crush her against him, so great was his relief that she was safe, but he saw the men closing about them, and grasped her hands, holding her away from him.

"You came back," he said roughly.

"He brought me back," Kassia gasped. "I thought he would rape me or kill me, but he did not! He was kind, Guy! He brought me home!"

"What," Guy said, startled by her strange words, "are you talking about?"

"Where is Graelam? He is all right, is he not?"

"He is searching for you. I expect him to return shortly."

"Blount! Rolfe!" she cried, pulling away from Guy. "How good it is to see you again!" She had no time in her excitement to realize that the men were gaping at her, for she saw Blanche standing on the steps leading up to the great hall, her son, Evian, at her side.

"Blanche! Are you all right? I was so worried for you!"

Kassia started toward her, but Guy grabbed her arm. "Wait," he said tersely.

She responded to his voice, and turned slowly to face him, confusion darkening her eyes. "What is the matter, Guy? Did everyone believe me dead? I was afraid, but he wasn't evil as I thought at first. Indeed—"

She broke off, hearing the thundering sound of approaching horses. She felt Guy take her arm and hold her still beside him. Why had Blanche not come to welcome her? Why were the men regarding her like she was a ghost?

Graelam rode at the fore of his dozen men into the inner bailey. He was so bloody tired he could scarce see straight. His face was gray with worry, and fear, and anger. He raised his head, his hand upraised to halt his men, and saw her standing beside Guy. He felt a spurt of sheer relief, before rage flowed through him.

He leapt off Demon's back, his hands clenched into fists. He held himself still for an instant, drawing on his waning control.

Kassia pulled free of Guy and ran toward her husband. "Graelam! I am home! I am safe!"

He caught her arms and stared down at her.

"You are unharmed?"

She nodded happily. He closed his eyes a moment, nearly choking on his rage. "Aye," he said very calmly, "I see that you are quite unharmed. Why did you come back, my lady?"

She cocked her head to one side in question. "He brought me back, my lord. He did not harm me, I promise you."

Graelam was aware that every servant and all of his men were watching. He should take her inside, away from all his gaping people, but he could not seem to bring himself to move. He saw Blanche from the corner of his eye, her face white, her hand clutched over her breast. "He, my lady?" he asked coldly, turning back to her. "The man you hired to help you return to Brittany brought you back?"

"Hired . . ." Kassia repeated blankly. "I do not understand, my lord. I was kidnapped, but the man, Edmund is his name, felt . . . sorry for me, I think. He brought me back."

Graelam swallowed convulsviely. He took her arm, saying as he drew her forward, "Come, we shall go into the hall." He heard Guy call to him, but he ignored him.

Kassia took double steps to keep up with him. What had he meant about her hiring men? She darted a glance upward to his set profile. She could see the lines of weariness on his face, and felt a spurt of hope. He had been searching for her. He must care something for her.

He released her suddenly, and gently pushed her down into a chair. He stood over her, frowning down at her thoughtfully. He said very pleasantly, "So you think, wife, to return to me, and have me smile at you and forget what you did?"

She shook her head, trying to clear her mind, but she blurted out her thoughts. "You searched for me."

"Aye," he said, "I have spared nothing trying to find you. That appears to please you."

His voice was calm, but his eyes, dark as a cloudless night, were cold, so cold that she shivered.

"It . . . surprises me," she said quietly.

Graelam's eyes narrowed to black slits. Abruptly he turned away from her and called out sharply, "Blanche!"

Kassia felt a wave of relief to see Blanche walk slowly toward them.

"Blanche," Kassia said, "you are all right? That man, Edmund, he did not harm you?"

Blanche smiled at her gently, a sad, pitying smile. "The man did not harm me, Kassia," she said. She is like a cat, Blanche thought, always landing on her feet. By God, what was she to say, how was she to act? What would Graelam do if he discovered the truth? That made her still any guilt she felt. Why, she wondered, does everything I do end up in disaster? She had no choice now but to brazen her way through this.

"Tell her, Blanche," Graelam said, "what you told me."

She looked down at Kassia again, and said slowly, "Perhaps I was wrong, Graelam. Perhaps she did not hire those men. It simply appeared so to me."

"What are you saying, Blanche?" she whispered. "You

know I did not hire those men. How could you ever believe that?" Her voice rose in her disbelief. "You saw them come after us. Surely you knew that they meant us harm. Their leader, Edmund, he raped you! Surely you realized they—"

"Yet you are returned safe and unharmed," Graelam interrupted her smoothly.

"Kassia," Blanche said urgently, "you are here again, safe. It is obvious that they meant you no harm." She shrugged. "I was not certain if you were fleeing from them when they rode toward us. I thought that you were . . ." She paused, leaving a delicate, damning silence.

"That I what, Blanche?" Kassia said harshly, disbelieving what she was hearing.

"That you had hired them to help you escape Wolffeton and your husband. Forgive me if I misjudged you."

Kassia stared at the circle of disbelieving faces around her. Edmund had warned her, but she had not understood. "But the man raped you, Blanche. How could you believe that they would do less to me?"

"He did not rape me, Kassia. No man save my husband has ever touched me. He merely . . . . fondled me for a moment, and that made me scream. I believed he was in a hurry to return to you." That, she thought frantically, must surely have been the truth!

"Kassia," Graelam said very quietly, "you will cease your act."

Act? What am I acting?

She struggled to her feet and looked at the faces around her. She saw Guy reach out to take her hand, saw her husband shove him away.

"Listen to what she has to say," Guy said to Graelam.

"I will listen," Graelam said. "Sit down, my lady. And talk."

Kassia sat down again in the chair, her eyes staring blankly ahead. It was a nightmare, she thought vaguely. In a moment, she would awake, and she would be safe and warm.

"Speak," she heard Graelam say.

She raised her eyes to her husband's cold, set face and said very softly, "Blanche and I went riding yesterday morning. We were without escort, but on Wolffeton land. Three men came toward us. We tried to escape them, but they caught us. The leader, Edmund, told me he had raped Blanche and let her go. He took me up on his destrier. I thought he would rape me or kill me, or hold me for ransom, but he did nothing. He was . . . kind to me. He brought me home."

Graelam regarded her silently. "Such a pitiful little tale," he said finally. "Surely you had ample time to invent something more believable." He turned to Guy. "Well, chivalrous knight, have I given her enough of a hearing?"

Guy had been watching Blanche's face. He saw fear and something else in her eyes. Kassia's story had been so unbelievable as to be the truth. He said quietly to Graelam, "If Kassia hired these men to return her to her father, what did she pay them?"

Blanche smiled, her relief so palpable that she quickly lowered her head so no one would see it.

"And why did she have them return her to you, my lord? If indeed she did hire them to escape you, the fact that she changed her mind must mean something."

"Perhaps," Blanche said, knowing that she must say something, hating herself for the damning words even as she spoke them, "she paid the men with her body."

"No!"

Blanche scented victory. She must not succumb to pity or regret now. She said calmly, her eyes thoughtful on Kassia's face, "And perhaps they did not like the bargain and thus let you go."

You have been such a fool, my girl. Such a fool. Kassia gazed at Blanche helplessly. Slowly, the words forced from her mouth, she said, "My lord, I did not try to escape you."

"I have heard enough for the moment, my lady," Graelam said calmly. "Go to our bedchamber. I will come to you soon."

Guy, who knew his lord much better than did Kassia, felt shuddering alarm at Graelam's passionless voice. He touched his hand to Graelam's sleeve. "I believe her," he said.

"Do you indeed, Sir Guy? Do you not question why a man would kidnap a woman only to return her unharmed? It is foolishness."

"I believe her," Guy repeated, more firmly this time.

"You," Blanche hissed at him, wanting to strike him for his obvious concern for Kassia, "are a besotted fool."

Kassia grabbed up her skirts and fled up the stairs to his bedchamber. I should have begged Edmund to send me to Brittany, she thought. She shook away the thought. No, she would convince Graelam of the truth. After all, she was his wife. Surely that must mean something!

19

Graelam listened to the furor of voices raging around him, but said nothing. Had he been capable of it, he would have smiled to hear Blount, that hard-nosed old goat, who never gave an inch, vociferously defend his lady. And Guy. Aye, had she come back because she could not bear to be separated from the young knight?

He rose from his chair and said in an emotionless voice that chilled Rolfe to his bones, "You will go about your duties now." He saw the worry etched in many of the faces, and added shortly, "I have heard all of you. Go now."

He did not wait to see if they obeyed him. It was only Kassia who had ever dared to disobey him. He walked up the stairs to his bedchamber. He paused a moment, hearing Kassia's old nurse, Etta, sobbing loudly.

"Why, my baby?" the old woman was pleading, her voice hoarse from her crying. "Why did you do it?"

"Etta," Kassia said, sighing softly, "I did nothing. You, of all people, should believe me."

Graelam pushed open the door. He said nothing, merely motioned to the old nurse to leave. She slithered past him, her eyes puffy with weeping.

He stood quietly for a moment, looking at his wife. She was pale, but that little chin of hers was lifted in stubborn defiance. He wanted to wrap his fingers around her slender throat, but instead he asked, "Did the men rape you?"

Kassia shook her head. "Nay, I told you that they did not harm me."

"I would think that such ruffians as Blanche described to me would not leave such a tempting morsel as yourself with her legs together and her belly empty."

She winced at his crudeness, but said firmly, "Their leader, Edmund, was no ruffian. Indeed, his men called him 'my lord.' "

"I know of no Edmund who is a lord in these parts."

"I do not believe it was his real name."

"Tell me, Kassia, what did this Edmund look like?"

She took heart at the quiet, interested tone of his voice. "He was not of your size, my lord. When I saw him closely, I was reminded of sand. His hair and eyes and brows were all of that strange hue. He knew of you. Indeed, I believe he feared you."

Despite himself, Graelam searched his memory for a man of that description. There was none that he knew of. "And that is why he returned you to me? He feared retribution?"

"Nay," she said honestly. "I told you, 'tis my belief that he felt sorry for me." She paused a moment, then blurted out, "He asked me if I would prefer going to Brittany or returning here."

"And what was your reason for returning, my lady?"

"He told me that even if I returned to Belleterre,

you would still hold claim. That if you wished it, you could wage war upon my father for your rights. I could not allow that to happen."

"Ah, behold the sacrificial little lamb."

The menacing sneer in his voice made her close her eyes. "Please," she whispered, desperate now, "you must believe me, Graelam."

He regarded her thoughtfully, watching her pitiful defiance begin to crumble.

He said very softly, "Do you recall, my lady, what I told you I would do to you if you ever again tried to escape me?"

She remembered suddenly, and without thought, realizing what a ridiculous fool she was, she dashed frantically toward the door.

She felt his powerful arm lock around her waist and heave her up as if she were naught but a bag of feathers. If she struggled against him she would only hurt herself. She knew it well, but could not stop herself. She tried to twist from his grasp, but he only tightened his hold, and for an instant she felt the breath squeezed from her body.

Graelam eased her down upon her back on the bed. He sat back and regarded her intently, his fingers lightly touching her throat.

"You do not wish me to have you," he said, his voice almost meditative. "Did you enjoy this Edmund's caresses? Did he give you a woman's pleasure?"

He saw the look of utter incomprehension in her wide eyes, and knew at least that she had told the truth about not being raped.

Kassia gulped. "Why will you not believe me? I have never lied." Her expression flickered, and she quickly amended, "At least I have not lied since I was a child."

He ignored her words. "Kassia, what did you use for payment?"

"There was no payment! Why will you not believe me?"

He frowned suddenly. "Do not move, my lady." He rose from the bed and strode purposefully to his large chest. He jerked open the lid and riffled through the contents. Beautiful cloth rippled through his impatient fingers. He delved to the bottom and pulled up a large leather case. His fingers trembled as he opened it. The necklace, worth a king's ransom, was gone. All hope dissolved in that moment. The depths of his disappointment startled him. He had wanted to believe her. But she had lied.

He slowly replaced the leather case in the bottom of the trunk, slowly straightened all the glittering cloth, and shut the lid.

Without a word, he strode back to the bed. "You were a fool to come back," he said.

"I . . . I do not understand."

"The necklace is gone."

"What necklace?" She gazed at him, bewildered.

He did not even show that he had heard her. He leaned over her and ripped away the skirt of her gown.

Kassia gasped and tried to jerk away from him, but she was no match for his strength, and he had but to use such a small portion to subdue her. She watched him, wide-eyed, as he tore the wool into strips. He clasped her hands and drew them over her head.

"Graelam," she began, "what are you going to do?"

"I told you, told you quite specifically before you left me again."

"No!" she shrieked, but he tied her wrists securely above her head.

He rose and stared down at her for a long moment. He saw the terror in her eyes, the pleading. Her small breasts were heaving violently against the cloth of her tunic.

He quickly subdued her thrashing legs and spread them wide, binding each ankle. He drew his dagger, and sat down beside her.

"Please," she whispered, nearly beyond reason, "do not hurt me."

Slowly he sliced the dagger blade through the material. He cut each layer from her body, until she lay naked, sprawled helplessly on her back.

He straightened over her and let his eyes rove over each inch of her. "You have filled out a bit," he said dispassionately. He lightly touched a fingertip to her breast, and felt her quiver in fear.

"I wonder if that tiny little belly of yours will ever fill with my child."

Kassia closed her eyes against his words, against what she knew he was going to do to her. Fool, she screamed at herself. Such a fool.

She heard him disrobing, felt the bed sink down as he eased beside her. His hand splayed over her belly, and she moaned softly, helplessly.

Graelam gazed at the slender straight legs drawn so widely apart, followed their woman's shape to the soft curls between her thighs. He touched her lightly, and she whimpered, but not with desire. Never with desire for him. What do you expect, you stupid whoreson?

Damn her! The devil take her and all women! He lurched up between her legs and grasped her hips. She was bound so securely that she could not struggle against him. He did not mean to take her, merely to frighten

her, merely prove to her that he would not allow her to
make a fool of him.

He drew away his hands and sat back on his haunches,
looking at her face. It was bloodless. Tears were streaming from her tightly closed eyes. He jerked away from
her, her distress burning deep into him. He picked up
a blanket and smoothed it over her trembling body.

He turned away from her, wishing he could close out
the sound of her choking on her own tears. He cursed
loudly and fluently, grabbed a towel, and wiped her
face with it.

"Stop it," he growled at her. "Stop those damned tears!"

She sniffed, and unwittingly brushed her cheek against
his hand. He felt her hot, salty tears wet his palm.

He could not bear it. He untied her wrists and ankles, cursing himself for a weak bastard, even as he
rubbed feeling back into her numbed flesh.

She lay passively, her sobs now noisy hiccups.

He rose. "At least you did come back," he said, "for
whatever reason."

"I never left," she said in a deadened voice.

He turned and quickly dressed, cursing his trembling
hands. He strode to the chamber door, paused, and
said over his shoulder, "You are mistress of Wolffeton,
my lady. I expect a decent meal. Rouse yourself and
see to it."

He heard her quickly indrawn breath, and added
harshly, "And bathe yourself. You smell of horse sweat."

And fear, he added silently. She smelled of fear.

"Did you hurt her?" Guy demanded.

Graelam drew a sharp breath. "If I killed her, 'twould
be no more than she deserved," he said, eyeing his
knight coldly.

"My lord, she told the truth. There is naught but honesty in her. If I can see it, you, as her husband, cannot be blind to it."

"Guy, you are a fool," Graelam said wearily, forgetting his jealousy of the younger man. "The necklace is gone."

"The necklace from Al-Afdal's camp?"

"Aye," Graelam said shortly. "Damn her," he added softly. "I would have given it to her."

Guy studied his master's face. He is suffering, Guy realized, shocked with his insight. For the first time in his life, he is suffering for a woman. He said no more, wanting to think. If Kassia had not taken the valuable necklace, then who had? The answer was not long in coming to him.

The evening meal, if not excellent, was at least more palatable than it would have been had Kassia not been at Wolffeton. But her movements, her instructions, were mechanical. She saw vaguely that there was pity and concern in some of the eyes that looked at her. In others, there was puzzlement. Nan regarded her with contemptuous triumph.

And there was Blanche. It had taken her benumbed brain several hours before she had realized the perfidy of the other woman. She didn't know what to do. If she confronted Blanche, she most likely would sneer at her and call her a liar. If she told Graelam what she believed . . . She shuddered. In his eyes, Blanche was everything Kassia was not. Never would he believe her. She didn't know what to do.

Her silence that evening in the great hall was seen by most as the proper response of a chastised wife. She avoided Graelam's eyes, not wanting to see the distrust, even the hatred he must feel for her. She ate little, unable to stomach the blandest of the vegetables.

"So, you will dwindle away with your sulking?"

Her head snapped up at her husband's taunting voice.

"I do not sulk," she said, and quickly amended, "at least I haven't for some five years now."

"Just as you do not lie. Then eat." He eyed her closely, and added on a harsh drawl, "When I told you you had filled out a bit, I did not mean that you had grown presentable. You still scarce have a woman's body."

She flinched. So that was why he had not forced her. He found her so repulsive that he could not bring himself to take her, even in his rage.

She knew she should be ecstatic, but tears sparkled on the tips of her thick lashes.

"If you cry in front of everyone, I shall truly give you cause to do so."

"You already have," she said, gulping down the hated tears.

"You amaze me, Kassia," he said, leaning back in his chair, his arms crossed over his chest. "Do you never tread warily?"

She said nothing, merely stared fixedly into her goblet of wine.

"Perhaps I should return you to your father. At least your absence would bring me some peace."

The response he knew he would gain from his words was swift in coming. "Nay, please do not."

"Ah, anything to save your father. Anything to save Belleterre. This man who felt so sorry for you, Kassia, you say it was he who told you that to return to Belleterre would lose all?"

"Aye, that is what I said to you." She raised weary

eyes to his mocking face. "Why do you torment me? I have told you everything." But she was lying, not telling him about Blanche, and he saw the lie in her eyes.

A surge of rage swept through him, and he gripped the arms of his chair until his knuckles showed white.

"Leave me," he said finally, his voice harsh, "and know, my lady wife, that I can make your life a hell if you do not admit to your lies."

Blanche ate daintily, savoring every bite of the tender pork. I am safe, she thought. She was so relieved that she could not long sustain her fury at Dienwald de Fortenberry. Graelam would never believe his wife. And of course Kassia, little fool that she was, was too proud, too unbending to convince her husband otherwise. Blanche had looked closely at Kassia, searching for bruises. It had surprised her to see none, for she would have sworn that Graelam was furious enough to kill her. Again she stilled her guilt. Kassia had returned safely, and Blanche had but to bide her time.

"I had not realized that you knew of Lord Graelam's treasure trove."

Blanche's heart skipped a beat at Guy's words, but none of it showed on her lovely face. She arched an eyebrow. "You spoke, Sir Guy?"

"Aye, Blanche. You took the Saracen necklace and you hired those men to remove Kassia from Wolffeton. Did you expect them to kill her?" He shook his head thoughtfully. "No, you are not without some pity. But you wanted them to take her back to Brittany, did you not? Were you dismayed to see Kassia returned with nary a scratch?"

"Your imagination rivals the minstrels', Guy. Pray, Sir Knight, have you other, equally interesting tales?"

Never, he knew, would he succeed in getting her to tell the truth. He would have to do something else. He stroked his jaw with his shapely hand, realizing that Blanche was single-minded, if nothing else. She had failed this time to rid herself of Kassia. He had no doubt that she would try again, and that frightened him. How could Graelam be so damnably blind? He said very softly, "Blanche, even if Kassia were dead, Graelam would not wed you."

She gave a soft, tinkling laugh. "Ah, Guy, is that jealousy I hear in your voice?"

He looked at her for a long moment. "Jealousy, Blanche? Mayhap, lovely lady, you are onto something."

"'Tis a message from the Duke of Cornwall. He comes within the week."

Kassia quickly set aside the ledger of accounts, uncertain of Graelam's reaction to what she was doing, and forced a tentative smile to her lips. Blount certainly delighted in her skills, but she wasn't at all sure what her husband's reaction would be. "I shall see to his comfort, my lord."

"You may recall that his retinue is vast."

"Aye, I remember."

Graelam eyed her with growing irritation. "Must you leap out of your white skin whenever I am about?"

She looked at his darkly handsome face and felt a small wrench of pain. "I believed you wished proper submissiveness in your wife."

"You are about as submissive as my destrier. You cannot even play the role well."

She said nothing, her eyes on her hands that lay clasped in her lap.

"What are you doing?"

He leaned to the table and picked up the ledger, riffling through it. "Ah yes," he said, "I had forgot that your father taught you to read and write. Does Blount know that you poach on his preserves?"

"Aye," she said softly.

He tossed the ledger back onto the table. "Does it please you to make fools of us all? Nay, do not say it again, Kassia. Your lies have filled my craw to overflowing."

He strode from the small workroom, not looking at her again. She returned to her figures, wishing she could tell him that Wolffeton was becoming a rich holding. But hearing her say it would only anger him, for he would doubtless believe that she was angling for new gowns, jewels, or the like. She finished her task and called all the indoor servants together in the great hall.

She looked at their faces, some of them dear to her now, others, like Nan's, implacably hostile. Seeing Blanche sitting near the great fireplace, her expression chillingly serene, Kassia felt herself shudder. She told them of the duke's impending visit. "Marta," she said to an older widow who was now in charge of the spinning and weaving, "we will speak of new clothing for the women. We have enough surplus cloth now to see to our own needs."

All but Nan smiled at that.

"Aye, my lady," Marta said, beaming at her new importance.

"Bount will give up his chamber to the duke. Nan, Alice, you will see to its thorough cleaning. I hope to have finished new cushions for the duke's chair."

She heard Nan muttering, but ignored her. She gave other orders, then dismissed the servants, all save the cooks. She spent another hour planning meals with them.

Kassia rose and rubbed her neck. She wanted to ride,
but doubted Graelam would allow it. Indeed, she
thought, he would likely humiliate her in front of his
men if she even tried.

"Kassia."

She jumped, startled, for she had not noticed Guy
entering the hall.

"I have news, my lady. You shall be the first to
congratulate me."

She smiled. "What is your good fortune?"

"My father has died. His lands and keep near Dover
are now mine." He raised his hand, seeing the shock in
her eyes. "Nay, do not give me your condolences on his
demise. He was a rotten old lecher, mean-spirited and
cruel. It is a relief to all his men and servants, and to
my poor sister who lived with him."

"Then I do congratulate you, Guy. You are now a
knight of substance. You will leave us?"

"Aye. The keep is nothing to compare to Wolffeton,
of course, but it is a beginning." He paused a moment,
a smile lighting his blue eyes. "I begin to believe in
fate," he said at last.

Kassia cocked her head to one side in question, waiting for him to explain his strange words, but he only
shook his head and smiled at her.

"Aye," he said, "'tis indeed fate."

To Kassia's relief, Graelam showed no hesitation in
his well wishes to Sir Guy. The ale and wine flowed to
the early hours of the morning. Graelam, good-humored
in his drunkenness, tried to press Nan on Guy, but the
young knight refused, shouting to the company that he
doubted his ability to raise either his interest or his
member.

Kassia quietly left the hall, hopeful that her husband

would fall asleep below. She turned on the stairs at the sound of rustling skirts.

"How sad for you that the handsome, so malleable Guy leaves us."

"'Tis sad for all of us," Kassia said calmly. "I suggest you find your bed, Blanche. You are slurring your words as badly as the men."

Kassia could tell that Blanche would have liked to mock her, or taunt her, but the wine and ale had dulled her wits. She left her, shaking her head at her own stupidity. Blanche, her friend!

Blanche was indeed dull-witted. She glared at Kassia's retreating back, then made her way carefully to her own small bedchamber. It was close and warm, but she was too befuddled to slide the shutters away from the one window. She undressed clumsily and slipped into her bed. Her head was swimming and her thoughts were warm and wishful. It was almost as if she had willed him to come, she thought, watching the door open slowly. In the darkness, she could only make out the form of a man, a tall man.

"Graelam," she whispered, a woman's promise in her husky voice.

He quietly closed the door and stood a moment, tall and straight. Then he was coming toward her, shucking off his clothing.

"I knew you would come," she said, and held out her arms toward him.

"Aye," he said softly, "I came."

20

Blanche shuddered when he took her into his arms and pulled her onto his lap. He found her willing mouth, and kissed her deeply, thoroughly, until she was trembling with her need for him, and her triumph.

His flesh beneath her questing fingers was smooth as silk, contrasting with the rock-hard muscle beneath.

"It has been so long," she whispered, her hand caressing down his chest to his belly.

"No man since your husband died?" he asked softly, his words punctuated with nipping kisses down the side of her neck.

"Nay. And he was a beast."

"I am not," he said. He pressed her onto her back and lay down beside her. "What a woman you are," he said, his voice husky, as his fingers found the softness between her thighs.

"So long," Blanche whimpered, arching up against his hand, wanting him so much she could scarce restrain herself. She found him, hard and ready, and inhaled sharply at the feel of him.

"You will have me in your bed every night," he said. "Never will you want for a man again."

Her mind reeled with his promise, and she pulled him down over her, opening herself willingly to him.

His fingers drove her to the brink of madness before he very gently eased into her. He sucked in his breath at the enveloping heat of her body, and thrust deep.

"Now," Blanche managed between gasping breaths. She met his every thrust, drawing him deeper and deeper until he was beyond himself. But he held himself back until her soft cries of pleasure filled the stillness of the chamber.

He took his own release and fell heavily over her, his head beside hers on the pillow.

Blanche's tumbling thoughts, scattered by her searing pleasure, slowly came back into focus. He is inside me, his seed is filling me, she thought, and felt a moment of panic. She wanted to shove him away, to cleanse herself, but he would not move. She felt him kissing her lightly on her ear, and smiled into the darkness.

"You are mine at last," she whispered. Oddly enough, even though she had found great pleasure with him, she was thinking hazily of another, a knight with golden hair and bright blue eyes. You are naught but a silly fool, she chided herself. "When will you send her back to Brittany?" she asked, stroking her hands over his chest.

He said softly, still kissing her, "You will never worry about her again, Blanche. You will be mistress of my keep, and my wife. Very soon now. Very soon." She felt him growing hard within her once again, and she was surprised when her body leapt in response.

He took her more slowly this time, until she was pleading with him in soft, mewling cries.

He laughed, and gave her what she wanted. She fell asleep in the crook of his arm, so sated that she was beyond words, beyong caring that his seed still filled her, beyond the niggling feeling that she wished it had been another to share her bed. I have won, she thought. At last I have won. I am safe, my son is safe.

Blanche awoke the next morning with no splitting headache from her overindulgence the previous night. Graelam was gone, but that did not surprise her. She bathed herself thoroughly, so pleased that worry of him seeding a child within her was only a minor thought. She dressed herself in her most becoming gown, a russet wool with a golden-threaded belt that emphasized her full breasts and narrow waist.

She hummed softly as she made her way to the hall. She saw Kassia seated alone, nibbling on a slice of bread. She frowned, wondering how she should act. Had Graelam told Kassia that he was setting her aside? She remembered his words. Very soon, he had told her. Very soon. She decided to hold her peace. Kassia would discover the truth soon enough.

Kassia raised tired eyes to Blanche, mentally preparing herself for sarcastic taunts, but Blanche, to her utter surprise, only smiled at her.

She noticed Blanche's lovely gown and frowned, wondering why the woman was thus attired. She herself was wearing an old gown of faded gray, for she planned to oversee the cleaning of the stables herself. And the jakes. They were foul and needed a river of lime to depress the smell.

"You look like a serving wench," Blanche observed,

unable to keep the touch of triumph from her voice. After all, she defended herself silently, I have never won anything worthwhile before.

"Aye," Kassia said, raising her chin slightly. "But then, I am mistress of Wolffeton, Blanche. 'Tis my responsibility to see that all is ready for the duke."

Blanche laughed; she could not help herself. Blind little fool! So Graelam had said nothing to her as yet. It was on the tip of her tongue to tell Kassia that her brief stay was soon to be over, when she heard Graelam's deep voice. He was speaking to Guy about the final repairs on the eastern outer wall.

"Will you break your fast, my lord?" Kassia asked, rising from the bench.

"Aye," Graelam said. "And a goblet of ale to clear my aching head."

Kassia immediately left the hall to do his bidding.

Graelam stretched. His eyes fell upon Blanche. There was a gentle smile on her face, and he nodded at her.

"You have the look of a cat who has been well fed," Guy said in a bland voice.

"Aye," Blanche said, keeping her eyes soft upon Graelam's face.

"One should never allow a cat to go hungry for too long a time," Guy remarked as he sat himself beside Graelam.

Blanche looked at him uncertainly, wondering if he knew of his master's visit to her chamber. Somehow the thought made her cringe with shame. "Is there anything I can do to see to your comfort, my lord?" she asked Graelam.

"Nay," Graelam said shortly, turning again to Guy.

Why does he not say something? Blanche wondered,

eyeing him with mounting frustration. Why does he not ask to speak to me alone?

She looked up to see Kassia, a serving wench following in her wake, carrying a large tray.

Kassia motioned for the girl to set it in front of Graelam. "I have brought enough for you also, Guy," she said.

"Thank you, my lady," Guy said. "I need to keep up my strength."

"When must you leave us, Guy?"

Graelam thought he heard distress in his wife's soft voice, and slewed around to look at her. He saw only weariness in her eyes, and dark smudges beneath them, attesting to the fact that she had not rested well the previous night. What the devil did she want? he wondered, attacking the cold beef with a vengeance. After all, he hadn't bothered her.

"I will leave when the duke does, my lady," Guy said calmly. "I cannot in good conscience remove myself until Graelam has found another warrior to protect Wolffeton. I fear what would happen if I did go."

"Conceited fool," Graelam said without heat. "You know I have written to the duke. 'Tis likely he will have a knight in his train who is a landless lout, just as you were."

"How . . . sorry we will be to see you go," Blanche said.

"It warms me to hear you say so," Guy said.

Kassia heard the soft taunt in Blanche's voice, and something else as well that she couldn't define. She herself would miss Guy terribly, but of course, she could say nothing, especially in front of Graelam. Her one protector. She shuddered at the thought of the loneliness she would know.

"What ails you?" Graelam asked sharply.

She shook her head.

"Have you eaten?"

"Aye, my lord. If you will excuse me, there is much that needs my attention."

He nodded, and watched her walk slowly from the hall, her head bent. She is thinking of Guy, he thought, his brow puckering into a frown. She continues to elude me, to treat me as if I were naught but a heavy burden to be borne. He turned and bestowed a wide smile upon Blanche.

The night was dark and mysterious as the depths of a woman, he thought. But still he waited until he knew she would be asleep. Quietly he eased open the door to her small chamber and peered inside. He could hear her gentle breathing and knew she was deep in sleep. A long candle was close to gutting on the small table beside her bed. So she had waited for him. He undressed quickly and leaned over to blow it out.

Blanche lay on her side, one leg drawn up to her chest, her face pillowed by her open hand. She is beautiful, he thought, able at last to make out her outline in the darkness.

He eased beside her, lifted her heavy hair, and began kissing her neck, his hands softly caressing down her back. Blanche stirred, stiffened at first, then smiled.

"I did not think you would come to me," she murmured softly, parting her lips for his kiss.

"I told you that you would never sleep without me again," he whispered.

Blanche frowned a moment. Her mind was clear of sleep now and there was no wine to tangle her thoughts. His voice sounded odd. A searing bolt of pleasure spread through her loins, and she sighed and gave herself over to him.

"Allow me to rise," she said when he was done.

"Nay, love. You will go nowhere."

"I must!"

He nibbled on her breast, a smile forming on his lips as he realized the reason for her urgency. "Nay, Blanche, my seed will spring to life in your beautiful belly. You will give me sons, many sons."

She froze at the laughing taunt she heard in his soft voice. "But there is Evian," she began, only to feel him pushing deeper inside her, holding her still.

She lay exhausted, and still he moved within her. Something wasn't right, and it nagged at her. He seemed more lean than she remembered. She fell asleep even as her hand roved over his thigh, searching for the long, jagged scar.

Blanche eyed Kassia closely the next day, noting her pallor, the pinched look about her mouth. Graelam has told her, she thought, finally. "You do not look well, Kassia," she said, staring down at the wan girl.

"I did not sleep well," Kassia said, not looking at her.

"What you require is some exercise. Since it no longer matters, why do you not go riding?"

What no longer matters? Kassia wondered. She shook off Blanche's question, and nodded. "Indeed, 'tis what I wish to do. All is ready for the duke."

Still she hesitated, and Blanche said, "Graelam will not mind, I promise you. Mayhap this time you will not return."

Kassia looked at her wearily. "You will never tell him the truth, will you?"

"The truth?" Blanche arched a beautifully plucked brow.

"What was his name, Blanche? Not Edmund, I think."

"You surprise me," Blanche said. "He is not a gentle man, at least by repute, yet he released you. Certainly it was not because of your womanly endowments."

"Nay," Kassia said flatly. "And he was gentle, and quite kind to me. What is his name, Blanche?"

"I am tempted to tell you, now that it makes no difference. Graelam no longer cares. Mayhap he would even ask him to take you away again."

"I am going riding, Blanche." Kassia turned and walked quickly from the hall. She nodded to the men she met in the inner bailey, noted a scattered pile of refuse in a mud puddle from the brief shower the night before, and called to one of the servants to clean it up.

She raised her face to the bright morning sun. Even now, she thought, unhappiness searing through her, my father is gazing upward, just as am I. The sun is warming his face. She thought of Blanche's odd words about Graelam, and knew them to be true. If she rode out and never returned, he would not care.

To her utter surprise, the stable groom, Osbert, a feisty old man with grizzled hair and a hook nose, shook his head at her request. "Forgive me, my lady, but my lord said ye were not to ride out, not without him."

"When did he give you this order, Osbert?"

"Yesterday, my lady, again. He told me he'd stretch my neck if I bowed to your . . . pretty face."

Pretty face! She wanted to laugh. "Where is Lord Graelam?"

"Here, my lady."

She spun about, paling as she saw him leaning against the open doorway, his arms crossed over his massive chest. She ran her tongue over her suddenly dry lips, her eyes falling to the strewn hay at her feet.

"You wish to ride out?"

She wanted suddenly to demand where he had spent the past two nights. But when she raised her face, she saw that he was frowning at her, his dark eyes narrowed.

"Aye," she said. "If it pleases you, my lord," she added, hating the pleading in her voice.

He straightened and nodded toward Osbert. "Ready her mare. You may come with me, Kassia." She forced herself to stand quietly as he approached her. "Guy will ride with us," he said. "That is certain to please you."

Guy! She blinked, thinking absurdly that she was a bone, and two dogs were fighting over her. "Aye," she said, tilting her chin upward. "That would please me."

He made a growling sound deep in his throat, and wheeled away from her. "I will await you outside," he said, and left her.

There were six men in their party. Rolfe told her they were to visit the merchant Drieux in the newly chartered village of Wolffeton. To Kassia's surprise, Graelam said nothing when Guy reined his destrier beside her.

Guy smiled at her gently. "I was telling my master," he said, leaning toward her in the saddle, "that the jakes are no longer offensive to the nose."

"Lime," she said shortly.

"The duke will be pleasantly surprised," Graelam said, looking back toward Wolffeton. "Have you finished cushions for him?"

She nodded.

"His old butt will be well content," Guy said, laughing.

"You have done well, my lady," Graelam said.

She felt herself flushing with pleasure at his unexpected praise.

"Gallop with me, Kassia," he said, and slapped the flat of his gloved hand to Bluebell's rump.

She laughed aloud with pleasure, feeling the soft summer breeze tangling through her hair. She breathed the salty sea air deeply.

When they slowed to a walk, Graelam turned to her. "I had intended that you come with me this morning. Now that your cheeks are red and your eyes bright, you do not look so ill."

"I am not ill," she said.

"Tell me his name, Kassia."

She felt a deadening pain in her chest. "I asked Blanche," she said, "but she would not tell me."

"Blanche!" His hands tightened on the reins, and Demon snorted, dancing sideways.

She saw his face darken with anger, and drew in her breath. But he said nothing, merely dug his heels into his destrier's sides and galloped away from her.

The village of Wolffeton lay nestled in a valley not two leagues from the castle. A dozen men were building the defensive wall that would rise some eighteen feet into the air, shielding them from sea attacks. The ground was deeply rutted and muddy, and piles of refuse were stacked around at least a dozen tents. The only completed structure was the merchant's house. Drieux stood in the doorway waiting for them. He was an ascetic-looking man, his face thin, his pale eyes deeply set, and nearly the age of her father. He had been exquisitely polite to Kassia when he had met her some weeks before at the castle.

"My lord, my lady," he said, bowing deeply from the waist.

Graelam nodded, gracefully dismounting. "All goes well, I see," he said, gazing about the growing village.

"You do need more men," he added, pointing toward the wall.

"A dozen more families will be arrriving within the week," Drieux said. "By the end of the year, we will be self-sufficient."

Graelam turned to Guy, and Kassia watched him and the men ride toward the wall.

"I have brought my wife to see the goods we settled upon," Graelam said.

Goods! What goods? Kassia felt Graelam's hands close about her waist as he lifted her gently off her mare's back and set her on the ground. "Come, Kassia."

Graelam had to bow his head as they entered Drieux's house. Actually, Kassia saw, the main chamber housed his goods. The beamed ceilings were high, the floor still earth-covered. All smelled of freshly cut lumber. There were several long trestle tables, and on each were piles of material, boxes of spices and herbs and shining new tools. "'Tis a beginning," Drieux said wryly. "Here is the carpet, my lord."

Kassia sucked in her breath as a young boy helped Drieux unroll a magnificent red wool rug.

"Oh, Graelam, 'tis beautiful!"

He smiled down at her, his eyes lightening at her obvious enthusiasm. "Does it match your cushions?"

She turned glowing eyes to his face. "I will make new ones if it does not!"

He watched her finger the thick wool, exclaiming to the merchant as she traced each swirling pattern. "From Flanders?" she asked.

"Aye," said Drieux.

"And the other, for our bedchamber." Graelam said.

The other carpet was a vibrant blue, so soft that Kassia could imagine her bare feet sinking into it. "It is so very fine," she breathed. Suddenly she frowned, thinking of the cost, thinking of the valuable necklace stolen from Graelam's chest.

"It does not please you?"

She flinched at his harsh tone, and swallowed. "We really do not need it, my lord. It is so very valuable."

"It matters not. I want it."

She smiled up at him shyly, and he returned her smile, until he realized that he was playing the fool, seeking to please her.

"Shall we put it in the duke's bedchamber until he leaves?"

"An excellent idea," he said shortly. "The duke will doubtless believe that you are just the mistress Wolffeton needed."

He left her then, to see to the village's fortifications.

Kassia followed him outside and stood quietly, watching the men work on the wall. Drieux came up to stand beside her. "The carpets are indeed from Flanders, my lady," he said.

"However did you get them so quickly?"

"From a rich merchant in Portsmouth. Lord Graelam wanted them quickly."

Kassia smiled up at him. "Doubtless you will become a wealthy man, monsieur."

"With Lord Graelam's strength and protection, I believe it will be so."

Graelam returned and helped Kassia into the saddle. After giving Drieux instructions to have the carpets brought to Wolffeton that afternoon, he wheeled Demon about.

As they neared Wolffeton, Graelam sent Guy and his men to the castle and motioned for Kassia to follow him.

He saw her hesitate briefly, and raised a brow. "You do want to ride, do you not?"

He led her to the protected cove, the place where he had taken her virginity many weeks before.

"I wish to speak to you," he said.

He lifted her from her saddle, tethered the horses, then left her to walk along the rocky beach. He gazed out over the billowing waves, watching them crash, sending spumes of white over the jutting rocks.

He turned back to her and said suddenly, "When I asked you the man's name, you said that Blanche would not tell you. Why do you bring her into this, Kassia?"

Her chin rose, but she managed to say calmly enough, "Because it had to be she who hired those men. I did not guess it until you told me of the missing necklace. I knew then that it had to be someone within the keep. Since it was Blanche who accompanied me that day, there was no one else. I asked her to tell me the man's name, but she merely laughed at me and refused."

"That is ridiculous," he said coldly. "There is no reason for Blanche to do such a thing."

"Aye, there is. She wishes to wed you, and she loves her son mightily and seeks to ensure his future."

Graelam was silent a moment. He remembered the night Blanche had come to his bedchamber, into his bed.

Kassia knew that he didn't believe her, but she said nonetheless, "I do not know if Blanche hired them to kill me. I trust it is not so."

"You weave fantasies, Kassia," he said harshly. "It is not me Blanche desires, it is Guy. Indeed, Guy will announce their betrothal this evening. He has spent the last two nights in her bed."

Kassia swayed where she stood. Guy and Blanche! "No!" she whispered.

"Aye, that distresses you, does it not, my lady? Your gallant Guy desires another woman. And Blanche is a woman, with a woman's needs, and a woman's soft body."

"But she is older than Guy!"

"Two years. 'Tis nothing. She will breed him many sons, which, of course, is the only reason for a man to wed, that and to add to his coffers or land to his holdings. He could not ask her before, since he owned no land. As I said, Blanche is a woman, and she is honest in her need for a man."

Kassia was beginning to doubt her sanity. If Blanche loved Guy, then why would she hire those men to take her away from Wolffeton? There was no answer to her silent question.

Graelam saw the changing thoughts on her expressive face. He remembered Guy telling him the previous evening, "It is best for your wife if Blanche is gone from Wolffeton," but he said nothing to Kassia. He saw the unhappiness in her eyes, unhappiness she would not hide at losing Guy, and wanted to hurt her. Even as he spoke, he knew he was being unfair and unnecessarily cruel. "Guy is lucky, is he not? He is wedding a woman who is soft and giving. A woman who welcomes him gladly to her bed." He saw her stiffen, and her chin rise again.

"I believe it time for you to breed me sons, my lady. Even though you are a frigid child, you will do your duty by me." He clasped her slender shoulders and drew her against him. He cupped her face in his large hands, holding her firmly, and kissed her roughly. Her lips were cold and tightly pursed.

"Please," she whispered against his mouth, "do not hurt me again. I have done nothing to deserve it."

He cursed softly and pushed her away from him. "Have you not? Perhaps I should send you back to Belleterre and get myself a wife who is also a woman."

His thrust made her blind with fury. "Perhaps you should," she said quite coldly.

"Enough!" he roared at her. "Mount your mare, wife. At least there is something you are good at. You may return to Wolffeton and order preparations for a feast tonight. You would not want Guy to feel . . . unappreciated, would you?"

She shook her head, mute, and climbed on Bluebell's back.

21

Kassia stood quietly while Etta tightened the soft silk belt around her waist, drawing in the bright blue silk tunic. She would have preferred dull gray wool, but knew Graelam would be furious with her if she did not appear well-garbed this evening. She had seen nothing of Blanche during the day. It was probably just as well, she thought, wincing as Etta drew her tortoise shell comb through her hair, tugging at a tangle, for there was no reason at all for Blanche to tell her the truth. She bit her bottom lip. What was the truth?

"'Tis lovely you look, my baby," Etta said fondly, stepping back to admire her mistress. "The duke does not arrive until tomorrow. Why do you wear your best gown tonight?"

Kassia gave her a pained smile. "You will see, Etta. Be in the hall."

Blanche, as had been her habit the past two days, also appeared in one of her best gowns, and looked utterly beautiful, even to Kassia's jaundiced eye. No wonder Guy loved her.

271

Blanche eyed Kassia closely, an arched dark brow winging upward. She asked in a honey-sweet voice, "You have nearly the look of a gentlewoman this evening, Kassia. May I ask why?"

"To honor your betrothal, of course," Kassia replied.

Blanche blinked rapidly and drew in her breath. "You know? Graelam has spoken to you?"

"Aye, he did this morning. I suppose that I must congratulate you."

Blanche felt that the world had taken a faulty turn. "Are you not upset? You did understand what Graelam said?"

"Aye, I understood, and I am only upset because it seems . . . an unlikely match, at least to me. I had no idea you cared for each other."

Blanche was momentarily speechless, wondering if the little snit was blind. She was not loath to gloat, just a bit. "And I had thought that you cared for him. It was all an act? Come, I do not believe you!"

"I do care for him." Kassia shrugged. "However, since I have no say in the matter, it is foolish to rant and rave. It is his decision, after all." She raised her chin. "I hope, Blanche, that you will be a good wife to him."

"You may be certain that I shall. He has been quite pleased to share my bed the past two nights."

"Aye, I know. Graelam also told me of that."

Blanche could only shake her head. She wanted to gloat a bit more, but in the face of Kassia's calm acceptance, she was left without a word to say. "You are mad," she managed, and left her.

Mad, am I? Kassia frowned in some confusion at Blanche's back, then turned to direct the servants. The hall filled quickly, the men seating themselves along

the long trestle tables. Blanche hung back a moment,
until Guy smiled at her and motioned her to her place
beside him.

"I don't know," she began, trying to gain Graelam's
attention. But he was speaking to Kassia and did not
heed her.

"Sit down, Blanche. You will see, 'tis better so."

She could scarce eat a bite, her gaze continually
going to the high table, questions tumbling through her
mind. When will he tell everyone? Why is he waiting?
What is he saying to Kassia?

"Patience, Blanche," Guy said softly, slanting her an
amused look.

At least, she thought, turning to the young knight,
she could show him her triumph. If Graelam had told
Kassia, 'twas likely Guy also knew. "Everything has
worked out just as I said it would," she said, her voice
sounding shrill and defensive to her own ears.

"I think so," Guy said blandly.

"There is nothing you can do about it!" she hissed at
him. "In a few minutes Graelam will make the announcement." Why did he seem so indifferent to what
had happened, so uncaring?

"He told me he would," he said.

She cursed him softly under her breath, her unspoken disappointment making her say angrily, "It is your
hope to take Kassia yourself? Will you volunteer to see
her back to her father in Brittany?"

"No," he said evenly.

Blanche turned at the sound of Graelam's bellow for
silence. At last, she thought, straightening. At last!

Graelam rose from his chair. "Attend me," he called
out. He paused a moment until the hall was quiet. "I

have happy news to give you. Blanche, will you please come here? And Guy, of course."

Why Guy? she wondered. She walked gracefully to the raised dais, Guy beside her.

"Everyone wish the couple well," Graelam said, grinning at Guy. "Blanche and Guy will be wed the day after tomorrow, in the presence of the Duke of Cornwall."

"No!" The small word readied to erupt from her mouth, but Guy grabbed her and kissed her heartily, smothering her cry.

There was a chorus of shouts and congratulations and calls for more ale. "It is done, Blanche," Guy said into her mouth.

"You whoreson!" she spat at him, her mind still reeling. She tried to pull away from him, but his arms were like iron bands.

"You didn't think that when I was in your bed," he whispered. "Indeed, you enjoyed yourself much, Blanche. And I did promise you that you would never sleep alone again. You are well caught, my love. Graelam is pleased. You will not gainsay me now."

"No," she moaned, still unable to believe what had happened.

Guy heard shouts and kissed her again, allowing his hand to slip down her back. "Mayhap my son already grows in your belly, my love. Chitterly is not so grand as Wolffeton, but you will grow contented, you will see. Now, Blanche, smile, else when I come to your bed tonight, I will take you without thought to your pleasure."

"You planned this," she gasped, feeling his hand upon her hips. "May you rot in hell, Guy! I will never wed you, never! 'Tis Graelam I want, and I shall have him!"

Guy was profoundly grateful for the lecherous calls

and lewd jests from the men, and Graelam's oblivious presence. "I think, my love, that you and I will leave the hall for a moment. There is much that you must come to understand." Without another word, Guy hoisted her onto his shoulder and strode through the laughing men out of the hall.

She struggled mightily, but it was no use. She was panting in fury when he set her down and took her arm, pulling her along with him into the inner bailey. He took her into the warm, dark stable. Only Osbert was there, and Guy dismissed him quickly.

He gave her a light shove and she fell onto a pile of hay. He stood over her, hands on his lean hips. "Listen well, Blanche. It is my intention to turn you into a sweet, loving wife. If you fight me, I shall beat you, doubt it not." He saw the rippling fury in her eyes, and hastened to add, his voice harsh, "Graelam does not want you. He never has. How you could be so blind astonishes me. You know as well as I that there are . . . problems between Graelam and Kassia, but you will not be here to add to Kassia's unhappiness, or, I might add, my love, to hire more men to rid Wolffeton of her presence. No, do not bother to deny it. Now, I believe it time to . . . consummate our betrothal."

He began shedding his clothing, and for a moment Blanche simply stared at him. Pain filled her, and she whispered, "You told Graelam that I willingly bedded you?"

"Aye." He puased a moment and regarded her closely. "'Tis odd. Graelam still believes you modest and submissive. That you managed to keep him blind for so long is amazing to me." He laughed heartily. "I assured him that you were quite a woman in my bed."

"You do not want me," she said, her eyes against her

will going over his body as he bared himself. "It is that little slut you want. You know Graelam does not want her! Damn you, you know it!"

He stood before her, naked. "Graelam wants her, all right," he said softly. "He merely does not know it yet. And with you gone from Wolffeton, my lady, he will come to understand her quickly enough, and himself. Do you like my body, Blanche? Last night you searched for the scar on my groin before you fell into a sated sleep. And Graelam is a much larger man. I was surprised that you did not recognize me last night, for you were drunk only on lust, and not on wine."

"I was a fool," she said dully.

Guy didn't like the defeat in her eyes. "'Tis likely," he said coolly, dropping down beside her on the hay. "But you have won me, Blanche. You do account me a good lover, do you not?"

"I believe you a nasty, cocky whoreson," she spat him. He smiled and pressed her upon her back. "You are a feisty little witch, do you know that? Come now, Blanche, I know you are not indifferent to me, no more than I am to you." He kissed her deeply, his hand gliding downward over her belly. He felt the ripple of pleasure in her as she arched her hips up toward him. "No," he whispered into her mouth, "not indifferent at all. You are a delightful bargain, my love. I will easily make you forget Graelam and Wolffeton."

"You could pretend that you are pleased," Graelam said, looking sharply at his wife.

Kassia gave him a wan smile. "I will miss Guy," she said. "He has been kind to me."

"Aye, so many men are *kind* to you. Even Drieux

sings your praises." He leaned closer to her. "Have you entertained the good merchant in your bed?"

"Since my bed is also yours, my lord," she said coldly, "you know you speak only to fan your dislike of me." She shrugged. "Of course, since you have not been in your bed for several nights, you cannot really know, can you?"

She felt gooseflesh rise on her arms at his deep laugh, and wished she had kept her mouth shut. Why did she allow him to bait her? "You sound lonely, my lady. But I wonder how that can be so, when you are still a child, and have no use for men." He sat back in his chair, his arms folded over his chest. "I imagine that at this very moment Guy is thrusting deep between Blanche's lovely thighs. That bothers you, does it not?"

She shook her head, not looking at him.

"Kassia, you believe I dislike you. Damn you, look at me when I speak!"

She obeyed him. "Aye, I believe it," she whispered. "Not at first, but you changed."

"I, wife? 'Tis only that I discovered my sweet, innocent wife was a deceitful bitch."

Was there never to be an end to it? she wondered wearily. "I did not hurt you, my lord. Nor have I ever been deceitful."

He cursed very softly, aware that Blount was looking at him.

"May I be excused, my lord?"

He waved her away. He watched her walk gracefully through the hall, stopping to speak to various of his men, and felt his irritation grow. He thought again of the conversation he had had with Drake, his armorer, that afternoon. He admitted to himself that he had been wavering in his beliefs until Drake had matter-of-factly stated in his even, emotionless way that women, even the best of them, couldn't help themselves. "They spin tales, my lord," he said as if he were calmly discussing the weather. "Lady Kassia lied to you, but again, she is but a woman. How could she tell you the truth?" Drake shrugged, and spat into the corner of the armory.

"Mayhap," Graelam heard himself say as if from a great distance, "she did not lie."

"She is young, my lord. Wolffeton is vastly different from her home in Brittany. Why did she try to escape you? Why did she come back? Why, my lord, does any woman behave in ways that make our heads spin?" He picked up a hauberk and began to pound methodically at the iron fastenings. "You might as well forget it, my lord. Accept your lady for what she is."

Graelam knew that he should have cut off Drake's impudence, but he had wanted to hear what he had to say. He was a man who had lived many years and known many women. He treated Kassia's duplicity as if it were naught. Damn her, he thought now, draining the remainder of his wine.

"Well, well, my lord," the Duke of Cornwall said to Graelam as he gazed about the great hall of Wolffeton, "'Tis quite an improvement. Even a carpet." He turned a kindly smile upon Kassia.

"You have done more than I thought possible, my lady. It appears you have tamed this big brute. Ah, even cushions on the chairs. Aye, Graelam, you chose your wife wisely."

Graelam grunted and Kassia kept her head lowered.

She felt the duke's bony fingers cupping her chin and slowly raised her head. "And you, my lady, have much

benefited from your husband, I see. More meat on your
delicate bones. No babe as yet?"

Kassia, her eyes held by the old duke's piercing gaze,
could only shake her head.

"You'll see to it, my lord," the duke said, and patted
her cheek. He turned slowly, his joints creaking in his
own ears, and called out, "Sir Walter! Come and meet
your new lord!"

Kassia watched the tall, thin knight stride forward.
He was well-garbed, and as she listened, she realized
that he said all the right words, showing due deference
to Graelam. But there was something about him, something that she distrusted and disliked. When he at last
turned to her, she realized that it was his eyes. They
were dark blue, but cold and flat, without feeling.

"My lady," Sir Walter de Grasse said smoothly.

She felt naked, even her thoughts stripped bare before him. She thrust up her chin, angered at herself for
such fancifulness. "Sir Walter," she said in a crisp voice.
"Welcome to Wolffeton."

"Sir Walter comes from Cornwall," the duke said,
"Now, unfortunately, he must make his own way."

Sir Walter said, "Aye, 'tis true. My family's home
was destroyed by the father of that viper Dienwald de
Fortenberry."

Graelam gazed at the man thoughtfully. He heard
venom in his voice, and saw the gleam of hatred in his
eyes. He said very calmly, "Whatever de Fortenberry
has done, Sir Walter, he has not come near to Wolffeton.
I do not count him an enemy. I pray you will not forget
that."

Sir Walter bowed slightly. Kassia shivered. She became aware of her husband's eyes upon her, and immediately broke into speech. "My lord duke, we have

prepared a chamber for you that has its own carpet. Allow me to show you."

When told later at dinner of Sir Guy's betrothal, the duke beamed with pleasure. "A good lad, and worthy. The lady Blanche, I understand, is Graelam's sister-in-law?"

"His first wife's half-sister," Kassia corrected smoothly.

"The boy, Evian," the duke continued to Graelam, "is he not Blanche's son?"

"Aye. Sir Guy has decided that the lad will remain here at Wolffeton. He is performing his duties quite well. I have hopes that one day he will squire me."

Kassia wondered how Blanche felt about leaving Evian at Wolffeton. They had not seemed particularly close, but still, shouldn't Blanche be the one to decide the future of her son?

"Likely the boy will have many brothers and sisters," the duke said, casting his rheumy eyes toward Blanche and Sir Guy. "The lady looks to be a fine breeder."

"At least she is a proven breeder," Graelam said dryly.

"Do you consider wives to be as cattle and horses, then, my lord duke?" Kassia asked, and immediately bit her lip. Graelam's opinion of women she knew well. Likely now she had insulted the duke.

"Nay, my dear wife," Graelam said very softly, leaning toward her. "Cattle and horses know but one way to mate. Wives, if they but show a little interest, can find breeding very pleasurable."

The duke overheard Graelam's words and laughed loudly. "Well said, my lord. But forget not that your lady has many other talents as well." He patted the cushion and sighed in contentment. "My old bones feel like they've melted and gone to heaven."

When at last the sweetmeats and fresh fruit were set in front of the duke, he turned to Graelam, a wide smile on his face, and said, "I've a surprise for you, Graelam. Quiet the men, and I will announce my news."

Kassia cocked her head to one side, wondering wearily if the duke had another heiress for Graelam.

The Duke of Cornwall rose and stood quietly for a moment, then burst out heartily, "Edward the First, King of England, returns shortly! His coronation and his queen's will take place in Westminster Abbey in October! My lord Graelam, your presence is requested at the ceremony."

There was wild cheering, and Kassia discreetly motioned for the servants to bring in more ale and wine. Her head whirled with excitement for Graelam. She turned excitedly to her husband. "Graelam, you will go, will not you? I must sew you new tunics. You have but one fine one. And a new robe, of purple velvet, I think. For the king, you must look very grand!"

Graelam felt a smile tugging at his mouth at her enthusiasm.

"And what of you, Kassia? Do you not have need of new gowns and the like?"

She raised wide, questioning eyes to his face. "Do you mean that you wish me to accompany you?"

He felt a brief wrenching pain at the pitiful stirring of hope he saw in her eyes. "Of course you will come with me," he said curtly. "Who else would see to my comfort?"

Any of the female servants, she wanted to yell at him, but her excitement at traveling to London quickly overcame her ire at his words. "I will really meet King Edward and Queen Eleanor?"

"Aye, you will meet them. And you do have need of

some new gowns, Kassia. Unfortunately, the duke, as usual, gives us little time to prepare."

"I will do it," Kassia said. "Whatever needs to be done will be done."

Graelam fiddled with his wine goblet for a moment, frowning at himself even as he spoke. "There is a bolt of gold-threaded silk in my trunk. You will sew yourself a gown from it."

Her jaw dropped in surprise, and she blinked at him.

" 'Tis a pity you gave the necklace away, for you could have worn it with the silk."

He saw the light go out of her eyes as if he had struck her. St. Peter's bones, he thought furiously, why should he feel guilty? She was the one who had played him false. She was the one who persisted in her lies.

"Nan!" he called. "More wine!"

Kassia sat very quietly. In her excitement, she had forgotten momentarily how much he disliked and distrusted her. But of course he would not forget. He would never forget.

She lay curved into a small ball some hours later, the raucous laughter from the hall below softening in her dream. A man's voice spoke, saying very softly, " 'Tis time to see if my little wench can breed." She sighed and turned onto her back. Suddenly she could hear the man's breathing. She blinked and abruptly came awake.

"Hold still," Graelam said, his hands on the belt of her bedrobe.

He was drunk, she thought frantically. "Please, Graelam," she whispered, pressing her hands against his bare chest.

"Hold still," he repeated. He jerked up her bedrobe, giving up on the knot at her waist, and fell on top of her. He grasped her head between his hands and kissed her, his tongue thrusting deep into her mouth. Kassia felt his swollen manhood against her thighs. She knew she couldn't fight him, and lay perfectly still.

He raised his head until he could focus on her face in the dim light. Her eyes were tightly closed. "Damn you," he said softly. He felt her quiver beneath him, and smiled bitterly. "I will make you respond," he muttered. He mustered his waning control and eased himself off her.

Her eyes flew open, and she drew a shattered breath at his harsh face above her, his mouth set in a grim line.

"You want me to force you," he said. "Then you can hate me all the more."

"I don't hate you."

He lightly stroked his hand over her throat. "Take off the bedrobe, Kassia."

He controls me, she thought. He will do just as he pleases with me, despite my wishes. A flicker of rebellion rose within her. "You tell me I am a child, that I do not have a woman's feelings. Why do you bother? Why do you not return to your mistress? Does it please you to hurt me? If so, then just get it over with!"

Graelam felt the haze of drunkenness gripping his mind, but he was sober enough to make sense of her tumbled words. He realized vaguely that he was likely too drunk to make her respond to him, and that now her mind was locked against him. He rolled off her and rose. "Very well," he said, reaching for his bedrobe. Oddly enough, he felt no anger at her for spurning him. "If I return during the night, you need have no fear of me." He turned on his heel and strode from the bedchamber.

22

Kassia turned away from the cooking shed, mulling over again the words she had overheard Sir Walter say to Guy just before Guy and Blanche had left Wolffeton. "It is a pity that I do not have a father to die and pass me his estates." Guy, who was distracted, had said only, "Aye, 'tis unfortunate."

"But there are other ways," Sir Walter had continued after a moment. "Soon, I believe, I will not longer be landless. I will gain what should have always belonged to me."

Kassia shivered now, remembering how coldly and emotionlessly he had spoken, though, objectively, they could simply reflect Sir Walter's ambition. She wished she could tell Graelam of her feelings, but she guessed he would simply look at her like she was a stupid woman and dismiss her out of hand. She paused a moment, gazing at Drake, the armorer, at his work. She missed Guy. Her brow puckered as she recalled his words at his leave-taking. "Now, my lady," he had said, lightly touching her cheek, "the way is clear for you to live at Wolffeton happily and safely." Her eyes flew to his face, but he had shaken his head at her, smiling. "Blanche is a handful, never doubt it, Kassia, but she will please me. You may be certain of that!"

Kassia was not so certain that would be the case. Although there seemed to be a new softness about Blanche, she nonetheless stared through Kassia, ignoring her completely when they took their leave of Wolffeton.

Kassia paused a moment, hearing her husband's forceful voice from the practice field. He had not returned to their bed that night nearly a week before, and since then he had slept with her every night without attempting to touch her. She imagined that after taking his man's pleasure with Nan, he wanted the comfort of his own bed. She wanted to shrug, but could not manage to do it.

She made her way to Blount's accounting room and began another coward's letter to her father. Not wanting to worry him, she had never mentioned her unhappiness or her husband's obvious distrust of her. She paused a moment over the piece of parchment, thinking about his last letter to her. "Geoffrey is quiet," he had written. "Too quiet. Like a snake that is slithering about until he can find a protected place from which to strike." The rest of his letter had merely recounted the day-to-day events at Belleterre. Kassia told him of the upcoming coronation, and left it at that.

"Ye believe ye're so above us all, don't ye, my fine lady?"

She turned at Nan's sneering voice, and frowned. The girl stood in the doorway, her hands on her hips, her hair tossed back, long and thick down her back.

Normally she did not allow Nan's insolence to bother her, for after all, the wench did bed with Graelam. But this attack was both unexpected and beyond the line.

"What do you want, Nan?" she asked crisply, rising.

"That old crone Etta told me ye wanted me to scrub down the trestle tables."

"Yes, that is what I wish you to do."

"We'll see about that!" Nan muttered, and flounced away.

Kassia frowned. She frowned again several hours later when she finished sewing on her silk gown and went into the great hall. The trestle tables hadn't been cleaned. Furthermore, Nan was sitting in Kassia's chair, waving her hands, giving outlandish orders in a loud, shrewish voice in an effort to mimic her. Kassia felt a surge of rage, and strode into the hall.

The other servants saw her before Nan, and quickly lowered their heads, bending more ardently to their tasks.

"Get out of my chair," Kassia said in a cold voice. "Now."

Nan jumped, and slithered out of the chair, responding to the voice of authority. But she quickly straightened and faced Kassia.

"You will do your assigned tasks, Nan, else you will go into the laundry shed or the fields."

"Nay, my lady," Nan said, eyeing her with open contempt. "Ye haven't the power to do that. My lord would never allow it." She ran a hand through her gleaming long hair. "Aye, ye haven't the power. 'Tis hard work, cleaning the trestle tables. My lord wouldn't want me to use my energy and become too tired for him."

Kassia heard a soft snicker behind her. She closed

her eyes for a brief instant. She was the mistress of Wolffeton. This little slut could not be allowed to speak to her thus, else she would lose all control. She drew herself up to her full height.

"You will still your insolent mouth, Nan, and do the work I ordered you to do. Now."

"Nay, my lady. 'Tis too hard a task. My lord won't want me to harm his child." She clasped her arms about her belly, her eyes challenging Kassia.

Child! Graelam's child! Kassia felt a wave of dizziness wash over her. Her eyes traveled over Nan, and even she could now see the slight bulge at her waist. If she had had a knife, she would have stabbed it into Nan and then into Graelam.

Graelam stood in the shadows of the great oak door. Nan's startling words surprised him, but it was not she who held his attention. Kassia looked both ill and furious. He knew that he could not allow Nan to gainsay her mistress, knew it as well as he suspected Kassia did. He strode forward, drawing all eyes.

Kassia saw him and wondered dully how much he had overheard. She stood numbly, waiting for him to complete her humiliation.

"My lord!" Nan cried, and started toward him.

Graelam raised a hand. "What is happening here, my lady?" he asked Kassia.

He knows exactly what has happened, she thought, and he is baiting me. He will make me say what I believe in front of the servants, then say exactly the opposite. She forced herself to meet his dark gaze. She said in a cool, clear voice, "I have given Nan a task, my lord. She does not wish to do it because she carries a child." *Your child*.

"I see," he said. He turned to Nan. "What is this task that would be so wearing on you?"

"Scrubbing the trestle tables, my lord. The duke's men were pigs, and left them filthy."

Graelam gazed back toward his wife. He saw her hands fisted against her sides. He smiled slightly. "Begin the task, Nan, as your mistress instructed. My lady, you will please accompany me now."

Begin the task. Kassia looked at him warily. Nan cocked her head to one side, but realized enough to keep her mouth shut. Perhaps he simply didn't wish to embarrass his skinny wife in front of all the servants. She probably should have told him of the child before she attacked Kassia.

"Very well, my lord," she said sweetly. "I shall begin the work."

"Come, Kassia," Graelam said, and walked from the hall.

Kassia knew she had no choice. She trailed after him, her shoulders square and her chin raised.

He waited until she had entered their bedchamber, then quietly closed the door. He said nothing for a long moment, merely watched her. That little chin of hers, he noticed, was raised again for battle.

"It is your child, of course," Kassia said, hearing the tremor of anger in her voice.

"I suspect so," he said calmly.

"I suppose you expect me to thank you for not humiliating me in front of the servants."

"You could, but I doubt that you will."

His utter disinterest riled her beyond reason. "I am the mistress of Wolffeton!" she shouted at him.

"Are you?" he asked calmly. "In some ways I suppose that you are. In others, my lady, you are sorely lacking."

"Just as are you, my lord!"

To her surprise, he nodded. "It is true. Now, you will heed me well, my lady. I put a stop to Nan's insolence for the moment. I will handle the wench to your satisfaction if you will agree to become the mistress of Wolffeton in all ways."

"Wh-what do you mean?"

"I see I have your full attention. Here is the bargain I propose, my lady. You will come to me willingly in my bed. You will no longer act the outraged maiden or the passive victim. If you refuse, I imagine your life could be particularly unpleasant."

He expected her to draw back in disgust, but she didn't move. Her eyes remained wide and questioning on his face. "What do you mean that you will handle Nan to my satisfaction?"

"Ah, the terms of the agreement. You are wise to have everything clear before agreeing or disagreeing. I will marry the wench off and remove her from Wolffeton. You will never have to deal with her insolence again. That is, if you agree."

Kassia could easily imagine what would happen if Nan gained the upper hand. She raised her chin even higher. "I do not think that it is your right to interfere at all in how I manage the servants. And that includes your precious mistress."

"Then I take it that you do not agree to my . . . bargain?"

He thought he heard her curse, and it made him want to smile.

"You have not the right! Will you take everything from me?"

"On the contrary," he said smoothly. "I wish to give

you more. A woman's pleasure, for example. Such pleasure truly does exist, I promise you."

"Give it to your slut, damn you!"

He regarded her calmly and said, "How I envy Guy. I heard Blanche's cries of pleasure on their wedding night. Would you grant to Guy what you refuse to grant to me?"

"I would grant none of you anything!"

"Enough, Kassia. What is your answer?"

"If I refuse, will you release Nan from all her duties and make her the mistress of Wolffeton?"

Of course he would not, but he saw that Kassia did not realize that. He merely shrugged, looking bored and impatient.

She looked away from him, her hands clenching and unclenching in front of her. "I don't know what to do!" she cried.

"All I desire is your . . . cooperation. I will teach you the rest. Come, wife, my men await me. What is your answer?"

"I . . . I agree," she said in a whisper.

He made no move toward her. "Very well. Now you will come with me back into the hall and give Nan her orders. I will endeavor to find her a husband."

Kassie followed him, her thoughts in a whirl. Why did he even bother? Why was it so important to him that she enjoy coupling? She did not understand him.

Nan gasped in disbelief, her eyes pleading on Graelam's face. She pleased him, the whoreson, she thought venomously, and now he was choosing his skinny wife over her! It occurred to her that she had pushed Kassia too hard, challenged her too openly. She saw it in the eyes of the other servants. They were enjoying her downfall, rot them! She had to speak to Graelam alone.

Graelam took Kassia's hand and drew her with him to the inner bailey. "You will begin to fulfill your bargain this night, wife." He squeezed her hand slightly, and left her to stare after him, gooseflesh rising on her arms.

Later Graelam watched Sir Walter wash down his head and torso at the well. "All goes well, Walter?"

"Aye, my lord."

"I wish you to ride with three men tomorrow morning to the demesne farm that lies due west three miles. The farmer's name is Robert, I believe, and he has recently lost his wife. I want you to bring him to Wolffeton."

Walter readily agreed, not caring why Graelam wanted the farmer brought to Wolffeton. He only wished he could travel farther than the three miles, toward Dienwald de Fortenberry's stronghold.

Graelam decided wisely not to speak to Nan until the following day. He had no real faith that Kassia would hold to the bargain. He felt nothing in particular about Nan or the fact that she carried his child. He would provide support, of course, and pay the farmer well to marry her. It was his second bastard. The first, a girl, had died in her first year of life. His father had bragged about the wenches he had gotten with child, and claimed more than a dozen children. However, Graelam had never seen any resemblance to himself in any of the peasants around Wolffeton. He thought of Kassia's small belly filled with his child and felt an intense jolt of pleasure. I am becoming a half-wit, he told himself, and roared furiously at one of his men-at-arms who had bungled his lance.

"Your hair is growing quickly, my baby," Etta said as she brushed through the shiny tresses. "I believe it is thicker than before your illness. Still, you should not wear a wimple or even a snood."

Kassia looked into the polished silver mirror. Her chestnut hair fell in soft curls nearly to her shoulders. "Aye," she said in a clipped voice, "I begin to look like a female again." *In just a few minutes, I will have to pretend that I like being one!* Oddly enough, she remembered how she had liked her husband touching her and kissing her, until he had hurt her. Until he had shown how much he despised her. How could anything be different now?

"Your lord dealt well with that little slut, Nan," Etta continued as she straightened the chamber from Kassia's bath. "You will no longer have to put up with her tantrums."

"No, I will not," Kassia said.

"I have also heard that the new knight, Sir Walter, is not as popular with the men as was Sir Guy."

"Where did you hear that?" Kassia asked sharply.

Etta shrugged. "From one of the men, likely. I do not remember. I find him a cold lout, and a secretive one."

"I wonder what Graelam thinks of him," Kassia said, more to herself than to her old nurse.

"Your lord is an astute man. If Sir Walter is not what he appears, he will soon be ousted."

"I trust you are right, Etta."

"Right about what?" Graelam asked as he came into the chamber.

Etta replied readily enough, "Right about Sir Walter."

"Perhaps," Kassia essayed bravely, "he is not what he appears to be."

Graelam's brows drew together in a mighty frown. "Has he bothered you?"

Kassia blinked at him. "Nay, my lord, it is just that I do not completely trust him. He reminds me somehwat of Geoffrey."

"I see," Graelam said. He dismissed Etta and stood quietly watching his wife fidget about the room, her hands going again and again to the sash at her waist.

"Are you still of the same mind, my lady?" he asked quietly.

She swallowed and nodded, not meeting his eyes.

"I promised you once that I would not force you again. You still believe that you will have to bear pain and pretend to enjoy me, do you not?"

"I have known nothing else," she said, her eyes focused on her bare feet, sinking down into the soft carpet.

"You will tonight."

"I . . . I will try, Graelam."

There was a soft rap on the door and Graelam opened it. Evian handed him a tray upon which stood wine and two goblets.

"You do not have to make me drunk, my lord!"

He smiled at her. "Nay, but I do think you need to relax a bit, my lady. Here." He handed her a goblet of wine, then poured himself one.

She sipped at the cool sweet wine slowly, wondering vaguely how it slipped down her clogged throat. She felt her face grow warm as she downed a second goblet. Everything seemed softer, her tongue loosened, and she spoke her thoughts aloud. "Why is it important to you that I . . . that I like coupling with you?"

"I do not want my child conceived in fear," he said, knowing he wasn't being honest with her.

"Does it matter?"

"To me it does." He did not want to probe his own

reasons, and said abruptly, "Enough wine, Kassia. Get into bed now."

She obeyed him, forcing herself not to burrow under the covers.

He watched her from the corner of his eye as he quickly undressed. Indeed, he thought, why did it matter what she felt? She was but a woman, and his wife. But it did matter, and for whatever reason, he was pleased that he had thought of a way to ensure her compliance. He saw her face pale when he eased into the bed beside her. She thinks I will savage her now, he thought. He smiled wryly, stretched upon his back, and pillowed his head with his arms. After a moment he asked, "Did Nan do your bidding?"

"Aye, but unwillingly."

Her reply was barely above a strangled whisper. It was time, he decided, to see if she would hold to the bargain. "Kassia, come here."

He did not look at her, but felt the bed sink down as she moved toward him. "Now," he said quietly, turning his head to look at her, "I want you to kiss me."

Kassia frowned a moment, wondering at him. He hadn't moved. His hands were still pillowed beneath his head. Slowly she rose on her elbow, leaned down, and quickly pecked him on his mouth.

"Excellent," he said gravely. Still he did not move. "Now I want you to kiss me again, only this time, part your lips just a bit."

He felt her warm breath, sweet from the wine, as her lips brushed his mouth again. He looked up into her eyes and smiled. "That wasn't so terrible, was it?"

She shook her head.

"I want to feel your tongue on my mouth. It will not hurt, I promise you."

As Kassia, filled with embarrassment and wariness, did as he bid her, she became aware, very slowly, of her body pressed against him. He is so large, she thought vaguely, for the first time feeling his tongue lightly touch hers. She drew back an instant, but as he made no move, joined her tongue with his. It is the wine that is making me feel warm, she thought. She was unaware that her hand now rested on his chest, and her fingers were tentatively winding in his thick mat of hair.

When she raised her head, she was panting slightly, and there was a look of profound worry in her eyes. He wanted to laugh and at the same time to crush her against him, but he did neither. "Again, Kassia," he said softly.

He allowed her to do just as she wished, and was delighted when she deepened the kiss, her hand now on his shoulder, her fingers digging into his flesh. He felt her soft breasts pressing against his chest, and wondered if he could control himself. Very slowly he brought one hand from beneath his head to rest lightly on her back. He felt her start and draw back, wary again. He began to stroke her soft hair, steeling himself against the raging desire she was raising in him.

He thought he would explode when her hand drifted over his chest, downward to his belly.

"Do you like the way I feel?" he asked her, the words warm in her mouth.

Her answer was a small gasp as she whipped her hand away. She did not know why she had wanted to touch him. It was as if her body was no longer taking orders from her mind.

"I . . . I do not mind kissing you," she managed after a breathless moment.

"I am pleased," he said, hearing the rough huskiness in his voice. St. Peter's bones, he thought, barely stifling a groan, this was a torture he could never have imagined.

She was kissing his chin now, her fingers sliding beneath his head to bring him closer to her.

When she made another foray into his mouth, he felt her quiver when his tongue touched hers. Her bare thigh was rubbing lightly against his, and he could feel her tentative urgency. If he allowed her to continue, he knew that he would lose control.

He gently brought his other hand down and clasped her shoulder, pushing her away from him. "You have done well," he said, looking closely into her vague eyes. "Go to sleep now, Kassia."

She stared at him stupidly, aware of the coiling heat in her belly, aware that her breasts felt tingly and swollen, aware that she did not want to stop what she was doing. "I . . . I don't understand," she gasped.

"Go to sleep," he repeated. He pushed her gently away from him and rolled over onto his stomach, his head turned away from her. He knew that she had not moved. He smiled painfully, and added quietly, "I want you to take off your bedrobe. When you become cold during the night, I want you to come to me for warmth. Good night, wife."

Kassia's numbed fingers pulled at the belt, flinging it away from her. She slipped out of the bedrobe, and with a deep, confused sigh, curled up on her side. "I will never understand you," she said into the darkness.

Perhaps, he thought, still striving to calm his breathing, he would never understand himself.

23

The farmer Robert was delighted with the offer of a new wife. That she carried the lord's child bothered him not a bit. She was a comely wench and quite young. With the sons she would doubtless bear him, his farm would prosper, and him along with it. As for the lord's child, that one would be well taken care of. He realized quickly that she was not at all pleased with the prospect of becoming his wife, but he thought tolerantly that would quickly change.

Nan was at first disbelieving, then utterly furious. She shot venomous glances at Kassia, saving her pleading looks for Graelam. But it was all to no avail. As for the farmer, she hated him on sight, though, objectively, he was neither old nor ill-looking.

Wolffeton's priest, Father Tobias, married the couple with dispatch, and Graelam presented the farmer with a cask of his finest wine, as well as a dowry for Nan.

If Kassia believed Graelam to be rather cold-blooded about casting off his mistress, she had to admit to overwhelming relief that the girl would be gone. Even during the brief ceremony, she found her thoughts going over and over what had happened the previous night. It both galled and frightened her that she had felt something whilst she had kissed him, something that made her feel very warm and . . . urgent. Yet Graelam had pushed her away. Rejected her. This morning when she had awakened, he was gone, and he had greeted her in the hall as if nothing out of the ordinary had occurred between them. For a moment she had felt an overwhelming urge to kick him.

She stood quietly beside him, watching Nan and her new husband ride in an open cart from Wolffeton, the cask of wine set up beside Nan like a plump child. She toyed briefly with the notion that she would tell him the bargain was off. He could no longer threaten her with Nan's insolence. She bit her tongue. She was no longer certain that she didn't want the bargain to continue, if continue it would. Why, she berated herself silently, hadn't she asked her father to explain men to her?

Graelam wished fervently for a fight. His energy was inexhaustible, his mood violent. He would have even welcomed Dienwald de Fortenberry pillaging his lands if only he could meet the man in battle. Since his wish wasn't to be granted, at least that day, he rode off with a dozen men to the village of Wolffeton, and worked frenetically to finish the defensive wall. He was utterly exhausted when he returned late that afternoon, pleased that he had exorcised his wife from his thoughts during most of the day.

But he didn't feel as exhausted as he had believed when Kassia entered their bedchamber while he was bathing.

"I have come to assist you, my lord," she said, not quite meeting his eyes. He was relieved that the water level hid his desire from her.

"You may wash my back," he said abruptly, and leaned forward.

Kassia stared at the broad expanse of back. She could feel the movement of sinewy muscle beneath the bathing cloth. To her surprise, she felt a rising warmth, coming, she believed, directly from her belly.

"What did you do today?" Graelam asked rather desperately, trying to distract himself.

"I have finished your new tunic. I trust you will approve."

"What about your gown?"

"I will begin it shortly."

Her hand dipped down below the water toward his hips, and he whipped his head around. "That is enough, Kassia. Go see to our meal."

He thought he saw a flicker of hurt in her eyes, but it was quickly masked.

"I will be down shortly."

She nodded, unable to speak, for there was a knot of misery forming in her throat. She left the bedchamber, and severely berated a serving wench when she carelessly dropped a silver platter.

Sir Walter de Grasse turned his gaze again to the raised dais, to Lady Kassia. He sensed her dislike of him, and found it angered him. So proud she was, the lord's wife, who had willingly taken up with Dienwald de Fortenberry. He had heard the description of the man Edmund she had given her husband in her attempts to appease him. Features the color of coarse sand. Aye, it could be none other than de Fortenberry.

Just how she had managed to meet him was beyond
Walter, but he supposed that women were devious and
more capable of deceit and cunning than most men
believed. He leaned forward, resting his elbows on
either side of his trencher. Soon, he thought, as soon as
he had the opportunity, he would bring de Fortenberry
here to Wolffeton. He wondered how the proud Kassia
would react when she saw her lover. He frowned a
moment, thinking of the men who had professed to
believe her unlikely tale. No, he was certain she had
lied. He only wondered why Lord Graelam seemed so
gentle with her. Had she been his wife, he would have
beaten her to death for such an offense.

He wondered if he should simply tell Graelam the
identity of the man. Graelam's rage would likely lead
him against de Fortenberry. Sir Walter downed his
goblet of ale and continued his thinking.

"Do you wish to play a game of chess with me?"
Graelam asked Kassia.

"I think so," she said, fiddling with a piece of bread.

He laughed softly. "You are not certain? As I recall,
you have beaten me more times than not."

She remembered wanting to kick him, and said more
strongly, "Aye, I should enjoy it, my lord."

When they sat across from each other in their bedchamber, the chess table between them, Graelam leaned
back in his chair, watching Kassia concentrate on the
position of her pieces. Very slowly he stretched out his
legs, allowing his thigh to brush against her. She jumped,
her eyes flying to his face.

"See to your bishop, Kassia," he said blandly, ignoring her reaction.

"My bishop," she repeated, tearing her eyes away
from his face.

"Aye, your queen's bishop." He smiled at her, seeing her abstraction. He stroked his chin, his eyes gleaming. "Why do we not make the game more interesting?"

"How?"

"We have yet to trade even a pawn. Let us say that every piece you lose to me, you will kiss me."

Kassia became very still. Her lips twitched. "And what would happen, my lord, were you to lose a piece to me?"

"Ah, in that case, I suppose I shall just have to kiss you."

She glanced warily at the board between them. "Do you really wish to?"

"Wish to what? Kiss you?"

She nodded, still not looking at him.

"Let us just say that you will suffer my kisses as I will yours. Agreed?"

"I . . . Very well."

On Graelam's next move, he took her king's knight. He sat back, watching the myriad expressions flit over her face. "Well, wife?" he asked.

"That was not a wise move, my lord," she said stiffly. "You will lose both a bishop and a pawn."

"I will suffer the consequences," he said, and patted his thigh. "Come and pay your forfeit, Kassia."

What disturbed Kassia as she slowly rose from her chair was that she wanted to kiss him. She stood beside him a moment, then allowed him to draw her onto his lap. She closed her eyes tightly and pursed her lips. She felt his large hands holding her loosely about her waist. Slowly she leaned forward and pecked him on his mouth.

"That, Kassia," he said, his dark eyes mocking, "is hardly a kiss. Try again."

She ran her tongue nervously over her lower lip. "I believe," she said, "that this game could last a very long time."

"Aye," he said softly.

She looked deeply into his eyes, very aware of him. She wanted to ask him why he was being so kind to her. Was it possible that he finally believed that she hadn't stolen the necklace, that she hadn't tried to escape him? She parted her lips slightly and leaned against him. He allowed her the kiss, leaving his hands about her waist, not forcing her at all. He felt her small breasts pressing against his chest, and wondered as her tongue touched his lips if she could feel his hardness beneath her hips.

She was breathing more quickly when she broke off her kiss. He made no move to continue it, merely smiled at her. "I believe you are learning," he said.

He felt her leaning toward him again, her eyes upon his mouth. He quickly tightened his hold about her waist and lifted her off his lap. "Onward, wife. I believe it is your move."

Kassia felt slightly dazed. She shook her head as she sat again in her chair, forcing her attention back to the chessboard.

Her wits cleared, and she gave him an impish smile, the dimples in her cheeks deepening. "'Tis now your move, my lord!" she said.

"Perhaps not such a long game," Graelam said. She had not taken his bishop, merely moved her king pawn forward another square.

Without a thought, he took her pawn, laying himself open to at least a check. He said nothing, merely patted his thighs again.

When Kassia leaned away from him this time, she

wondered vaguely if he could hear her heart pounding. She squirmed a bit on his thighs, and felt his muscles tighten beneath her. She flushed at what she had done, and hung her head. "I . . . I don't know what's wrong with me," she whispered.

"We will see," Graelam said, and again lifted her off his lap.

She was forced at last to take one of his pieces. She raised her head. "I do not believe I can hold you in my lap, my lord."

She looked so very worried that he was hard pressed not to laugh. "Then you must come here, I suppose."

When she was settled again on his thighs, he said softly, "Remember, wife, this is my kiss. You are not to caress me or move against me."

"But I didn't!" she began, only to draw in her breath when his mouth closed over hers. She felt his hand on the back of her head, tangling in her hair, bringing her closer. "Just relax," he murmured in her mouth. "You have nothing to do but close your eyes and let me kiss you."

He didn't press her, merely deepened the pressure slowly, as he felt her begin to respond to him. Very slowly he eased his hands around toward her breasts. To his utter delight, when he gently cupped her breasts in his hands, she moaned softly into his mouth, arching her back. He released her immediately.

Never, he thought, somewhat dazed himself, had he seen such a look of disappointment on a woman's face. Woman. Aye, he thought, tonight he would make her a woman. As he watched her move shakily back to her chair, he wondered if she wouldn't attack him before the game was through.

He continued to study her as she regained her wits

and gazed at the board. He remembered, with some pain, how she had been so open and trusting of him before he had forced her. Would she admit the truth to him once he regained her trust? He wanted her to beg him to take her. His jaw tightened, and the next kiss he gave her was quick and passionless.

After some fifteen more minutes, Kassia had lost all but her king and two pawns.

"An exciting game," Graelam said. "I am tired," he continued, rising and stretching. "I wish to go to bed." He saw her look warily at him, but ignored it. "Unless you wish for another game?"

"Nay," she said quickly, plucking nervously at the folds of her gown.

"One final kiss for the winner. Come here, Kassia."

She walked slowly toward him, her eyes never leaving his face. He gathered her gently to him, leaned down, and lightly touched her lips. She parted her lips without any instruction from him, and despite his intentions, his hands stroked down her back to cup around her buttocks. He drew her up until her belly was pressed against his swollen manhood. She wrapped her arms about his neck, unthinking now, only feeling. And wanting to feel more, much more. "Please," she whispered.

"Please what?" he asked, molding her more tightly against him, his fingers caressing the curve of her hips.

"I . . . I don't know."

Her voice was nearly a wail.

"And if I give you what you want, will you finally admit the truth to me?"

She stared up at him blankly; then her face flooded with color, and her arms fell away from him.

If he could have kicked himself, he would have. She was stiff and cold and withdrawn.

"Come to bed," he said harshly, and turned away from her.

He lay on his back, staring up into the darkness. He heard her sobbing in harsh little gasps, and imagined that she had stuffed her fist into her mouth. He listened until he could bear it no longer.

"Kassia," he said softly. "Come here. I promise I will not hurt you."

He waited patiently until she rolled toward him. He drew her into his arms, feeling the wet of her tears against his chest.

Her sobs eased as he gently stroked her back.

"I will say nothing more about it," he said finally.

But you will never believe me!

"I want to come inside you, Kassia. I don't think I can hold back another night."

He felt her quiver at his words, but he did not know whether it was in fear or in anticipated pleasure. He had spoken the truth. His body was aching for release. He quickly pulled off her bedrobe and groaned with the pleasure of her naked body against his.

"You are so small, so delicate," he whispered against her temple as his hands stroked over her breasts and belly. "Part your legs, Kassia."

She felt his finger ease inside her and her muscles clenched convulsively. "You are ready for me," he said. When he withdrew his finger, she felt her own wetness against her belly.

He wanted to caress her, to make her cry out for him, but his body was wound tight as a bowstring. When she moved against him, he thought he would lose control. "I cannot wait," he gasped, and moved between her legs. Gently he eased inside her, feeling her stretch for him, feeling himself slide easily into her. He moaned at the unbelievable sensation, and thrust his full length into her. He leaned over her, cupping her face in his hands. He wished he could see her eyes. "Am I hurting you?" he asked softly into her mouth.

She shook her head. "It feels . . . odd." Actually, she thought, as he moved slowly over her, if coupling were always this way, it was quite bearable. The thought was surprising, but more surprising was the slow ache that was building low in her belly, separate from him, yet also a part of him.

"Graelam, I . . ." Her voice suspended in bewilderment when he thrust his tongue into her mouth, just as his manhood was delving deeply into her belly. The urgent heat was building deep within her, and she moved beneath him, arching her back upward, her arms tight around his waist.

"Kassia, do not!" But it was too late. He could no longer hold back. He moaned raggedly, deep in his throat, and thrust into her. For an instant, as she felt his seed explode within her, filling her, she felt a pounding need to respond. But as he quieted over her, the need slowly faded, leaving her vaguely disappointed, not knowing what it was that she sought.

She stroked her hands over his back, kneading the thick hard muscles, enjoying the feel of his man's body. She heard his breathing slow, felt his body relaxing over her. His weight was great, but she did not mind. No, she thought drowsily, coupling was not too bad. It didn't hurt.

Graelam raised himself on his elbows and looked down at her shadowed face. He knew he had moved too quickly, that she had not gained a woman's release. He cursed softly at his loss of control. She stiffened.

"I'm sorry," she whispered. "I do not know what to do."

"Hush," he said softly, "'tis I who am as fledgling as an untried boy."

He felt her shake her head against his shoulder.

"You are soft and pleasing, Kassia, and I wanted you very much. Soon, I promise you, you will want me equally."

He could picture the bewildered question in her eyes at his words. He kissed her gently, and rolled onto his side, bringing her with him.

She fell asleep with the very strange feeling of his manhood resting inside her.

Kassia awoke at dawn, her eyes drawn to the bright slivers of pinkish light coming through the shutters. She stirred slightly, and quieted quickly, aware that she was half-lying on Graelam, his thigh between her legs, her cheek pillowed against the mat of thick hair on his chest. She blinked away the remnants of sleep, allowing a procession of images from the night before to flow slowly through her mind. With the intimate images came a flood of feelings. She blinked, startled at herself, but still did not move. She felt the thick muscles in his thigh pressing up against her and the feelings were no longer memories. She felt a stirring deep within her, awakening her body as surely as she had awakened with the dawn, making her move slowly and quietly against him. She slid the palm of her hand over his chest, and felt the slow, regular pounding of his heart. She breathed deeply, relieved that he slept. She should move away from him, she thought, but her body had no intention of obeying her. Her hand slipped down through the hair on his chest to his flat, hard belly. Her fingers stroked the ridges of smooth muscle, and moved still lower. Feeling the edge of the scar at his groin, she followed its roughness over his thigh. When her arm brushed against his manhood, lying soft against him, a surge of warmth spurted through her, making her move once more against his thigh. She squeezed her eyes shut at the unbelievable sensations it brought. Her breathing quickened, and her body continued its sensuous movements, knowing instinctively what to do.

She realized that she wanted to touch him, to feel the texture of his flesh, to try to understand why his body, with no effort from him, was making her feel the way she was. Slowly, tentatively, her heart pounding loudly in the silence of the chamber, her fingers closed around him, and she cradled him in her hand.

She did not realize that she was moving rhythmically against his thigh, deepening the pressure. But Graelam did. He did not move. When her fingers closed over him he thought he would jerk upward, but he held himself still. He lifted his thigh very slowly, and the pressing, upward motion brought a small cry from her lips. Never had she taken the initiative, and he smiled with pleasure, then grimaced in the next moment, not certain how long he could remain quietly under her touch.

In a moment her hand could no longer close over him. Her head flew up to his face, and she saw him regarding her intently.

"You are awake," she said stupidly.

"Aye," he said, forcing himself to hold still.

A soft moan came unbidden from her mouth, and she

flushed, her eyes widening in bewilderment and embarrassment. "I . . . Your leg, it makes me feel so . . ."

He moved his thigh against her, feeling the growing moistness, and reveling in it. "You feel so what?"

She smiled, ducking her head and pressing it against his chest. "I do not think I can stop moving against you," she whispered.

Her fingers fell away from her manhood, and he drew in a deep breath in disappointment. He thought vaguely that men were utterly physical, with no modesty over their bodies—born, it seemed, with the need to have a woman stroke them and caress them. Whilst women . . . The thought left him when Kassia moaned softly again, now kneading her fingers in his belly.

He gently lifted her onto her back. Her eyes flew to his face, but he only kissed her lightly on her mouth, teasing her with his tongue, but not forcing himself upon her. His hand cupped her breast, his thumb stroking over her nipple, and still she stared up at him, unmoving. He smiled down at her, knowing well what she needed. His fingers found her, and he sucked in his breath at the warmth and wetness of her. His stroking was rhythmic, his fingers pressing deeply, then lightly teasing her, making her wail in mounting frustration.

"Graelam," she cried, clutching his shoulders frantically.

"Aye?" he asked softly, watching her face.

"I . . . I cannot bear it," she gasped. Her hips lurched upward against his fingers, and he moved more quickly and surely against her.

He had pleasured women many times in this fashion, but never had he felt so . . . involved, as if all he felt depended upon her feelings. He felt the tenseness in

her legs, and slowly thrust his tongue into her mouth.
She gasped with the pleasure of it.

"Kassia," he murmured, and the sound of her name
on his lips sent her spinning into a realm of sensation
that she had never imagined existed. She writhed against
him, sharp cries bursting from her throat.

He watched every expression on her face, from the
utter surprise in her eyes to the dazed, vague sheen
when the deep pleasure tore through her, making her
unaware of him, unaware of everything except the pounding, radiating sensations coming from beneath his fingers. At the height of her release, she cried out his
name, and he moaned softly with the pleasure of it.

For a moment, she seemed senseless. He kissed her
gently, feeding on her soft mouth, enjoying her small,
jagged gasps of breath. To his immense delight, he felt
her quiver anew when he cupped his hand over her,
gently pressing his palm against her. She seemed hardly
aware that she was moaning softly again, arching her
back upward, moving jerkily against him. He brought
her to pleasure again, and this time she clutched him to
her, sobbing into his shoulder.

She was filled with passion, he thought, so utterly
responsive to him. He wondered if he could bring her
to pleasure yet again, but decided against it this time.
She was unused to the feelings that were rampaging
through her body. Soon, he thought, gathering her
against him and stroking her back, he would test the
depths of her passion.

He realized that he had not thought of his own need
even once. You are becoming a half-wit, he told himself, yet he was smiling when he gently kissed her ear
and pressed her against the length of his body. He did

not fall asleep again, but Kassia did, a deep, sated sleep.

. . . whilst women, his thinking of many moments before continued, women were more complex. At least Kassia was. He realized that she had to trust him completely before her body could open to him. But what man cared about a woman's trust? What man cared if a woman enjoyed coupling? He did, unfortunately, and he knew well that he could not retreat from her now.

24

Graelam smiled at the sound of Kassia's bright laugh. No longer was she the pale, silent little ghost of the week before. She was full of energy, full of laughter, and full of desire for him. He had never before wanted to be with a woman, other than to couple with her, but everything seemed different now. He enjoyed her teasing, enjoyed watching her care for Wolffeton and all its people, enjoyed the softened look in her eyes whenever she met his gaze. Invariably when that happened, she blushed, and he would smile wickedly and whisper intimate words to her, causing her to blush even more furiously.

He learned that she could not respond to him in bed if something was on her mind, a problem with a servant perhaps, or a new project taking shape in her thoughts. Thus it was that he was beginning to learn how she thought, how she felt about her thoughts, and how she came to decisions about problems within the keep. He smiled ruefully, recalling the first time he had wanted

312

nothing more than to fling her onto the bed and love her until she was panting for him. She had not refused him, but he saw a frown on her forehead as he was kissing her most expertly. At first he was insulted and infuriated with her, and had snapped, "What is wrong with you, Kassia? Where is your mind?"

She cocked her head at him, a soft smile on her lips. "It is Bernard," she said ruefully. "I don't know what to do about him, and I must do something!"

"Bernard," he repeated blankly, finally picturing the quiet, shaggy-looking boy who had come to the castle to tend the dogs after ten years with his father's sheep.

She nibbled thoughtfully on her lower lip, then burst into a wide smile. "Why did I not ask you immediately? You will know what to do!"

Thus it was that they discussed the problem of Bernard and his odd and painful reaction to dog lice until they found a solution that pleased them both. Her response to him afterward was something he could not have imagined.

He gave her free access to all the material in his trunk, telling her to do with it as she wished. But of course she did not. She always asked him, and he knew it would take a long time for her to forget his initial reaction when she had taken material to make him a tunic.

He realized also that he liked his wife. It was a terrifying, nonsensical thought, and one he did not wish to consider. A wife sees to her husband's comfort, both in his keep and his body, most men of his acquaintance believed and parroted religiously. He turned again, hearing her laughter, and realized that it was coming from the practice field. Whatever would Kassia be doing among his men? He strode to the wide field and drew to an abrupt halt. There she sat, wearing a white wool cloth over her hair and a faded green wool gown, his men gathered around her. If he had not recognized her laugh, he would have thought her a serving wench.

"Nay, Bran," he heard her say, the laughter still in her voice, "the remaining pie is for my lord. You have already had your share!"

He saw that she was holding a tray and his men were either eating or wiping their mouths.

Her lord. Any thought of chastising her for interrupting his men disappeared from his mind. When she saw him she skipped toward him, startled pleasure at seeing him in her eyes.

"I had thought you buried with Blount," she said gaily. "Here, my lord. It is an apple tart, freshly baked."

He accepted the pastry from her, realizing belatedly that his expression was probably just as besotted as the rest of his men's.

He wiped his mouth and smiled down at her. "It was delicious, my lady. But I do not believe that these stupid louts are deserving of your consideration."

He heard loud guffaws from behind him. Kassia was laughing with the rest of them. Without really wishing to, he lightly touched his fingers to her smooth cheek. "Go now, little one," he said softly. "Else I might be tempted to toss you over my shoulder and show you how delicious you are."

She flushed, disclaimed, smiled wickedly at him, and sped from the practice field. Sometime later, Rolfe said to him, "You are a lucky man, my lord. Aye, very lucky."

"Aye," Graelam said blandly, wiping the sweat from his brow and gazing toward the fortified eastern wall. "Wolffeton is a castle to be proud of. The jakes no longer stink, and Bernard does much better in the stables with the horses." He stretched, eyeing his master-at-arms from the corner of his eye. Rolfe could not recognize a jest if it kicked him in his lean butt.

Rolfe cleared his throat. "Aye," he said slowly, "that is true, my lord, but I was speaking of your lady wife." He drew himself up, frowning at the slight smile on his master's lips. "She brings joy to us, my lord. It pleases me—all the men—to see her smile again."

She didn't betray you! He immediately quashed the thought. He had decided many days before that he had been as much to blame as she for her leaving him. And, he had thought over and over, she had returned to him. *But why will she not tell me the truth?*

He shook his head, realizing vaguely that it brought him a measure of pain to think about it. He said aloud, "There is enough pain in life without adding to it."

Rolfe pulled on his ear. "She is a dear child," he said at last.

"Nay, my old friend. She is not a child," Graelam said.

Late that night as he caressed her soft belly, feeling her rippling response to him, he said quietly, "You are no longer a child, Kassia."

Her answer was a moaning cry that made his loins tighten. He wanted to bury himself within her. He pushed her to the edge of her climax, then thrust into her. Her release was immediate and rending. She cried out helplessly into his mouth, her back arched up against him, so beyond herself in that long moment that she could think of nothing, only feel. He was held spellbound in her pleasure before his own need consumed him. He moved slightly, afraid that his weight was too much for her.

He felt her slender arms clutching around his back. "Nay," she whispered, "do not leave me."

He slipped his arms around her and rolled onto his back, bringing her on top of him. She laughed, surprised, for he was still deep inside her. "You are now to be ridden, my lord?"

"Aye," he said, cupping her face in his hands and bringing her lips down, "in a moment, Kassia. In a moment."

"I feel so . . ." She paused, her eyes caressing his face, as her lips curved into a smile. "Not so full as I did!"

He lightly slapped her hips. "Mouthy wench." He stroked his hands over her back. Gently he eased her off him and laid her on her back. He leaned over her, balanced on his elbow.

Kassia felt embarrassed at his scrutiny, and brought her hand up to cover herself.

"What is this?" he asked, surprised. He pushed her hand away. "You are filling out nicely, Kassia."

His callused fingers roved lightly over her breast. "Very nicely," he murmured, and leaned down to caress her with his mouth.

"Do you really think so?"

He raised his head.

She flushed. "I mean . . . I was so skinny!"

He looked down the length of her, his eyes pausing a moment on the soft triangle of curls between her thighs, still damp from their passion. "You are," he said, his voice rough and deep, "as I want you to be."

"As are you, my lord," she said softly.

Dammit, he did not want to leave her! He eyed the messenger from Crandall, knowing he had no choice but to return and stem the rebellion there. I'll take her with me, he thought, only to reject his decision almost immediately. He wanted her kept safe, above all. Damn Raymond de Cercy, nephew of the former castellan. He had not been overly impressed with the man, yet more fool he, he had made him governor of the small keep on the southern edge of Wolffeton. What had the fool done to bring the peasants to revolt so quickly?

He dismissed the tired messenger and strode to their bedchamber. He found her there, seated by the window, sewing. He remembered suddenly the last time he had left her, and flinched at the memory. He had been back less than two days before he had hurt her.

"I must leave," he said without preamble.

She jabbed her finger with the needle, and cried out softly.

"I am clumsy," she said, watching a drop of blood well up.

He dropped to his knees beside her chair and took the finger in his hand. Gently he lifted the finger to his mouth and licked away the blood.

"Where do you go, my lord?" she asked, her voice breathless.

He lightly kissed the finger and rose. "To Crandall. De Cercy's messenger tells of a revolt amongst the peasants."

She felt a spurt of fear for him. "Will there be danger?"

"Perhaps, but not likely," he said, shrugging his shoulders indifferently.

Kassia was not fooled. She saw the gleam of anticipation in his dark eyes. "How long will you be away?"

"A week, perhaps longer. If de Cercy is the fool I begin to believe him to be, I will have to find another man to be castellan of Crandall."

"May I come with you, Graelam?" She saw that he would tell her no, and immediately burst into tangled speech. "I can care for you, you will see! I don't tire easily, and I will not bother you. I can cook your—"

He leaned down and lifted her out of her chair. "Hush, Kassia," he said, and drew her against his chest. "I will take no chance with your safety." Her arms clutched at him, as if she wanted to become part of him, and he felt a wave of protectiveness so strong he trembled with it. He grasped her arms and gently pushed her away.

He saw the bright glimmer of tears in her eyes. "Do not," he said, trying to sound stern, but failing woefully.

"I . . . I will miss you," she managed, sniffing.

He cupped her chin with his hand. "Will you really?" he asked.

Kassia rubbed her cheek against his palm, and he felt the wet of her tears on his flesh.

"I will not leave until the morrow," he said, and pulled her against him.

"You look like a lost lamb," Etta scolded her. "This is no way to behave, my baby! What would your lord say if he saw you wandering about pale and silent?"

"It has been four days!" Kassia wailed. "And I have heard nothing! Nothing! He promised to send me word."

"So," Etta said, her rheumy eyes narrowing on her mistress's face, "it has finally happened."

Kassia abruptly stopped her pacing and whirled around to face her old nurse. "What has happened?" she snapped.

"You love your husband," Etta said calmly.

"Nay! That is, perhaps it is just that . . ."

"You love your husband to distraction," Etta said again.

To Etta's surprise, Kassia looked at her blankly, turned on her heel, and walked quickly from the chamber.

She went to the stable and asked Bernard to saddle Bluebell for her. Sir Walter stood in the inner bailey when she emerged from the stable leading her mare.

"Sir Walter," she said stiffly.

"You wish to ride, my lady?"

"As you see."

"Lord Graelam bade me never to leave your side if you rode out of the keep."

She paused a moment, chewing on her lower lip. She wondered why Graelam had left Sir Walter at Wolffeton whilst he took Rolfe with him to Crandall. Was it because he did not wish the man to fight beside him? She wanted very much to be alone, but it appeared she had no choice but to suffer Sir Walter's company. She nodded. "Very well," she said.

She pushed Bluebell into a gallop, leaving Sir Walter and his three men behind her. At the protected cove, she dismounted and stared out over the churning water. A summer storm was building to the north. It would strike tonight, she thought, while she would be alone in the great bed. She shivered.

"If you are cold, my lady, perhaps we should return to Wolffeton."

She jumped, for she had not heard Sir Walter approach. She shook her head. "Nay, I wish to walk about for a while."

"If you wish," he said, and offered her his arm.

She ignored him and walked to the edge of the cliff.

"Is it your lord you miss, my lady?"

At his snide tone, she stiffened. Her hand itched to

strike him, but she said only, "My feelings are none of
your business, Sir Walter."

"Perhaps not, my lady, but I heard about your . . .
misadventure. Perhaps you did not plan your escape
well enough."

"I wish to return to Wolffeton," Kassia said, and
walked quickly away from him.

Sir Walter wanted to shake her and wring her proud
neck. Little bitch, treating him as if he were vermin, of
no worth at all! He watched one of the men help her
into her saddle. Soon, my lady, he thought, smiling.
Very soon now.

Kassia felt a brief surge of excitement as she stood at
her post in the crenellated embrasure in the eastern
outer wall, watching the riders come nearer. She sighed
deeply, recognizing Sir Walter riding at their head. He
had left the day before, claiming that there had been an
attack on a demesne farm. She had not believed him,
and seeing him now, she wondered where he had gone
and what he had done.

One man was huddled over his saddle as if he were
hurt, and three men were obviously dead, slung over
their horses' backs like bags of wheat. As they drew
nearer, she could see that the hurt man was bound with
heavy rope. Speeding down the narrow stairs, she made
her way into the inner bailey. As Sir Walter shouted to
the porter, she prepared to step forward, but something she could not explain stopped her. She waited in
the shadows of the cooking shed and watched the men
enter the inner bailey. The wide smile on Sir Walter's
face made Kassia shiver.

He pulled the bound man off his horse. The man
staggered, then stood straight. "Behold," Sir Walter

called out to the gathering men. "We have caught a prize!" He pulled the hood back from the man's head. "Dienwald de Fortenberry, knave, murderer, and . . . taker of other men's women!"

Kassia felt herself go cold. It was Edmund! She remembered Sir Walter's venomous words about de Fortenberry, remembered clearly Graelam telling him that de Fortenberry had made no forays onto Wolffeton land, and was thus of no interest to him. *Taker of other men's women.* Somehow Sir Walter had discovered that Dienwald de Fortenberry was the man who had taken her. Her head spun. She saw Sir Walter draw back his fist and smash it into Dienwald's ribs. That decided her. She ran forward.

"Hold, Sir Walter!" she yelled.

Sir Walter spun around, as did the other men.

"My lady," he said, bowing to her deeply, the sarcasm in his voice clear for all to hear.

"Is it a knight's code to strike a bound man, Sir Walter?"

"It is a knight's code to crush vermin, my lady."

She drew herself up to her full height. "I believe you called this man Dienwald de Fortenberry. I remember my lord telling you that he was no threat to Wolffeton. Why have you brought him here, Sir Walter?"

He could denounce her in front of everyone, Sir Walter thought. But no, he quickly decided. The proud little bitch was too popular among the men and the servants, and he couldn't be certain of their backing. Oh no, he would wait for Graelam to return. Graelam would be enraged; he would kill the miserable de Fortenberry for him, and, Sir Walter thought, he would be thankful to him for bringing the whoreson to him. Land, he thought, his chest expanding in anticipation;

Graelam would doubtless award him land and his own keep.

"I have brought him here, my lady," he said, quite calmly now, "to be held for Lord Graelam's return."

Kassia felt a surge of relief. Dienwald de Fortenberry would tell Graelam that it was Blanche who had hired him. At last he would know the truth. At last he would believe her.

She turned to Dienwald de Fortenberry, who was struggling to regain his breath. She wanted to go to him, to help him, but she knew she would be a fool to do so.

Dienwald knew that several of his ribs were broken. He met Kassia's worried gaze for a moment before a surging pain ripped through him and he crumpled to the cobblestones.

Kassia listened numbly, her fingernails digging into palms, as Sir Walter ordered the men to carry de Fortenberry to the dungeon.

"Sir Walter," she said in a loud, calm voice, "I trust that Dienwald de Fortenberry will be alive when my lord returns."

"Slut," Sir Walter hissed between his teeth. Did she believe she had that much power over Graelam? Tales of Graelam de Moreton's prowess were legendary. He could not imagine such a warrior allowing his wife to escape unscathed when he was confronted not only with her lover but also with the man she had hired to help her escape him.

Kassia went directly to her bedchamber, closed the door, and sat in her chair to think.

At the evening meal, she appeared serene and concerned only with the taste of the roast pork and the fresh green peas. She chatted easily with Blount and

Father Tobias, aware that many eyes were observing
her, watching her very closely. She could feel the dislike emanating from Sir Walter, but she could also
sense his uncertainty at her calm behavior. You will pay
for this, she vowed silently. It was odd, she thought as
she replied to a question from one of the serving
wenches, but she should be thanking him. Were it not
for his hatred and his bitterness, she would never have
known that Edmund was Dienwald de Fortenberry.

She returned to her bedchamber to wait. It was near
to midnight when Etta slipped into the chamber, nodding silently.

"There was but one guard?"

"Aye, my baby, and soon he will be fast asleep.
There is no need for any guards down there," she
continued, shivering. "The saints could not escape from
that place."

"Sir Walter is taking no chances," Kassia said. "How
very surprised that knave will be when Dienwald tells
my lord the truth of the matter!"

Etta gripped Kassia's arm. "Must you go to him, my
baby? Can you not wait for Lord Graelam's return?"

"Dienwald de Fortenberry is many things, Etta, I
know that, but he was kind to me. Had Blanche paid
another man to take me, I would likely have been
raped and killed. If he dies from his wounds, I will gain
nothing. And I must speak to him. I must be certain
that he will speak the truth to Graelam."

Etta knew she could not sway her mistress. "All the
men are asleep. I heard no one."

"Excellent," Kassia said stoutly, though she felt gooseflesh rising on her arms in her fear. "I do not wish you
to wait for me, Etta. Go to bed now."

She waited until her old nurse had left, then drew on

her cloak. Saying a silent prayer, she slipped from her
bedchamber and made her way out of the great hall.
The dungeon was in the base of the southern tower.

Soundlessly she moved beyond the thick oak door,
sucking in her breath when she saw the guard. But he
was fast asleep, his head cradled on his arms. Carefully
she eased the huge iron keys from his tunic and dropped
them into the pocket of her cloak. Then, clutching the
lone candle, she walked down the deeply worn stone
steps to the lower level. The air became more fetid and
foul, and she could hear the rats scurrying from her
path. It smelled of human misery, she thought, though
she knew that no prisoner had been held here for many
years. Her hand shook as she fitted one of the keys into
the rusting lock. It grated so loudly that she whipped
about, expecting to see all of Sir Walter's men bursting
in upon her.

But only rats were about.

The door swung open and she stepped into the cell,
holding the candle high. She felt nausea rise in her
throat at the stench. The stone walls were green and
slimy with dampness, the earth floor was strewn with
ancient straw reeking of human excrement. She raised
the candle higher, gasping when she saw Dienwald de
Fortenberry. His arms were pulled away from his body,
his wrists manacled to the walls.

"Dienwald," she said softly.

Slowly he raised his head. For a long moment he
stared at her blankly. Then a slow smile twisted his
mouth into a painful grimace.

"Little chick," he whispered. "Why did you send me
a message begging that I help you?"

25

Kassia stared at him. "I do not know about any message," she said finally.

A spasm of pain wiped his mind of words and it was some moments before he said, "No, I do not suppose that you do. I was a fool, and now I will pay for it."

"No, you won't!" She rushed to his side and quickly unlocked the heavy rusted manacles from his wrists. He managed to steady himself and sank down onto the straw.

"It was Sir Walter," she said, dropping to her knees beside him. "He hates you, but I had no idea that it was you he hated."

He raised his head and smiled at her. "Only I would know what you mean, little chick."

"When my lord returns to Wolffeton, all will be well, I promise you, Edmund . . . Dienwald." She touched her hand to his shoulder. "You will tell him it was Blanche who hired you, will you not?"

"You have had a difficult time making your husband believe you?"

"Very few people here believe that I am innocent, but now, Dienwald, they will know the truth."

"Ah, little chick, you are so innocent and trusting."

"No," she said firmly, "no longer. I will see that my lord punishes Sir Walter for what he did to you. Where are you hurt?"

"Several ribs are broken. Sir Walter is a vicious man. I begin to see now why he did not simply kill me as he did my men."

"I do not understand."

He lifted his hand and touched his fingers to her soft hair. "No, likely you would not understand. I will explain it to you. Sir Walter doubtless wants land. What landless knight does not? And it is true that my father killed his and took his birthright, though from what I remember, his action was justified. But had Sir Walter killed me there would have been no reward for him, no gain at all if, that is, he kept his neck in place. Your husband, little chick, is a very powerful man with very powerful friends. Were he to kill me, there would be no retribution, and Sir Walter would most likely gain from his trickery."

Kassia shook her head, saying vehemently, "Graelam would not kill you."

Dienwald gave her a tender look that held pity. Slowly he drew her forward, and before Kassia knew what he was about, he had fastened one of the heavy manacles about her wrist.

"Little chick," he said ruefully, "I beg you will forgive me, but I do not wish to die. If I stay, your husband will kill me without a second thought. Even if I were able to fight him with all my strength, he would still likely put an end to me."

"He has no reason to kill you. Please, Dienwald, you must not leave me!"

"Kassia, listen to me, for I must escape, and very soon. Your husband believes that you paid me to help you escape him. If I were to tell him it was Blanche, he would still kill me, for I accepted his barbaric necklace as payment to rid Wolffeton and Blanche of your presence." He gave a pained laugh. "Were I your husband, I would kill me. I know that when you are found here, in my cell, you will be blamed for releasing me. I am sorry for it, but your husband will not kill you. Were there another way, little chick, I would not leave you. But there is no choice for me. Forgive me, Kassia."

She looked at the harsh manacle about her wrist. "I forgive you," she said. "But you have sentenced me to hell."

He grasped her chin in his palm and lightly kissed her. "I can take you with me, little chick."

He saw the helpless pain in her eyes, and drew back. "Ah, so that is the way it is." He rose and stood over her a moment. "Graelam de Moreton is a harsh and ruthless warrior. He can have no understanding of something as delicate and honest as you. Please, little chick, do not scream until I am gone."

"It would do no good," she said dully. "My old nurse drugged the only guard. Evidently Sir Walter believed no more guards were necessary."

"I will leave you the candle," he said. "Good-bye, little chick." She watched him slip through the cell door and pull it closed behind him. She leaned back against the damp wall as the rats moved closer to her, their small eyes orange in the wavering candlelight. When the candle sputtered out and the cell was plunged into blackness, she whimpered softly and drew her legs up to her chest.

She heard heavy boots approaching, and then the cell door was shoved violently open. A rushlight torch filled the darkness with blinding light. Kassia had prayed that Etta would come for her, but her prayer was not answered. For a moment her dazed eyes could only make out the outline of a man. Sir Walter, she thought dully. What would he do to her?

"Kassia."

She froze and pressed herself closer to the slimy wall, moaning softly in her throat. "What are you doing here?" she asked finally.

Graelam gave a harsh laugh. "No, I do not suppose you expected me until tomorrow night. I missed you and pushed my men to return." He laughed again, a cruel sound that made her flinch. He handed the torch to a man behind him and strode toward her. She cowered away from him. He dropped to his knees and unlocked the manacle.

"Did your lover really need to chain you? Could not even he trust you?"

Kassia rubbed her bruised wrist, concentrating on the slight pain to block the terrible words from her mind.

"Look at me, damn you!" Graelam grasped her shoulders and shook her.

"I am looking now," she said, staring directly into his furious eyes.

"Dienwald de Fortenberry. Did he appreciate your calling him Edmund, my lady? How very surprised you must have been to see him. Sir Walter is something of a fool, unfortunately. He never dreamed that my soft, fragile lady would be so daring as to release her lover. He is now . . . distraught."

"Dienwald de Fortenberry is not my lover," she said quietly, hopelessly.

His fingers tightened about her shoulders and he felt her small bones twisting beneath his strength. Damn him for a fool! He had ridden back to Wolffeton like a maniac, his only thought of Kassia and holding her, seeing her, listening to her laugh, feeling her soft body beneath him, opening to him. His fingers ground harshly into her shoulders and she whimpered from pain. He released her abruptly and stood.

"Come," he said roughly. "I do not wish you to die from a fever."

She staggered to her feet and pulled her cloak more closely about her. She saw Sir Walter standing in the narrow doorway, a look of hatred contorting his features. She said in a loud, clear voice, "Did Sir Walter tell you how he managed to capture Dienwald de Fortenberry? Did he tell you how he beat him viciously whilst he was bound and could not defend himself?"

Graelam turned slowly to face his knight.

"Did he tell you that he trusted you to kill de Fortenberry and then reward him for bringing him to you?"

Graelam said in a cold voice, "I will speak to Sir Walter, wife. Now, my lady, you will come with me."

He drew away from her a moment and spoke in a quiet voice to Sir Walter. The man nodded and withdrew. He hates me because I am a woman and thus not to be believed or trusted, she thought. She said aloud, "I did not betray you, Graelam. I have never betrayed you."

She saw the fury building in his dark eyes. She threw

back her head, raising her chin. "Will you kill me now? Just as you would have killed Dienwald?"

He looked at that proud tilted chin of hers and turned quickly away, his hands clenched at his sides. He did not want to strike her, for if he did, it would likely kill her.

"That is why he escaped, Graelam. It is true that I released his chains, but my thought was only to spare him more pain. I trusted him to tell you the truth, that it was Blanche who had paid him the necklace to be rid of me, but he said you would kill him regardless of what he told you. He did not wish to die."

"So he left you here, chained, to face me. An honorable man."

"Was he right? Would you have killed him?"

"Come, Kassia," he said, striding to the cell door.

She followed him silently, feeling blessedly numb. She did not wonder about the future; it could be naught but the cold misery of the present.

There was utter silence as she walked beside her husband through the great hall. She felt the servants' eyes upon her. She imagined that she could even feel their fear for her. But she felt no fear. She felt nothing. Everything was over now.

Graelam paused a moment and gave orders for hot water to be brought to their bedchamber. She saw the lines of fatigue in his face for the first time, and the filth of his chain mail and tunic. She wanted to ask him if he was all right, then almost laughed aloud at the wifely spurt of concern she felt for him.

When they reached their bedchamber, Graelam ignored her. Evian helped him strip off his armor. After he dismissed the boy, he peeled off the rest of his

clothes and sank down naked into his high-backed chair.
Still he said nothing.

Two serving wenches came into the room and poured
hot water into the wooden tub. Graelam rose and walked
to the tub even as they filled it, seemingly oblivious of
his nakedness. He dismissed them with a curt nod and
climbed into the tub.

He felt the hot water seep into his muscles, easing
his soreness and bone-weariness. He wondered vaguely
whether Sir Walter would have left her locked in de
Fortenberry's cell if Graelam had not returned until the
following night. No, the knight would not have dared.
Graelam sighed, easing his body deeper into the water.
Thoughts of his joy at seeing Kassia mingled with knowledge of her deception, and he felt suddenly old and
very tired. His father was right. Drake, his armorer,
was right. He had been a fool to have begun to doubt
his sire's wisdom. Women were good for breeding, and
only if a husband kept his wife away from other men to
ensure whose seed filled her belly. Had de Fortenberry
taken her before he had escaped? He sat up in the tub
and turned his head to see her sitting quietly, as still as
a statue, in a chair. "Kassia," he said quite calmly, "take
off your clothes. I wish to see if de Fortenberry's seed
is in your body or still clinging to your thighs."

She could only gape at him, furious color flooding her
face, as his words gained meaning in her mind.

"Damn you, do as I say!"

"Graelam," she said, clutching the arms of the chair
until her knuckles showed white, "please, you must
believe me. Dienwald de Fortenberry was not my lover!"

"If you do not obey me, I will rip off your clothes."

"Why won't you believe me?"

His jaw clenched. He quickly washed his hair and his

body and just as quickly rose from the tub and dried himself. From the corner of his eye he saw her rise from the chair and dart toward the chamber door. He caught her as her hand touched the brass handle.

"Please," she panted, "for once, please believe me!"

"Do you want me to rip your clothes off?"

She stared up at him, knowing he was implacable. She would not let him cow her again. Slowly she shook her head. "You will not humiliate me," she said. "My only crime was feeling concern for a man who was kind to me." Her chin went up. "I am glad he was wise enough to escape. I am glad he did not stay so you could kill him."

He drew back his hand, but then got a grip on himself and slowly lowered it to his side. Very slowly he turned away from her. He said over his shoulder, "If you leave this room, you will wish you had not."

He tossed on his bedrobe, belted it, and returned to her. "Take off your clothes," he said very softly.

"Nay," she said, her voice a croak.

He shrugged, and very deliberately tore away her olive-green wool gown. She tried to struggle against him, but it was useless and she knew it. She would only hurt herself. When she was naked and trembling before him, he stepped back, a cruel light in his dark eyes, and thoughtfully began stroking his chin. "Aye, you have become quite the woman, have you not, wife? Such lovely breasts you have now. And that soft little belly of yours."

She did not try to cover her body from his eyes. Instead, she clapped her hands over her ears to block out his cruel words.

He laughed, picked her up in his arms, and carried her to the bed. He tossed her down upon her back.

"Hold still," he said coldly. There could be no greater humiliation, she thought, as he pulled her legs apart and looked down at her. She flinched when he ran his hand over her.

"So," he said, straightening. "if a child does grow in your belly, it will be mine. At least this time."

Kassia rolled over onto her side and drew her legs up. Great sobs built up, pounding against her chest, tearing from her throat.

Graelam stared down at her, hating himself for the pain he was feeling at her suffering, hating himself for wanting to gather her into his arms and stroke her and soothe her and caress her.

"Get under the covers," he said harshly. When she did not move, he lifted her roughly and placed her beneath them himself.

"There is no choice, my baby. You cannot remain here longer."

Kassia sighed and nodded, knowing Etta was right.

Still, she clutched Etta's arm before she stiffened her back and walked down into the great hall. She heard the clatter of horses' hooves from the inner bailey and wondered with a mixture of relief and pain if Graelam were leaving again. She stood quietly at the top of the steps and watched Sir Walter and three men preparing to ride out. Had Graelam dismissed the man from his service? Hope leapt in her breast. She started forward, only to stop abruptly when Graelam, as if sensing her presence, turned to look at her. The bright morning sun gleamed down on his thick dark hair. For a brief moment she saw him as she had when he had held her so tightly against him, whispering love words whilst he gave her pleasure. Her hands clenched, remembering the feel of his flesh, the tautness of his muscled body. He strode toward her and she remained where she was, watching him in wary silence.

He said nothing, merely looked at her, his face expressionless. Finally he said, "Do you not wish to know where Sir Walter goes?"

"Aye," she said.

He remained silent and she burst out, "Have you dismissed him?"

He gave a brief, harsh laugh. "Nay, wife, I have made him the new castellan of Crandall. He goes to relieve Rolfe, who now holds the keep."

"You have . . . rewarded him? After all that he did?"

"Tell me, Kassia," he said quietly, striding up the steps toward her, "tell me once again why you had Dienwald de Fortenberry return you to Wolffeton. Tell me why you did not stay with him or have him take you back to your father. Tell me why you did not leave with him last night."

She closed her eyes against the dull anger in his dark eyes. "I never left you, Graelam. When he asked me if I wished him to take me to Brittany, I told him that I wanted to go home." Her voice was singsong, as if she was reciting a litany.

"And did he refuse to take you with him last night?"

She shook her head.

"Ah, so he did want to take you with him when he escaped?"

She stared at him like a wounded animal who knows that the hunter taunts, waiting to deliver the killing blow. She nodded. The blow came quickly.

"Why did you not go with him?"

"I told him that he was sentencing me to hell if he escaped."

"Why did you not go with him?" The repeated words, though softly spoken, held such menace that she shivered.

It did not occur to her to lie. She said quietly, "I could not go with him because you are my husband, and I love you."

Graelam sucked in his breath as if he had been struck in the belly. For an instant, something deep inside him seemed to expand, filling him with inexplicable joy. The feeling quickly shriveled and died. "That was quite good, my lady," he said, the sneering sarcasm in his voice making her flinch. "So, your handsome lover did not ask you to go with him. Did he suggest to you that you might tell me that lie to calm my . . . ire?"

"No," she whispered.

"Lies, quite good ones actually, flow so easily from your pretty mouth, my lady. Such a pity that you did not wed a man who is a gullible fool."

Anger flowed through her and she thrust her chin up. "I did not marry any man. If you will recall, my lord, I had no choice in the matter. And it appears that my husband is a fool!"

"Get out of my sight," he said in a deadly voice. "Go, before I thrash you."

She clutched her gown in her hands and fled back up the stairs.

Kassia did not see him until the early-evening meal. The tension among the men was palpable, as thick and tangible as the slabs of beef on the trays. Graelam said nothing to her, and she listened while he and his men discussed the situation at Crandall. There had been some fighting by the few soldiers loyal to the castellan, de Cercy, who held the keep.

She heard Ian, a young man-at arms who worshiped

Graelam, say reverently, "You dispatched that whoreson so quickly, my lord. He was no match for your
strength."

Who, Kassia wondered. De Cercy?

"He had become lazy from greed," Graelam said in a
dismissing voice.

She wanted to ask him what he expected Sir Walter
to do, but she held her tongue. As the men recounted
in great detail each bout with the enemy, Kassia lost
what little appetite she had. She left the table very
quietly while Graelam was held in close conversation
with Blount.

The gown she was sewing awaited her, but she did
not touch it. Why should she? There would be no place
she could wear such a beautiful garment. And it was
beautiful, special. Blue satin, its sleeves long and closely
fitted, its skirt flowing, fitted to her waist with a leather
girdle threaded with gold and silver. She paced across
the thick carpet, her thoughts in a blank whirl.

"I thought I had made it clear to you, Kassia, that
you were not to leave unless you had secured my
permission."

How could he walk so silently, she wondered frantically, and he was so large?

"Forgive me," she said. "You appeared very interested in your talk. I did not wish to disturb you."

Graelam said nothing. His eyes lit upon the luxurious
blue satin material, and he walked to it and lifted it,
stroking it in his hands. "You will look quite lovely in
this. I told you, did I not, that the cloth came from
Acre?" He continued to caress the material, looking
thoughtful. Suddenly he tossed the material aside. "You
will need some ornament to wear with it. I believe this

will look quite dramatic." He pulled something from the inside of his tunic and tossed it to her.

She caught it, and stared down at the heavy golden necklace studded with gems of incredible beauty. "It is lovely," she began. She raised bewildered eyes to his set face. "Why do you give it to me, my lord?"

"Will you forever playact with me, my lady? I fancy you recognize the necklace. You should. It has caused you a great deal of difficulty."

She sucked in her breath, dropping the necklace as if it were a snake that had bitten her. "It is the necklace Blanche gave to de Fortenberry," she said dully, staring at the tangled heap of gold on the carpet at her feet. The gems winked up at her, taunting her. "Where did you get it?"

"A groom found it in de Fortenberry's cell, hidden in some straw. I imagine that it must have dropped from his clothing. I also imagine that he was bringing it back to you."

Kassia raised pain-filled eyes to his face. "Aye," she said slowly. "He must have forgotten about it."

Graelam regarded her silently. He was a fool, he realized, to feel cold and sad at the sight of her pain. He said finally, "Have you bathed away the stench of the dungeons?"

She nodded blankly.

"Get into bed. I have gone many days without a woman."

She did not argue with him, or attempt to plead with him. It would gain her naught, she knew. Slowly she removed her clothes, folding each item carefully. She slipped into bed, naked, and closed her eyes.

She felt his hands stroking over her cold flesh. She thought he would simply force her quickly and be done

with it. But he did not. He was undemanding, finding
her mouth and kissing her slowly, gently, while his
hand cupped her breast, his thumb caressing her nipple. To her horror, she felt her body leap in reponse.
He had taught her well, too well, and her body was not
in her mind's control.

Graelam felt her slender arms go around his back,
and he smiled grimly as he kissed her throat. He knew
how to arouse her, and he watched her face as his
fingers found her moist softness. She moaned softly,
arching up against him. He moved down her body,
touching and stroking every inch of her soft flesh. When
he gathered her hips in his hands and lifted her to his
mouth, he looked at her face. He could see the building
passion in her eyes, and something else, a flicker of
pain. He lowered his head and brought her closer to
her release. She cried out, thrashing wildly, her head
arched back against the pillow.

But he did not allow her release. He left her abruptly,
raised himself above her, and thrust into her. He cupped
her face between his hands, holding her still, willing
her to look at him.

"Tell me the truth, Kassia. Tell me, and I will forgive
you."

Her body froze, and all pleasure disappeared as if it
had never awakened.

"Tell me," he said more harshly, his voice matching
the rough thrusting into her body.

"I have told you the truth!" she wailed.

He had filled her, made himself a part of her, and
she hated it and him and herself. She lay like cold
marble beneath him, suffering him in silence, unmoving. She was separate, apart from the helpless woman
who lay beneath the man.

Graelam cursed her, his words catching in his throat as his seed exploded deep within her. He rolled away from her immediately and lay panting on his back.

"Your love is short-lived, I see," he said, not turning toward her.

"Yes," she whispered. "I suppose it must be. How can love survive cruelty and distrust?"

He cursed again softly.

Kassia rose shakily from the bed, walked to the basin, and quickly bathed herself. She knew he was watching her, but she said nothing, did not acknowledge him. She hugged the side of the bed, pulling the covers to her chin, but she could not get warm. She realized vaguely that the coldness was coming from deep within her. She would probably be cold for the rest of her life.

26

"Edward's coronation is in a week and a half."

"When will you leave, my lord?" Kassia asked, finishing the fresh peas from her trencher.

"I, my lady? Do you not recall that the both of us are invited? Do you find my company so distasteful that you would even forgo such an exciting event?"

She raised pitifully hopeful eyes to his face. He watched her pink tongue flicker over her lower lip, and cursed himself silently for wanting her, wanting her simply because she sat beside him, and in a hall full of people!

"I am to come with you, my lord?"

"I do not dare risk leaving you here," he drawled, effectively dampening the sharp edge of his desire for her. He saw a flash of anger in her eyes, and added lazily, his eyes roving over her body, "And do eat more, wife, else I will have naught but sympathy from Edward when he sees I am wed to such a skinny child."

He watched with great interest when her hand closed

about the stem of her goblet. "Go ahead," he taunted her softly. "Toss your wine in my face. I at least would enjoy my retaliation."

Her hand fell away from the goblet as if it had burned her.

He laughed harshly. "It matters not, Kassia. Coupling with you gives me little enough pleasure. If you continue as you are, you will soon enough look like a boy. Then perhaps I will think of myself as a pederast."

She gritted her teeth until her jaw ached.

"What?" he mocked. "You will not even raise that little chin of yours?"

Kassia picked up a ribbed piece of pork. She raised it to her mouth and slowly began to nibble off the meat. She heard him suck in his breath, and let her tongue lick the gravy from the bone. She eased it deeper into her mouth, sucking at the tender meat.

Once, so long ago, it seemed, he had taught her to give him pleasure. He had laughed at her, teased her at her clumsy efforts until he had moaned, and laughed again at her obvious delight. She saw his eyes fastened on her mouth, and felt the momentary power of revenge. She withdrew the bone and tossed it carelessly to her trencher. She raised her chin.

"Bitch," he said softly.

He rose abruptly from the table and strode from the hall.

It had begun to rain, and she nearly called to him. You are such a stupid fool, she chided herself, worrying that he will take a chill!

Graelam strode at a furious pace up the winding wooden stairs to the ramparts. He leaned forward against the harsh cold stone and looked toward the sea, but the sliver of moon showed him no more than an occasional white-topped wave. The rain was warm on his face. At least, he mocked himself silently, it cools my passions.

He realized that he was tired, tired to the depths of his being of baiting Kassia, tired of watching her show alternately her fear and her hatred of him. None of it was his fault, damn her! But he knew that it was. She would never have left him if he had not driven her to it. The events of the past months careened through his mind. The weeks of warmth and caring they had shared when he had decided to forget what she had done, forget her lies, excusing her by blaming himself. Dienwald de Fortenberry. The knight's name rang like a death knell in his mind. *I did not leave with him because I love you*. His eyes darkened, anger at himself flowing through him for believing her even for a moment.

Graelam pounded his fist hard against the stone. He hated himself for his feelings of deep uncertainty. He had never experienced the emotions she had evoked in him. If Edward called for another crusade, he would have agreed immediately. On the heels of that thought he saw her face, her dimples deepening as she smiled at him, saw her eyes widen with bewildered astonishment when he had first brought her pleasure.

"Saint Peter's bones, but I am weary of all this!" he muttered. He strode back into the keep, shaking off the rain like a huge mongrel dog.

It would take them six days to travel to London, but Kassia didn't mind. She was filled with excitement, and even her husband's distance did not overly upset her. He had simply ignored her, leaving all preparations to her. The string of details and decisions to be made allowed her to bury her feelings for him, and her hurt, until she lay in bed at night, listening to his even breathing. The day before they were to leave, Graelam had walked into their bedchamber unexpectedly. He paused a moment, watching Kassia twirl around in her new blue satin gown. She looked utterly beautiful, despite her fragile slenderness. Her hair lay in thick soft curls about her small head, now falling to her shoulders. Her laughter died in her throat when she saw him.

"My lord?"

"The gown becomes you, my lady," he said harshly.

Her face went carefully blank. "Thank you, my lord."

"You will wear the necklace with that gown." He could see the frisson of distaste in her eyes before she lowered her head.

He walked to his trunk and dug it out. He held it up, watching the precious gems gleam in the sunlight that poured through the small windows. "Come here," he said.

She walked slowly to him and turned around, lifting her hair off her neck. She felt the weight of the necklace as it rested upon her chest, felt the chill of the thick gold against her bare neck. He fastened the clasp and stepped back.

She looked like a barbaric princess, he thought. He watched her lift her hand and lightly touch her fingers to the necklace. It did not particularly surprise him when her fingers fell away from it as if it burned her.

"You will be thus gowned for the coronation," he said, and left the bedchamber.

He took her that night, quickly but not roughly, and she thought she heard him curse her when he stiffened over her. She lay very still even after he had rolled off her. When she made to rise to bathe herself, he closed his hand around her waist, pulling her back.

"Nay," he said, "you will not wash my seed from your body."

She was shocked when she quivered at his words, and had to remind herself that he saw her now as naught but a brood mare. She tugged and he released her wrist.

"Go to sleep, wife, we leave early on the morrow."

Is there no way I can reach you? she cried out silently.

They arrived in London a full week later, filthy and weary, their horses and wagons splattered with mud. Kassia had ridden most of the way, even when it had rained, once she had convinced Graelam that riding in a wagon made her ill.

She didn't know what to expect, but the sight of so many people packed into such a small area made her blink with surprise. And the filth! There was a constant stench of human excrement and rotting food. And there was so much noise from vendors screeching at the top of their voices at passersby.

"All towns of any size are like this," Graelam said when he saw her cover her nose. "It is not so bad where we will stay. The compound is on the Thames, but north of the city."

"This is the house the Duke of Cornwall gave to you?" she asked.

"Aye, he deeded it to me upon my betrothal to Lady Joanna," he said dryly.

Her eyes flew to his face.

"He insisted I keep it once he had deemed you worthy."

A fine, misting rain was falling steadily and the ground

was slushy mud. Bluebell slipped and Graelam's hand
shot out to grasp the reins and steady the mare.

Kassia started to thank him, but he said merely, "You
are filthy enough. I do not wish you to have a broken
leg as well."

"Then you would have to wear that wretched necklace yourself," she muttered under her breath.

"There," Graelam said to her, pointing to his left, "is
Westminster Abbey, where Edward will have his
coronation."

"It is beautiful," Kassia said.

"Aye, King Henry spent much money to reconstruct
it. He is buried there."

They passed the White Tower, where Edward and
Eleanor were now staying. "I do not know when Edward returned to London," Graelam said. "But I imagine that immediately the Duke of Cornwall heard he
was coming, he set the coronation into motion."

Kassia was weaving in the saddle, so weary she could
no longer appreciate the vivid sights. At last they reached
a high-walled fortress. A thick-barred iron gate swung
slowly open and their caravan passed into a muddy,
utterly dismal yard. The two-story wooden building in
front of them was square and looked gray and uninvit-
ing in the growing darkness.

"You will see to the inside, my lady," Graelam said as
he lifted her off Bluebell's back.

She nodded, imagining with growing depression what
awaited her within. To her utter astonishment, once
inside the house there were scores of lighted candles
and a huge fire burning in a fireplace at the far end of
the long, narrow lower chamber.

"Lady Kassia?"

A plump gray-haired woman approached her and proffered a deep curtsy.

"I am Margaret, my lady. The duke told us to expect you."

"I am so pleased you are here," Kassia told the woman with a tired smile.

Margaret clucked around her, much in Etta's manner, and Kassia allowed herself for some minutes to be cosseted. She was led upstairs to a comfortable chamber, where another fire burned.

"For you and your lord," Margaret said.

There were fresh reeds on the stone floor and a tapestry of vivid colors covering one wall. A large bed was set upon a dais, and there were several high-backed chairs surrounding a small circular table.

"I believe I have died and gone to heaven!" Kassia exclaimed.

"I will kiss the duke's feet," Etta said fervently.

"I will have the wenches bring you hot water for a bath," Margaret continued placidly. "My husband, Sarn, will assist your lord to see to the horses and wagons. You need do naught, my lady, but see to yourself."

Etta hurrumphed when Margaret started to assist Kassia out of her wet cloak, and the woman merely smiled, curtsied again, and left the chamber, saying over her shoulder, "The duke sent an entire pig for your first meal. After you have rested, my lady, we will have the evening meal."

"Etta," Kassia scolded her old nurse, "you are wet through! You see to yourself. I am not helpless, you know."

Kassia was immersed to her chin in a wooden tub filled with blessedly hot water when Graelam entered the chamber.

She forgot the restraint between them, forgot she was naked, and said happily, "The duke must be the most thoughtful man in all of England! I do not even have to see to the preparation of dinner! And this room is so pleasant and so very warm! Was all as you wished, my lord?"

He smiled at her wearily. "Aye, everything is fine. I will give you five more minutes in that tub, Kassia."

She flushed, and quickly ducked her head underwater to wet her hair. When she emerged from the tub, Graelam was wearing his bedrobe, seated in front of the roaring fire. She quickly toweled herself dry and wrapped a small linen towel about her wet hair.

"I was very dirty, Graelam," she said, eyeing the bathwater.

"I called for clean water," he said, not turning.

Kassia heard the heavy footsteps outside their chamber and scurried to pull on her bedrobe, drawing the belt tight about her waist.

She was combing out her hair in front of the fire when Graelam said from the tub, "We will have our meal here this evening. Tomorrow we will go to the tower."

Kassia paused a moment in her combing and said tentatively, "I should like to see everything, my lord. I fear I was too tired today to appreciate England's capital."

"Aye," he said, closing his eyes, "it has been a long time since I was here. I remarked changes. We will see everything you wish to see."

"Thank you," she said softly. "Do you wish me to assist you, my lord?"

"Bring me a towel," he said, rising.

She tried to avoid looking at his body, but failed dismally. Her fingers itched to tangle themselves in the thick mat of black hair on his chest, to stroke over the velvet smoothness of his back. It had been so long! Her mind warred with her body, and in that moment she hated him for teaching her pleasure, for teaching her body to respond to him. Her eyes fell to his groin and she felt heat suffuse her loins. But he hated her, she reminded herself, forcing her eyes upward. She met his dark gaze and gulped.

"The towel, Kassia," he said, holding out his hand.

She thrust the towel at him and quickly turned back and sat before the fire.

She knew he had seen the desire in her eyes, and she wanted to kick herself. She heard him say very calmly from behind her, "I will part your sweet thighs, my lady, and caress you until you scream with pleasure, if you will but admit, finally, the truth to me."

She wanted to yell at him, to plead her innocence yet again. But it would do no good. Why not simply tell him what he wanted to hear? She froze at the thought, for she knew what the result would be. He would possibly forgive her, but he would never trust her. He could never really care for her if he distrusted her. At least, she sighed, there would be peace of a sort between them. From the corner of her eye she saw him remove the towel and stand quietly, stretching in front of the fire, oblivious of his nakedness. His manhood was jutting outward, and she gulped, quickly turning her face away from him. He would slake his desire in another woman's body. The thought made her jump to her feet, the pain of her spirit shimmering in her eyes.

"Graelam, I—"

There was a knock on the chamber door. She closed her eyes, and trembled with the knowledge of what she had been about to say to him.

"Enter," she called, her voice high and shrill.

Two serving wenches came into the chamber, carrying trays. Their eyes went immediately to Graelam, who was languidly reaching for his bedrobe. Both the women eyed him openly. Would he take one of them?

"Set the trays here," Kassia said harshly, pointing to the small table.

She gritted her teeth as one of the women, quite pretty, with thick black hair and full breasts, gave Graelam an open invitation with her dark eyes.

"You may leave now," she said sharply, stepping in front of her husband.

He watched her, a gleam of satisfaction in his eyes. But he said nothing until she was seated across from him, her mouth full of roast pork.

"That was quite a display of wifely jealousy, my lady," he said.

She choked, and downed half the wine in his goblet. She could not speak for several moments as she gasped for breath. But she shook her head violently.

"Odd," he continued calmly. "I had the impression that you were about to tell me something of great interest when the wenches interrupted us."

She said nothing, staring down at the wooden plate. Her face was very expressive, and Graelam saw the myriad emotions clashing there. Was it pride that kept her silent? he wondered.

"You are very young, Kassia," he said after a moment, remembering Drake's words. "When one is young, one makes mistakes. And one is . . . reluctant to admit to mistakes."

"Do not older people also make mistakes, Graelam?" she asked quietly.

"Aye," he agreed easily, sitting back in his chair and

crossing his arms over his massive chest. "But heed me, wife, I do not intend to hear more mewling protests from you. They now weary me and bore me."

"Very well, my lord," she said, "I will say nothing."

The decision was made. Was it pride that kept her silent? Honor? Stupidity?

In the next instant he was towering above her, jerking her out of her chair.

"No," she whispered, leaning back as far as she was able.

He laughed and swept her over his shoulder. "Would you prefer that I bed that pretty wench who brought our meal?"

"Aye!" she shouted. "I care not what you do!"

He dropped her onto her back and stripped off her bedrobe. When he released her to rid himself of his own bedrobe, she rolled onto her knees and tried to escape him. He caught her by her ankle and flipped her again onto her back.

"No," he said, his voice mocking to her ears, "I am not yet sated with your sweet body. But there will be no pleasure for you, my lady." He pulled her legs apart and thrust into her. His eyes widened and flew to her face, for she was moist and ready for him.

Kassia stared at him. She felt him deep and throbbing inside her, felt him grinding against her belly, and she cried out, beyond herself, her body exploding in harsh, rippling pleasure.

It would not stop, and cry after helpless cry burst from her throat.

Graelam felt her fingers clutching at his shoulders, felt the furious arching of her hips to match his rhythm. He kissed her deeply, and moaned his own release into her mouth.

He crushed her against him, utterly confused by her passionate response to him. The punishment he had wished had failed abysmally. It both angered him and, oddly enough, pleased him.

Damn her! He said, his voice a mocking taunt, even as his hands stroked and caressed her hips, "So yielding and passionate, dear wife. Did you think of him when I came into you?"

He felt her quiver and stiffen, but he would not release her. "Go to sleep, Kassia. I will not allow you to bathe yourself. My seed will stay in your belly."

Graelam finally fell into an exhausted sleep, the wet of her tears on his shoulder.

27

I must remember everything, Kassia thought as she gazed upward at the high vaulted cathedral, for someday I shall tell my grandchildren that I attended the coronation of King Edward the First of England. She avidly took in the gorgeously arrayed lords and ladies and the splendid stained-glass windows. All was overladen with religious solemnity. The prelates, their flowing robes as beautifully sewn as those of the king and queen, recited the ceremony in Latin, their voices hushed and reverent. Kassia leaned forward when Edward accepted his scepter and crown. All too soon, the ceremony was over. The new king and queen of England were whisked away, and the lords and ladies moved quietly out of the abbey. Kassia heard Graelam give a deep sigh of relief. She gazed up at him uncertainly, but he merely nodded at her, saying only, "At least our king is home. Now, Kassia, we will shuck all the religious trappings and you will meet Edward and Eleanor."

She looks beautiful, Graelam thought, unconsciously

comparing Kassia to the other noble ladies assembled in the huge lower chamber of the White Tower. "Do not look so awestruck," he said quietly to her, "else everyone will believe you a country maid."

"I am trying to memorize everything," she said quite seriously.

"We will doubtless come to London again."

She nodded, and spoke before she could censor her thought, "Aye, but this is the coronation. We will be able to tell our grandchildren about it." Her hand flew to her mouth in consternation. She waited for his taunting response.

"I had not thought of that," he said, his dark eyes suddenly opague. "Come, Kassia, there are many people for you to meet."

It was indeed odd, Kassia thought after meeting so many lords and ladies, that her mouth seemed frozen into a permanent smile, but she had not felt at all intimidated as she had expected to. Graelam was playing the husband's role well, pretending he was pleased to have all his friends meet his wife. And it was also the necklace, she thought. Although she hated its weight on her neck and all the pain it had brought her, it nonetheless gave her a very rich, slightly exotic appearance that, strangely, gave her confidence.

"By all that's precious! Look what Cornwall has spit up, Chandra! My lord Graelam!"

Kassia raised her eyes to meet the merry blue ones of one of the most handsome men she had ever seen. He was nearly as tall as Graelam, wide of shoulder and lean of waist and hip. His hair was burnished gold and his face lightly tanned and exquisitely formed. Standing next to him was a very beautiful lady, the perfect mate for such a man. She felt suddenly skinny, ugly, and tongue-tied, her confidence utterly destroyed compared to this unbelievable creature with her long golden hair and her utterly perfect woman's body.

"So you and Chandra have traveled from the northern wilds for the great occasion," Graelam said, slapping the other man on his muscled arm. "Chandra," he continued, his voice dropping slightly as he grasped her hand, "how is it you manage to appear more beautiful each time I see you?"

Chandra laughed lightly. "This beast, Jerval, has kept me off the practice field for the past month so I would not embarrass him at court with my bruises and scratches."

Practice field. What, Kassia wondered blankly, was she talking about?

"I pray you will not believe that tale, Graelam," Sir Jerval said, his long fingers lightly caressing his wife on her slender shoulder. "The only thing that has slowed her down at all was the birth of our son but four months ago."

"I do not suppose," Graelam said in a mock-pensive voice, "that you named the lad after me?"

"Not likely, Graelam," Chandra said. "He is Edward. Jerval believed that there should be an Edward in London and one in Cumbria. I had no choice in the matter."

"And for once she was flat on her back, too tired to argue with me," Sir Jerval said. He lowered his voice to a lecherous whisper. "Of course, I learned that technique of gaining her compliance long ago."

Kassia blinked at their banter, wishing Graelam would introduce her to these people, yet afraid of making a fool of herself if he did so. She felt so insignificant!

"The necklace! My God, Graelam, I had forgot all about it!"

It was as if, Kassia thought, her husband had just remembered her presence. "Aye," he said easily, " 'tis the same one, from Al-Afdal's camp. And the little one wearing it is Kassia, my wife."

Lady Chandra gasped, her expressive blue eyes widening in surprise. "Good heavens, Jerval, you and I now have a son, but Graelam has got himself a wife! My dear, I trust you buffet this great beast at least twice a day. He doubtless tries to play the tyrant over you."

Kassia felt bereft of speech at this unexpected advice, but Lady Chandra continued smiling at her openly, and she gulped, and blurted out, "I suspect he is as much a tyrant as he ever was."

"Kassia," Graelam said, his voice clipped, "this is Sir Jerval de Vernon and his wife, Lady Chandra."

"My wife," Sir Jerval said kindly to Kassia, "is always offering advice that she herself ignores. She adores me so mightily that I am always having to lift her from her knees—"

Lady Chandra poked him in the ribs. "You are a fiend and a miserable liar, my lord! Pay him no heed, Kassia. He is like most men, crowing his conceit and praying others will believe him!"

"Ha!" Sir Jerval said.

Chandra ignored him, and continued to Kassia, "Has Graelam told you of our adventures in the Holy Land? How long ago it seems! The history of the necklace you are wearing is particularly . . . precarious. I had thought we would be saying our last prayers!"

"You tried to kill me, Chandra, then saved my miserable life," Graelam complained ruefully. "Neither tale bears repeating, particularly to a wife who—" He broke

off, not really knowing what he would have said, and
fearing that it would show his bitterness.

"Well," Chandra said comfortably, "I shall tell her all
about it."

"You . . . you tried to kill my husband?" Kassia asked.
She saw Chandra's eyes fly to Graelam's face.

"'Twas a long time ago," Lady Chandra said finally.
"And of no importance at all now."

"Jerval, Chandra, how long do you remain in London?" Graelam asked.

"Another week or so," Jerval said. "Chandra has accepted a challenge from Edward on the archery range.
I fear I am relegated to the role of holding her quiver."

"'Twill be an alarming contest," Graelam said. "I
will bear you company and the two of us will cheer her
on." He turned to his wife. "Come, Kassia, 'tis time
you met your king."

"Lady Chandra will go against the king?" Kassia asked,
disbelief so clear in her voice that Graelam laughed.

"Indeed," he said. "Chandra is a warrior."

"But she is so beautiful!"

"I learned with her that the one only enhances the
other. She is a woman who holds honor dear. And at
last it appears that she holds her womanhood dear as
well."

The tone of his voice altered slightly, and Kassia
frowned down at her blue leather slippers. She remembered him telling her that a lady had given him the scar
on his shoulder. Chandra? she wondered. Had he loved
her? Did he still love her? At the very least, she thought
miserably, he much admired her. She is everything I
am not. I would not know the end of an arrow from its
beginning.

They entered a line of nobles that would pass in front

of the newly crowned King Edward and Queen Eleanor. Kassia smiled, curtsying to a Sir John de Vescy, another noble who had been with Graelam in the Holy Land.

Thank the Lord for the coolness of the October day, Kassia thought, for with the press of people, heat would have made it unbearable.

She moved closer to her husband, comparing him to the other noblemen. He looks as magnificent as a king, she thought, as he threw back his black head and laughed aloud at a comment from a gaunt-looking man with bushy black eyebrows. His robe was of rich gold velvet, full-cut, its flowing sleeves lined with ermine. About his waist was a thick black belt from which hung a slender gem-studded sword. The robe fit across his massive shoulders perfectly. She had sewed many hours to make it thus.

"Ah, my lord Graelam!"

Graelam bowed deeply. "Sire, welcome home! Your throne has grown dusty in your absence, and your barons morose without a king to complain about!"

"Aye," the king said, smiling widely, "but I venture you have told them enough stories to blacken my reputation! My love, here is the Wolf of Cornwall to greet you!"

Queen Eleanor gasped with pleasure. "Graelam! So many friends come to see us! You look more handsome than my poor lord, Graelam! I fear foreign lands have added gray to his hair!"

"But who is this, my lord?" Edward said, his penetrating blue eyes going to the small woman at Graelam's side.

"Allow me to present my wife, sire, Kassia de Moreton."

"My lady," Edward said smoothly, and took her small hand into his large one.

"Sire," Kassia said, curtsying. She blurted out, "You are so tall! I had believed my lord the largest of men, yet you can see over his head!"

Eleanor laughed. "He has oft told me that he grew to such a height to better intimidate all his nobles. My lord's uncle, the Duke of Cornwall, has told us of you, Kassia. So romantic and dramatic a story. We will speak, for I wish to hear all about you and your taming of the Wolf of Cornwall."

Taming! Ha, Kassia thought as she walked beside her husband to greet other acquaintances.

The afternoon faded into evening and by the time the great banquet was served, Kassia felt herself trembling with weariness. She toyed with the vast variety of foods, sampling only the delicious stuffed pheasants and the creamed potatoes. The wine, she was certain, came from Aquitaine.

"The queen is very gracious," she said to Graelam when he turned away from conversation with Lord John de Valance.

"Aye," Graelam said. "'Tis the only love match amongst royalty I have heard of. Eleanor saved Edward's life in the Holy Land when he was attacked by an assassin with a poisoned dagger."

"She killed the assassin?" Kassia asked, her eyes wide.

"Nay, Edward killed the man and collapsed. She sucked the poison from his arm. I was not present, but Jerval and Chandra were. Edward's physicians were supposedly furious at the queen's interference."

She toyed for a moment with her goblet. "You knew Lady Chandra before she wed Sir Jerval?"

Graelam studied her averted profile. "Aye," he said shortly.

" 'Twas she who stabbed you in the shoulder?"

"She did not stab me. Actually, she flung the dagger from a goodly distance. Had she been less furious and closer to me, I would likely be dead."

"How . . ." Kassia began, but Graelam's attention was drawn back to Lord John. Questions flew about in her mind, but she had no opportunity to speak privately to Graelam until they arrived at their compound. To Kassia's delight, Margaret had hot spiced wine awaiting them in their chamber.

"I feel like royalty with all this attention," she said as she carefully removed the necklace.

Graelam stretched, rubbing his neck. "The ceremony went well. I am pleased that Edward is home again. We return tomorrow to the tower. I will be meeting with Edward along with many other nobles. You, Kassia, will become better acquainted with the ladies."

He paused a moment. He had seen Lady Joanna, but had managed to avoid her. He supposed he was a fool for worrying that she would not be kind to Kassia.

"Graelam, would you tell me about Lady Chandra?"

He shrugged, and sat down in one of the high-backed chairs. "There is little to tell, but if you wish it . . . I had wanted to marry her, but her father, a Marcher baron—" he broke off a moment, seeing her confusion. "A Marcher baron is a noble whose holdings and fortresses defend the border of England from the Welsh. In any case, Lord Richard refused me. Through trickery, I managed to capture both Chandra and their castle of Croyland. She would have wed me, for I held her younger brother, save for the timely arrival of Jerval. I was routed and managed to leave with but a wound in my shoulder. Chandra's father then forced her into marriage with Jerval, the son of a close friend of his."

She was staring at him. "But you are all friends!"

"Now we are. Much happened in the Holy Land to . . . reconcile our differences. And from what I can tell, that is where Chandra decided to become a woman and return her husband's love."

Kassia fiddled with the fastenings on her gown. "Did you love her?"

Graelam stared into the glowing coals in the fireplace. "It was a long time ago. No, I did not love her, but I wanted her. She is unlike any woman I have ever known. She knows a man's honor and a man's loyalty." He raised brooding eyes to her face. "She is capable only of truth. Aye, rare in a woman."

Kassia sucked in her breath at the pain his words brought her. She walked slowly to the far corner of the chamber and began to remove her clothes. He watched her from beneath slitted eyelids, feeling a pang of guilt. He had spoken the truth about Chandra, but not all of it. Before she had fallen in love with Jerval, she had been more unbending than the most ruthless of men, spurning the meaning of compromise. Even now, Graelam imagined that Jerval waged a constant battle with his beautiful wife to keep control.

He sipped the warm wine, waiting for Kassia to get into bed. It was odd, he thought, but when he had seen Chandra, he had felt no rush of desire for her. Indeed, he had felt nothing save friendship for both her and Jerval. He saw a flash of soft white flesh before Kassia pulled the covers over herself. He shifted in his chair, angry at himself for the desire he felt for his wife. He thought about the intense passion he had felt for her the evening before, passion he had forced himself to ignore.

After a while Graelam rose to his feet and stripped off his clothes. He strode to the bed, lifting the lone candle high, and stared down at his wife. Her soft hair was spread about her head on the pillow, her mouth slightly open as she breathed evenly in sleep. Could he blame Dienwald de Fortenberry for being taken with such an apparently guileless, fragile girl? He slipped into bed, forcing himself to stay a goodly distance away from her.

Queen Eleanor sat among her chattering ladies in the solarium. The interested, attentive smile never left her face as she looked toward Kassia de Moreton. She continued to weave the intricate tapestry, watching the girl from the corner of her eye as Chandra de Vernon approached her.

Events might well prove interesting, she thought. Her ears perked up when she heard a snide comment from Lady Joanna, daughter of the Earl of Leichester.

"You should have seen her," Joanna was saying to Lady Louise de Sanson, "when she first arrived at Wolffeton. I could tell that Lord Graelam was appalled, but of course there was nothing he could do about her."

"He really married her on her deathbed?" Louise asked, her sloe eyes lighting avidly.

"Aye," Joanna said. "The look on his face when the skinny little thing arrived, looking for the world like a dirty little boy! And her hair so short!"

"Scandalous," Louise agreed.

"You can see that she has not much improved," Joanna said maliciously.

Eleanor, seeing that other ladies were beginning to listen and then cast furtive glances toward Kassia de

Moreton, decided it was time to intervene. "I think her quite lovely," she said in a soft, quite clear voice. "Lord Graelam is most lucky."

Joanna paused a moment, judging the waters. She said in a hushed whisper that carried a goodly distance, "But that is not what Lord Graelam thinks, your highness. I was told by Lady Blanche de Blasis, the half-sister of Graelam's first wife, that Lady Kassia even tried to escape him. It would not appear that he made such a good bargain."

The whispering had reached Kassia's sensitive ears and she was flushed with anger even as she tried to heed Lady Chandra's words. Suddenly Chandra's strong fingers closed over her arm. "Leave the bitch to me," Chandra said, and strode toward the little group.

"Ah, Lady Joanna! I understand that you were to be married. How very unfortunate for you that the groom escaped."

Queen Eleanor hid a smile behind her hand.

There was a loud rustling of silk skirts as the ladies moved closer.

Joanna knew of Chandra only by reputation. She had believed that she must be an Amazon, but faced with the beautiful creature staring at her with contempt, she was forced to revise her opinion. "My father is relieved that I did not marry Lord Graelam." She gave a small shudder. "He did not wish me to be immured in Cornwall."

"But how terribly embarrassing for you, dear Joanna," Chandra continued in mock sympathy. "To be turned away from your first choice."

"Graelam had no choice!" Joanna said in a shrill voice. "He was forced to keep her!"

Kassia moved quietly to stand beside Chandra. She

could not allow Chandra to defend her, as if she were naught but a frightened little mouse!

"He did have a choice, Joanna," Kassia said. "You see, our marriage had not been consummated."

"Then why did you try to escape him?" Louise said, honestly confused.

"I believe," Kassia said slowly, "that Lady Blanche claims this as a fact. It is not true. I owe my . . . loyalty to my husband and always will."

"How you have changed your stance!" *Why am I still baiting her? Do I so fear that Graelam will learn that I was the one responsible?* It was true, Blanche admitted to herself as she watched Kassia whirl about at the sound of her sarcastic words. She feared Graelam would take revenge upon Guy.

"Blanche . . ." Kassia murmured.

Very soon, Eleanor thought, this gathering will degenerate into a true debacle. She set aside her thread and rose from her chair. "Ladies, I believe it is time for me to tell you of the court in Sicily. And I will show you some of the treasures I brought back with me."

"Come," Chandra said quietly to Kassia. "If I stay longer, I will break Joanna's neck! And perhaps Blanche's arm!"

"Why did you defend me?" Kassia asked. "You do not know me."

"A penchant for fairness," Chandra said. "Joanna. from what I hear, is a vicious, mean-spirited bitch. Graelam would likely have killed her had he married her."

Kassia said slowly, "You sound as though you have forgiven Graelam for what he tried to do to you."

"So he told you about that, did he?"

"Aye, I asked him last night. He much admires you."

"Well," Chandra said after a moment, "had we wed, I do not know who would have survived! Graelam is used to ruling all within his power. He will not tolerate his wishes gainsaid. And unfortunately, he cannot seem to accept a woman's going against him in anything. Am I right?"

"Aye," Kassia said forlornly, "you are right. There was a time when I believed that he—" She broke off, biting her lip. "It matters not. Nothing will change his opinion of me now."

"Walk with me," Chandra said. "I would hear about this adventure of yours."

". . . and so I cannot blame Dienwald for escaping," Kassia concluded after some time. "Graelam would have killed him. And now Blanche is here, and still persists in despising me. There is nothing I can do or say to convince him otherwise!"

"Hmmm," Chandra said.

"If I were more like you," Kassia burst out, "he would likely love me! At least he might believe me, for he spoke about your honor and your honesty."

Chandra smiled down at Kassia. "I have an idea," she said. "Why do you not come with me to the archery range. I have a contest with the king tomorrow and must practice. And while I am at it, I can show you how to shoot."

28

"You are meddling, and I do not like it."

Lady Chandra de Vernon snuggled closer to her husband. "But she is innocent, Jerval," she protested mildly, drawing in her breath as her husband's hand roved down over her belly. "I only wish to help."

"She does bring out one's protective instincts," Jerval said.

"Aye, but do not think she is a fragile helpless little flower. There is a core of strength in her, I think. She will bend, but will not break. If only Graelam were not such a—"

"Proud, cynical, arrogant, distrustful—"

"All of those things, I suppose," Chandra said on a sigh. "You should have seen her on the archery range this afternoon. She looked at my bow as if it were a snake that would bite her. But she quickly got over that! She hasn't much physical strength, but she does have a good eye and a steady hand."

"So you would turn her into a warrior?"

"If you laugh, Jerval, I will take a dagger to your . . . well, you will regret it!"

"Just remember, my love," Jerval said softly, drawing her into his arms, "if that dagger of yours strikes, you will lose also. I will make you a bargain. I will speak to Graelam tomorrow, and also Sir Guy de Blasis. He seems a decent man."

"I cannot say that much for his wife!"

"Hush now, woman. I wish to have my way with you."

"I wonder," Chandra said before succumbing to her husband, "what Blanche is saying to her husband. Do you believe he knows the truth?"

Sir Guy knew all there was to know about his bride. He had realized even before he had tricked her into marrying him that her relentless pursuit of Graelam had been primarily because of her fear for her son's future. Well, perhaps not entirely, he quickly amended to himself, grimacing a little. But Evian's future was now assured. Guy felt a good deal of affection for her, even enjoyed her tirades, for he knew that once in bed, she would forget everything but him. She was a passionate woman, one who was not always logical, and, unfortunately, quite single-minded. But that would change. He smiled at her now, lazily, listening to her rant. She never bored him.

"I do not want to be pregnant!"

"But you are, my dear," he said mildly, "and you will remain that way. After you have given me two or three sons, I will allow you to take that vile potion again."

"You are a beast!"

"A virile beast, it appears. I should keep you in bed

all the time—it would save your temper and my ears and patience."

"I do not want to be ugly, fat, and swollen! I do not want the pain of birthing another child!"

"Blanche," he said, leaning over the small table between them, "I am truly sorry about the birthing pain. If I could prevent it, I would, but I cannot. As to your appearing ugly, you are being foolish. You will see that my desire for you will not diminish. You are my wife and my lover. It will remain thus, I promise you."

"I am not a fool, Guy," she said in a low, taut voice.

"I trust not, at least not anymore."

She jumped to her feet, splaying her hands on the table. "I know why you married me! 'Tis that skinny little girl you love, not me!" She paled as the words poured out of her mouth, and she whirled about, presenting him her back.

Guy leaned back in his chair, clasping his hands behind his head. "At last," he said with deep satisfaction. "You have finally admitted it."

"I . . . I have admitted nothing! Admitted what?"

"That you love me, of course. It warms my heart, Blanche. Do you not realize there is no need for you to insult Kassia further?"

At her silence, he added softly, "Please turn around, my love."

Blanche slowly swung about, but she kept her face lowered, her eyes on her soft leather slippers.

"You are doubtless the most stubborn woman in England. Come, love, at least yell at me."

"I am not stubborn, and she was with that bitch Chandra de Vernon!"

"Are all the ladies at court bitches, Blanche? My poor love, how very trying for you."

"I must admit that I did not like being in Joanna's company," she said grudgingly.

"Forced to take sides, my dear? And, it appears, you have chosen the wrong one, again."

She wanted to tell him that she had baited Kassia because she was afraid for him. Afraid of what Graelam would do if he discovered her perfidy. *I have been fine and fairly won*, she thought. *I love him, yet I am afraid to tell him so. Afraid that he really thinks me a spiteful witch*.

Guy rose and walked to her, clasping her shoulders in his hands and shaking her a little. "Listen to me, wife. It is time for you to forget Graelam, Kassia, and Wolffeton. To forget your disappointment. It is time, you know, for you to accept me as your husband." He paused a moment, examining his thoughts to make them into words. "I do not love Kassia. I felt protective of her, for a more innocent maid I have yet to see. But I wanted you, Blanche, despite what you did." He shrugged, and added honestly, "I gained you, and saved Kassia from further of your . . . machinations."

Her eyes flew to his face. "I . . . I did nothing!" *Can I never cease lying?*

He lightly caressed his fingertips over her lips. "I am not blind, love. There is no reason for you to pretend to me. I will admit that it would please me mightily if you would willingly go to Graelam and tell him the truth." His eyes darkened, narrowing in thought. "Of course, Graelam, being as blind as he appears to be when it comes to women, would likely assume that I put you up to it. And seeing you soft and lovely from my attentions, I could not blame him. Perhaps 'tis best to leave matters as they are, at least for the time being. I have a feeling that they will work out things between them without any more of your interference, or mine. But attend me, Blanche. I will not allow you to direct any more mischief toward Kassia. Do you understand me?"

"I cannot help but understand you! You are a brute and a braggart, but I won't believe you!"

He did not release her, but sighed deeply. "Perhaps in five or ten years you will come to believe me. Together, Blanche, you and I will build Chitterly into a great holding." He chuckled, and leaned down to kiss her lips lightly. "Our children will never believe their mother a spineless wench."

"You mock me, Guy," she muttered, "and you are slippery as the wettest fish. I do not like you."

"Nay, but you love me. I will accept that for a while. I trust that you will not go against my wishes."

"You would likely beat me if I did."

He touched his hand to her slightly rounded belly. "No, but I would find other ways to punish you."

She buried her face against his shoulder. "I do not mean to say bad things, Guy," she whispered. "I was just so . . . afraid."

He kissed her temple. "But not now. Not ever again. And, love, I enjoy your fishwife's tongue." He felt her stiffen in protest, and quickly said, "Now I will take you to bed and make you forget everything but your passion and your love for me."

The afternoon was clear and sunny, the air crisp. Lords and ladies were gathered in the huge tower courtyard to see the competition between King Edward and Lady Chandra de Vernon. Graelam left Kassia with the queen and joined Jerval de Vernon and his friend Sir Mark. There was much good-natured jesting and prodding until Jerval tore off part of his tunic sleeve.

"An adequate favor for my lady?" he asked, and the men dissolved into more laughter.

"My lord is quite cocky," Queen Eleanor said with a smile, "but I think he will soon become quite serious about it all. You watched Chandra practicing yesterday, Kassia?"

"She is unbelievable," Kassia said. "I never dreamed that a woman could be so . . ." She sought vainly for a word.

"Complete?" Eleanor supplied.

"Perhaps. And she is so beautiful."

"Actually, Kassia, her completeness came only when she fell in love with her husband. She was not always as happy as she is now."

But her husband always loved her, Kassia wanted to say. Instead, she spoke of the match. "She is concerned that the third round will do her in. The distance requires a great deal of strength, and she says that only the king can shoot so far with accuracy."

"Aye, I know," Eleanor said. "I believe my lord insisted upon it. He does not like to lose."

Kassia laughed. "At least he is honest about it!" She looked toward Chandra, who was laughing as her husband wrapped a piece of material about her arm as his favor. I would be like her, Kassia thought. If I could but learn a little of what she does so effortlessly, perhaps Graelam would admire me. She gasped at the thought of herself wielding a lance, riding a mighty war-horse. Nonetheless, the thought stayed with her.

Eleanor turned to speak to the Countess of Pembroke. Kassia looked about her and smiled at a slight, light-haired girl whose belly was rounded with child. "You must be tired," she said. "Come and sit beside me."

"Thank you. I do not have the energy that I used to have."

Kassia felt a brief twinge of envy, then looked toward Chandra. "Does she not look utterly beautiful?"

"Aye. You should see her in her armor, though. 'Tis a sight that taxes the mind. I grew up with Chandra, you see."

Kassia's thoughts whirled and she said abruptly, "Were you at Croyland when Graelam de Moreton came to take her?"

The girl stiffened, but answered quietly enough, "Aye, I was there."

"Did Lady Chandra truly hurl a dagger at Graelam?"

The girl nodded. She turned at the sound of a bright child's laughter. "Ah, my daughter, Glenda." She took the child from a nurse and lifted her in her arms. "Glenda, I would like you to meet a lovely lady." She looked inquiringly at Kassia.

"Kassia is my name. She is a lovely child. You are very lucky." Kassia gazed at the little girl's thick dark hair, then into her large gray eyes. Suddenly Glenda leaned toward Kassia, her small hand clutching at the ermine of her cloak. The child laughed as she stroked the fur, and Kassia froze. The expression was Graelam's.

"Are you all right, Kassia? You look very pale."

Kassia gulped. "I do not believe I know your name," she managed at last.

"Mary. My husband, Sir Mark, is yon, standing with Sir Jerval and . . . Graelam de Moreton."

The pause in her voice boomed in Kassia's mind. Was Mary a former lover of Graelam's? It seemed impossible. Mary appeared so sweet, her face so gentle and innocent.

Mary's voice broke into her confused thoughts. "I

hear that Lord Graelam has wed. She is, I am told, an heiress from Brittany."

"Aye, she is from Brittany."

"I cannot but feel sorry for her," Mary said in a low voice. "I cannot imagine that Lord Graelam is an easy man."

"No, he is not," Kassia said. "Your daughter, does she resemble her father?"

"I do not believe so," Mary said after a brief pause. "Why do you ask?"

Kassia closed her eyes a moment as she whispered, "My name is Kassia de Moreton."

"I . . . I see," Mary said in a voice so low Kassia barely heard her. "Do you see such a resemblance, then? I did not want to bring her to London, but my husband said no one would notice. He assured me that Glenda looks not one whit like Graelam."

"It is not her features, but the expression when she laughed. Forgive me for making you uncomfortable. I will say nothing, I promise you."

Mary forced a smile. "Thank you. Look, Chandra is preparing to shoot!"

To Kassia's amazement, Chandra won the first round. The straw-filled circular targets stood at a distance of thirty feet. For the second round, the distance was doubled. The king won, by dint of a very lucky shot that split one of Chandra's arrows. Kassia heard Chandra's bright laughter as the targets were moved to an even greater distance.

"Sire," she cried, "you have much improved! You are at last providing me with decent competition!"

"Ho, my lady!" the king said, drawing himself up to his full giant's height. "We will see now who is the better."

"I need my husband to provide some brawn," Chandra said, shading her eyes as she looked at the distant targets.

Edward's smile lasted only until he stepped forward. His eyes narrowed in concentration and his arm was steady. His arrow arched through the air and landed near the edge of the black center of the target.

"'Tis a pity the target is so distant," Sir Jerval said to Graelam as he watched his wife prepare to shoot. "She has the eye of an eagle but not the strength for this distance."

Chandra released her arrow and it soared gracefully toward the target, landing close to Edward's.

"Well done!" Jerval shouted.

More haggling bets were laid, and Edward had to shout for silence before he took his next turn. There was a loud thud as his arrow embedded itself once again just inside the black center.

Chandra's next arrow was carried by a sudden shift of the slight breeze to the outside edge of the target.

"I can hear her cursing from here," Jerval said.

The same shifting breeze caught Edward's arrow, and it missed the target altogether.

"By all the saints," Graelam said. "I did not believe it possible!"

There was utter and complete silence as Chandra released her final arrow. It landed with a light thud near her first arrow, at the edge of the black center. Loud applause and shouting followed.

Edward grinned at her and blew her a kiss. "Forgive me, my lady," he said, and released his final arrow. It smacked in the middle of the bull's-eye, its feathered tip vibrating for some moments at the power of the shot.

"I do not suppose, sire," Chandra said, "that you will believe I allowed you to beat me?"

Edward tossed his bow to one of his men, clasped her about her slender waist, and twirled her high above his head. "My lady," he said, lowering her gently to the ground, "I would believe anything you chose to tell me!"

"You are too much the sporting winner, sire. Nay, the victory is yours."

"Jerval, you lucky hound, come and rescue your wife before I abduct her!"

Kassia saw the glint of admiration in Graelam's eyes as he watched Lady Chandra. A knot of resolve formed in her. He will look at me like that, she swore to herself. She turned about, but Mary was gone, her small daughter with her.

"I see that your bitch protectress is well-occupied," Lady Joanna said from behind Kassia.

Kassia's hand itched to slap her face, but her voice sounded quite mild. "Must you show your jealousy, Joanna? It makes your face appear quite plain, you know."

She felt a moment of satisfaction when Joanna quickly raised her hand to her face, as if to assure herself that every feature was still in place.

"Kassia!"

Graelam's dark eyes glittered with anger at Joanna, but his smile was gentle as he gazed down at his wife. "Come, Edward wishes to celebrate his victory."

She walked quietly beside him, her thoughts on the little girl, Glenda.

"Do not let her distress you," Graelam said.

"She is like a bothersome insect," Kassia said coolly. "I do not heed her."

"Then why is your face flushed?"

Kassia stopped, turned slowly, and studied her husband's face. "I met your daughter."

If she expected to see guilt ravage his features, she was doomed to disappointment. Graelam merely looked at her blankly, a black brow raised in silent question.

"Did you meet Sir Mark, a friend of Sir Jerval's?"

"Aye, but what has that to do with this daughter of mine?"

"His wife, Lady Mary, grew up with Lady Chandra. She was at Croyland when you took the castle."

Slowly memory righted itself. "It was long ago," Graelam said slowly. "A very long time ago."

"Was she your mistress?"

"Nay. I took her by force to gain Chandra's compliance."

Kassia gaped at him, shocked. "You forced a lady?"

He flushed, and it angered him. A man could do whatever he wished, without the condemnation of his damned wife! A muscle jumped in his jaw. "That is enough," he said coldly. "It was a long time ago, as I told you, and I do not wish to hear you rant at me anymore." He added, seeing the horror still in her eyes, "I am sorry for it. I was very angry at the time, and frustrated."

"As angry and frustrated as you were with me?" Kassia asked quietly.

Again his face darkened, but he did not respond. After a long moment he said stiffly, "I seem to do little that pleases you. Will this news send you plotting again to escape me?"

She shook her head.

He gave a growl of laughter. "At least you no longer protest your innocence. Do not tell me that Chandra is teaching you the value of keeping your spiteful tongue

behind your teeth? Ah, there are Sir Guy and his lovely
bride."

"You are looking well, Kassia," Guy said, briefly touching
her small hands.

"And you, Guy. Does all go well with you?"

"Aye, and soon I will be a father."

Kassia was surprised at the twisting jealousy she felt
at his words. She turned to Blanche and said quietly,
"Congratulations, Blanche. You are very . . . lucky."

Guy saw the uncertainty in his wife's eyes, and quickly
pulled her against him, hugging her close. He kissed
her cheek, whispering as he did so, "Easy, my love.
Let Graelam and Kassia see your winsome side."

"Thank you," Blanche said. Then, to her own surprise,
she smiled widely, her eyes going inadvertently
to her husband's face.

"Guy," Graelam called, "bring your conceited ass
here. I wish you to meet Sir Jerval."

Blanche gazed after her husband, shaking her head as
if to clear her thoughts. "You do not look well, Kassia,"
she said. "Joanna remarked it to me yesterday."

"Joanna remarked many things. Indeed, she dominated,
did she not, with her vicious tongue?"

"Aye," Blanche said honestly, "she did."

"Are you happy now, Blanche?"

Blanche narrowed her eyes on Kassia's face, but could
see no hidden meaning there. "A husband is a husband,"
she said, shrugging, her words sounding utterly
false even to her own ears.

"Nay, I find Guy most accommodating."

"He is *my* husband," Blanche said sharply.

"I know. Please, Blanche, I have never taken anything
of yours." Kassia did not realize that Blanche's
words were spurred by jealousy, and added, a touch of

sarcasm in her voice, "Incidentally, Dienwald de Fortenberry sends you his greetings."

Kassia heard Blanche's hissing breath, but she merely nodded and turned away.

Graelam remained occupied with his friends, and it was Rolfe who accompanied Kassia and Etta on a tour of London. So many beautiful things, she thought, fingering bolts of exquisite material. But she had no coin, and was too ashamed to admit it to Rolfe.

Late that evening Kassia lay huddled in the soft bed, wondering where Graelam was. When she at last heard the door to their bedchamber open and close, she closed her eyes tightly. She felt the bed sink under Graelam's weight, and tried to calm her breathing, to pretend sleep.

"I know you are awake, Kassia," he said, his words slightly slurred from too much ale.

"Aye," she admitted. "I am awake."

"Tell me, wife, when I left you alone with Blanche, were you again unkind to her? I saw her standing alone, her head bowed, after you so callously left her. What did you say to her, Kassia?"

She sucked in her breath. "I said nothing untoward to her!"

"Why do I not believe you?" he snarled at her softly.

Kassia could no more prevent her actions than stop the sun from rising. Lurching up, she drew back her arm and slapped him as hard as she could. He looked at her with blank surprise, then his eyes darkened in fury. She cried out and rolled off the bed. Naked, she ran toward the bedchamber door.

He caught her about the waist and jerked her around to face him. His fingers bit into her soft flesh but she made no sound. She stared numbly at his hair-covered chest and waited.

"If I thrust myself between your lovely legs, will I again find you warm and ready for me?" His voice was softly taunting.

She shook her head, afraid to speak, afraid of what would come from her mouth.

He entwined his fingers in her hair, pulling her head back.

"Will you howl your pleasure before I have scarce begun to couple with you?"

She saw the vague imprint of her palm on his cheek. "Will you strike me?" she asked.

"You deserve it," he said, his eyes falling to her small white breasts. "But no. There is a more effective punishment for you, is there not? I must simply ensure that your fear of me douses your passion."

She trembled. "You will force me again, rape me like you did poor Mary?"

"Why not?" he asked harshly, hating himself for the desire he felt for her. "I can do anything I wish with you. You are my wife."

"Please, Graelam," she whispered, trying to pull away from his searching hands, "do not hurt me."

He lifted her and carried her to the bed. "No, I will not hurt you, but neither will I allow you pleasure." He pressed her onto her stomach and spread her legs. She heard his jerking breathing, and closed her eyes against the humiliation. She knew he was staring down at her, and when his fingers touched her, she quivered and cried out softly. Suddenly he released her.

"Go to sleep," he said harshly. "I do not want you."

She curled into a ball, drawing the covers to her

chin. She felt tears sting her eyes, and quickly and angrily dashed them away.

One moment she was sleeping soundly, and the next, she was moaning softly into the darkness. Her legs were quivering with the exquisite feelings, and there was an inescapable burgeoning glow of pleasure deep within her. She felt his mouth, hot and wet, kissing her, caressing her, and both sleep and the humiliation she had felt fled her mind.

He took her, and her body dissolved into a torrent of pleasurable sensations.

Her body was utterly sated, but her thoughts tumbled in confusion. How could she respond to him so easily after what he had said and done? I am nothing but a simple fool, she thought.

29

The heavy cloak made her clumsy, but she ignored it and took another arrow from Evian. She set it in its notch and slowly drew it back until her bunched fingers touched her cheek. She released it, her eyes never leaving the target. To her immense pleasure, she heard a satisfying thud and saw the arrow embedded firmly in the straw target.

"Well done, my lady!" Evian said, clapping his hands.

She wanted to shout her own pleasure at her meager prowess. She would never be Chandra, but she had hit the target, and from twenty feet.

"I have improved, have I not?" she asked, her eyes sparkling. The boy nodded enthusiastically. Kassia saw that he was shivering with cold. "Oh, Evian," she said, "you are freezing! It is enough."

But Evian saw her gazing wistfully toward the remaining arrows in the leather quiver. "Nay, my lady," he said firmly, "you have six more arrows to shoot."

"I can see your breath even as you speak," she chided him.

"We will not have sunlight for much longer," he said, and handed her another arrow.

Rolfe rubbed his arms as he rounded the naked-branched apple trees in the orchard. Saint Peter's bones, he thought, it is getting cold! He started to speak, then stopped and watched Kassia shoot three arrows. All three hit the target firmly, one of them close to the dark blue center. He smiled ruefully, remembering his shock when Kassia had approached him during their return trip from London. She had pulled her mare in beside him, and he felt her eyes upon him, studying him.

"My lady!" he asked, turning in his saddle to face her.

"Rolfe," she said, "will you teach me to use a bow and arrow?" The words had rushed out of her mouth and he would have laughed had he not seen the intense, pleading look in her eyes. He was not stupid. His young mistress had met the exquisite Lady Chandra, had watched her with all the other nobles in her match with the king. He had been in Lord Graelam's service when he had decided he wanted to wed Chandra de Avenell, the warrior princess, as he called her. He had accompanied him to Croyland and witnessed the first success and final failure of his plan to wed the girl.

He asked very gently, "Why do you wish to learn a man's skill, my lady?"

Her eyes fell for a moment; then that resolute little chin of hers rose defiantly. "I wish to be complete," she said. She knew it odd of her to speak thus to her husband's master-at-arms, but she did not have a choice.

She doubted he would help her if she was not honest with him.

He pondered her words for a long moment. "A lady such as you is complete. You manage a great keep, help Blount with the accounts—aye, he told me that—direct the preparation of meals that keep our bellies happy, and play an amazing game of chess."

"It is not enough," she said quietly. He saw the flash of pain in her fine eyes, and wished for a moment that he could kick his master off his destrier and pound some sense into his thick head.

Rolfe said finally, hoping his young mistress wouldn't take offense, "She was nothing more than a dream, spun in my lord's imagination and fed by the minstrel's foolish songs. I doubt that she has acquired your skills, my lady."

Kassia did not pretend to misunderstand him. "She is all that Graelam wants and admires, Rolfe. Nay, please do not look away from me. I must speak what is in my mind. He told me about her, of course, when I asked him. He spoke of her honor, of her honesty, and of her amazing skills as a warrior. In his eyes, Rolfe, I have none of those things. Perhaps if I acquire some skill, the other qualities will follow." She lowered her head a moment and Rolfe saw her clench the reins tightly in her small hands. "I must do something!"

But not mold yourself into Lady Chandra's elusive image, he thought. "In most of the men's eyes, my lady, you are all that is good and honest and honorable. Very few believe that you betrayed Graelam."

"He does," she said harshly.

Rolfe said honestly, before he could stop himself, "He is a fool, particularly when it concerns a woman."

"He is also my husband. If I cannot change his thinking, it is likely that I will betray him and return to my father. I cannot bear the pain of it, you see."

Rolfe sucked in his breath in anger. He wanted to demand if Graelam had beaten her, but he could not. Even speaking to her so honestly was improper.

"He knows great anger at me." She gave him a sad smile. "I do not blame him for what he believes. Sometimes I wonder if I did not imagine it all."

Rolfe looked between his horse's ears, wishing yet again that he could beat some sense into his ruthless master's head. To his surprise, he saw Graelam turn in his saddle, a look of suspicion narrowing his dark eyes. My God, Rolfe thought, startled, he is jealous! Of me, an old man! He thoughtfully chewed his lower lip. "My lady," he said finally, smiling at her, "I will teach you."

"Graelam must not know of it."

"Nay, he will not know, not until you have the skill to impress him."

"Thank you, Rolfe!" She gave him a radiant smile, and he was stunned at the pure sweet beauty of her face.

Rolfe waited now until she had shot her final arrow, then strode forward. He could see his breath in the still, cold air. Fallen leaves crunched under his booted feet. He worried that she would catch a fever, standing for so long in the silent winter afternoon. But he also knew that to say so would wipe the pleasure off her face. He said evenly, "You must hold your right arm more stiffly. Here, let me show you."

He helped her until he felt the cold seep through his thick clothes. She must be freezing, he thought, and stepped back from her. "That is enough, my lady. My old bones need the warmth of a fire."

"And some hot ale!" Kassia exclaimed happily. "For you too, Evian."

Evian tucked her bow and the leather quiver beneath his arm, as if it were he who was practicing so faithfully. Rolfe had told him only that his lady's practice was to be a surprise for Lord Graelam.

Kassia entered the great hall, a pleased smile still on her face. She drew up abruptly at the sight of Graelam, his arms crossed over his chest, watching her. He had returned the evening before from a visit to Crandall. He had not asked her to accompany him, and she had said nothing. It had given her nearly a week to practice without worrying if he would come upon her. She felt a deep, lurching pleasure as she stared at him. He looked vigorous, and splendidly male, his thick black hair tousled around his head. Her face became a careful blank at his harshly asked question.

"Where have you been?"

Her eyes fell. He had been so busy with Blount. It had not occurred to her that he would miss her, and she had practiced but an hour.

"Would you care for some mulled wine, my lord?" she asked carefully.

"What I would care for, my lady, is an answer from you."

She raised her chin. "I was walking in the orchard."

She saw the blatant distrust in his eyes, and hastened to add, "Evian was with me. I am thinking about planting some . . . pear trees in the spring."

Graelam wondered why she was lying to him. Pear trees, for God's sake! "Come and warm yourself," he said, his voice roughening with concern. "Your nose is red with cold."

She obeyed him willingly after she had given orders for some mulled wine.

"Sir Walter," she said, relieved that Graelam did not question her further, "how fares he at Crandall?" It was difficult to keep the dislike from her voice.

"He is a bit overbearing with the peasants, but I doubt not that he will settle in."

Kassia had hoped that Sir Walter would show his true colors to Graelam, but it appeared that he hadn't yet. She said, "Did Blount show you the message from the Duke of Cornwall?"

"Aye, and it worries me. All his talk about growing old! One would think that with Edward safely on the throne, the duke would relax a bit and enjoy life."

"He has no more responsibilities to keep him young. It would seem, as you have said, that once the heavy burdens are lifted, a man could enjoy his peace. But it is not so. Sometimes I think that Geoffrey and his threats of treachery keep my father healthy, though I pray it is not true."

"Let us hope that your father has enough to keep him busy during the winter. If Geoffrey plans something, he will not execute it until spring."

"How I pray that Geoffrey will forget his disappointment! I cannot bear the thought of Belleterre being threatened." She moved closer to the huge fireplace and stared into the leaping flames. Her father and Belleterre had been the two constants in her life. Geoffrey had always seemed but a mild nuisance. Belleterre and her father were her refuge, even now, if Graelam no longer wanted her. Two tears spilled onto her cheeks and trailed quickly downward. She did not have the energy to brush them away.

"Stop crying," Graelam said. "You are not a child, Kassia, and there is no reason to worry about Geoffrey."

His tone sounded harsh and cruel to his own ears. Oddly enough, he understood vaguely what she was feeling. He cursed softly when she raised her face and looked at him with such hopelessness.

He gathered her into his arms, pressing her face against his warm tunic. "Hush," he said more gently, his strong fingers kneading the taut muscles in her slender shoulders.

He felt a surge of desire for her. He well understood lust, but what he felt for Kassia was tempered with other emotions, deep, swirling emotions that he was loath to examine. Damn her, he thought, holding her more tightly. He had bedded several serving wenches during his stay at Crandall, hoping that the next one would give him release and wipe Kassia's image from his mind. But after his stark passion had peaked and receded he had lain awake staring into the darkness even as the woman who had pleasured him lay sleeping blissfully beside him.

He felt the delicate bones in her shoulders, so fragile beneath his strong fingers. He closed his eyes, breathing in the sweet scent of her. No other woman smelled like her, he thought somewhat foolishly. He lowered his head and rubbed his cheek against her soft hair. Lavender, he thought. She smells of lavender. His hands dropped lower, cupping her hips. He felt her stiffen. He gave a low, mocking laugh and pushed her away from him. His voice was a familiar taunt. "I will not take you here, my lady. Dry your tears and see to our evening meal."

Kassia brushed away her tears, cursing herself for desiring his strength and his comfort even for a moment. "Aye, my lord," she said quietly, and left him. She smiled and spoke throughout the long evening, seeing to Graelam's needs, while wishing that she could creep away someplace and shroud herself in the bleakness of her spirit. She listened to him speak to his men, listened to him laugh as they traded jests. He had not touched her the night before, and she knew that he would take her this night. She wanted him to take her, she realized, make her forget, if only for a moment. But not in anger. Not as a punishment.

She excused herself and went to their bedchamber. It took her some time to rid herself of Etta. She bathed in hot scented water, forcing herself to accept the conclusion she had fought against for so long. Pride and truth yield but empty misery. She thought of all her practice with the bow and arrow, and laughed aloud at her foolishness. Perhaps Graelam would admire her, but likely it would not bring him to trust her, to believe in her. Only a lie would change how he treated her.

When Graelam entered much later, she was lying in their bed propped up against the pillows.

"I had expected you to be asleep," he said as he stripped off his clothes.

She smoothed the bedcovers under her shaking hands. "Nay," she said quietly. "I have missed you," she blurted out.

His heat shot up. She saw the gleam of pleasure in his dark eyes before he quickly made his expression impassive. "Why?" he asked bluntly.

He stood by the bed, naked, his eyes intent upon her face.

"I do not want strife between us, Graelam," she whispered, trying not to gaze so hungrily at his body.

But she failed, and he knew it. "You know what I

demand from you," he said as he slipped into bed beside her.

"Aye, I know." *Do not cry, you stupid fool!* "You said you would forgive me."

"I will forgive you," he said, his voice flat and cold.

"Then it was as you believe."

He felt a searing wave of contempt at himself, and a surge of disappointment as well. He had wanted her to admit her quilt, admit that she had hired Dienwald de Fortenberry and given him the necklace, but facing the fact of her doing it made him almost physically ill. He rose on his elbow beside her and gazed down into her pale face. He saw tears shimmering in her eyes.

"I told you I would forgive you if you but spoke the truth. Why do you cry?"

I am so lonely! I cannot bear my loneliness! I will gladly take whatever part of you you wish to give me.

She could think of nothing to say to him. With a small, helpless cry, she flung herself against him, wrapping her arms about his back and burrowing her face against his shoulder.

"So," he said, his bitterness sounding in his voice, "it is my body you wish." He felt her soft mouth pressing light kisses against his chest.

"Please," she whispered, "no more anger. I can bear no more anger from you."

"It is not anger I feel for you now, Kassia. I will give you your woman's pleasure, and we will speak no more about the past." He gently pressed her onto her back and drew the covers down to her waist. Her heart was pounding so loudly she thought he must hear it. She felt his eyes roving over her body, and it both alarmed and excited her.

"Your breasts seem fuller," he said. Very gently he

stroked a fingertip around a pink nipple. She sucked in her breath.

"You do not find me . . . too skinny?"

Oh no, he thought, stifling an angry laugh. I find you all that I want. "You are fine," he said. He lowered his head and gently kissed her. His hand slipped under the covers and began kneading her soft belly. "I like the feel of you."

"Please, Graelam," she gasped, lurching upward as his fingers probed lower.

His fingers touched her soft, moist swollen flesh. "You are so delicate," he said into her mouth. "And you are ready for me." She felt his fingers deepen their primitive rhythm.

Kassia was shuddering with need. "Please, love me. I cannot bear it."

To her surprise, Graelam rolled onto his back and brought her with him. "I would have you ride me," he said, laughing softly at her uncertain expression.

She felt him deep inside her, felt his hands about her waist, lifting her and lowering her. "Draw up your legs," he instructed her. "You may move over me as you wish."

Kassia had never imagined that such feelings could come from her body. When his fingers found her, she lost all hold on reason and cried out, her head thrown back, her back arched.

She vaguely heard him gasp her name, felt his fingers tense over her even as her body convulsed in the almost painful pleasure. He was deep inside her when she felt his seed filling her. She fell forward, her mind emptied of all regret and pain, holding now only the aftermath of complete belonging.

Graelam held her close to him and gently straightened her legs. She fell asleep, covering his body, her hand nestled in the hollow of his throat. He stroked her tousled hair and tried to close his mind to its tortured thoughts.

It is not enough, Kassia thought, aware yet again that Graelam was watching her, his expression brooding. He wants to hate me, but his honor keeps him to his promise. She wanted to shriek and cry at the same time, but she could not. She had done it to herself, and must now live with it.

He continued to be kind to her. At night she could imagine that he loved her as he gently took her body. She was so aware of him that if his eyes darkened, her body leapt in response. And he knew it. She wondered if he hated her for that too.

It is time to concentrate, Kassia, she told herself. She urged Bluebell forward into a gentle gallop, drew back the bow, and released the arrow at the target. It hit the center, and she turned in the saddle at Evian's shout of congratulation.

They were on the beach, a good mile from Wolffeton. She did not want to take the chance that Graelam would come by chance upon her. In this, she would surprise him. He would be pleased with her prowess. He must be pleased. It was the only thing that kept her practicing so diligently.

But he had missed her. She immediately saw the distrust and anger in his eyes.

"You plan more trees for the orchard?" he asked her, watching her dismount from Bluebell's back.

Her chin rose. "Nay, my lord," she said brightly. "I plan a surprise for you!"

His eyes narrowed. "Explain yourself."

She shook her head, forcing teasing laughter from her throat. "Nay, my lord. You must wait!"

"I promised to forgive you the past, not the present," he said.

She could only stare at him. "But I have done nothing to displease you."

"Have you not?" he asked, then turned on his heel and left her.

If she had had a rock in her hand, she would have hurled it at his back. "I will show you," she hissed between her teeth.

Three days later, on a bright, cold afternoon, Kassia calmly planned to surprise him. She felt excited, hopeful, and proud of herself.

30

"Rolfe! You promised!"

Rolfe scratched his head, wishing suddenly he was anywhere but here at Wolffeton. "I don't think it is a good idea," he said lamely, no match for the pleading in her eyes.

"But Graelam will be surprised and . . . pleased. You know he must be, Rolfe." *I will be just like Lady Chandra and he will admire me,* she added silently to herself. *If naught else, that must be true.* "You said yourself that I have improved beyond all your expectations. You have already arranged the competition."

"Aye, I have," he said helplessly. "I will probably be hanged for a fool."

"Mayhap," she said, ignoring his words, "the minstrels will hear about me and write their *chansons* to praise my prowess."

"I don't know what will come of this," Rolfe grumbled.

What will come of this is that Graelam will admire me. Perhaps he will even come to truly care for me, a small, wistful voice said.

"I must change my clothes." She lowered her voice to a conspiratorial whisper. "Do not forget what you will say to my lord!"

Rolfe watched her run up the stairs into the great hall. He scuffed the toe of his leather boot against a cobblestone and cursed softly.

"So, Rolfe," Graelam said with some amusement to his master-at-arms as they walked side by side toward the practice field, "do you also expect me to give a prize to the winner?"

"The men have practiced hard," Rolfe said in a neutral voice. "Some sort of recognition from you would not be amiss."

"Then I shall think of something." Graelam shaded his eyes and gazed over the course. "You are lucky it hasn't rained in a week," he said. "The targets are arranged wide apart," he continued, scanning the course. "I think most of the men will complete it with a perfect score. Why is it so easy?"

So your lady won't break her neck! "The men competing have little practice in shooting their arrows from horseback," he said smoothly. "I wanted to be as fair as possible to them."

Graelam cocked a thick black brow at him. "I believe you grow soft in your old age," he remarked. He saw his men lined up on the far side of the course, drawing lots to determine the order. He moved into position beside Rolfe, waiting for the competition to begin.

Rolfe saw him glance back toward the keep and wondered if his master was looking for his wife.

"Kassia takes great pleasure in surprising the men," Graelam said, as if in answer to Rolfe's thoughts. "I wonder if she will bring the winner a tray of pastries."

Rolfe grunted, his eyes on Kassia, dressed in boy's clothes, sitting proudly astride a bay stallion. She was wearing a short mantle that fastened with a broach over her right shoulder, its hood drawn up and clipped securely over her chestnut curls. It had not occurred to either of them until the day before that Graelam would immediately recognize Bluebell if she rode her mare in the competition. Thus the bay stallion, Ganfred. Rolfe watched the stallion prance sideways, and closed his eyes in a silent prayer. The horse was not as placid and obedient as Bluebell, and Kassia had ridden him but once. She had not seemed at all concerned, but Rolfe was not deceived.

"Only eight men to compete?" Graelam asked, turning to Rolfe. "Have I counted aright?"

The other men had moved away to take positions along the course. The truth was out. "Aye, 'tis primarily the men who have not done much of this." Indeed, he had handpicked the men who would not make Kassia look like a complete graceless child. Most of them were big men, clumsy with a bow, men who were trained to the lance and mace.

"I imagine," Graelam said acidly, "that I am about to be most impressed," for he had begun to recognize the men, even from this distance. "I did not know that Joseph even knew how to notch an arrow."

"He has been practicing," Rolfe said. "Come, my lord, I believe they are ready to begin."

They had erected a small dais, wide enough for only two men. Graelam jumped into it and gave Rolfe a hand.

He turned at a shout and watched the first man, Arnold, ride into the course, his bow aimed at the first target. The arrow struck the target with more strength than accuracy, and Graelam shook his head. By the time Arnold had completed the course he had managed to hit the bull's-eye on six of the twelve targets.

There was much good-natured laughing and cheering from the men.

"Arnold the ox!"

"He'll eat the targets he missed for his dinner!"

"Most fascinating," Graelam said sarcastically to Rolfe. "I grow more excited by the minute."

The next two men did no better than Arnold, and Graelam was beginning to believe that Rolfe had arranged this ridiculous competition as a jest. He started to say as much to his master-at-arms, but Rolfe was staring fixedly toward the next rider.

Graelam did not recognize the man—boy, rather, he quickly amended to himself. But the stallion, Ganfred, was from his stable.

"At least the lad shows more ability than the rest," he said, watching the boy draw his bow smoothly back and gently release the arrow. It hit the center. He frowned. "Who is he, Rolfe? A new fledgling you wish to take under your wing?"

"He does well," Rolfe said, trying to postpone the moment of reckoning as long as possible. "Look, my lord, another bull's-eye!"

Rolfe felt himself swell with pride. She was doing well, despite the problems she was having with the stallion. By the end of the course, she had struck nine bull's-eyes out of twelve.

"The boy is undersized," Graelam said, watching him ride back to the far side of the field. "I begin to believe that you arranged this competition just to make him look good. You gave him Ganfred to ride? Who is he, Rolfe?"

"My lord, look! Here is Bran!"

Graelam shot a sideways glance at Rolfe. Something was brewing. He decided to wait and see and simply enjoy himself in the meanwhile. The wiry, graceless Bran made Arnold look like a master archer. Graelam joined the laughter as Bran finished the course, smiling widely, showing the huge space between his front teeth.

"I will challenge any jongleurs to beat this act!" Graelam said.

Perhaps, Rolfe thought, he shouldn't have picked such utter dolts to compete. Even if Lady Kassia won, it wouldn't be much of a victory. He realized that the men competing had, of course, recognized her, for their performance became even worse. All the men were very fond of her, and were shielding her. He saw the men whispering to each other, passing the word along, and he realized that he had made a grave mistake in allowing this. Graelam would skin him alive.

He cleared his throat nervously. "The lad appears to have won the first round, my lord," he said as the men slapped Kassia on the back, congratulating her. "The men will pair up in the second round and compete for the targets."

"I can barely contain my excitement," Graelam said dryly.

Rolfe saw that Kassia was paired with Bran, the worst of the lot. He waited until the two of them rode toward the first target, jockeying for position as they drew close.

"The lad, my lord," he said, touching Graelam's sleeve to gain his attention, "he did win the first round."

"Aye, and he does not do so badly in this one. But he had better watch Bran's horse. The brute hates Ganfred."

Rolfe drew in his breath in consternation. The plan had been to have Kassia ride smartly up to her husband, pull back her hood, and demand the prize from him. He watched helplessly as Bran's horse reared up, kicking his hind legs at Ganfred just as Kassia, as vulnerable as possible, raised her bow to shoot at a target.

"We must stop this!" Rolfe shouted.

"Why? You are growing soft as an old man, Rolfe. Let's see how much talent the lad does have."

"The lad, my lord, is your wife! She did not ride Ganfred until yesterday!"

"You are mad," Graelam said between his teeth. "The jest goes too far, Rolfe."

But Rolfe had jumped from the dais and was running toward the course, waving his hands. The men had quieted, watching Bran try unsuccessfully to rein in his mount. The stallion, his eyes rolling with challenge, bit Ganfred on the neck, reared again, and smashed his hooves into Ganfred's sides.

Graelam was running, all thought frozen. Fear coursed through him, raw and cold. He watched helplessly as Kassia's bow and arrow went flying from her hands to the ground. He saw her desperately try to pull away from the maddened stallion, but she did not have the strength to control him. Ganfred turned on the other horse and attacked.

"Kassia, jump off!" He heard his own shout, knowing it was lost in the shouts of his men.

Kassia was not afraid, she was furious. She must have been born under an unlucky star. "Bran, pull the beast away!" she cried out. When Ganfred reared up and attacked, she realized that all had gone awry. She struggled to bring the huge stallion under control, but it was no use. She felt Ganfred jerk the reins from her ineffectual hands at the same time she heard Graelam shout at her.

But she knew if she jumped she might be crushed under the horses' hooves. She hung on, clutching frantically at Ganfred's mane.

"Bran," she croaked, "pull him away!"

Ganfred gave a mighty heave, rearing up again to attack, but the other stallion was running away. He snorted in fury and dashed after him. Kassia lost her hold. She realized that she should roll once she hit the ground, but when the hard earth crashed against her side she was stunned, unable to move, the breath knocked from her.

She lay perfectly still, trying to clear her wits and regain her breath.

"Kassia!"

She looked up to see Graelam above her. "It is not fair," she panted. "I would have won! It is not fair!"

He dropped to his knees beside her, his hands roving methodically over her body. "Can you move your legs?"

"Aye," she whispered, feeling suddenly dizzy and nauseous. "Graelam, I would have won!"

His hands were bending her arms, then prodding at her belly.

She sucked in her breath, not wanting to retch. That would be the ultimate humiliation. She saw the shadows of the men above her, heard them talking.

Graelam clasped his hands about her shoulders. "Kassia," he said, gently pulling her up. "Look at me. Can you see me?"

"Of course," she said. "I am all right."

Graelam lifted her gently into his arms. "The competition is over," he said harshly to the men.

She closed her eyes against the waves of dizziness,

her head falling back against his arm. "I was not afraid," she muttered. "If it had not been for that wretched horse . . ."

"Hush," Graelam said. He carried her to their bed-chamber, shouting for Etta. After laying her on the bed, he gently straightened her legs. She closed her eyes tightly, and he saw the tensing around her mouth.

He felt utterly helpless.

"My baby!" Etta scurried to the bed, ignoring Graelam as she sat beside her mistress.

"I am going to be sick, Etta," Kassia whispered.

When the spasms passed, she lay pale and weak. Her head ached, but the waves of dizziness were growing less.

"I will prepare her a potion, my lord," Etta said, and slowly rose.

"Will she be all right?" Graelam asked harshly.

"I trust so," Etta said. "It is just that—"

"Just what?"

"Naught of importance," Etta muttered, and hastened from the bedchamber.

Graelam sat beside his wife, took her small hand in his, and noticed the calluses on the pads of her fingers for the first time. His wrenching fear was lessening. But he said nothing, merely watched her pale face for signs of pain.

Kassia opened her eyes and looked into her husband's worried face. "I would have won," she repeated, sounding a litany.

"Why did you do it?" he asked, his grip tightening on her hand.

"I wanted to make you admire me as you do Lady Chandra," she said simply. "I thought if I won you would be pleased."

"I do not want my wife aping men!"

His words cut through her, and she stared up at him, hopelessness in her eyes. "I wanted only to gain your approval, to make you proud of me. I could think of nothing else to make you care for me, to make you forget that you so dislike me."

Graelam said nothing. Guilt flooded him. "I do not dislike you," he said finally. "But what you did was foolish beyond permission."

"Please do not blame Rolfe," she whispered. "Nor any of the men. They could not have known that Bran's stallion would attack Ganfred."

He wanted to bash all their heads in, but he saw the pleading in her eyes and said, "Very well." He gently unfastened the brooch and pulled off her mantle. "You will likely be sore for a while from your fall." He fell silent, then smiled at her ruefully. "Compared to the dolts in the competition, you did very well indeed. This was my surprise?"

She nodded. "They were not real competition," she said, rallying. "Rolfe did not believe I could gain your attention if I went against the better men. He did not want me to look bad."

"You did not look bad. Did Lady Chandra give you this idea?"

"Nay, not really, though she showed me how to handle a bow. She is so beautiful."

"Kassia," he said very gently, "I wanted her, I told you that. But I did not love her. There was no reason for you to be jealous of her skills." He lightly touched his palm to her forehead, and relaxed. She felt cool to the touch. "Kassia," he continued after a moment, "does it matter so much to you what I think?"

She gazed at him, remembering that she had once

told him she loved him. Had he simply disregarded her words? Believed that she was telling but another lie? And now, of course, since she had admitted that she had lied to him, he would likely believe nothing she said. She said only, "Aye, it matters to me."

"There has been much between us," he bagan, only to break off as Etta came into the bedchamber. He moved aside and watched her give Kassia the vile smelling potion.

Etta straightened. "She will sleep now, my lord. I did not know what she planned, else I would never have allowed her to do it. I pray that she will be all right."

"I will stay with her until she sleeps," he said. "I will call you if she worsens, Etta."

He took her hand in his and stroked his fingers over her soft flesh. Her lashes fluttered and closed. He listened to her breathing as it evened into a drugged sleep.

He undressed her, smiling whimsically at the boy's clothes. Gently he eased her beneath the covers, pulling them to her chin. He found himself studying her, comparing her to Chandra. There was, he decided, no comparison at all, and he was pleased.

Kassia slept the afternoon away, awakening briefly in the evening. She felt oddly heavy, and dull.

"It is the potion Etta gave you," Graelam told her. "I fear that you must rest a few days before you again take up your bow and arrow."

"You do not mind?"

"Nay," he said, smiling at her. "In fact, I will give you better competition than poor Bran. The fellow is frantic with worry. You must get well and reassure him."

"Aye, I will." She fell asleep again, hope filling her at his words.

She awoke to darkness, her throat dry and scratchy. She slipped from the bed and made her way slowly to the carafe of water on the table. She reached for the water, only to whip her hand to her belly at a sudden fierce pain. She felt wet stickiness gushing from her body. She looked at herself, not understanding, then doubled over as another cramping pain ripped through her. She cried out.

Graelam heard her cry and bounded out of the bed. He quickly lit a candle and strode toward her.

"Kassia, what is it?"

"Graelam, help me! I'm bleeding!" She gasped as another pain clutched at her.

He saw the streaks of crimson on her white chemise, the rivulets of blood flowing down her legs. Her monthly flow, he thought blankly. No, it was not that. He felt a searing fear turn his guts cold.

He grabbed her to him. Her hands clutched at his shoulders, and she stiffenend with another cramp. "Help me," she whimpered. "What is happening to me?"

He knew then that she was miscarrying a babe. He heard himself saying to her quite calmly, "You will be all right, Kassia. Let me help you into bed. I will get Etta."

He lifted her gently into his arms and laid her on the bed. She stared up at him, her eyes wide with fear.

"You will be all right," he repeated, more for himself than for her. "Do not move."

She watched him stride to the door, jerk it open, and bellow for Etta.

Etta paid no heed to Lord Graelam's nakedness. She was panting with exertion, still pulling on her bedrobe.

"Blood," Graelam told her. "I fear she is losing a babe. Is she with child?"

Etta felt the blood drain from her face. "Aye," she whispered. She looked down at Kassia, saw her mistress lying in a pool of blood, and uttered a distressed cry. "Oh, my baby," she said, clutching at Kassia's hand.

"What can I do?" Graelam asked from behind her.

Etta pulled herself together. "Clean cloths, my lord, and hot water. We must make certain she does not bleed her life away."

Graelam turned immediately, pausing only when he heard Etta call after him, "My lord, your bedrobe!"

31

"You knew she was with child?"

Etta's kind face contorted with pain. "Aye, I knew, my lord, and I was going to tell her if she did not come to the knowledge soon."

"It is a pity that you did not tell before she played the man today."

"You had no knowledge of it, my lord?"

Graelam made a slashing motion with his hand. It was on the tip of his tongue to shout at her that he was a man and paid no heed to women's concerns. But he held himself quiet. It should have occurred to him that she had had no monthly flow. And had he not noticed that her breasts seemed fuller?

"How far along was she?" he asked instead.

"Early days," Etta said. "Two months, I should say."

He looked down at his wife, asleep now from another potion Etta had given her. She was so pale that her face looked as if it had been drained of blood. Her chemise, stained with streaks of crimson, lay wrapped in cloths on the floor. He swallowed convulsively. "She will be all right?"

"Aye, the bleeding is stopped." Etta rubbed her gnarled hands together helplessly. "I should have told her. I thought that since she was now a married lady, and you a man of experience, she would realize that—"

Graelam cut her off. He felt impotent and angry. "I married a child," he said harshly. "How could anyone expect her to know a woman's function?"

"She has had other concerns of late, my lord," Etta said, looking directly at him.

"Aye, riding astride and learning men's sports!"

"'Twas not her fault," Etta said steadily.

"I do not suppose that she finally admitted to you that she lied? About everything?"

"My lady does not lie, my lord."

Graelam gave a snorting laugh. "Little you know her. It matters not now. Go to bed. I will call you if she awakens."

Etta gave him a long look, tempted to tell him he was a fool, but she saw the pain in his dark eyes and held her tongue. He did care for Kassia, she thought, but how much? She shuffled from the chamber, her bones creaking with tiredness.

Kassia awoke, blinking into the bright sunlight that streaked into the bedchamber. Memory flooded back and she tensed, waiting for the terrible pain, but there was none. She felt tired and sore, as if her body had been bludgeoned. She smiled wryly, remembering well that it had. But the blood. What had happened to her?

"Here, drink this."

She turned her head slowly on the pillow at the sound of her husband's voice. She felt his hand slip behind her head to lift her, and sipped the sweet-tasting brew.

"How do you feel?" Graelam asked as he carefully eased her down again.

She gave him a wan smile. "I feel as though you must have beaten me, my lord. But I do not understand. All the blood, the pain in my belly."

"You lost our . . . a babe."

She stared up at him blankly. "I was with child?" At his nod, she felt herself grow cold. She whispered brokenly, "I did not know. Oh no!"

Tears filled her eyes and fell onto her cheeks, but she did not have the strength to dash them away.

Graelam wiped them away with the corner of the bedcover. He wanted to comfort her, but bitterness flowed through him and he said coldly, "I daresay even your mentor, Chandra, knew enough to curb her men's sports when she was with child."

The unfairness of his words numbed her. Did he believe that she lied about not knowing? Did he believe that she had willfully endangered their babe? It was too much. She slowly turned her face away from him and closed her eyes tightly against the damnable tears. I will weep no more, she told herself. "Perhaps," she said so softly that he had to lean closer to hear her, "it would have been best had I died."

Graelam sucked in his breath. "Do not speak nonsense," he said sharply. "There will be other babes."

Would there? she wondered silently.

"You will not blame Rolfe? He did not know, I swear it."

"I am not a monster," he said coldly, forgetting for a moment the tongue-lashing he had given his master-at-arms. "You must rest now and regain your strength.

Your nurse is hovering outside to attend you. I will see you later."

She watched him stride toward the door, so powerful, so unyielding. He did not look back at her.

The evening meal Etta served her was temptingly prepared for an invalid's flagging appetite.

"Come now, my baby. The cook made the stewed beef especially for you, using the herbs and spices just as you taught him. And here is hot, freshly baked bread with honey."

Kassia ate. When she was too exhausted to lift the spoon, she leaned back against the fluffed pillows. "Where is Lord Graelam?"

"In the hall," Etta said carefully, eyeing her mistress. "Everyone is very worried about you. Poor Rolfe was ready to kill Bran."

"'Twas not Bran's fault," Kassia said, closing her eyes. "He blames me," she said flatly after a long, silent moment.

Etta did not pretend to misunderstand her. "Your lord is most concerned for your welfare," she began.

"Do not spin tales, Etta. He believes a wife's only worth is in breeding children. I was stupid, and forgot that."

"You will carry another child, my baby. I could see no harm done."

"Aye, it is my duty to do something my lord approves of," she said dully. "I will not be so stupid as to want something more—ever again."

"You will cease this silly talk!" Etta said sharply, her brow furrowed with worry. "'Tis a man's kingdom," she continued after a moment, searching for the right words. " 'Tis men who rule, men who make the rules."

"Aye, and it is a woman's duty to give birth to more

of them so they may subjugate the lot who have the misfortune to be born girls!"

Etta tried frantically to think of something soothing to say, for Kassia was becoming flushed. Her thinking halted abruptly at the sound of Lord Graelam's voice. Oh my God, she thought frantically, how much had he heard?

"You speak the truth, my lady, but your words are overly harsh and bitter. Men rule because they are the only ones fit to do so. A woman does have worth, you are right, for men cannot continue unless women birth them."

"Now I have no worth," Kassia said matter-of-factly. She felt oddly devoid of feeling, and blessedly numb.

"I did not say that," Graelam said evenly. "I trust only that you now will see to your woman's duties."

She looked at him straight, all hope in her quashed, and said very calmly, "If I but knew how to get a message to Dienwald de Fortenberry, I should be tempted to offer him that wretched necklace to take me away. That would please you. 'Tis a pity that Blanche is no longer here to wed you."

He clenched his teeth, feeling a muscle in his jaw jump convulsively. "But you do know how to reach Dienwald de Fortenberry, do you not?"

"My lord," Etta said, rising to face him, "she is overly tired and knows not what she says. She must have rest!"

Graelam smiled grimly, remembering how he had come to comfort her, to spend time with her while she mended. But her drawing words had wrenched anger from him. "I will leave her to your tender ministrations," he said, and left the chamber.

"You must not say things like that," Etta scolded her gently.

"Why? It matters not, Etta. Nothing matters, not anymore."

The inked quill hovered over the parchment, but she knew she could not write to her father of the despair in her heart. She inquired after his health and the winter weather in Brittany, then detailed inanely all the household improvements she had made. She did not ask him about Geoffrey, knowing that if he were to plan anything, her father would send a message to Graelam, not her. She wrote nothing of the lost babe or the state of calm indifference that existed between her and Graelam. She had just finished sprinkling sand on the parchment when Blount entered the small chamber.

"You write your father, my lady?"

"Aye, 'tis done, Blount."

He looked at her and then down at the parchment. "My lord will read what you have written, my lady," he reminded her in gentle warning.

She took his meaning well, but merely smiled wearily at him. "I know. There is naught within to anger him." She rose and shook out the skirt of her wool gown. "Indeed, it is so boring, perhaps my lord will think it useless to send." She walked slowly to the small window and drew back the wooden shutters. "It does not feel like the end of February. There is the sweet smell of spring in the air."

"Aye, 'tis uncommonly warm today." Blount eyed his mistress, worry drawing a deep furrow in his brow. "Why do you not ride out, my lady?" he suggested gently.

"Perhaps I shall," Kassia said, turning. "Aye, 'tis a good idea."

Though the weather was mild, Kassia dressed warmly, choosing a velvet mantle lined with miniver. A month, she thought, walking slowly to the stables, a month waging a war without fighting. She smiled grimly. She should be used to it by now. During her short marriage she had endured more bitter than sweet, and now the bitter seemed unending. She greeted servants and Graelam's man-at-arms, all of whom, had she but noticed, held sympathy in their eyes.

Bran was in the stables. At the sight of her his face turned pale and he rushed to her. "My lady, you must forgive me! Those damned horses, and 'twas all my fault!"

Kassia raised a hand. "You will not blame yourself, Bran. 'Twas my decision to compete and my decision not to ride my mare. No, say no more. It is over and best forgotten. I am well again. Indeed, I am riding out now to enjoy the lovely weather."

No one tried to stop her. She waved to the porter, but did not slow Bluebell's gentle canter. The sky was a vivid blue with fleecy clouds drifting slowly overhead. The slight breeze grew stiffer the closer she drew to the sea. She threw back her head and breathed in the crisp, salty scent of the water. She guided Bluebell down the rocky path to the small cove, the place where Graelam had taken her so slowly, and held her so gently. No, she would not think of that. She slid from Bluebell's back and tethered her to a bare-branched yew bush that thrust out of a rocky crevice.

Kassia walked along the beach, watching the water slowly rise closer as the tide came in. It was so peaceful here. If only, she thought, raking her hand through her hair, she could know this peace all of the time. She sat down on an outjutting boulder, tucking her feet beneath her to protect them from the encroaching waves that pounded against the lower rocks, spewing white mist upward. Her mind flitted to many things, always returning to Graelam and the bitterness of her life with him. She accepted that she loved him, knowing she was a fool to do so, but unable to change the feelings that seemed so deeply embedded within her. He would always blame her for losing the babe. After all, what else was she good for? She gave vent to a mirthless laugh. She should not allow herself to forget what excellent meals he and his men now enjoyed.

And he would always believe her guilty of trying to escape him and of freeing Dienwald. After all, had she not stupidly admitted guilt to him? All to spare further anger, further recriminations. What a fool she had been! Dienwald. His face formed in her mind and she did not allow it to fade. Peace, she thought; she could hope for nothing more now. Brittany and her father. The irony of this thought made her smile bitterly. She rose slowly to her feet and shook out her velvet mantle. Her idea burgeoned and she nourished it, not thinking for the moment how she would accomplish it. Her slender shoulders straightened and her chin rose with new determination. She thought of the barbaric necklace, and laughter gurgled from her throat. If Blanche could manage it, then so could she!

Graelam read the message from the Duke of Cornwall, bidding him to come to him. He frowned, for the duke gave no indication of any urgency. Damn, he was a warrior, trained to fight. Affairs in England had been more interesting when he was a lad. Aye, he would even be pleased were one of his neighbors to try some mischief. He sighed, wondering what the duke wanted. He decided to leave immediately, for there was nothing to hold him here. Having made his decision, he called Rolfe, gave instructions, then went in search of Kassia. She was not in their bedchamber, nor could he find her in any of the outbuildings. He saw Bran approach him and paused.

"My lord," the man began, "I hear you search for Lady Kassia. She went riding, I know not where."

Graelam felt his jaw tighten, for he had given orders to Osbert that she was never to ride out without his permission. The man had obviously disobeyed him. He was on the point of striding to the stable when he saw Kassia's still face in his mind. She was not foolish enough to ride from his lands. Let her mend, he thought, let her regain her health and her spirit. When he returned from the Duke of Cornwall's, he would go more gently with her. She had not, after all, known she was with child; though she had been foolish . . . Here his thinking stopped. She had tried to impress him, believing he would admire her if she could be like Chandra. He felt a gnawing pain, and flinched from it. It made him feel uncomfortable, because it made him feel uncertain about himself and what he wanted. A man who was soft with women was weak and despicable. He shrugged, forcing his mind to picture her lovely body, the silkiness of her flesh, the warmth of her when he was deep within her. He would once again enjoy her in his bed and see her smile.

Kassia still had not returned when he left Wolffeton, twenty of his men with him. He instructed Blount merely to tell her that he was visiting the Duke of Cornwall and would return to Wolffeton soon.

He looked back at Wolffeton once before a steep hillock obstructed his view. He would miss her, he realized, but it was for the best that he be apart from her for a while. Being with her constantly made him want her. And it was still too soon. He wanted her well first.

Kassia felt a crushing emptiness when Blount, unable to meet her eyes, told her what Graelam had instructed him to. For a moment she could not seem to draw enough breath into her lungs. Graelam had left. He had not cared enough even to see her, to tell her of his business or when he would return. Any niggling doubts she had felt were gone. She cursed him softly, and it made her feel better.

She rode with Bran and an escort of six men the same afternoon to the village of Wolffeton. The merchant Drieux would help her. The small wrapped package would indeed be delivered as soon as possible to Dienwald de Fortenberry, Drieux assured her. That the package contained the necklace and letter to Dienwald would remain her secret.

To Bran's pleased surprise, his mistress laughed deeply on their ride back to Wolffeton.

# 32

"Little chick, may I say that you have surprised me more than I ever believed possible?"

Kassia smiled at Dienwald de Fortenberry, quite unaware that it was a sad smile, one that tugged at his heart. "But you did come," she said.

"Aye, though I was tempted to believe it another ruse on the part of that whoreson Sir Walter."

"My husband rewarded Sir Walter by making him castellan of Crandall," she said stiffly. "At least he is no longer at Wolffeton. He disliked me as much as he did you, I believe."

Dienwald looked at her closely for a long moment, then moved his destrier closer to her mare. "Your message said only that you needed me, little chick. I see you have some baggage with you. And you sent me the necklace. What is it you wish?"

Kassia drew a deep breath. "I want to return home to Brittany, to my father. The necklace is payment."

Dienwald stared hard at her, saw that she was quite

serious, then threw back his head and roared with laughter. He quieted quickly enough. "So," he said slowly, "that fool husband of yours has finally driven you away. The irony of it can't have escaped you, little chick."

"Aye, it has made me laugh as well. I would have been much wiser to let you return me to Belleterre the first time."

He could not miss the bitterness in her voice. He noticed the bruised shadows beneath her expressive eyes, and said in a savage voice, "Did that bastard beat you?"

Kassia shook her head wearily. "I lost a babe through my own foolishness. I cannot really blame him for being angered, though I did not know I was with child."

He saw her hands tug convulsively at her mare's reins. "I am most sorry, Kassia. If you are certain this is what you wish, I will take you to your father."

"It is what I must want," she said quietly.

"He will come after you."

"Perhaps, but I beg leave to doubt it. He is blessed with many powerful friends. It is more likely that he will have our marriage dissolved and marry a proper English lady. One who will most willingly accept her place."

Dienwald cursed fluently, making the men behind him stare at him in surprise. She was so damned helpless and vulnerable and trusting. St. Peter's teeth, how he wished he could knock some sense into Graelam's thick head! He knew well enough that she loved her husband, else he would have begged her to let him care for her, to wipe the sadness from her eyes. He grew silent.

"Will you help me, Dienwald?"

"You are not content with what he gives you," he said flatly. "What is the place you cannot accept?"

"Being treated as though I had no more importance than a brood mare . . . No, that is not precisely true." She slashed her hand through the still air. "He does not love me and never will. I thought perhaps I could gain his trust, his esteem, but it was for naught. I can bear no more. I ask you again, Dienwald. Will you help me?"

"Aye, little chick." He smiled ruefully. "It seems to be my fate to have my life intertwined with yours. I do not want the necklace, Kassia. I think the damned thing is cursed."

"Nay, it is yours. I fancy that it will cost you much to get me to Brittany."

He glanced at her oddly for a long moment. "You trust me not to take advantage of you?"

She looked surprised and cocked her head to one side. "Should I not trust you?"

"I did leave you in my cell at Wolffeton to face your husband."

"Aye, but I understood. I would likely have done the same in your place. It is over now, and there is no need to speak of it again."

"Very well, my lady. We will return to my keep for supplies. I will have you safe in your father's hands within two weeks, I promise you."

"Thank you, Dienwald. Please, keep the necklace. Any merchant will pay you greatly for it." Her voice rose with cold determination as she saw him still hesitate. "I wish never to see it again."

He nodded, then asked curiously, "How did you manage to leave Wolffeton without your husband's knowledge?"

She gave a short, bitter laugh. "He left to visit the Duke of Cornwall, for what reason I know not. He was growing restless at Wolffeton. Perhaps there is some dispute the duke wishes him to settle. I did not even see him."

Dienwald ignored the pain in her voice. "Good. Now I do not have to look over my shoulder! Come, little chick. We have some distance to go!"

"So, Graelam, you came more quickly than I had expected," the Duke of Cornwall said as he eyed the younger man over his wine goblet.

"As your loyal and dutiful vassal, is it not what you would expect?" Graelam asked dryly.

The duke chuckled. "Aye, you are in the right of it, of course. Actually, I wished to have your opinion on Edward's grandiose plans."

"Ah, he chafes already under the weight of his kingly robes? I take it he is ready to journey to Wales?"

"Aye, I imagined he had spoken to you of it. He is ready to begin building. Unlike his father, his plans do not include cathedrals."

"It is well," Graelam said, sipping at the sweet red wine in his golden goblet. "The Marcher barons have not the strength to keep the Welsh raiders in check." He grinned at the duke. "Now that you have my opinion, my lord duke, you wish me to leave?"

"Nay, you impudent rascal. Actually, I have planned a tourney and wish you to take part. Does that interest you?"

Graelam rubbed his hands together, his dark eyes lighting up. "It interests me. I have grown bored with naught to do but see to the reparations of Wolffeton. When will the tourney take place?"

"I had thought of April. It gives me no pleasure to think of knights floundering about in foot-deep snow and slush."

"Will Edward deign to come?"

"Can you doubt it, Graelam? This building of his will cost dearly, and his nobles, of course, must dig into their coffers."

"I imagined as much. Still, it is wiser to have his nobles bashing each other's heads in a tourney sponsored by the king's uncle than attacking each other without his permission."

"What do you think your lady would say to your fighting, my lord? She would accompany you, would she not?"

Graelam stiffened, his dark eyes narrowing. He forced himself to ease, and sipped negligently at his wine again before answering. "She has been ill. We will have to see when the time grows near."

"Ill? Does the child do better now?"

"She lost our babe," Graelam said evenly. "She is well now, at least in body."

"A pity, but she is young and appears quite healthy. She will bless you with many sons."

Graelam held himself silent, and the duke continued after a moment. "I have heard from Sir Guy. It appears that his new bride, Blanche, is with child. He is most pleased."

"I will visit him soon. He is a good man and a valiant warrior. I miss him sorely."

"But it pleases you that he is now landed, does it not?"

"Aye, it pleases me."

"How did your lady lose her babe?"

Taken off guard, Graelam said, his voice filled with

anger, "She was playing at being the man. My master-
at-arms, Rolfe, had taught her how to shoot the bow.
He arranged a competition with the most clumsy of my
men, to make her look good, of course. One of the
horses attacked her mount and she was thrown."

The duke leaned forward in his chair, a questioning
smile on his face. "I do not understand. What made her
do such a thing?"

"She met the Lady Chandra at Edward's coronation.
She was most impressed with Chandra's prowess. She
thought to . . . impress me."

"And did she?" the duke pressed quietly.

Graelam sighed, the truth coming easily now, for he
was beset with guilt. Still, his voice was hesitant. "Aye,
but 'twas not necessary. I was coming to admire her
without such ruses."

The duke felt as though the world had taken a faulty
turn. He knew he was staring, but he could not help it.
He had always believed Graelam a warrior without
equal, a proud man, a man who took what he wanted,
be it possessions or women. But there was always a part
of Graelam he knew to be lacking. He said quietly, "My
lord, to love a woman does not weaken a man or make
him a mewling fool. The stronger the man, the more
gentle he is with his lady. Your father was quite wrong,
you know."

Graelam gave a snort of disdain. "You sound like the
troubadours, my lord duke. Can you see me kneeling
before a lady and vowing her eyes are brighter than the
stars and her complexion a rival to the fairest rose?"

"Does your wife demand such nonsense?"

Graelam ran his hand over his brow, smoothing out
the troubled frown. "Nay, but she demands more of me
than I am able to give." Even as he spoke the words, he

knew they were not true. What had she demanded of
him? Naught save gentleness and kindness and affection. An angry inner voice repeated the refrain he had
struggled with for months. *She left you. She lied. She is
not to be trusted. She lost your babe.* He rose abruptly
and paced about the duke's solarium, the confusion of
his thoughts clear on his face. He stilled momentarily at
the sound of the duke's voice. "And just what, Graelam,
does your gentle wife demand of you?"

I should have known the old man would pry, he
thought. "I believe," he heard himself say, voicing his
inner thoughts, "that she wants me to love her." He
slammed his fist against his open palm. "Damn her! I
told her I forgave her lies!"

The duke raised a bushy gray brow. "Lies? What is
this?"

Graelam saw no hope for it. He eased himself into
the high-backed chair opposite the duke and quickly
related the happenings at Wolffeton, omitting nothing.
When he had finished, the duke was silent for many
moments. "Odd," he said finally, "I would have thought
that Dienwald de Fortenberry would be a merciless,
rutting beast, even with a gently bred lady. But no
matter. Why, my lord Graelam, do you not believe
your wife?"

"Do you know," he said slowly, astounded at the
words that were taking form, "I have come to think that
it matters naught, not anymore." But for the first time,
he allowed himself to consider that Kassia had been
telling him the truth.

"Excellent. I might add that it is possible you saw
Blanche as she wished you to see her. I myself received the impression that she was not at all what she
seemed, at least in her dealings with you." The duke

actually had no idea if this were true or not. But he had overheard Queen Eleanor say something to her husband of Blanche's unkindness to Kassia.

Graelam shrugged. "I did not come here to speak of my marital problems, my lord duke. She is my wife and will remain so, no matter what her feelings."

"And what of your feelings, my lord?"

"Dammit! I wish to speak no more of it. Mayhap I will fall in your damned tourney. If you believe my wife to be such a paragon, you may take her!"

The duke merely smiled, pleased with what he saw. They proceeded to discuss in detail Edward's plans, then enjoyed an excellent meal. The duke offered Graelam a girl for his bed, and to his amusement, Graelam refused. The more unyielding the warrior, the duke thought, the more mightily he succumbs.

Graelam did not leave the duke's fortress for a week. During the days, he forced his thoughts to planning the duke's tourney, but at night, alone in his bed, he could not prevent Kassia's image from coming into his mind. He could practically feel the softness of her slender body, hear her passionate cries as he gave her pleasure, smell her delicate woman's fragrance. He jerked upright in his bed, his body taut with need, his hands clutching at the bedcovers. He thought to rut the girl the duke offered him. He shook his head in the darkness. Nay, there was but one woman who would satisfy him. The admission surprised him, and at the same time brought him a great measure of peace. *I love her.* He began to laugh, seeing himself for the first time as Kassia must have seen him. Gentle and loving one day, harsh and unforgiving the next. How could she have come to love him when he had treated her thus? He flinched, remembering his rape of her so long ago. Yet she had forgiven him that. *And you, you bloody fool, you were so magnanimous in offering to forgive her!*

He jumped from the bed and strode naked to the shuttered windows. He opened them, and breathed in the crisp cold night air. The moon was a silver sliver in the black sky, as clear from Wolffeton as it was from here. Are you thinking of me now, Kassia? Is there anger at me in your mind? I will win you back when I return to Wolffeton.

It was a woman's place to yield, to surrender; a man's place to demand and dominate. He had spent nearly thirty years without a thought to a woman's needs. Oh, her physical needs, to be sure, for that but added to his sense of dominance. It chilled him to admit that he had acted the ass, utterly selfishly. Telling himself it was not too late, he felt a surge of confidence. Soon he would yield to her. The unexpected thought gave him great pleasure.

Dienwald rode beside Kassia up the winding path to Belleterre. He had journeyed in easy stages, trying not to weary her too much. He felt the tension mount in her as they neared the mighty keep.

"Be easy, little chick," he said gently. "All will be well, you will see."

Nay, Kassia thought, nothing would ever be well again. She thought of Etta's likely anguish at finding her gone from Wolffeton, even though she had tried to explain her actions in a message to her old nurse. Would Graelam care? She shook her head. It did not matter. She must put him behind her. She must look to the future.

The muted gray stone of Belleterre gleamed in the afternoon sunlight. Kassia tried to take pleasure in her homecoming. She gazed at the naked-branched trees she had climbed in her childhood, at the deep-cut embrasures in the wall along the north tower where she had played so many years before. What would her father say? Would he forgive her? Would he insist she return to Graelam? She shivered, refusing to consider those possibilities.

They pulled to a halt in front of the mighty gates.

"I will leave you now, little chick," Dienwald said. "I do not intend to wait and see if your father wishes to thank me or slice my head from my body. I am not, after all, your esteemed husband."

Kassia turned in her saddle, her gratitude to him shining in her eyes. "I am lucky to have a friend such as you," she said. She reached out her hand and he grasped it in his. "Thank you. God go with you, Dienwald."

"Good-bye, little chick. If ever you have need of me, I will come to you."

With those words he whirled about his destrier and galloped down the winding path to where his men waited.

Kassia looked up and saw the surprised faces of the men who had known her since she was a child. Shouts of greeting rose even as the great iron-studded gates swung open to admit her. She rode into the inner bailey, forcing a smile to her lips. These were her people. They loved her, trusted her, and respected her. Children cavorted around Bluebell and she leaned down to speak to each of them. She was dismounting from her mare she heard a welcoming shout from her father.

"Kassia! You are here, child!" He gathered her into his arms, squeezing her so tightly that she yelped. She felt her father's love flow into her, and began to know again a measure of peace and comfort.

"Where is Graelam, poppin?" He held her back as he asked his question, studying her weary face.

Kassia's eyes dropped. "Can we speak alone, Father? 'Tis a long story, and one that should be talked of in private."

"As you wish," Maurice agreed. His arm tightened about her slender shoulders as they entered the great hall. "My love . . ." he began, then paused, clearing his throat. "There is something I must tell you."

"Aye, Papa?" she prompted as he again paused, her head cocked to one side.

"I was on the point of sending you a message."

"What message?" Kassia stared at her father.

"I have someone I wish you to meet," he said gruffly. "She is my wife."

"*Wife!*"

Maurice nodded, not quite meeting her eyes. "Her name is Marie, and she hails from Normandy. I met her in Lyon, actually. She is a widow . . ." He drew to a relieved halt at the sight of Marie. "My dear," he called, relieved to have assistance.

Kassia's mind was reeling with her father's completely unexpected news. She had a stepmother! She watched a graceful woman of some thirty-five or so years walk toward them. Her hair was as black as a raven's wing, her eyes a soft brown, her complexion fair. There was a questioning smile on her face.

"My love," Maurice said, releasing his daughter. "This is Kassia, come for a visit!"

"How very lovely you are!" Marie said, holding out a beautiful white hand. "Maurice speaks so much of you—

and your husband, of course." She gazed around expectantly.

"My husband did not accompany me," Kassia said, feeling tears choke in her throat. She would not make a fool of herself in front of her father's new wife!

"No matter," Marie said complacently, as if a wife traveling without her husband were the most common occurrence. "I hope we may be friends, Kassia. Come, my dear, I will take you to your chamber. You must be weary from your journey." She smiled gently at her husband. "We will join you a bit later, Maurice."

"You are quite a surprise," Kassia said frankly as she accompanied her new stepmother up the winding stairs to the upper chambers.

"Your father and I just returned to Belleterre three weeks ago. I believe he intended to send a message to you and your lord in the next day or so. Oh dear, I had hoped we would have a few moments of quiet!"

Three children, two young boys and a girl, were racing toward them.

"My children," Marie said, lifting her dark brows in comic dismay. "I fear now we shall have little peace."

"They are beautiful!" Kassia exclaimed as she stared down at a doe-eyed little girl of about seven years. The two boys hung back. "How very lucky you are."

"Now I am," Marie said quietly. "Gerard, Paul, come and greet your sister. And you, Jeanne, make your curtsy."

"Oh dear," Kassia said, bursting into merry laughter. "I am overcome!"

"My lord, there is an encampment ahead."

Dienwald drew in his destrier. "Are they French? Did you see a standard?"

"Aye, my lord. Three black wolves, upright and snarling against a background of white."

Dienwald shook his head, bemused. "The Wolf of Cornwall," he said softly. Graelam. Well, he had told Kassia her husband would come after her. It would be easy enough, he thought, to ride unseen around Graelam's camp. It was on the tip of his tongue to give that order, but he did not.

Graelam stretched out on his narrow cot, pulled a single blanket over himself, and commanded his weary body to sleep. Tomorrow, he thought, watching the lone candle spiral its thin light to the roof of the tent, he would see Kassia. His fury at her disappearance had faded, leaving only a numbing emptiness within him. He though again of her message, and it chilled him. "You must not worry about my safety, my lord," she had written, "for I will be well-protected." By whom? he wondered, but the answer gnawed clearly in his mind. She had hired Dienwald de Fortenberry once; likely she had done it again. "It is likely that my father will not blame you for my failure. Belleterre will doubtless be yours in any case. I trust, my lord, that you will find a lady who will please you."

And that was all. Nothing more. Did she really expect him to let her go? Did she really think so little of herself that she believed Belleterre the only reason he had kept her as his wife? Damned little fool!

He gave not two farthings for Belleterre at the moment. He wanted his wife. He wanted to beat her, kiss her and crush her against him. He wanted to hear her tell him that she loved him, that she forgave him. He laughed mirthlessly. How he had changed, and all of it wrought by a skinny little girl whose smile would

melt the heart of the most hardened warrior. Except
yours, you fool! Until now.

Graelam heard a soft rustle as the tent flap raised. He
sat up, instantly on guard, and reached for his sword.

"Hold, my lord Graelam," he heard a man's deep
voice say. He saw a flash of silver steel.

"What is this?" Graelam growled, not loosing his
fingers from his sword.

"I mean you no harm, my lord. I am not your enemy.
I have too healthy a wish to keep my body intact."

"Who the devil are you?"

"Dienwald de Fortenberry. Your wife spared me the
only other opportunity I had of meeting you."

Graelam sucked in his breath, his eyes glittering in
the dim light. So he had been right. The bastard had
taken Kassia back to her father. "Just how did you get
past my men?" he asked, his voice coldly menacing.

"A moment, my lord. I beg you not to call for you
men. I have no wish to run you through."

Graelam released his sword, and Dienwald watched
it fall to the ground. "Thank you," he said. He looked at
Graelam de Moreton closely. He was naked, save for
the blanket that came only to his loins. He was a
powerful man, his chest mightily muscled and covered
with thick black hair. Dienwald could see the ribbed
muscles over his flat belly. Aye, he thought, a man
women would admire, and desire. His eyes roved over
Graelam's face. It was not a handsome courtier's face,
he thought, but it was strong, proud, and at the moment harsh, the dark eyes narrowed on Dienwald's
face. His mouth was sensual, the lower lip full, his
teeth gleaming white and straight. Dienwald was probably a fool to take this chance, slipping into this man's
camp, but he had decided it was a debt he owed to

Kassia. He shook himself from his examination, aware that Graelam was studying him just as closely.

Graelam eyed the man. His features are the color of sand, he remembered Kassia telling him. It was true. "What do you want?" he asked coldly. Oblivious of his nakedness, he rose and poured two goblets of wine. He quirked a black brow toward Dienwald.

Dienwald accepted the goblet of wine. "Please sit down, my lord. You must excuse my distrust, but I am not the fool I must seem. When my men told me of your encampment, I was pleased that you came so quickly for your wife. Of course, she did not believe me. She fancied you would be pleased to see no more of her."

Graelam tensed, his eyes narrowing. He wanted to leap at the man and tear his heart from his chest with his bare hands. But Dienwald held the upper hand, for the moment at least, and Graelam had no idea how his men were situated outside his tent.

"You have interfered mightily in my life," he said after a long moment, his voice a sneer. "So she paid you yet again to take her from me."

Dienwald gently caressed the razor-sharp edge of his sword. "You are a fool, my lord. Your wife's gentle heart is pure and honest. If she would have me, I would willingly take her from you. I crept into your camp for one reason only. I owe a debt to your wife."

"What did she use for payment this time?" Graelam hissed. "The necklace again?"

"Aye," Dienwald said, his lips a twisted smile. "I did not want the damned thing, but she insisted. I have laughed at the irony of it, my lord. Now, you will heed me, for I imagine that I have not much more time. Your wife has never lied to you, at least to my knowledge. 'Twas Blanche who first paid me the necklace to rid herself of your wife. But I could not do it. When I asked her what she wished, she told me to return her to Wolffeton, to you, her husband. Then that whoreson Sir Walter captured me by a ruse, using Kassia's name. She released the manacles, my lord, because she hated to see me in pain. She was, of course, too trusting. I had to leave her there, for I had no wish to die by your hand." He paused a moment, then said in a self-mocking voice, "I asked her to come away with me, but she would not. She loves you, though I do not think you deserve it."

Graelam stared at the man whose words rushed through his mind in a torrent. "You could be lying for her even now," he said, his voice a menacing snarl. "Perhaps you are even her lover, as I have always suspected."

Dienwald smiled, encouraged at the fury in Graelam's face. "I could certainly have ravished her. Perhaps 'tis what Blanche expected, even wished me to do. But I found that even I, a rough and conscienceless rogue, could not harm so gentle and trusting a lady. It is you she loves, my lord, though by all the saints in heaven you do not deserve such tender feelings from her." He fingered his sword edge for a long moment. "I first believed her the most gentle, biddable of creatures. But 'tis not so. There is a thread of steel in her, my lord, and a pride that rivals any man's. She left you because she could see no more hope for herself living as your wife. Her sadness would smite the most closed of hearts. As I said before, you are a great fool."

To Dienwald's utter surprise, Graelam looked straight at him and said, "Aye, you are right. I realized it myself but days ago. It is more ironic than you believe, de

Fortenberry. I found I no longer cared if she had lied to me or not. I want her, and if I can convince her of the truth of my feelings, I will take her back to Wolffeton with me, as my true wife."

Very slowly Dienwald sheathed his sword. "I trust you have a smooth tongue, my lord, for she is adamant."

"She will obey me!"

"I foresee a battle royal. Forget not, my lord, that she is in her father's keep, not yours. I imagine he would protect her from your . . . ah, demands."

Graelam began to pace furiously about the small space, his powerful naked body gleaming in the gentle candlelight. Suddenly he turned to Dienwald and smiled. "Aye, you've the right of it. But she will obey me. I am her husband." Graelam paused a moment, chewing at his lower lip. "How did her father greet her?"

"I did not enter the fortress with her, fearing some retribution from her father. I have learned never to count on a peaceful welcome from a stranger."

"It goes against the grain to thank a man I have always considered my enemy. Now that you are no longer a stranger to me, Dienwald de Fortenberry, I will welcome you at Wolffeton. Keep your sword sheathed."

Dienwald smiled, shaking his head. "Can I really be assured that you will not wish to see my body severed in bloody pieces for your sport?"

Graelam stretched out his hand to Dienwald. "I call you friend. And I thank you for protecting my wife. You are welcome at Wolffeton, I swear it."

"Thank you, my lord."

"May I now know how you managed to get into my camp and into my tent without any of my men noticing?"

Dienwald chuckled. "'Tis not so difficult for a lone

man to enter where he wishes, my lord. But leaving intact is a different matter. I am mightily relieved you do not wish to see the color of my blood!"

"Nay," Graelam said, smiling easily now, "your blood can remain in your body, at least until the tourney. It would please me to face you on the field."

"A tourney, my lord?"

"Aye, the Duke of Cornwall plans one for April."

"Then I shall see you there. I bid you good-bye and good luck, my lord."

Graelam stood motionless as Dienwald slipped quietly from his tent. He shook his head, bemused, and returned to his cot. If only, he thought, snuffing out the gutting candle, he had known the truth months ago. Now it didn't matter. He pondered on the vagaries of fate before he fell into the first sound sleep he had enjoyed in more than a week.

33

The evening meal was boisterous, Maurice having allowed his stepchildren to join them. The men-at-arms
pelted Kassia with questions she did not precisely answer, and all the servants stayed close, wishing to tell
her all that had occurred to them during her absence.
No one mentioned her husband. Kassia felt her father's
eyes on her, but she resolutely kept a happy smile pinned
to her lips. Indeed, she was inordinately pleased to see
him so blantantly happy with himself and his new family.
Marie appeared as good-natured as Kassia had first suspected; that she loved Maurice, Kassia did not question.

"The stewed beef does not please you, Kassia?" Marie asked her after some time of watching her new
stepdaughter push the food about on her trencher.

"Oh, of course, Marie. 'Tis just that I am too excited
to eat. Truly, I shall be ravenous on the morrow."

Marie was silent for a moment, then leaned close to
Kassia. "I trust, my dear, that you are not displeased
with your father's marriage."

432

Kassia blinked in surprise, and said honestly, "I am happy that my father has found someone to care for. My mother died so long ago, and I fear he has been particularly lonely after I left for England. And the children bring new life to Belleterre."

"I would not have you or your husband concerned that Belleterre will pass from you to my children," Marie continued quietly. "Indeed, both my boys will have lands of their own, bequeathed to them by my late husband. As for Jeanne, she will have sufficient dowry."

"My husband will be pleased that he will not lose Belleterre," Kassia said evenly.

"Maurice has told me much of Lord Graelam, particularly about your lord saving his life in Aquitaine. He holds him in great esteem."

"As do I," Kassia said, her eyes on her trencher. She waited tensely for Marie to ask her the obvious question, but her new stepmother said nothing further, merely spoke of the servants and their efficiency and kindness to her, their new mistress.

It was very late when the great hall quieted. Kassia saw Marie nod to her husband; then she approached Kassia and hugged her gently. "I will bid you good night, Kassia. If you are not too tired, I think your father would like some private words with you." With those calmly spoken yet ominous words, she left, shooing her very tired children in front of her.

"You are to be congratulated, Father," Kassia said with a tired smile. "Marie is enchanting, as are the children. You are most lucky."

"Aye, I know it well. I am pleased, and relieved, that you approve, poppin." Maurice slicked his hand through his gray hair in seeming agitation, then turned a gentle eye to his daughter. "Kassia, do you wish to tell me why you have come to Belleterre alone?"

"I did not come alone, Father," she said. "A dear friend brought me. My safety was never in question."

"My men told me about this 'dear friend' of yours, poppin. Why did he not come to greet me?"

"He is not my husband. He feared you would not be overly pleased to see him."

"Aye, likely," Maurice said. "Come and sit down, Kassia. My old bones are weary, and you are looking none too spry yourself."

Kassia did as he bid her, and eased into the chair opposite her father's "Does Marie play chess?" she asked.

"A bit. She has not your quickness with the pieces or your strategy of the game."

Maurice studied her for a long moment, noting the dark shadows beneath her expressive eyes and the tenseness of her hands, now clutched together in her lap. "You have left your husband" he said.

Kassia could only nod. Were she to speak, she knew she would burst into tears and shame herself.

Maurice sighed deeply, and turned his gaze to the dying embers in the fireplace. "I hope you will forgive me, poppin. 'Tis all my fault, wedding you to a man I knew scarce a week. But I truly believed him honorable, my love."

"Papa, you believed I was dying," Kassia said sharply, hating his spate of guilt. "And Lord Graelam is honorable. It is just that . . ."

"That what, poppin?" Maurice pressed gently.

"He does not love me," she said quietly.

Maurice had always believed his daughter one of the most beautiful girls he had ever seen. He tried now to see her objectively, to see her as a stranger might. Her glorious hair was in loose curls to her shoulders, thick and lustrous. She had filled out again, but she was still very slender, almost fragile in appearance. But the impish, whimsical quality about her was lost. "Then I must believe," Maurice said slowly, "that Graelam is something of a fool."

"Nay, Papa," she said quickly, wondering at herself for defending her husband, "he simply has no place in his heart for a female. And I miscarried our babe."

Maurice sucked in his breath. "Are you well?" he asked harshly.

"I am well. Indeed, I did not even know I was with child." She rose clumsily to her feet. "Please, Papa, I do not wish to speak more about it now. He will not come after me. He is likely well-pleased that I left him."

He heard the harsh pain in her voice, and felt utterly helpless.

"May I stay here, Papa? I swear to you that I will not interfere with anything Marie does."

"Of course. This is your home, Kassia."

"Thank you, Papa."

"You are weary, my love. We will speak more about this when you are rested." He drew her to him and gently hugged her. He felt her womanly curves, her woman's softness. It amazed him that he had not noticed earlier that his little girl had matured. Had Graelam abused her? he wondered, his body tensing. He pictured the huge man naked with his daughter, taking her as a man took a woman, and gritted his teeth. He leaned his head down and gently kissed her cheek. It was wet with her tears.

"Kassia," he murmured softly. "Do not cry, poppin. All will be well now, you will see."

"I do not deserve you," she said, sniffing back the hated tears.

"Well, we are even, for your husband does not deserve you." He patted her back and released her. "In the morning, poppin. Everything always looks brighter in the sunlight."

Kassia smiled. It had always been one of her father's favorite sayings. She turned to go, when his voice halted her in her tracks.

"Do you love Graelam?"

She turned slowly back to face him, and Maurice sucked in his breath at the tragic sadness in her expressive eyes. She said very quietly, "I am sick with love for him, Papa." She gave a harsh, derisive laugh that made him wince. "I am a fool." She turned quickly, lifted her skirts, and fled up the stairs to the upper chambers.

Maurice stood still for many long moments, listening to her light footfalls on the stairs. He had met Marie and lost his heart to her. How could any man not do the same for his daughter? Was Graelam so hardened a warrior that there was no giving, no softness in him? Maurice shook his head and walked slowly to his chamber, knowing that Marie would be there in his bed, ready to comfort him with all the kindness in her heart.

There were no more conversations with her father. Kassia knew she was purposefully avoiding him. She saw the questions in his eyes when she chanced to look at him, but it was too soon. The pain was too sharp within her. She spent the next day to herself, walking about Belleterre, searching out all her old childhood haunts. She spoke to all her old friends, savoring their words, for they evoked happier times, when her life was simple and filled with love. How odd, she thought, walking up the steep wooden steps to the eastern tower, that she had always taken everyone's love and approval for granted. Several times the servants had come to her with questions, out of long habit, she assumed, and she had sent them to Marie. She had no intention, just as she had assured her father, of wresting the management from her new stepmother.

She gained the watchtower and threw back her head to savor the gentle breeze from the sea and the bright afternoon sunlight on her face. She heard the men-at-arms joking with each other on the practice field. In other days, she would have skipped happily down to watch them, never questioning that she was welcome.

Her eyes widened at the sight of a group of men riding toward Belleterre. Her heart began to pound, and her breath grew short. No, it could not be he! Still, her feet moved along the walkway toward the great gates of Belleterre. She stood motionless, watching the clouds of dust kicked up by the horses' hooves. She recognized Graelam's standard, recognized his mighty destrier. He looked utterly resplendent in his silver mail and black velvet surcoat. He had come. But why? To assure himself that Belleterre would still be his upon her father's death?

She stood directly above the gates, looking down at her husband as he halted his men. She heard Pierre, the porter, shout down, "Who are you, my lord? What do you wish at Belleterre?"

She watched Graelam jerk off his helmet and pull back the mesh hood from his head. "I am Graelam de Moreton. I have come for my wife," he shouted upward, his voice firm and commanding.

Kassia felt a wave of dizziness flood through her. It could not be true, she thought, doubting it even as it passed through her mind. Her husband was a possessive man. Had her leaving him hurt his pride?

"I am here, my lord," she shouted down at him, leaning forward so he could see her.

Graelam looked upward, and to her consternation, a wide smile crossed his face. "Madam wife," he called up to her. "I trust you are well after your harrowing journey."

"It was not at all harrowing," she said coldly. "Dienwald was most careful of my well-being."

There, she thought, let him realize the truth. She waited to see the fury turn his face to stone. His smile, to her utter surprise, did not falter.

"Have your men open the gates. My men and I are weary."

She stood a moment, irresolute. He had but a dozen or so men with him. He could not force her to return with him. Her father would protect her. She called to the porter. "Allow my lord to enter, Pierre."

She found herself smoothing her hair, wishing that she was garbed in a more becoming gown. Fool! she chided herself. It matters not if I look like a dairy maid. She flung back her head, her chin up, and marched down the stairs to the inner bailey.

He rides in like a conquering master, she thought, her eyes narrowing as she watched him. Her chin rose higher.

Graelam drew Demon to a halt some feet from his wife and dismounted. He handed the reins to one of his men, then looked back at her. It was not going to be easy, he thought, so pleased to see her that he had to hold himself back from grabbing her and crushing her

against him. He was aware of men and servants closing
about them, all of them ready to club him to death if he
threatened her in any way. Their show of loyalty pleased
him.

"My lady," he said, halting in front of her.

"Why are you here, Graelam?" she asked without
preamble.

"It is as I said, Kassia. I have come to bring you
home to Wolffeton."

"There was no reason for such an action, my lord. I
assured you that you would not lose Belleterre."

"I do not give a flying damn about your father's
possessions, my lady," he said very softly.

Her chin rose even higher. "Dienwald de Fortenberry
brought me here. I paid him with the necklace."

"Aye, I know it well." He reached out his hand so
quickly she had not time to jerk away from him. He
cupped her chin in his palm. "Your pride pleases me,
wife. Now, I would like something to drink, my men
also. We have ridden hard this day."

He released her chin, and she backed away. "You
will follow me, my lord."

Graelam watched her walk stiffly, her slender shoulders squared, up the steep oak stairs into the great hall.

What are his plans? she wondered, her mind spinning. Will he continue toying with me?

Graelam's eyes narrowed upon the black-haired woman
who approached them.

"My stepmother, Marie, my lord," Kassia said in a
clipped voice. "Marie, this is my . . . husband, Lord
Graelam de Moreton."

Marie eyed the huge man. He looked utterly fierce
and unyielding. "My lord," she said quietly. "Kassia,

your father is in the solarium with his steward. Would you care to fetch him?"

Kassia nodded, thankful to Marie for the chance to escape.

"So," Graelam said agreeably after Kassia had left, "Maurice has found himself a new wife."

"And three stepchildren, my lord."

Graelam remembered Maurice telling him that his seed was lifeless. He had done well for himself. "Excellent," he said

"Will you not be seated, my lord?"

Graelam sat himself in Maurice's chair, and watched Marie give quiet orders to the serving wenches. He wondered idly what Kassia thought of her father's new wife.

"My lord." Graelam rose from his chair to greet his father-in-law. Maurice was looking at him warily, uncertain, Graelam imagined, just how he should greet his son-in-law.

"Maurice, it is a pleasure to see you again." He clasped the older man's shoulders and hugged him briefly.

"You have come to see your wife?"

"Aye, more than that. I am come to take her home to Cornwall."

"Why?"

It was Kassia who had spat the word at him. He shifted his gaze from Maurice and drank in the sight of his wife. She was regarding him as warily as her father.

"Because," he said quietly, "you are mine and will always be so. Your father gave you to me." He saw her eyes narrow with fury, and smiled at her. "However, I understand your wish to visit with your father and your new stepmother for a while. If it pleases your father, we will remain here at Belleterre for several days before we return to Wolffeton."

Kassia looked helplessly toward her father. Maurice, for the first time in his life, had not a clue as to what he should do. He had to admit to great admiration for Graelam, for the man had ridden up to Belleterre, seemingly without a worry in the world. He would have known, of course, that Maurice's men could have cut down him and his men had he wished it. But there was his daughter to consider. It was Marie who spoke in her gentle voice.

"We are pleased to welcome you, my lord. You may, if Kassia wishes it, speak to her."

Maurice added more forcefully, "Aye, Graelam, but you'll not force my daughter to do anything she does not wish to."

"It is not my intention ever again to force Kassia to do what she does not want to do."

I do not believe you! Kassia wanted to yell at him.

Marie said, "Would you care to bathe, my lord? The evening meal will be ready soon."

Graelam nodded. "Thank you, my lady." He sought out his wife. "Would you please show me to the proper chamber?"

Maurice saw Kassia hesitate, but he knew that Graelam had no power in Belleterre. "Aye, daughter," he said crisply. "Accompany Graelam."

Kassia bit her lip, knowing she had no choice. She tossed her head and marched toward the stairs. She heard Marie giving orders for a bath. She led him to her chamber, pausing a moment inside the room.

"Come in, Kassia," Graelam said. "I need assistance with my armor."

"I am not your squire!"

"True, you are my wife. Surely the sight of my body will not surprise you or offend you."

She felt a wave of heat suffuse her face. It had been so long. She cursed him silently for teaching her passion. Then she dropped to her knees and untied his cross-garters. He pulled off his chaussures and stood naked in front of her. He did not move to cover himself when two serving girls entered, bearing buckets of hot water.

I will not look at him, Kassia swore to herself. She watched the tub filled with steaming water. When he stepped into the tub, she tossed him a bar of lavender-scented soap.

Graelam did not appear to notice the gentle scent. He leaned back in the tub and closed his eyes. "Ah," he sighed, beginning to rub the soap over his broad chest, his eyes still closed. "You have led me a merry chase, Kassia."

She said over her shoulder, still not looking at him, "Nay, my lord. I did nothing but leave a most unhappy situation."

"With Dienwald de Fortenberry," he added mildly.

"Why not?" she flung at him. "After all," she continued in a snide voice, "he has helped me on previous occasions. Surely you cannot doubt our . . . devotion to each other."

"I certainly do not doubt his devotion to you."

"Then why are you here?" she snapped. "I have proved to you that I am not trustworthy, that I have no honor, indeed, that I have lied to you from the very beginning."

"I suppose I could regard it in such a light."

He was toying with her! She gritted her teeth. "I will not return with you, Graelam. I will no more suffer your foul humor and your indifference to me. I will not play brood mare to your stallion."

Graelam opened one eye and regarded her flushed face. "But, my dear wife, you have not yet proved to me that you can even fulfill that role."

She sucked in her breath in fury. "I have no intention of playing any role for you, my lord! And you cannot force me. My father will protect me!"

"I imagine that Maurice would," Graelam said lazily. He began to lather his hair, as if he had no other concern in the world.

"I repeat, my lord, why are you here?"

He did not reply, merely continued washing his hair, then rinsing it, cupping his hands in the hot water, and splashing it liberally. He shook his head, sending droplets of water flying toward her, then asked, "Will you scrub my back, Kassia?"

"No! Your dirt is your own, my lord. I will have nothing to do with it."

He sighed. "You left Wolffeton in something of an uproar, my lady. Your nurse was so noisy in her tears that she could only hand me your message to her. As for yours to me . . ." He shrugged. "Well, it made me want to thrash you, but very gently."

"You will not touch me, my lord!"

He cocked a thick wet brow at her. "I would not be too certain of that, Kassia."

Before she could frame a reply, he rose in the tub, and her unruly eyes coursed down his body. She gulped, for his manhood was swollen. She whirled about, clutching her arms over her breasts.

"You are quite beautiful," she heard him say softly behind her. "I have found that more generously endowed women no longer appeal to me." She felt his fingers touch her hair. "So soft. You will give me a daughter, Kassia, endowed with your beauty."

"Stop it! Please, Graelam, I do not want—"

His arms closed around her, and he gently drew her back against his chest. His powerful arms prevented any escape. She stood stiffly, willing herself not to succumb. He did not love her. She was a woman, and he merely wanted her as such.

"Release me, my lord."

He did, much to her bemused disappointment. "Have you a bedrobe for me, Kassia?"

She shook her head mutely.

"No matter. I am weary, wife, and wish to rest for a while." He took her arm firmly and drew her toward the bed.

"I will not let you take me, Graelam," she spat at him. "It will have to be by force. But then again, you are quite uncaring of how you take a woman."

She heard him draw in his breath sharply. "I have not been a very loving husband to you," he said slowly, turning her to face him. "But that will change. You see, Kassia, I have never before wanted a woman as I want you. I never believed a man could truly love a woman, yield to her without losing the essence of his strength." He gently stroked his hands over her arms, and his voice deepened. "I have not known much gentleness in my life, Kassia, yet I know now that I would never willingly hurt you again. I love you, and because I love you, I want you to come home with me."

She gazed up at him, her breath caught in her throat. "But you cannot love me," she cried. "You do not trust me!"

"I would trust you with my life," he said simply.

"Has . . . has Blanche finally admitted the truth to you?"

"No, I have heard nothing from Blanche."

"Then why? Why are you acting this way? Why are you saying these things to me? I told you that you would not lose Belleterre! Do you wish my father also to assure you of that fact?"

His grip on her arms tightened slightly. "I see that if there is trust to be gained, it is you to learn that I can be believed. No, do not raise that little chin of yours at me, though it is a delightful part of you. Will you consent to believe me, Kassia?"

She stared at him numbly, her eyes wide with confusion.

"Will you consider forgiving me for all I have done to you? Can you still love me?"

She lowered her head from his intense gaze. "I have no choice but to love you. But . . . but I am not Chandra! I have not the talent to be as she!"

He drew her close, gently pressing her cheek against his chest. She could feel the deep rumbling of laughter as he stroked his hands down her back. "I once told Guy that Chandra is a prince among women. I wish to be with a princess, my lady. I wish to love you, watch you smile and laugh, watch your small belly grow with our children.

"I want to hear you cry out your passion for me when I love you. Kiss me, Kassia."

She felt her heart expand with such happiness that she could scarcely think straight. Mutely she raised her head. She felt his hands cup her buttocks and raise her from the floor, fitting her belly against him. He kissed her very gently, lightly nipping at her lower lip. She gasped with the pleasure of it, and parted her lips to his tongue.

She felt his powerful body tremble with need for her. Her breasts felt swollen, as if he had caressed them. "Graelam," she whispered softly into his mouth.

He laid her on her back onto the bed. "Will you let me love you now, Kassia?"

He made no move to touch her, but waited patiently for her to answer him. "Aye," she said. "I want you to love me. It has been so long . . . and you taught me too well."

She saw his dark eyes leap at her words. Slowly, as if she were a precious treasure, he undressed her, pausing as he removed each article of clothing to caress and kiss her. When her breasts were bare to his gaze, he smiled down at her. "You are more beautiful than I remembered. So delicate." Slowly he began to kiss her breasts, circling her taut nipples, teasing her. When he heard her moan softly, he eased the rest of her clothes from her body. "By all the saints," he said in a husky, deep voice, his hands following his eyes to stroke her ribs and belly, "you are the most lovely of God's creations."

"Not so beautiful and perfect as you are," she said, her eyes sweeping down his body.

"And just how many men have you seen naked?" he gently mocked her.

"If ever I see another man naked, I should likely laugh, for no man could look as you do."

His fingers found her, and she gasped, her hips arching up of their own volition.

"You are so warm, so ready for me," he said, fitting himself beside her. He continued to caress her rhythmically as he looked directly into her eyes. He watched

them grow smoky with burgeoning desire, and felt his
entire being expand with pleasure when she cried out
softly for him. But he held himself back. Slowly, with
infinite care, he eased himself between her legs. He
lifted her hips in his hands and lowered his mouth to
her. She jerked upward, crying out. He reveled in her
pleasure. She was shuddering in the rippling aftermath
when he slowly rose over her and eased into her. She
raised her hips to receive him, and gasped as he filled
her. She whimpered softly, her hands clutching his
back as he thrust into her. She repeated his name again
and again, and when he tensed over her, she felt herself opening even more to him, welcoming the seed
that burst from his body deep within her.

She welcomed his weight, holding him tightly against
her.

"Nay, love," he said softly, "I am too heavy for you."
Gently he eased out of her and turned her on her side
to face him.

"Thank you," Kassia said, turning her face into his
shoulder.

"For what?"

"For loving me."

"You will never doubt it again. Now I will let you
sleep before I hear you moan with pleasure again. The
shadows under your eyes are interesting, but I would
prefer you lost them."

"I too," she murmured. She fell asleep in a cocoon of
warmth. She woke slowly, disoriented, until she felt a
surge of pure pleasure warm her belly. Graelam was
deep inside her, still facing her, his fingers stroking
her.

"I love you," she whispered, and pressed herself
tightly against him.

He gently drew her hand down between them and let her feel his fingers caressing her. Her embarrassment was a brief illusion. "Feel how you want me," he murmured softly against her lips.

She moaned in his mouth and felt him smile. She moved her fingers away from his grasp and touched him. At his sharp indrawn breath, she smiled. "I feel how you want me, my lord."

 **34**

They walked together in the gentle sunlight, Graelam's arm about his wife's waist, his head lowered to hear her speak.

"Graelam, my father knew! He looked at me so oddly this morning!"

Graelam chuckled. "At least he did not believe that I was holding you in your bedchamber, thrashing you. The glowing smile on your face testified to my innocence."

"Speaking of smiles, did you see how Rolfe looked at us? And the rest of the men?"

"Aye, they are most pleased, and relieved that I am no longer a braying ass."

Her eyes twinkled at him, and her dimples deepened. "Aye, my lord, as am I!"

Graelam was silent for a moment, his gaze resting thoughtfully on the bare-branched trees in Belleterre's orchard. "I wish to tell you something, Kassia."

She tensed at his tone, and he felt it. "Nay, love, 'tis not a bad thing, but a confession of sorts. I wish there only to be truth between us." He paused a moment, then lifted her in his arms and kissed her soundly on the mouth. "That is to assure you that my feelings have not changed and never will."

She wrapped her arms about his neck and pressed herself against him. "I need no confession, my lord."

He set her down. "Nay, little wench. Listen to me. When I left Wolffeton to visit the Duke of Cornwall, many things became clear to me. I will admit to you that the duke, the interfering old goat, did call me a fool whilst we spoke of you. But he did speak the truth. To love a woman well, to yield to her, does not weaken a man. It has been a difficult truth for me to accept, but accept it I did. When I returned to Wolffeton, I intended to tell you of what I felt for you. But you were gone.

"Two nights ago I was lying in my tent, as miserable as a man can be, when Dienwald de Fortenberry entered. When he told me who he was, I was ready to break his neck. He told me, Kassia, that he owed you a debt, and to pay it meant he must speak the truth to me. We parted friends, my love. No, do not draw away from me. Had he told me that you had hired him a dozen times to remove you from my hold, it would have changed naught. You see, it no longer mattered. It was up to you to forgive me my distrust, my blind conceit, not the other way around. So you see, Dienwald or no Dienwald, it made no difference in my feelings for you."

Graelam chuckled softly. "I think he would have liked to return that damned necklace to me."

"He has been kind to me, Graelam," Kassia said, "and I hoped that when Sir Walter brought him to Wolffeton, he would tell you the truth then. I released him only to spare him pain. But he had to escape. He felt very guilty about it, I think."

"He did indeed. Do you believe me, Kassia? Believe that I did not change my feelings for you because of his words?"

"I believe you, my lord." Her eyes narrowed. "Now, if I could see Blanche. How I should love to sever her tongue!"

"Why not ask her and Guy to visit Wolffeton? You can then challenge her to an archery match."

She giggled, and because she was so happy, threw her arms about his waist, squeezing him with all her strength.

"Attacked by a fly," Graelam said, leaning down to nibble at her ear. "Ah, my love, I see your father eyeing us. Shall we assure him that I am not coercing you?"

Geoffrey could scarce credit his man's words. Graelam de Moreton, his enemy, the only man who stood between him and Belleterre, was in Brittany! Over the past months he had ground his teeth in frustration, especially when it had become clear to him that to assassinate Graelam in Cornwall was a plan doomed to failure. The man was always too well-protected, his men too loyal. But now he was here, and with but a dozen men guarding him.

Geoffrey knew every hillock in Brittany, every likely spot for an ambush. He wondered idly if Kassia would care if he butchered her husband. If she did, it would take him a bit more time to bring her around. If she threatened to denounce him, he would simply lock her away and beat her, for he would force her to wed him immediately. He smiled at the thought. His proud little

cousin would not long berate him. He was, after all, a
man who knew women well. They were simple and
easily led.

He rode purposefully away from his keep, wanting to
avoid his mother. He had not seen her for many weeks
now, having just returned from the court in Paris, for
her acerbic tongue was enough to drive any man to
distraction. She would change her stance once Kassia
was his wife, and Belleterre would be his after his uncle
had died.

Graelam and Kassia left Belleterre three days later.
Early-spring weather blessed their journey, a sign,
Graelam assured Kassia, straight from the Duke of Cornwall. That wily old man believed he had the direct ear
of the Lord Almighty.

"Mayhap Papa also talks into that same ear," Kassia
said. "I have never seen him so pleased!"

"Do not forget your winsome stepmother. I vow it
was her influence that kept your father from beating
down your bedchamber door that first evening I arrived. Aye, a wise woman. She doubtless recognized
me as your proper master, and knew you would succumb quickly enough to me."

"Conceited brute!" Kassia said in high good humor.

"I was forced to tell her that you would not allow me
out of your bed," Graelam continued in great serious-
ness. "Likely she was concerned that your woman's
appetites would exhaust me."

Kassia flushed a rosy pink. She saw that he would
continue to tease her, and decided it was her turn.
"You know, my lord, I must admit that suffering your
great body is a mighty chore."

He was not to be drawn. "And a nightly one, Kassia.

I also have wondered how your skinny little parts ac-
commodate me so nicely. I think you forget my mighty
size once you are mewling with pleasure."

She reached out and struck his shoulder, laughing as
she did so.

Rolfe nodded, a wide, amazed smile parting his lips
as he watched his master and mistress. Never had he
believed Lord Graelam could be so much at his ease
with a woman. Life was much improved, he thought,
aye, much improved indeed. In the next moment, all
thoughts of improved life fled his mind, at the sound of
one of the men screaming in pain.

"Brigands!" Rolfe shouted at the top of his lungs,
twisting around in his saddle, his hand already upon his
sword hilt. "An ambush!" He looked wildly about at the
narrow passage, at the boulders rising high into the air,
surrounding them.

Long years of training kept panic at bay. Graelam
coolly analyzed their situation, a fraction of a second
passing before he shouted orders.

"All of you, dismount and press under the overhangs
in the cliffs! The whoresons will have to come in to get
at us!"

Graelam grabbed Kassia off Bluebell's back, protecting her with his body. An arrow tore through the chain
mail at his side, but did him no harm. He pulled her to
an indentation between two mighty boulders and shoved
her inside. "Crouch down and cover yourself with your
cloak!"

Kassia obeyed him, her mind whirling with sudden
fear. Brigands! She winced at the scream of a horse.
Graelam moved swiftly away from her, his back pressed
against the stones, until he was crouched next to Rolfe
and three of his men.

"We must discover the leader," he said tersely. "James there is a small cleavage between those boulders yon. Think you that you can ease through it? See the number of men who are there?"

"Aye, my lord," James said, fear and excitement flowing through him. He was fairly new to Lord Graelam's service, and now he would prove himself. He inched away, licking his tongue over his suddenly dry lips, and squeezed his slender body upward through the narrow passage.

Kassia felt a frisson of terror at the sudden utter silence. The horses had calmed, for there were no more arrows raining down. She began to pray, calling upon every litany she had learned since childhood.

The wait seemed an eternity. Graelam held himself perfectly still, listening to any sound that would give him information. He heard a slithering noise and twisted about to see James slip down beside him.

"'Tis some sort of lord," James said. "I saw him seated on his destrier, dressed in gleaming armor, a man beside him holding his standard. An eagle, my lord, its beak blood-red."

Graelam frowned. Something Kassia had said many months ago stirred in his memory. "Do not move, any of you."

He moved like a stalking panther, slipping in and out of the protective crevices until he reached Kassia.

"It is all right, love," he quickly assured her, seeing her utterly white face. "A standard, Kassia, one with an eagle on it."

"Geoffrey," she whispered, scarcely believing her own words. "I do not understand, Graelam. 'Tis madness."

"I know," he said quietly. "Stay here, Kassia. All will

be well, I promise you." He kissed her swiftly, and was gone.

He moved in the shadow of the boulders until he was nearly at the end of the narrow passage. He shouted out, "Geoffrey! Geoffrey de Lacy! Show yourself, you scum coward!"

Geoffrey jumped at the sound of his name on his enemy's lips. One of his men had suggested he not fly his standard, even that he not garb himself in armor. He had scoffed, and done as he pleased. Now he was frowning. If he did nothing, and waited, perhaps Graelam and his men could slip out under cover of darkness. He bit his lower lip. Damn the overhanging cliffs and the protection they provided from his men's arrows! Why had not one of his damned men told him they offered enough protection from arrows?

"Your father whelped a voiceless coward as well!" Graelam shouted. "Fight me, you mewling whoreson! Do you have guts only to clear the food in your belly?"

Geoffrey gave a roar of fury. "You come to me, Englishman! I will show you how a true warrior fights!"

Graelam gave a derisive laugh. "What, coward? And have your men cut me down? Your treachery is widely known, spineless cur."

"Damn you, pig of an Englishman! You shall not keep what is mine!"

Graelam was silent a moment. The man evidently did not know of Maurice's marriage, that it was no longer just he who stood between Geoffrey and Belleterre.

"You bray like an ass, Geoffrey! Go home to your own keep, for it is all you will ever own. Maurice has remarried and has blessed himself with two healthy stepsons!"

"A likely tale!" Geoffrey shouted. "I heard nothing of such a marriage! You are a coward and a liar, Englishman!"

Kassia could keep quiet no longer. "It is true, Geoffrey. I swear it to you. Leave us go in peace!"

Geoffrey gnawed at his lower lip, uncertainty flowing through him. The unfairness of it all surged through him, making him tremble with its force.

"My lord," one of his men muttered beside him. "Mayhap it is the truth."

Geoffrey growled fluent obscenities at the hapless man. Thoughts swirled through his mind, until finally he smiled. "Kassia," he called, "come to me, in safety, and tell me to my face."

Graelam froze in his hunkered stance. "Kassia," he hissed, but he was too late. He saw his wife move away from her hidden spot and rise to her full diminutive height, in full view of all of Geoffrey's attacking men.

"Here I am, Geoffrey," she called out in her sweet, clear voice. "Let this foolishness cease. If you cannot believe me, I will ride back with you to Belleterre and you may meet my father's new wife and children."

Graelam determined at that moment to thrash her buttocks. Without a thought to his own safety, he rushed out and grabbed her. He felt a searing pain go through his arm, and looked vaguely at the arrow embedded through the chain mail. He tossed her to her knees and dragged her back into the shadowed overhang.

"You little fool," he ground out.

But Kassia wasn't heeding him. She stared conscience-stricken at the arrow in his upper arm. "Hold still, my lord," she said, wondering at the calmness of her own voice. She closed her eyes a brief moment, then drew a deep breath and laid her hands about the arrow's thick shaft. Quickly she jerked it out. Graelam made not a sound. He watched her lift the skirt of her gown and rip off material from her chemise. She bound it securely about his arm.

"Do not think that this wound weakens me, wife. You disobeyed me. I shall thrash you for it, for you imperiled your own life."

"But I only wished to spare you his treachery! I knew he would not dare to harm me." She saw quickly enough it was not a reason he would savor. "Very well, Graelam," Kassia said docilely. "What shall we do now, my lord?"

"Wait," Graelam said tersely, "until it grows dark. Then I will take great pleasure in killing that fool."

"Perhaps if I did return with him . . ." Kassia began, only to swallow the remainder of her words at the fierce look from her husband.

As the time dragged on slowly, Kassia began to think about how thirsty she was. Graelam had slipped away from her to confer with his men. The sun was setting in the distance, casting golden slivers of light over the rough-hewn boulders. Suddenly Kassia sat upright. She could not believe her ears. It was indeed her Aunt Felice's loud voice!

"You fool!" she heard Felice screech. "Lucky for you, imbecile, that one of the men told me of your lunatic plan! Since when do you act without consulting me?"

Kassia could not make out Geoffrey's reply, but she did feel a brief instant of pity for him. It was not right for a mother to belittle her son in front of his men.

"They spoke the truth!" Felice screeched out again. "Damn, Geoffrey, I have wept enough tears for the both of us! It is over."

Kassia turned to see Graelam slip down beside her. There was a wide grin on his face. "Another prince among women," he said, laughing softly, "and this one a termagant beyond belief!"

"Kill the Englishman and you gain naught!" they heard her screech. "Do you wish to wed with your cousin so badly? She would come to you without any dowry, young fool! Think of your own neck, Geoffrey. The Englishman is powerful. There would be retribution."

Geoffrey stared impotently at his mother. "But he deserves to die," he said sulkily.

"Fool," Felice said scornfully. "You will listen to me now, Geoffrey. When I discovered that Maurice had wed Marie de Chamfreys of Normandy, I began to change my thinking. I have found you a lovely girl, my boy, one who will bring us—you—valuable lands. Leave the Englishman with his skinny twit of a wife."

"What is her name?"

"Whose name? Oh, the girl. 'Tis Lady Joanna. She is English and the daughter of the Earl of Leichester. She is ripe for the plucking, and I have had my good friend Orland de Marston speak to her father. He will dower you with rich lands in Normandy. You are to travel to London to meet your betrothed. Soon, Geoffrey."

Geoffrey heaved a despondent sigh. "Very well, Mother," he said.

Felice nodded her head, not expecting any other reply. "Now, it would give me great pleasure to tell Lord Graelam what we—you—have gained."

She rode to the end of the narrow passage, pulling in roughly on her mare's reins. "My lord Graelam," she called out.

"Lady Felice," Graelam said in greeting. "Have you come to take your puppy home?"

"Do not become too amused, my lord," she continued coldly. "I wish my son to take no chances with his. . .

health. He has far greater advantages offered to him. My lord, he will shortly wed Lady Joanna, the Earl of Leichester's daughter! She will bring him great wealth, and her beauty is renowned! Take your silly chit of a wife and leave Brittany!"

Felice jerked her mare about and rode back to her son.

Graelam turned to look at his wife. Kassia was trying valiantly not to laugh, but it was no use. Graelam roared with laughter. His laughter grew even louder as the guffaws from his men met his ears.

"Oh, it is too much!" Kassia gasped.

"Joanna and Geoffrey!"

"Nay, my lord! Joanna and Geoffrey and Felice!"

"Oh, my God! It is a fitting fate for your cousin, my love, and the precious Joanna!"

"We must, my lord," Kassia said primly, "send my cousin and his betrothed a wedding gift."

"Aye," Graelam said thoughtfully, pulling her against him. "Mayhap a whip and manacles. I vow I would wager on Joanna's success."

Kassia raised her head at the sound of the departing band of horses. "Now, my lord, I wish to see properly to your arm."

"And I, my lady, once properly seen to, wish to thrash you soundly." Graelam drew her up agianst him and gently caressed his hand downward over her soft hips. "Mayhap I could bring myself to do it in fifty years or so," he said, and kissed her.

Epilogue

Graelam quietly opened the shutters and breathed in the crisp early-summer air. A year and a half it had been, a year and a half since he and Kassia had returned to Wolffeton. And now he had a son. He turned slightly, a smile touching his lips as he stared at Kassia, suckling their son, Harry, at her milk-swollen breast. Her hair was much longer now, curling softly about her shoulders. The color of gold and brown and copper, he thought, the colors of autumn.

He shook his head, suddenly remembering how such a short time before he was in an agony of worry that she would die in childbirth. He spoke his thoughts aloud. "Four hours, my lady, and you present me with a wailing son. I believe there is much peasant stock in you."

Kassia looked up, her eyes twinkling. "You wanted a good breeder, my lord, and now you complain that I was not sufficiently delicate!" She scarce believed that the pain had ended so quickly. Even now it was becoming a receding memory, now that she held her son in her arms and she was well and getting stronger, and so very happy that she wanted to shout her joy to all of Wolffeton. "He is beautiful, is he not, Graelam?"

"Aye, he will rival the vigorous looks of his father when he is a man, though I fear his eyes will be black as that rogue, Roland." Graelam looked thoughtful for a moment. "I wonder how Roland managed in Wales. He was going there, you know, to perform some sort of rescue."

"Roland is a man who lands on his feet because his tongue is so agile. Now, my lord, I wish to speak more of my beautiful son," Kassia said, putting Harry to suckle at her other breast. "I cannot see that he carries even the smallest bone of his sweet mother in him. Even his hair will be black as all the sins of Satan."

But Graelam didn't smile. He was back into his agonizing memories. "You scared the very devil out of me," he said, drawing close to the bed, his voice hoarse. "I was about to swear I would never touch you again if you but survived. And in the next moment, just before I was to take an eternal vow of celibacy, you smiled at me and bade me look at the miracle you accomplished."

"I wonder," she mused aloud, "if you would have kept that vow. 'Tis a mystery never to be solved." She hugged Harry to her and he looked up with blurry eyes, making her laugh. "He is a miracle, is he not, Graelam? He will be a great powerful man, just like his father."

"Let us trust so—if he is to protect the sisters he's certain to have in the next couple of years."

Kassia merely smiled at that, all the pain of Harry's birthing not yet relegated to the past. She lifted her now-sleeping son from her breast. Graelam took him, placing him gingerly in the crook of his arm. "I cannot believe I was once this small and fragile. It's alarming."

"And so dependent upon a woman's care."

"Ah, that I can believe. 'Tis a lesson I learned late in life from a mouthy little wench." He raised his eyes from his son's wrinkled face to study his wife. "You are feeling all right now, Kassia?"

"Aye," she said, and stretched lazily. "But it is a pity he must look so much like you. It does not seem fair when I did all the work."

"Mayhap his eyes will become an impudent hazel."

"Ha! You're right—they'll be as black as Roland's. Mayhap he will have dimples. I like the thought of that."

He grinned at her and gently laid his son into his cradle. He lightly stroked his finger over the child's smooth cheek, feeling a knot of pride so strong he could not speak. In that moment he vowed silently that his son would never know the coarseness and cruelty he had known. When he sat beside Kassia on their bed he looked uncommonly serious.

"Very well, my lord," Kassia said, laughter in her voice. "He will not have dimples. I meant not to distress you so."

"He can have dimples on his ass for all I care," Graelam said, his voice gruff. "He will be a strong man, Kassia, but he will also learn that women are to be esteemed and protected."

"He could have no better teacher, my lord."

Graelam shook himself and smiled crookedly. "I grow overly serious, love, and I had meant to make you laugh. We have a message from your father."

Kassia's eyes sparkled. "Since you want me to laugh, I assume he is quite healthy?"

"Aye, as are Marie and the children. It concerns Geoffrey."

When he only grinned at her, she pummeled his shoulder. "Graelam, tell me! What has happened?"

"It seems your Aunt Felice and Joanna have formed something of an alliance. Geoffrey, a bridegroom of only three months, has fled to Paris to escape their plans to improve him."

Kassia's merry laughter filled the chamber. "I can almost feel pity for him. Poor Geoffrey!"

"Well, he did not leave until he got Joanna with child. At least he did something that must please that mother of his."

"Speaking of children, when will we see Guy's son?"

"Soon, I expect. Unfortunately, Blanche will not accompany him for she is breeding again." Graelam sighed deeply. "Such an accommodating, submissive woman. So gentle and understanding of her master's needs and wants."

Kassia eyed him severely, but humor lurked in her eyes, for it was a jest of long standing between them. "Aye, you may keep nurturing that illusion, Graelam, though it crumbles so easily at but a touch or at the smallest word."

As she spoke, he gently cupped his hand under her breast, weighing its heaviness. "Did I tell you how beautiful you are, Kassia?"

"Not since yesterday, I think. But—"

She grew silent yet again as her husband pulled down her shift, lowered his head, and gently suckled at her breast. She felt a ripple of pleasure that brought a delicate flush to her face.

She caressed her fingers through his thick hair and held him close. He raised his head and stared at her for a long moment. "I cannot believe," he said in a thick voice, "that my greedy son received as much pleasure from his mother as I just did. Your milk is warm and sweet, like the rest of you."

"I pray you will always feel thus, my lord," she said, her voice breathless.

"I think it likely, my lady. Very likely."

To Carol Steffens Woodrum
Bright and beautiful and loved very very much by
her auntie Catherine.

1

Beauchamp Castle
Cornwall, England
April 1275

"You must wed me, you must!"

Philippa looked at Ivo de Vescy's intense young face with its errant reddish whiskers that would never form the neat forked mustache he hoped for. "No, Ivo," she said again, her palms pressed against his chest. "You are here for Bernice, not for me. Please, I don't want you for a husband. Go now, before someone comes upon us."

"There's someone else! You love another!"

"Nay, I do not. There is no other for me right now, but it cannot be you, Ivo, please believe me."

Philippa really did expect him to leave. She had told him the truth: she didn't love him and didn't

7

wish to marry him. Instead of leaving her chamber, instead of releasing her, he simply stood there staring at her, his arms loose now around her back.

"Please leave my chamber, Ivo," she said again. "You shouldn't have come. I shouldn't have let you in."

But Ivo de Vescy wasn't about to leave. "You will wed with me," he said, and attacked.

Philippa thought, even as he lifted her off her feet and tossed her onto her back on her narrow bed, that a man bent on winning a lady was not best served using rape as an argument. She jerked her face back as he wetly kissed her cheek, her jaw, her nose. "Please, this is absurd! Stop, now."

But Ivo de Vescy, newly knighted, newly pronounced a man by his stringent sire, saw his goal and dismissed the obstacles to his goal as more pleasurable then risky. Philippa would want him soon, he told himself, when he pressed his manhood hard against her, very soon now she would be begging him to take her. He finally found her mouth, open because she was primed to yell at him, and thrust his tongue inside.

It was like putting flame to dry sticks. He was breathing heavily, wanting her desperately, pinning her now-struggling body under his full weight. He got his hand under her long woolen gown, shoved aside her thin linen shift, and the feel of her smooth flesh relieved him of his few remaining wits.

Philippa twisted her head until his tongue was out of her mouth—not a pleasant experience, and one she didn't care to repeat. She wasn't worried until Ivo managed to slither his hand over her knee. His fingers on her bare thigh turned him into a heaving, gasping creature whose body had become rigid and heavy on top of her.

"Stop it, Ivo!" She wriggled beneath him, realized quickly that this would gain her naught—indeed, would gain her even more of a ravening monster—and held perfectly still. "Listen to me, Ivo de Vescy," she whispered into his ear. "Get off me this minute or I will see to the destruction of your precious manhood. I mean it, Ivo. You will be a eunuch and I will tell my father and he will tell yours why it happened. You cannot ravish a lady, you fool. Besides, I have as much strength as you, and—"

Ivo groaned in his dazed ardor; he unwisely thrust his tongue into her mouth again. Philippa bit him hard. He yowled and raised his head to stare down at the girl he wanted so desperately. She didn't yet look as if she wanted him, as if she was ready to beg him for his ardor, but it didn't matter. He decided he would try a bit of reason even as he thrust his member against her in a parody of the sex act.

"No, Philippa, don't try to hurt me. Listen, 'tis you I want, not Bernice. 'Tis you and only you who will bear my sons, and I will take you now so that you will want to be my wife. Aye, 'twill happen. Don't move, sweeting."

His eyes were glazed anew, but Philippa tried again, speaking slowly, very distinctly. "I won't marry you, Ivo. I don't want you. Listen to me, you must stop this, you—"

He moaned and jerked his belly repeatedly against hers. They were of a height, and every male part of him fitted against her perfectly, at least in his mind. Philippa decided it was time to

do something. She was loath to harm him; he
was, after all, Bernice's suitor and perhaps future
husband. Her sister wouldn't want him to be a
eunuch. But he was in her chamber, pinning her
to her narrow bed, breathing into her face, and
planning to force her.

When his fingers eased higher on her thigh,
she yelled into his ear, and he winced, his eyes
nearly crossing, and moaned again—whether from
passion or from the pain of her shrill cry, Philippa
didn't know.

"Stop it!" she yelled once again, and pounded
his back with her fists. Ivo touched her female
flesh, warm and incredibly soft, and thought that
finally she wanted him, would soon be begging
him. Her legs were so long he'd begun to wonder
if he would ever reach his goal. Ah, but he'd
arrived, finally. He pressed his fingers inward
and nearly spilled his seed at the excitement of
touching her. He was panting now, beyond himself. He would take her and then he would marry
her, and he would have her every night, he
would . . .

"You bloody little whoreson! Devil's toes and
St. Andrew's shins, get off my daughter, you stupid whelp!"

Lord Henry de Beauchamp was shorter than his
daughter, blessed with a full head of hair that he
was at this moment vigorously tugging. His belly
well-fed, but when aroused to fury, he was still
formidable. He was nearly apoplectic at this
point. He clutched Ivo's surcoat at his neck, ripping the precious silk, and dragged him off Philippa. But Ivo didn't let go. He held tightly to
Philippa's waist, his other hand, the one that had
touched her intimately, dragging slowly back

down her thigh. She pushed and shoved at him and her father tugged and cursed. Ivo howled as he fell on the floor beside her bed, rolled onto his back, and stared blankly up at Lord Henry's convulsed face.

"My lord, I love Philippa, and you must—" He shut his mouth, belated wisdom quieting his tongue.

Lord Henry turned to his daughter. "Did the little worm harm you, Philippa?"

"Nay, Papa. He was lively, but I would have stopped him soon. He lost his head."

"Better his head than your maidenhead, my girl. How comes he to be in your chamber?"

Philippa stared down at her erstwhile attacker. "He claimed to want only to speak to me. I didn't think it would become so serious. Ivo forgot himself."

Ivo de Vescy had more than forgotten himself, Lord Henry thought, but he merely stared down at the young man, still sprawled on his back, his eyes now closed, his Adam's apple bobbing wildly. Lord Henry had nearly succumbed to a seizure when he'd seen Ivo de Vescy atop his daughter. The shock of it still made the blood pound in his head. He shook himself, becoming calmer. "You stay here, Philippa. Straighten yourself, and, I might add, you will keep silent about this debacle. I will speak to our enthusiastic puppy here. Mayhap I'll show him how we geld frisky stallions at Beauchamp."

Lord Henry grabbed Ivo's arm and jerked him to his feet. "You will come with me, you randy young goat. I have much to say to you."

Ivo deserved any curse her father chose to heap on his head, Philippa thought, straightening her

clothing, and her father had an impressive reper-
toire of the most revolting curses known in Cornwall. She thought of Ivo's hand creeping up her
leg and frowned. She should have sent her fist
into his moaning mouth, should have kicked him
in his spirited manhood, should have . . . Philippa paused, wondering exactly what her father
would say to Ivo. Would he tell him to forget
about Bernice? Would he order Ivo out of Beauchamp Castle? This was the *third* man who'd
acted foolishly . . . well, not so foolishly as Ivo,
and it wasn't amusing, not anymore. Bernice
didn't think so, and neither did their mother,
Lady Maude. Lord Henry wouldn't order Ivo
away from Beauchamp; he couldn't. Bernice
wanted Ivo Vescy very much. Lady Maude wanted
him for Bernice. Philippa wanted him for Bernice
as well.

Philippa felt a thick curl of hair fall over her
forehead and slapped it away, then sighed and
tried to weave it back into its braid. Life wasn't
always reasonable; one couldn't expect it to be.
But there had been five suitors for Bernice's well-
dowered hand. Two of the men had swooned
over Bernice, but she hadn't shared their enthusi-
asms. The other two had preferred Philippa, and
Bernice, unaccountably to her sister, had decided
it was Philippa's fault. And now Ivo de Vescy,
the young man most profoundly desired by Bernice, the one with the sweetest smile, the clever-
est way of arching only one eyebrow, and the
most manly of bodies, had turned coat.

What was Lord Henry saying to him? Philippa
couldn't allow Ivo to be turned out of Beauchamp.
Neither Bernice nor Lady Maude would ever forgive her. They would both accuse her of trying

to gain Ivo's affections for herself. Bernice would probably try to scratch her face and pull out her hair, which would make life excessively unpleasant.

Philippa didn't hesitate a moment. She hurried quietly down the deeply indented stone stairs from the Beauchamps' living quarters into the great hall with its monstrous fireplace and a beam-arched ceiling so high it couldn't be seen in the winter for all the smoke gushing upward. She didn't stop, but speeded up, slipping out of the great hall into the inner ward and running toward the eastern tower. She climbed the damp stone stairs, slowing down only when she reached the second floor and the door to her father's private chamber. His war room, it was called, but Philippa knew that her father frolicked away long winter nights in that room with willing local women. Without hesitation she eased the door open a crack, just enough for her to see her father standing near one of the narrow arrow slits that gave out over the moat to the Dunroyal Forest beyond. Ivo de Vescy, his shoulders attempting arrogance, stood straight as a rod in front of him. She heard her father say sharply, "Have you no sense, you half-witted puppy? You cannot have Philippa! Bernice is the daughter who is to be wed, not Philippa. I will not tell you this again."

Ivo, sullen yet striving with all his might to be manly, squared his shoulders until his back hurt and said, "My lord, I must beg you to reconsider. 'Tis Philippa I wish to have. I beg your pardon for trying to . . . convince her of my devotion in such . . ." He faltered, understandably, Philippa thought, easing her ear even closer.

"You were ravishing her, you cretin!"

"Mayhap, my lord, but I wouldn't have hurt her. Never would I harm a hair on her little head!"

"Hellfire, boy, her *little* head is the same height as yours!"

That was true, but Ivo didn't turn a hair at the idea of having a wife who could stare him right in the eye. "Lord Henry, you must give her to me, you must let me take her to wive. My father will cherish her, as will all my family. Please, my lord, I wouldn't have hurt her."

Lord Henry smiled at that. "True enough, young de Vescy. She wouldn't have allowed you to ravish her, you callow clattermouth. Little you know her. She would have destroyed you, for she is strong of limb, strong as my hulking squire, not a mincing little bauble like other ladies." There was sudden silence, and Lord Henry stared at the young man. There came a glimmer of softening in his rheumy eyes and a touch of understanding in his voice. "Ah, forget your desire, young Ivo, do you hear me?" But Ivo shook his head.

All softening and understanding fled Lord Henry's face. His fearsome dark brows drew together. He looked malevolent, and even Philippa, well used to her sire's rages, shrank back. Surely Ivo would back down very soon; no man faced her father in that mood. To her shock and Lord Henry's, Ivo made another push, his voice nearly cracking as he said, "I love her, my lord! Only Philippa!"

Lord Henry crossed his meaty arms over his chest. He studied Ivo silently, then seemed to come to a decision. Frowning, he said, "Philippa is already betrothed. She is to wed on her eighteenth birthday, which is only two months from now."

"Wed! Nay!"

"Aye. So be off with you, Ivo de Vescy. 'Tis either my lovely Bernice or—"

"But, my lord, who would claim her? Whom would you prefer over me?"

Philippa, whose curiosity was by far greater than her erstwhile ravisher's, pressed her face even closer, her eyes on her father's face.

"She is to wed William de Bridgport."

De Bridgport!

Philippa whipped about, her mouth agape, not believing what she'd heard. Then she caught the sound of her mother's soft footfall and quickly slithered behind a tapestry her grandmother had woven some thirty years before, where only her pointed slippers could be seen. She held her breath. Her mother passed into the chamber without knocking. Philippa heard some muttered words but could not make them out. She quickly resumed her post by the open door.

Philippa heard her mother laugh aloud, a rusty sound, for Lady Maude had not been favored with a humorous nature. "Aye, Ivo de Vescy, 'tis William de Bridgport who will wed her, not you."

Ivo stared from one to the other, then took a step back. "William de Bridgport! Why, my lord, my lady, 'tis an old man he is, a fat old man with no teeth, and a paunch that . . ." Words failed Ivo, and he demonstrated, holding his hands out three feet in front of his stomach. "He's a terror, my lord, a man of my father's years, a—"

"Devil's teeth! Hold your tongue, you impudent little stick! You know less than aught about anything!"

Lady Maude took her turn, her voice virulent. "Aye, 'tis none of your affair! 'Tis Bernice we offer, and Bernice you accept, or get you gone from Beauchamp."

Philippa eased back, her face pale, images, not words, flooding her brain. De Bridgport! Ivo was right, except that de Bridgport was even worse than he had said. The man was also the father of three repellent offspring older than her—two daughters, shrill and demanding, and a son who had no chin and a leering eye. Philippa closed her eyes. This had to be some sort of jest. Her father wouldn't . . . There was no need to give her in marriage to de Bridgport. It made no sense, unless her father was simply making it up, trying to get Ivo to leave off. Aye, that had to be it. Ivo had caught him off-guard and he'd spit out the first name that had come to mind in order to make Ivo switch his ardor to the other sister.

But then Lady Maude said, her voice high and officious, "Listen you, Ivo de Vescy. That giant of a girl has no dowry from Lord Henry, not a farthing, hear you? She goes to de Bridgport because he'll take her with naught but her shift. Be glad de Bridgport will have her, because her shift is nearly all Lord Henry will provide her. Ah, didn't you know all call her the Giant? 'Tis because she's such a lanky, graceless creature, unlike her sweet-natured sister."

Lord Henry stared in some consternation at his pallid-faced wife whose pale gray eyes hadn't shone with this much passion since their first wedded night, a very short wedded night, and slowly nodded, adding, "Now, young pup, 'tis either you return to York and your father or you'll take my pretty Bernice, as her mother says, and you'll sign the betrothal contract, eh?"

But Ivo wasn't quite through, and Philippa, for a moment at least, was proud of him, for he mouthed her own questions. "But, my lord, why? You don't care for your daughter, my lady? I mean no disrespect, my lord, but . . ."

Lord Henry eyed the young man. He watched his wife eye de Vescy as well, no passion in either eye now, just cold fury. Even her thin cheeks sported two red anger spots. Ivo was being impertinent, but then again, Lord Henry had been a fool to mention de Bridgport, but his had been the only name to pop into his mind. And Maude had quickly affirmed the man, and so he'd been caught, unable to back down. De Bridgport! The man was a mangy article.

"Why, my lord?"

There was not only desperation but also honest puzzlement in the young man's voice, and Lord Henry sighed. But it was Maude who spoke, astonishing him with the venom of her voice. "Philippa has no hold on Lord Henry. Thus she will have no dowry. She is naught to us, a burden, a vexation. Make up your mind, Ivo, and quickly, for you sorely tax me with your impertinence."

"Will you now accept Bernice?" Lord Henry asked. "She, dulcet child, tells me she wants you and none other."

Ivo wanted to say that he'd take Philippa without a dowry, even without a shift, but sanity stilled his impetuosity. He wasn't stupid; he was aware of his duty as his father's eldest son. The de Vescy holdings near York were a drain at present, given the poor crops that had plagued the area for the past several years. He must wed an heiress; it was his duty. He had no choice, none at all. And, his thinking continued, Philippa wasn't small and soft and cuddly like her sister. She was too tall, too strong, too self-willed—by all the saints, she could read and cipher like a bloody priest or clerk—ah, but her rich dark blond hair was so full of colors, curling wildly around her face and making an unruly fall down her back, free and soft. And her eyes were a glorious clear blue, bright and vivid with laughter, and her breasts were so wondrously full and round and . . . Ivo cleared his throat. "I'll take Bernice, my lord," he said, and Lord Henry prayed that the young man wouldn't burst into tears.

Maude walked to him, and even smiled as she touched his tunic sleeve. " 'Tis right and proper," she said. "You will not regret your choice."

Philippa felt like Lot's wife. She couldn't seem to move, even when her father waved toward the door, telling Ivo to repose himself before seeking out Bernice. In an instant of time her life had changed. She didn't understand why both her parents had turned on her—if turn they had. She'd always assumed that her father loved her; he worked her like a horse, that was true, but she enjoyed her chores as Beauchamp's steward. She reveled in keeping the accounts, in dealing with the merchants of Beauchamp, with settling disputes amongst the peasants.

As for her mother, she'd learned to keep clear of Lady Maude some years before. She'd been told not to call her "Mother," but as a small child she'd accepted that and not worried unduly about it. Nor had she sought affection from that thin-lipped lady since she'd gained her tenth year and Lady Maude had slapped her so hard she'd heard ringing in her ears for three days. Her transgression, she remembered now, was to accuse Bernice of stealing her small pile of pennies. Her father had done nothing. He hadn't taken her side, but merely waved her away and muttered that he was too busy for such female foolishness. She'd forgotten until now that her father hadn't defended her—probably because it had hurt too much to remember.

And now they planned to marry her to William de Bridgport. They wouldn't even provide her with a dowry. Nor had anyone mentioned it to her. Philippa couldn't take it all in. From a beloved younger daughter—at least by her father—to a cast-off daughter who wasn't loved by anyone, who had no hold on her parents, who was of no account, who had only her shift and nothing more . . . What had she done? How had she offended them so deeply as to find herself thus discarded?

Even as Ivo turned, his young face set, she couldn't make herself move. Finally, when Ivo was close enough to see her, she did move, turned on the toes of her soft leather slippers, and raced away. The toes of the slippers were long and pointed, the latest fashion from Queen Eleanor's court, and they weren't meant for running. Philippa tripped twice before she reached the seclusion of her chamber. She slid the bolt across the thick oak door and leaned against it, breathing harshly.

It wasn't just that they didn't want her. Nor was it that they simply wanted her away from them and from Beauchamp. They wanted to punish her. They wanted to give her to that profane old man, de Bridgport. Why? There was no

answer that came to mind. She could, she supposed, simply go ask her father why he and her
mother were doing this. She could ask him how
she had offended them so much that they wanted
to repulse her and chastise her.

Philippa looked out the narrow window onto
the inner ward of Beauchamp Castle. Comforting
smells drifted upward with the stiff eastern
breeze, smells of dogs and cattle and pigs and the
lathered horses of Lord Henry's men-at-arms. The
jakes were set in the outer wall in the western
side of the castle, and the wind, fortunately,
wafted away the smell of human excrement today.

This was her home; she'd never questioned that
she belonged; such thoughts would never have
occurred to her. She knew that Lady Maude cared
not for her, not as she cared for Bernice, but Philippa had ignored the hurt she'd felt as a child,
coming not to care over the years, and she'd tried
instead to win her father, to make him proud of
her, to make him love her. But now even her
father had sided with Lady Maude. She was to
be exiled to William de Bridgport's keep and company and bed. She felt a moment of deep resentment toward her sister. Bernice, who'd been the
only one to garner the stingy affections Lady
Maud had doled out as if a hug or a kiss were
something to be hoarded.

Was it because Philippa was taller than her
father, a veritable tower of a girl who had not the
soft sweet look of Bernice? Lady Maude had told
Ivo that she was called the Giant. Philippa hadn't
known; she'd never heard that, even from Bernice
in moments of anger.

Was it because she'd been born a girl and not
a boy?

Philippa shook her head at that thought. If true, then Bernice wouldn't be exempt from displeasure, surely.

Philippa wasn't really a giant, just tall for a female, that was all. She turned from the window and looked blankly around her small chamber.

It was a comfortable room with strewn herbs and rushes covering the cold stone floor. She had to do something. She could not simply wait here for William de Bridgport to come and claim her.

It occurred to Philippa at that moment to wonder why Lord Henry had gone to such pains to educate her if his intention were simply to marry her off to William de Bridgport. It seemed a mighty waste unless de Bridgport wanted a steward and a wife and a brood mare all in one. Philippa had been Lord Henry's steward for the past two years, since old Master Davie had died of the flux, and she was becoming more skilled by the day. What use was it all now? she wondered as she unfastened her soft leather belt, stripped off her loose-fitting sleeveless overtunic of soft pale blue linen and then her long fitted woolen gown, nearly ripping the tight sleeves in her haste. She stood for a moment clothed only in her white linen shift that came to mid-thigh. Then she jerked the shift over her head. She realized in that instant that she'd seen something else in the inner ward of the castle. She'd seen several wagons loaded high with raw wool bound for the St. Ives April Fair. Two wagons belonged to the demesne farmers and one to Lord Henry.

She stood tall and naked and shivering, not with cold, but with the realization that she couldn't stay here and be forced to wed de Bridgport. She couldn't remain here at Beauchamp and

pretend that nothing had happened. She couldn't
remain here like a helpless foundling awaiting her
fate. She could hear Bernice taunting her now:
. . . *an evil old man for you, a handsome young man
for me. I'm the favorite and now you'll pay, pay* . . .

She wasn't helpless. In another minute Philippa
had pulled a very old shapeless gown over an
equally old shift and topped the lot with an over-
tunice that had been washed so many times its
color was now an indeterminate gray. She
replaced her fashionable pointed slippers with
sturdy boots that came to her calves. She quickly
took strips of linen and cross-gartered the boots
to keep them up. She braided her thick hair anew,
wound it around her head, and shoved a woolen
cap over it. The cap was too small, having last
been worn when she was but nine years old, but
it would do.

Now she simply had to wait until it grew dark.
Her cousin Sir Walter de Grasse, Lady Maude's
nephew, lived near St. Ives. He was the castellan
of Crandall, a holding of the powerful Graelam
de Moreton of Wolffeton. Philippa had met Walter only twice in her life, but she remembered him
as being kind. It was to her cousin she'd go.
Surely he would protect her, surely. And then
. . . To her consternation, she saw the farmers
and three of her father's men-at-arms fall in
beside the three wagons. They were leaving now!

Philippa was confounded, but only for a
minute. Beauchamp had been her home for nearly
eighteen years. She knew every niche and cavity
of it. She slipped quietly from her chamber, crept
down the deep stairs into the great hall, saw that
no one noticed her, and escaped through the
great open oak doors into the inner ward.

Quickly, she thought, she must move quickly. She ran to the hidden postern gate, cleared it enough to open it, and slipped through. She clamped her fingers over her nostrils, shuddered with loathing, and waded into the stinking moat. The moat suddenly deepened, and her feet sank into thick mud, bringing the slimy water to her eyebrows. She coughed and choked and gagged, then swam to the other side, crawled up the slippery bank, and raced toward the Dunroyal Forest beyond. The odor of the moat was now part of her.

Well, she wasn't on her way to London to meet the king. She was bent on escape. She wiped off her face as best she could and stared down the pitted narrow road. The wagons would come this way. They had to come this way.

And they did, some twenty minutes later. She pulled her cap down and hid, positioning herself. The wagons came slowly. The three men-at-arms accompanying the wagons to the fair were jesting about one of the local village women who could exercise a man better than a day of working in the fields.

Philippa didn't hear anything else. From the protection of her hiding place she flung several small rocks across the road. They ripped into the thick underbrush, thudding loudly, and the men-at-arms reacted immediately. They whipped their horses about, drawing the craning attention of the farmers who drove the wagons. As quickly as she could move, Philippa slipped to the second wagon and burrowed under the piles of dirty gray wool. She couldn't smell the foul odor of the raw wool because she'd become used to the smell of the moat that engulfed her. The wool was coarse and scratchy, and any exposed flesh was instantly miserable. She would ignore it; she had to. She relaxed a bit when she heard one of the men-at-arms yell, " 'Tis naught!"

"Aye, a rabbit or a grouse."

"I was hoping it was a hungry wench wanting to ride me and my horse."

"Ha! 'Tis only the meanest harlot who'd take you on!"

The men-at-arms continued their coarse jesting until they heard one of the peasants snicker behind his hand. One of them yelled, "Get thee forward, you lazy lout, else you'll feel the flat of my sword!"

2

St. Erth Castle, Near St. Ives Bay
Cornwall, England

The sheep were dead. Every last miserable one of them was dead. Every one of them had belonged to him, and now they were all dead, all forty-four of them, and all because the shepherd, Robin, had suffered with watery bowels from eating hawthorn berries until he'd fallen over in a dead faint and the sheep had wandered off, gotten caught in a ferocious storm, and bleated themselves over a sheer cliff into the Irish Sea.

Forty-four sheep! By Christ, it wasn't fair. What was he to do now? He had no coin—at least not enough to take to the St. Ives Fair and purchase more sheep, and sheep that hadn't already been spring-shorn. He couldn't get much wool off a spring-shorn sheep. He needed clothes, his son

25

needed clothes, his men needed clothes, not to mention all the servants who toiled in his keep. He had a weaver, Prink, who was eating his head off, and content to sit on his fat backside with nary a thing to do. And Old Agnes, who told everyone what to do, including Prink, was also doing nothing but carping and complaining and driving him berserk.

Dienwald de Fortenberry cursed, sending his fist against his thigh, and felt the wool tunic he wore split from his elbow to his armpit. The harsh winter had done him in. At least his people were planting crops—wheat and barley—enough for St. Erth and all the villeins who spent their lives working for him and depending on him to keep them from starving. Many lords didn't care if their serfs starved in ditches, but Dienwald thought such an attitude foolhardy. Dead men couldn't plant crops or shoe horses or defend St. Erth.

On the other hand, dead men didn't need clothes.

Dienwald was deep in thought, tossing about for something to do, when Crooky, his fool, who'd been struck by a falling tree as a boy and grown up with a twisted back, shuffled into view and began to twitch violently. Dienwald wasn't in a mood to enjoy his contortions at the moment and waved him away. Then Crooky hopped on one foot, and Dienwald realized he was miming something. He watched the hops and the hand movements, then bellowed, "Get thee gone, meddlesome dunce! You disturb my brain."

Crooky curtsied in a grotesque parody of a lady and then threaded a needle, sat down on the floor, and mimed sewing. He began singing:

My sweet Lord of St. Erth
Ye need not ponder bare-arsed or
Fret yer brain for revelations
For you come three wagons and full they be
Ready, my sweet lord, for yer preservations.

"That has no sensible rhyme, lackwit, and you
waste my energies! Get out out of my sight!"

My sweet lord of St. Erth
Ye need not go a-begging
In yer humble holey lin-en
There come three wagons full of wool and
But a clutch of knaves to guard them-in.

"Enough of your twaddle!" Dienwald jumped
to his feet and advanced on Crooky, who lay on
the rush-strewn floor smiling beautifully up at his
master. "Get to your feet and tell me about this
wool."

Crooky began another mime, still crouched on
the floor. He was driving a wagon, looking over
his shoulder; then fright screwed up his homely
features. Dienwald kicked him in the ribs. "Cease
this!" he bellowed. "You've less ability than the
bloody sheep that slaughtered themselves."

Crooky, exquisitely sensitive to his master's
moods, and more wily than he was brain-full,
guessed from the pain in his ribs that his lord was
serious. He quickly rolled to his knees and told
Dienwald what he'd heard.

Dienwald stroked his hand over his jaw. He
hesitated. He sat down in the lord's chair and
stretched out his legs in front of him. There was
a hole in his hose at the ankle. So there were
three wagons of raw wool coming from Beau-

champ. Long he'd wanted to tangle with that overfed Lord Henry. But the man was powerful and had many men in his service. From the corner of his eye Dienwald saw his son, Edmund, dash into the great hall. His short tunic was patched and worn and remarkably filthy. His hose were long disintegrated, and the boy's legs were bare. He looked like a serf.

Edmund, unconcerned with his frayed appearance, looked from his father to Crooky, who gave him a wink and a wave. " 'Tis true, Father? Wool for the taking?"

Dienwald looked again at the patches that were quick wearing through on his son's elbows. He shouted for his master-at-arms, Eldwin. The man appeared in an instant and Dienwald knew he'd heard all. "We'll take eight men—our most ferocious-looking fighters—and those wagons will soon be ours. Don't forget Gorkel the Hideous. One look at him and those wagon drivers will faint with terror. Tell that useless cur Prink and Old Agnes that we'll soon have enough work for every able-bodied servant in the keep."

"Can I come with you, Papa?"

Dienwald shook his head, buffeted the boy fondly on the shoulder, a loving gesture that nearly knocked him down into the stale rushes. "Nay, Edmund. You will guard the castle in my absence. You can bear Old Agnes' advice and endless counsel whilst I'm gone."

The stench was awful. By the evening of that first day, when the wagons and men camped near a stream close to St. Hilary, Philippa was very nearly ready to announce her presence and beg mercy, a bath, and some of the roasting rabbit

she smelled. But she didn't; she endured, she had
to. They would reach St. Ives Fair late on the morrow. She could bear it. It wasn't just the raw, bur-
filled wool, but the smell of moat dried against
her skin and clothes and mingled with the odor
of the raw wool. It didn't get better. Philippa had
managed to burrow through the thick piles of
wool to form a small breathing hole, but she
dared not make the hole larger. One of the men
might notice, and it would be all over. They
would sympathize with her plight rightly enough,
and let her bathe and doubtless feed her, but then
they would return her to Beauchamp. Their loyalty and their very lives were bound up with Lord
Henry.

She pictured her cousin Sir Walter de Grasse
and tried to imagine his reaction when she suddenly appeared at Crandall looking and smelling
like a nightmare hag from Burgotha's Swamp. She
could imagine his thin long nose twitching, imagine his eyes closing tightly at the sight of her.
But he couldn't turn her away. He wouldn't. She
prayed that she would find a stream before arriving at Crandall.

To make matters worse, the day was hot and
the night remained uncomfortably warm. Under
the scratchy thick wool, adding sweat to the
stench, the hell described by Lord Henry's priest
began to seem like naught more than a cool summer's afternoon.

Philippa itched but couldn't reach all the places
that were making her more desperate by the
minute. Had it been imperative that she jump into
the moat? Wasn't there another way to get to the
forest? She'd acted without thinking, not used her
brain and planned. "You think with your feet,

Philippa," Lord Henry was wont to tell her,
watching her dash hither and yon in search of
something. And she'd done it again. She'd certainly jumped into the moat with her feet.

How many more hours now before she could
slip away? She had to wait until they reached the
St. Ives Fair or her father's men would likely see
her and it would have all been for naught. All the
stench, all the itches, all the hunger, all for
naught. She would wait it out; her sheer invest-
ment in misery wouldn't allow her to back down
now. Her stomach grumbled loudly and she was
so thirsty her tongue was swollen.

Her father's guards unknowingly shared their
amorous secrets with her that evening. "Aye,"
said Alfred, a man who weighed more than Lord
Henry's prize bull, "they pretend it pains them
to take ye—then, jist when ye spill yer seed and
want to rest a bit, they whine about a little bauble.
Bah!"

Philippa could just imagine Alfred lying on her,
and the thought made her ribs hurt. Ivo had been
heavy enough; Alfred was three times his size.
There were offerings of consolation and advice,
followed by tall tales of conquest—none of it in
the service of her father against his enemies—and
Philippa wanted to scream that a young lady was
in the wool wagon and her ears were burning,
but instead she fell asleep in her misery and slept
the whole night through.

The next day continued as the first, except that
she was so hungry and thirsty she forgot for
whole minutes at a time the fiery itching of her
flesh and her own stink. She'd sunk into a kind
of apathy when she suddenly heard a shout from
one of Lord Henry's guards. She stuck her nose

up into the small air passage. Another shout; then: "Attack! Attack! Flank the last wagon! No, over there!"

Good God! Thieves!

The wagon that held Philippa lurched to a stop, leaned precariously to the left, then righted itself. She heard more shouting, the sound of horses' hooves pounding nearer, until they seemed right on top of her, and then the clash of steel against steel. There were several loud moans and the sound of running feet. She wanted to help but knew that the only thing she could possibly do was show herself and pray that the thieves died of fright. No, she had to hold still and pray that her father's men would vanquish the attackers. She heard a loud gurgling sound, quite close, and felt a bolt of terror.

There came another loud shout, then the loud twang of an arrow being released. She heard a loud thump—the sound of a man falling from his horse. And then she heard one voice, raised over all the others, and that voice was giving orders. It was a voice that was oddly calm, yet at the same time deep in its intensity, and she felt her blood run cold. It wasn't the voice of a common thief. No, the voice . . . Her thinking stopped. There was only silence now. The brief fighting was over. And she knew her father's men hadn't won. They would tell no tall tales about this day. She waited, frozen deep in her nest of wool.

The man's voice came again. "You, fellow, listen to me. Your guards are such cowards they've fled with but slight wounds to nag at them. I have no desire to slit any of your throats for you. What say you?"

Osbert wasn't amused; he was terrified, and his

mouth was as dry as the dirty wool in the wagon, for he'd swallowed all his spit and could scarce form words. But self-interest moistened his tongue, and he managed to fawn, saying, "My lord, please allow this one wagon to pass. Thass ours, my lord, my brother's and mine, and thass all we own. We'll starve if ye take it. The other two wagons are the property of my lord Henry de Beauchamp. He's fat and needs not the profits. Have pity on us, my lord."

Philippa wanted to rise from her bed of wool and shriek at Osbert, the scurvy liar. Starve indeed. The fellow owned the most prosperous of Lord Henry's demesne farms. He was a free-man and his duty to Lord Henry lightened his purse not overly much. She waited for the man with the mean voice to cut out Osbert's tongue for his effrontery. To her chagrin and relief, the man said, " 'Tis fair. I will take the two wagons and you may keep yours. Say nothing, fellow," the man added, and Philippa knew he said those words only to hear himself give the order. Her father's farmers would race back to Beauchamp to tell of this thievery, and likely bray about their bravery against overwhelming forces—and take her with them, if, that is, she was in the right wagon.

Suddenly the wagon moved. She heard the man's voice say, "Easy on the reins, Peter. That mangy horse looks ready to crumple in his tracks. 'Twould appear that Lord Henry is stingy and mean."

Philippa wasn't in the right wagon. She was in one of the stolen wagons and she had no idea where she was going. For that matter, when the farmers returned to Beauchamp they wouldn't have any idea who'd attacked them.

Dienwald sat back on his destrier, Philbo, and looked upon the two wagons filled with fine raw wool, now his. He rubbed his hands together, then patted Philbo's neck. The guards had fled into Treywen Forest. They would be fools to ride back to Beauchamp. If they did, Lord Henry would have their ears cut off for cowardice. Other parts of their anatomy would doubtless follow the ears. The farmers would travel to St. Ives. He knew their sort. Greedy but not stupid, and liars of superb ability when their lives were at stake. He imagined them playing the terrified and guiltless victims very well. He imagined them carrying on about this monster at least seven feet tall whose face was nearly purple with scars, who'd threatened to eat them and spit them out in the dirt. And they wouldn't be far off the mark. That was the beauty of Gorkel; he hadn't said a word to the terrified peasants; he didn't have to. Perhaps Lord Henry would even let them keep the proceeds from the sale of their wool—well, not all, but enough for their efforts. And St. Erth now had enough wool for Old Agnes to weave her gnarly fingers to the bone; and in addition, he had two new horses. Not that the nags were anything wonderful, but they were free, and that made them special. It wasn't a bad outcome. Dienwald was content with his day's work. He would remember to give Crooky an extra tunic for his information.

"Don't dawdle," he called out. "To St. Erth! I want to reach home before nightfall."

"Aye, my lord," Eldwin called out, and the wagon lurched and careened wildly as the poor

nag broke into a shuffling canter. Philippa fell
back, bringing piles of the filthy wool over her
face. She couldn't breathe anything save her own
stench until she managed to burrow another
breathing hole. Where was St. Erth? She'd heard
of the place but didn't know its location. Then
her stomach soured and she thought only to keep
herself from retching. The nausea overpowered
her and she clawed through the layers of wool
until her head was clear and the hot sun was searing her face from overhead.

Philippa kept drawing deep gulping breaths,
and when her stomach eased, she grew brave
enough to look around. The man driving the
wagon had his back to her. She craned her neck
and saw the other wagon ahead, and beyond the
first wagon rode six men. All were facing away
from her. Which one was the leader, the lord?
They were all poorly garbed, which was odd, but
their horses seemed well-fed and well-muscled.
Philippa, her stomach snarling even more loudly,
tried to ignore it and take stock of her surroundings. She had no idea where she was. Gnarled
oak trees, older than the Celtic witches, grew in
clumps on either side of the pitted dirt road. She
fancied she would get an occasional sniff of the
sea from the north. Mayhap they were traveling
directly toward St. Ives. Mayhap all was not lost.

Philippa continued thinking optimistically for
another hour. They passed through two small villages—clumped-together huts, really, nothing
more. Then she saw a castle loom up before them.
Set on a high rocky hill, stunted pine trees clus-
tered about its base, was a large Norman-style
castle. Its walls were crenellated and there were
arrow loops, narrow windows in the four thin

towers and walls at least eight feet thick. It was
gray and cold, an excellent fortress that looked
like it would stand for a thousand years. It stood
guard like a grim sentinel over mile upon mile of
countryside in all directions. As the wagons drew
nearer, Philippa saw there was no moat, since the
castle was elevated, but there was a series of
obstacles—rusted pikes buried in the ground at
irregular intervals, their sharp teeth at a level to
rip open a horse's belly or a man's throat if he
fell on them. Then came the holes covered with
grass and reeds, holding, she imagined, vertical
spears. The wagons negotiated the obstacles without hesitation or difficulty.

Philippa heard a loud creaking sound and saw
twenty-foot gates made of thick oak slowly part
to reveal a narrow inner passage some thirty feet
long, with withdrawn iron teeth of a portcullis
ready to be lowered onto an enemy. The wagons
rolled into an inner ward filled with men, women,
children, and animals. It was pandemonium, with
everyone talking at once, children shrieking, pigs
squealing, chickens squawking. There were more
people and animals here than in the inner ward
at Beauchamp, and Beauchamp was twice as big.
Even the chickens sounded demented.

Philippa barely had time to duck under the
wool again before the wagons were surrounded
by dozens of people cheering and shouting congratulations. She heard the thick outer gates grind
close again, and it seemed a great distance away.

Philippa felt her first complete shock of fear.
Her optimism crumbled. She'd done it this time.
She'd truly acted with her feet and not with her
brain. She'd jumped into a slimy moat and then
into a wagon of filthy raw wool. And now she

was alone at a stranger's castle—a prisoner, or worse. She was so hungry she was ready to gnaw at her fingers.

The wagon lurched to a sudden jolting halt. Dozens of hands rocked the wagon. Philippa felt them grabbing at the wool, felt their hands sifting through the layers, nearer and nearer to where she was buried.

Then she heard the leader's voice, closer now, saying something about Gorkel the Hideous and his magnificent visage, and then her stomach announced its rebellion in no uncertain terms and she fought her way up through the wool until she flew out the top, gasping, gulping the clean air.

"God's glory," Dienwald said, and stared.

A little boy bellowed, "What is it, Papa? A witch? A druid ghost? Thass hideous!"

Gorkel shuddered at the apparition and yelled, " 'Tis more hideous than I! God gi' us his mercy! Deliver us from this snare of the devil's!"

Dienwald continued to stare at the daunting creature lurching about, its arms flapping, trying to keep its balance in the shifting wool. The creature was tall, that much was obvious, its head covered with wool, thick and wild and sticking straight out. Then the great wigged hag gained its footing and turned toward him downwind, and he gagged. The noxious odor surpassed that of his many villeins who didn't bathe from their birth until their death.

The creature suddenly began to shake itself, jerking away clumps of wool with its grubby fingers, until its face was cleared and he saw it was a female sort of creature staring back at him with frightened eyes as blue as the April sky that was just beginning to mellow into late afternoon.

His people were as silent as mourners at a
pope's tomb—an achievement even St. Erth's
priest, Cramdle, had never accomplished in his
holiest of moments—all of them staring gape-
mouthed and bug-eyed. Then slowly they began
to speak in frightened whispers. "Aye, Master
Edmund has the right of it: thass a witch from
the swamp."

" 'Tis most likely a crone tossed out for
thievery!"

"Nay, 'tis as Gorkel says: thass not human,
thass an evil monster, a punishment from the
devil."

Edmund yelled, " 'Tis a witch, Papa, and she's
here to curse us!"

"Be quiet," Dienwald told his son and his people. He dug his heels gently into Philbo's sleek
sides. He got within five feet of the ghastly female
and could not bear to bring himself closer. He
fought the urge to hold his nose.

"I'm no witch!" the female shouted in a clear
loud voice.

"Then who are you?" Dienwald asked.

Philippa turned to stare at the man. She wasn't
blind. She saw the distaste on his face, and in
truth, she couldn't blame him. She touched her
fingers to her hair and found that her cap was
long gone and the thick curls had worked free of
the braid and were covered with slime from the
Beauchamp moat and crowned with clumps of the
squalid wool. She could just imagine what she
looked like. She felt totally miserable. People were
making the sign of the cross as they stared at her,
horror and revulsion on their faces, calling upon
a dizzying array of saints to protect them.

And she was Philippa de Beauchamp, such a

wondrous and beauteous girl that Ivo de Vescy had tried to force her so she would wed him. It was too much. By all the saints, even William de Bridgport wouldn't want her now. She imagined herself standing before him covered with slime and wool, her smell overwhelming. Surely he would shriek like the little boy had. She pictured de Bridgport turning and running, his fat stomach bouncing up and down. She couldn't help herself. She laughed.

"I am in obvious disarray, sirrah. Forgive me, but if you would allow me to quit your very nice castle, I will be on my way and you won't have to bear my noxious smell or my company further."

"Don't move," Dienwald said, raising his hand as she moved to climb over the side of the wagon. "Now, answer me. Who are you?"

It was the man with the mean deep voice, and her brief bout of laughter died a quick death. She was in a very dangerous situation. It didn't occur to her to lie. She was of high birth. No one with any chivalry would hurt a lady of high birth. She threw back her wild bushy head, straightened her shoulders, and shouted, "I am Philippa de Beauchamp, daughter of Lord Henry de Beauchamp."

"A witch! A lying crone!"

"I am not!" Philippa shouted, furious now. "I might look like a witch, but I'm not!"

Dienwald gazed at the hideous apparition, and it was his turn to laugh. "Philippa de Beauchamp, you say? From my vantage, 'tis barely female you appear, and such an unappetizing female that my dogs would cringe away from you. In addition, you have likely spoiled some of my wool."

"She will curse us, Papa!"

"*Your* wool? Ha! 'Tis my father's wool and you

are nothing more than a common thief. As for you, you loud crude boy, I am mightily tempted to curse you."

Edmund shrieked, and Dienwald began to laugh. His people looked at him, then at the female creature, and they began to laugh as well, their chuckles swelling into a great noise. Philippa saw a misshapen fellow standing near the steps to the great hall, and even he was cackling wildly.

She wished now she'd lied. If she'd claimed to be a wench from a village, perhaps he'd simply have let her leave. But no, she'd told the truth— like a fool. How could she have imagined chivalry from a man who'd stolen two wagons of wool? Well, there was no hope for it. Up went her wool-clumped chin. "I am Philippa de Beauchamp. I demand that you give me respect."

The moment the creature had opened her mouth, Dienwald realized she wasn't an escaped serf or a girl from the village of St. Erth. She spoke like a gentlewoman—all arrogant, and loud, and haughty—like a queen caught in the jakes with her skirts up, yelling at the person who'd seen her. What the devil was this damned female doing hidden in a wool wagon, stinking like a hog's entrails, and covered with slime?

"I have long thought Lord Henry to be a red-nosed glutton whose girth makes his horses neigh in dread of carrying his bulk, but even he couldn't have been cursed with such as you. Now, get you down from the wagon." Dienwald watched her weave about, gain her balance, and climb down. She was very tall, and his villeins moved away from her, especially those unfortunate enough to be downwind of her. She stood on the ground, watching him, looking so awful it would curdle

the blood of the unwary. He let Philbo back away
from the fright and shouted at her, "Don't move!"

Dienwald dismounted, tossed the reins to his
master-at-arms, Eldwin, and strode over to the
well. He filled a bucket, then returned to the
wagon. Without hesitation, he threw the bucket
of water over her head. She wheezed and
shrieked and jerked about, and some of the wool
rolled off her body and tunic. He could see her
face now, and it wasn't hideous, just filthy.
"More water, Egbert!"

"Water alone won't get me clean," Philippa
said, gasping from the shock of the cold water.
But she was grateful; she could now sniff herself
without wanting to gag. She licked her lips and
gratefully swallowed the drops of water that
remained.

"I can't very well strip you naked here in my
inner ward and hand you a chunk of lye soap. I
mean, I could, but since you claim to be a lady,
you would no doubt shriek were your modesty
defiled."

A howl of laughter met this jest, and Philippa
tried not to react. She said, calm as a snake sun-
ning itself on a warm rock, "Couldn't I have the
soap and perhaps go behind one of your
outbuildings?"

"I don't know. My cat has just had kittens back
there, and I hesitate to have her so frightened that
her milk dries up." Dienwald felt the laughter billowing up again. He yelled for lye soap; then
added, "Egbert, take the creature behind the
cookhouse and leave her be. Look first for Eleanor. If she and her kittens are there, take the creature behind the barracks. Agnes, fetch clean
clothes for her and attend her. Then bring her

to me—but only when she no longer offends the nose."

"But, Papa, she's a witch!"

"Officious little boy," Philippa said as she turned on her bare heel—her boots were buried somewhere in the wool—and followed the man with the wonderful bucket of water.

"Careful what you call the creature, young Edmund," Crooky said, hobbling up. "It might cast a foul spell on you. Thass a relic from Hades, master." He threw back his head and cleared his throat. Dienwald, recognizing all too well the signs, yelled, "Keep your lips stitched, fool! No, not a word, Crooky, not a single foul rhyme out of your twitching mouth.

"As for you, Edmund," he continued to his son, "the creature isn't a relic. Relics don't turn your stomach with their stench, nor have I ever seen a relic that talked back to me. Now, let's have our wool begin its progress into cloth and into tunics. Prink! Get your fat arse out here!"

3

"The well will go dry before the creature is clean enough for mortal viewing and smelling," Dienwald said, rubbing his jaw as he spoke.

"Aye, thass the truth," said Northbert, who was sniffing the wool. " 'Tis not a virtuous smell, my lord," he added, picking up a clump of wool and bringing it to his nose, an appendage flattened some ten years before by a well-aimed stone.

"We'll let Old Agnes deal with it," Dienwald said.

"There she comes!" Edmund shouted.

Dienwald looked up at his son's yell. Indeed, he thought, staring at the female vision striding toward him, barefoot, the rough gown nearly threadbare and loose everywhere except her breasts. Her hair was a damp wild halo around her head, hair the color of dark honey and fall leaves and rich brown dirt, and growing curlier by the minute as it dried.

She walked up to him, stopped, looked him squarely in the eye, and said, "I am Philippa de Beauchamp. You are a thief, but you also appear to be master of this castle and thus my host. What is your name?"

"Dienwald de Fortenberry. Aye, I am lord of this castle and master of all those herein, including you. Now, I have much to say to you, and I don't wish to speak in front of all my people. Follow me."

He turned without another word and strode across the dusty inner bailey toward the great hall. He was tall, she saw, following in his wake, some three or four inches taller than she was, and straight as a lance and just as solid. She couldn't see a patch of fat on him. He was also tough-looking and younger than she'd first thought when she heard him giving orders after his theft of the wool wagons. He wasn't all that much older than she, but he was treacherous—he'd already proved that. He was naught but a thief without remorse. She had still to see if he had the slightest bit of chivalry.

Dienwald de Fortenberry. She turned pale with sudden memory and was grateful he wasn't looking at her to see her face. She'd heard tales of him since she was ten years old. He was known variously as the Rogue of Cornwall, the Scourge, and the Devil's Blight. When de Fortenberry chanced to plunder or rob or pillage close to Beauchamp lands, Lord Henry would shake his fist in the air, spit in the rushes, and scream, "That damnable bastard should be cleaved into three parts!" Why *three* parts, no one at Beauchamp had

ever dared to ask. She should never have told
him who she was. She'd been ten times a fool.
Now it was too late. He was master of this castle.

The great hall was shadowed and gloomy, with
smoke-blackened beams supporting the high ceiling, and only a half-dozen narrow windows covered with hides. The floor rushes snapped and
crackled beneath her bare feet, and several times
she felt one of the twigs dig into her sole—a twig
or mayhap a discarded bone. There wasn't much
of an odor, just a stale smell. She watched the
man wave away poorly garbed servants, several
men-at-arms, the crooked-backed fellow, and the
small boy whom she assumed was his son. Where
was his wife? He had a son; surely he had a wife.
On the other hand, what woman would want to
be wedded to a scourge or a blight or a bastard?
Philippa watched him sit down in the lord's chair,
a high-backed affair of goodly proportions that
had been made by a carpenter with some skill
and a love of ornamentation. "Come here," the
Scourge of Cornwall said, and crooked his finger
at her.

No one had ever crooked a finger at her in such
a peremptory way. Not even Lord Henry in his
most officious moments.

Philippa forgot for a moment where she was
and who it was who'd commanded her. She
straightened her shoulders with alarming force.
Her breasts nearly split the center seam of her
gown. She nearly wailed with humiliation as she
quickly hunched forward.

Dienwald de Fortenberry laughed.

"Come here," he said again.

Philippa walked forward, keeping her eyes on
his face. It wasn't a bad face. She would have

thought a scourge's face would be pitted by the pox, that he'd be wild-eyed and black-toothed, not hard and well-muscled and with eyes of light brown ringed with gold, with hair and brows the identical shade. There was a deep dimple in the center of his chin. Mayhap that was a mark of the devil. But if it were a devil's mark, why didn't he wear a beard to hide it? Instead he was clean-shaven, his hair worn longer than was the current fashion, with tight curls at his nape. He didn't look like a rogue or a devil's blight, but hadn't he stolen her father's wool without a by-your-leave?

"Who are you?"

"I am Dienwald de Fortenberry—"

"I know that. I mean, are you truly a devil's tool? Or perhaps one of his familiars?"

"Ah, you have realized my identity. Have you heard mind-boggling tales of me? Tales that have me flying over treetops with my arms spread like great wings to escape Christian soldiers? Tales that have me traveling a hundred miles from Cornwall in the flash of an eye to kill and butcher and maim in the wilds of Scotland?"

"No, I have heard my father curse you mightily when you have raided near Beauchamp, but you are always just a man to him, even though he roars about scourges and blights and such."

" 'Tis true. I am of this earth, not above it or below it. I am but a simple man. Do you, Philippa de Beauchamp, consider this earthbound man of sufficient prominence to sit in your august presence?"

"I don't think you care at all what I think. Moreover, I'm lost."

Dienwald sat forward in his chair. "You are in my castle, St. Erth by name. As to your exact whereabouts, I believe I shall keep that to myself for a time. Sit you down. I have questions for you, and you will answer them promptly and truthfully."

Philippa gazed about. There was no other chair.

He pointed downward at his feet. "On the floor."

"Don't be absurd! Of course I won't sit on the floor."

Dienwald stood up, still pointing to his feet. "Sit, now, or I will have my men fling you down. Perhaps I shall plant my foot on your neck to keep you down."

Philippa sat down on the floor, folding her long legs beneath her. She tried to straighten the skirt of her borrowed gown, but it was too narrow and too short and left her knees bare.

Dienwald resumed his seat, crossing his arms over his chest, negligently stretching his long legs in front of him. She noticed for the first time that his tunic and hose were in shameful condition.

She looked up at him. "May I please have something to drink? I am very thirsty."

Dienwald frowned at her. "You aren't a guest," he said, then in his next breath bellowed, "Margot!"

A thin young girl scurried into the hall, managed a curtsy, and waited, her eyes on the now-clean creature barely covered by a tattered garment of dull green belonging to one of the cookhouse wenches.

"Ale and . . ." He eyed the seated female, whose knees were showing. Nice knees connected to very nice legs. "Are you hungry as well?"

Her stomach growled loudly.

"Bread and cheese as well, Margot. Be speedy, we don't want our guest to collapse in the rushes."

Philippa could have hugged him at that moment. Food, at last. *Food!*

"Now, wench—"

"I am not a wench. I am Philippa de Beauchamp. I demand that you treat me according to my rank. I demand that you . . . well, you could begin by getting me a chair and then a gown that isn't so very rough and worn and old."

"Yes? What else? That isn't all you wish, is it?"

She ignored his sarcasm. "I know I am tall, but perhaps one of your wife's gowns would fit me."

"I have no wife. I had a wife once, but I don't have one now, nor have I had one for many a year, thank the saints. The gown Old Agnes found for you is doubtless precious. There isn't a single hole in it. It deserves your thanks, not your disdain."

"I meant no insult and I do thank you and the gown's owner. May I please borrow a horse? A nag, it matters not. I will see that it is returned to you."

"Why?"

To lie or to speak more foolish truths? Philippa settled for the middle ground. "I was traveling to see my cousin, who lives near St. Ives. I was riding in the wool wagon to the fair and then I planned to walk the rest of the way to my cousin's keep. Now, of course, I am here, and 'tis probably still too far away for me to walk."

Dienwald looked at the female and realized she was quite young. The wild hair and the ill-fitting gown had deceived him. The hair was now dry and a full glorious fall down her back. There were more shades than he could count, from the palest flaxen to dark ash to deepest brown. He frowned at himself. "All right, I believe you are Philippa de Beauchamp. Why were you hiding in a wool wagon?"

Margot appeared with a wooden tray that held ale, bread, and a chunk of yellow cheese. Philippa's mouth began to water. She stared at the food, unable to tear her eyes away, until Dienwald, shrugging, rose and pointed her toward the long row of trestle tables that lined the eastern side of the great hall.

He kept further questions to himself and merely watched her eat. She tried to be dainty and restrained, but her hunger overcame her refined manners for a few minutes. When she chanced to look up, her mouth full of bread, to see him watching her, she quickly ducked her head, swallowed, and fell into a paroxysm of coughing.

Dienwald rose and leaned over the trestle table, and pounded her back. He handed her a cup of ale. "Drink."

Once she'd gotten her breath back, he was sitting again, silently watching her. If she'd been in that damned wool wagon all the way from Beauchamp, she hadn't eaten or drunk anything for nearly two days. It also seemed to Dienwald that she'd acted without much thought to any consequences, a usual feminine failing.

"You have a lot of hair."

She unconsciously touched her fingers to the tumbled curls. "Aye."

"Who is this cousin you were traveling to see?"

"I can't tell you that. Besides, it isn't important."

"How old are you?"

"Nearly eighteen."

"A great age. At first I had believed you older. Why were you running away from Beauchamp?"

"Because my father wanted me to marry a—" Philippa stopped cold. She dropped a piece of cheese onto the trestle table, then jumped to retrieve it. She fought with all her better instincts not to stuff it into her mouth. She bit off a big chunk.

"You were so against this marriage that you jumped into the moat, then buried yourself in my wool, making both it and you stink like a marsh hog?"

She nodded vigorously, her mouth full of the wonderful cheese. "Truly, I had to. If you don't mind, I should like to keep running."

"It won't work, you know. A lady of your tender years and wealth doesn't go against her father." He paused, giving her a long, brooding look, a look Philippa didn't like a bit. "A daughter should never go against her sire. As for marriage, 'tis to increase the family's wealth and lands and political influence. Surely you know that. Weren't you raised properly? What is wrong with you? Have you taken the minstrels' silly songs to heart? Did you fall in love with some silly fellow's eyebrows? Some clerk who read you romantic tales?"

She shook her head, thinking about her family gaining lands and wealth. Marrying her to William de Bridgport wouldn't bring any of those benefits. "Truly, sir, I can walk, if you'll just tell me the direction to St. Ives."

Dienwald continued brooding and looking. Finally he rose and returned to his chair, saying over his shoulder, "Well, come along. Sit on the floor."

Philippa grabbed the last piece of bread and the last morsel of cheese and followed. When she sat, the tunic slid up above her knees. She chewed on the bread, watching him, praying he wouldn't ask anything until she'd swallowed the rest of her food. But his next words nearly made her choke again.

"There are many things to consider here. I could ransom you. Your father is very wealthy, from what I've heard. Beauchamp is a formidable holding, and has been since William gave it to Rolfe de Beauchamp two hundred years ago. And your father has some influence at court, or so I heard some years ago." He paused, looking away, and Philippa's gaze followed his. He said, "Ah, I believed myself too lucky to be alone. Come here, Crooky, and join in my musings. What do you think the wench would bring in ransom?"

Crooky hobbled up, looked Philippa up and down, and said. "Thass a tall wench, master, even sitting, a strapping big wench. Those legs of hers just don't stop. By Saint Andrew's nose, 'tis yer height she be, or nearly, I'll wager ye."

"No, no," Philippa said, "he is taller than I, by at least four inches."

"Yes, that's true," Dienwald said, ignoring her. "This is Crooky," he added after a moment to Philippa, "my fool, my ears, and a great piece of impertinence a good deal of the time. But I suffer his presence." He saw her nose go up. It was a nice narrow nose. It was also an arrogant and supercilious nose.

Fitting for a Philippa de Beauchamp.

To Philippa's surprise, Crooky suddenly broke into song.

What be she worth?
This wooly-haired wench?
Jewels for a ransom?
Not with her stench.
She looks like a hag
She brays and she brags—

"You're blind, clattermouth," Dienwald interrupted. "She's clean and wholesome and I've
even fed her so her ribs are no longer clanking
together. Come here so I can kick you in the
ribs."

Crooky cackled and backed quickly away. "A
bath did her good, sweet lord. Aye, ransom the
wench. She'll bring you coin, much-needed coin.
Mayhap we'll need more weavers for all that
wool. Let de Beauchamp pay dear to fetch the
little partridge back into his fold. God gi' ye grace,
madam." And the strange little man who bellowed off-key gave her a crooked-toothed grin.

"That was a horrid rhyme," Philippa said.
"You've no talent at all. My mare neighs more
agreeably than you sing."

"Slit her throat," Crooky said to his master.
"She's got a bold tongue and she's naught but a
pesky female. Of what earthly good is she?"

"You're right, Crooky. A deadly combination,
surely, and of no use." Dienwald reached for the
dagger at his belt.

Philippa gasped, sudden fear causing her to
jump to her feet and back away. With her hunger
and thirst slaked, she'd let herself forget who this
man was, had let down her guard and behaved
as she would have at home, and now look what
her tongue had gotten her into.

Dienwald drew his dagger and fingered the

sharp edge. He rose slowly. "Have a care, lady. This is not your domain. You have no power here, no authority. Moreover, you are naught but a female, a big strapping female with more wit than most, but nonetheless you are to keep your mouth closed and your tongue behind your teeth. Aye, I will ransom your hide, now that it is white again and sweet-smelling. I will have my steward write to your father telling him of your status. Have you an idea of what he'll pay for your return? A clean and hearty wench he'll get, I will promise it, a wench ready for him to flail with his tongue and his belt. Both of which you deserve."

Philippa shook her head. Fear clogged her throat. Fear of this unpredictable man and fear of the truth. Perchance the truth in this instance would serve her well. On the other hand, perhaps it wouldn't. She didn't know what to do. She said finally, "My father doesn't want me back. He won't pay you anything. He will be pleased never to see my face again in this life. He didn't want me. That's why I ran away."

"That's not hard to believe, what with the face you had when I first beheld you. He would have believed himself in hell, faced by the devil's mistress."

"I told you that I jumped into our moat and that I ran away. It was foolish, I admit, but I did it and I can't now undo it."

Philippa heard a gasp and saw a plump big-breasted girl staring at them, her face pale. Then she saw the direction of the girl's eyes, and saw the girl was staring at the man's dagger. He was still holding it, caressing the blade with the pad of his thumb. Philippa had forgotten the dagger. Would he slit her throat? Wasn't he possessed of any chivalrous instincts? She very quickly returned to the floor, folding her legs under her as far as she could manage.

"It begins to rain, my sweet lord," Crooky said. "I'll see the wool is kept dry. Come along, Alice, the master is busy counting coins in his head. He'll make you happy later, once he's rid himself of this extra wench."

"Aye," Dienwald said, not looking toward the big-breasted girl. "Go. Leave me. I will make you happy tonight."

Philippa stared. Her father had mistresses; she and all at Beauchamp knew it. But he pretended otherwise; he was discreet. Of course this man had no wife to shriek at him. She turned back and saw that Dienwald was speaking to an old woman.

"Aye, master, that old fool Prink has sickened suddenly, taken to his bed, he has, yelling that he's dying."

Dienwald cursed, then said, "I'll wager Father Cramdle is at his bedside even now, just in case. His list of sins is long enough for three days."

Then the little boy strode up and bellowed, "Hers a witch, kill her, Papa, stick your dagger in her gullet!"

Philippa looked at the boy standing out of her reach, legs apart, an expression on his face that was remarkably like his father's.

"Not *hers* a witch," Philippa said. "Can't you speak properly? It's *she's* a witch." Of the boy's father she asked, "Have you no privacy here? And I'm not a witch."

"Very little privacy," Dienwald said, and waved Edmund away. "Go see to our wool. And keep out of mischief. Aye, and speak properly!"

Philippa added her coin. "Why don't you go visit the water and the lye soap?"

"I shan't. You're a lanky spear with a wooly head!"

"Officious little clodpole!"

"Enough! Edmund, get thee gone now. You, lady, keep your tongue behind your teeth or you will surely regret it." Again he pointedly fingered his dagger, and Philippa, not liking the sharpness of that blade, nor the tone of his voice, lowered her head and shut her mouth. She'd been a fool, but she didn't have to continue being one.

"I had great need of the wool," Dienwald said, looking down at his frayed hose. "I lost forty-four sheep before shearing, and all of us are ragged. That's why I took the two wagons." He glanced up, straight at her, and seemed startled that he'd explained his theft.

"Your need is quite evident. But thievery will bring you only retribution from my father, doubt you not."

"Ah, you think so? Let me tell you something, Lady Lackwit. Those dauntless farmers with the other wagon will continue to the fair at St. Ives. They will sell the wool and hide well their profits. Then they will go bleating to Lord Henry about the theft of all three wagons. Moreover, they have no idea who robbed them. Now, in addition, you are my prisoner, as of this minute. If I decide to ransom you, I can always say I found you creeping along a road. And if you, wench, tell your sire the truth, think you those brave farmers will say they lied and robbed your father and were cowards? Now, I was considering treating you like a guest, but I think that isn't what you need. You are too bold, too brazen for a female. You want mastering and proper manners. Perhaps I shall take on the chore. You will remain at St. Erth until I decide what to do with you. You will leave me now."

"I would like to leave you forever! My father will discover the truth and crush you like the pestilence you are!"

Dienwald smiled. "It will make a jongleur's tale that will cause the beams of the hall to creak with mirth."

"You are the only lackwit here. I told you, my father wants nothing more to do with me."

"Then perhaps I can instead discover the name of the man he wished you to marry. I can send a message to the clothhead and *he* can ransom you."

"Nay!"

She'd actually turned white, Dienwald observed. Let her skin creep with the thought. He wondered who the man was.

"Arrogant fool," Philippa said as she looked out the narrow window of her cell down into the inner ward. The sky was leaden in the late afternoon, and fog rolled over the castle walls. It had stopped raining some minutes before.

Dienwald de Fortenberry was striding across the now-muddy ward toward the stables, three dogs at his heels, followed by two small children and a chicken with sodden feathers. He'd ordered her taken by Northbert, a man with a very flat nose, to a tower chamber and locked in. Chamber, ha! 'Twas a cell, nothing more. At least he hadn't locked her down in the granary. Philippa watched him until he disappeared into the stables. Only the chicken followed him inside. The

children and dogs were stopped by a yelling stable hand with the blackest hair Philippa had ever
seen. Although he spoke loudly, calling the children little crackbrains, she could barely hear him
over all the other people in the inner bailey. So
many people, and so noisy, each with an opinion
and a loud voice. The men yelled and shouted,
the women yelled and shouted, and the children
and chickens squawked and shrieked. It was a
cacophony of head-splitting noise and Philippa
turned away from the window slit and surveyed
her room. It was narrow and long and held only
a low bed with a rank-smelling straw-stuffed mattress and a coarse blanket. There was no pillow,
no water to drink; there was a cracked pot under
the cot in which to relieve herself, but nothing
more.

It was heaven-sent compared to her residence
in the wool wagon, but it still wasn't at all what
she was used to. She'd always taken Beauchamp
and all the luxuries it had afforded her for
granted. It had been her home, and all the people
there were known to her and trusted. Now she
was nothing more than a prisoner. All her wondrous escape had netted her was a dank cheerless
room in the keep tower of a man more unpredictable than the Cornish weather and, by reputation,
a thoroughly bad lot.

"Thass good quality, master," Old Agnes was
saying to the thoroughly bad lot, her gnarled fingers caressing the wool. "Jes' lovely."

"Aye," Dienwald agreed. "Pick what wenches
you need to help you clean and weave the wool
and tell Ellis. I'll have Alain hire weavers immediately. The first new tunic is for Master Edmund—
aye, a new tunic and new hose."

Old Agnes looked sour at that order but didn't say anything. "What about the creature, master?"

"The what? Oh, her. She'll be gone before you can give her a new gown. Let her return home in what we gave her. 'Tis a gift."

"Thass a lady, master, not a scullion."

Old Agnes sometimes forgot herself, Dienwald bluntly informed her. Old Agnes gave him a toothless grin and a mirthless cackle and returned to picking filth from the wool. Dienwald left the stables, nearly stumbling over a chicken. The bird squawked, deftly avoiding the kick of a foot.

Dienwald sniffed the heavy air. White fog hung over his head in patches. It would shower again soon. There was time enough to practice with the quintains, since today was Tuesday, but he felt unsettled and restless. He made his way to the solar, where there were three small rooms, one used for St. Erth's priest and Edmund's tutor, Father Cramdle. He eased open the door to the sound of his son's penetrating voice: "Thass naught but silly tripe for peasants!"

4

Father Cramdle's voice, normally the model of patience and tolerance, was a bit frayed. "Master Edmund, peasants can't read, much less cipher. Listen, now, 'tis what your father wants. If I add eleven apples from this barrel to the seven bunches of grapes in this barrel, what is the result?"

"Purple apples!"

Dienwald's first response was to laugh at his son's wit, but he saw the pained look on Father Cramdle's homely face. Edmund not only looked like a villein's child, he was as ignorant as any of them.

"Answer Father Cramdle, Edmund. Now."

"But, Papa, thass a foolish problem, and—"

"*That is*, not *thass*. I don't want to hear that from you again. Answer the problem. Speak properly." He remembered Philippa's correction, made without thought. Had his son become so ill-managed? He wanted Edmund to read at least enough so he wouldn't be cheated by merchants or his own steward in the future. He wanted him to cipher so that he would know if he'd gotten the correct measure of flour from the miller. Dienwald could sign his name and make out words if he spoke them aloud slowly, but little more. It wasn't something he regretted very often, just at times like this when he saw the proof of ignorance in his son.

It required all of Edmund's fingers and toes and painstaking counting, but finally the correct answer came from his mouth.

"Excellent," Dienwald said. "Father, if the boy needs the birch rod, tell me. He will learn."

"Papa!"

"Nay, little gamecock. You will remain here studying with Father Cramdle until he sees fit to release you. It is what I wish of you, and you will obey me."

Dienwald left the room knowing that the kindly and very weak-willed Father Cramdle didn't have the spirit to control a nine-year-old boy. Dienwald would have to involve himself more. As for Alain, the steward, he could control the boy, but Edmund hated Alain. Though he would never say why, he avoided him, slinking away whenever Alain came into the vicinity.

As Dienwald left the solar, he glanced over to the east tower. He saw Philippa de Beauchamp at the narrow window, looking down. He hoped she was scared out of her wits wondering what he was going to do to her. He would give her until the following afternoon to become appropriately submissive. She was too proud. She was

also too big, too tall, too curly-haired. He had no
complaint about her legs, which seemed to go on
until they reached her throat, just as Crooky had
pointed out. Her breasts seemed more than ample
as well. But she wasn't . . . He forced his thinking
away from that channel. Kassia de Moreton was
delicate and small and sweetly soft. And she
would never belong to him. It wasn't fated to be.
Pity that he liked her hulking warrior husband
nearly as much as he cared for her, else he would
be tempted to slit Graelam's throat some dark
night and relieve him of his wife.

Dienwald sighed. He admired everything about
Kassia—her gentleness, her shy humor and guileless candor, her fierce loyalty to her husband, her
daintiness, even the smallness of her bones and
her delicate wrists . . . Ah, well, it was hopeless.
At least she was his friend, delighting in his company, though now she was determined to find
him an heiress—to save him from mold and damp
and ruin, she'd say, and pour him some of her
father's precious wine from Aquitaine. She wanted
Dienwald to become respectable, a concept that
thoroughly irritated and frightened him. But not
for long. After all, what family would want to be
allied with a rogue like him? It was just as well.
The Scourge of Cornwall liked life just as it was.
With the acquisition of the wool, the days would
continue to be as entertaining as they'd been
before the mindless sheep had plunged off that
cliff.

It occurred to him a few moments later why he
was so restless. He needed a woman. He didn't
delay, simply asked to have Alice sent to his
chamber. When she arrived, plump and smiling,
her arms held forward a bit to further push out

her breasts, Dienwald waved her closer. When she stood in front of him, he started to sweep her onto his lap. But her smell stopped him cold. "When did you last bathe?"

Alice flushed. "I forgot, master," she said, eyes cast down. She knew to avert her eyes, because if she looked at him, he just might see the amazement on her face. All this insistence upon rubbing her body with water and soap! It was beyond foolish.

Dienwald wanted her, but even her breath smelled of the stuffed cabbage she'd eaten the previous night.

"I won't have you again in my bed until you wash yourself—all of you, do you understand, Alice? With soap. Even between your legs and under your arms. And cleanse your teeth."

He sent her away, calling out, "Use the soap!" He'd first herded her into his bed only two weeks before. She'd learn, he hoped, that he liked a woman's body to be free of odor and her breath sweeter than that of his wolfhounds.

He waited, tapping his fingertips impatiently on the arms of the single chair in his chamber. When Alice appeared thirty minutes later, her hair wet from its washing but smooth from a good combing, and her breath pure as a spring breeze, he smiled and patted his thighs.

She came to him willingly, and when he brought her to stand between his thighs, she again pressed her breasts forward. He wondered who'd taught her to do this. Normally it amused him. Now, however, he wanted only release, and quickly. He slipped her coarse gown over her head, to find her naked beneath. She hadn't dried herself completely, and his hands slid over her moist flesh.

He clasped her hands down to her sides and looked at her. She was white and plump and smooth as an egg. She would also be quite fat in no more than five years, but that didn't disturb him one whit. She was merely pleasingly bountiful now, the flesh between her legs soft and damp, and she was nearly the same age as his long-legged prisoner in the east tower.

He kissed Alice's mouth, tentatively at first, until he knew that she'd cleansed her teeth; then he became more enthusiastic. When at last he eased her down onto his manhood, groaning at the feel of sinking deep into her body, he leaned back his head, closing his eyes. Finally he played with her hot woman's flesh until she squirmed and arched her back and cried out. Then he allowed himself relief, and it was sweet and long and good.

He left her asleep on his bed and quit his solar, stretching and contented, every restless feeling stilled. Night had fallen and the evening meal was late, as usual. Dienwald thought about his prisoner, alone and probably so hungry she was ready to gnaw on the cot in her chamber. He decided he was feeling benevolent and told Northbert to have her fetched. She would doubtless be grateful to him for feeding her.

When she appeared beside Northbert, he motioned her to the chair beside his.

"Thass the witch," Edmund said, waving a handful of bread toward the approaching Philippa.

"She's not a witch. And it's *that is*, not *thass*. Mind your manners, Edmund. She's a lady, and you will treat her politely."

Edmund grumbled, and Dienwald, giving him a very pointed look, added, "One insult, and you will spend your evening with Father Cramdle reading the holy writ."

The threat brought instant obedience. Dienwald studied his prisoner again. She didn't look like a lady, of course, in that shapeless coarse gown, bare feet, and thick curling hair loose around her head.

"God's greetings to you, lady," he said easily to Philippa. "Sit thee here and take your fill."

"What? The master offers me a chair rather than the dank floor?"

He eyed her. Some show of gratitude. He should have guessed. She wasn't one whit broken; not a shadow of submissivenes. She was still insolent. He should have held to his original plan and left her in that chamber alone for twenty-four hours. He continued, still tolerant, lounging back in his chair, "There are no females at St. Erth as great-sized as you, lady, so moderate your appetite accordingly, for there are no more gowns for you."

"God bless your sweet kindness, sir," Philippa said with all the gratitude of a nun who'd just been made an abbess. "You have the charitable soul of Saint Orkney and the pious spirit of a zealot."

"There is no Saint Orkney."

"Is there not? Why, with your example, kind lord, there should be. Yes, indeed."

Philippa smiled at him, her dimples deep, so pleased with herself that she couldn't help it. Then she smelled the food. Her stomach growled loudly. She forgot Dienwald de Fortenberry, forgot that her situation was fraught with uncertainty, and looked down at her trencher, on which lay a thick slab of bread soggy with rich gravy and decorated with large chunks of beef.

Dienwald watched her attack the meal. A bold wench with a ready tongue. No wonder she thought her father didn't want to ransom her. Who would want such a needle-witted wench in his keeping? Unaccountably, he smiled. When she mopped up the trencher with her last chunk of bread, he said, "Will you eat all my mutton and pigeon as well? Every one of my boiled capons, with ginger and cinnamon, and all of my jellied eggs?"

"I don't see the jellied eggs." There was stark disappointment in her voice.

"Perhaps you ate them without seeing them. Your hands and your mouth toiled very diligently."

She turned to him. "And surely you wouldn't have mutton, would you? Didn't you lose all your sheep?"

Dienwald had to pause a moment on that one. He saw her dimples deepen again, and realized she was enjoying herself mightily at his expense. One could not allow a woman to have the last word. It was against the laws of man and God. It was as intolerable as a kick to the groin.

He shook himself. "What wear you beneath that gown?"

A man, Philippa thought, used whatever weapons available to him. Her father was a master at bluster. His nose turned red, his eyes bulged, and he raged long and loud. Her cousin Sir Walter de Grasse, if she remembered aright, turned sarcastic and cold when he was in a foul temper. Her father's master-at-arms never thought, just struck out with his huge fists. As for this man, at least his dagger still lay snug in its sheath at his belt, so a show of violence wasn't on his mind. It relieved her that he wished to best her with words, even though they were meant to shrivel her with embarrassment. Unfortunately, she'd taken a sip of the strong ale when he'd spoken, and now she choked on it. He slapped her on the back, nearly sending her face into a wooden platter of boiled capon.

"I can feel nothing," Dienwald said as he leaned down close to her. His fingers splayed wide over her back. "No shift? No pretense at modesty?"

Philippa felt the urge to violence—after all, she was her father's daughter—and she acted instantly. Quick as a snake, she reached for his dagger. She felt his hand lock around her wrist until her fingers turned white from lack of blood.

"You dare?"

She'd thought with her feet again, and the result had brought his anger on her head. She shook her head.

"You *don't* dare?"

But there was no anger in his tone, not now. He seemed amused. That was surprising, and vastly relieving as well. He loosened his grip on her wrist and pressed her hand palm-down against his thigh. Her eyes flew to his face, but she didn't move.

"I have decided to give you a choice, lady," Dienwald said.

Philippa wasn't at all certain she wanted to hear of any choices from him.

"Not a word? I don't believe it." He paused a moment, cocking a brow at her. She remained silent.

"You tell me your father won't ransom you. You also refuse to tell me the name of your unpleasant suitor. You balk at telling me the name of this cousin you were running to. Very well, if you aren't able to bring me pounds and shillings and pence, the very least you can do is repay my hospitality on your back. It is doubtful, but perhaps I'll find you acceptable in that role, at least for a limited time."

She'd been right: she *hadn't* wanted to hear his choices.

"You don't care for the thought of me covering you?"

Surely a man who allowed children, dogs, and a chicken to follow him about couldn't be all that bad. There were still no words in her mind.

"Wrapping those long white legs of yours around my flanks? They're so long, mayhap they'll go around me twice. And plucking your virginity? Doesn't that give you visions of delirious pleasure?"

"Actually," she said, looking out over the noisy great hall at all the men and women who sat at the trestle tables eating their fill, laughing, jesting, arguing, "no."

"No, what?"

Philippa reached for a capon wing with her left hand and took a thoughtful bite. She couldn't let him see that he'd stunned her, demolished her confidence, and made her nearly frantic with consternation. Wrapping her legs around his flanks? Plucking her . . . Philippa wanted to gasp, but she didn't; she took another bite of her capon wing. Dienwald was so surprised at her nonchalance, her utter indifference, that he released her wrist. She shook her hand to get the feeling back, then reached for another piece of capon. Before she brought it to her mouth, she dipped it deep in the ginger-and-cinnamon sauce.

Dienwald stared at her profile. More thick tendrils had worked loose from her braid, a braid as thick as Edmund's ankle, and curled around her face.

She turned back to him finally, dipping her fingers into the small wooden bowl of water between their places. " 'Tis very good, the capon. I like the ginger. No, my father won't ransom me. I should have lied and told you he would, but again, I didn't think, I just spoke."

"True. Your point, lady?"

"I don't want to be your mistress. I don't want to be any man's mistress."

"That won't be up to you to decide. You are a woman."

"That is a problem I share with half the world. What will you decide, then?"

"Must you persist in your picking and harping? Must you nag me with questions until I am forced to put my dagger point to your white neck?"

"Nay, but—"

"Swallow your tongue! I shall have the name of your betrothed, and I shall have it soon. I will even demand less ransom if he will have you back."

"No!"

Dienwald picked up her long braid and wrapped it around his hand, drawing her face close to his. "Listen, wench—"

"I am not a wench. My name is Philippa de—"

"You will do my bidding in all things, no matter you're the Queen of France. Now, what is the poor crackbrain's name?"

Philippa swallowed. She smelled the tart ale on his breath, felt its warmth on her temple. His eyes were darker, the flecks of gold more prominent. "I won't tell you."

"I think you will. You lack proper submissiveness and obedience. You need training, as I told you earlier. I think I should begin your lessons right now." He looked quite wicked as he said, "Take off your gown and dance for my people."

She stared at him. "Your priest would not approve."

Dienwald took his turn at staring. " 'Tis true," he said. "Father Cramdle would flee to meet his maker."

"Very well. If my choices are between being your mistress and telling you the name of that awful man my father wished me to wed, and if you then plan to ransom me to that horrid old man and make me suffer his presence for the rest of my life, then my answer is obvious. I will be your mistress until you don't want me anymore."

It took a moment for her flow of words to make sense. When they did, he refused to let her see how stunned he was. Was her intended husband that repulsive? Or had she simply no womanly delicacy? No, she was just toying with him, first telling him nay, then changing her tune.

"I could give you over to my men," he continued thoughtfully. "You are really not to my taste, with your big bones and your legs as long as a man's. Have you also feet the size of a man's?"

Philippa was frightened; she didn't understand this man. Unlike her father, who would have been purple-faced with rage and yelling his head off by now, this man's agile tongue cavorted hither and yon, leaving her mind in disarray. She didn't want to have to prance atop the trestle table naked. She didn't want Father Cramdle to clutch his heart with shock. All the power she'd felt whilst they fenced with words had been an illusion at best. The fact that this man didn't kick children or dogs or chickens didn't automatically endow him with an honorable nature. Now he was showing his true colors. Now he was getting down to serious business. She opened her mouth, but what came out was unbidden and unsanctioned.

"You make me sound like an ugly girl."

She was appalled that such errant vanity could come from her brain, much less from her mouth. But his insults, piled up now as high as the stale and matted rushes on the cold stone floor, had cut deep.

He laughed, an evil laugh. "Nay, but a gentle soft lady you are not. Now, let me see. There must be something about you that is . . . You do have very nice eyes. The blue is beyond anything I have ever seen, even beyond the blue speckles on robins' eggs. There, does that placate your female vanity?"

Philippa managed to say nothing. To her surprise, she saw the fool, Crooky, who'd been crouched beside Dienwald on the floor beside her chair, leap to his feet and sing out a coarse lyric about the effect a woman's blue eyes could have on a man's body.

Dienwald burst into loud laughter, and at the sound, the remaining fifty people in the great hall guffawed and thumped their fists on the tables until the beams seemed to shake with their raucous mirth.

"Come here, Crooky, you witless fool," Phil-

ippa called out over the din, caution again tossed
to the four winds, "I want to kick your ribs."

Dienwald looked at the girl beside him. She
was laughing, and she'd mimicked him perfectly.

Philippa, basking in her temporary wit, failed
to notice that utter silence had fallen. She further
failed to notice how everyone was gazing from
her to Dienwald with ill-disguised consternation.

Then she noticed. If he didn't cut her throat,
he'd throw her to his men. She didn't doubt it.
He hadn't a shred of honor, and she'd crossed
the line. Without a word, she quickly slipped out
of the chair, jumped back, and ran as fast as she
could toward the huge oak doors of the great hall.

5

Windsor Castle

Robert Burnell, Chancellor of England and King Edward's trusted secretary, rubbed a hand over his wide forehead, leaving a black ink stain.

" 'Tis time to take your rest," King Edward said, stretching as he rose. He was a large man, lean and fit, and one of the tallest man Robert Burnell had ever seen. Longshanks, he was called fondly by his subjects. A Plantagenet through and through, Burnell thought, but without the slyness and deceit of his sire, Henry, or the evil of his grandfather, John I, who'd maimed and tortured with joyous abandon anyone who chanced to displease him. Nor was he a pederast like his great uncle, Richard Coeur de Lion—thus the string of children he and his queen, Eleanor, had assembled to date. And that brought up the matter at hand. Robert wondered if his broaching the topic would call forth the Plantagenet temper. Unlike his grandfather, Edward wouldn't fall to the floor and bash his fists and his heels in bellowing rage. No, his anger was like a fire, perilous one moment, cold ashes the next, a smile in its place.

"I work you too hard, Robbie, much too hard," Edward said fondly, and Burnell silently agreed. But he knew the king would continue to use him as a workhorse until he met his maker, thanks be to that maker.

"Just one more small matter, your highness," Burnell said, holding up a piece of parchment. "A matter of your . . . er, illegitimate daughter, Philippa de Beauchamp by name."

"Good God," Edward said, "I'd forgotten about the girl. She survived, did she? Bless her sweet face, she must be a woman grown by now. Philippa, a pretty name—given to her by her mother, as I recall. Her mother's name was Constance and she was but fifteen, if I remember aright. A bonny girl." The king paused and his face went soft with his memories. "My father married her off to Mortimer of Bledsoe and the babe went to Lord Henry de Beauchamp to be raised as his own."

"Aye, sire. 'Tis nearly eighteen she is, and according to Lord Henry, a Plantagenet in looks and temperament, healthy as a stoat, and he's had her educated as you instructed all those years ago. He reminds us 'tis time to see her wedded. He also writes that he's already been beleaguered for her hand."

The king muttered under his breath as he strode back and forth in front of his secretary's table.

"I'd forgotten . . . ah, Constance, her flesh was

soft as a babe's . . ." The king cleared his throat.
"That was, naturally, before I became a husband
to my dear Eleanor . . . she was still a child . . .
also, my daughter is a Plantagenet in looks . . .
not a hag then . . . excellent, but still . . ." He
paused and looked at his secretary with bright
Plantagenet blue eyes, eyes the same color as his
illegitimate daughter's. He snapped his fingers
and smiled.

"My dear Uncle Richard is dead, God rest his
loyal soul, and we miss the stability he provided
us in Cornwall. For a son-in-law, Robbie, we must
have a man who will give us unquestioning loyalty, a man with strength of fist and character and
heart, but not a man who will try to empty my
coffers or trade on my royal generosity to enrich
himself and all his brothers and cousins."

Burnell nodded, saying nothing. He wouldn't
remind the king that he, his faithful secretary,
hadn't received an increase in compensation for a
good five years now. Not that he'd ever expected
one. He sighed, waiting.

"Such a man is probably a saint and in residence in heaven," the king continued, giving Burnell another Plantagenet gift—a smile of genuine
warmth and humor that rendered all those in his
service weak-kneed with the pleasure of serving
him. "I don't suppose Lord Henry has a
suggestion?"

"No, sire. He does write that suitors for his
other daughter tend to look upon Philippa instead,
as likely as not. He tires of the situation, sire.
Indeed, he sounds a bit frantic. He writes that
Philippa's true identity becomes more difficult to
keep a secret as the days pass, what with all the
young pups wanting her hand in marriage."

"A beauty." Edward rubbed his large hands together. "A beauty, and I spawned her. All Plantagenet ladies are wondrous fair. Does she have golden hair? Skin as white as a sow's underbelly? Find me that man, Robbie, a man of strength and good heart. In all of Cornwall there must be a man we can trust with our daughter and our honor and our purse."

Robert Burnell, a devout and unstinting laborer, toiled well into the dark hours of the night, burning three candles to their stumps, examining names of men in Cornwall to fit the king's requirements. The following morning, he was bleary-eyed and stymied.

The king, on the other hand, was blazing with energy and thwacked his secretary on the shoulders. "I know what we'll do about that little matter, Robbie. 'Tis my sweet queen who gave me the answer."

Was this another little matter he didn't know about yet? Burnell wondered, wishing only for his bed.

"Yes, sire?"

"The queen reminded me of our very loyal and good subject in Cornwall—Lord Graelam de Moreton of Wolffeton."

"Lord Graelam," Burnell repeated. "What is this matter, sire?"

"Lackwit," Edward said, his good humor unimpaired. " 'Tis about my little Philippa and a husband for her fair hand and a sainted son-in-law for me."

Burnell gaped at the king. He'd discussed his illegitimate daughter with the queen, with his *wife*?

He swallowed, saying, "Lord Graelam's wedded, sire. He was atop my list until I remembered he'd married Kassia of Belleterre, from Brittany."

"Certainly he'd wedded, Robbie. Have you lost your wits? You really should get more rest at night. 'Tis needful, sleep, for a sprightly brain. Now, Lord Graelam is the one to ferret out my ideal son-in-law. You will readily enough wring a list of likely candidates out of him."

"I, sire?"

"Aye, Robbie, certainly you. Whom else can I trust? Get you gone after you've had some good brown ale and bread and cheese. You must eat, Robbie—'tis needful to keep up your strength. Ah, and write to Lord Henry and tell him what's afoot. Now, I must needs speak to you about the special levy against those cockscomb Scots. I think that we must—"

"Forgive me, sire, but do you not wish me to leave for Cornwall very soon? To Wolffeton? To see Lord Graelam?"

"Eh? Aye, certainly, Robbie. This afternoon. Nay, better by the end of the week. Now, sharpen your wits and recall for me the names of those Scottish lords who blacken the Cheviot Hills with their knavery."

6

St. Erth Castle

Philippa heard shouts behind her. One great bearded man grabbed at her, ripping the sleeve from her tunic, but she broke free. She heard a bellow of laughter and a man shouting, "Ye should have grabbed her skirt, rotbrain! Better a pretty bare ass than an arm!"

It was as dark as the interior of a well outside the great hall. Philippa dashed full-tilt across the inner bailey toward the stables, hoping to get to a horse and . . . And what? The gates were closed. There were guards posted on the ramparts, surely. The night was cold and she was shivering in nothing but a ragged one-sleeved gown to cover her.

Still, her fear kept her going. The stables were dark and warm and smelled of fresh hay, dung, and horses. They were also deserted, the keepers, she supposed, in the great hall, eating their evening meal with all the rest of the denizens of this keep. She stopped, pressing her fingers to the stitch in her side. She was breathing hard, and froze in her tracks when she heard her captor say from nearby, "You are but a female. I accept that as a flaw you can't remedy—God's error, if you will—yet it would seem that you never think before you act. What were you planning to do if you managed to get a horse?"

Philippa slowly turned to face him. Dienwald de Fortenberry was standing in the open doorway of the stable, holding a lantern in his right hand. He wasn't even breathing hard. How had he found the time to light a lantern?

"I don't know," she said, her shoulders slumping. "You have so many people within the keep, I hoped mayhap the gates would be open, with people milling in and out, that mayhap the guards and porters wouldn't notice me, but they all appear to be in the great hall eating, and—"

"And mayhap the moon would make an appearance and guide you to London to court, eh? And thieves would salute you and blow you sweet kisses as you rode past them, your gown up about your thighs. Stupid wench, I would not have gained my twenty-sixth year if I'd been so heedless of myself and my castle. We are quite snug within these walls." He leaned down and set the lantern on the ground. Philippa backed up against a stall door as he straightened to look at her.

"If you don't begin to think before you act, I doubt you will gain your twentieth year. You ripped off a sleeve."

"Nay, one of your clumsy men did that." She remembered another man's coarse jest and felt suddenly quite exposed, standing here alone with him, her right arm hanging naked from her shoulder. "Please, my lord, may I leave? I'm thinking clearly now. I should be most grateful."

"Leave? Tread softly, lady. Your position at present is not passing sweet. I think it more fitting that I should beat you. Tie you down and beat you soundly for your audacity and disrespect—something your father never did, I suspect. Do you prefer a whip or my hand?"

"Stay away!"

"I haven't moved. Now, you told me that you didn't want to be my mistress. Then, like a female, you danced away to a different tune and said you would prefer my using you as my mistress rather than wedding the man your father selected for you. Have I the sequence aright?"

She nodded, her back now flat against the stall door. "I should prefer Satan's smiles, but that doesn't seem to be an available choice. You told me you would give me choices but you didn't."

"Don't keep pushing against that stall door, wench. Philbo, my destrier, is within. He isn't pleased with people who disturb him, and is likely to take a bite of your soft shoulder."

Philippa quickly slid away from the stall door and looked back at the black-faced destrier. He had mean eyes and looked as dangerous as his master.

"Are you a shrew?"

"Certainly not! 'Tis just that de Bridg—" She broke off, stuffed her fist in her open mouth, and gazed at Dienwald in horror.

"William de Bridgport?" Interest stirred in

Dienwald's eyes. He got no response but he saw that she'd terrified herself just by saying the man's name. He imagined anyone could eventually get everything out of this girl. She spoke without thinking, acted without considering consequences. She was a danger to herself, a quite remarkable danger. He wondered if she would yell in passion without thinking. "He is a repulsive sort," Dienwald said. "Fat and rotten-toothed, not possessed of an agreeable disposition."

"Nay, 'tis someone else! I just said his name because he looks like . . . your horse!"

"My poor Philbo, insulted by a wench with threadbare wits." He became silent, watching her, then said, "You would prefer my using your fair body to wedding him. I know not whether to be flattered or simply amazed. Are you certain Lord Henry won't ransom you? I really do need the money. I would prefer money to your doubtless soft and fair—but large—body."

Philippa shook her head. "I'm sorry, but he won't. You must believe me, for I don't lie, not this time. I overheard him tell my mother and a suitor for my sister's hand who tried to ravish me that I would have no dowry at all."

"Your sister's suitor tried to ravish you? How was this accomplished?"

" 'Twas Ivo de Vescy. He's a sweet boy, but he fancied me and not my sister. My father pulled him off me before I hurt him, which I would have done, for I am quite strong."

Dienwald laughed; he couldn't help it. He'd come after her with violence in mind, but she'd disarmed him, first with her pale-faced fear, then with her artless candor. He looked at the long naked white arm. She was so young . . . Nay, not so young. Many girls were married with a babe suckling at their breast by her age.

"Your father told de Vescy that he was marrying you to de Bridgport?"

She nodded. "I didn't know—he'd never said a word to me about de Bridgport. At first I couldn't believe it, wouldn't believe it, but then . . ."

"And then you didn't think, just acted, and jumped in the moat, then into the wool wagon. Well, 'tis done. Come along, now. You've gooseflesh on your naked arm, and it's powerfully unappetizing. I think I'll take you to my chamber and tie you to my bed. I will be careful not to rip your gown further, since it is the only piece of clothing you have."

Beauchamp Castle

"She's a deceitful bitch and I hope she falls into a ditch! I hope she's been set upon by pillaging soldiers. I hope she's imprisoned in a convent. At least dear Ivo doesn't want her—at least, he'd better not."

"Bernice, quiet!" Lord Henry roared. "I must write to the king immediately . . . again. God's nails, I will lose Beauchamp, he will tear my limbs from my body."

Lady Maude quickly ordered Bernice from the solar. Her daughter whined and balked, for her curiosity was at high tide, but her mother's hand was strong and she was determined. Bernice would not find out her supposed sister's true parentage, not if Lady Maude had any say about it, which she did.

"My lord," she said upon returning to her

spouse, "you must moderate your speech. Aye, you must write to the king again, but don't tell him the girl is missing. Nay, a moment." Lady Maude stared toward the ornate *prie-dieu* in the corner of the chamber. "We must think. We mustn't act precipitately. Philippa must have overheard our talk of marrying her off to de Bridgport."

Lord Henry groaned. "And she fled Beauchamp. Why did I think of that whoreson's name, much less spew it out to de Vescy like that? God's eyebrows, the man's a braying ass, and I've proved myself a fool."

Lady Maude didn't disagree with his assessment of himself, but said loudly, "I think William de Bridgport a man to make a girl a fine husband."

Lord Henry stared at his thin-lipped wife. When, he wondered, had her lips disappeared into her face? He seemed to remember years before that she'd had full, pouting lips that curved into sweet smiles. He stared down her body and wondered where her breasts had gone. They'd disappeared just like her lips. Through her endless prayers? No, that would just make her bony knees bonier. He thought of little Giselle, his sixteen-year-old mistress. She had magnificent breasts, and *her* lips hadn't disappeared. She also had all her teeth, which nipped him delightfully.

He groaned again, recalling his current problem. The king's daughter was gone; he had no idea where, and he was terrified that she would be killed or ravaged. His mind boggled at the possible fates that could befall a young, beautiful girl like Philippa. More than that, Lord Henry was quite fond of her. For a girl, she was all a father could wish. Nay, she was more, for she was also his steward.

She wasn't filled with nonsense like her sister. She wasn't particularly vain. She could read and write and cipher, and she could think. The problem with Philippa was that she didn't think when things were critical. Oh, aye, set her to solving a dispute between two peasants and she'd come up with a solution worthy of Solomon. But face her with a crisis and she turned into a whirling dervish without a sensible thought in her head. And she'd heard de Bridgport's name and panicked.

Where had she run?

Suddenly Lord Henry's eyes widened. He'd been stupid not to think of it before. The wool wagons bound for the St. Ives Fair. Philippa wasn't altogether stupid; she hadn't merely thrown herself out on the road and started walking to God only knew where. He grinned at his wife, whose nostrils had even grown pinched over the years. Would they eventually close and she'd suffocate?

"I know where Philippa went," he said. "I'll find her."

St. Erth Castle

Dienwald hadn't completely lost his wits. Unlike Philippa de Beauchamp, he tended to think things through thoroughly before acting—if he had the chance, that is—and in this matter he had all the time he wanted. And he did want to punish the wench for dashing out of the great hall the way she had, making him look the fool in front of all his people. He held firmly to her naked white arm as he walked her back across the inner bailey. A donkey brayed from the animal pen behind the barracks; two pigs were rutting happily in refuse, from the sound of their squeals; and a hen gave a final squawk before tucking in her feathers and going to sleep.

Philippa was frightened now, and he felt her resistance with every step. It was a chilly night and she was shivering. "Hurry up," he said, and quickened his pace, then slowed, realizing her feet were bare. She was going to try to escape him on bare feet and in a flimsy torn gown? She was an immense danger to herself.

Silence fell when he strode into the great hall with her at his side. He yelled for his squire, Tancrid. Tancrid, a boy of Philippa's years, was skinny and fair, with soft brown eyes and a very stubborn jaw. He ran to his master and listened to his low words, nodding continuously. Dienwald then turned on his heel and left. He pulled Philippa up the outside stairs to the solar.

"You're not taking me back to that tower cell?"

"No. I told you, I'm taking you to my bed and tying you down."

"I would wish that you wouldn't. Cannot you give me another choice?"

"You have played your games with me, wench—"

"Philippa. I'm not a wench."

Dienwald hissed between his teeth. "You begin to irk me, you wench, harpy, nag, shrew . . . The list of seemly names for you is endless. No, keep quiet or I will make you very sorry."

As a threat it seemed to lack unique menace, but Philippa hadn't known him long enough to judge. She bit her lip, kept walking beside him up the solar stairs, and shivered from the cold. His fingers were tight about her upper arm, but he hadn't hurt her. At least not yet.

They passed three serving maids and two well-armed men, bound, evidently, for guard duty. Dienwald paused, speaking low to them, then dismissed them. He took Philippa to a large bed-chamber that hadn't seen a woman's gentling touch in a long time. There was a large bed with a thick straw mattress and a dark brown woolen spread atop it. There were no hangings to draw around it. There were two rough chairs, a scarred table, a large trunk, a single wool carpet in ugly shades of green, and nothing else. No tapestries, no wall hangings of any sort, no bright ewers or softening cushions for the chair seats. It was a man's chamber, a man who wasn't dirty or slov-enly, but a man to whom comforts, even the smallest luxuries, weren't necessary. Or perhaps he simply hadn't the funds to furnish the room properly. Still, whatever the reason, Philippa didn't like the starkness of the chamber at all.

She wished now that there weren't any privacy. She wished there was an army camping through-out the solar. She wished there was a chapel in the chamber next to this one filled with praying priests and nuns. But the chamber was empty save for the two of them. He released her arm, turned, and closed the chamber door. He slid the key into the lock, then pocketed the key in his tunic. He lit the two tallow candles that sat atop the table. They illuminated the chamber and had a sour smell. Didn't the lord of St. Erth merit can-dles that were honey-scented or perhaps laven-der-scented?

"There is little moonlight," he said, looking

toward the row of narrow windows, "as you'd
have noted if you'd paused to do any planning at
all in your mad dash for escape."

Philippa said nothing, for she was staring.
There was glass in the windows, and that surprised her. Lord Henry had glass windows in the
Beauchamp solar, but he'd carped and complained at the cost, until her mother had threatened to cave in his head with a mace.

Dienwald smiled at her then and strode toward
her. "No," Philippa said, backing away.

He stopped, as if changing his mind. "I asked
Tancrid to bring us wine and more food. I assume
you're yet hungry? Your appetite seems endless."

To her own surprise, Philippa shook her head.

"You dashed out of the hall before you ate any
boiled raisins. My cook does them quite nicely, as
well as honey and almond pastes." He was prat-
tling on and on about food, and all she could do
was stand there looking petrified. He smiled at
her, and if possible she looked even more
alarmed.

There came a knock on the door. She nearly
collapsed with relief, and Dienwald frowned.
"You like having someone besides my exalted self
with you? Well, 'tis just Tancrid with wine and
food. Don't move."

The boy entered bearing a tray that was dented
and bent but of surprisingly good craftsmanship.
He set it upon the table and fiddled with the
flagons.

"Go," Dienwald said, and Tancrid, with a curious look at Philippa, took himself off.

"They all wonder if I'm going to ravish you,"
Dienwald said with little show of interest, and sat
at the table. "That, or poor Tancrid is afraid you'll

stick a knife between my ribs." He didn't sound at all concerned. He poured himself wine, sat back in his chair, and sipped it.

"Are you?" She swallowed convulsively. "Are you going to ravish me?"

Dienwald stretched. "I think not . . . tonight. I have already lain with a very comely wench, and have not the urge to do it again, particularly with a girl of such noble proportions and such—"

"I'm not ugly! Nor am I oversized or ungainly! I have had three very fitting men want my hand in marriage. How dare you say that I'm not worth your energy or that I am not to your taste or to your—"

Dienwald burst out laughing. Here she was, heedless as a squeaking hen, taking exception to his refusal to ravish her. He continued to laugh, watching her face turn alarmingly pale when she realized finally what she was doing.

Very suddenly she sat down on his bed, covered her face with her hands, and started crying. Not dainty feminine tears, but deep tearing sobs that racked her body and made her shoulders jerk.

"By god! I have done nothing to you! Stop your tears, wench, or I'll—"

She jerked up at his words and said through hiccups, "I am not a wench, I'm Philippa de—"

"I know, you're Goddess Philippa, Queen Philippa, Grand Templar Philippa. Be quiet. You'll sour my stomach. Now, no more crying. You have no reason to cry. I have done nothing to harm you. Indeed, I saved you from death. Thank me, Empress Philippa."

"Thank you."

Dienwald hadn't expected that. Perhaps she

wasn't such a little tartar after all. He rose and watched her jump from the bed and scurry back against the far wall. He smiled and leaned down to unwrap the stout cross garters that wrapped securely about his calves.

When he rose to face her again, he waved the long cross garters. "Come here and let me tie you down. I won't tie you tightly."

"Nay!" she whispered.

Dienwald merely smiled and reached for her, a length of cross garter in his hand. She ducked away from him, stumbled and fell to her hands and knees on the floor. He winced for her, knowing that the rough stones were hard as a witch's kettle.

He grabbed her around her waist, realizing as he hauled her up that he liked the feel of her. Her waist was narrow and . . . He had no more time for female appraisal because Philippa turned on him. She screamed, making his ears ring, and her fist caught his jaw, sending his head snapping backward with the force of her blow.

He released her and she fell onto her back. He came over her, ready to thrash her, but her dirty foot caught him squarely in the belly, kicking him a good three feet back. He grunted and landed in a heap on the bed. Dienwald had blood in his eyes. He managed to stop himself, managed to remind himself that he, unlike this raving wench, thought before he acted. Slowly, very slowly, he sat up on the bed and looked at her.

Philippa scurried up to her knees, jerking the gown back into place. She stared back at him, her breath hitching, her breasts heaving deeply.

"Come here."

"Nay."

Dienwald sighed and smiled an evil smile at her. "Come to me now or I will tell Tancrid, who is doubtless outside my chamber door, his ear pressed against the oak, to fetch me three of my most foul men. They, wench, will strip you and have their sport with you. In front of me, I think. I should enjoy watching."

His threat this time was quite specific, and Philippa, without another contrary thought or word, struggled to her feet. She stiffly walked over to him, afraid, but still wanting to smash her fist into his face. He motioned her closer, and she stood between his spread legs, her head down.

"Put your hands together."

She shook her head, but at his look she slapped her palms together, watching as he wrapped the long narrow leather cross garter around her wrists.

"I can't take the chance you will be stupid enough to try to escape me again. Now, don't struggle."

He clasped his hands beneath her hips and lifted her onto the bed, dropping her on her back. He wrapped the other cross garter through the knot at her tied wrists and tethered her to a post at the top of the bed. Her arms were pulled above her head, but not tightly. She stared up at him, and he saw that she was very afraid. He didn't blame her; she was completely helpless.

Her gown had tangled up about her thighs, and the expanse of white flesh was annoying his groin. He pulled a blanket over her, bringing it to her chin. "Now, keep quiet."

It was an unnecessary command. She was silent as a tomb.

Within moments the bedchamber was as silent

as she was. Dienwald snuffed out the single candle, then quickly undressed. He stretched out naked beside her. She could hear his breathing. He'd made no move to touch her. She gave the leather strap a tentative tug; nothing happened. She lay there trying to decide what she could do.

Dienwald said, "Were William de Bridgport here, he would have tied you down as well. The difference is, he would have pulled your white legs wide apart and pinched you with his dirty fingers and leered at you, whereas I, wench, will stroke your white flesh with clean fingers and a warm mouth and—"

"I have to relieve myself!"

"I'm powerfully comfortable and you've quite tired me out. Do you really have to relieve yourself or are you again lying to me?"

"Nay, please."

He cursed, lit the single candle again, then released her wrists. "The pot is beneath the window, yon. I will leave you for a minute or two. Don't dally." He pulled on his bedrobe as he spoke.

Philippa didn't look at him. She didn't move until he'd closed the chamber door behind him. She raced from the bed to the chamber pot without bothering to light the tallow candle. She could see well enough.

The chamber door opened some minutes later, and for a moment Dienwald was silhouetted in faint light. He closed the door behind him. "Get back into bed and stretch your hands above your head so I can tie you again."

He heard a deep hitching breath close to him, far too close, but he wasn't fast enough. The chamber pot hit him squarely atop the head and he dropped like a stone.

Philippa stared down at him. He looked dead, and she felt the shock of fear and guilt. She dropped to her knees and pressed her palm against his chest. "Don't you dare die, you scoundrel!" His heartbeat was steady and slow. She got to her feet and stood over him. Her mind began to function again as she stared down at the unconscious man.

Now what was she to do?

She'd thought with her feet again, only this time her actions could well prove to be worse than jumping into the Beauchamp moat.

Tancrid. She had to get the squire out of the way. Perhaps she could take him as a hostage. Yes, that's what she'd do. And she could take his clothes and his shoes and . . . Her mind squirreled madly about.

A hand curled around her ankle and pulled hard. Philippa's legs went out from under her and she went down hard on her bottom. Dienwald, his head spinning, threw himself on top of her, pinning her down with his weight.

She was larger than most women, but she couldn't push him off her. His eyes accustomed themselves to the dim candlelight and he stared down into her face.

"I didn't hit you hard enough."

"Aye, you did. I'm seeing four of you, and believe me, wench, even one of your sort is too many."

Dienwald became suddenly aware of her full breasts and her soft body beneath him. His lust sprang full-blown into life, and with it his manhood. Without thinking, he pressed himself against her.

"You're a menace," he said, hating the fact that he wanted to jerk up her gown and ride her until she was yelling with the pleasure of it and his own pleasure was washing over him. Instead he said, "You're a foolish girl who hasn't a thought for consequences, and I'm tired of it."

"What are you going to do to me?"

Dienwald didn't answer. His vision cleared, as did his lust. Cleansing anger took its place. He pulled himself off her and hauled her up with him. He strode to the bed, dragging her behind him, then pulled her down over his thighs. He held her down with one arm and lit the candle with the other. Then he yanked up her gown, baring a very lovely bottom. And brought the flat of his hand down as hard as he could on the white flesh.

For an instant, Philippa froze. No, he couldn't be spanking her, not like this, with her buttocks as bare as the day she'd come from her mother's womb. He struck her again, and she shrieked in rage and pain and tried to rear up.

He smacked her again, harder this time, then again and again. She was sobbing with pain and impotent fury, struggling with all her strength, when she felt his fingers pressing inward, pushing her legs more widely apart, touching her. She let out a small terrified cry.

Just as quickly, Dienwald flung her off him, onto her back on the bed. He wrapped her wrists again, tying her more securely this time.

She gave a pitiful sob.

"Don't you dare accuse me of hurting you. Edmund would laugh at a hiding that tender."

He hated that word the moment it came from his mouth. It brought to mind the violent lust he'd felt for her moments before.

Her sobs died in her throat. "Your hand is hard and callused. You did hurt me."

"You can't even lie convincingly. Would you prefer a chamber pot on your head, you stupid wench? Thank St. George's lance you hadn't relieved yourself in it first!"

"Of course I hadn't used it! I'm not a—"

"Quiet! You will drive me to lunacy and back! Enough. Go to sleep."

Philippa's bottom felt hot and her flesh was stinging. Her tears were drying on her cheeks and itching. There was nothing she could do about it.

Dienwald was so irritated he couldn't remain silent. "I don't know why I don't simply take you. Why don't—"

"My father would see to it that you were sent as a eunuch to Jerusalem if you forced me."

"What know you of eunuchs and the Holy Land?"

"I am not an ignorant girl. I have learned much. I've had lessons since my eighth year."

"Why would your father waste good coin to educate you, a silly female? That makes no sense at all."

"I don't know why," Philippa said, having wondered the same thing herself. Bernice fluttered about with her ribbons and clothes and her extravagantly pointed slippers, given no opportunity for learning with Father Boise—not, of course, that she'd ever desired to read the *Chanson de Roland*. "Perhaps he thought I could be of use to him. And I have been of use to him. Our steward died nearly two years ago, and I have taken his place."

"You're telling me that you, a female, did the duties of your father's steward?"

"Aye. But my mother also insisted that I learn to manage the household. She didn't enjoy my instruction, but she did it—as an abbess would with an indigent nun."

This entire evening was odd in the extreme, Dienwald decided, exhausted by her nonsense, her violence, her female softness. He snuffed out the candle beside him, and turned onto his back.

"What am I going to do with you, wench?"

"I'm not a wench, I'm—"

Dienwald turned on his side away from her and began snoring very loudly.

"I'm Philippa de Beauchamp and—

Philippa got no further. He rolled over atop her and kissed her hard. She felt his manhood swell against her belly, felt the heat of him, and opened her mouth to protest. His tongue was her reward, and without thought, she bit him.

He yelped, drawing back.

"I should have known you'd try to make me into a mute. Damned stupid wench, I . . . No, don't you dare say it, lady, else I'll pull up your gown and—"

"You already did! And you looked at me and you hit me!"

He stopped, and even though she couldn't see his face clearly, she knew his expression was filled with evil intent.

He rolled off her and pulled up her gown. She was naked to the waist, her hands tied above her head, as helpless as could be.

"Now," Dienwald said, sounding quite pleased,

"let's continue this conversation. What is it you wanted to say to me, *wench?*"

She shook her head, but he couldn't see it, and that infuriated him. All he'd done this night was to light and snuff candles, protect himself, curse her, and have his rod swell with lust.

He lurched over to the far side of the bed and lit the tallow candle again. It had nearly burned down to the mottled brass holder. He rested on his knees, the candle held high, and looked down at her. For a very long time Dienwald didn't say anything. He was pleasantly surprised, that was all, nothing more. This was to be her punishment, not his, damn her. He stared at her flat belly, then lower, at the profusion of curls that covered her woman's flesh. Curls the color of her head hair, rich and dark, with gleaming browns mingling with strands of the palest blond and . . .

". . . dirt, rich dark dirt."

His words took her so much by surprise that she forgot her terror of him, forgot he was staring at her, seeing her as no man had ever seen her before.

"What is like dirt?"

"Your woman's hair," he said, and cupped his hand over her, pressing his fingers inward.

She yelped like a wounded dog, and he lifted his hand and sat back.

He reached out and splayed his fingers over her flat belly. He stretched out his fingers, watching them nearly touch her pelvic bones. "You're made for birthing babes." He felt something within him move, and lifted his hand as if from a scalding pot. He looked at her face and schooled his expression into a cruel mask. "Remember what I can do to you, wench. Are you such an innocent that I must explain it to you? No? Good. Now, have you anything more to say to me? Any more carping? Any more nagging?"

She shook her head.

"You finally show some wisdom. Good night, wench."

He snuffed the candle yet again, burning his fingers, since the candle had burned down to a wax puddle, then rolled onto his back. He forgot his burning fingers, still seeing her lying there, naked to the waist, those long white legs spread; he could still feel the softness of her flesh, feel the tensing of the muscles in her belly beneath his splayed fingers.

He cursed, grabbed the blanket, and pulled it over her.

When he was nearing the edge of sleep, he heard her whisper, "I'm Philippa de Beauchamp and I will awaken and this won't really be happening."

He grinned into the darkness. The wench had spirit and fire. A bit of it was interesting; too much, painful. He rubbed the back of his head. He hoped it hadn't cracked the chamber pot. It was the only one he owned.

7

The next morning, Dienwald wasn't grinning. His weaver, Prink, was very seriously ill with the ague, and much of the wool had already been cleaned and prepared and spun ready for weaving. Dienwald stomped about, cursing, until Old Agnes plucked at his worn sleeve.

"Master, listen. What of the fine young lady ye've tied to yer bed, eh? Be she really a lady or jest enouther of yer trollops?"

Dienwald ceased his ranting. He'd left Philippa asleep, but he'd untied her wrists, frowning at himself as he brought her arms down to her sides and rubbed the feeling back into her wrists. She'd never even moved. He imagined her bottom was still soft and white, without the mark of his palm, whereas his head ached abominably from her blow with the chamber pot.

"You mean, old hag, that she could weave, mayhap? Direct the women, instruct them?"

Old Agnes nodded wisely. "Aye, master, she looks a good girl. Thass what I mean."

Dienwald remembered Philippa's words about her household instruction. He took the solar stairs two at a time. When he opened his bedchamber door it was to see Philippa standing in the middle of the room staring around her.

"What's the matter?"

She pointed toward the corner of the bedchamber. "The chamber pot. I broke it when I struck your head with it. I need to . . ." She winced, then burst out, "I must relieve myself! You locked me in and—"

His only chamber pot, and she'd destroyed it. "Satan's earlobes! Get you here, wench." He directed her to a much smaller chamber, waving her inside. " 'Tis Edmund's room. Use his pot, then come down to the hall. 'Tis not a lovely hand-painted pot, merely a pottery pot, but it will do. After this, use the jakes. They're in the north tower; you won't get lost, you'll smell them. Don't tarry."

Why did he want her in the great hall? She dreaded it, knowing there would be snickering servants looking at her and knowing that she was now their master's mistress. When he'd burst into the chamber she'd momentarily forgotten what he'd done to her the previous night—smacking her, toying with her, stripping her, *looking* at her. She didn't understand him and was both relieved and afraid because she didn't. It was a good thing that she wasn't to his liking; otherwise she would no longer be a maid and no longer worth much to her father. That thought brought forth the vision of William de Bridgport, and she prayed that all her maneuvers and ill-fated stratagems wouldn't lead to marriage to him. When she left Edmund's small chamber and made her way down the outside solar stairs, her ears were nearly overcome by the noise. There were men and women and children and animals everywhere. All were shouting and squawking and carrying on. It seemed louder than the day before; it was, oddly, comforting.

"Come wi' me, lady."

She turned to see Gorkel the Hideous, the fiercest-looking and ugliest man she'd ever beheld, obviously waiting for her. Odd, though, he didn't seem quite so gruesome of mien as he had yesterday.

"I'm Gorkel, iffen ye remember. Come wi' me. The master wants ye."

She nodded, wishing she had shoes on her feet and cloth covering her naked right arm. She'd combed her fingers through her hair, but she had no idea of the result. Gorkel could have told her that she was as delicious a morsel as a man could pray for, if she'd asked. The master was lucky, he was, and about time, too. A hard winter, but they'd outlasted it, and now it was spring and there was wool and the master had this lovely girl to share his bed. Gorkel left her at the entrance to the great hall, his task completed.

Dienwald saw Philippa, nodded briefly in her direction, and went back to his conversation with Alain, his steward. The man who'd given her dirty looks the evening before. He looked at her now, and there was contemptuous dismissal in his eyes.

Philippa waited patiently, although her stomach was growling with hunger.

It was as if Dienwald had heard her. "Eat," he called out, waving toward the trestle table. "Margot, fetch her milk and bread and cheese."

Philippa ate. She wondered what was going on between Dienwald and the steward Alain. They seemed to be arguing. As she studied the master of St. Erth, she wondered at herself and her reaction to him. She felt no particular embarrassment upon seeing him this morning. In fact, truth be told, she'd rather been looking forward to seeing him again, to crossing verbal swords with him again. She felt a tug on her one sleeve and turned to see the serving maid, Margot, looking at her with worry.

She lifted an eyebrow.

" 'Tis the master," Margot said as low as she could.

"He's a lout," Philippa said, and took a big bite of goat cheese.

"Mayhap," Dienwald said agreeably, dismissing Margot with a wave of his hand. "But I'm the lout who's in charge of you, wench."

That was true, but it didn't frighten her. He hadn't ravished her last night, and he could have. She'd been completely helpless. She thrust her chin two inches into the air and fetched forth her most goading look. "Why do you want me here?"

Dienwald sat in his chair, noted her look, sprawled out to take his ease, and watched her eat, saying nothing for some time.

"You told me your mother taught you household matters. Is this true?"

"Certainly. I'm not a liar. Well, not usually."

Dienwald had a flash of memory of another lady speaking to him candidly, without guile. Kassia. That was absurd. This girl was no more like the gentle, loyal Kassia de Moreton than was a thorn on an apple tree.

"Can you weave?"

Philippa very nearly choked on the cheese in her mouth. No ravisher or ravening beast here. "You want me to weave my father's wool that you stole?"

"Yes. I want you to oversee the weaving and train the women, although several of them already know a bit about it, so Old Agnes told me."

Philippa grew crafty, and he saw it in her eyes and was amused by it. He was also impatient and on tenterhooks. He needed her help, but he couldn't afford to let her see that. She said with the eye of a bargainer at the St. Ives Fair, "What will you do for me if I help you with the wool?"

"I will allow you the first gown, or an overtunic, or hose. Just one, not all three, though."

Philippa looked down at the wrinkled, stained woolen gown that hung about her body like an empty flour bag. The bargain seemed like an excellent one to her. "Will you let me go if I do it for you?"

"Let you go where? Back to your father's household? Back into the repulsive arms of de Bridgport?"

She shook her head.

"Ah, to this other person, this alleged cousin of yours. Who is it, Philippa?"

She shook her head again.

"The gown or the overtunic or the hose. That's all I offer. For the moment, at least."

"Why?"

"Yea or nay, wench."

"I'm not a—"

"Answer me!"

She nodded. "I will do it." She looked him straight in the eye. "How will you behave toward me?"

He knew exactly what she wanted him to say, but he was perverse and she irritated him and amused him and she'd nearly felled him with a chamber pot.

"I will keep you in my bed until I tire of you." He spoke loudly, and Alain looked up, his contempt now magnified.

Philippa grabbed Dienwald's arm and pinched him, hissing, "You make it sound as if I'm already your mistress, damn you!"

"Aye, I know. In any case, you will remain in my bed. I can't trust you out of my sight. Now, 'tis time for you to earn your keep."

He yelled for Old Agnes and brought her over to Philippa. Old Agnes was older than the stunted oak trees to the north of the castle, and mean as the dung beetles that roamed about the stables. He stood back, crossing his arms over his chest.

Philippa ate another piece of cheese, slowly, as she looked the old woman over.

To Dienwald's amazement, Old Agnes fidgeted.

Philippa drained her flagon of milk, then said, "I shall see the wool after I've finished my meal. If it isn't thoroughly cleaned and treated, I shan't be pleased. The thread must be pure before it's woven. See to it now. Where is your weaving room?"

Old Agnes drew up her scrawny back, then

sagged under Philippa's militant eye. " 'Tis in the outbuilding by the men's barracks . . . mistress."

"I will need you to pick at least five women with nimble fingers and with minds that rise above the thoughts of useless men and, can learn quickly. You will assist me, naturally. Go now and see to the quality of the thread. I will come shortly."

Old Agnes stared at this young lady who knew her way quite well, and said, "It will be as you say, mistress."

She shuffled out, her step lighter and quicker than it had been in two decades. Dienwald stared after her. This damned girl had wrought a miracle—and she'd not been nice, she'd been imperious and arrogant and haughty and . . .

He became aware that Philippa was looking at him, and she was smiling. "She needs a strong hand, and more, she wants a sense of worth. She now has both." Then Philippa began whistling.

Dienwald turned on his heel and strode from the great hall, bested again by a girl who'd already smashed his head. He cursed.

Philippa silently thanked her mother, whose tongue was sharper than an adder's when it suited her purpose. But, Philippa remembered, her mother's tongue was also sweet with praise when it served her ends. Old Agnes would do more work than all the others combined, and she'd drive them in turn. Philippa turned back to her place, only to see a slight shadow hovering over her.

"Philippa de Beauchamp. I am Alain, Lord Dienwald's steward."

He was speaking to her. She hadn't expected it, given the dislike she'd felt coming from him. She raised her head and kept her face expressionless.

"If you will but tell me this cousin's name, I will see that you are quickly on your way out of this keep and away from Dienwald de Fortenberry."

"Why?"

His good humor slipped. "You don't belong here," he said, his voice loud and vicious. He immediately got hold of himself. "You are an innocent young lady. Dienwald de Fortenberry is a villain, if you will, a rogue, a blackguard, a man who owes loyalty to few men on this earth. He makes his own rules and doesn't abide by others'. He raids and steals and enjoys it. He will continue to hurt you, he will continue to use you until you are with child, and then he will cast you out. He has no scruples, no conscience, and no liking for women. He abused his first wife until she died. He enjoys abusing women, lady or serf. He cares not. He will see that you are cast out, both by him and by your family."

His venom shocked her. She'd smashed a chamber pot over the lord's head the previous night, but that had been different. That was between the two of them. Dienwald hadn't ravished her, and he could have. He hadn't abused her, even when she'd angered him to the point of insensibility. She'd hurt *him*. She thought suddenly of the thrashing he'd given her, but then again, what would she have done to him had he smacked her over the head with a chamber pot? But this steward of his, who should be praising his master, not maligning him—it was beyond anything she'd ever seen.

"Why do you hate him, sirrah?"

Alain drew back as if she'd struck him. "Hate my master? Certainly I don't hate him. But I know what he is and how he thinks. He's a savage, ruthless, and a renegade. Leave, lady, leave before you die or wish to. Tell me this cousin's name and I will get you away from here."

"Yes," she said slowly. "I will tell you."

She watched him closely, and saw immense relief flood his face. His eyes positively glowed and his breath came out in a whoosh. "Who?"

"I shan't tell you today. First of all I must earn a new gown for myself. That was my bargain with your master. I cannot go to my cousin as I am now. You must understand that, sir."

"I think you are a stupid girl," he said. "He will grunt over you and plow your belly until you carry a bastard, then will kick you out of here and you will die in a ditch." He turned on his heel with those magnificent words and strode away, anger in every taut line of his body.

Philippa brooded a moment. This was a peculiar household, and the lord and master was the oddest of them all. She rose from the wooden bench, replete with cheese and bread, and made her way to the weaving building.

Old Agnes had assembled six women, and silence immediately fell when Philippa entered the long, narrow, totally airless room. There were three old spinning wheels and three looms, each of them more decrepit-looking than its neighbor. Philippa looked at each of the women, then nodded. She spoke to each of the women, learned their names and their level of skill, which in all

cases but two was nil. Then she tackled the
looms. A shuttle had cracked on one; a harness
had come loose on another; the treadle had
slipped out of its moorings on yet another. She
sighed and spoke to Old Agnes.

"You say that Gorkel knows how to solve these
problems?"

"Aye, 'tis a monster he is to look at, but he has
known how to repair things since he was a little
sprat."

"Fetch Gorkel, then."

In the meanwhile Philippa inspected the spinning wheels and the quality of thread the women
had produced from the wool. Given the precarious balance of two of the spindles and the wob-
bling of the huge wheels, the results were more
than satisfactory. She smiled and praised the
women, seeing her mother's face in her mind's
eye.

Two hours later, the women were at their
looms weaving interlacing threads into soft wool.
They worked slowly and carefully, but that was
to the good. As they gained confidence and skill,
the weaving would quicken. Old Agnes was
chirping over their shoulders, carping and scolding, then turning to Philippa and giving her a
wide toothless grin. "Prink—he were the weaver,
ye know, milady—well, a purty sod he were, wot
with his proud ways. Said, he did, that females
couldn't do it right, the weaving part, only the
spinning. Ha!" Old Agnes looked toward the
busy looms and cackled. "I hope the old bugger
corks it. Thass why none of the females knew
aught—the old cockshead was afraid to teach
them. Make him look the fool, they would have
done."

Philippa wanted very much to meet Prink before he corked it.

All was going well. Philippa de Beauchamp, lately of Beauchamp, was busy directing the weaving of her father's wool into cloth for the man who'd stolen it. She laughed aloud at the irony of it.

"Why do you laugh? You can't see me!"

"I should have known—how long have you been watching, Edmund?"

"I don't watch women working," Edmund said, planting his fists on his hips. "I was watching the maypole!"

"Nasty little boy," she remarked toward one of the looms, and turned her back on him.

"I'll tell my papa, and he won't let you use my chamber pot again!"

Philippa whipped around, pleading in her eyes and in her voice as she clasped her hands in front of her. "Ah, no, Master Edmund! I must use your chamber pot. Don't make me use the jakes, please, Master Edmund!"

Edmund drew up and stared. He was stymied, and he didn't like it. He assumed a crafty expression, and Philippa recognized it instantly as his father's. She whimpered now, wringing her clasped hands.

"My papa will make you sorry, and thass the truth!"

"*That's*, not *thass*."

She'd spoken without thinking, and watched the little boy puff up with fury like a courting cock. "I'll speak the way I want! No one tells me how to say things, and thass—"

"*That's*, not *thass*."

"You're big and ugly and my papa doesn't like

you. I hope you get back into a wagon and leave." He whirled about, tossing back over his shoulder, "You're not a girl, you're a silly may-pole!"—and ran straight into his father.

"I should expire with such an insult," Dienwald said, staring down at his son. "Why did you say such a thing to her, Edmund?"

"I don't like her," the boy said, and scuffed at the dirt with a very dirty foot.

"Why aren't you wearing shoes?"

"There's holes in them."

"Isn't there a cobbler here in the castle?" Philippa asked, wishing she could have shoes on her own very dirty feet.

Dienwald shook his head. "Grimson died six months ago. He was very old, and the apprentice died a week after, curse his selfish heart. I haven't hired another."

Philippa started to tell him to send his precious steward to St. Ives and hire a cobbler, when she remembered he didn't have any coin. She searched for a solution. "You know," she said at last, "it's possible to stitch leather if your armorer could but cut it to size for the boy. Also, I'll need very sturdy thick needles."

Dienwald frowned. Meddlesome, female. Edmund was right: she didn't belong here. He looked again at his son's filthy feet and saw a small scabbing sore on his little toe. He cursed, and Edmund smiled in anticipation of his father's wrath.

Philippa said nothing, merely waited.

"I'll speak to my armorer," Dienwald said, and took Edmund by the arm. " 'Tis time for your lessons, Edmund, and don't carp!"

Edmund looked at Philippa over his shoulder as his father dragged him from the room. His look was one of astonishment, fury, and utter bewilderment.

8

Philippa was sweating in the airless outbuilding. All the weavers were sweating as well, their fingers less nimble, their grumbling louder now than an hour before. Swirls of dust from the floor hung in the hot air, kicked up by the many feet. Even Old Agnes looked ready to drop in the corner and hang her scraggly head.

The master had demanded too much too quickly, a habit, Philippa learned from one of the main grumblers, that was one of his foremost traits. Philippa finally called out, "Enough! Agnes, send someone for water and food. 'Tis the afternoon. We all deserve it."

There were tired smiles from the women as they flexed their cramping fingers. The morning couldn't have gone much worse, Philippa was thinking as she walked around praising the cloth that had been woven. If Philippa had believed in divine retribution for sins she might have been convinced that the morning's calamities stemmed from some mortal act of heinous proportions on her part. The wretched looms, ill-cared-for by the infamous Prink, kept breaking, their parts were so old and worn. She'd become closer to Gorkel the Hideous than to anyone else during the long morning. He'd worked harder than she had, tinkering with the ancient treadle, tying together the spindle whose wood kept cracking from dry rot, balancing the loom when it kept teetering. Even Gorkel now looked ready to tumble to the ground. But even at his worst scowls, Philippa was no longer afraid of him or repelled by his face.

Excellent quality wool, though, Philippa thought as she examined the cloth woven by Mordrid, the only woman Prink had taught anything. Mordrid, Old Agnes had whispered to Philippa, had let the old cootshead into her bed, and thus he'd had to teach her something as payment.

Philippa could see that the woven wool was stout and strong enough to last through winters of wear, and would have fetched a good price at the St. Ives Fair. She didn't want to wait for the wool to be dyed before she set other servants to making a gown for herself. Perhaps an overtunic as well, one with soft full sleeves and a fitted waist. Dienwald wouldn't have to know.

Then she saw Edmund in her mind's eyes. The little ruffian dressed and spoke like the lowest villein. She sighed. His tunic was a rag.

Then she saw Dienwald, the elbow poking out of his sleeve, and sighed again.

It occurred to her only then that he was her captor and that she owed him nothing. He could rot in the worn tunic he was wearing. Her clothing came first. Then she would escape and make her way to Walter, her cousin.

After everyone had eaten bread, goat cheese, and some cold slices of beef, Philippa reluctantly herded the women back to the looms. Nothing improved. The fates were still against her. The remainder of the day passed with agonizing slowness and heat. The looms continued to break, one part after another. Gorkel was taxed to his limits and was looking more bleak-browed as the afternoon wore on. The lord and master didn't show himself again. He'd set her the task and the responsibility and then proceeded to absent himself, curse him.

It was late, and Philippa was so tired she could barely stand. She rose from the loom where she was working, told the women to be back on the morrow, nodded to Old Agnes, then simply walked out of the weaving building. Long shadows were slicing across one-third of the inner bailey. She spoke to no one, merely walked toward the thick gates that led to the outer bailey. She weaved her way through squawking chickens, several pigs, three goats and a score of children. She just looked straight ahead, as if she had an important errand, and didn't stop.

She'd nearly reached the inner gates when she heard his voice from behind her. "Do my eyes deceive me? Does my slave wish to flee me again? Shall I tether you to my wrist, wench?"

So, now she knew. He must have set up a system whereby he would be told immediately if she did something out of the ordinary. Walking to the inner-bailey gates must meet that requirement. Well, she'd tried. She didn't turn around, merely stood there staring at the gates. She said over her shoulder, still not turning, "If you tether yourself to me, then you must needs sweat until you want to die in that dreadful weaving room. I doubt you wish to do that."

"True," Dienwald said, regarding her thoughtfully. Her face was flushed, but not, he thought, from his threat, but from the heat in the weaving room.

"And I'm not your slave."

He smiled at her defiance. Her hair was bound loosely with a piece of leather and lay thick and curling between her shoulder blades almost to her waist. Her shoulders weren't straight and high, but slumped. She looked weary and defeated. He didn't like it, and frowned, then said, "I will have the pieces of leather for you soon. My armorer is cutting them. He will measure your feet as well."

"I doubt he has so much leather in single pieces."

"I did ask him to be certain. I wouldn't want him to measure your feet, only to discover that he couldn't cover them after all. I don't wish you to be humiliated."

"My feet aren't that large!"

"But they are dirty, nearly as dirty as my son's. Should you like to bathe now? The day is nearly done. Actually, I was on my way to the outbuilding to see to your progress. How goes it? Prink is trying his best to overcome his ague. He's furious that *women* are doing the weaving and that a woman is directing the proceedings. He is accusing poor Mordrid of base treachery."

"Old Agnes said he was about to cork it," Philippa said, so diverted that she turned to face him, smiling despite herself.

He was garbed in the same clothes as yesterday, and he looked hot and tired. His hair was standing a bit on end. Perhaps he'd had reason not to see to the work during the day. Then she happened to look at his long fingers, and she closed her eyes over the vision of his hands on her body.

This was absurd. He'd looked at her but hadn't wanted her. If he had tried to ravish her, she would have brought him low—naturally, she would have fought him to her dying breath. "You don't need me anymore. Old Agnes is adept at battering the women. Mordrid is capable of teaching them. Gorkel can repair the looms, even when they break every other breath. Your wonderful Prink is a sluggard and a fool. The looms should have been burned and new ones made ten years ago, and . . . Oh, what do you care?" Philippa threw up her hands, for he was simply looking at her with casual interest, the sort of look one would give a precocious dog. "Truly, all the women can weave passably now. I want my gown, and then I want to leave and go to my cousin."

"What did you say his name was, this so-called cousin of yours?"

"His name is Father Ralth. He's a dour Benedictine and will garb me as a choirboy and let me have a small cell of my own. I plan to meditate the rest of my days, thanking God for saving me from de Bridgport and villains like you."

"You will be known as Philippa the castrato?"

"What's a castrato?"

"A man who isn't a man, who's had his manhood nipped in the bud, so to speak."

"That sounds awful." Her eyes went inadvertently to his crotch, and he laughed.

"I would imagine it isn't a fate to be devoutly sought. Now, wench, come with me to my bedchamber. The both of us can bathe. I tire of my own stench, not to mention yours. I shall consider letting you scrub my back."

Philippa, as much as she wanted to exercise an acid tongue on his head, couldn't find the energy to do it. A bath sounded wonderful. Then she looked down at the old gown, dirty and sweat-stained, and sighed. Dienwald said nothing. He turned on his heel, firmly expecting her to follow after him like a faithful hound, which she did, curse his eyes.

They passed Alain. Philippa saw the steward give Dienwald an approving nod and wondered at it. Why had he so openly attacked his master to her just this morning? Something was decidedly wrong. Philippa had never before considered herself to be of an overly curious nature, even though her parents had accused her of it frequently, but now she wanted very much to shake Master Alain and see what fell out of his mouth.

It didn't occur to her to wonder how the bathing ritual would take place until Dienwald had locked the bedchamber door, tossed the key into the pocket of his outer tunic, and turned to say, "I'll exercise some knightly virtue and let you bathe first. You see, chivalry still abounds in Cornwall."

"I'm so dirty you'll need another tub. Also, you can't stay in here. Will you wait outside?"

"No." Frank enjoyment removed the tiredness from Dienwald's eyes. "No, I want to see you

naked. Again. Only this time, all of you at one
time, not just parts."

Philippa sat on the floor. She eyed the copper-
bound wooden tub with steam rising from it and
felt a nearly murderous desire to jump in, but she
didn't move. She wouldn't move, even if she had
to rot here. She wouldn't allow him to humiliate
her anymore. She wouldn't play the partial trollop. To her surprise, Dienwald didn't say anything, didn't threaten her with dire punishments.
He rose from the bed and calmly stripped off his
clothes.

She didn't look at him, but after several minutes
had passed and she heard no further sound, no
movement, she couldn't stand it anymore. When
she raised her head, it was to see him standing
by the tub, not three feet away from her. She'd
seen naked men before; only girls who had been
raised by nuns in convents hadn't. But this was
different; *he* was different. He was hard and lean
and hairy, his legs long and muscled, his belly
flat and sculptured. She looked—and couldn't
look away. His manhood swelled from the thick
bush of hair at his groin, and she stared with
open fascination as it grew thicker and longer.

She felt something quite odd and quite warm
low in her belly. Philippa knew this wasn't right;
she also knew she was losing control of a situation she somehow no longer wanted to control.
She swiveled about and faced away from him.

Dienwald laughed and climbed into the tub.
He'd seen her stare at him, felt his sex rise in
concert with her interest, seen her interest rise as
well and her confusion. He reveled in her reactions—when they didn't irritate him.

He lathered himself, feeling the grime soak off,

and said, "Wench, tell me of your progress. And don't whine to me about all your problems or of the heat in the outbuilding or of Old Agnes' carping. What did you accomplish?"

Philippa turned back, knowing the height of the tub would keep her from further inappropriate perusal of his man's body. His hair was white with lather, as were his face and shoulders. She couldn't see any more of him.

"It has been nearly nothing *but* problems, and I'm not whining. I may skin Prink alive if the ague doesn't bring him to his grave first. Oh, we now have wool, curse you. I was thinking, mayhap the first tunic should be for Edmund. He looks ragged as a villein's child."

Dienwald opened his eyes, and soap seeped in. He cursed, ducking his head under the water. When he'd cleansed his eyes of the soap he turned to her and nearly yelled, "Nay, 'tis for you, foolish girl. That was our bargain. I am an honorable man, and though you, as a woman, can't understand bargains or honor, I suggest you simply keep your ignorance behind your tongue. I dislike martyrs, so don't enact touching gestures for me. And you simply haven't looked at the villeins' children. They're nearly naked."

"You're taking your anger out on me because you were clumsy with the soap! You're naught but a tyrant and a stupid cockshead!"

"Not bad for a maiden of tender years. Should I improve upon your insults? Teach you ones more spiteful and less civil?"

He saw her jump to her feet and knew what was in her mind. He said very calmly, even though his eyes still burned from the soap and he wasn't through with her, "Don't, Philippa.

Leave the key where it is. You're not using your brain. Tancrid is outside the door. If you managed to trip him up and smash his head with something, there would still be all my men to be gotten through. Sit down on the bed and tell me more of your day. If you must, you may whine."

She sat down on the bed and folded her hands in her lap. He resumed his scrubbing. She looked at his discarded outer tunic, the one that held the bedchamber key. She sighed. He was right.

"We will begin dyeing the wool tomorrow."

He nodded.

"If there are skilled people, then the first of the cloth will be ready for sewing into garments the next day."

He was washing his belly. Philippa knew it was his belly—or flesh even more southerly—and she was looking, she couldn't help herself. She wondered what it would feel like to touch him, to rub soap over him . . . He looked at her then and smiled. "I will order clean water for you. I have blackened this."

"Will you stay to watch me?"

Dienwald imagined that she'd choose to remain dirty if he said yes. He shook his head. "Nay, I'll leave you in peace. But if you try anything stupid I will do things to you that you will dislike intensely."

"What?"

"You irritate me. Close that silly mouth of yours and hand me that towel. 'Tis the only one, so I will use only half of it. Thank me, wench."

"Thank you."

Wolffeton Castle, near St. Agnes

"That damned whoreson! He *knew*, damn him, the scoundrel *knew* full well that wine was bound for Wolffeton from your father. I'll break all his fingers and both his arms, then I'll smash his nose, stomp his toes into the ground—"

Graelam de Moreton, Lord of Wolffeton, stopped short at the laughter from his wife. He eyed her, then tried again. "We have but two casks left, Kassia. 'Tis a present from your sire. It costs him dear to have the wine brought to Brittany from Aquitaine, then shipped here to us. Care you not that the damned whoreson had the gall to wreck the ship and steal all the goods?"

"You don't now that Dienwald is responsible," Kassia de Moreton said, still gasping with laughter. "And you just discovered today that the ship had been wrecked. It must have happened over a sennight ago. Mayhap it was the captain's misjudgment and he struck the rocks; mayhap the peasants stole the goods once the ship was sinking; mayhap everything went down."

"You're full of mayhaps! Aye, but I know 'twas he," Graelam said, bitterness filling his voice as he paced away from her. "If you would know the truth, I made a wager with him some months ago. If you would know more of the truth, our wager involved who could drink the most Aquitaine wine at one time without passing out under the trestle table. I told him about the wine your father was sending us. When we'd gotten the wine, Dienwald and I would have our contest. He knew he would lose, and that's why he lured the captain to his doom, I know it. And so do you beneath all that giggling. Now he has all the wine and can drink it at his leisure, rot his liver! Nay, don't defend him, Kassia! Who else has his skill and his boldness? Rot his heathen eyes, he's won because he stole the damned wine!"

Kassia looked at her fierce husband and began to laugh again. "So, this is what it is all about. Dienwald has bested you through sheer cunning, and you can't bear being the loser."

Graelam gave his wife a look that would curdle milk. It didn't move her noticeably. "He's no longer a friend; he's no longer welcome at Wolffeton. I denounce him. I shall notch his ears for him at the next tourney. I shall carve out his gullet for his insolence—"

Kassia patted her hair and rose, shaking the skirts of her full gown. "Dienwald is to come next month to visit, once the spring planting is undertaken. He will stay a week with us. I will write to him and beg him to bring some of his delicious Aquitaine wine, since we are neighbors and good friends."

"He's a treacherous knave and I forbid it!"

"Good friends are important, don't you agree, my lord? Good friends find wagers to amuse each other. I look forward to seeing Dienwald and hearing what he has to say to you when you accuse him of treachery."

"Kassia . . ." Graelam said, advancing on his wife. She laughed up at him and he lifted her beneath the arms, high over his head, and felt her warm laughter rain down upon his head. She was still too thin, he thought, but her pregnancy was filling her out, finally. He lowered her, kissing her mouth. She tasted sweet and soft and ever so willing, and he smiled. Then he hardened.

"Dienwald," Graelam said slowly, evil in his eyes, "must needs be taught a lesson."

"You have one in mind, my lord?"

"Not yet, but I shall soon. Aye, a lesson for the rogue, one that he shan't soon forget."

St. Erth Castle

At least she was clean, Philippa thought, staring about the great hall, a stringy beef rib in her right hand. The dirty tunic itched, but she would bear it. She wouldn't be a martyr; Dienwald was right about that. She wanted clean soft wool against her flesh; it was all she asked. She didn't even consider praying for silk. It was as beyond her as the moon. Her eyes met Alain's at that moment and she nearly cringed at the malice she saw in his expression. She didn't react, merely chewed on her rib.

She heard Crooky singing in a high falsetto about a man who'd sired thirty children and whose women all turned on him when they discovered he'd been unfaithful to them, all nine of them. Dienwald was roaring with laughter, as were most of the men in the hall. The women, however, were howling the loudest as Crooky graphically described what the women did to the faithless fellow.

"That's awful," Philippa said once the loud laughter had died down. "Crooky's rhymes are a fright and his words are disgusting."

"He's but angry because Margot refused to let him fondle her and the men saw and laughed at him."

Philippa chewed on some bread, saying finally

to Dienwald, "Your steward, Alain. Who is he?
Has he been your steward long?"

"I saved his life some three years ago. He is
beholden to me, thus gives me excellent service
and his loyalty."

"Saved his life? How?"

"A landless knight had taken a dislike to him
and was pounding his head in. I came upon them
and killed the knight. He was a lout and a fool,
a local bully I had no liking for in any case. Alain
came to St. Erth with me and became my steward."

Dienwald paused a moment, gazing thoughtfully at her profile. "Has he insulted you?"

She quickly shook her head. "Nay, 'tis just that
. . . I don't trust him."

She regretted her hasty words the moment
they'd escaped her mouth. Dienwald was staring
at her as if she had two heads and no sense at
all.

"Don't be foolish," he said, then added, "Why
do you say that?"

"He offered to help me get away from you."

"Lies don't become you, wench. Tell me no
more of them. Don't ever again attack a man
who's given me his complete fealty for three
years. Do you understand?"

Philippa looked at Dienwald, saw the banked
fury in his eyes, making his irises more gold than
brown, and read his thought: A woman couldn't
be trusted to give a clear accounting, nor could
she be trusted to be honest. She calmly picked up
another rib from her trencher and chewed on it.

Dienwald was reminding himself at that
moment that only one woman in all his life hadn't
been filled with treachery and guile, and that was
Kassia de Moreton. For a while he'd been unsure

about Philippa. She had seemed so open, so blunt, so straightforward. He shook his head; even a woman as young as Philippa de Beauchamp was filled with deceit. He should simply take her maidenhead, use her until he wearied of her, then discard her. It mattered not if she was ruined; it mattered not if her father kicked her into a convent for the remainder of her days. It mattered not if . . . "Perhaps Alain distrusts you, perhaps he fears you'll try to harm me. That is why he wishes you gone from St. Erth, if, of course, he truly said that to you."

Philippa found she couldn't tell him of the steward's venom. Perhaps he was right about Alain's motives. But she didn't think so. She merely shook her head, then turned to Edmund.

"What color would you like your new tunic to be?"

"I don't want a new tunic."

"No one asked you that. Only whether you wish a certain color."

"Aye, black! You're a witch, so you can give me a black tunic."

"You are such an officious little boy."

"You're a girl, and thass much worse."

"*That's*, not *thass*."

Dienwald overheard this exchange, smiling until he heard her correct Edmund. He frowned. Meddlesome wench. But even so, he didn't want his son speaking like the butcher's boy.

"You will not have a black tunic. Do you like green?"

"Aye, he'll have green, a dark green, to show less dirt."

His father's voice kept Edmund quiet, but he stuck his tongue out at Philippa.

She looked at him with a wondering smile. " 'Tis odd, Edmund, but you remind me of one of my suitors. His name was Simon and he was twenty-one years old but acted as if he were no more than six, just like you."

"I'm nine years old!"

"Are you truly? My, I was certain you were no more than a precocious five, you know, the way you act, the way you speak, the—"

"Do you want more ale, wench?"

So Dienwald had some protective instincts toward his son. She turned and smiled at him. "Aye, thank you."

She sipped at the tart ale. It was better than her father's ale, made by the fattest man at Beauchamp, Rolly, who, Philippa suspected, drank most of his own brew.

"How much more ale do you need?"

She took another sip before asking, "Why do you think I need more? For what?"

"I think, wench, that I will take your precious maidenhead tonight. It taunts me, wench, that maidenhead of yours, just being there. And you do belong to me, at least until I tire of you. But who knows? If you please me—though I doubt you have the skill to do so—I will let you stay and see to the sewing of all the woolen cloth into clothing. What say you to that?"

Philippa, without a thought to the precariousness of her position, tossed the remaining ale from her flagon into his face.

She heard a gasp; then the hall suddenly fell silent as one by one the men and women realized something had happened. Oh, dear, Philippa thought, closing her eyes a moment. She'd thought with her feet again.

Dienwald knew he'd taunted her to violence, and actually, the ale in his face was a minor violence—nothing more or less than he'd expected of her. He supposed he should have waited until he had her in his bedchamber to mock her. Now he would have to act; he couldn't be thought weak in front of his villeins and his men. He cursed softly, wiped his palm over his face, then shoved back the heavy master's chair. He grabbed her arm and dragged her to her feet.

He saw the fear in her eyes, saw her chin go up at the same time, and wondered what the devil he should do to her for her insolence. For now, he needed a show worthy of Crooky. He turned to his fool, who'd come to his feet and was staring avidly at his master like all the others in the great hall.

"What, Crooky, is to be her fate for throwing ale in her master's face?"

Crooky stroked his stubbled jaw. He opened his mouth, looking ready to burst into song, when Dienwald changed his mind. "Nay, do not say it or sing it."

" 'Tis not a song, master, not even a rhyme. I just wanted to ask the wench if she would make me a new tunic as well."

"Aye, I will sew it myself," Philippa said. "Any color you wish, Crooky."

"Give her another flagon of ale, master. Aye, 'tis a good wench she be. Don't flog her just yet."

"You're not to be trusted," Dienwald said close to her ear. "You'd promise the devil a new tunic, wouldn't you, to keep me from your precious maidenhead?"

"Where *is* the devil tonight?" Philippa asked,

looking around. "In residence here? There are so many likely candidates for his services, after all."

"Come along, wench. I have plans for you this long and warm night."

"No," she said, and grabbed the thick arm of his chair with her left hand. She held on tight, her fingers white with the strain, and Dienwald saw that he'd set himself a problem. He looked at the white arm he held, then at the hand holding the chair arm for dear life. "Will you release it now?"

She shook her head.

Dienwald smiled, and she knew at once that she wasn't going to like what followed.

"I will give you one more chance to obey me."

She stared up at him, knowing all the people in the hall were watching. "I can't."

She didn't have to wait long. He smiled again, then lifted his hand, grasped the front of her gown, and ripped it open all the way to the hem.

Philippa yelled, released the chair arm, and jerked at the ragged pieces, trying to draw them over her body.

Dienwald locked his hands together beneath her buttocks and heaved her over his shoulder. He smacked her bottom with the flat of his hand and strode from the great hall laughing like the devil himself.

9

"You note, wench, I'm not breathing hard, even carrying you up these steep stairs."

Philippa held her tongue.

She felt his hands on her buttocks, caressing her, and felt him press his cheek for a moment against her side.

"You smell nice. A big girl isn't such a bad thing—there's a lot of you for me to enjoy. You're all soft and smooth and sweet-smelling."

She reared up at that, but he smacked her buttocks with the flat of his hand.

"Hold still or I'll take you back into the great hall and finish stripping off that gown of yours."

She held still, but thought that his priest would surely die of shock were he to do that. When Dienwald reached his bedchamber, he carried her inside and dropped her onto the bed, then strode across the room and locked the thick door.

When he turned, Philippa was already sitting on the side of the bed, clutching the frayed material together over her breasts.

She fretted with the jagged edges, not looking at him. "I must sew it. I have nothing else to wear."

"You shouldn't have thwarted me. You forced me to retaliate. It was a stupid thing to do, wench."

"I was supposed to let you tread on me like rushes on the floor? I'm not a wen—"

"Shut your annoying mouth!"

"All right. What are you going to do?"

He kicked a low stool across the bedchamber. One of its three legs shuddered against the wall and broke off. He cursed. "Get into bed. No, wait. I must tie you up first. I'll wager you'd even try to escape nearly naked, wouldn't you?"

Philippa didn't move. "I want to sew my gown."

"On the morrow. Hold out your hands." When she didn't, he merely stripped off his clothes. He shrugged into his bedrobe, and when he turned back to her, he was holding a leather cross garter in his right hand.

"No, I won't do it. It's like demanding a chicken to willingly lay its neck on the chopping block. I'm not witless."

"I'm not at all certain of that, but you're right about one thing. Remove the torn gown first."

"Please . . ." she said, and swallowed. "I've never done anything like that before. Please don't make me do it."

"I've already seen you," he said slowly, the man of patience and reason. "I don't suppose you've perchance grown a new part to interest me?"

She shook her head.

He stared down at her bent head. He wanted her very much, but he wasn't about to give in to his appetite for her. It would do him in, mayhap irreparably. It would be stupid—and extremely pleasant. As much as Dienwald hated the notion of denying himself something because an outside authority would disapprove, he wasn't completely witless. If he ravished her, her father would sooner or later hear of it and come to St. Erth and besiege him until there was nothing left but rubble. Also, Dienwald didn't want to get a bastard on her. There were some things he simply couldn't bring himself to do. He wouldn't dishonor her and he wouldn't end up ruined. What he felt was only lust. Lust, he understood. Lust, like a thirst, could be quenched from any available flagon. He said nothing more. He wanted no more than to simply lock her in, but that would allow her to believe she'd gained the upper hand.

He took her off-guard, knocking her backward on the bed. He was fast and he was determined. Within moments the torn gown was on the floor and Philippa was naked beneath him. He saw that she was terrified and, oddly, seemingly curious. He saw it in her eyes. She was curious because she was a maid and he was the first man to treat her in this way. He knew she could feel his increasing interest. Well, let her feel it. It didn't matter. He rolled off, grabbed her wrists, and bound them together.

After he'd tethered the other cross garter to the bed, he stood beside her and looked down at her dispassionately. "You're quite beautiful," he said after a long study, and it was the truth. "You have large breasts, full and round, and your nipples are pale pink. Aye, I like that." He looked down at the curling triangle at the base of her belly. He'd like to sift his fingers through that hair and hear her cry out for him . . . He forced his eyes downward to those magnificently long legs, sleek with muscle and white as pale snow and of a shape to make a man groan with pleasure. Even her arched feet were elegant and graceful. He leaned down and lightly flicked a finger over her nipple. She tried to jerk away but couldn't move out of his reach. "Has a man ever looked at you this way before, wench?"

Philippa was beyond words. She'd watched him look at her, watched his eyes narrow. She could only shake her head, staring at him like a trapped animal, a trapped animal nearly incoherent from the strange sensations flooding its body.

"Have you ever had a man suckle your breast?"

She shook her head again, but he could see in her eyes not only the shock of his words but also the possible effect of the action.

He leaned down and took her nipple in his mouth. She tasted sweet and female and he felt her nipple tighten as he caressed her with his tongue, then suckled her more deeply. He felt his sex throbbing and pressing against his bedrobe. He had to stop this, or . . . "Do you like that?"

He expected a vehement denial—an obvious lie—mayhap a hysterical denial, but to his surprise, she said nothing. He felt a quiver go through her before he forced himself to rise. He tried desperately to keep his look dispassionate. "Has no man ever before touched his fingers to the soft woman's flesh between your thighs?"

"Please," she whispered, then closed her eyes, turning her head away from him.

He frowned. Please *what*? He didn't ask, but merely grabbed a blanket and covered her. He'd tortured himself quite enough.

"I will go relieve myself now with a willing woman," he said, and strode toward the door of the bedchamber.

"You make a woman sound like a chamber pot!"

"Nay, but she is a vessel for my seed." To his surprise, his own words made him all the randier. He was aching, his groin heavy. He wanted Margot or Alice—it didn't matter which—and he wanted her within the next three minutes.

"I hope your male parts rot off!"

He paused, not turning, and grinned. "I will find out soon enough if your curses carry more than the air from your mouth," he said, and strode back down the solar stairs and into the great hall. He saw Margot sitting close to Northbert. He frowned at the same moment she saw him, for he realized he was wearing naught but his bedrobe. A wondrous smile spread over her round face, making her almost pretty. She jumped to her feet and hurried over to him.

"I want you now," he said, and Margot smiled a siren's smile. She followed him outside, then bumped into his back when he came to an abrupt halt. Dienwald didn't know where to take her. Philippa was bound to his bed. He quivered. Damned female. Where, then?

"'Come," he said, grabbed her hand, and nearly ran to the stables. He took her in the warm hay in a far empty stall. And when she cried out her pleasure, her fingers digging into his back, he

let his seed spill into her, and in that moment he
saw Philippa, and could nearly feel her long white
legs clutching his flanks, drawing him deeper and
deeper. "Curse you, wench," he said, and fell
asleep on Margot's breast.

She woke him nearly three hours later. She was
stiff and sore, bits of hay sticking into her back
and bottom, and he'd sprawled his full weight on
top of her, flattening her.

Dienwald straightened his clothes and took
himself to his bedchamber after giving Margot a
perfunctory pat on the bottom. He'd left the single candle lit and it had burned itself out. He
could make out Philippa's form on the far side of
the bed as he stripped off his bedrobe and eased
in beside her. He untied the cross garter that tethered her to the bed and lowered her arms and
pulled her to him. With a soft sigh, she nestled
against him. Fortunately for his peace of mind
and Philippa's continued state of innocence, he
fell asleep.

When Philippa awoke the following morning,
she was alone, which was a relief, and her wrists
were free. Her ripped gown was gone, and in its
place she found a long flowing gown of faded
scarlet, the style from her childhood, its waist
loose and its sleeves tight-fitting to the wrists.
With it was an equally faded overtunic with wide
elbow-length sleeves and a fitted waist. She felt a
jolt when she realized that the faded clothing
must have belonged to Dienwald's long dead
wife.

The gown was too short and far too tight in the
bosom, but the material was sturdy despite its
age, and well-sewn, so she needn't fear the seams
splitting.

Her ankles and feet were bare, and she imagined that she looked passably strange in her faded too-small clothes, the skirt swishing above her ankles.

It was thoughtful of Dienwald to have had the clothes fetched for her, she thought, until she remembered that it was he who had ripped the other gown up the front, rendering it an instant rag. She hardened her heart toward him with ease, though the rest of her still felt the faint tremors of the previous night, when he'd looked down at her, then kissed her breast. Those feelings had been odd in the extreme, more than pleasant, truth be told, but now, alone, in the light of day, Philippa couldn't seem to grasp them as being real.

She made her way to the great hall, drank a flagon of fresh milk, and ate some gritty goat's cheese and soft black bread. It didn't occur to her not to go to the weaving shed to see to the work. Old Agnes, bless her tartar's soul, was berating Gorkel the Hideous for being slow to repair one of the looms. Philippa watched, saying nothing, until Old Agnes saw her and exclaimed as she shuffled toward her, "Gorkel's complaining of wood mold, but I got him at it again. Prink is threatening to come upon us today and whip off our hides. He didn't cork it! Mordrid said he ate this morning and was up on his own to relieve his bowels. May God shrivel his eyeballs! He'll ruin everything."

"No, he won't," Philippa said. She wanted a fight, and Prink sounded like a wonderful offering to her dark mood. She discovered when she called a halt for the noonday meal that Dienwald and a half-dozen men had left St. Erth early that morning, bound for no-one-knew-where. That, or no one would tell her.

Now was the time to escape.

"Ye look like a princess who's too big fer her gown," said Old Agnes as she gummed a piece of chicken. "That gown belonged to the former mistress, Lady Anne. Small she were, small in her body and in her heart. Aye, she weren't a sweetling, that one weren't. Master Edmund's lucky to have ye here, and not that one who birthed him. She made the master miserable with her mean-spirited ways. When she died of the bloody flux, he was relieved, I knew it, even though he pretended to grieve."

Old Agnes then nodded as Philippa stared openmouthed. "The master'll fill yer belly quick enough. Then he'll wed ye, as he should. Yer father's a lord, and that makes ye a lady—and all will be well, aye, it will." Old Agnes nodded, pleased at her own conclusions, and shuffled away to where Gorkel squatted eating his food.

Philippa walked outside the shed, Old Agnes' words whirling about in her mind. Wed with the master of St. Erth? The rogue who'd stolen her father's wool and her with it? Well, it hadn't quite been that way, but still . . . Philippa shook her head, gazing up at the darkening skies. Evidently he had to get her with child first before such notions as marriage would come to him. She didn't want him; she didn't want his child. She wanted to leave, to go to . . . Where? To Walter's keep, Crandall? To a virtual stranger? More of a stranger than Dienwald was to her?

"It'll rain and we'll have to rot inside."

She turned to see Edmund, his hands on his hips, looking disgruntled.

"Rain makes the crops grow. The rain won't last long, you'll see. We'll survive it." She grinned down at him. "And aren't you supposed to be at your lessons?"

He looked guilty for only an instant, but Philippa saw it. "Come along and let's find Father Cramdle. I haven't yet met him, you know."

"He won't want to see you. He'll go all stiff like a tree branch. My father ripped off your gown last night and carried you off. You're only my father's mis—"

"I don't think you'd better say it, Edmund. I am not your father's mistress. Do you understand me? I'm a lady, and your father doesn't dare to . . . harm me."

Edmund seemed to think this over for a half-dozen steps before finally nodding. "Aye," he said, "you're a big lady. And I don't need lessons."

"Of course you do. You must know how to read and to cipher and to write, else you'll be cheated by your steward and by anyone else who gets the chance."

"Thass what my father says. *That's!*" he said before she could.

Philippa smiled. "Tomorrow you'll have a new tunic. Also study new shoes and hose. You'll look like Master Edmund of St. Erth. What do you think of that?"

Edmund didn't think much of it. He scuffed his filthy toes against a rock. "Father went a-raiding. He's angry at a man who hates him and who struck last night and burned all our wheat crop near the south edge of St. Erth land."

"Who is this man?"

Edmund shrugged.

"How long will your father be away?"

"He said mayhap a week, longer or shorter."

"How did your father find out about the burned crops?"

"Crooky. He sang it to him at dawn. Father nearly kicked his ribs into his back."

"I can imagine. How does Crooky find out things so quickly?"

"He won't tell anyone how he does it."

"If he provides useful information, I suppose one can forgive his miserable rhymes."

"Aye, but Father said that only he could kick Crooky because Crooky was *his* fool and no one else's and had his protection. So no one touches Crooky." Edmund shrugged. "Crooky always finds out everything first. I think mayhap he's a witch, like you, except he's not a silly girl."

So much for a little peace talk, Philippa thought.

"There's Father Cramdle," Edmund said as they came in sight of the priest.

Philippa made his acquaintance, and was pleased when he looked her squarely in the eye and was polite to her. She gave him Edmund with the admonition, "You will do as Father Cramdle tells you, Edmund, or you will answer to me."

"Maypole! Woolly head! Witch!"

Philippa didn't turn around when she heard Edmund's fierce whispers; she merely smiled and kept on going. She met with the armorer, a ferocious old man whose name was Proctor and who had only one eye and that one rheumy. He'd cut leather for many pairs of shoes, including a pair for her. She delivered the leather to Old Agnes, and she, in turn, set others to stitching the leather into shoes.

It was late afternoon when Philippa thought again of escape. Why not? She stopped cold. She'd acted all through the day, she realized suddenly, as if she were chatelaine here at St. Erth, and that was absurd. She was a prisoner; she was as good as a serf; she was a *wench*.

She stopped her ruminations at the sight of Alain. He was speaking with a man she hadn't noticed before. The conversation looked furtive to her sharp eyes, and the steward gave something to the man. She watched silently until the man melted away behind the soldiers' barracks. Alain then mounted a horse and rode out of St. Erth. Most curious, she thought. Without hesitation Philippa went into the great hall, through the side chambers, until she found the steward's small accounting room.

There were wooden shelves built against the walls, and in the small cubicles were rolled parchments tied with bits of string. There were also larger sections in which bound ledgers were kept. Quills and ink pots and a thick pile of foolscap lay atop the table, as well as large dust particles. There were books stacked on the floor in front of the shelves, a narrow cot against one wall, and a low trunk at the foot of the cot. Nothing more. Evidently Alain both worked and slept in this room.

Philippa took one of the large ledgers from a shelf, moved to his desk, and opened it. It was a record of the past three years' crops—what was planted in which section of land, the price of the grain, the sale of the product, and a log of the villeins who'd worked each section, including the number of hours and days. Another bound book contained birth and marriage records of St. Erth.

Philippa returned to the first book and read it through. She sought out another book that held all the records of building and repairs done at St. Erth in the past three years—the tenure of Alain's stewardship.

It took Philippa only an hour and a half to discover that Alain was a thief. No wonder Dienwald had had to steal the wool: there was no coin available because Alain had stolen it all. Why didn't Dienwald know this? Didn't he go over his steward's records?

Philippa rose and rearranged all the steward's materials the way she'd found them and left the small airless room. He still hadn't returned. Where had he gone? Who was the man to whom he'd been speaking? What had he given the man? She had no answers.

Philippa went back to the weaving shed, saw that all work was progressing satisfactorily, then went in search of Crooky. She found him curled up in a corner of the great hall—sleeping off a huge meal, Margot told her, glaring down at the snoring fool.

Philippa walked over to him and lightly stuck a toe in his ribs. He jerked up, his mouth opened, and he started singing:

> Ah, my sweet lord,
> don't cuff your loving slave;
> He slumbers rarely in your service,
> like a toothsome wench who—

"Don't finish that atrocious rhyme," Philippa said. "Stand up, fool. I'll have words with you."

Crooky blinked and staggered to his feet, scratching his armpit. "What want you, mistress?"

"I suppose 'mistress' is better than 'wench.' "

"My sweet lord isn't here, mistress."

"I know it. I need your help, Crooky. I want to ask you several questions, but please don't sing your answers, just speak them like sensible people."

Crooky rubbed his ribs. "You've a sharp toe, mistress."

"It'll be sharper if you don't attend me."

"Oh, aye, I'm whetted."

Ten minutes later Philippa left the fool to resume his sleep. He'd given her more food for thought than she wished to consume. The greatest shock of all was the fact that the Lord of St. Erth could make out written words, but only slowly and with difficulty. He could write only his name and cipher only the most simple of problems. Not that all that many men could, and no more than a handful of women. She was foolish to be so surprised. She'd just thought that Dienwald, who, despite his stubbornness, his arrogance, was intelligent and seemingly learned . . . No wonder he was firm about Edmund's lessons with Father Cramdle. He knew it was important; he felt the lack in himself.

Philippa was very angry. She also realized when she saw Alain ride back into the inner bailey that she had less than no power at all. She was a prisoner, not the mistress of St. Erth.

She had to bide her time.

Unfortunately, Alain sought her out at the evening meal. He, she quickly discovered, played the master in Dienwald's absence, with Dienwald's permission, evidently. She knew she must tread

EARTH SONG 139

warily. He sat beside her in the master's high-backed chair, ignored her for a good long while, then turned and gave her a leer a man would give a worn-out trollop of no account at all. She said nothing, didn't change her expression, merely sank her white teeth into a piece of pigeon pie, a delicious concoction that included carrots and turnips and potatoes.

"I see you stole the dead mistress's clothes."

So, Philippa thought, the steward wanted to bait her. He couldn't keep his dislike of her to himself. He really wasn't very good at the game. Not nearly so accomplished as his master. She smiled. "Do you see that, really? I'd thought you here only three years, *Master* Alain. The mistress, I'd heard, died shortly after Edmund's birth."

His right hand crushed a piece of bread. "Don't think you to insult me, whore. Dienwald will plow your belly, but he will show you no favors. You are but one of many, as I told you before. He will toss you to his men when he's through with you. You look a fool in the gown—'tis far too small for you. Your breasts look absurd, flattened like that. And your legs stick out like two poles, it is so short."

" 'Tis better than wearing nothing."

"Aye, all of us saw him rip your clothing off you, then carry you to his bed. You must have angered him mightily. Did he ravish you until you screamed? Or did you enjoy his plunging member inside you?"

"Nay," Philippa replied, as if considering the matter.

Alain laughed, sopped up some gravy from his trencher with the large piece of bread he'd crushed in his hand, and stuffed it into his mouth.

"You really don't look good in his chair," Philippa said, looking at his bulging cheeks. "It is too large for you, too substantial, too important. Or perhaps 'tis you who are just too meager, too paltry, for Dienwald's place." She thought he would spit out the bread in his anger at her, but he managed to keep chewing and swallow.

It was then she saw the shift in his expression. He'd realized that what he was doing wouldn't get him what he wanted. He was prepared to retrench. She waited. "We argue to no account," he said finally, and he sounded the reasonable man, not the furious brute who wanted to strike her. "Truly, Philippa de Beauchamp, you must leave St. Erth while there is still time. I will help you return to your father. You must go before Dienwald returns."

He wanted her gone, and very badly. Why? She was a threat to him now that she knew him for a thief, but he couldn't know that she'd discovered the truth about him. Why, then? "I've a notion to stay here and wed the Lord of St. Erth. He is a man of worth, and comely. What think you, steward?" The moment the words were out, Philippa was appalled at herself. But she wouldn't take them back. She watched, fascinated, as his face mottled with rage—and something else, something sly and frightening. His hand shook.

"I'll have you whipped, whore," he said very quietly. "I've a fancy to wield the whip myself. God, how I'd enjoy it. I'd see those breasts of yours heave up and down when you scream and try to escape the whip, and I'd mark that back of yours with bloody welts."

Edmund suddenly slipped out of his place at
the trestle table and quickly moved to her side
even as Philippa said, "No you won't, Master
Alain. You have no power here either. If Dienwald only knew that you—" She bit her lower lip
until she felt the sting of her own blood. She'd
very nearly spit at him that he was a liar and a
thief and a scoundrel and probably even worse.

At that moment Crooky rose from the floor
beside Alain's chair and moved to stand on Philippa's other side. He yawned deeply, stared
blankly at the steward, then sprawled back onto
the rushes.

Alain didn't look pleased. He eyed Edmund,
who looked for all the world like a mangy little
gamecock. "The boy can't protect you, whore, nor
can the fool, who's an idiot, a half-wit. He's
naught of anything, and Dienwald keeps him
here only because he finds it amusing to endure
him. Now, what were you going to say, whore?
You were going to accuse me of something? Make
up lies about me?"

"My name is Philippa de Beauchamp. I am a
lady. You're naught but offal."

"You're no more a lady than the fool is a poet.
You're a silly vain trollop." Without warning, the
steward raised his hand and struck her hard
across the face. Her head snapped back from the
force of it and she felt tears burn her eyes. Oddly,
she noticed ink stains on his fingers, and wondered when he'd last bathed.

"Damned slut!" He raised his hand to strike her
again, but suddenly, to Philippa's bewilderment,
his chair began to shake, tip backward, then go
crashing to the floor, the steward with it, landing

on his back, his head striking the carved chair back.

Philippa, her hand pressed to her flaming cheek, could only stare at the fallen steward. Edmund stood over him, rubbing his hands together and crowing with laughter. The hall had fallen silent.

Alain scrambled to his feet, his face blotchy with rage, his thin body trembling. He waved his fists toward Edmund, yelling, "You damned little cockscomb! I'll hide you for that!"

Philippa was out of her chair and standing in front of Edmund in a flash. "You touch the boy and I'll kill you. Doubt me not."

The steward drew up short, looking at the woman who was at eye level with him. She was strong, but she wasn't strong enough to do him damage. Her words meant nothing; she'd cringe away at the first threat of violence, like every other woman he'd known. He wanted to spit on her, he wanted to wring her neck. No, he had to keep control. "Stand aside, whore."

He raised his hand when Philippa didn't move. There came a deep grumbling sound from behind the steward. Slowly, very slowly, Alain lowered his arm, turning toward the sound as he did so. Philippa stared at Gorkel the Hideous. He was the most terrifying sight she'd ever seen. His bony face, with its pocked surface and puckered scars, its stubbled jaw and thick beetle eyebrows that met over his nose, looked like a vision from hell. And there was that low growl coming from his throat, like an animal warning its prey.

"Get ye gone, little man," Gorkel said finally, and his lips barely opened.

Alain wanted to tell the codshead take himself

to hell, but he was afraid of Gorkel; the man could easily break his spine with but little effort of his huge hands. He looked at Philippa, then at the boy, who was standing there with his hands on his hips, his chin thrust forward. He'd get her; then he'd punish the boy. The steward turned on his heel and strode from the hall.

Crooky suddenly jumped to his feet and burst into wild song, the words following the enraged steward from the hall:

> A varlet he'll be to the end
> A stench that rots in the walls
> Next time he'll not have the gall
> When the master's back in the hall.

Philippa looked down at Edmund. "Thank you."

"He's a bully. Father doesn't see it because Alain's always careful around him. Why does he hate you? You're naught but a girl. You've never done anything to him, have you?"

"No, I haven't. I truly don't know why he hates me, Edmund."

"You will stay away from him. I can't always be around to protect you."

"I know." She looked up and met Gorkel's eyes. She smiled at him and he nodded, a deep rumbling sound in his throat. He scratched his belly, turned, and strode back to his place below the salt.

Noise filled the hall again. Crooky sprawled once more to the rushes. Edmund crammed bread into his mouth, and Philippa, her cheek still stinging, merely sat back into her chair, wondering what she was to do now.

For the next three days she kept close to Gorkel. He didn't seem to mind, and his presence kept Alain well away from her. He even disdained to sit beside her at the lord's trestle table. Gorkel didn't tell her that it was the master's order that he keep close to her. It would be Gorkel's head were the wench to escape St. Erth. In those three days Philippa learned more about St. Erth, met all its inhabitants, sewed Edmund a tunic of forest-green wool, and began one for Dienwald. Hers could wait a bit longer. Philippa became so used to all the noise that she could even identify what squawks came from what chicken. One pig in particular chose her as its mother and followed her everywhere, making Gorkel laugh. Philippa named the pig Tupper.

On the morning of the third day, Philippa, her step buoyant and carefree, entered the weaving shed to be greeted by pandemonium. A gaunt middle-aged man with tufts of gray hair sticking straight up on his head was screaming at Mordrid. He was quaking with rage, shaking so violently that his clothes, hanging loosely around him, were in danger of leaving his body.

He yelled, "Bitch! Slut! Treacherous cow! I lie on my deathbed and ye take my job. I'll kill ye!"

10

Philippa stared at the man, then shouted, "Hold! Who are you? What do you do here?"

The man whirled about. He looked Philippa up and down and sneered, and his eyes seemed to turn red. "Aye, so ye're t' witch who's beleaguered t' master. Ye're t' one who's made him think of naught but plungin' into yer belly and givin' ye wot's mine!"

"Ah," Philippa said, crossing her arms over her breasts. "You must be Prink. Fresh from your deathbed. I see you are still with us."

Her bright, very polite voice stalled Prink, but only for a moment. He felt ill-used, betrayed, and he wanted to leap on the wench and tear the hair from her head. It was her size that held him back. He didn't have his full strength back yet. He drew himself up. "I'm here t' do my work. Ye're not welcome, wench. Out wi' ye, and take all these

145

stupid women wi' ye." He grabbed Mordrid's arm
and twisted it. "I'll keep this one—she deserves
a hidin', she does, and I'll gi' it to her."

"Prink," Philippa said very slowly, "you will
release Mordrid, now."

The weaver looked fit to spit. His hold tightened on Mordrid's arm until the woman moaned
with pain.

Philippa wondered where Gorkel was. During
the past three days he'd been where she'd been.
Well, he wasn't here and she had no one but herself to handle this predicament. Even mouthy Old
Agnes was hiding behind a huge woven piece of
cloth newly dyed a bright yellow. Philippa
stepped up to the furious weaver, saw his pallor,
saw the spasms that shook his muscles, and knew
him still to be very ill. She said calmly, her voice
pitched low, "You aren't well, Prink. Here, allow
me to help you back to your bed."

He squealed like Philippa's worshipful pig,
Tupper, but he did drop Mordrid's arm. He gave
Philippa his full attention. "Ye're naught but t'
master's slut, and ye've taken wot's mine and—"

"Your face is gray as the sky this morning,
Prink, and sweat drips off your forehead. Do you
wish to remain here and fall on your face in a
faint, in front of all the women?"

Prink didn't know what to do. He'd exhausted
himself with his rightful indignation. He wanted
to wring the wench's neck, but he hadn't the
strength. He mumbled curses at Mordrid and
walked slowly, his muscles cramping, toward the
door of the outbuilding. At that moment Gorkel
appeared, looking from the weaver to Philippa.

"Do help him back to his bed, Gorkel, and see

that he remains there until he's completely well again. I will speak to you later, Prink."

The instant the weaver disappeared, Old Agnes bounded out of her hidey-hole, squawking with fury. "Old codshead! How dare he try to ruin everything, the stinking poltroon!"

Philippa ignored Old Agnes. "Mordrid, are you all right? Did he hurt your arm?"

The woman shook her head. "Thank you, mistress." She fretted a moment, then said, "Prink's a good man, he is, a proud man. The cramping illness makes him feel less than a man."

Would a woman forgive a man absolutely anything? Philippa wondered as she watched the work settle back into its placid routine. When Gorkel reappeared, he merely nodded to Philippa and took his post by the door.

The following afternoon, Philippa was hot and tired and feeling lonely. She was walking across the inner bailey, the pig, Tupper, squealing at her bare feet in hot pursuit, when the porter, Hood, called out to her that a tinker was coming. Did she want him to enter? Excitement flowed through Philippa as she yelled back that, yes, she wanted him to come. A tinker meant trinkets and ribbons and thread and items the keep sorely needed. Perhaps the tinker even had gowns, sold or bartered to him on his travels. She didn't stop to think that it was odd for her to be asked permission by the porter.

Men and women were gathering in the inner bailey, buzzing with excited conversation. Children, feeling their parents' anticipation, stayed close. Even the animals quieted as the stranger came through the huge gates. Philippa greeted the tinker and her eyes glistened with enthusiasm at the sight of the two pack mules he led, each one carrying more packages than she'd ever seen.

It was when she was fingering two long lengths of pink ribbon that she realized she had no coin.

She had nothing, either, with which to trade.

She wanted to cry.

A soft voice sounded in her ear. "You agree to leave St. Erth, and I'll buy you all the ribbons you want. Mayhap even a gown and some shoes. The tinker has everything. Ah, yes, you silly girl, those ribbons would go very nicely with your hair. Do you want them?"

She expelled her breath, turning to see the steward standing close beside her, his leer as pronounced as ever.

Anger filled her and she very nearly screamed that she knew he was a thief and that was why the master had no coin. She stopped herself in the nick of time. She had to keep quiet. She had to wait until Dienwald returned. She tilted her head back so that she was looking down her nose at him. "Nay, sir steward, there is nothing I wish."

"Liar."

She stepped back then and watched the people of St. Erth buy and trade goods with the tinker.

She wanted to weep when she handed him back the ribbons. It was foolish, but she wanted them desperately. They were as pale a pink as the sunrise in early May, and matched a gown she owned back at Beauchamp.

The tinker remained the night and Crooky proved to be in fine fettle, singing until he was hoarse, the words of his songs so colorfully crude that Father Cramdle was forced to clear his throat several times. When Philippa finally left the great hall, Gorkel beside her, she was still smiling.

"I told the tinker to circle back this way when the master is here," Gorkel said as he left her beside her bedchamber door.

"It truly doesn't matter," Philippa said, and swallowed a bit hard.

"Keep the door locked," Gorkel said as he'd said each preceding night. She did as he'd said, then turned with her candle to set it down. Standing in front of her was Alain, holding a knife.

Philippa rushed back to the door and turned the large brass key in the lock, yelling, "Gorkel! Gorkel! *A moi! A moi!*"

The steward was on her in a second, his arm closing around her throat as he jerked her back against him. His right hand rose and the sharp point of the knife pointed down at her breast. Philippa couldn't scream now; his arm was cutting off her breath. She clawed at his arm with her nails, but he was strong—and strong with purpose.

He didn't slam the knife into her breast. She realized that he didn't want to kill her here. It would be far too dangerous for him. The knife was to ensure her obedience. His arm tightened and she felt the chamber spinning as white lights burst before her eyes. She jerked at his arm and felt the tip of the knife prick into her throat. She felt a cold numbing followed by the slick wetness of her own blood.

"Hold still, whore, or I'll gullet you now. As for Gorkel, that cretinous idiot can't hear you. The doors are thick. But you'll keep quiet or all that will come from your mouth is a bloody gurgle."

Philippa held still as a stone, dropping her arms to her sides.

"Good. Now, come here."

He half-dragged her over to Dienwald's bed and shoved her down onto her back. He came down next to her, holding the knife over her throat. She swallowed, looking up at him.

" 'Tis past time for you to escape from St. Erth. Aye, you'll be long gone by the time the master returns. And he'll blame Gorkel, the hulking fright. Not me. He'll never even think about me."

She said nothing, letting her brain work rather than her mouth. It was a novel approach.

"You wonder why I want you gone so badly from St. Erth—I can see it in your silly female's eyes. Those eyes of yours . . . they're familiar, the shape and the color, aye, that shade of blue has bothered me . . . I have seem them before, somewhere . . . but no, I have no time for such nonsense. I wouldn't have killed you had you left before, but now you give me no choice. Stupid sow, you should have left when I first offered you the chance.

"But you didn't, did you? You wanted the master, wanted to believe his lies. Did he tell you that he wanted you more than any other female? He deceives women well. You should have left. But now 'tis too late, far too late."

He was rambling on and on, bragging and insulting Dienwald, and it seemed to Philippa that he must be mad.

"Why?" she whispered, not moving because the knife was still pressed so deep, its tip already bathed in her blood.

"Why? Should I tell you, I wonder? Well, soon

you'll be dead and gone, so it matters not. I know who you are."

That made no sense. She said slowly, "I'm Philippa de Beauchamp. Everyone knows that."

"Aye, but you see, I sent my two men after the third wagon of wool, the one my foolish master left to the farmers because he felt pity for them. Aye, my men got them, and before they killed the luggards, they found out all about you. The farmers didn't know you'd been hiding in one of their wagons, but they were ready to talk all about you once knives were at their hearts. My men found out you were your father's favorite, that you were his steward in fact and in deed, that it was you who had set the price of the wool and sent them to the St. Ives Fair to get that price. Which means that you can read and write and cipher, unlike my master, who believes whatever I tell him.

"So you must die. You wonder why Dienwald trusts me, don't you? Aye, I can see it in your eyes. Dienwald saved me from a knight I'd swindled, and then he killed my master, who'd sided with the knight, after I told him how I'd been cheated and beaten. Then he brought me to St. Erth, where I've become a rich man. He believed he had earned my gratitude, the pathetic fool.

"Dienwald believes himself a rogue, a scoundrel, a rebel who can wave his fist in the face of higher authority, but deep in his soul he holds beliefs that can and will do him in. So you see, I can't let you remain, for I also know you visited my chamber. You left papers and documents just the way you found them, but one of my spies saw you. Aye, he saw you leaving, looking furtive and wary. So you found out the truth, did you, and were just waiting for the proper moment to tell Dienwald.

"And he set Gorkel to keep you from escaping, not realizing that he was at the same time protecting you from me. You didn't know that, did you? Gorkel has stayed close, and I didn't know how to get you until tonight. Then it came to me, and I knew I must be bold. You know, Philippa de Beauchamp, I hated you the moment I first saw you. I knew your purpose to be contrary to mine."

Before she could say a word, before she could draw another breath, Alain brought the bone handle of the knife down against her temple, hard. She saw a burst of lights, felt a sharp pain, and then there was blackness.

Philippa awoke with the earthy smells of the stables filling her nostrils. Her hands were bound tightly behind her, but her legs were free. She lay perfectly still, waiting for the dizziness to clear. When it did, she realized she couldn't breathe easily. A blanket covered her. She gripped an edge with her teeth and pulled it off her face. She seemed to be alone, but it was very dark in the stables and she couldn't be certain. She couldn't hear anyone moving about or speaking. Where was Alain?

Now, she thought, now was the time to think. Not with her feet, though they were the only free part of her, but with her brain. What to do? Alain had nothing to lose; he had to remove her from St. Erth. Snatches of songs sung by the jongleurs paraded through her mind in those moments, songs about mighty heroes rescuing fair maids from degrading and frightful situations. There wasn't a mighty hero anywhere to be found. The fair maid would have to save herself.

She tried to loosen the ropes at her wrists, but the effort did nothing but shred her skin. She rolled over and managed to rise to her feet, peering from the stall where she'd been left unconscious. She nearly fainted from the pain in her temple where the knife handle had struck, but she held on. She had no choice but to hold on. She couldn't have much time left now. Alain would be coming back for her soon. And he'd kill her; she didn't doubt it for an instant.

Philippa managed to free the latch on the stall and push the door open. It squealed on its rusted hinges, and she froze. Where was the steward?

It was at that moment that she heard two men speaking in low voices in the stableyard. The steward's men. Standing guard until he returned. From where?

Philippa drew a deep breath of relief. She'd been on the point of rushing out of the stables at full tilt, screaming for help. She'd been fully ready to think with her feet again. She looked around carefully, her eyes now used to the darkness, and saw an old scythe, sharp and deadly, hanging from a hook on the wall.

Her bonds didn't take long to cut through, but the edge of the scythe was sharp and she felt her own blood, sticky and slippery, covering her palms before she was free. Once she was loose, she stooped down and eased back to the stable door. The two men were still there, still speaking in low voices.

Now, she decided, she could take them by surprise and run as far as the great hall before they caught up with her.

"Well? Heard you aught out of the whore? Is she still unconscious?"

Alain had returned. Philippa shrank back, her heart pounding so loudly they must hear it. No matter. Let them come. She pulled the scythe from the wall and clutched it to her breast.

She heard one of the men say, "Nay, t' wench is still quiet. T' blow will keep her unconscious until we cut her throat. Can we split her afore we kill her?"

Philippa swallowed convulsively. She realized suddenly that her bloody hands were making the scythe handle slick. She picked up some hay at her feet and rubbed it over the handle and over her palms. The pain was fierce, but she welcomed it. As long as she felt pain, she was alive. And as long as she had the scythe, she had a chance.

"You can do whatever you wish to her. But you must kill her afterward, make no mistake about it, and make certain her body's never found. The wench is conniving, so take care if she comes to herself again. Now, I've spoken to Hood, the porter, and told him that I'm sending some supplies to the master. The man's not stupid, so be careful. You'll load the girl on a pack mule and take her away from St. Erth. When you return, you'll be paid. Now, go."

Then Alain was leaving; she heard his retreating footsteps. Only his two accomplices remained, then.

All she had on her side was surprise.

She raised the scythe over her head and waited. One of the men was coming into the stables, saying to the other, "Wait here and I'll fetch t' wench."

The other man protested, "Nay, ye'll take her in t' stall, ye bastid!"

They were fighting over who was going to ravish her first. Her hold on the scythe handle tightened. Filthy villains. One appeared in the doorway, moonlight framing his head. Philippa drew a sharp breath and brought the scythe down hard. It was only the blunted, curved edge of the blade that hit him, but the force of her blow cracked the man's head open and he didn't even cry out, but fell, blood spewing everywhere, to the hay-strewn floor.

The man behind him cried out, but Philippa, like a blood-spewed vision from hell, screamed and came at him, the scythe raised over her head.

The man bellowed in fear, his eyes rolling in his head, and turned on his heel. Philippa drew up for an instant, her mouth gaping in surprise. The man had run from her, terrified. She quickly ran across the inner bailey and up the steps of the great hall. She flung the doors open and rushed in. As always, there was the loud noise of general conversation. Then a few people noticed her standing there, the scythe in her hands, covered with blood, her hair wild about her pale face.

There was an awesome silence. Then Alain jumped to his feet and yelled, "Kill the whore! By the devil's knees, she's butchered our people! Look at her, covered with blood! Murderess! She's stolen the master's jewels! Kill her! Strike her down quickly!"

Philippa looked around her and raised the scythe. The silence was deafening and paralyzing. No one was moving yet. Everyone was staring as

if at a mummers' scene. "Gorkel," she said, her
voice just above a croak, "help me."

Alain, seeing that no one had moved, bounded
to his feet, screaming as he ran toward her, "Kill
the damned witch! That's what she is, a cursed
witch!"

He grabbed one of the men-at-arms' swords
and ran straight toward her.

"Kill her!" another man's voice roared with the
steward's. "Aye, she's a witch who steals men's
jobs!" It was Prink, still pale and sweaty but ready
to do her in. "Slay her where she stands!"

Eerily, Philippa now heard each voice sepa-
rately. Every sound came singly and loudly and
obscenely. She heard Father Cramdle praying
loudly, she heard Edmund screech like one of her
mother's peacocks as he dashed toward her. "No,
Edmund, stay back!" But her words were just an
echo in her mind. Northbert, Proctor, the
armorer, Margot, Crooky, Alice—all of them were
rushing at her. To aid her? To kill her?

She shuddered and backed away. She knew
Alain's other henchman was out there in the
inner bailey somewhere, just waiting to kill her if
she came out. And here was Alain, fury and
hatred burning him, ready to kill her even as she
stood here in a hall filled with people.

She wasn't a coward. She raised the scythe.

"Nay, mistress."

It was Gorkel and he was moving slowly
toward her, a look of abandoned joy on his terrifying face. His teeth were bared in a smile, and
in that instant Philippa felt a bolt of pity for Alain.

Gorkel caught the steward's arm just above the
elbow and simply squeezed. Alain's sword clanked
harmlessly to the floor.

Then the steward was screaming and begging and pleading. Philippa saw that Gorkel was twisting the steward's elbow back and up, even as Alain's screams grew louder and louder.

Finally, seemingly without emotion, Gorkel closed the thick fingers of his other hand about the steward's neck. He raised him with one arm, the fingers tightening, and the steward dangled above the floor. He couldn't scream now; his voice was a mere liquid gurgle in his throat, as Gorkel shook him until his neck snapped—an indecently loud noise in the silent hall.

Gorkel grunted and flung the quite-dead steward to the rushes.

Philippa dropped the scythe, covered her face with her bloody hands, fell to her knees, and burst into tears.

She heard voices, felt hands touching her gently.

Then she heard a little boy's voice, Edmund's voice, and it brought her face out of her hands, for he said, "Stop those silly female tears."

She looked at him, and, surprising herself, smiled. "You are a mean little boy, with no more sympathy than a bug, but the sight of you right this moment pleases me."

"Aye," Edmund said. "That's because you're a female and need to be protected. You're filthy and covered with blood. Come along."

"Go with the boy," Gorkel said. "You did well, mistress, very well."

"There's another man, Gorkel. I killed his partner—he's in the stables—but the other man ran. I don't know who he was, but I would recognize his voice."

"It was probably the cistern keeper, a scurvy ruffian," Gorkel said. "He's been hanging about the steward. Aye, I'll have him fetched, and the master can see to his punishment when he returns."

"What about him?" Old Agnes screeched, pointing at Prink. "He's a filthy traitor!"

The weaver was swaying on his feet, looking sick and afraid as Gorkel advanced on him.

"Leave him be," Philippa called. "Don't kill him, Gorkel. He's just stupid and foolish from his illness. Leave him be."

"I'll give him a taste of pain," Gorkel said. "Just a little taste of pain so he'll remember not to make another mistake like this one."

Philippa watched him lift the weaver high above the floor and shake him like a mongrel. Then he sent his fist into the weaver's stomach, dropping him, kicking his ribs, and saying softly, "Ye touch the mistress again, ye say one word out of the side of yer mouth to her, and I'll kick ye until yer ass comes out yer ears."

Philippa turned away. Edmund took her hand. "Come along, Philippa. I'll take you to your chamber."

Edmund was whistling as he walked beside her up the solar stairs.

Wolffeton Castle, Cornwall

Graelam de Moreton wiped the sweat from his brow and greeted his visitor. "Aye, Burnell, 'tis a pleasure to see you again. Is our king well? And Eleanor? Is our kingdom healthy?"

The two men spoke as Burnell, weary to the tips of his worn leather boots, trudged beside the lord of Wolffeton Castle. He was met by Graelam's wife, Lady Kassia, a charming, slight lady with large eyes and a laughing mouth. He found her delightful but wondered how such a small female dealt with the huge warrior that was her husband.

"What brings you here, Burnell?" Graelam asked finally, waiting for their guest to refresh himself with a bit of the remaining excellent Aquitaine wine.

"Actually, my lord, 'tis a mission for the king. He wishes your advice."

Graelam's dark brows shot upward. "Edward wants *me* to advise *him*? Come, Burnell, 'tis nearly May and the king must want to march against the Welsh or the Scots, and I imagine he wants more men and more money for a campaign. Come, now, and tell me the truth—"

" 'Tis true, my lord. The king has a daughter and he wants to find her a husband, one here in Cornwall."

"But Edward's daughters are far too young, and the king couldn't want an alliance with only a baron," Lady Kassia protested.

"His daughter isn't a princess, my lady," Burnell said to Kassia, who was sitting in her husband's vast chair. Graelam was standing beside her. It was then that Burnell noticed that she was heavy with child.

"What is she, then?"

"Kassia, my love," Graelam said, grinning down at her, "methinks I scent a royal indiscretion. Edward must have been quite young, Burnell."

" 'Tis true. Her name is Philippa de Beauchamp. She's nearly eighteen and 'tis past time for her to be wedded."

"De Beauchamp! But Lord Henry's daughter—"

"She's the king's illegitimate daughter, my lord, raised by Lord Henry as his own."

Both Graelam and Kassia were staring with fascinated eyes at the king's secretary. Slowly Robert Burnell gave them all the facts and the king's request. ". . . So you see, my lord, the king wants a man who won't try to bleed him, but also a man of honor and strength here in Cornwall."

Graelam was frowning. He said nothing.

Burnell, hot and tired, said with some desperation, "He wants you to give him a man who would be worthy of his daughter's hand, my lord, so—"

"I may know the man the king seeks," Graelam said with his first spark of enthusiasm, and Kassia saw the evil intent in her husband's eyes.

"You do?" she asked, staring at him.

"Aye, mayhap I do."

"His present rank isn't important, my lord. The king will make him an earl."

"An earl, you say? 'Tis something to think about. You will remain until tomorrow, Burnell?"

Robert Burnell would have happily remained in a soft feather mattress for a week. After visiting Lord Graelam, he would have to stop at Beauchamp and speak to Lord Henry and tell him, hopefully, that there would be a groom for Philippa shortly.

"Good. I will tell you my opinion on the morrow. Aye, advice for the king."

That night, Graelam was laughing heartily in bed beside his wife. Kassia was chiding him sharply. "You cannot, Graelam! Truly, you cannot!"

"I told you I would bring that whoreson down, Kassia. This will do it." And Graelam continued to laugh, finally holding his belly.

"But Dienwald despises authority—you know
that. His father-in-law would be the King of
England! Dienwald wouldn't accept it. He'd travel
to the Pope to plead for his freedom, or escape
to the Tartars, or even pray to the devil if need
be. And to be made an earl. Dienwald disdains
such trappings. He hates respectability and
responsibility and tending to his name and his
holdings and his *worth*. Oh, my lord, he bested
you, but this revenge would make him miserable
forever. He could no longer raid when it pleased
him. He could no longer brag about being a rogue
and a scoundrel. He is proud of his reputation!
And what if the girl is a hag? What then?"

Graelam laughed harder.

Kassia just looked at her husband and thought
about the casks of Aquitaine wine that Dienwald
had probably stolen from the wrecked ship. She
thought of Dienwald as an earl, his father-in-law
the King of England himself. Hadn't Burnell mentioned that the girl, Philippa, looked every inch a
Plantagenet?

Kassia started laughing herself. "He'll murder
the both of us," she said, "if Edward takes your
advice."

St. Erth Castle

It was the middle of the night and Philippa was
dreaming that she felt a warm hand lightly stroking through her hair, rubbing her scalp, and it
felt wonderful. Then a man's mouth was touching
her cheek, her jaw, nipping at her throat, licking
over her lips; then a man's tongue was stroking
rhythmically over her lower lip. She sighed and

stretched onto her back. She loved the dream, cherished it, held it tightly, now feeling the man's fingers caressing her breasts, his callused fingertips stroking her nipples.

When the man's fingers rubbed over her ribs, curved in with her waist, then stroked her belly, her muscles contracted with pleasure. Then he was pressing her legs open and delving through her hair to find her, and she sighed, then moaned deeply, wanting more, lifting her hips, and wanting, wanting . . .

She opened her eyes to see the man wasn't a dream. It was Dienwald, and she looked at him until she could make out his features in the darkness. He looked tired and intent and he was breathing hard as he stared down at her.

"It wasn't a dream," she said.

"No, wench, it wasn't a dream. You feel like the softest of God's creatures." She felt his fingers caressing her flesh and knew she was wet beneath his fingers and swelling, her flesh heating. Then he eased his middle finger inside her, and she cried out, jerking up, feelings she'd never before imagined welling up inside her.

"Hush," he said, and pressed his palm against her belly to push her down again, and then his finger eased more deeply within her, and more deeply still. "Does that pain you, wench? I can feel you stretching for my finger. Ah, there it is, your badge of innocence. Your precious maidenhead. Intact, ready for my assault." He shuddered, his whole body heaving, and for a moment he laid his face against her, his finger still inside her, not moving now, soothing and warm. "You almost died tonight, Gorkel told me. I'm sorry, Philippa. I thought you well-protected—from yourself, truth be told—yet my trusted man was an enemy of the worst sort. I'm so sorry." He kissed her belly, licked her soft flesh, and his finger pressed more deeply into her, testing the strength of her maidenhead. He moaned, a jagged raw sound, and withdrew his finger.

He came over her and his mouth covered her, and Philippa, excited and quiescent in the dark of the night, yielded completely to him.

His tongue was inside her mouth, tasting her, savoring her, and she touched the tip of his tongue with hers. Then, once again, without warning, he rolled off her, leaving her abruptly.

"Please," Philippa whispered, holding her hand toward him. She felt nearly frantic with longing—for what, she knew not.

"Nay, wench," he said, sounding as though he'd been running hard. "Nay, 'tis just that I've been without a woman for a week and my loins are fit to burst with lust. Get you back to sleep."

She cried out at his words, hating them, hating him for making her realize yet again that she was nothing to him, nothing but a vessel, nothing more. She heard him leave the chamber and slam the door.

She turned onto her side and wept, her sobs a faint sound in the quiet darkness.

When Dienwald returned some time later, she pretended to be asleep. He made no move to touch her when he climbed into the bed beside her. She listened to his breathing even into sleep and knew she had to leave him and St. Erth.

As soon as she could find a way.

11

The next morning, Philippa awoke to the slap of a hand on her naked buttocks and lurched up.

"You're awake. 'Tis time I had some answers from you, wench. I leave my castle in fine fettle, only to return and find my steward dead and everything in an uproar. Get you up and come into the great hall."

Dienwald smacked her bottom one more time and left her alone. She lay there wondering what would happen to her if she cracked his head open with a scythe. The cockscomb.

She rolled onto her side and tried to go back to sleep, but it was impossible.

In the great hall, Dienwald was staring at his fool, stretched on his side on the floor. "Tell me again what happened, Crooky, and say it in words that make sense. No rhymes, no songs."

Crooky looked at Dienwald. His master was

tired, ill-tempered, and had obviously ridden back to St. Erth in haste. Why? To see the mistress? He'd missed the girl? Crooky hadn't seen him the previous evening when he'd stormed into the hall yelling his head off because the porter had screeched about Philippa being covered with blood and dead bodies everywhere.

Crooky grinned at his master. "Methinks you grow cockhard, master."

"I grow what? Listen, you damnable mule offal, I don't—"

"You caught the bastards who burned the crops?"

Dienwald tore into a piece of bread with his strong teeth. "Aye, three of them, but curse their tongues, they were already dead and couldn't tell me who'd sent them."

" 'Twas Walter de Grasse, the slimy serpent."

"Aye, in all likelihood." Dienwald chewed another piece of bread, not speaking again until he'd swallowed. Then he bellowed, "Margot! Bring me ale!"

"Let the mistress tell you of her adventures, master. 'Twill make your hair stand up in fright."

"You dare to call the wench 'mistress'? It's mad! I should kick you—"

Crooky quickly rolled away from his master's foot and came up onto his knees. "She's good for St. Erth," he said. "And stouthearted. She saved herself."

Margot brought the ale, giving Dienwald a wary look as she served him. "What's the matter with you?" he demanded, then waved an irritable hand when she paled at his words.

He turned back to the hapless fool. "You were

here, damn your ears! I want to hear what happened."

"Oh, leave him alone," came Philippa's irritated voice from behind him. "The last thing I want to listen to is Crooky singing at dawn."

Dienwald turned about and eyed her. It required all his will not to smile at her. It took him only a few moments more to tamp down on the wild relief he felt upon seeing her whole and ill-tempered. " 'Tis about time you deign to come to me," he said. "You look like a snabbly hag."

Actually, she looked tousled and soft and very, very sweet. He eased back into his chair, stretching out his legs in front of him, folding his hands over his chest. He'd fetched her another old gown worn by his first wife, this one a pale gray, frayed and baggy. It stopped a good three inches above her ankles.

"Thank you for the gown. There is no overtunic?"

"I didn't even have the chance to see you in the other gown I gave you. This one doesn't fit you at all, but there was nothing else. And don't whine. Why haven't you yet sewn yourself a new gown and overtunic?"

"I should have," she said, wanting to kick him. He'd touched her and caressed her and kissed her, then left her to find himself another female vessel. And now he was baiting her and insulting her. But she also remembered how he'd laid his head on her stomach and told her how he'd been afraid when he'd heard what had happened. Had she dreamed that? He didn't seem at all concerned about her this morning, just bad-tempered. She raised her chin. "I think I shall begin immediately." She picked up a piece of bread and begin to chew it with enraging indifference.

"Tell me what happened, wench. Now."

She chanced to look down at her wrists. They were bruised and raw but there wasn't much pain now.

Dienwald hadn't yet noticed her wrists; now he did, and sucked in his breath. His irritation rose to alarming heights. "I don't believe this," he bellowed at her. "I leave my keep, and look what happens. Have Margot wrap up your wrists." He added several lurid curses, then sat back, closing his eyes. "Tell me what happened whilst I was gone."

Philippa looked at him closely, decided he'd calmed himself sufficiently, and said, "Not all that much happened at the beginning. We spun nearly all the wool into cloth, and now we've gotten most of it dyed. The sewing has begun, just yesterday. Oh, just one small happening out of the ordinary—Gorkel had to break your steward's neck, but Alain deserved it. I have determined that you are the most pious of saints when compared to the loathsome departed Alain."

"I see. Now, before I take you to my chamber and thrash you, you will tell me why my loathsome steward wanted you dead."

Philippa just shrugged. She knew it infuriated him, and, unable to stop herself, she shrugged again.

He rose swiftly from his chair, walked to her and grabbed her beneath the arms, and lifted her off the bench. He held her eye-to-eye. "Tell me what happened, else you'll be very sorry."

"What will you do? Will you continue what you did to me in my sleep during the night?"

A spasm of some emotion Philippa couldn't identify crossed his face; then his expression was closed again. "Give over, Philippa, give over. I am weary and wish to know what happened."

His serious voice, empty of amusement, brought her eyes open. "I'll tell you. Put me down."

Dienwald very slowly lowered her to her bare feet. He walked back to his chair, pressing his hand against the small of his back. "Your weight strains even my strength," he remarked to the black-beamed ceiling, and sat down again, waving his hand at her.

She told him of what she'd found in the steward's chamber. "I didn't trust him, even from that first day I was here. He hated me, and there was no reason I could see. Well, my lord, he's been cheating you all the time he's been here, and when he held the knife to my throat in your chamber, he admitted it and insulted you and me and said he was going to kill me."

He made a strangled sound but said nothing. Philippa, swallowing against the remembered fear, spoke in a clipped and precise voice, emotionlessly telling him of coming to in the stables, of killing one of the men with the scythe, of running into the great hall, and of Gorkel's killing of the steward. "Alain also sent his men out to take the other wool wagon. He had the farmers killed. It was from them that he learned that I could read and write and that I'd acted as my father's steward."

Dienwald said nothing for a very long time. He merely looked beyond her, over her right shoulder, she thought, as she waited tensely for him to say something, anything. To show concern perhaps for her safety, as he had in the dark of the night. To tell her of his undying gratitude. To tell her that he was glad she wasn't hurt, to tell her he was sorry it had happened. To exclaim over the perfidy of his steward. To thank her for her diligence, her concern for him and for St. Erth. To tell . . .

He exploded into her thoughts, nearly yelling, "What in the name of St. Andrew am I to do now? I have no steward because you ensured that he'd die, curse you! Poor Gorkel had no choice but to dispatch him, and 'tis all your fault!"

Philippa stared at him, nearly choking on the piece of buttered bread in her mouth. "He was *cheating* you! Didn't you attend me? He was a filthy knave! Didn't you hear me? Don't you care?"

Dienwald merely shrugged, causing her to leap to her feet and throw the remaining bread at his head. He ducked, but some of the sweet butter hit his cheek in a yellow streak.

"You ungrateful fool! You—"

"Enough!" Dienwald rose from his chair, wiping the butter from his face with his hand.

"I repeat, wench, what will I do for a steward?"

She stuck out her chin, squared her shoulders, and readied herself for his insults. "I will be your steward."

It didn't take him long to produce the insults she expected at her announcement. "You? A female? A female who has no more sense than to spy on a man and be caught and nearly butchered for her stupidity? Ha, wench, ha!"

"That's not true. I was careful when I searched through his chamber. I saw him ride away before I went into the room. It was just bad fortune that he had spies and one of them saw me. And what about his dishonesty? You, so astute, such a keen and intelligent male, didn't even begin to realize he was robbing you down to your last tunic, to your last hay straw, to your last . . . You, a brave male, didn't realize anything at all. You might even now give a thought to the fact that Alain's spies are very likely still here. Ha!"

"Females don't have the brains to resolve problems and keep correct records of things."

Philippa just stared at him, her bile spent, her rage simmering down to weary resentment.

"Females," Dienwald continued, waxing fluent now, "don't know the first thing about organizing facts and making decisions. Females have one useful role only, and that is—"

"Don't you dare say it!"

"They should see to the weaving and the sewing and the cooking. They are useful for the soft things, the things a man needs to ease him after he's toiled a long day with both his body and his brain."

"You're a fool," Philippa said, and without another word, for she'd spent even her anger now, turned on her bare heel and strode toward the oak doors.

"Don't you dare leave, wench!"

She speeded up, and was through the door within moments. She raced across the inner bailey, dodging chickens and Tupper, who squealed with berserk joy at the sight of her. She felt his wet snout against her ankle as she ran. Children called to her, women stared, and men just shook their heads, particularly when the master emerged from the great hall, his face a storm, his temper there for all to see.

"Come back here, you stupid wench!"

Philippa turned to see him striding toward her. "By the saints, you are a miserable clod!" She ran now, holding the frayed gown to her knees. Her legs were long and strong and she ran quickly—right into Gorkel.

"Mistress," Gorkel said. "What goes?"

"I go," she said, and jerked away from his huge hands. "Release me, Gorkel!"

"Hold her, Gorkel. Then, if you wish, you can watch me thrash her hide."

Gorkel gave a mournful sigh and shook his ugly head. "Ye shouldn't prick t' master."

"He's a fool and I'd like to kick him hard."

Dienwald winced at that mental imagine. At the same time, he felt an unwanted sting of distress at her words, but shook it off. "Come with me," he said, and grabbed her arm.

"Nay."

He stopped, looked from Gorkel back to Philippa, who was pale with fury. "You'll but hurt my back if you force me to carry you again."

Philippa drew back her right arm and swung with all her strength. Her fist struck his jaw so sharply that his head snapped back. He lost his balance and would have gone down in humiliation into the dirt had not Gorkel grabbed him and held him until he regained his balance.

Dienwald looked at Philippa as he stroked his sore jaw. "You're strong," he said at last. "You're really very strong."

She raised her fist and shook it at him. "Aye, and I'll bring you down again if you try anything."

Dienwald looked beyond her, his eyes widening. He shook his head, and Philippa snapped about to see what or who was behind her. In the next instant, she was flung over his shoulder, head down, her hair nearly trailing the ground as she yelled and screeched like hens caught in a rainstorm.

He laughed, and strode back toward the great hall. He took the solar stairs, aware that all his people were watching and talking about them and laughing, and the men, ah, they were shouting the most explicit and wondrous advice to him.

When he reached the solar he tossed her on her back onto his bed. "Now," he said. "Now."

"Now what?"

"I suppose you expect me to give you wages?"

She stared at him, her brain fuzzy from hanging upside down.

"Well?"

"Wages for what?"

"For being my steward, of course. Have you no brain, wench?" Suddenly he smacked his palm to his forehead. "I cannot believe what I'm saying. A female who has so little sense that she escapes in a gown reeking of a moat in a wagon of wool. And this female wants to control all that happens at St. Erth."

"My father trusted me." Philippa came up onto her elbows. She looked wistfully toward the empty chamber pot on the floor beside the bed. Old Agnes had seen that it was mended.

Dienwald said absently, "Don't do it, wench, else you'll regret it. Now, just be quiet. I must think."

"The pain it must cause you!"

He ignored her remark, saying finally, "I suppose you will demand to sleep in the steward's chamber as well as do the work there."

"Aye, of course. Certainly. To be free of you is—"

He grabbed her arms and kissed her hard. She didn't fight him. It didn't occur to her to do anything but ask him to kiss her again.

"Did you not beg me last night, wench?" he said when he raised his head. "Beg me to take you? You wanted me to relieve you of your maidenhead, didn't you? Well, sleep in your cold bed by yourself. You'll miss me, you'll want my hands and mouth on you, you know it. But enough. I won't miss you. I will sleep sweetly as a babe. Now, straighten yourself and sew yourself something to wear. I can't abide the way you look." He dropped her back onto the bed and strode from his bedchamber.

Nearly an hour later, her hair combed and fastened at the nape of her neck with a piece of cloth, bathed and sweet-smelling, Philippa visited the steward's chamber—now her chamber, she amended to herself. She arranged papers and moved the table some inches to the right. She asked Margot to bring fresh rushes for the floor, then returned to Dienwald's bedchamber. He was in bed, asleep, snoring loudly. On the floor beside the bed were her blood-stained clothes. She'd looked at them briefly, hoping they could be saved, but saw now that it was impossible.

Then she looked at Dienwald. He was sprawled on his stomach, one arm hanging over the side of the bed. Clutched in his hand was the nearly finished tunic she'd sewn for him. Philippa slowly eased it out of his fingers and shook out the wrinkles.

"I should burn it," she said, and left the chamber, needle and thread in her other hand.

Crandall Keep, near Badger's Cross,
Cornwall

Lord Henry wiped his hand across his sweating brow and listened to his destrier blow loudly. The trip had been long and hot and wet and altogether miserable. Three days to get to this damned keep, and what if he were wrong? What if Philippa hadn't run here to her cousin? He took a deep drink from the water skin and handed it back to his servant. His men had just spotted Crandall Keep, where his nephew Sir Walter de Grasse was castellan. All appeared calm. Lord Henry motioned his men forward again.

Crandall was a prosperous keep, he saw, noting the green fields that surrounded the low thick walls. But its defenses were meager, the reason being that Crandall paid obeisance to Lord Graelam de Moreton of Wolffeton. An attack on Crandall would mean swift and awful retribution from Lord Graelam.

Philippa had to be here, she simply had to be. Lord Henry wiped his brow again. There was no other place for her to escape to. She was either here or she was dead. His farmers had been found dead, all the wool wagons disappeared, the guards gone—fled or dead, he didn't know. No sign of his daughter. He'd put off Burnell, the king's tenacious chancellor and secretary, but the man wasn't stupid and would want to see Philippa. He would want to give a personal report to the king. He would want to tell Lord Henry the name of the man the king had selected to be Philippa's husband. Lord Henry raised his eyes to the heavens. Philippa had to be here with her cousin, she had to be.

Sir Walter de Grasse was playing draughts in the hall with his mistress, Britta. She knew the game well, as well as she knew him. She always managed to lose just when he became frustrated, a ploy that pleased Sir Walter. He was informed that his uncle, Lord Henry de Beauchamp, was approaching Crandall. What was his uncle doing here? He thanked the powers that he'd returned two days before from the raid on the southern lands of that whoreson Dienwald de Fortenberry. He'd lost three men, curse the luck. But he'd burned the crops and razed peasants' huts and killed the villeins. All in all it had been worth the price the three men had paid. De Fortenberry must be grinding his teeth by now. The bastard was helpless; he would know who was behind the attack. Oh, he could guess, but Lord Graelam wouldn't act against him, Walter, unless there was proof, and Walter was too smart for that. Luckily the three men had died before Dienwald could question them.

Sir Walter frowned and lightly patted Britta's cheek in dismissal. She removed the draught board and herself, giving him a look over her shoulder designed to excite him. Walter frowned after her. He wished he'd had some warning of his uncle's visit. The keep could be in better condition, fresh rushes strewn on the floor and the like, but it was well enough. It wasn't his overlord, Lord Graelam, thank the saints.

The two men greeted each other. Lord Henry had never been particularly fond of his wife's nephew. Walter was thin and tall and his nose was very long and narrow. His eyes were shrewd and cold and he had no sense of humor. He hated well, but to Lord Henry's knowledge, he'd never loved well.

As for Walter, he thought his uncle by marriage a fat buffoon with more wealth than he deserved. He should have been Lord Henry's heir, but there were the two stupid girls instead. When they were finally alone, Lord Henry wasted no more time. "Your cousin Philippa has run away from Beauchamp. Is she here?"

Now, this was a surprise, Walter thought, staring at his uncle. Slowly he shook his head. "Nay, I haven't seen Philippa since she was a gangly girl with hair hanging to her knees."

"She's no longer gangly. She's nearly eighteen, long since ready to be wedded."

Suddenly, to Walter's surprise, Lord Henry lowered his face into his hands and began to sob. Not knowing what to do, Walter merely stared at his uncle's bowed head, saying nothing.

"I fear she's dead," Lord Henry said once he'd regained control.

"Tell me what happened."

Lord Henry saw no reason not to tell Walter the entire truth. After all, it hardly mattered now. He spoke slowly, sorrow filling his voice.

"She's *what*?"

"I said that Philippa is the king's illegitimate daughter. He is at this moment selecting a husband for her."

Walter could only stare. Damn! What had happened to the girl?

Lord Henry soon enlightened him about the rest of it.

"I know not who killed the farmers or who stole the wool, but Philippa is now likely as dead as the farmers."

Lord Henry wiped his eyes. His sweet Philippa, his stubborn-as-a-mule Philippa. Dead. He couldn't bear it. He'd lost a daughter, a steward, and, most terrifying, he'd lost the king's illegitimate progeny. It wasn't to be borne.

"I shouldn't be too certain, Uncle," Walter said, stroking his rather pointed chin gently. "I hear things, you know. I can find out things too. Return to Beauchamp and let me try to discover what happened to my dear little cousin. I will send you word immediately, of course, if I find her."

Lord Henry left Crandall the following day, Sir Walter's assurances ringing hollow in his ears. Walter had already dispatched men to scout out information. Empty words, Lord Henry thought, but they had lightened his burden, if just for a little while.

As for Sir Walter, he was rubbing his hands together by the following afternoon. The cistern keeper of St. Erth had escaped to Crandall, arriving just that morning with news that Walter's steward, Alain, was dead, unmasked by a big female with lavish tits and bountiful hair whose name was Philippa. Walter nearly swallowed his tongue when he realized how very close Philippa had been to dying by the steward's order.

Now he knew where his dear cousin was, his dearest cousin, the girl he would wed as soon as he got his hands on her. Oh, aye, she'd want him. After all, in all likelihood she'd been on her way to him when she'd been captured by that miserable Dienwald de Fortenberry. Walter could just imagine how Dienwald had treated the gently bred girl—ravishing her, humiliating her, shaming her . . . But why and how had she uncov-

ered the steward's perfidy if she'd been thus
shamed?

It didn't matter. The cistern keeper had probably confused things. Walter would marry the
king's illegitimate daughter. She was his gift
horse and he would have her. He prayed she
wasn't carrying de Fortenberry's bastard in her
womb. Perhaps he could rid her of the brat—if
there was one—when he got his hands on her.

Walter sighed with the pleasure of his contem-
plations. At last he would be somebody to reckon
with. He would starve out de Fortenberry and
have him torn limb from limb. He would regain
St. Erth, the inheritance he should have had, the
inheritance his father had lost to Dienwald's
father so many years before. He would spit on
Lord Graelam—behind his back, of course—and
leave this pigsty Crandall. He would be overlord
of all Cornwall and Lord Graelam would be his
vassal, with his father-in-law's agreement and
assistance. He would almost be a royal duke! He
would then look south to Brittany. Aye, his
grandfather had held lands there, now stolen
away by that whoreson de Bracy of Brittany. Aye,
with the king's help, with the king's money, with
the king's men, he would take back what was his,
all of what should have been his in the first place.
And he could add to it if he were wily and
cunning.

Sir Walter hummed as he made his plans. He
wondered briefly what Philippa looked like. If she
were a true Plantagenet, he thought, she must be
beautiful. The cistern keeper spoke of her tits and
hair. What color? he wondered. He liked big
breasts on a woman. He couldn't let himself forget, though, that she was a bastard, after all, and

thus tainted, despite her royal blood. He wouldn't forget that, nor would he allow her to forget it. Aye, she would welcome him, her dear cousin. After her doubtless brutal treatment at de Fortenberry's hands, she'd come leaping into his waiting arms.

St. Erth Castle

Philippa sat in the steward's chamber, her head bowed, entering inventories of the crops in a ledger. Her back hurt from sitting so long, but there was much to be done, much to be corrected and adjusted. Alain had created fiction, and it must be set aright, and quickly.

Dienwald's new tunic of deep blue, so soft that it slithered over the flesh, was finished and lay spread smooth over the back of the only other chair in the small chamber. She was a fine needlewoman, and the thread, thankfully, was stout.

She looked up then and smiled upon the tunic. He would look very nice wearing it, very nice indeed, fit to meet the king thus garbed. She hoped she'd made the shoulders big enough and tapered the waist inward enough, for he was lean. She hoped he thought the color nice and . . .

She stopped herself in mid-thought. Here she was thinking like the mistress of St. Erth again. As if this were her home, as if this were where she belonged. She'd entertained no thought of escape in more hours than she cared to reckon.

She laid down the quill and slowly rose, pushing back from the table. She was nothing more than his servant. For the past two days she'd worked endless hours in this small airless chamber, and for what?

For the joy of wearing an ill-fitting gown belonging to his long-dead first wife? For the joy of helping him, the man who'd lain atop of her, his finger easing into her body, making her hot and frantic and . . .

"Stop it, you stupid wench!"

"I thought your name was Philippa."

She could have gladly removed her own tongue at that moment. Dienwald stood in the doorway, amusement lighting his eyes.

" 'Twas a private exhortation," she said. "It had naught to do with you."

"As you will, wench. How goes the work?" He waved toward the stacks of foolscap on the table.

"It is an abominable mess."

"I imagined as much."

"You do not read," she said, and unknowingly, her voice softened just a bit.

"Nay, not very much. 'Twas not deemed important by my sire. Few read or cipher—you know that. Why ask you?"

She shrugged. "I merely wondered. You insist upon Edmund's learning from Father Cramdle."

"Aye. The world changes, and men must change with it. It is something Edmund must know if he is to make his way."

Philippa had seen no sign of change in her brief lifetime, but she didn't disagree. She realized belatedly that she was staring at him, hunger in her look, and that he was already aware of it.

He grinned at her. "Come have your dinner. That is why I am here, to fetch you."

She nodded and rounded the table. He caught

her hand and pulled her against him. "You miss me, wench?"

She more than missed him. She lay awake at night, thinking of how much she wanted him lying beside her.

"Of course not. You are arrogant and filled with conceit, my lord."

"You don't miss my hands stroking you?"

One arm kept her pressed against his chest. She felt his other arm lower, his fingers parting her, pressing inward. She tried to draw away—a paltry effort, they both knew.

Her breathing hitched. She felt the heat of his fingers, the heat of herself, and there was only the thin wool of her gown between the two.

Then he released her, turned, saying over his shoulder, "Come and have your dinner now, wench."

"I'm not a—" she yelled, then stopped. He was gone, the door closed quietly behind him.

That evening she learned from Northbert that the cistern keeper had escaped but that several men were out searching for him.

"Alain worked not by himself, so thinks the master," Northbert said, then wiped his bread in the thick beef gravy on his trencher.

" 'Tis a varmint named de Grasse the cistern keeper has run to," Crooky announced, his mouth bulging with boiled capon.

Philippa grew instantly still. "Walter de Grasse?" she asked slowly. Her heart was pounding, her hand squeezing a honey-and-almond tart.

Dienwald heard her and turned, saying, "What know you of de Grasse?"

"Why, he's my cousin," she said without thinking.

12

Dienwald's face was pale, his eyes dark and wild. "Your *cousin*? Lord Henry's *nephew*?"

He didn't sound angry, merely incredulous, and Philippa felt emboldened to add freely, "Nay, Walter is my mother's nephew. My father doesn't like him, but I do." She raised her chin, knowing that Dienwald wouldn't be able to keep his opinion to himself, and that it would be contrary to hers.

"I don't believe this," was all he said. He rose, slamming his chair back, and left the great hall.

Crooky looked at Philippa and shook his head.

"He is always slamming out of here like a sulking child!"

"Nay," Gorkel said. "He leaves because he is angry and he doesn't wish to strike you."

"Strike me? I have done nothing. What is

wrong with him this time? I cannot help that Sir
Walter is my kin."

"It matters not," Crooky said. "You, mistress,
you say that you like this serpent, this vicious
brute . . . well, what do you expect the master to
do?"

"But—"

Crooky cleared his throat, and Philippa closed
her eyes against the discordant sounds that
emerged loud and clear from the fool's mouth:

> A villain, a coward,
> A knave without shame.
> De Grasse maims and he destroys
> And takes no blame.
> He lies and he steals
> And he slithers out to kill.
> My sweet master will slay him,
> Come what will.

"Why do you keep calling him 'sweet master'?"
Philippa asked, irritated and frightened and wondering all the while what her cousin had done to
earn such enmity.

Crooky gave her a small salute with a dirty
hand and said with a wink, "Think you not that
he is a sweet master? The females hereabouts
think him more than sweet. They like him to bed
them, to push apart their thighs and—"

"Hush!"

"Forgive me, mistress. I forget you are yet a
maid and unknowing of the ways of men and
women."

Edmund, hearing this outpouring from Crooky,
frowned at Philippa and said, "Are you truly a
maid? Still? I know you were before, but . . . You

still aren't my father's mistress, even after all the times he's carried you off to his chamber? You said that—"

"I'm not his mistress. I'm naught but his drudge, his captive . . ." Philippa ground to a halt. She was also St. Erth's steward. "Why aren't you wearing your new tunic? You don't like it? I know that it fits. Margot told me it did. 'Tis well made, and the color suits you. And the hose and shoes. Why don't—"

"I don't like them. Besides, my father doesn't wear anything new. Until he makes me, then I'll stay the way I am."

"You are such a stubborn little irkle."

" 'Tis better than being a maypole."

"Edmund, if you do not wear your new tunic on the morrow, I will come to your chamber, hold you down, and put it on you. Do you understand me?"

"You won't!"

She gave him a look to shrivel any male. He ducked his head, and she saw that he was quite dirty, his fingers and fingernails coated with grime. He looked like a villein's child; he looked like he'd been wallowing in mud with Tupper. She had to speak to Dienwald about this. He forced his son to learn to read and write and cipher but allowed him to look like a ragged little beggar.

"Yes," she said, "yes, I will. And you will bathe, Master Edmund. When was the last time your hands were in soap and water?"

"There ban't be any soap, mistress," Old Agnes shouted to Philippa. The old woman had amazing hearing when it suited her. "No one thought to make it," she added, quick to defend herself should the need arise. "The master said aught."

Philippa called back, "But that is absurd. I have used soap in the master's chamber."

"Aye, thass the last of it. The master likely didn't realize it was the last of it."

"We will make soap on the morrow," Philippa said. "And you, you pigsty of a boy, will be the first to use it."

"Nay, I won't!"

"We'll see."

Philippa had much to consider that night when she closed the door to her small chamber. She'd just pulled the frayed tunic over her head and laid it carefully over the back of the single chair when she heard his voice say softly, "Put it back on. I don't wish to enjoy you here. I want you in my bed, where you can warm me when it grows cold near dawn."

"I'm not your mistress! Go away, Dienwald!"

"I've already enjoyed a woman this night. I have no pressing need for another, be she even as soft and big and, in truth, as eager as you. Come along, now."

Her eyes had adjusted to the dimness of the chamber and she saw him now, holding her discarded gown, his hand stretched out to her. She was standing there quite naked, just staring at him. Philippa grabbed the gown and pulled it over her head. In the next moment he had her hand and was pulling her after him, out of the steward's chamber.

There were still a dozen or so people milling about the great hall, and two score more sleeping on pallets lining the walls. "Hush," he said, and pulled her after him. Everyone saw. No one said a thing. Not a single man yelled advice. Philippa wanted to kick him, kick *all* of them, hard.

She tugged and pulled and jerked, but it was no use. He turned on her then, frowning, and said, "No more carrying you. You come willingly or I will drag you by the hair."

"You will pay for this, Dienwald, you surely will." She gave him an evil smile. "I will send word to my dear cousin Sir Walter—aye, and I'll tell him what a cruel savage you are, a barbarian, a—"

"I'm already paying, wench. But I beg of you not to tell your precious cousin that I'm a ravisher of innocent maids. Nay, do not, even though it would please you mightily were I to take you." It was at that instant she realized he'd drunk more ale than usual. He didn't slur his words like Lord Henry did, nor was his nose flaming red. He walked very carefully, like a man who knows he's drunk but doesn't want anyone else to know. She wasn't at all afraid of him, drunk or sober. She found that she was rather anticipating what he would do.

Once inside his bedchamber, Dienwald went through the now-familiar routine of pushing her onto the bed. "Now," he said, looking down at her, "now you can remove the gown. It is ugly and offends me. Haven't you yet finished something for yourself?"

She lay there staring up at him, not moving, marshaling her strength. "I made you a tunic. 'Tis down in my chamber."

He paused. "Did you really finish it? It disappeared, and I believed you'd destroyed it in your ire at me."

"I should have." She began inching away to

the far side of the bed. "You have drunk too much ale."

"Philippa," he said quietly, "there are no more gowns, not another stitch of anything for you to wear. Take care of the only one you have, else you will be naked. Aye, I have drunk more than I usually do, but 'tis done. Take off the gown now."

"Blow out the candle first."

"All right." He snuffed the candle, throwing the chamber into gloom. Moonlight came through the one window, slivering clear light directly across the bed. There was nothing she could do about it. Still, she wasn't at all afraid of him or of what he could do to her if he so chose. Philippa eased out of the gown and laid it at the foot of the bed. Then she slid beneath the single blanket.

"It's deep spring now," Dienwald said, and she knew he was taking off his clothes as he spoke, even though she wasn't looking at him. His voice deepened, grew absent and thoughtful. He didn't sound at all drunk. "That's what we call it here. Deep spring. Very late April and early May. My grandmother told me of deep spring when I was but a boy, told me this was what men called it a very long time ago when priests ruled the land and everyone worshiped the endless force of spring, the timeless renewal of spring. She said they saw the wheat shoving upward, ever upward toward the blazing gold of the sun, all the while deepening its roots into the soil, into the darkness. Opposites, this light and darkness, yet bound together, eternal and endless.

"She called it by the old Celtic words, but I cannot remember them. Whenever I say 'deep spring' now, I think about how a woman takes in a man and holds him, then empties him and yet renews him and herself with his nourishment, just as spring is infinite yet predictable in its sameness, just as spring always renews the earth, and the light and the dark exist together and complement each other." He turned to face her now. "I like thinking about you in that way—how you would empty me and renew me and yourself with my seed.

"But you are Walter de Grasse's cousin, and that makes you my enemy, not just my slave or my captive or my mistress. Nay, my enemy. I loathe the very thought of the man. I wonder, wench, should I punish you for his evil? For his wickedness? Does the foulness of his blood run in you? In your soul?"

Philippa was shaken. He'd shown her another side of himself that drew her and made her want to weep, but it had also called forth his hatred, his bitterness. Was he speaking so freely only because he'd drunk too much to keep his thoughts to himself?

"What did he do to you that you hate him so?"

"I lost much with the burning of my crops. And not just the crops, but all the people who worked them, *my* people. All of them butchered, the women ravished, the children piked on swords, the huts destroyed, burned to the raw earth. And it was your cousin who ordered it done."

"But you are not certain? You could catch no one to tell you?"

"Sir Walter de Grasse was once a landless knight. He still is, though Lord Graelam de Moreton made him castellan of Crandall, one of his keeps to the southwest of St. Erth. It is not enough for Sir Walter; he believes it his right to have more. The man hated me before I even knew of his existence. My father won St. Erth from his father in a tourney in Normandy when I was a small boy. Walter screams of dishonor and trickery. He demands back his supposed birthright. King Edward wouldn't give him heed, yet he still seeks my death and my ruin. He nearly succeeded once, not long ago, but I was saved by a beautiful artless lady who holds my loyalty and my heart, aye, even my soul. So there it is, wench. Sir Walter will do anything to destroy me, and you are his kin."

Philippa felt a lance of pain go through her. She swallowed, and licked her dry lips. "Who is this lady? How did she save you?"

Dienwald strode toward the bed then and laughed, a drunken laugh, one that was sharp yet empty, raw yet thick. She saw his body in the shaft of clear moonlight and she thought him beautiful—a strange word surely to describe a being who was sharply planed and angled and shadowed and hard, but it was so. He stood straight and tall and lean, and still he laughed, and it hurt her to listen.

Yet she wanted to hear his story, and he, free-speaking from the ale, said, "You wish her name? She is a lady, a sweet, loving, guileless lady, and her name is Kassia. She hails from Brittany. I cannot have her, though I tried."

"Why can't you?"

"She is wedded to a powerful man who is also my friend and a mighty warrior—the same overlord of your precious Walter, Lord Graelam de Moreton."

"You . . . you love her, then?"

Dienwald eased down onto the bed, lifting the

blanket. She could feel the heat from his body, hear the steady rhythm of his breathing. She didn't move. He was silent for a very long time, and she believed him asleep, finally insensate from the ale he'd drunk.

"I know not of love," he said, his voice low and slurred now. "I just know of feelings and passions, and she took mine unto herself and holds them. Aye, she holds them gently and tenderly because she could do aught else. She is like that, you see. You are very different from her. She is small and delicate and fragile, yet her spirit is fierce and pure. Her smile is so sweet it makes you want to weep and protect her with your life. Aye, she came to womanhood, but she went to him—her body and her heart both went to Graelam. Go to sleep, wench. I grow weary of all this talk."

" 'Tis you who have done all the talking!"

"Go to sleep."

"I am not your enemy. I am merely your captive."

"Perhaps. Perhaps not. I will think about it. God knows, I think of little else. You are a problem that irritates like an itch that can't be reached. Perhaps I will send word to Lord Henry that I have you and will return you if I am given Sir Walter in your place. Perhaps I will demand his head upon a silver platter, like that of St. John, though Walter is about as righteous as a dung beetle. What think you? Would your esteemed father send me Sir Walter's head to have you returned?"

"My esteemed father won't even dower me. My esteemed father seeks to wed me with de Bridgport. My esteemed father probably doesn't even care that I am gone. I have told you this before. I didn't lie."

"It seems the answer is no, then. I am to be cursed with the eternal itch. What am I to do with you?"

"I am your steward."

He laughed again, low and deep, and she wanted to strike him, but didn't move. Only then did she realize she hadn't demanded that he release her and let her go free.

"Well, I suppose you cannot do a worse job of it than Alain. You will ruin me in your ignorance and innocence just as he was doing in his dishonesty and thievery. Or will you cheat me as well for your own revenge, since I stole from your father?"

"I'm not ignorant. Nor will I cheat you."

"So you say. Come here, wench. I'm cold and wish your big body to warm me."

When she didn't move, Dienwald rolled against her, drawing her to his side. "Hush and sleep," he said, his breath warm against her temple as he pressed her cheek against his chest. She smelled the sweet ale on his breath as he said, his words low and indistinct, "Do not berate me further. My brain is calm for the moment."

Nay, she thought, there was nothing she had to say now.

Philippa didn't sleep for a very long time. She thought of a lady whose name was Kassia, a lady who was small and delicate and sweet and loyal. A lady who had saved Dienwald's life.

And Philippa was a naught but an irritant that made his brain itch.

He, the drunken brute, was asleep almost at once, his snores uneven rippling sounds, like his dreams, she thought, aye, like his ale-filled dreams. She hoped monsters visited him that night. He deserved them.

Wolffeton Castle

Robert Burnell wrote industriously as Graelam de Moreton spoke of the man he believed would be the ideal husband for King Edward's bastard daughter.

"He is strong and young and healthy. He is comely and has excellent teeth and all his hair. He's an intelligent man who cares for his villeins and his lands. He was wedded once and has a son, Edmund, but his wife died many years ago. Is there aught else, Burnell?"

Robert accepted a flagon of milk from Lady Kassia, smiling up at her. "The day brightens now that you are here, my lady," he said, and nearly choked on his words, so unlike him they were. But something deep inside had leapt to speak to her poetically. Mayhap it was the sweetness of her look, the soft curve of her lips as she smiled. Burnell quickly recovered his wits and sent an agonized look to Lord Graelam, but that intimidating warrior merely cocked his head at him, his look ironic.

"I thank you, sir," Kassia said. She moved slowly because of her swollen stomach, and sat down. "You are telling Robert of Dienwald's excellent qualities?"

"Aye, but there are so many, my head buzzes with the sheer number of them. What say you, Kassia?"

"Dienwald de Fortenberry is loyal and trustworthy and kind. He enjoys a good jest and loud talk, as do most men of spirit. He has wit and is facile with words. He fights well and protects what is his."

"He begins to sound like a possible saint," Burnell said, "and a man you perhaps praise more than he deserves."

"Ha!" Graelam said. "I have many times wanted to trounce him into the ground and crush his stubborn head beneath my heel and give the imbecile a kick in the ass—"

"But always," Kassia interrupted easily, "my lord and Dienwald are grinning at each other and slapping each other's shoulders in great friendship after they've decided not to kill each other. We do not overpraise him, sir, for Dienwald is a good man, sir, a very good man."

"Despite all his shortcomings," Graelam said.

"I must needs hear some of these shortcomings, my lord. Edward is sure to be suspicious if I give him only this glowing praise."

Graelam grinned, and Burnell saw the answering smile on his lady's face.

"He is stubborn as a mule, grandiose in his gestures, poor in his material belongings, and doesn't care. He revels in danger and enjoys treading the narrow path. He is crafty and sly and cunning as a fox. He isn't greedy, however, so Edward need have no fear of his coffers. As I said, he doesn't lust after earthly things. Further, there is no family, so Edward need have no worry that he will be pressed for endless favors. Dienwald is also a shrewd, ruthless, occasionally disgraceful man who will do anything to gain what he wants."

"Ah," said Burnell, writing again. "He becomes human at last, my lord."

"The lady, Philippa de Beauchamp," Kassia said. "Is she a pretty girl? Sweet-tempered?"

"I know not, save what I have been told, my lady. That is, she is a Plantagenet and thus must be considered beautiful. Since his majesty said that, it is a matter of close-held opinion and not be contested."

Kassia laughed. "And her disposition?"

"I know not. She was raised by Lord Henry and she still believes him her father. I know aught about the Lady Maude. The king, very young then, ordered that if the child survived her infancy, she be taught to read and write and cipher. She does these things well, I was told. She is perhaps too well-learned for Dienwald de Fortenberry—or mayhap for any man, no matter his rank or his leanings toward kindness and tolerance. She is possibly too set in her own ways of thinking to be content with a master's heavy hand, but truly, I know not for certain."

"Dienwald needs a woman of strong character," Graelam said. "A woman who can kick his groin one minute and salve his wounds the next."

"I travel to Beauchamp upon my return to London. I will see the girl then and report all to the king. De Fortenberry sounds like a man the king might wish for his daughter. Does the king know de Fortenberry?"

"I don't think so," Graelam said. "Edward hasn't been long in England yet, nor has he come to Cornwall to see his vassals. Dienwald is not a man to travel to London to wait upon his majesty. He is a man who holds to himself."

"I suppose that could show that he is not a leech. It is also true that his majesty has not long been home, but Edward is so overwhelmed with all the needs of England."

"Aye, and there are Wales and Scotland to be ground under the royal foot."

Robert Burnell gave Lord Graelam a thin smile. The lord was criticizing, though his tone was light and his sarcasm barely touched the ear, but Burnell wouldn't tolerate it. He harrumphed as his eyes narrowed, and said, "Did I tell you, my lord, that it was the queen herself who suggested that you be consulted? The *queen*! She advised him on his illegitimate daughter."

"The queen," Graelam said, "is a lady of honest and gracious ideals. Edward gained another part of himself when he wedded with her. Mayhap the best part."

At these last words, Lord Graelam smiled yet again at his wife as Burnell sipped his milk and looked on.

St. Erth Castle

Dienwald avoided his prisoner. He remembered, the next morning, what he'd said in his drunkenness. God's ribs, had he truly gone on and on about deep spring? What nonsense! Had he truly told her of Kassia and of his feelings for her? What idiocy! He despised himself so much that he'd welcomed the violent retching. He'd been a blockhead and a loose-mouth. The next thing he knew he'd be singing to her in rhyme like his fool.

Thinking of Crooky, Dienwald wondered where he was and went in search of him. He asked Hood, the porter, but he hadn't seen the fool. He asked the armorer, who merely spat and shrugged. It was Old Agnes who told him.

"Aye, the little mistress is fitting him for a tunic, master. She told him she would have two sewn for him if he would but promise not to sing to her for a month."

"She's not little," Dienwald said, and strode away. Damn the wench's eyes, he thought, interfering in everything, sticking her big feet in where they didn't belong. If his fool's elbows stuck out of his clothes, it wasn't her mission to give him a new tunic. He looked down at his own nearly worn-through tunic. He had yet to see the one she'd made for him, sewed it herself, he remembered, and for an instant he softened. But only for that brief moment. He'd told her about Kassia, blathered on about a pagan belief that, in his mind at least, fitted cleanly with Father Cramdle's heaven and its multitude of saints. Then he'd gone on and on about Walter de Grasse, a man he'd sworn to kill, a man who'd given him no choice but to try to kill him. He'd made an ass of himself. It wasn't to be borne.

Everywhere he looked these days, the women were sitting in small groups, gossiping whilst they sewed. They'd see him and giggle, and he wanted to bellow at them that Philippa wasn't their damned mistress.

How had things gotten so twisted up? She'd jumped out of the wool wagon looking like a fright from hell itself, and then she'd proceeded to take over. It wasn't to be tolerated, despite the fact that she slept in his bed and he touched her and caressed her whenever he wished to—but it was harder now, because it was no longer the game it had started out to be. He wanted her,

wanted her more than he'd ever wanted any of
the women who'd always welcomed him when
he'd had the need. But because the witch was still
a maid and because he had somehow come to
regard her as more than just another female to
be treated according to his whims, he couldn't,
wouldn't, suffer the obvious consequences of
taking her maidenhead. He wasn't that great a
fool.

His thoughts were interrupted by a shriek from
his son, near the cistern by the weaving shed.
Dienwald didn't worry about it until he heard
Philippa yell, "Hold still or I'll break your ear!
Edmund, hold still!"

Interfering again, and this time with his son.
What was she doing now? He broke into a trot.

"You rancid little puffin! Hold still or I'll cuff
you!"

Dienwald rounded the corner of the weaving
outbuilding to see Philippa holding Edmund's
arm and dousing him with a bucket of water. She
quickly picked up a block of soap once she'd gotten him wet, and now she was scrubbing him
with all her strength, which was considerable.
Edmund was squirming and fighting and yelling,
but he couldn't break away. He was also naked,
his ragged clothes strewn on the ground.

Philippa wasn't unscathed, however. She was
sopping wet, her hair loose from its tie at the
nape of her neck and flying out in a wild nimbus
around her head. Her frayed gown was plastered
against her breasts. She and Edmund were standing in a growing mud puddle from all the water
she was throwing on him.

Dienwald watched Philippa pull Edmund back
against her, and now she scrubbed him with both

hands—his face, his hair, even his elbows. He was shrieking about his burning eyes, but she just kept saying over and over, "Edmund, stop fighting me! It will go easier with you if you just hold still."

Edmund went on howling like a gutted hog.

Dienwald came closer but kept out of range of the deepening mud puddle. His people were wandering by, not paying much attention, but there was Father Cramdle, his arms crossed over his chest, looking pious and quite pleased. The pig, Tupper, was squealing near Philippa, coming close to her, then retreating quickly when threatened with flying streams of water from the bucket.

Dienwald kept quiet until Philippa had doused Edmund with another bucket of water to rinse him off. Then she wrapped him in a huge towel— one newly cut, he realized—and lifted him out of the mud and rubbed him until he was dry.

She kept him wrapped up, then lifted him onto a plank of pine and hunkered down to her knees in front of him. "Listen to me, you wretched little spittlecock. 'Tis done, and you're clean. Stay away from all this mud and filth. Now, you will go with Father Cramdle and garb yourself in your new clothes. Do you understand? And then you will have your lessons."

Dienwald heard a muffled shout of, "I hate you, Maypole!" coming from beneath the towel that covered Edmund's head.

"That's all right. At least you're clean and I don't have to watch you stuff food in your mouth with filth under your fingernails. Go, now."

Edmund's head emerged from the towel. He glowered at Philippa, but she didn't change expression. Edmund was about to retire from the field when he saw Dienwald.

"Father! Help me, look what the witch did to me!" And on and on it went as Dienwald just stood there, wanting to laugh, yet furious that Philippa had forced cleanliness upon his son, and wondering how she'd enlisted Father Cramdle in her task, for the priest was surely on her side.

Meanwhile Edmund kept shrieking and complaining, dancing about on his clean feet. Finally Dienwald, seeing that the result was to his liking, even if Philippa's pushing ways were not, said in a voice that brought his son to instant silence, "Edmund, I fancy that I hear your mother in you, which is distressing. You will go with Father Cramdle and clothe yourself. I had no idea you had become such a filthy little villein. Keep your shrieks behind your teeth or you will feel my hand."

Edmund, head down and silent as a pebble, trailed after Father Cramdle, the towel wrapped around him like a Roman toga.

"Thank you," Philippa said to Dienwald. He said nothing for a moment, just watched her try to straighten her hair, pulling it back, away from her face.

He strode up to her. "Hold still yourself, wench."

She did. He smoothed her hair and retied it with the bit of leather. He frowned at the dirty strip of hide. She needed a proper ribbon, a ribbon of bright color to complement her hair, something . . .

"You look worse than Edmund. Much worse. Like a dirty wet rag. Do something with yourself." With those pleasing sentiments duly expressed, Dienwald turned on his heel. He heard a loud whoosh, but not in time. A half-filled bucket of water struck him squarely between the shoulder blades and he went flying forward from the force of it, hitting a goat. The goat reared back and kicked Dienwald on the thigh. He cried out, grabbing his leg, which caused him to lose his balance and fell sideways into a deep patch of black mud. He came up on his hands and knees, but for a moment he didn't move. He had no intention of moving until he'd regained complete control of himself. Slowly, very slowly, he rose and turned to see Philippa standing there like a statue yet to be finished, a look of mingled horror and defiance on her face. People had stopped their conversations and were converging and staring. Then Gorkel, with a low rumbling noise, came forward, stepped squarely into the mud, and began to brush off his master.

" 'Twere an accident," Gorkel said as he grabbed gobs of mud from Dienwald's clothing and flung them away. "The mistress acts, then thinks—ye know that, master. Aye, but she's—"

"You damnable monster, don't defend her! Be still!"

Gorkel obligingly shut his mouth and continued scraping off mud.

Dienwald shook himself free of his minion's help and strode over to Philippa, who took one step back, then stopped and faced him, squaring her shoulders.

"You struck me!" The incredulity in his voice equaled the outrage. "You're a *female*, and you struck me. You threw that damned bucket at me."

"Actually," Philippa said, inching a bit further

back, "it was the bucket that struck you, not I. I didn't realize I was such a marksman, or rather, that the bucket was such a marksman." Then, to her own astonishment, she giggled.

Dienwald drew several very long, very deep breaths. "If I throw you into that mud, you will have nothing to wear. You haven't yet sewed anything for yourself, have you?"

She shook her head, not giggling quite so loudly now.

He looked at her nipples, taut against the wet tunic. The material also clung to her thighs.

He smiled at her, and Philippa felt herself shrivel with humiliation. "Throw me in the mud," she said. "Do that, but please don't do what you're thinking."

"And what is that, pray? Ripping off that rag and letting my people see the shrew beneath it?"

She nodded and tried to cover her breasts with her hands. "I'm not a shrew."

"All right," he said, and without another word, moving so quickly she had only time to squeak in surprise, Dienwald grabbed her about the hips, lifted her, and strode to the black puddle and dropped her. She landed on her bottom, arms and legs flying outward, and mud spewed out in thick waves, hitting him and Gorkel. She felt it squishing over her legs, felt it seep through the gown, and she wanted to laugh at the consequences that she'd brought upon herself, but she didn't. She now had nothing to wear, nothing save this now-ruined gown.

She looked up at Dienwald, who stood in front of her, his hands on his hips. He was laughing.

Philippa saw red. Tears clogged her throat, but her fury was stronger by far. She managed to come to her feet, the mud clinging and making loud sucking noises. She flung herself at him, clutching his arms and yanking him toward her. She locked her foot behind his calf and he fell toward her, laughing all the while. Together they went down, Dienwald on top of her, Philippa flat on her back, the mud flying everywhere.

Dienwald raised himself on his hands, his fingers clenching deep into the muck. He slowly raised one mud-filled hand and opened it against her face and rubbed. She gasped and spat, but then he felt her knees against his back and he was falling sideways as she rolled against him, knocking him onto his back, pounding her fists at him, her muddy hands sliding over his face, slapping him with it.

He dimly heard people laughing and shouting and cheering for him, cheering for Philippa. Wagers were screamed out, and even the animals were dinning, for once louder than the children. Then Tupper leaped into the mud, not three inches from Dienwald's head, snorting loudly, poking his snout into Dienwald's face.

It was too much for a man to suffer. Dienwald spread his arms in surrender and yelled at the bouncing fury astride him, "I yield, wench! I yield!"

Tupper snorted and squealed and kept the mud churning.

Philippa laughed, and as he looked up at her, he wanted her right then—muddy black face, filthy matted hair, and all.

"Master, pray forgive me." Northbert stood on the edge of the mud puddle, consternation writ on his ugly face.

Dienwald cocked an eye at him. "Aye? What is it?"

"We have visitors, master."

"There are visitors at St. Erth's gates?"

"Nay, master. The visitors are right here."

13

Philippa was shocked into numb silence. She didn't move, but of course, she had no drier place to move to. Dienwald looked behind Northbert and saw Graelam de Moreton striding toward them, tell and powerful and well-garbed and clean, and he was staring toward Dienwald as if he'd grown two heads. And then he was staring at Philippa.

"God give you grace, Graelam," Dienwald said easily. His eyes went to Kassia, standing now beside her husband, wrapped in a fine ermine-lined cloak of soft white wool. She looked beautiful, soft and sweet, her chestnut hair in loose braids atop her head. He saw she was trying very hard not to laugh. "Welcome to St. Erth, Kassia. I hope I see you well, sweet lady."

Kassia couldn't hold it back. She burst into laughter, hiccuping against her palm as she gasped

out, "You sound like a courtier at the king's court,
Dienwald, suave and confident, while you lie
sprawled in the mud . . . Ah, Dienwald, your
face . . ."

Dienwald looked up at Philippa, who'd turned
into a mud statue astride him. "Move, wench,"
he said, grinning up at her. "As you see, we have
visitors and must bestir ourselves to see to their
comfort."

Kassia, Philippa was thinking, her mind nearly
as muddy as her body. Kassia, the lady that Dienwald held so dear to his wretched heart. And
Philippa could understand his feelings for the
slight, utterly feminine confection who stood well
out of range of the mud puddle. That exquisite
example of womanhood would never, ever find
herself sitting astride a man in a mud puddle.
Philippa's eyes went to Lord Graelam de Moreton, and she saw a man who would never yield,
a man both fierce and hard, a man who was Kassia's husband, bless his wondrous existence. She
remembered now seeing him once at Beauchamp
when she was very young. He'd been bellowing
at her father about a tourney they were both to
join near Taunton.

"Wench, move," Dienwald said again, and as
he spoke, he laughed, circled her waist with his
hands, and lifted her off him. He carefully set her
beside him in the mud.

She felt the black ooze sliding up her bottom.

"Graelam, why don't you take your very clean
wife into the hall. I will scrub myself and join you
soon."

" 'Twill take all the water in your well," Graelam said, threw back his head, and laughed.
"Nay, Dienwald, sling not mud at me. My lady

just stitched me this fine tunic." He laughed and
laughed as he took his wife's soft white hand in
his and led her away, saying over his shoulder,
"All right, but I begin to cherish that black face of
yours. It grows closer to the color of your heart."

Dienwald didn't move until Graelam and Kassia, trailed by a half-dozen Wolffeton men-at-
arms, had disappeared around the side of the
weaving shed. He could hear Kassia's high giggles and Graelam's low rumbles of laughter.

Philippa hadn't said a single word. She hadn't
made a sound, merely sat there in the mud, a
study of silent misery.

Dienwald eyed her, then yelled for another
bucket to be brought. "Get up, Philippa," he said,
and when she did, he continued, "Now, step out
of the mud," and when she did, he threw a
bucket of cold water over her head. Philippa
gasped and shivered and automatically rubbed
the mud off her face. The late-April air was chill,
but she hadn't realized it until now.

After three more buckets she was ready for the
soap.

"You will have to remove the tunic soon," he
said, then called for Old Agnes to fetch two blankets. He looked at the score of people staring at
them, laughing behind their hands, and roared,
"Out of here, all of you! If I see any of you in
two seconds, you'll feel the flat of my sword on
your buttocks!"

"Aye," Crooky yelled, "but the wenches would
much enjoy that kind of play."

Dienwald bellowed again, and soon he and
Philippa were alone standing on the plank of lumber, scrubbing themselves with the newly made
soap. Dienwald had simply stripped off his

clothes. He looked up at Philippa, his face clean
and grinning. "I've dismissed everyone, wench—
you heard and saw. Take off the gown now."

She did, without comment, seeing no hope for
it, and together they washed and scrubbed and
threw water on each other. At one point Dienwald paused, looking at her, beautifully naked in
the April sunshine, and pulled her against him.
He didn't kiss her, merely soaped his hands. Philippa felt his large hands soaping down her back
and over her buttocks. She felt his soapy fingers
sliding between her legs and tensed, but his touch
seemed impersonal.

It wasn't, but Dienwald wasn't about to let her
know that. When he'd finished, Philippa cleaned
his back, her touch more tentative than his had
been. He stared at the mud puddle, then thought
of the eyes that were probably watching them at
this very minute.

Once dry, they wrapped themselves in the
blankets. Dienwald looked at Philippa, her face
scrubbed pink, her hair plastered around her
head, and he thought her exquisite. He said
instead, looking once again toward the mud puddle, "You made me feel very young with our
play. Do you wish to come into the hall and meet
our guests?"

Speak to Lady Kassia, Philippa thought. She
would feel like a great bumbling fool, like a huge
ungainly blanket-wrapped beggar gawking next
to a snow princess in her white cloak. She shook
her head and swallowed her misery.

"They are my friends," Dienwald said, not
seeing the misery, only the stubbornness.

"Not yet, if it pleases you."

"Very well," he said, her respectful tone softening him. "But if you wish to meet them, I would ask that you not tell them your name or that you're my prisoner."

"Then what am I?" she asked, irritation now writ clear in her voice.

Dienwald paused at that. So much for respect and deference from her. "My washerwoman?"

"No."

"My weaver?"

"Nay. I would be your steward."

"Graelam would burst his bladder laughing at that notion. No, you can be my mistress. You begin to look passable again, so that would not strain his credulity. Does that please you, wench?"

"Doesn't it worry you that I might beg Lord Graelam to return me to my father? That I might tell him you're naught but a miserable scoundrel and thief?"

"Why should it worry me? You'll not do that. You have no wish to return to your father. Don't forget that that toad William de Bridgport awaits you with widespread fat arms and foul breath."

That was true, damn him. She chewed on her lower lips. "I could ask him to send me to his vassal, Sir Walter, since I am his cousin and since that is where I was bound in the first place."

"Aye, you could do that, but it would displease me mightily. You know, Philippa, Sir Walter wouldn't treat you well. He is not the man you think him."

"Of course he would treat me well! I'm his cousin, his kin. I won't be your mistress."

He raised his hand and lightly touched his fingertips to her cheek. "You're a snare, Philippa. Of the devil? I wonder."

He said nothing more, merely turned on his

bare heel and strode away from her. He should have looked ridiculous, walking barefoot and wrapped in an ugly brown blanket, but he didn't.

Philippa followed more slowly, and she saw faces and heard laughter and knew that she and Dienwald had been observed whilst they bathed. Was there nothing private in this wretched castle? She knew the answer was no, just as it had been at Beauchamp.

How could Dienwald ask her to meet Kassia, the woman who was the most precious of all God's female flock? The woman who'd saved his life, the woman who was so lavishly guileless, the essence of purity and perfection?

Philippa wanted to be sick.

Instead, she walked up the solar stairs, the blanket wrapped close like a shroud, and locked herself in Dienwald's chamber. He'd already come and gone. His blanket was a heap on the rushes. She fretted about what he was wearing, wishing she'd given him the tunic she'd made for him. It looked every bit as fine as the one Lord Graelam was wearing, the one the beautiful Kassia had sewn for him.

In the great hall, Dienwald, garbed in a tunic and hose that were tattered and faded from their original gray to a dirty bile green, finally greeted his guests.

Graelam and Kassia were speaking with North-bert and Crooky, drinking ale and tasting the new St. Erth cheese that Dienwald had directed made from his own recipe, passed to him by his great-aunt Margarie, now long dead.

"Where is my wine, you whoreson?" Graelam asked without preamble upon Dienwald's appearance.

Dienwald looked at him blankly. "*Your* wine? What wine? That's not wine, it's ale, and made from my own recipe. I would have offered you wine had I some, but I don't. I have naught but ale, and no coin to purchase wine. God's bones, Graelam, I always bring myself to Wolffeton when I wish to reward my innards."

Graelam's dark eyes narrowed with suspicion. "You're a convincing liar when it pleases you to be so."

"What cursed wine?" Dienwald nearly shouted, flinging his arms wide.

Kassia laughed and placed her hand on his forearm. "You don't remember the wager between you and my lord? The Aquitaine wine my father was shipping to us? The ship was wrecked on the rocks and all the cargo disappeared. You didn't do it? You didn't steal the wine?"

Dienwald just shook his head. "Of course not. Are you sure, Kassia, that your wondrous lord didn't do it? He feared losing the wager to me, you know, and was at his wits' ends to find a way out of humiliating himself."

"Nay, don't try to win her to your side, you sly-lipped cockscomb."

Kassia laughed. "The both of you be still. 'Tis obvious that another rogue stole the wine, my lord. Drink your ale and forget your wager."

"But who?" Dienwald said as he accepted a flagon from Margot.

"Roland is in Cornwall," Graelam said.

"I don't believe it! Roland de Tournay! He's really here?"

"Aye, he's here. I heard it from a tinker who'd traveled the breadth of Cornwall."

"Aye, the tinker was here not long ago, but I was not." More's the pity, he thought, that the fellow hadn't as yet returned. He was seeing that strip of dirty leather tying Philippa's hair back. A narrow ribbon of pale yellow would be beautiful with her hair color. "He told you of Roland?"

"It seems that Roland stopped him, brought him to his camp in the forest of Fentonladock, and instructed him to tell me of his coming—not the why of it, but just that he would be at Wolffeton. I do wonder what he wants. You and Roland were boys fostering together, were you not? At Bauderleigh Castle with Earl Charles Massey?"

"Aye, we were. Old Charles was a proper devil, mean and evil and hard, but we both survived to become mean and evil and hard. I've not heard from Roland in five years."

"He went with Edward to go crusading, as did I. I didn't see him much in the Holy Land, but he survived, thankfully."

"I wonder how he does and what he wants with you."

"I am to meet him at Wolffeton in two weeks' time. He will tell me then. I was told that he used his talents spying for Edward whilst in the Holy Land. A Muslim he was, becoming so like them they never guessed he was an Englishman. He was an intimate of the sultan himself, so it was said."

"He's a dark-skinned bastard, looks like a heathen."

Graelam shrugged. "Aye, and his eyes are as black as a fanatical priest's and his tongue as smooth as an asp's."

Dienwald was thoughtful, then said without

thinking, "I should like to see him. Mayhap I could bring the wench with me. She would enjoy—" The instant it was out of his mouth, Dienwald wanted to kick himself.

Graelam, a man of subtlety when he so wished, inquired mildly, "Who is the wench, Dienwald? She was the one astride you, I gather? Sporting in the mud with you?"

"Aye."

"No more? No explanations? Is she clean? Where is she now?"

"She has no clothes, not a stitch, the muddy gown was old—it belonged to my first wife—and it was the last one. The wench is wearing a blanket now, and is in my bedchamber."

Kassia cocked her head to one side. "Wench? What is her name?"

"Morgan," Dienwald said without hesitation, then nearly swallowed his tongue. Well, he'd said it. He said it again, looking Graelam right in his eye. "Her name's Morgan and she's my mistress."

"She's a villein?"

He shook his head vigorously, and said, "Yes."

Graelam snorted. "What goes on here, Dienwald? Don't try to lie to me, I'll know it. You're clear as a spring pond."

"You said I was a fine liar just a moment ago."

"I exaggerated."

"Both of you relieve your minds and shut your mouths! Now, the female we saw, her name is Morgan, you say. An odd name, but no matter. I shall go visit her. I have no extra clothing with me, but I can have gowns and other things sent to her."

"She is a maypole, a giant of a girl. Nothing you own would fit her big body."

Kassia merely frowned at him, shook out the
skirt of her finely woven pale pink gown,
smoothed the sleeves of the delicate white overtunic, and walked slowly from the great wall. It
was then that Dienwald saw her big belly.

He was suddenly very afraid. He turned to
Graelam and saw his friend nodding.

"I shield her as best I can. She is so small, and
the child grows large in her belly. She insisted
upon coming to St. Erth today. She grows bored
and restless at Wolffeton—the women won't let
her do a thing within the castle, and even my
men hover about her when she is in the bailey—
and I couldn't deny her. You should see Blount,
my steward—he feels a quill is beyond her
strength. She frets."

"How much longer before the babe comes?"

"Not until June. I die each day with the thought
of it." Graelam then cursed luridly, and Dienwald, looking hopeful and thoughtful, said, "She
appears well and is beautiful and laughing."

"Aye," Graelam said, and drained his flagon.
He eyed Dienwald. "I wish you wouldn't speak
of my wife as though you were her lover. It irks
me. Now, 'tis true you didn't steal the wine from
Kassia's father? You didn't have the ship wrecked
with false warning lights from the point?"

"I wish I'd thought of it," Dienwald said, his
voice gloomy with regret.

"Roland, then," Graelam said, nodding in satisfaction at his conclusion. "I'll break two of his ribs
for his impertinence."

"That I should like to see," Dienwald said.

Kassia slowly climbed the solar stairs. She held
to the railing, careful, as always, of the babe she

carried. She felt wonderful and healthy and very alive. If only Graelam would but believe her and stop his worrying and his endless agitation. It was driving her to distraction. And there was her father, now threatening to come to Wolffeton and watch over her. Between the two of them she'd go mad, she knew it.

She reached Dienwald's bedchamber and knocked softly on the solid door. Then she turned the handle. It was locked. She called out, "Please, Morgan, let me in. 'Tis Kassia de Moreton."

Philippa stared at the door from her huddled spot in the middle of Dienwald's bed.

Morgan!

Who in the name of St. Andrew was Morgan? She rose, wrapped the blanket securely about her, and padded on bare feet to the door. She opened it and smiled.

"Come in, my lady."

"Thank you. Oh, dear, I see Dienwald was speaking true. You have no clothes."

Philippa simply shook her head.

"You are no villein's daughter, are you? What prank does Dienwald play now?"

"What did he tell you?"

"That you are his mistress."

Philippa snorted and tossed her head. Her hair was nearly dry now, and curled wildly down her back.

"Your hair is beautiful," Kassia said. "I've always wished for hair such as yours. Not long ago I was very ill and my head was shaved. My hair has grown back thicker, but not like yours. Do you mind if I sit down? My burden is heavy."

Philippa realized as the small lady walked across Dienwald's bedchamber that this female

was very nice and probably hadn't a mean bone
in her very feminine body. She was also heavy
with child. She was married to that huge warrior.
For an instant Philippa imagined that huge man
covering this very small female. It didn't seem
possible. But it didn't matter. This Kassia was
safely out of the way; Dienwald was safe from
her perfection.

It was an unspeakable relief.

"Forgive me," Philippa said. "Would you care
for some milk perhaps? I don't imagine that Dienwald thought of that."

"Nay, I am fine as I am, and no, he didn't. He
is a man much like my dear lord. Tell me, what
is your real name?"

Philippa wanted to spit it out, all of it, but she
paused. She realized that she didn't want Dienwald to be put upon or doubted or questioned,
even by his friends. Nor did she want to go to
her cousin Walter. She wanted to stay right here.
"Morgan *is* my name," she said, and her chin
went up.

Kassia thought: You're a truly awful liar. She
merely smiled at the tall, very lovely girl who sat
on Dienwald's bed, a blanket wrapped around
her. What was she doing here? It was a mystery,
and Kassia was quickly fascinated. Then she
thought of Robert Burnell's visit and of Dienwald
as the husband of Edward's illegitimate daughter
and how she and her husband had praised Dienwald's very eyebrows to Burnell. She felt a frisson
of worry, but shook it off. If Dienwald loved this
girl, then he would simply say no to Edward if
he offered him his daughter's hand in marriage.
Dienwald would say no to anybody, even the
Pope. He would laugh in the king's face if it

pleased him to do so. No, Dienwald couldn't be coerced into doing anything he didn't wish to do. She wouldn't worry. Everything would work out as it was meant to.

"I have come to offer you clothes, Morgan. I have none with me, but if you will let me see your size, then I can have some sent to St. Erth on the morrow."

Philippa had sunk into guilt over the truly violent thoughts she'd harbored toward this elegant lady. "I have woven wool. I merely haven't had time to see to clothes for myself. There were Edmund and Dienwald, even the fool, Crooky. He was so worn and ragged and so . . . so *accepting* of it. I couldn't bear it. I will sew myself something this evening. But I thank you, truly. You are kind."

"This is very interesting," Kassia said, cocking her head to one side.

"What is, my lady?"

"You and Dienwald. He is not, in the usual course of everyday events, a man in the habit of giving much of his attention to ladies."

That's because he's thinking of you. "Is that true?" Philippa said, noncommittal.

"Aye. Don't mistake my words. He has always enjoyed women, that is true, but not for longer than it takes him to relieve his needs with them. He's a complicated man, and obstinate, yet loyal and true. He is also a rogue, sometimes quite a scoundrel, and he much enjoys being unpredictable."

"I know."

"You do? Well, that is even more interesting. Do you know him well, then? You've been at St. Erth a long time?"

Philippa raised her chin. Was this lady toying with her? Showing her that it was she, not Philippa, who held Dienwald? No covering it up with fresh rushes, she thought, and said with the most emotionless voice she could dredge up, " 'Tis you, my lady, who holds Dienwald's interest, not me. 'Tis you he worships and admires, not me. 'Tis you he bleats on about, not me. He finds me unwomanly, ungainly, clumsy. But he speaks of you as if you were a . . . a *shrine*, and he wishes to fall on his face and worship at your feet."

"By all the saints' waggery, that is wondrous stupid," Kassia said, and burst into laughter. "And not at all like Dienwald."

"Dienwald is a man," Philippa said when Kassia had subsided into only an occasional giggle.

"Aye," Kassia said slowly, "he is, is he not? He is just like my lord. A man who dominates, a man who must rule, a man who yells and bellows when one dares cross his will or challenge him, and a man who will cherish and protect those weaker then he with all his strength."

"I'm just barely weaker than Dienwald."

"I doubt that, Morgan."

"He doesn't cherish me at all. He knows not what to do with me. I am a thorn in his flesh." Philippa's chin went up yet another notch. "But I am also his steward, though he doesn't wish to tell anyone, the obstinate cockscomb. He said were your husband to know, he would burst his bladder with laughter."

"His steward? Tell me, please. What happened to Alain?"

Philippa's dam burst, and words poured out of her mouth. She didn't tell Kassia de Moreton who she really was or how she came to be at St. Erth, but she told her of Alain's perfidy and how he'd tried to kill her and how she had since taken his place because Dienwald had no one else of the *proper* sex to do it.

Kassia stared at this rush of confidences, but before she could speak, the door burst open and Dienwald catapulted into the chamber, yelling even before his two feet were firmly planted on the floor, "Don't believe a word she says!"

Philippa jumped to her feet. "Morgan!" she shouted. "Who the devil is this Morgan?"

Dienwald drew up, frowning. "I don't know. The name merely popped into my mind. I like it. It has a certain dignity."

"What is your name, then?" Kassia asked.

" 'Tis Mary," Dienwald said quickly. "Her name is Mary. A nice name, a simple name, a name without pretense or deceit."

"I wouldn't say that," Graelam de Moreton said as he came through the bedchamber door. He looked over at his grinning wife. "I once knew a Mary who was as cunning and devious as my former mistress, Nan. You remember, Kassia? Ah, perhaps you don't wish to. You wonder why I'm here, sweetling? Well, Dienwald feared what the girl was telling you and bolted out of the hall. What was I to do? All that was of interest was here, so I followed."

"This is the wench, Mary," Dienwald said, and he gave Philippa a look that would rot off her toes if she dared to disagree with him.

"You don't look like a Mary," Graelam said, coming closer. He studied Philippa, his dark eyes intent. Then he looked troubled, questioning. "You look familiar, though. Your eyes . . . aye,

very familiar, the blue is brilliant, unique. I wish
I could remember—"

"She doesn't look familiar," Dienwald said,
stepping in front of Graelam. "She isn't at all
unique. She looks only like herself. She looks like
a Mary. Nothing more, just a simple Mary."

"She looks clean," Graelam said, and turned to
his wife. "Kassia, have you learned all of Dienwald's secrets? Did he steal my Aquitaine wine?"

"Dienwald isn't a thief!" Philippa turned red
the moment the words flew out of her mouth, but
proceeded to make matters worse: "He isn't
except when necessity forces him to be, and—"

"Ph . . . Mary, be quiet! I don't need you to
plead my innocence before this hulking behe-
moth. I didn't steal your puking wine, Graelam."

Kassia rose slowly to her feet. "This is quite
enough. Now, I suggest that we have our meal up
here, since Mary can't come to the hall wearing
naught but a blanket. What say you, Dienwald?"

What could he say? he wondered, both his
brain and belly sour, even as he nodded.

The evening meal, all cozy in Dienwald's bedchamber, passed off more smoothly than Dienwald could have hoped. Philippa held her tongue
for the most part, as did Kassia. The men spoke
of men's things, and though Philippa would have
liked to join in, because she was, no matter what
Dienwald said, St. Erth's steward, she kept still.
She was afraid she would inadvertently give
something away. Neither Graelam de Moreton
nor his lovely wife was stupid.

Why had Graelam looked at her so oddly?
Could he believe she looked familiar because he
remembered seeing her very briefly at Beauchamp
some years before?

Graelam sat back in his chair, a flagon of ale between his large hands. "Kassia and I will return to Wolffeton on the morrow. She wished merely to see that you were all right."

"Why? Nay, Graelam, your lie contains more holes than a sieve. You wished to see if I was drinking your wine."

"That as well." Graelam paused a moment, then continued easily, "Let us go for a walk, Dienwald. I have something to discuss with you."

Kassia shot him a questioning look, but he only smiled and shook his head.

What was going on here? Philippa wondered. She watched the two men leave the bedchamber. On the threshold, Dienwald turned, saying, "Mary, we will give our bed over to Graelam and Kassia tonight. Tell Edmund that he is to sleep with Father Cramdle. No, wait—we will sleep in your small bed in the steward's chamber." That taken care of to the master's satisfaction, Philippa was left sitting on the bed, her face red with anger and embarrassment.

"I will surely kill him, the miserable bounder," she said to no one in particular.

To her surprise, Lady Kassia laughed.

Graelam made a decision as he and Dienwald walked down the solar stairs and into the inner bailey. He wouldn't tell Dienwald of Burnell's visit. Kassia was right: leave things alone. Dienwald delighted in doing precisely what he wanted to do, and King Edward at his most cajoling or his most threatening wouldn't change his mind once he'd set himself a course. The two men walked toward the ramparts and climbed the ladder to the eastern tower.

"Your steward stole everything?" Graelam asked, leaning his elbows on the rough stone.

Dienwald nodded. "Bastard. Gorkel the Hideous broke his neck. But Alain had a spy who managed to flee St. Erth. My fool, Crooky, somehow knows such things—his ways of finding out things both amaze and terrify me. He believes Alain was involved with Walter de Grasse and that one of the men who tried to kill Ph . . . Mary is even now at Crandall. He is the cistern keeper."

Graelam said nothing for several moments. Finally: "I know of the hatred between the two of you, needless to say! And yes, I heard about the burning of your crops on the southern border and the butchering of all your people. You have no proof that Sir Walter was behind it, though, do you?"

Dienwald admitted that he had none. Thus, he was surprised when Graelam said, "I have decided to remove Walter. I will tolerate no more discord. If we discover that he burned your crops and destroyed your people, I will kill him. Now, my friend, bring out my wine—I'm convinced you have it hidden."

Dienwald could but stare at Graelam; then he bellowed for Northbert. "Bring out the wine!"

It wasn't Aquitaine wine, but it wasn't vinegar either. There was but one cask, and it hailed from a Benedictine abbey near Penryn.

When Dienwald entered the steward's small chamber in the early hours of the morning, not at all drunk, for he hated wine, he smiled toward the lump on the narrow bed.

He walked silently to the bed and went down on his knees, setting his lit candle on the floor beside him. He said nothing, merely lifted the blanket that covered Philippa. She was naked, lying on her side facing away from him, one leg stretched out, the other bent, and all the beauty of her woman's flesh was there for him to see. He swallowed and didn't wait another moment. Lightly he touched his fingertips to her inner thighs, then moved them up slowly, very slowly, until he felt the warmth of her. He drew in his breath, aware that his sex was swollen and aching. Slowly, he eased his middle finger inside her. She was very tight and he loved the feeling of his finger stretching her and he imagined how it would feel to have her around his manhood, so tight, squeezing him until he wanted to die with the wonderful feelings. His finger deepened. Her body was responding, dampening, easing for his finger.

He leaned forward and kissed her hip even as he let his finger ease more deeply. He heard her moan and felt her tighten convulsively. He would spill his seed right here in this damned darkened room. He quickly withdrew his finger and tried to calm his frantic breathing. He rose and stripped off his clothes. He lay beside her, feeling her buttocks against his swelled sex. He began to knead her belly then let his fingers go once more where they ached to. He found her woman's flesh in the soft curls and moaned deep in his throat as he began to stroke her, gently exploring.

When her hips jerked and she moaned in her sleep, he rolled her onto her back and came over her.

14

Philippa was whimpering even as she opened her eyes. Then she shrieked into the shadowed face above her.

Dienwald cursed, bent down, and kissed her mouth. He gave her his full weight for an instant, then raised himself on his elbows, still kissing her wildly.

He was between her legs, his sex stiff and hot and hurting. He reared back onto his knees and parted her thighs with his hands, looking down at her. "You would make me debauch you," he said, his voice low and raw. "You're a witch, a siren, and you would take me and wring me out and make me feel things I don't want to feel."

Philippa's mind finally cleared. She was still throbbing, deep in her belly, but she saw him clearly now and heard his words and understood them and was enraged. All unwanted sensations

223

quickly fled her body. "*I* make *you* debauch *me*? What about your grandmother's deep spring and all that religious nonsense of renewal and light and dark and how you thought of me as being deep and fulfilling and renewing you and . . . I am in my own bed, you insensate brute! 'Tis you who seek to dishonor me! I am a maid and not your wife. 'Tis you who make me feel things I shouldn't feel. 'Tis you who wish to desecrate me—a prisoner with no voice in anything, a wretched captive who has no clothing even!"

"A fine volley of words you fling at me—but naught but peevish rantings. You have no voice, you say? You beset me, wench, your mouth is nearly as bountiful as your ass!"

She saw red, fisted her hands, and smashed them against his chest even as he shouted, "You make yourself sound like a shrine, a relic to heedless virgins! Desecrate? You came to me through foul mischance, wench—that, or God sent you as my penance—" He was still holding her thighs when she hit him again as hard as she could.

Dienwald growled a half-dozen curses even as he teetered sideways and fell to the stone floor beside the bed. He didn't release her, and she came crashing down on top of him. When her head hit his as he was trying to rise, and he was plunged back, she heard the ugly thudding sound of his head against the leg of her steward's table.

His head lolled on the stone floor and he was still. Philippa was frozen for an instant, trying to comprehend what had happened; then she knew bone-deep fear, rolled off him, and flattened her palm against his chest. His heartbeat was slow and steady. She brought the single candle closer and examined his head. A lump was beginning

to swell over his left temple. Well, it served the
slavering ravisher right. He'd come to take her
even as she slept, so she wouldn't fight him; then
his wayward mouth had accused *her* of debauching *him*, or some such nonsense. She wanted to
hit him again, but didn't. Instead she sat on the
cold stone floor, crossed her legs, and eased his
head onto her thighs. She didn't feel the chill of
the stones against her flesh; rather she felt the
heat from his shoulders, the warmth of him
beneath her hands. She leaned against the bed
and gently stroked his forehead. She was conscious only of him and her worry for him. After
a while she also found that she was staring, and
discovered he quite delighted her. His sex wasn't
hard and throbbing now; quite the contrary. His
long legs were sprawled out, slightly parted. She
smiled and laid her hand on his belly. Slowly she
traced the ridges of muscle, then let her fingers
stray to the thick brush of dark hair at his groin.

"You are such a churlish knave," she said.
"What am I to do with you?"

He didn't reply, nor did he stir. Philippa sang
him a soft French ballad her mother had taught
her when she was four years old. Then she
stopped and sighed. More to the point of course
was what *he* would do with *her*. She forced her
fingers away from him. She couldn't begin to
imagine how he would taunt her were he to know
what she had done whilst he lay unconscious.

"St. Gregory's chilblains, wench, your voice
sounds like a wet rag slapping against the side of
a sleeping horse."

"You're awake," she said, her voice flat. "A
minstrel who sojourned at Beauchamp just last

year told my parents that my voice was dulcet and silvery, like a turtle dove's."

"Dulcet dove? The fellow lied, and is worse with words than Crooky." Dienwald fell into melancholy silence, for he'd realized that his head lay in her lap, that if he turned his face inward he could kiss the soft flesh between her legs. He didn't want to do that. Why must she offer him such wondrous fodder for his weakness? It wasn't to be borne. He turned his face against her, his lips seeking.

Philippa sucked in her breath and shoved him away. He moaned, and immediately she felt guilty. "You shouldn't have done that. You'll hurt yourself again."

He moaned again, dramatically, and Philippa gritted her teeth against laughing. "Come, you must get up now. You're naked."

"I'm pleased you noticed. So are you, wench." Dienwald struggled to his feet, stood there weaving for a moment, then collapsed onto her narrow bed.

Philippa looked down at him. He gave a loud snore. She cursed and covered him with a blanket.

"I'm cold and will die of watery lungs brought on by your cruelty if you leave me."

"I like the sound of your snores better," Philippa said even as she eased down beside him. "Nay, I shan't let you touch me again. It isn't right you should do that, and well you know it. I'm not your mistress. I shan't ever be your mistress." She grabbed another frayed blanket and wrapped it about herself. "Go to sleep, master, else I'll fling you off my bed again."

Dienwald sighed. "Big wenches are difficult."

"I know," she said, her voice nasty. "You'd much prefer your precious *little* Kassia, your so-perfect *little* princess who doubtless sighs and swoons all over you—a *big* warrior."

He laughed.

"Well, you can't have her, you ass! She's well-wedded and she's with child and she's not for you, so you might as well forget her."

"How well you extol her person," he said. "Mayhap you are right. I will think about it. Big wenches are even more difficult when they're jealous." He began snoring again and soon, much sooner than Philippa, he was truly asleep.

Jealous, was she? He turned onto his side away from her and soon she was snuggled against his back. She wondered what he'd do if she bit him. Probably just laugh at her again. She fell asleep finally, feeling warm and secure, damn him.

Graelam stood in the open doorway of the steward's chamber early the next morning, staring toward the narrow bed that held his host and the wench whose name wasn't Mary. The girl's face was pressed against Dienwald's naked back, but the rest of her was protected from him by an old blanket, a blanket that, he saw, separated the two of them. An eyebrow cocked upward. So the girl whose name wasn't Mary also wasn't Dienwald's mistress either. Kassia would find this fascinating.

Suddenly Dienwald groaned and turned onto his back, flinging his arm over his head. Philippa, jerked from a sound sleep, was nearly thrown off the narrow bed onto the floor. Dienwald groaned again, muttering, "My God, you've nearly killed me, wench. My head, it's swollen and hurts and—"

"And has put you in particularly good humor," Graelam said, stepping into the chamber.

Philippa's eyes flew open and fastened in consternation upon the intruder. He merely smiled. "God give you a good morrow, Mary. I am sorry to disturb your slumber, but my wife and I must take our leave soon. This door was open and I did tap my fist upon it, but there was no reply."

Dienwald opened an eye, and complaints issued rapidly from his mouth. "The wench nearly killed me. I've a lump on my skull the size of my foot."

Philippa was less than sympathetic. "You deserved it, you disgusting lout!"

"Lout? God's knees, you randy wench, all I did was think about letting you debauch me, nothing more." He smiled guilelessly up at her.

Philippa reared up, quickly jerked the blanket over her breasts, and sent her fist into his belly. "My lord," she said, turning immediately toward Graelam, "I cannot rise to see to you and your perfect wife's needs. But this attempted defiler of innocent maids can, and he will, once he stops acting like he's been flayed by a band of Saracens."

"I've never known him for a coward, thus it must be your superior strength and cunning, Mary. Dienwald, rise now, and pay your homage to my lady. Kassia wishes to bid you adieu." Graelam's eyes suddenly widened. "*Perfect* wife?" He guffawed. "I shall tell Kassia, it will amuse her. *Perfect!*" He shook his head. "The little witch—*perfect!*" Still laughing, Graelam left the steward's chamber, closing the door behind him.

"*You* think she's perfect," Philippa said.

"Feel the lump on my head. Tell me if I will survive rising from this bed."

Philippa leaned over and gently examined his head. "The lump will grow if you stay in this bed. You will survive it, so get thee gone, I tire of you."

He sighed and rolled over her, coming to his feet beside the bed. He was naked and quite unconcerned about it. He grinned down at her and said, "Don't stare, wench, else my manhood will rise like leavened bread." He gave a heartfelt sigh. "And 'twill make my hose uncomfortable. It will also bring the stares of all your gentle rivals— in short, most of the wenches here at St. Erth. What say you?"

"I grant you good morrow," Philippa said, then turned away from him and stared at the wall.

Dienwald knew well enough that his body pleased her. Although he wasn't a massive warrior like Graelam, he was big enough, well enough made, muscled and lean and hard, not a patch of fat on him. He leaned down and quickly kissed her cheek, then straightened, began whistling, and dressed himself. He was out of the steward's chamber in but a moment, still whistling.

Philippa spent her morning sewing herself a gown from soft wool dyed a light green that Old Agnes had brought to her; she hummed to herself as she sewed. She jumped at the knock on her door, then smiled when Edmund burst into the room. He drew to a halt, planted his hands on his hips, and said, "What think you, Maypole?"

She studied him silently for several minutes, until he began fidgeting about. "Very nice, Master Edmund. Come here and let me inspect you more closely."

Edmund swaggered over to where Philippa sat draped in her blanket. He was proud, that was clear to see, he'd even combed his fingers through his hair, and Philippa was pleased. "What says your father?"

"He just looked at me and rubbed his chin. Lord Graelam thought I would become a fine knight, and Lady Kassia asked that I carry her favors when I am in my first tourney."

Perfect Kassia had done it again, Philippa thought, had said just the right thing at the right time. Curse the woman.

"Father said that soon I will go to Wolffeton to foster with Lord Graelam. I will be his page, then, soon, his squire. I will prove myself and my loyalty."

"Do you wish to go to Wolffeton?"

Edmund nodded quickly, but then he fell silent. " 'Tis not far from St. Erth, no more than a half-day's hard ride. I shall go and I shall earn my spurs very soon."

"You will not, however, be an ignorant knight, Edmund. Few pages can read or write, but you will. Few men of any class can read or write, save priests and clerks. Lord Graelam will thank God the day you come to Wolffeton. Now, Father Cramdle awaits you. Go and leave the maypole to sew something to cover herself."

It wanted only Edmund's father, Philippa thought, watching Dienwald come into the small room after his son had left. She nearly filled it, and with him in here as well, it was suffocating. "What do you want?"

"I wish to tell you that my son is mightily pleased with himself."

Philippa merely nodded.

"Thank you, wench."

She swallowed a lump in her throat and said

in an offhand manner, "Shall you also be pleased with your new tunic? 'Tis finished." Before he could answer her, Philippa eased out of her chair, her blanket firmly in place around her, and handed him the tunic she'd sewn for him.

Dienwald took it from her outstretched hand and stared down at it, running his fingers over the tiny stitches, feeling the soft wool, marveling that she had made it for him and that it was so fine, the most excellent tunic he'd ever owned. It was too special to wear on this ordinary day, but he said nothing, merely pulled off his old tunic and pulled this one over his head. It felt soft against his flesh, and it fitted him perfectly. He turned to face Philippa and she smiled at him. " 'Tis very well you look, Dienwald, quite splendid." She reached out her hand and smoothed the cloth over his chest. Her breathing quickened and she suddenly stilled.

Dienwald stepped back quickly. "I'm leaving and I wanted to tell you to stay close to St. Erth."

Her stomach cramped tight. "Where go you? Not into danger?"

He heard the forlorn tone and the fear, and frowned at it. "I go where I go, and 'tis none of your affair. You will stay here and not move one of your large feet from St. Erth. When I return, I will decide what to do with you."

"You make me sound like entrails tossed out of the cooking shed."

Dienwald merely smiled at that, touched his fingertips to her cheek, then leaned down and kissed her mouth. Still smiling, he jerked the blanket from her breasts, gazed down at them, kissed one nipple, then the other.

"Don't do that!"

He straightened, gave her a small salute, and strode from the room.

He began whistling again as the door closed firmly behind him. Philippa just stood there, the blanket bunched around her waist. He'd worn his new tunic.

Dienwald didn't think of her as anything remotely close to "entrails," but he didn't know what to do with her. What he wanted to do, in insane moments, was take her again and again until he was sated with her. And the insane moments seemed to be coming more and more often now; in fact, were he to count his errant thoughts, the moments would melt together.

He cursed and gave Philbo a stout kick in the sides. The destrier snorted and jumped forward. Northbert, surprised, kicked his own destrier into a canter, as did Eldwin, who rode on his left side.

Dienwald could remember the fragrance of her sweet woman's scent, and something else more elusive—perhaps 'twas the essence of gillyflowers, he thought, dredging the scent from his childhood memories.

The wench had bewitched him and beset him, curse her for the guileless siren she was. And somehow she'd made him like it and want more of it, more of her. He'd very nearly taken her maidenhead the previous night, and he hadn't even drunk enough ale to account for such stupidity. No, he'd just thought of her, seeing her in his mind's eye sleeping in her narrow bed in the steward's chamber, and he'd left Graelam to stare after him, their chess game still undecided. He would have taken her had she not awakened with that loud shriek in his face.

What was he to do with the damned wench?

He sighed, now picturing his son strutting about in his new clothes, bragging about the Maypole. His son, who just this morning hadn't carped and crabbed quite so much about being sacrificed to studies with Father Cramdle.

The wench was taking over St. Erth. Everywhere he saw her influence, her touch. It was irritating and disconcerting. He didn't know what to do about it.

It was Northbert who pulled him from his melancholy thoughts. "Master, what do you expect to find?"

"We didn't search before. We buried the dead and came back to St. Erth. I wish to find something to prove that Sir Walter ordered the burning and the killings. That or find someone who mayhap saw him or recognized one of his men."

Northbert chewed on that for several miles. Finally he said, "Why not just kill the malignant bastard? You know he's responsible, as do all the rest of us. Kill him."

Dienwald wanted to kill Walter, very much, but he shook his head. He wanted things done right. He wanted to keep Graelam's trust and his friendship. "Lord Graelam needs proof; then we will argue together to determine who gets to scatter the bastard's bowels."

"Ah," said Northbert, nodding his ugly head. "Lord Graelam includes himself now. 'Tis good, methinks."

They reached the southern acres of St. Erth late that afternoon. The desolation was shattering. There was naught but emptiness and black ruins. There was only the occasional caw of a rook. Curls of smoke still rose from some of the burned huts. There were a few peasants prodding the burned remains in leveled hovels, and Dienwald drew up and began to ask his questions.

Philippa was bored. More than bored, she'd discovered what Dienwald's errand was and she was worried, despite the fact that he was a trained fighter and no enemy was supposed to be where he was going.

She accepted without question that her cousin Sir Walter de Grasse was a black villain. She just wished there was something she could do.

She wore her new gown that afternoon and she looked proud and very pretty, so Old Agnes told her, very much the proper mistress. Then Agnes sought confirmation from Gorkel, who looked at Philippa and grunted, his hideous face achieving a repellent smile. She'd cut a narrow piece of wool and tied it around her hair. As for Crooky, he was feeling expansive in his own new clothes, which were still very clean, and praised her to her eyebrows. Philippa expected the worst and wasn't disappointed:

She sweetly sews for all of us, this lovely
maid whose name's not Mary.
Our sweet lord who stole her wool aches to
drink from her sweet dairy.
She made him a tunic and kissed it pure
Our sweet lord wonders what to do with her.

Philippa cheered loudly and the other servants in the hall quickly joined her. "It rhymed, truly," she said, wiping her eyes with the back of her hand. "Though your sentiments don't do the master justice."

Crooky, in a new mood of self-doubt, merely

said, "Nay, mistress, 'twas hideous. I must do better, aye, I must tether my wayward thoughts and bring them to smoothness and pleasure to the ear. Aye, I will beg Father Cramdle to write it down for me."

Philippa said, "You have lightened me for a few moments, Crooky, and I thank you. Now, before you go to the priest, tell me when the master will return."

"No one knows," Gorkel said, stepping forward. "He's gone to the southern borders."

She knew that, and sat there worrying her thumbnail. She paced the great hall. In a spate of feverish activity to distract herself, she had lime dumped down the privy hole in the guardroom. She spaded the small garden near the cistern, willing the few vegetables to grow. She watched the women sewing, always sewing, and she praised them, and joined in herself for an hour, making another tunic for the master. Old Agnes ran her arthritic fingers over it and gave her a sly smile. Philippa went to the cooking shed and spoke with Bennen, a stringy old man who knew more of herbs than anyone she had ever known and presided over the cooking with what Philippa's mother had called the "special touch." He got along well with St. Erth's withered cook, which was a good thing, because no one else seemed to get along with him. She spoke of several dishes she herself liked, and Bennen committed them to memory, and called her "mistress" and smiled at her, his toothless mouth wide. If Dienwald wanted to feel trapped, he needed only listen to his own people. She even visited Eleanor the cat and her four kittens, all healthy and mewing loudly.

The night was long, and Philippa wished Dienwald were there, kissing her, fighting with her, trying to fit himself between her legs even as he fought himself.

The next morning, Edmund said to her after watching her crumble a particularly fine hunk of cheese and toss it to one of the castle dogs, "You didn't sleep well, Maypole. You look sour and your eyes are all dark-circled. My father has a nice palfrey that should be big enough for a female your size. Come riding, Philippa. You won't miss my father so much." He added after a little thought, "Aye, I miss him as well. We will both ride."

"I don't miss him, but I should like to ride."

The palfrey's name was Daisy and she was docile and well-mannered. Philippa, her gown hiked up to her knees, her legs and feet bare, sat her horse, smiling down at Ogden, the head stableman. He was wildly red-haired and so freckled she couldn't make out the tone of his flesh beneath.

Gorkel approached and said, "You'll want men with you, mistress. The master ordered me to . . ." He faltered, and Philippa could only stare, it was so unexpected of the man who'd without hesitation snapped the steward's neck.

"I understand," she said. "The master doesn't want me perchance to lose myself in the wilds of Cornwall."

Gorkel beamed at her. "Aye, mistress, thass it. I don't ride well, but I'll fetch men who will accompany you."

The afternoon was sunny, only a light breeze stirring the air, and the countryside was wild and hilly, trees bowed from the fierce winds and

storms that blew from the Irish Sea just to the
north—but not now, not during Dienwald's fanciful deep spring.

Edmund allowed that she looked less testy
upon their return to St. Erth some three hours
later.

"You must take care with your flattery, Master
Edmund, else I may mistake your sweet words
for affection."

To which Edmund snorted in disgust and said
with a dignity that sat well on his boy's shoulders, "I am not a churl."

"Not today, at least," she said, and grinned at
him.

Edmund didn't retort to that because they'd
just crossed into the inner bailey and he was staring at a pack mule loaded with bundles, three
men in Wolffeton colors lolling around the mule.

Perfect Kassia, the little princess, the glorious
little lady, had sent clothing, just as she'd promised. An entire mule-load of clothing. Philippa
gasped as she unwrapped the coarse-wool-
wrapped garments. Gowns, overtunics, fine hose,
shifts of the softest cotton and linen, ribbons of
all colors, even soft leather slippers large enough
for her, the toes pointed upward in the latest
fashion from Eleanor's court. It was too much and
it was wonderful and Philippa felt like the most
sour-natured of wretches. She read the letter from
Kassia, handed to her by one of the men. Mary
was thanked for the hospitality of St. Erth, and
Philippa could practically see Kassia smiling as
she penned the words. The close of the letter
made her frown a bit: ". . . do not worry if things
transpire somewhat awry. Dienwald makes his
own decisions and he is strong and unswerving.

Don't worry, please do not, for all will be as it should be.''

Now, what did that mean? Philippa wondered as she rolled the sheet of foolscap and retied it. She looked at the clothing spread out on the trestle table in the great hall. So much, and all for her. Odd how she'd forgotten how much she'd owned at Beauchamp, and how dear one simple gown had now become to her.

She hummed and arranged the clothing in the steward's room. Then she began to work, quickly and happily, still humming. She sent Gorkel to direct the children to collect fresh rushes after she measured him for a new tunic. She asked Bennen for rosemary to scent it. More lime was dumped down the privy, for the easterly winds were strong.

The following morning, she and Edmund rode out from St. Erth again, this time with three men in attendance. Gorkel was master in Eldwin's absence, and he was directing the remaining men in the practice field. As they rode out, she could hear the men's shouts and yells and the dull thuds of the lances as they rode against the quintains. She wanted to see the cattle in the northern pastures, to make a count so she could be certain that her steward's ledgers were correct. She was garbed anew and felt like a very fine lady surrounded by her courtiers. Then it rained and she worried and fretted that her new clothing would be ruined. The cattle counted, they returned to St. Erth, Philippa to her steward's books.

On the third morning, she wore the gown she'd sewed for herself and left her legs bare. It didn't matter, for the day was warm and the master wasn't here to see her and perhaps smile at her with lecherous intent. Ah, but she missed him and his hands and his mouth and the feel of his hard body. She missed his smile and his volley of words. She missed arguing with him and baiting him. She thought suddenly that debauching him was an interesting notion—folly, to be sure, but seductive folly. Her fingers flexed as she remembered holding his head on her lap that morning and how he'd turned his face inward and kissed her. She doubted she would have time to debauch him before he'd already done the debauching. She laughed aloud, and Edmund stared at her.

As to her future, she refused to think about it. As to St. Erth's future, it looked much brighter. With luck, there would be some cattle to sell and coins in Dienwald's coffers. She would need to check on the pigs just as she had on the cattle. She wanted nothing left to chance or hearsay. Her entries in her steward's ledgers grew longer, by the hour, it seemed, and she felt pleasure for St. Erth's master as she worked. Repairs were needed in St. Erth's eastern wall. Soon, perchance this fall, there would be enough coin to hire them done. She whistled and worked faster.

She turned her attention back to Edmund as he demanded to know why she, a heedless maypole of a girl, could read and write and cipher. "Because my father wished it, I suppose," she said, frowning as she spoke the words, the same reply she'd given Edmund's father. "I do wonder, though, why he wished it. My sister, Bernice, has naught but space in her head, that and visions of chivalrous knights singing praises to her eyebrows. Aye, she's a one, Master Edmund."

"Is she a maypole like you?"

Philippa shook her head. "She's short and plump and has a pointed chin and very red lips. She pouts most virtuously, having practiced before a mirror for the past six years."

"And she had all your suitors?"

"Must you keep asking me questions? All right, there was Ivo de Vescy, and he was wildly in love with me."

"His name sounds shiftless. Did he truly wish to wed with you? Was he a giant? You're almost as tall as my father." Edmund paused, then shook his head. "Mayhap not."

"You're naught but a little boy. How can you possibly tell from down there? I come nearly to your father's nose."

"He likes small women, *short* women. Just look at Alice and Ellen and Sybilla—"

"Who are Ellen and Sybilla?"

Edmund shrugged. "Oh, I forgot. Father married Ellen to a peasant when he got her with child, and Sybilla sickened with a fever and died. But Alice is small, not like you."

Philippa wanted to cuff his ears and stuff one of her new leather slippers into his mouth. She wanted to scream so loud that it would chase the cawing rooks away. Edmund's flowing child's candor had smitten her deep, very deep, with pain; she wanted to weep. Of course Dienwald had made no secret of his couplings. He'd said merely that they saved her maidenhead. And she'd not cared then because he was a stranger she hadn't come to know yet. But now she had and she wanted to send her fist into his belly and hear him bellow with pain. She wanted . . .

"Father will send you back to Lord Henry. He

has no choice. He doesn't want to wed, ever. Thass what he tells everyone."

"*That's,*" Philippa said automatically. "Why do you believe that?"

Edmund shrugged. "I heard him tell Alain once that women were a man's folly, that if a man wished more than a vessel, he was naught but a windy fool and an ass."

"Your memory rivals a priest's discourse in its detail."

This was greeted with another shrug. "My father knows everything. Thass . . . *that's* why he doesn't use you as he does the others. He'd be ashamed, perchance worried that he would have to wed you. Is your father very powerful?"

"Very powerful," Philippa said. "And very mean and very strong and—"

It was then that Edmund grunted and jerked at his pony's reins. "Look yon, Philippa! Men, and they're coming toward us!"

15

Philippa saw the men and felt her heart sink to her toes. They were riding hard, and even from a distance they looked determined. Who were they?

"Your father, Edmund?"

"Nay, I don't recognize Father or Northbert or Eldwin, and they ride the most distinctive destriers. I don't know who they are. We must flee, Philippa."

The man-at-arms, Ellis, turned to Philippa, consternation writ clear on his face. "There are too many of them, mistress. Ride! Back to St. Erth. We can't fight them."

Philippa, without a word, jerked on her palfrey's reins and dug her bare heels into the mare's sides. She looked sideways at Edmund and realized that his pony didn't have the endurance to keep pace with the rest of them. Their pursuers' horses were pounding toward them, ever closer,

their hooves kicking up whorls of dust into the
clear air. Who were they?

It didn't matter. Philippa lowered her head and
urged her palfrey faster. When Edmund's pony
faltered, she'd simply bring him onto Daisy's back
with her. Daisy was strong and stout of heart.
Philippa gently tugged Daisy's reins to the right
and drew closer to Edmund.

Sir Walter de Grasse looked toward the fleeing
men, the girl and young boy protected in the
midst of them. His destrier, a powerful blooded
Arabian, couldn't be outrun, particularly by that
muling mare Philippa was riding. He really didn't
care about the others. Walter was pleased; he
smiled and felt the wind tangle his hair and make
his eyes tear. At last. He'd waited and planned
and waited. Finally she'd ridden this way, and
that whoreson peasant Dienwald wasn't with her.
He was back scrounging about in his burned
southern acres, finding nothing because Walter
never left anything to find. Dead bodies were the
only witnesses. Walter urged his destrier faster.
If only Philippa knew that it was he, her own
cousin, in pursuit, she would wave and flee from
Dienwald's men. He noticed the little boy beside
her on his laboring pony and wondered who he
was.

He wished he could make out her face, but
from this distance all he could see for certain was
her wildly beautiful hair rippling out behind her
head, atop the slenderness of her body. It was
enough. If she had no teeth, he would still crave
her above all women, this king's daughter who
would shortly be his wife. He thought of St. Erth
and how it would be his within the year, he
doubted not. How could King Edward deny his

son-in-law his own castle, stolen from his father
by Dienwald's thieving sire?

Philippa could hear the pursuing horses. They
were very close now. She knew all was lost. They
were still a good two miles from St. Erth. The
countryside around them held only a few peasants' huts, low pine trees and scrubby hawthorns
and yews, and indifferent cattle. No one to help
them. She saw the fierce look on Ellis' face, attesting to his impotent rage. Their pace was frantic
and the horses were blowing hard, their flanks
lathered white. She saw Edmund's pony stumble
and she acted quickly, jerked Daisy close, dropped
the knotted reins, and grabbed Edmund even as
his pony went down. He was heavy, heavier than
she'd imagined, but she pulled him onto Daisy's
back. "My pony!" he yelled, nearly hurtling himself off Daisy's back.

Philippa fought to steady him. "The pony will
make its way back to St. Erth. Worry not for the
pony, but for us."

Edmund quieted, but he was breathing in quick
sharp gasps, his small body shuddering.

"Your pony will go home," she said again,
this time in his ear, hoping he heard her and
understood.

He made no sign. His small face was white and
grim.

She held him close and urged her mare faster.

Suddenly, without warning, Ellis screamed, a
tearing raw-throated sound. Philippa saw an arrow
bedded deep between his shoulder blades, its
feathered shaft still vibrating from the force of its
entry. Ellis lurched forward, gasping, then fell
sideways, his foot catching in the stirrup. He was
dragged along, blood spewing from his back onto

his maddened horse. Philippa tried to hide Edmund's head, but he watched until Ellis' foot worked free of the stirrup and he fell to the hard ground, rolling over and over, the arrow's shaft going deeper into his body.

Edmund made no sound; Philippa held him tighter, swallowing convulsively.

The other two men closed around her, and one of them yelled at her to keep down, to hug her mare's neck, but even as the words left his mouth he slumped forward against his horse's back, an arrow through his neck.

Philippa knew it was no use. "Flee," she shouted to the third man, whose name was Silken. "Go whilst you can. 'Tis I the men want, not you. Go! Get help. Get the master."

The man looked at her, his eyes sad and accepting. He drew his horse to a screaming halt, whipped him about, and drew his sword. "I won't die with a coward's arrow in my back," he yelled at Philippa. "Nor will I die a coward's death in my soul by escaping my fate. Ride hard, mistress. I'll hold them as long as I can. Keep the boy safe."

"Nay, Silken, nay!" Edmund shouted, and Philippa knew that she couldn't leave the man, knew that even if she rode away, she would manage to save neither herself nor Edmund. She pulled Daisy to a halt. "Stay back behind me, Silken," she yelled at him. "Keep your sword to your side!"

The men were upon them in moments. Dust flew, blurring the air, making Philippa cough. She couldn't have been more horrified or surprised when one of the men yelled, "Philippa! My dearest cousin, 'tis I, Walter, here to save you!"

Silken whirled on Philippa, his face gone white, his mouth ugly with sudden rage. "*You*, mistress! You brought this bastard cur upon us! You got word to him!"

"Find the master, Silken. Here, take Edmund with you, quickly!"

But Edmund wouldn't budge, shaking his head madly and clutching at the mare's mane. Silken waited not another moment, but rode away as only a desperate man can ride, and Walter, intent for the moment upon the object of his capture, allowed the man to gain distance. Then he yelled for two of his men to bring him down. Philippa prayed hard, as did, she imagined, Edmund. Silken was their only chance. He disappeared over a rise, the two men in pursuit.

"Philippa," Walter said as he rode up to her. "Ah, my dearest girl, you are safe, are you not?"

Philippa stared at her cousin Walter, a man she hadn't seen for some years. He wasn't a handsome man, but then, neither was he ill-looking. But he did look different to her. She had remembered him as very tall and thin. He wasn't thin now; he was gaunt and wiry, his face long, his cheekbones high and hollow, his eyes more prominent. She remembered thick dark brown hair fashionably clipped across his forehead. His hair was thinner now but still clipped across his forehead. She hadn't remembered his eyes. They were dark blue, and they looked hot with triumph, with success. She quickly assessed matters and got control of herself. He believed he'd rescued her, saved her. She whispered to Edmund, "Hold your peace, Edmund. Do as I do."

The boy was white with fear, but he nodded. She squeezed him comfortingly.

"Walter, 'tis you?"

"Aye, Philippa, 'tis I, your dearest cousin. You have changed and grown into a woman and a beautiful creature. You are most pleasing to mine eyes. And now you are safe from that knave." Walter paused a moment, noticing Edmund, it seemed, for the first time.

"Who is this? The bastard's whelp? Shall I dispatch him to heaven, Philippa? Surely that is where the angels would carry him, for he is yet too young to have gleaned the foul wickedness from his sire."

"No, leave him be, Walter. He is but a child, too young for heaven, unless God calls him. Leave him to me. He cares not for his sire, for he foully abuses him." She prayed Edmund would keep his small mouth firmly closed. He started, stiffening against her, but said nothing.

"Aye, that I can believe. The cruel traitor not only abused his own child, but you as well, I doubt not. You are both safe with me, Philippa, at least until I decide what to do with the boy. Aye, I'll ransom him. His father is coarse of spirit, but the boy is of his flesh and his heir. Aye, we'll all return to Crandall now."

"I'll tear out his lying tongue!"

"Shush, Edmund, please, say nothing untoward!"

Philippa turned Daisy about, saying as she did so, "What is the distance to your keep, Walter?"

"Two days hence, fair cousin."

"My palfrey is lathered and blowing."

"Leave the beast and take that one. Dienwald's man needs it no more." And Walter laughed, pointing to Ellis' body sprawled in a ditch beside the dusty road.

"Nay, leave me the mare, just keep our pace slow for a while."

Walter felt expansive. Everything had come about as he'd planned. Philippa was beautiful and she was gentle and yielding, her expressive eyes filled with gratitude for him. "I'll grant you that boon, Philippa." He rode forward to speak to one of his men. Philippa whispered in Edmund's ear, "We must pretend, Edmund, and we must think. We must exceed Crooky's most talented fabrications."

"I will kill him."

"Perhaps I shall be the quicker, but hold your tongue now, he returns. Say naught, Edmund."

"We will ride until it darkens, sweet cousin. I know you are tired, but we must have distance from St. Erth." He turned and looked behind them, and she knew he was at last worried that his men hadn't returned to report Silken's death. She prayed harder.

"We will do as you wish, Walter," she said, her voice soft and low. "You're right—we're too close to the tyrant's castle." He seemed to expand before her eyes, so pleased was he at her submissiveness.

"Shall I carry the boy before me?"

"Nay, he is afraid, Walter, for he knows you not. He can't abide me—he follows his sire's lead and insults me and abuses me—but at least I am a known adversary. Leave him with me for the moment, if it pleases you to do so."

It evidently suited Walter, and he turned to speak to a man who rode beside him.

"You act the flap-mouthed fool," Edmund said, his child's voice a high squeak. "He cannot believe you, 'tis absurd!"

"He doesn't know me," Philippa said. "He wants to believe me soft and biddable and as submissive as a cow. Fret not, at least not yet."

It wasn't until late that afternoon that the two men who had followed Silken caught up with them. Philippa held her breath as they pulled their mounts to a halt beside Walter. She waited, still with apprehension. To her wondrous relief, Walter exploded with rage. "Fools! Inept knaves!"

"Silken escaped," Philippa said into Edmund's ear. "Your father will come. He will save us."

Edmund frowned. "But he is your cousin, Philippa. He won't harm you."

"He's a bad man. Your father hates him, and for good reason, I think."

"But you mocked my father about him and—"

" 'Tis but our way—your father and I must rattle our tongues at each other, goad and taunt each other until one wants to smash the other's head."

Edmund said nothing to that, but he was confused, so Philippa just hugged him, whispering, "Trust me, and trust that your father will save us."

It came to dusk and the sky colored itself with vivid shades of pink. They rode inland a bit and stopped at the edge of a forest whose name Philippa didn't know. It was dark and deep, and she watched silently as two men immediately melted into the trees in search of game. Two other men went to collect wood.

Walter lifted Edmund down and paid him no more attention. Then he wrapped his hands around Philippa's waist and lifted her from Daisy's back. He grunted a bit because she wasn't a languid feather to be plucked lightly. She grinned. When her feet touched the ground he didn't release her, but held her, his hands lightly caressing her waist. "You please me, Philippa, very much."

"Thank you, Walter."

He frowned suddenly. "Your feet are bare. The gown you wear, it is all you have? That wretched bastard gave you nothing to wear?"

She lowered her head and shook her head. "It matters not," she said, her voice meek and accepting.

Walter cursed and ranted. To her horror, he turned on Edmund, and without warning, backhanded the boy. The blow sent Edmund sprawling onto his back on the hard ground, the breath knocked out of him.

"Foul spawn of the devil!"

"Nay, Walter, leave the boy be!" Philippa was trembling with rage, which she prayed her voice didn't give away. She quickly dropped to her knees beside Edmund. She felt his arms, his legs, pressed her hand against his chest. "Oh, God, Edmund, is there pain?"

The boy was white-faced, not with pain but with anger. "I'm all right. Get back to your precious cousin and show him your melting gratitude, Maypole."

Philippa gave him a long look. "Don't be a fool," she said very quietly. She got to her feet. Walter was standing there, absently rubbing his hands together.

"Come to the fire, Philippa. It will grow cool soon, and your rags will not protect you."

Her new gown wasn't a rag, she wanted to yell at him, but she held her peace. She gave Edmund another look and walked beside Walter. One of his men had spread a blanket on the ground, and she eased down, her muscles sore, her back aching from the long ride. "Let the boy warm himself as well," she said after some minutes had passed.

It was nearly dark before the two men returned with a pheasant and two rabbits. After they'd supped and the fire was burning low and orange, Philippa wrapped herself in a blanket, pulled Edmund down to the ground beside her, and waited. It took Walter not long to say, "I heard that de Fortenberry was holding you prisoner. I planned and schemed to get you free of him."

"Where did you hear that?"

Walter paused a moment, then said with a rush of dignity, "I am not without loyal servants, cousin. St. Erth's cistern keeper told me of your position." Walter paused a moment, then leaned over to take Philippa's hand in his. His was warm and dry. She said nothing, didn't move. "The man told me how his master had mistreated you, molesting you, holding you against your will in his bedchamber whilst he ravished you. He even told how Fortenberry had ripped your gown before all his people, then dragged you from the hall to rape you yet again. Then he told me how Alain, the steward, had wanted you killed and how he and another were to do it. He didn't realize that you, dearest heart, were mine own cousin. I killed him for you, Philippa. I slit his miserable throat even as the words gagged in his mouth. You need never fear him again."

The cistern keeper had deserved death, she would have killed him herself had she been able, but to hear of it done in so cold-blooded a fashion . . . And Walter believed she'd been abused, violated. It was, she supposed, a logical conclusion. "Does my father know?"

"You mean Lord Henry? Nay, not as yet."

"What else did he tell you?"

"That his master had stolen Lord Henry's wool and forced you to oversee the weaving and sewing, that he treated you as a servant and a whore. How was Alain found out?"

Philippa said this cautiously, not wanting Walter to realize that she'd discovered his treachery because she worried and fretted about St. Erth and its master. She said only, "He was a fool, and one of the master's men broke his miserable neck."

"Good," Walter said. "I just wish I could have done it for you, sweetling. Of course, I know why the steward feared you and wanted you dead. It was because you read and write and cipher and he knew you'd find him out. A pity he tried to kill you, for he was a good servant and bled St. Erth nearly dry of its wealth, and much of the knave's coin found its way to my coffers."

Philippa felt Edmund stir, felt fury in his small body, and she quickly laid a quieting hand on his shoulder. "Walter, will you return me to my father?"

"Not as yet, Philippa, not as yet. First I wish you to see Crandall, the keep I oversee. And you need clothes for your station, aye, soft ermine, mayhap scarlet for a tunic, and the softest linen for your shifts. I long to see you garbed as befits your position. Then we will speak of your father."

She frowned at him. What was going on here? Why was Walter acting loverlike? Her position? She was his cousin, that was all. Surely he didn't want her, since he believed she was no longer a maiden, since he believed Dienwald had kept her as his mistress. Had perchance her father gone to him? Promised him a dowry if he found her, thus promising her in marriage to her cousin? It seemed the only logical answer to Philippa. No man could possibly want her if he believed she lacked both a maidenhead and a dowry.

"Do we reach Crandall on the morrow?"

He nodded and yawned. He smiled upon her, seeing her weariness. "I will keep you safe, Philippa. You need have no more fear. I will make you . . . happy."

Philippa was terrified, but she nodded, her look as pleasingly sweet as she could muster it. *Happy!*

St. Erth Castle

"What say you, Silken? She what? That whoreson Walter killed both Ellis and Albe? *Both* of them? He took Edmund as well?"

"Aye, master. He took both the mistress and Master Edmund. We fetched Ellis' and Albe's bodies, and Father Cramdle buried them with God's sacred words."

Dienwald stood very still, weary from a long hard ride, his mind sluggish; he couldn't take it in. Two days had passed since Sir Walter de Grasse had taken his son and Philippa and killed Ellis and Albe. He himself had just ridden into St. Erth's inner bailey and learned what had happened from Silken. Dear God, what had Walter done to them? Had he taken them for ransom? Fear erased his fatigue.

Silken cleared his throat, his gnarled hand on Dienwald's arm. "Master, heed me. I have been filled with murderous spleen since my escape, but have wondered if what I first believed to be true was true or was the result of blind seeing."

"Make sense, Silken!"

"This Sir Walter greeted the mistress as if . . . as if she'd sent for him and he'd rescued her as she wished him to. As if he'd known she would be riding and he'd had but to wait for her to come in his direction. He was waving at her, smiling like a man filled with joy at the sight of her."

Dienwald stared blankly at the man, and his gut cramped viciously.

"Aye, she'd ridden out three days in a row, master, and that last day, only three men attended her and the young master."

"And was that her demand?"

"I know not," Silken said. "I know only that Ellis and Albe lie rotting in the earth."

The heavens at that moment opened and cold rain flooded down. Thunder rumbled and the sky darkened to night. Dienwald, his tired men at his heels, ran into the great hall. It was silent as a tomb. There were clumps of women standing about, but at the sight of him they became mute. Then Gorkel came to him, his hideous face working. With anger? With betrayal?

"Ale!" Dienwald bellowed. "Margot, quickly!"

He ignored Gorkel for the moment, his thought on his son, now a prisoner of Sir Walter de Grasse, his greatest enemy, his only avowed enemy. His blood ran cold. Would Walter run Edmund through with his sword simply because the boy was of his flesh and blood? Dienwald closed his eyes against the roiling pain of it, against the helplessness he felt. And Philippa . . . Had she betrayed him? Had she taken Edmund

riding with her on purpose so that Dienwald
wouldn't follow for fear his son would be killed?

He was tired, so tired that his mind went adrift
with frantic chafing, with uncertainty. Philippa
was gone . . . Edmund was gone, his only son
. . . two of his men were dead . . .

Gorkel drew nearer to speak, but Dienwald
said, "Nay, hold your peace, I would think."

It was Crooky who said in the face of his master's prohibition, "The mistress left her finery.
Surely if she'd wanted to be rescued by her loathsome cousin, if somehow she'd managed to send
him word, she would have taken the garments
sent her by Lady Kassia, nay, she would have
worn them to greet her savior."

"Mayhap, mayhap not."

"She knew you hate the man and that he hates
you."

" 'Tis true, curse the proud-minded wench."

"She would not endanger Master Edmund."

"Would she not, fool? Why not, I ask you.
Edmund calls her maypole and witch. She held
him by his ear and scrubbed him with soap. He
howled and scratched and cursed her. Surely she
can bear him no affection. Why not, I ask you
again."

"The mistress is a lady of steady nature. She
has not a sour heart, master, nor did she allow
herself to be vexed with Master Edmund. She
laughed at his sulky humors and teased him and
sewed him clothes, aye, and held him firm to
bathe him, as a mother would. She would never
seek to harm the boy."

"I don't understand women. Nor do you, so
pretend not that you possess some great shrewdness about them. But I do know their blood sings

with perversity. They become peevish and testy when they gain not what they want; they become treacherous when they believe a certain man to be the framer of their woes. They see only the ends they seek, and weigh not the means to achieve them. She could perceive Edmund as only a minor obstacle."

"You are the one who sees blindly, master."

"That is what Silken said. Oh, aye, I hear you. Get you gone, fool. Thank the heavens above that you did not sing your opinion to me. My head would have split open and my thoughts would have flowed into oblivion."

"I have known it to happen, master."

"Get out of my sight, fool!" Dienwald made a halfhearted effort to kick Crooky's ribs, but the fool neatly rolled out of reach.

"What will you do, master?"

"I will sleep and think, and think yet more, until the morrow. Then we will ride to Crandall to fetch my son and the wench."

"And if you find she deceived you?"

"I will beat her and tie her to my bed and berate her until she begs God's forgiveness and mine. And then . . ."

"And if you find she deceived you not?"

"I shall . . . Get out of my sight, fool!"

Windsor Castle

"Dienwald de Fortenberry," King Edward said, rubbing his jaw as he looked at his travel-stained chancellor. "I know of him, but he has never come to my court. Not that I have been much in evidence before I . . . But never mind that. I have been on England's shores for nearly eight months now and yet de Fortenberry disdains to pay his homage to me. He did not attend my coronation, did he?"

"Nay, he did not. But then again, sire, why should he? If all your nobles—the minor barons included—had attended your coronation, why then London would have burst itself like a tunic holding in a fat man."

The king waved that observation aside. "What of his reputation?"

"His reputation is that of knave, scoundrel, occasional rogue, and loyal friend."

"Graelam wishes an occasional rogue and a scoundrel to be the king's son-in-law?"

Robert Burnell, tired to his mud-encrusted boots, nodded. He'd returned from his travels but an hour before, and already the king in his endless energy wanted to wring him of all information. "Aye, sire. Lord Graelam wasn't certain that you knew Dienwald, and so he recited to me this man's shortcomings as well as his virtues. He claims Dienwald would never importune you for royal favors and that since he has no family, there are none to leech on your coffers. Lord Graelam and his lady call him friend, nay, they call him good friend. They say he would cease his outlaw ways were he the king's son-in-law."

"Or he would continue them, knowing I could not have my son-in-law's neck stretched by the hangman's noose!"

"Lord Graelam does not allow that a possibility, sire. I did question him closely. Dienwald de Fortenberry is a man of honor . . . and wickedness, but his wickedness flows from his humors, which flow from the wildness and independence of Cornwall itself."

"You turn from a shrewd chancellor into a honeyed poet, Robbie. It grieves me to see you babble, you a man of the church, a man of disciplined habits. De Fortenberry, hmmm. Graelam gave you not another name? You heard of no other man who would become me and my sweet Philippa?"

Burnell shook his head. "Shall I read you what I have writ as Lord Graelam spoke to me, sire?"

Edward shook his head, his thick golden hair swinging free about his shoulders. Plantagenet hair, Burnell thought, and wished he could have seen if Philippa was as gloriously endowed as her father.

"Tell me of my daughter," Edward said suddenly. "But be quick about it, Robbie. I must needs argue with some long-nosed Scots from Alexander's court, curse his impertinence and their barbaric tongue."

"I didn't see her," Burnell said quickly, then waited for the storm to rage over his head.

"Why?" Edward asked mildly.

"Lord Henry said she was ill with a bloody flux from her bowels, and thus I couldn't meet her."

"St. Gregory's teeth, will the girl live?"

"Lord Henry assures me the de Beauchamp physician worries not. The girl will live."

"I wish you had waited, Robbie, until you could have spoken with her."

Burnell merely nodded, but his soul was mournful. The king had abjured him to return as soon as he could. And he had obeyed his master, as he always did.

"Lord Henry showed me a miniature of the girl."

The king brightened as he took the small painting from Burnell's hand. He studied the stylized portrait, but saw beyond the white-faced expression of bland purity and the overly pointed chin to the sparkling Plantagenet eyes, eyes as blazing bright as a summer sky, eyes as blue as his own. As for her hair, it was nearly white, it was so blond, and her forehead was flawless, high and white with but thin eyebrows to intercede, but then again, an artist strove to please. He tried to remember the color of Constance's hair but couldn't bring it to mind. He couldn't recall that she'd had such flaxen white hair; no woman had hair that color. That much, he thought, was the artist's fancy. He placed the miniature in his tunic. "Let me think about this. I will speak to the queen. She will translate the artist's rendering, and her counsel rings true. I suppose if I agree, I must bring de Fortenberry here to Windsor to tell him of his good fortune." King Edward strode to the door, then turned back to say, "The damned Scots! Harangue me they will until my tongue swells in my mouth! You must needs rest, Robbie, 'twas a long journey for you, and wearying." The king turned again, his hand on the doorknob, then said absently over his shoulder, "Fetch your writing implements, Robbie. I must have you record faithfully their muling complaints. Then we shall discuss what is to be done with them."

Burnell sighed. He walked to a basin of cold water and liberally splashed his face. He was back in the royal harness, he thought, and smiled.

16

Crandall Keep

"You are beautiful, Philippa. The soft yellow gown becomes you."

"I thank you, Walter, for your gifts. The gowns and overtunics please me well." They were of the finest quality, and Philippa had wondered where her cousin had gotten them. Obviously from a woman who was short and had big breasts. Evidently she also had rather big feet for her height, for the soft leather slippers pinched Philippa's toes only slightly. Who and where was the woman? Surely she couldn't be pleased to have Philippa wearing her clothing.

"Crandall is a well-maintained keep, Walter, and since you are its castellan, it is to your credit alone. How many men-at-arms are there within the walls?"

"Twenty men, and they are finely trained. Lord Graelam does not stint on our protection, but of course 'tis I who have trained them and am responsible for their skills."

Philippa nodded, wishing there were only two, and those old and weak of limb. It didn't bode well for her and Edmund getting out or for Dienwald getting in. She hadn't spoken to any of the men, but she had spent a bit of time with several of the keep servants, and discovered that her cousin wasn't a particularly kindly master nor much beloved, but he did appear fair—when he wasn't brandishing his whip. "He's fast wi' t' whip," one of the servants, a bent old woman, had told her in a low voice. "Ye haf t' move fast when he's got blood in his eye and t' whip in his hand." Philippa had but stared at her. A whip! She remembered how several of the women had looked at her when they thought she wasn't paying heed, and they'd spoken behind their hands and looked worried, even frightened. Even now she could feel the female servants looking at her, judging her perhaps, and she wondered at it.

She said now to Walter as she accepted a hunk of bread from his hands, "These lovely garments, cousin—from whence did they come?"

" 'Tis not your concern, sweetling. I had them, and now they are yours. That is all you must needs know."

And Philippa could only wonder, and wonder yet more. He'd given her until yesterday to rest and be at her ease, and then he'd begun to woo her. Philippa couldn't be mistaken, particularly after enduring Ivo de Vescy's outpourings of affection. Walter was playing the besotted swain. Only he wasn't besotted; his words bespoke all the right sentiments, but his eyes remained cold and flat. At first Philippa couldn't credit it. There was no reason—no dowry, in short—for a man in Walter's position to be interested in marriage with her. And it was impossible that he could have fallen deliriously in love with her; he'd known her for but two days. No, her father was behind it; he had to be. But just how, Philippa couldn't imagine.

She toyed with the cabbage stuffed with hare and decided it was time to test the waters. "Walter, does my father know I am here?"

His eyes narrowed on her face, eyes that were always cold and flat when they looked at her. "Not as yet, Philippa. You care so much to return to Beauchamp?"

She shook her head, smiling at him, not chancing an argument because there was something in him that frightened her, something elusive, yet it was there, and she wanted to keep her distance from it.

Walter chewed thoughtfully on mashed chestnuts encrusted with boiled sugar, his favorite dish. Philippa wasn't what he'd expected. He saw flashes of contradiction in her, and although they surprised him, they didn't worry him unduly. Despite her hardy size, he could control her easily should the need arise. He would wed her by the end of the week. He had the time; he could afford to go gently with her, to bend her slowly to his will. Three days was enough time to bend the most rebellious woman to his will. He thought now that he could tell her some of the truth. Perhaps it would make her trust him all the more quickly, and it didn't really matter one way or the other to him.

"Your father was here, Philippa," he said, and watched her twist in her chair, her expression stunned. "He thought perhaps you had come to me when you escaped in the wool wagons, as you would have if that bastard hadn't captured you and taken you to St. Erth.

"At the time of Lord Henry's visit, I didn't know where you were. Lord Henry told me, Philippa, that he'd promised you to William de Bridgport in marriage. He was most adamant about it, even when I argued with him. I could not, nay, still cannot, imagine you wedded to that testy old lecher. But Lord Henry needs the coin de Bridgport will pay for you. You see, Philippa, as much as it hurts me to wound you, you must know the truth. Lord Henry holds his possessions more dear than he ever held you."

Philippa could only shake her head. So her father had come here. She'd shown surprise to Walter, guessing it was the correct response, but she'd already guessed her father's presence. Her insides felt cold and cramped. She wanted to scream that her father couldn't have told Walter that, he couldn't have, it wasn't true.

But it was true. Philippa had overheard him say it himself. It wasn't Walter's fault.

"You must still send a messenger to my father to tell him I am here. I would not wish you to be my father's enemy."

Walter started to shake his head, then thought better of it. He'd just been offered his best opportunity. "I think we still have some time, sweetling, before I do that. Three days, perhaps four." He saw her revulsion, her fear, and he moved swiftly to take advantage of it. He gently took her hand in his. There were calluses on the pads of her fingers, attesting to the labors Dienwald had forced her to, the mangy scoundrel. He felt her tense, but she didn't pull away. "Listen, Philippa," he said, his voice low and soft, "if you wed me, there is naught Lord Henry can do. You cannot be forced to wed de Bridgport. You will be safe as my wife, you will be secure. No one— not even the king himself—could take you from me."

There it was, Philippa thought, staring at her cousin. He wanted to marry her, but it made no sense. He believed her already ravished by Dienwald, so he couldn't expect a virgin's blood on the wedding sheets. More important, there was no coin forthcoming from her father. What was going on? She must continue her deceit until she discovered his plot. She kept her head modestly lowered and let her fingers rest against his.

"You offer me much, Walter, more than I deserve. You must allow me time to compose my thoughts. All this comes as a surprise, and my thoughts have gone awry." She raised her head and saw the frown of impatience in his eyes. She added quickly, "I am slow of reason, Walter, being but a woman, and your generosity, though a gift from God, leaves me tongue-tied, but just for a brief time. Until tomorrow, dear cousin— then I will speak to you of my feelings."

He gave her a grave nod and squeezed her fingers again before releasing her hand. Her tongue was smooth, her words gently flowing, respectful, filled with deference, but something bothered him. Perhaps it was that she hadn't asked of their close kinship, thus requiring special permission by the church. But she was but a woman and probably ignorant of such things. Aye, just a woman, but she could read and write and cipher. He didn't wish to tell her that he shared not one drop of her blood, that he knew her conceived of another man's seed, a seed most royal, but he wasn't at all certain of her reaction. No, he must hold his tongue. She was biddable, soft and comely, and she was endowed with beauty aplenty. She was too tall for his taste, but then again, there was Britta, hidden away now, but waiting for him, and he would continue with her when it pleased him to do so. Tonight, he thought, his loins tightening at the thought of her. He gave a small shudder. Were it not for Philippa, he would leave this instant and go to Britta. He saw that Philippa was looking about the hall, and said, "What troubles you, sweet cousin?"

"Naught, 'tis just that I see not the boy, Walter. Although I do not hold him dear, I have a responsibility for him, since he was with me when you rescued me. Have you yet sent a demand of ransom to Dienwald?"

Walter shook his head. He wouldn't send anything to anyone until he was her husband. Not even to his overlord, Graelam de Moreton. "The whelp keeps company with my stable lads. I do him a good service. 'Twill humble him to see how those beneath him live, and make him more stouthearted. He will learn what it is like to serve."

At least he wasn't locked away somewhere in the keep, but she worried that the villeins would abuse him. She said nothing, merely forced herself to eat another bite of the cabbage. It needed some of the wild thyme she'd just planted in her garden at St. Erth. *Her* garden. Philippa wanted to cry, odd in itself, but it was true: St. Erth had become home to her in a very short length of time and its master had become the man she wanted. But he didn't want her, had never lied about it, had even kept his manhood out of her body because he feared having to keep her, having to take her to wive because she was too wellborn to use at his whim.

She pushed Dienwald and his perversity from her mind. She had to escape Walter, and she had to take Edmund with her. She had not many more days before Walter pushed her into wedlock. She doubted not that he would bed her to force her hand. She was sleeping by herself in a tiny chamber off the great hall, a chamber, from the smell of it, that had held winter grain but days before her arrival. It was airless, but she didn't mind; the stuffiness kept her awake, and that allowed her to think. And she thought of St. Erth and its master and wondered if he were close even now. But she knew she couldn't simply wait for Dienwald to do something; she had to act to save herself and Edmund.

Walter kept her with him that evening, playing draughts, and when she won, forgetting that she was but a woman and thus inferior to male stratagems, he was sharp with her.

"You were lucky," he said, his voice edged with anger. "I allowed you too much time with your moves because of your sex. You deceived me, cousin, but . . ." He paused, and the light changed in his eyes. He shook his head, wagging a playful finger in her face. "Ah, Philippa, you won because of your sweet nature and your softness. You took me in with your gentle presence, your glorious eyes. You see me slain at your dainty feet. All my thoughts were perforce of you, my dearest. Would you sleep now, sweetling?"

He wasn't stupid, Philippa thought as she rose from her chair. He'd been furious because she'd beaten him, but quickly adjusted himself to a more favorable position in her eyes. He was still her gallant suitor. But for how much longer? She shuddered as she walked beside him to the small room. Before he left her, he grasped her upper arms and pulled her against him. "Beautiful cousin," he said, and kissed her ear because she jerked her head to one side. It was a mistake. She felt his fingers dig into her flesh, heard his breath sharpen with anger.

"Please, Walter," she said softly, "I wish . . ." Words failed her. She wanted to scream at him to remove his slimy person.

He drew a false conclusion. "Ah, 'tis because he abused you, because he forced you. I won't hurt you, cousin, never will I touch you amiss. I will always be your gentle master. You must trust me, and I will make you forget the knave's violence toward you." He leaned down and lightly touched his mouth to her forehead and released her arms. "Sleep well, my heart."

Philippa nodded, her head down, but she couldn't prevent the words that came spilling from her mouth. "Walter, you know me so little. You met me only as a child. Why do you wish to wed with me? You know I am no longer a maid. You know that my father will not dower me. Tell me, dear cousin, tell me why you so wish me as your wife."

She raised her head and knew that she'd again jumped with her feet; she hadn't thought. What if he turned on her, what if . . . . ? She waited, tense and still, hoping he would speak, yet fearful that he would simply rant at her and perhaps beat her with that whip of his.

Walter found himself at something of an impasse. Again he saw the contradiction in her. She was but a woman, full of softness and gentle smiles, and here she was questioning him, but, ah, so sweetly she questioned. He'd thought to slap her hard to show her that he wouldn't always tolerate inquiries from her, but now he thought better of it. That was doubtless how Dienwald had treated her. Aye, Dienwald had been violent and rough with her. Walter must prove to her that he was different. He would resort to more straightforward methods only if she pushed him to them.

"I have loved you since I first saw you five years ago, Philippa. I spoke to Lord Henry then, but he only shook his head and laughed and called me fool. I have corresponded with him over the years, but had almost admitted failure of my hopes when he came to me and admitted that you'd fled to escape the marriage with de Bridgport. I am a simple man, Philippa, with simple needs and only one desire that burns in my life, and that is you, to earn you for my wife."

"But I am used," she said, and looked at him straightly, wishing she could tell him his memory was faulty. He'd last seen her more than five years before. "He debauched me again and again. He used me unnaturally."

If only Dienwald had done a bit more debauching than he had, she thought now, watching Walter. He wasn't stupid, this cousin of hers, so when he leaned down and kissed her gently on the mouth, she wasn't overly surprised. Dis-

mayed, but not surprised. "It matters not to me,"
he said in a richly sincere voice. He turned and
left her, locking the door behind him.

"But you must needs lock me in," she said after
him.

There was but one candle to light the chamber.
She felt the shadows surround her, and they were
comforting. She made her way to the narrow bed,
stripped off her soft yellow overtunic and the
gown beneath. She stretched out on her back,
staring up into the darkness.

What, after all, could he have said to her? she
wondered now. But why did he wish to wed her?
Why? Sir Walter was a dangerous man, and she
recognized the threat in him. She saw the intensity in him, the will to drive himself, to drive others. The last thing that would be his main desire
was a woman, any woman.

She must go very carefully. She must give him
false security. She must hang around his neck
until he wished her to leave him alone. Then,
perhaps, she would find a way for her and
Edmund to escape Crandall. If they didn't escape,
she feared what would happen to them. She
would refuse to wed Walter and he would rape
her endlessly. She knew it. But *why?*

She dared not wait for Dienwald, for the way
things were progressing, he might well be too
late. But why, she wondered again and again, did
Walter want to wed her so badly?

Over and over she tortured her brain with possible motives Walter could harbor. Had her father
changed his mind and offered Walter money if he
found her and wedded her? Land? She shook her
head on that possibility. Her father never changed

his mind. Never. There were no answers, only more questions that made her head ache badly.

Near Crandall Keep

Dienwald scratched his chest. He was hot and dirty and disliked the fact. He hated the waiting but knew there was naught else to be done. He rose and began pacing the perimeter of his camp. They were withdrawn into a copse of thick maple trees, well-hidden from the narrow winding road that led to Crandall. His men were lolling about, bored and restless, arguing, tossing dice, recounting heroics and tales of their male prowess.

Where were the fool and Gorkel?

What of Philippa and Edmund? Worry gnawed at him, paralyzed his brain. What was the truth? Had Philippa betrayed him, or had she been caught as certainly as Ellis and Albe had been slain?

Only she could give him the answer. She or that whoreson peasant, Walter. Dienwald sat down and leaned against an oak tree older than life itself, and closed his eyes. What he wanted, damn her soft hide, was Philippa. He saw her sprawled in the mud, laughing, her eyes a vivid blue in her blackened face; then he saw her naked as he threw buckets of water on her and soaped her body with his hands. His loins were instantly heavy, his rod hard and hurting. He knew in that moment that he would have to return her to her father the moment he got his hands on her again. If he kept her with him, he would take her, and he wouldn't allow himself to do that. If he did, it would be all over for him.

He wouldn't allow himself to be caught. Allying himself to de Beauchamp—he couldn't bear the thought of it. Lord Henry was a pompous ass, arrogant and secure in his own privilege, in his immense power and dignity. No, Dienwald would remain free, unencumbered, answerable to no one other than himself, responsible for no one but himself and his son. If he needed wool, he'd steal it. He wished now he hadn't forgotten about the wine arriving from Kassia's father. He would have gladly planned the shipwreck and the theft of every cask. He would have laughed in Graelam's face, and taken a pounding if Graelam had pushed him on it. He wanted to be free.

He wondered what was happening at Crandall, and he fretted, bawled complaints to the heavens, and paced.

Crandall Keep

In Crandall's inner bailey, Crooky smiled and sang and capered madly about, drawing everyone's attention. He held Gorkel on a chain leash fastened about his huge neck with a leather band, and tugged at him, carping and scolding at him as though he were a bear to be alternately baited and cajoled. "Nod your ugly head to that fair wench yon, Gorkel!"

Gorkel eyed the fair wench, who was staring at him, fear and excitement lighting her eyes. He nodded to her and smiled wide, showing the vast space between his front teeth. He felt the fool tugging madly at his leash and growled fearsomely, making the females in the growing crowd

scream with fear and the men step back a pace.
The bells on his cap tinkled wildly.

The fool laughed and pranced around Gorkel,
kicking out but not quite touching him. "Fret not,
fair maids. 'Tis a brute, and ugly as the devil's
own kin, but he's a gentle monster and he'll do
as I bid him. Hark now, yon comely maid with
the soft smile, what wish you to have the creature
do?"

The girl, Glenda by name and pert by nature,
angled forward, preening in the center of all
attention, and sang out, "I wish him to dance. A
jig. And I want him to raise his monstrous legs
high."

Crooky hissed between his teeth, "Canst thou
jig for the maid, Gorkel?"

Gorkel never let his wide grin slip. His expression vacuous, his eyes blank, he began to hop
and jump. He ponderously raised one leg and
then the other and clambered about gracelessly.
Quickly Crooky began to sing and clap his hands
to a beat Gorkel didn't need. His eyes scanned
the crowd as he bellowed as loudly as he could:

All come to see the beastie prance
He'll cavort and jump, he'll do a wild dance
He's a heathen and a savage, ugly and black,
But withal he's merry, no matter his lack.

Crooky wanted to shout with relief when he
saw Edmund slip between two men and gape at
Gorkel. The boy was ragged and bruised and
filthy, but at the sight of him and Gorkel, he
looked happy as a young stoat, his eyes gleaming.
Thank St. Andrew that he was alive. Where was
the mistress? Was she imprisoned? Had Sir Walter

harmed her? Crooky's blood ran cold at the thought.

Crooky jingled Gorkel's chain, and he ceased his clumsy movements and stood quietly beside the fool, breathing hard and still grinning his frightening grin. He eyed Edmund and nodded, his eyes holding a warning. "Ah," yelled Crooky suddenly, "methinks I see another fair wench. A big fair wench with enough hair on her head to stuff a mattress! Come hither, fair maid, and let my gargoyle behold your beauty. He'll not touch you, but let him behold what God created after he made a monster."

Philippa's heart was pounding madly. She'd watched Gorkel do his dance, not at first recognizing him in his wildly colorful and patched garments, the fool's cap on his head and the mangy beard that covered his jaws. It had been Crooky's bellowing verses that had brought her, nearly running, to the inner bailey. Dienwald was here, close, thank God. And she saw Edmund, filthy but well-looking, and quite alive, thank God yet again. "I come," she called out, voice filled with humor. "Let the monster gawk at the fair wench."

She picked up her skirts and raced toward them. She saw Crooky's relieved smile stiffen and go flat. She didn't understand. She drew to a halt, thinking frantically. "I am here. I bid you good morrow, monster." She curtsied. "Behold me, a maid who frets and who wishes for the moon but sees naught but a melting sun that holds her in bondage and gives her to chaff endlessly."

Crooky beheld her closely, all the while Gorkel loped in a clumsy gait around her, stroking his big bearded jaw.

She was beautiful, Crooky thought, finely dressed as a maid should be, as a *beloved* maid should be. She was no prisoner, Sir Walter no warden. Had he rescued her at her wish? He thought through her words, elegant words that twisted and intertwined about themselves. Had she meant that she wanted to escape her cousin? Crooky knew the matter wasn't his to decide. Since his tenth year, when the tree had broken and fallen on him, he knew that he wouldn't survive unless it was by his wits. He learned that his memory was his strength. He now committed her every word to his memory.

"Well, lovely maid," he said after a moment, "God grant you no ingratitude or bitter wrongs. If you will seek the moon, I will tell you that like the sun, the moon must hide in its hour, then burst forth, when least expected, to glow fairly yet in stark truth upon the face that seeks it forth. The moon awaits, maid, ever close as its habit, waits till tide and time issue it out."

"What is this, cousin? A cripple and a beast to be held by its leash?"

Philippa smiled at Walter, beckoning him to her side. "Aye, Walter, a team that brings shrewd humor and light laughter to Crandall. The little crooked one here tells me of the moon and the sun and how each must await its turn, and the monster there, he bellows and dances for all your fair maids."

Walter cared not a whit for the two who stood facing him. "If they please you, dearest heart, then so let them frolic and rattle their tongues to rhymes that bring good cheer."

Crooky said loudly, "Fair and hardy maid, what wish you for Gorkel the Hideous to do?"

"Why, I believe I wish to write him a love poem, not rhymed, for I have not your talent, but one to tell of beauty and love that ravaged the heart. What say you, beast? Wish you to have a love poem from me?"

Gorkel scratched his armpit, and Crooky, yanking hard at his leash, yelled, "Will you, monster? Nod aye, beast!"

Gorkel nodded and bellowed, and the crowd cheered.

Philippa nodded. "I shall hie me to my paper and write the poem for the monster. Give the crowd more laughter, then."

"I don't understand you," Walter said, and he sounded impatient and fretful.

"I amuse myself, Walter, as the beast has amused me. It pleases you not?"

She gave him that sweet, utterly diffident look that made him feel more powerful than a Palatine prince. It was on the tip of his tongue to tell her to write an immense tome, but he changed his mind. He mustn't give in to her female whims each and every time. "It doesn't please me this time, sweetling. Fret not." And before he left her, he raised his hand and lightly touched her cheek. As she looked at him, her smile frozen in place, his fingers fell to her throat, then to her breast, and before all of his people, he caressed her with his fingertips. He laughed and strode away.

Near Crandall Keep

"Tell me, and be quick about it."

Crooky, silent for once, looked at his master, uncertain how to begin.

"Did you see Edmund? The wench?"

"Aye, they're both alive," Gorkel said as he pulled off his belled cap. "The young master was dirty, his clothes rags, but he looked healthy."

"And the mistress?"

"She was finely garbed," Crooky said, looking over Dienwald's right shoulder. "Very finely garbed, a beautifully plumed peacock, a princess."

Dienwald felt his gut cramp. She'd betrayed him, damn her, betrayed him and stolen his son.

"Tell me everything. Leave nothing out or I'll kick in your ribs."

And Crooky related everything that had occurred. He recited faithfully what Philippa had said to him and to Gorkel. He paused, then ended, "She is no prisoner, at least it appeared not so. Sir Walter kissed her in full view of his people, and his hand caressed her breast."

Dienwald saw red and his fists bunched in savage fury. What had he expected, anyway? The wench had fled him, and that was that. "Tell me again her words." After Crooky had once more recited them, he said, "What meant she about the moon—am I the moon, silent and hidden, then bursting and malignant in her face? Bah! It makes no sense, the wench was playing with you, turning your own rhymes back on you, mocking you."

"She asked Sir Walter if she could pen a love poem to Gorkel, but he refused her. Mayhap she would have written of her plight, master."

Dienwald cursed with specific relish, saying in disgust, "She fooled you yet again! She would have penned her request for me to keep away, else she'd see Edmund hurt!"

Gorkel said, "Nay, master."

"What know you of anything!"

"Why did she keep the boy with her?"

"For protection, fool, what else? She isn't stupid, after all, for all that she's a female." He shook his fist in disgust at both of them, ignored his other men who looked ready to speak their opinions, and strode away from them all, disappearing into the maze of maple trees.

"He is sorely tried," Galen said, shaking his head. "He knows not what to think."

"The mistress wants rescuing," said Crooky, "despite all the plumage and display."

"And the boy," Gorkel added. "I fear what that whoreson will do to the boy, for he sorely hates the father."

17

Crandall Keep

Late that night Philippa lay in her bed thinking
furiously, an occupation that hadn't paled since
Walter had brought her to Crandall. She thought
of her excitement, her hope, when she'd burst
into the inner bailey to see Gorkel cavorting about
like a mad buffoon and Crooky twirling Gorkel's
leash while singing at the top of his lungs. But
what good had any of it done? Her attempt to tell
Crooky of her plight, her plea to write Gorkel a
love poem, all had been dashed when Walter had
shown his possession of her in front of everyone
by kissing her and caressing her breast. Crooky
would tell Dienwald, of a certainty. But still they
would attempt a rescue, if not for her, then for
Edmund. But how? What could Dienwald do? He
couldn't very well storm Crandall Keep. Walter

278

would kill Edmund without blinking an eye. No, Dienwald would use guile and cunning; she doubted not that he would succeed, but still, the thought of him being hurt terrified her. She knew well enough that Walter would kill him if but given a chance.

She had to do something, and she had to do it early on the morrow. She fell asleep, and her dreams, oddly enough, were of her first riding lessons at six years old on a mare named Cottie, a gentle animal Bernice had urged over a fence two years later, breaking the mare's leg.

Philippa came awake suddenly, tears still in her mind for the mare. She hadn't really heard anything, it was just a feeling that something wasn't right and she must pay attention now and wake up fully or she wouldn't like what happened to her.

Slowly, very slowly, Philippa turned her head toward the door. Walter had locked it as usual when he'd left her earlier, yet a key was turning in the lock and the door was opening slowly but surely.

It had to be Walter. He'd tired of waiting. He'd come to ravish her and be done with it. He didn't play the besotted swain very well.

So be it, Philippa thought, her muscles flexing to make her ready. She didn't move, just thought of what she would do to him to protect herself. She would fight him, and at the very least she would hurt him badly. She still wore her shift, one of soft linen that came to her thighs and left her arms bare. She wished now she had on every article of clothing Walter had given her, to make his task of ravishing her all the more difficult. She listened and strained her eyes toward the door.

Walter wasn't making any noise. Why? That made no particular sense. He wouldn't care, would he? He wouldn't care if she screamed or yelled. His men would do naught to help her.

The door widened, making no sound, the hinges not even creaking. From the dim light in the passage without, Philippa could at last make out the outline of the person.

It wasn't Walter. It was a woman.

Philippa didn't act immediately, as her nature urged her to. No, she held herself perfectly still, waiting to see what the woman would do, waiting to see what the woman wanted. Perhaps she wanted to free her. But how had the woman gotten the key to her chamber?

From Walter, of course. Walter was far too careful, far too possessive a man to allow others to keep something as important as the key to her chamber. So the woman must know him very well, must know him intimately. . . . Philippa gathered herself together and waited.

The woman was creeping across the narrow chamber now, and Philippa saw that she held a knife in her raised hand. The woman had come to kill her, not free her.

Philippa's astonishment was replaced by rage, and she jumped to her feet, yelling at the top of her lungs, "What do you want? Get away from me! Help! *A moi*! Walter . . . *A moi*!"

The woman lunged at her, extending her arm, bringing the knife down toward her chest. Philippa grabbed the woman's wrist, wrenching her arm back, but the woman was stronger than her meager inches would indicate. She was panting, gasping, fury making her as strong as Philippa, and she said, her voice vicious, filled with hatred,

"You damnable slut! You devil's spawn! You'll not have him! Do you hear me? Nay, never! I'll kill you!" And she jerked away from Philippa, her breasts heaving, staring at Philippa with hatred. Philippa slowly backed away from the furious woman and that very sharp knife.

She held up her hand in supplication. "Who are you? I've done nothing to you. What are you talking about? You're mad, wanting to kill me for no reason!"

"No reason!" the woman hissed, the words so harsh that spittle flew out of her mouth. "You damnable trollop, Walter is mine, only mine, and he'll stay mine. You'll not get him. He'll not wed you, no matter what you bring him! He loves me, wants me more than all the filthy riches you would bring him!"

But I wouldn't bring him anything, Philippa started to say, just as the woman lunged again, bringing the knife down in a brutal arc, sure and fast, and Philippa whirled to the side, away from the maddened woman, but she wasn't fast enough and she felt the tip of the knife slice through the flesh of her upper arm. She felt the coldness of it, then a quick numbness.

"You won't escape me, whore!"

Philippa, knowing there was no choice now, jerked about and struck out, backhanding the woman, her palm flat, ringing hard against her cheek. The woman yelled in pain and rage but didn't falter. She flew toward Philippa, the knife extended to the fullest.

Philippa saw the knife coming into her heart, stabbing deep, killing her, before she'd known what it was to really live, to love and be loved, and she whispered, "Dienwald . . ."

She could hear the air hiss as the knife sliced through it, and she dashed frantically toward the open door and into the arms of Walter de Grasse.

"What in God's name goes on here?"

Walter was shaking Philippa hard until he saw the blood flowing from her upper arm. He paled in the dim light, not wanting to credit it. Then he stared at the woman, half-crouched, the bloody knife dangling in her hand, and he whispered, "Britta . . . oh, no, why?" He pushed Philippa away from him and was at the woman's side, lifting her up, pulling her against him.

"Britta?"

She shook her head, her breath coming in painful gasps, her huge breasts heaving.

"She tried to kill me," Philippa said, watching with benumbed fascination as he caressed the woman. "Who is she? Why does she want me dead?"

She watched, silent now, as pain crossed Walter's face and it whitened, and she understood at last that this was the woman whose garments she wore, this was the woman who was her cousin's mistress, a woman who, incredibly, loved her cousin, and who couldn't, perforce, abide her. Philippa's mind clogged and she could but stare silently as Walter held the woman even more tightly, clutching her against him, speaking softly, so softly that Philippa couldn't make out his words.

Without further hesitation Philippa picked up a small three-legged stool, held it high over her head, and brought it down with all her strength on Walter's head. The woman cried out as Walter slumped against her, bearing her to the floor with his weight.

"Don't yell, you stupid fool!" Philippa hissed at the woman. "Just stay where you are and hold your peace and your lover. I'm leaving you and him and this cursed keep forever. He's yours until the devil takes him." Before Britta could push her lover off her, Philippa had grabbed the knife from her hand and jerked the keys from the pocket in her tunic.

"Just be quiet, you silly bitch, if you want him here and me gone!"

Philippa grabbed her gown and pulled it over her head even as she dashed toward the door. She locked it, then froze on the spot. Just around the corner, not three feet from where she stood, she heard two men in argument.

"I'll tell ye, thass trouble! I heard them wenches yelling and t' master runs in."

"Leave t' master be an' get back to yer bed."

"Oh, aye, there's trouble and it's yer ears he'll slice off, that, or he'll take his whip to yer back."

"Ye go back and I'll look."

Philippa flattened herself against the cold stone wall. She heard the one man still grumbling as he shuffled away. As for the other man, in the next instant he came around the corner to see a wild-eyed female with a knife in her hand and blood running in rivulets down her arm. He had time only to suck in his breath before the knife handle slammed into his temple and he crashed to the floor.

Slowly Philippa got enough nerve to peer around the corner. She saw sleeping men and women spread over the floor in the hall, and snores rose to the blackened rafters above. She crept as quietly as she could, inching slowly along the wall toward the large oak doors. Slowly, ever so slowly, she moved, knowing at any second a man or woman could rise up and shriek at her and it would be all over and perhaps Walter would kill her if his mistress didn't do it first. A dog suddenly appeared from nowhere and sniffed at her bare feet.

She didn't move, her heart pounding, letting the dog tire of her scent, then move on, praying the animal wouldn't bark. Then, without warning, she felt a spurt of pain in her arm and looked at it. So much blood, and it was hers. She had to slow it or she would faint. She slipped outside into the inner bailey and looked heavenward. There was no moon this night, and the sky was overcast, with no stars, no light whatsoever. She flattened herself against the wooden railing and ripped off a goodly section of the lower part of the gown. She wrapped it around her arm, using her teeth to tie the knot tightly. She felt the pain, felt it deeply, but it didn't matter. She had to find Edmund and they had to escape this wretched keep. She couldn't allow the wound to slow her. She had to be strong.

Fortune turned, and Philippa found Edmund close to the stable door, atop a heap of hay, sleeping on his side, his legs drawn up to his chest, his face resting on his folded hands. Philippa knelt beside him. "Edmund, love, come wake up." She shook him gently, ready to slap her hand over his mouth if he awoke afraid and cried out.

But Edmund awoke quickly and completely and simply stared up at her. "Philippa?"

"Aye, I'm here, and now we must leave. We'll need horses, Edmund. What think you?"

"Is my father here to save us?"

Philippa shook her head. "No, 'tis just us, but we can do it. Now, about those horses."

Edmund scrambled to his feet, excitement and a goodly dose of fear churning in his belly, and he grinned up at her. Then he was thoughtful, and Philippa waited. "We need to croak the two stable lads. We need—"

Philippa raised the knife handle. "It works," she said.

Edmund's eyes glistened and Philippa wondered if all men were born with the battle cry of war in their blood, with the love of violence and battle bred into their bones. "Show me where they are and then I'll . . ." She paused, then added, "You get the horses, Edmund. Pick well, for they must carry us to your father. He awaits out there somewhere."

"He can't be far away," Edmund said. "But we will come to him and not have to lie like helpless babes for him to rescue us. There is a difficulty, though, Philippa. I can't get the horses for us."

She stared down at him and saw the chain and thick leather manacle clamped about his right ankle. Those miserable whoresons! She wanted to yell in rage, but she said calmly, "Who has the key to that thing?"

"One of the stable lads you're going to croak," he said, and gave her an impudent smile.

They were good together, Philippa thought with surprised pleasure a few minutes later. She'd quickly found the key and released Edmund. She hadn't even paused before coshing the two stable lads on the head. They'd probably given Edmund his bruises, the malignant little brutes, and tethered him like an animal. No, she had no regrets that the both of them would have vile head pains on the morrow.

Edmund had brought out Daisy and the destrier that belonged to Walter. Should she dare? she wondered, then tossed her head. She dared. Her arm was paining fiercely now, and they weren't yet out of Crandall. She couldn't succumb to the pain, not yet, not for a very long while.

Edmund held the reins of the two horses, staying back in the shadows whilst Philippa sauntered like a whore in full heat and in need of coin toward the one guard who stood in a near-stupor near Crandall's gates. Three other sentries were patrolling, but they were distant now. She'd watched them, counting.

"Ho! Who are . . . ? Why, 'tis Sir Walter's mistress! What want you? Wh—"

She poked out her breasts and threw her arms around the man. He gaped and gawked and quickly grabbed her buttocks in his big hands, dropping his sword to fill his hands with her, and Philippa whipped out the knife and, leaning back, slammed the handle down on his head. He looked at her in mournful surprise but didn't fall. "You shouldn't ought to a done that," he said, and brought his hands up to her throat. He squeezed, saying all the while, "Ye're a handful, wench, but I'll show ye not to play wi' me." He squeezed harder and harder, and Philippa saw the world blackening before her eyes as the knife dropped from her slack fingers.

Then, as if from afar, she heard a voice saying, "You're a bloody coward, hurting a female like that . . . you whoreson, stupid lout with a mother who slept with infidels . . ." The fingers left her throat and she sagged to her knees, clutching her throat, gulping in air. She looked up to see the man turning, as if in a dream, turning toward Edmund, but Edmund was astride Daisy, and he was higher than the guard and brought a thick metal spade down as hard as he could on the guard's head. Philippa watched the man stare up at Edmund and shake his head as if to clear it. Then he made a small sound in his throat and fell in a heap to the ground.

Philippa staggered to her feet, grabbing the knife. Her throat felt on fire, and she croaked out, "Excellent, Edmund. Now we must go, quickly. The sentries will be returning in but moments now."

She raced to the keep gates and jerked at the thick beam levered from side to side of the large gate. It was heavy and she was getting weaker by the moment. She cursed and heaved, and finally the beam began to ease slowly upward until finally she managed to bring it fully vertical. "Now," she whispered, and pushed the gate open.

Philippa quickly mounted, grunting with effort, for there was no saddle and her right arm was now nearly useless. Suddenly she felt Edmund heaving her up, and she landed facedown against the destrier's neck, panting with exertion and pain.

Then Edmund was astride Daisy again and she cried, "Away, Edmund!"

The destrier was huge and fast and mean, and he quickly ate distance from Crandall. They needed to be fast. Philippa could imagine that Walter was already after them, unless she'd hit him so very hard that he was still unconscious and unable to give orders. The destrier pulled away even further, quickly outstripping Daisy. Philippa tried to pull him back, but her one strong hand wasn't enough. The destrier was in control.

"Edmund!" She turned back, her hair flying madly in her face.

"Hold, Philippa. I'm coming!"

But it wasn't Edmund who stopped the great destrier. It was a man flying out of the darkness astride a huge stallion, his head bare, his face averted, all his attention on the frantically galloping horse.

Other men appeared, shouting out, and she heard Edmund yell, "Father! Father, quickly, help Philippa!"

And she felt the reins jerked from her hand and then the destrier lurched up on his hind legs, whinnying frantically, his front hooves flailing, and she hard Dienwald's voice, soothing, calming the frenzied animal.

Then it was over and Philippa was weaving on the horse's back, her gown torn and pulled to her thighs, and she smiled at the man who turned to face her.

"The horse was maddened because of my smell," Philippa said, just content to stare at his face.

"You make no sense, wench."

"The blood . . . the smell of blood," she said. "It maddens animals to smell a human's blood." She slumped forward against the animal's neck. Before she fell unconscious, his arms were around her, drawing her close, and she sighed deeply, content now to give it up.

The burning pain brought her back. She tried to jerk away from it, cursing it in her mind, begging the pain to release her for just a few minutes longer, just a moment longer, but it was there and it was worse and she moaned and opened her eyes.

"Hold still."

She focused on Dienwald, leaning over her. He wasn't looking at her face, but looking grimly down at her arm. "Hello," she said. "I'm glad to see you. We knew you had to be close."

"Hold still and keep your tongue behind your teeth."

But she couldn't. There was too much to be said, too much to be explained. "Am I going to die?"

"Of course you're not going to die, you heedless wench!"

"Is Edmund all right?"

"Yes. Now, be quiet, you try me sorely with your babble."

"I fainted, I suppose, and I've never before fainted in my whole life. I was scared until I saw you, and then it was all right."

"Be still. Why is your voice so rough?"

"The guard tried to strangle me after I struck him with the knife handle. His head was powerfully hard, but Edmund told him his mother bedded infidels to get his attention from me, and then hit him with a spade and he finally fell. We got away from him, we got away from all of them. I counted the minutes, you know, and the other sentries were elsewhere. You knew we were at Crandall. Silken reached you safely."

"Aye, be quiet now."

"I prayed he would reach you. It was our only hope. Walter was stupid—he gave Silken time to outrun his men. I knew he would reach you, knew you would come."

"Wench, shut your irritating mouth."

"Walter's mistress tried to kill me, you know. Isn't that strange? And she kept screaming that she didn't care that I would bring him riches, 'twas she who would have him. I gave him to her freely, and I told her that. I also wanted to tell her that there were no riches, nay, not even a single coin. And he came in when I yelled my head off and he saw the blood on my arm, yet he went to her and held her and her name was Britta and it was her clothes he'd given me to wear. I struck him with a stool and he went down like a stone. It was a wonderful sound and he pinned the woman beneath him. I got her knife and the keys and locked them in."

"Philippa, you're weak from loss of blood and you're babbling. Now, be still."

"She has huge breasts," Philippa said, then closed her eyes at a particularly sharp jab in her arm. "Walter had given me her clothes and they were much too short for me and much too loose in the chest. Her breasts are of a mighty size. Gorkel and Crooky were wondrous funny." Dienwald drew in a deep breath at that moment and poured ale over the wound. Philippa lurched up, crying out softly, then fell back unconscious.

Dienwald stilled for a moment, then quickly placed his palm over her heart. The beat was slow and steady. He bound up her arm, then turned to see Northbert's legs. He didn't rise, just looked up at his man and said, "She's unconscious again, but the wound is clean, and if there is no poisoning, she will be all right."

Northbert nodded. "Master Edmund is overexcited, master, his tongue rattling about. Gorkel told him to go to sleep, but he can't close his mouth."

"She was the same."

Crooky hobbled up then. "The mistress wasn't a betrayer wi' her cousin, master."

"I suppose she wasn't, yet it strikes an odd chord."

"Aye, it does," said Gorkel in his low, terrifying rumble. "The boy refuses to sleep until he sees that the mistress is all right."

Dienwald looked surprised at that. "He *what*? Oh, the devil! Nothing is aright here, nothing! I let the two of them out of my sight for the space of a week, and everything goes topsy turvy. Bring Edmund and let him see the wench, I don't care."

Gorkel and Crooky exchanged looks, and Northbert merely shrugged.

Edmund knelt next to Philippa, and said softly as he stared down at her face, "She was very angry when she saw the manacle around my ankle. Her face turned all red and her hands shook. She'll be all right, truly?"

"Aye, she's too hardy to let this bring her down," Dienwald said. "You must sleep now, Edmund. At dawn we'll ride."

"You're not worried that the whoreson will come upon us tonight?"

His father grinned. "He'd never find us in this dark. There's not even a single star to guide him."

It was the middle of the night when Philippa awoke again. Her arm hurt, but not too badly. She was surrounded by darkness, which she'd become accustomed to in the small chamber at Crandall, but this was different. Sweet air touched her face and filled her nostrils, and she could hear the rustle of tree leaves in the gentle night breezes, and the deep breathing of a man. She opened her eyes and saw Dienwald stretched out next to her, his hand holding her wrist. He was snoring lightly.

She smiled and said, "Edmund and I escaped. Are you not pleased?"

His hand on her wrist tightened. Dienwald was dreaming of an explicitly passionate scene in which Philippa was naked, lying pliant in his arms, her hand was stroking down his belly, closing around his swelled rod and she was kissing him, her tongue thrust deep in his mouth and she was moaning as she kissed him and her fingers were caressing him and . . .

"Are you not pleased?"

He opened his eyes, startled, disoriented, and saw her beside him, not naked as he'd believed, but lying on her back, a blanket pulled to her waist. She was speaking of pleasure, but a pleasure different from the one of his dream. Philippa was really there with him, and he hurt with need for her, hurt with the urgency of it, and the reality melded into his dream and he didn't question it or the dark night or her beside him on the floor of a copse of maple trees.

"Philippa . . ." he said, his voice low as he rolled over until he half-covered her with his body.

"I'm so glad to see you, Dienwald," she said, and raised her hand to stroke his hair, to touch his jaw, his mouth. His tongue stroked over her finger, and she shivered. "Dienwald," she said again, and parted her lips, staring up at him as if he were the only man on earth, and she was so close to him, but a breath away from his mouth, and he couldn't bear it and leaned down and kissed her, gently at first, then more deeply because it was what she wanted and what he'd done in his dream, yet now the dream was real and his tongue was stroking her mouth. He didn't think, didn't consider his actions. He wanted her, wanted her more than he ever had.

He'd been terrified that Walter would kill her, and at the same time he'd hated her because she had perhaps betrayed him. He couldn't have borne that, but now she was here and it was all that mattered, and she was his at last.

The night was still and she was here, beneath him, and she wanted him. Her dream was his, and they were together. He stroked her face with urgent fingers, easing himself over her. He felt her part her legs, and he lay between them, hard against her woman's flesh, and she was making soft noises deep in her throat and her arm was around his neck, pulling him down, bringing him closer and closer.

She'd been hurt. God, she'd been hurt. Dienwald, his senses restored for an instant, drew back, saying, "Philippa, your arm, I can't hurt you. If your arm . . ."

She simply smiled up at him and said, "I will hurt more if you leave me. Don't leave me now. Please, Dienwald, debauch me. I've wanted you to for so long."

He laughed, he couldn't help himself. Then his laugh turned to pain as she said, "I didn't want to die, because if I did I would never have you, never know what it was like to have you come inside me."

He groaned now, her words burning deep, and he was drawn back into the intense feelings that were conquering all of him. But he realized even in his delirious state that she was a maid and he didn't want to hurt her more than was necessary. He saw his sex tearing through her maidenhead, and he moaned with the excitement of it, the triumph in claiming her, of possessing her, finally. He eased himself up until he grasped the hem of her gown, and he pulled it up and felt her naked flesh beneath his hand. Until he reached her upper thighs. She wore a shift, and it stymied him for a moment, for in his dream she'd been freely naked and open for him. He worked in growing impatience until she was naked to the waist, then came over her again, wanting only to feel her body against his, but he couldn't, for he was still dressed. He cursed, softly and foully, and came up onto his knees.

She was watching him, her eyes large and vivid as he clumsily jerked off his tunic, his cross garters, his hose, and then he was finally naked and she found him beautiful.

He was covering her again, his male flesh against her, and she was kissing him wildly, her tongue probing until she found his. He held her head between his hands and kissed her face, his words fast and frantic between kisses, telling her of his need for her, how he loved the feel of her, how he was happy she was still a maid and he would be easy with her, and how he wanted to come into her and meld into her flesh and stay there even as he spilled his seed in her.

She watched his face as he looked down at her, and she felt his fingers parting her flesh, then his sex pressing against her.

He threw back his head, his eyes closed. "Don't move," he said, and his voice trembled, for he

was coming very slowly into her, and despite his
instruction, she was lifting her hips for him,
wanting to feel all of him, now, this very moment.
He came deeper and she whimpered as he
stretched her and it hurt, but it was what she
wanted because he was what she wanted. She
could feel him so exquisitely, the hard smoothness of his member easing so gently, just a bit of
himself at a time, pressing into her.

In the next instant he felt her maidenhead
stretched against his sex. "Philippa," he said, his
eyes on her face, "look at me!" He had wanted
to be gentle at this moment, but he found he
could not. He thrust deep. She cried out at the
wrenching tear inside her. He fell over her, his
mouth covering hers, and he soothed her with his
tongue, even as he held himself still and deep
inside her, saying again and again, "No more
pain, my sweet Philippa, no more. Hold me and
feel me and let me lie deep inside you. 'Tis where
I belong."

Then slowly he began to move, his breath soft
and warm against her mouth. "Nay, love, accept
me now and hold me tight inside you. Aye, that's
it, lift your hips for me and bring me deeper . . .
ah, Philippa . . . no, don't move, I can't bear it,
and—"

She watched his beloved face distort with the
pain of his need, and he was heaving, delving
deep, his breath sharp and raw and her body
burned as he thrust again and again, his hands
drawing her up to meet him. She couldn't help
herself and cried out but he couldn't stop,
wouldn't stop. He threw back his head and she
felt his release, felt the wetness of his seed as he
emptied himself deep inside her body.

He was limp and weak, torpid in mind and drained in body, and he came over her and she welcomed his weight and he lay with his head beside hers and he was still deep within her.

He said, his voice echoing from the dream, "I'm sorry, Philippa. I wanted you badly. Hold still and the pain will fade."

Philippa regained her breath and her equilibrium. He was still inside her but there was only stinging now, not the tearing pain of before. It was strange, this lovemaking. She'd wanted him, very much, felt desire for him that overcame the pain in her arm, that, actually, made the pain as nothing, and she'd been whipped about with wild, urgent feelings, wanting to touch him, feel him, urge him to come to her, but the incredible feelings had fallen away when he'd come into her and ridden her so wildly. She'd been left stunned, bewildered, and hurting.

Not hurting now, she thought, smiling as she lightly stroked her hand over his naked back. His flesh was smooth and warm and she felt the muscle beneath and she said quietly, "I love you." And she said it again and again and she knew he didn't hear her for he slept soundly. She felt his member sliding out of her, and the wet of his seed and her wetness as well, she supposed.

She kissed his ear and settled herself beneath his weight. Soon she slept.

It was nearly dawn when Dienwald opened his eyes and came abruptly and horrifyingly awake. He was lying naked, half covering Philippa and he was cold and shivering in the night air, and his rod was swelled again and pressing against her. He cursed his randy sex, and gently and slowly eased himself off her, his mind still not accepting what had happened, for the dream was still strong in his mind, and it had become more, that vivid dream. He shook his head. What he'd done he'd done and it hadn't been a dream, but it had been in the dark of the night and he'd cleanly lost his wits. The early morning in the copse was an eerie grey and thick white mist hovered overhead. He could see her clearly though, her beautiful body bare from the waist down and her parted legs, parted for him when he pushed them apart to come over her, and there was her virgin's blood mixed with his man's seed smeared on her thighs, and he closed his eyes and swallowed.

He'd done himself in. He cursed softly, then smiled, feeling yet again the tightness of her, her urging hand, how she'd lifted her hips to him, how he'd driven into the depths of her, touching her womb. He wouldn't worry about it now. He looked down at her and wanted her again, powerfully, but he saw her wounded arm and the wound he himself had inflicted inside her. He would wait. He pulled a blanket over both of them and pulled Philippa into his arms. He would think soon, once the sun was shining down on his face, warming his brain. He would think of something, he would save himself and somehow he would at the same time protect her from dishonor. How, he didn't know, but an idea would come to him; it was still very early, his brain foggy with sleep. He slept again, holding her close, breathing in the scent that was uniquely hers, but only for a few moments.

He was brought painfully and abruptly to his senses by his son's outraged voice.

"Father!"

Dienwald opened an eye and saw Edmund standing over him and Philippa, his hands on his narrow hips, his eyes wide and disapproving.

"Father, you've taken Philippa."

"Well, perhaps . . . but perhaps not. Perhaps I am simply holding her, for she is hurt, Edmund—aye, very hurt and cold in the night and—"

"I won't allow you to dishonor her. You are holding her too close to just warm her, Father. And just look at her! She's hurt and yet she's asleep and she's smiling!"

Dienwald, startled, looked at the still-sleeping Philippa. She *was* smiling, her lips slightly parted, and the sight made him feel wonderful.

"Edmund, get you gone for a time. I am weary and the wench here will awaken soon and I must think—"

"You will wed her, Father. Aye, you must wed her. You've no choice now."

Dienwald looked with horror at his son and forgot that his men were all within hearing distance. "Wed her! God grant me death instead. 'Tis possible that she betrayed me, Edmund, aye, that she told her cousin to save her from me and took you as a hostage."

Edmund just shook his head and looked disgusted.

"You don't even *like* her! She bullies you and corrects your every word. You call her witch and maypole and you stick out your tongue at her and—"

"Father," Edmund said with great patience, "Philippa is a lady and you have taken her virtue. You must wed her."

Dienwald cursed and looked back down at Philippa. She was awake and staring up at him, and there where tears in her eyes.

18

"Why are you crying? For God's sake, cease your wailing this minute! I hate a woman's tears. Stop it, wench. Do you hear me?"

"She's not making a sound," Edmund said, peering down at Philippa.

Dienwald made no reply to this, simply kept staring down at Philippa.

Her tears didn't immediately do his bidding, and he turned further onto his side and leaned over her, his nose nearly touching hers. "Why are you crying? Did you hear Edmund and me, curse the boy's interfering habits?"

She shook her head and wiped her eyes with the back of her hand.

"Then why are you crying?"

"My arm hurts."

"Oh." Dienwald frowned at that. Her revelation was believable, yet somehow he felt insulted, and perversely he said, "Well, did you hear what my son demanded we do?"

Philippa lay on her back, looking up at the man she'd willingly given her innocence to during the night. His jaw was dark with whiskers, his hair tousled, and his naked chest made her heartbeat quicken. He looked beautiful and harried and vastly annoyed. He also looked worried, hopefully about her, which pleased her.

She smiled up at him then and raised her hand to touch his cheek. He froze, then jerked back.

"You're besotted," he said, his voice low, "and you've no reason to be. For God's sake, wench, I took your maidenhead but three hours ago, and you're smiling at me as if I'd just conferred the world and all its riches upon you. You got no pleasure from our coupling, I hurt you, and . . . ah, Edmund, you are still here, then?"

"Will you marry Philippa?"

"You know but one song, and its words more tedious than Crooky's. By St. Anne's knees, boy, the wench couldn't wish to wed with me, for—"

That was such an obvious falsehood that Philippa laughed. "Good morrow, Master Edmund," she said, facing him for the first time, her tears dry now.

The boy grinned down at her. "We must soon be on our way back to St. Erth," he said. "Northbert sent me to awaken you. *Both* of you," he added, meaning dripping from his voice. "Philippa, does your arm pain you sorely?"

She shook her head. "Nay, 'tis bearable, and thus so am I, unlike your father here, who must bring himself to the morning with foul words."

Dienwald said nothing, merely stared off into

the thick maple trees. "Go, Edmund, and strive to keep your opinions beneath your tongue."

Edmund frowned down at his father. "We are close to Crandall. Sir Walter could come this very very soon. Shouldn't we—"

Dienwald's expression changed suddenly. It was austere now, cold and forbidding, his eyes narrowed, and he said very softly, in such a deadly voice that Philippa could but stare at him, "I want the whoreson to come out from the safety of his walls. I owe him much, and the time has come to repay the debt. I've men carefully watching the road from Crandall. Aye, I want the bastard to come after you and Philippa, and 'tis I who will greet him."

Edmund grinned suddenly. "But Philippa struck him hard, Father. Perhaps he still lies in a heap."

Dienwald's expression lost its cruelty and he shook his head. "We'll see, but I doubt it. We will leave soon, Edmund, for St. Erth. The wench here needs to rest, and I can't very well wed her here in a forest. Search out Northbert and tell him that if Sir Walter hasn't shown his weedy hide within the next hour, we'll ride to St. Erth."

Edmund, swaggering with importance, took his leave. Dienwald stared after him, shaking his head, seemingly all thoughts of Sir Walter and his hatred of the man gone from his mind, for he said to Philippa, "I can't believe that my own son, a boy of good sense, would yell at me, and carp and bellow."

Philippa said nothing to that, and Dienwald, in a spate of ill-humor, flung back the blanket and jumped to his feet. For a moment it appeared he didn't realize he was naked, but not for a single instant was Philippa unaware of it. She stared at

him in the gray light of dawn and was pleased
with what she saw, very pleased. Before, she'd
admired him, but this morning, now that she
understood how men used their bodies to attach
themselves to women . . . well, now she had a
different way of looking at him, a softer way, a
more intimate way.

He scratched his belly, stretched, looked down
at himself and saw her blood on his member. He
cursed then turned to frown down at her. "Open
your legs."

"What?"

"Open your legs," he repeated, then dropped
down to his knees beside her. He pulled the blanket to her ankles, then without asking her again,
pulled her shift to her waist and pried her thighs
open. His seed and her maiden's blood were on
her inner thighs. Soft flesh, he saw, very soft,
and he wanted to touch her, to ease his finger
into her, feel her tighten about him. Curse her
and curse his member that hadn't the good sense
to remain calm and uninterested. Well, soon he
wouldn't have to deny himself. He could have
her again and again, as much as he wished and
whenever he wished it until his member stayed
quiet in exhaustion and his heartbeat stayed slow
and steady. He drew in his breath and said, "By
St. Peter's toes, there's no choice for me now.
We'll wed upon our return to St. Erth."

His duty done, at least in his mind, Dienwald
rose again and began pulling on his clothes. He
frowned and said, turning to look down at her,
"Don't fret about the blood, Philippa, 'tis your
virgin's blood and all females are so afflicted their
first time with a man. It won't happen again.
Now, pull down your clothes else I'll be tempted

to think you wish my rod between your thighs again.''

She thought it was a fine idea but jerked down her clothes. She could hear Dienwald's men moving about in the woods, very close to them. ''Wouldn't you at least like me to tell you what happened at Crandall?''

''You did,'' he said shortly. ''I couldn't force you to keep your woman's mouth closed last night and you babbled until you finally slept. I learned everything, finally. Are you very sore?''

''But I didn't get to sleep all that long, did I? You didn't wish me to! Sore where?''

He shook his head, giving her a sour look. ''Nay, it wasn't all my doing. You wanted me and you had me, curse my man's weaknesses. Your soreness is in your female brain and between your female thighs. You are small, Philippa, at least inside you are.'' He paused a moment, frowning toward her. ''I was dreaming about you, wench, empty-headed dreams they were, and then there you were, beside me, and holding out your arm to me, making me want to debauch you, and making all those whimpering noises in your throat—'' He stopped, finished fastening his cross-garters and took his leave of her, not looking back.

''Well,'' Philippa said aloud as she slowly got to her feet. ''He will wed me and he won't mind, once 'tis done.'' She could still see the appalled look on his face when his nine-year-old son had demanded that he marry her. Truth to tell, that had surprised her as much as it had Edmund's father.

The boy didn't seem to mind that she would be his stepmother. So be it. She clutched her arm and gently began to massage it. The pain was a steady throbbing now, but she could bear it. She looked down at herself and shook her head. Her single garment, the once beautiful yellow gown, was now fatally wrinkled, and rents parted its folds, material torn off to make a bandage for her wounded arm. But she had become so used to wearing rough clothing, even rags, that she gave it not much thought.

She was standing there wondering where she could go to relieve herself when Crooky appeared.

"God gi' you grace, mistress," he said, and sketched her a bow. "I hear from the lad that you will soon wed the master. 'Tis well done. I knew his lust for you would plant his body in his brain, and so it has. Strange that it struck him so swiftly and here in a wild forest, and with you hurt and all, but perhaps that's what pushed him, fear for you and seeing you hurt.

"But the master holds strong feelings for you and missed you, though he cursed you more than he sang of your bountiful beauty. Father Cramdle will speak wondrous fine words for your ceremony." He paused and added, "Don't mind the master. He'll get used to the idea once it seeps into that thick head of his. Aye, 'twill be fine." Crooky gave her another bow and took himself off. She was left standing alone in the small clearing.

Crooky's words had sounded to her like an attempt to convince himself. Well, perhaps Crooky's master didn't love her, but at the moment Philippa didn't care. But she did feel discomfort that she was nothing more than a waif, not a coin in her possession, her only clothes those Lady Kassia had sent her. Once she and Dienwald were wedded, she would dispatch a message to her father. He would have no choice but to send her possessions to her. She knew little about marriage contracts, dowries, and the like, but it seemed that there had been none for her, so how could her father complain? He'd had no intention of forming a grand alliance with another house of Beauchamp's stature. She no longer brooded on his reasons. Indeed, she no longer cared. Beauchamp seemed a lifetime ago, and surely that was another girl who'd had servants attending her every whim and clothes to suit her every mood. That girl had had a mother who didn't like her and a sister who carped constantly at her. Both the pleasant and the unpleasant were gone, forever.

St. Erth. She liked the sound of it on her tongue, the feel of it in her blood. St. Erth would be her home and Dienwald would be her husband. Her father could bellow until all Beauchamp trembled and his nose turned purple, but it wouldn't matter. Sir Walter had told her that her father had needed coin. She didn't believe it for a moment. However, she didn't know what to believe, so she left off all thought about it and consoled herself with the fact that even that repellent toad de Bridgport wouldn't want a bride who'd been bedded by another man. She smiled and sang a tuneless song as she prepared to return to her home with the man who would be her husband.

Her smile remained bright even when she faced all Dienwald's men, for they knew now that she would be the lady of St. Erth and there would be no more vile cursing from the master because he wanted to bed the maid. Now that he had, he would do what was right. She smiled until she was riding in front of Dienwald. She didn't turn to face him, not because she didn't want to but because his destrier, Philbo, took exception whenever she moved, cavorting and prancing, sending shafts of pain up her arm. The miles passed slowly and her arm throbbed.

"You cry again and I'll kick you off my horse. God's teeth, wench, you have me now. What more do you wish?"

"I'm not crying," she said, and stuffed her fist into her mouth.

"Then what are you doing? A new mime for Crooky's benefit? I suppose you'll tell me your arm pains you again?"

"Aye, it hurts. Your horse likes not my weight."

He snorted and stared over her shoulder between Philbo's twitching ears. "It's true you're a hardy wench and an armful. Still, Philbo hasn't bitten you—aye, methinks even he approves you for the mistress—so cease your plaints. You wanted me and now you've got me. I suppose your woman's ears beg to hear rhyming verses to the beauty of your eyes? That's why you're crying."

She shook her head.

" 'Tis too late to woo you, wench. You'll be a wife before you can congratulate yourself on your tactics, and then 'tis I who will show you that I am master at St. Erth and your master as well. I will do just as I please with you, and there will be none to gainsay me."

"You've always done precisely as you wished with me."

That was true, but Dienwald said nothing. His ill humor mounted and he sang out his own grievances. "Aye, I will wed you, and with naught to your name or your body save the clothes that Lady Kassia sent you. Your damnable father will likely come to St. Erth and demand my manhood for the insult to the de Beauchamps, since I am not of his importance or yours. You'll cry and carp and wail, and he'll lay siege, and soon—"

"Be quiet!"

Dienwald was so startled that he shut his mouth. Then he grinned at the back of her head. He fought against raising his hand to smooth down her wildly curling hair, and merely waited to see if she would continue. She did, and in a very loud voice, right in his face as she whirled about.

"I never cried, never, until I met you, you wretched knave! You are naught but an arrogant cockscomb!"

"Aye," he said mildly, and tightened his arms about her to keep her steady, "but you want to bed the cockscomb, so you cannot continue to carp so shrewishly.

"Should you prefer to be my mistress rather than my wife? Would you prefer being my chattel and my slave and my drudge?"

She jerked back against the circle of his arms and slammed her fist into his belly. Philbo snorted and reared on his hind legs. Dienwald grabbed Philippa, pulling her hard against him. He was laughing so hard that he nearly fell sideways, bringing her with him. He felt Northbert pushing against him, righting him once again.

"Take care, master," Northbert said. "The mistress isn't well. You don't wish her wound to open."

"God's bones, I know that. But the wound isn't in her arm, 'tis in her brain." He leaned against her temple and whispered, "Aye, and between those soft thighs of yours, deep inside, where I'll come to you again tonight. Think about that, wench."

She lowered her head, not in defeat at his words, but because she wanted to strike him again, but both of them would probably crash to the ground if she did so.

Dienwald said nothing more. He enjoyed baiting her, he admitted to himself. For the first time in his adult male life, he enjoyed talking, fighting, arguing—all those things—with a woman. Well, it was a good thing, since he would be bound to her until he shucked off his mortal coil.

He looked sideways at Northbert and saw that his man was frowning at him. Curse his interference! He said curtly, "No sign of de Grasse?"

Northbert shook his head.

Dienwald cursed. "You've got the men in a line behind us? At intervals, and hidden?" At his man's nod, Dienwald looked fit to spit. "The man's a coward." He cursed again. "I've wanted him for a long time now."

"Why?"

"Ah, you deign to speak to me again, wench?"

"Why?"

"I got a letter supposedly written to me by Kassia, but 'twas from him. He captured me when I went to see her, and I ended up in Wolffeton's dungeons. Kassia saved me, but not before the bastard had broken several of my ribs and killed three of my men. I owe him much. More than enough, since he took my son. Soon now I will repay him."

"And he took me."

"Aye, and you, wench."

So Kassia—perfect *small* Kassia—had saved him. Hadn't she other things to do? Like saving her own husband every once in a while? Curse the woman, she was a thorn in her side, nay, a veritable bush of thorns.

Well, there were those who'd wanted her as well, and she said now, "Why did Walter want to marry me?"

"Are you certain that he did?"

"Unlike you," Philippa said, her voice as bitter as the coarse green goat grass that grew beside the road, "he was most desirous of it. Indeed, he would have ravished me to ensure it, had I not escaped from him when I did. But it makes no sense to me."

"The man's mad."

Her elbow trembled, wanting to fling itself back into his belly. Finally she could bear it no longer and allowed her elbow to have its way.

He said nothing, merely grunted; then he closed his arms more tightly around her, higher now, his forearms resting under her breasts. He raised them a bit until they were pushing up her breasts, very high.

"Stop it, your men will see!"

"Then bait me not, wench."

She chewed thoughtfully on her lower lip, then said suddenly, "When the woman came to kill me, she screamed at me, something about how he—Walter—didn't want me, really, but the riches I would bring him. What could she have meant? My father must have visited Walter and promised him coin if he found me. I can think of no other reason."

"I don't know. We will find out soon enough. Your family must be told, once it is over."

"Then my father will come and cut off your manhood."

"Don't sound so vicious. 'Tis my manhood that endears me to you." To her surprise and to Dienwald's own astonishment, he leaned forward and kissed her ear. "I will give you pleasure, Philippa. And not only my manhood. The pain last night was necessary—'twas your rite of passage into womanhood, 'tis said."

"Who says?"

"Women. Who else?"

"Some arrogant male."

"Acquit me, wench. I want only to give you pleasure and to teach you how to pleasure me."

"I didn't give you pleasure last night?"

He grinned at the hurt tone of her voice. "A bit, I suppose. Aye, a bit. At least you were willing enough."

He felt her stiffen, and very slowly he eased his hand upward to cup her right breast. He caressed her, his fingers circling her nipple until he could feel the slamming of her heartbeat beneath his palm. "Shall I call a halt and tell my men that my bride wishes to have me here and now? Would you like that, wench? Shall I slip my hand inside your gown to touch your warm flesh and feel your nipple tighten against my palm?"

Her breathing was ragged, her breasts heaving. She wanted to feel his hands caressing her body. She wanted his mouth too, and his manhood, and so, without thinking, she said on a soft sigh as she leaned back against his chest, "Aye, if you will, Dienwald, 'twould please me very much, I think."

He forgot all his baiting, forgot everything save his desire for her, his seemingly endless need for her. The more she yielded to him, the more he seemed to want her. It was disconcerting and it was vastly annoying and it was so enjoyable his brain reeled.

He very gently eased his hand into her gown and cupped her breast. He could feel her breathing hitch beneath his palm. He saw her lips part, and her eyes never left his face. He knew it was ridiculous, what he was doing. Any of his men could come upon the mat any time. Northbert could draw alongside to tell him something . . . his son . . . St. Peter's toenails!

He pulled his hand out of her gown and slapped the wool back over her. "There'll be time for this later," he said, and turned her away from him. "Watch the trees and the hawthorns and the yew bushes. Colors are coming out now. Life is renewing." His words stopped abruptly, for he suddenly realized that he'd spilled his seed deep inside her but hours before—a new life could have already begun. An image flashed in his mind: a girl child with wildly curling hair streaked with many shades of brown and ash colors, tall and hardy, filled with laughter, her eyes a vivid summer blue.

He growled into Philippa's ear, "I suppose you'll give me more children than I can feed."

She just turned and gave him a beautiful smile.

Windsor Castle

King Edward nodded decisively. "Aye, Robbie, you must needs go and inform de Fortenberry of

his immense good fortune. The fellow probably
has gaps in his castle walls, he's so poor. His sire
had not a coin to bless himself with either. Aye,
I'll have St. Erth repaired. I don't want my sweet
daughter in any danger, so mayhap I'll have more
men sent."

Robert Burnell said, "But I thought you didn't
wish to acquire a son-in-law who would drain
your coffers, sire."

"Nay, not drain them, but we're speaking of
my daughter, Robbie, the product of my youth,
the outpouring of my young man's . . ." The king
grinned. "He has but a young son? All Plantagenet ladies love children. She will take to the
boy, doubtless, so we need have no worries there.
After you've gotten de Fortenberry's consent and
endured all his endless thanks and listened to all
his outpourings of gratitude, have Lord Henry
bring our sweet daughter here to Windsor. My
queen insists that my daughter be wedded here.
Philippa's nuptials will take place in a fortnight,
no longer, mind you, Robbie."

The king moved away from his chancellor, flexing his shoulders as he paced. "Aye, you must
go now, for there is much else to be done.
God's teeth, so much else. It never ceases. Aye,
we'll soon finish this business, and it will end
happily."

Robert Burnell, accompanied by twenty of the
king's finest soldiers, left the following morning
for Cornwall.

Not two days later, the king was sitting with
Accursi, plotting ways of wringing funds from his
nobles' coffers for all the castles he wanted to
build in Wales. Accursi, the son of a famous Ital-
ian jurist, was saying in his high voice, "Sire, 'tis

naught to worry you. Simply tell the nobles to open their hearts and thus their coffers to you. Your need is greater than theirs. 'Tis *their* need you seek to meet! They are your subjects and 'tis to your will they must bow."

Edward looked sour. He stroked his jaw. Accursi would never understand the English nobleman despite all his years in service with him. He thought them weak and despicable, sheep to be told firmly to shed their very wool. Edward was on the point of saying something that would likely send Accursi into a sulk when he heard a throat clear loudly, and looked up.

"Sire, forgive me for disturbing you," his chamberlain, Aleric, said quickly, "but Roland de Tournay has come and he awaits your majesty's pleasure. You gave orders that you wished to see him immediately."

"De Tournay!" Edward laughed aloud, rising quickly. A respite from Accursi. "Send him hence. I wish to see that handsome face of his."

Roland de Tournay paused a moment on the threshold of the king's chamber, taking it all in, as was his wont, and Edward knew he was assessing the occupants, specifically Accursi. Edward saw the very brief flash of contempt in Roland's eyes, an instinctual Englishman's reaction to any foreigner.

Edward said, grinning widely, "Come bow before me, de Tournay, you evil infidel. So our gracious Lord saw fit to save you to return to serve me again, eh?"

Roland strolled into the chamber as if he were its master, but it didn't offend Edward. It was de Tournay's way. It did, however, offend Accursi, who said in his high, accented voice, "See you to your manners, sirrah!"

"Who is this heathen, sire? I can't recall his face or his irritating manners. You haven't told the fellow of my importance?"

Edward shook his head. "Accursi, hold your peace. De Tournay is my man, doubt you not, and I'll not have him abused, save by me. 'Tis about time we see you in England, Roland."

"That is what I heard said of you, sire, you who wandered the world for two years before claiming your crown."

"Impudent dog. Come and sit with me, and we will drink to our days in Acre and Jerusalem and your nights spent wallowing in the Moslims' gifts. I hear Barbars gave you six women to start your own harem."

It was some two hours later when the king said to the man who'd done him great and loyal service in the Holy Land, "Why did you not come to my coronation October last? Eleanor spoke of your desertion."

Roland de Tournay merely smiled and drank more of the king's fine Brittany wine. "I doubt not the beautiful and gracious queen spoke of me," he said. "But, sire, I was naught but a captive in a deep prison, held by that sweetest of men, the Duke of Brabant. He, in short, demanded ransom for my poor body. My brother paid it, afraid not to, for he knew that you would hear of it if he didn't." Roland grinned wickedly. "Actually, I think it was his fair wife, lusty Blanche, who forced him to ransom me."

It took Edward only another hour before he slapped his knee and shouted, "You shall marry my daughter! Aye, the perfect solution!"

"Your daughter!" Roland repeated, staring blankly at the king. "A royal princess? You have drunk too much of this fine wine, sire."

The king just shook his head and told de Tournay about Philippa de Beauchamp. ". . . so you see, Roland, Robbie is on his way, as we speak, to de Fortenberry. I would rather it be you. You're a known scoundrel and de Fortenberry is an unknown one. What say you?"

"De Fortenberry, eh? He's a tough rascal, sire, a rogue, and worthy withal. I know naught ill of him as a man. But he's wily and likes not to bow to anyone, even his king. Why did you select him?"

" 'Twas Graelam de Moreton who suggested him. He's a force in Cornwall, a savage place still. I need good men, strong men, men I can trust. As a son-in-law I could trust his arm to wield sword for me. But you too could settle there, Roland. I would deed you property and a fine castle. What say you?"

"Will you make me a duke, sire?"

"Impudent cock! An earl you'll be, and nothing more."

Roland fell silent. It felt strange to be back in his own land, sitting with his king, discussing marriage to a royal bastard. He wanted no wife, truth be told, yet the truth hesitated on his tongue. Doubtless the king would regret his hastiness. The flagon of wine lay nearly empty between them. Roland would wait until the morrow.

" 'Twould enrage your brother, I vow," the king mused. "Himself the Earl of Blackheath, and to have his troublesome young brother be made an earl also and the king's son-in-law? Aye, 'twould make him livid."

That it would, Roland thought. But he didn't particularly like to rub his brother's nose in dung, so he slowly shook his head.

" 'Tis a generous offer, sire, and one that must be considered conscientiously and in absence of your good drink."

"So be it, Roland. Tell me of your harem," King Edward said, "before my beautiful Eleanor comes to pluck us away."

19

St. Erth Castle

On the last day of April, under the flowering apple trees in the St. Erth orchard, Father Cramdle performed a marriage ceremony crowned with enough ritual to please even the Archbishop of Canterbury himself. The sweet scent of the apple blossoms, musk roses, and violets filled the air, the bride looked more beautiful than the yellow-and-purple-patterned butterflies that hovered over the scores of trestle tables laden with food and ale, and the bridegroom and master of St. Erth looked like he wanted to frown himself into the ground. Father Cramdle ignored the bridegroom. The ceremony was right and proper. All the people of St. Erth were happy. The master was doing his duty by the maid.

The soon-to-be-mistress of St. Erth looked as

excited as any other girl at her own wedding, Old
Agnes thought as she watched Philippa de Beauchamp become Philippa de Fortenberry, the master's helpmeet and steward and keeper of the
castle. Aye, she was lovely in her soft pink gown
with a dark pink overtunic—both garments among
those sent to her by Lady Kassia de Moreton, a
fact that had seemed, for some unknown reason,
to annoy the mistress.

She wore her richly curling hair long and thick
down her back, with flowers twined together into
a crown on her brow. She was a maiden bride,
and if anyone thought differently, he was wise
enough to keep silent.

The master looked a magnificent animal as well,
clothed in the new bright blue tunic the mistress
had sewn for him, his long lean body straight and
tall. But he also looked uncommonly severe and
forbidding, something Old Agnes didn't understand but hadn't the courage to ask about. As for
the young master, he was grinning like a fatuous
little puppy after a big meal.

Since they were wedded here at St. Erth, no
dowry or bridal gifts involved, Dienwald spared
himself and his bride the ceremonial stripping.
He knew his bride was very nicely formed and
he knew that she thought well of his body as
well. He chewed his thumbnail and wished Father
Cramdle would finish with his array of Latin,
words spoken so slowly that Dienwald didn't
know where one word began and another left off.
Nor did he understand any of the words, so it
really didn't matter.

Neither did Philippa. She just wanted it over
with. She wanted to turn and smile at her new
husband and watch him smile back at her. They'd

returned the evening before, and to Philippa's surprise and chagrin, Dienwald hadn't come near his own bedchamber. She'd slept alone, wondering at his sudden bout of nobility—if, indeed, it were a case of nobility.

Perhaps, she thought, as Father Cramdle droned on, he'd not found her particularly to his liking that first time. Perhaps he didn't . . .

The ceremony was over, and there was suddenly loud, nearly riotous cheering from all the people of St. Erth. Gorkel had set Crooky on his massive shoulders and the fool was leading the people in shouts and yells and howls of glee.

" 'Tis done."

Philippa, her brilliant smile in place, turned to her new husband, but she didn't get a smile in return. He was staring beyond her at nothing in particular as far as she could tell.

"Aye," she said with great satisfaction, "you are now my husband. What is it? Is something the matter? Something offends you?"

"All my people," Dienwald said, still staring about him, "are shouting their heads off. And it is because they believe you to be good for their well-being. They make me feel I've been a rotten tyrant in my treatment of them."

"Mayhap," she said with a grin, "they believe I'll temper you rottenness and make you as sweet and ripe as summer strawberries. As for me, husband, I shall try to be good for our people. Mayhap they also believe I'll be good for their master. I had much food prepared. Indeed, everyone wished to help. Look at the tables, I vow they are creaking with the weight of it. There are hare and pork and herring and beef and even some young lamb—"

"Aye, I know." He struck his fingers through his hair. "Edmund," he bellowed. "Come hither!"

The boy was still grinning even as he came to a halt in front of his father and announced with glee, "You are wedded to the maypole."

Philippa laughed and cuffed his shoulder. "You weedy little spallkin! Come, give me a kiss."

Edmund came up to his tiptoes and hugged her, then raised his face, his lips pursed. She kissed him soundly. "Can you call me something a bit more pleasing, Edmund?"

Edmund struck a thoughtful pose. Crooky came up then and Edmund said, "A name, Crooky, I must have a comely name for my father's wife."

"Ah, a name." Crooky slewed a look at his master. "Mayhap Morgan? Or Mary?"

"Shut your teeth!" Dienwald bellowed, and cuffed Crooky, sending the fool tumbling head over arse to the ground in a well-performed roll.

"I think," Edmund said slowly, "that I wish to think about it. Is that all right?"

"That is just fine. Now, husband, would you like to partake of your wedding feast?"

There was enough feasting and consumption of ale to keep the people of St. Erth sick for a week. And that, Philippa thought, smiling, was probably the reason they'd cheered her so vigorously— enough food and drink and dancing to make the most sullen villein smile. Even the blacksmith, a man of morose habits, was laughing, his mouth stuffed with stewed hare and cabbage. Everyone was frolicking.

All but the master.

He danced with her; he picked at the roasted hare and pork Philippa served on his trencher, but he didn't try to pull her away to kiss her or fondle her on his lap. And that, she knew, wasn't at all like Dienwald. His hand should have been on her knee, moving upward, or caressing her breast, a wicked gleam in his eyes. She wished she had the courage to stroke her hand up his leg, but she didn't.

When the time came, Philippa allowed Old Agnes and the other women to see her to the master's bedchamber. Margot combed her hair and the women took off her clothes and placed her in Dienwald's big bed. Then, with much giggling and advice that Philippa found interesting but quite unnecessary, they left.

"Aye," Old Agnes called back, "we'll send up the master soon, if he isn't too sodden to move!"

Margot laughed and shouted, "We'll tell him stories to stiffen his rod! Right now 'tis too full of ale to do more than flop about!"

Now that, Philippa thought, was an interesting image to picture.

The night was dark, and but one candle flickered in the bedchamber. Philippa waited naked under the thin cover, for it was warm this night, her wedding night. Her arm was still bound in a soft wool bandage, but it scarce bothered her. She wanted her husband to come to her, she wanted him to touch her with his hands, with his mouth, and she wanted his rod to come inside her and fill her. She wanted desperately to hold him to her as he moved inside her. She loved him and she wanted to give him everything that she was, everything that she had, which, admittedly, were only her love and her goodwill for him, his son, and his castle.

Time passed and the candle gutted. She fell

asleep finally, huddled onto her side, her hands beneath her cheek.

The door crashed open and Philippa came instantly awake and lurched upright. Her new husband was standing in the open doorway holding a candle in his right hand. He was scowling toward her, and she saw that he wasn't happy.

He stepped into the chamber and kicked the door shut with his heel, then strode across the chamber and came to a halt beside the bed. He looked down at her. She pulled the blanket over her breast to her chin.

"Good," he said.

"Good what?"

"You're naked, wench—at least you had better be under that flimsy cover. The women were giggling enough about your fair and willing body, ready for me. Now that I've enslaved myself and all I own for you, now that you've gotten everything you wanted, I think I will take advantage of the one benefit you bring me."

He was pulling off his clothes as he spoke. Philippa stared at him, realizing that he was drunk. He wasn't sodden, but he was drunk.

She just looked at him. She wasn't afraid of him, but still she said, "Will you hurt me, Dienwald?"

That brought him upright. He was naked, standing with his arms at his sides, his legs slightly spread, and he was staring down at her. "Hurt you, wench?"

"I am not a wench, I'm your wife, I'm Philippa de Fortenberry, and—"

"Aye, I know it well . . . too well. Come, lie down and shut your woman's mouth and open your legs. I wish to take you, and if there is much more talk, I doubt I'll be able. Nay, I'll not hurt you if you obey me."

She didn't move for a very long time. Finally she said slowly, "You said you would give me pleasure."

He frowned. He had said that, it was true, but that was before he'd drunk so much ale he felt he'd float away with the Penthlow River. He felt ill-used, but he supposed it wasn't her fault, not really. No matter how he railed and brawled, he had taken her, and all because of that cursed dream of her he'd been having. That and the fact that he'd wanted her for longer than he could remember.

And so he said in a voice that was fast becoming sober, "I'll try, by all the saints' sweet voices, I'll try to bring you pleasure."

She smiled at that, all the while looking at him. He was tall and lean and hard, and so beautiful she wanted to cry. Her body was taut with excitement and soft with a need she knew lay buried within her, a need he would nurture into being. " 'Twill be fine, then, my husband."

She lay on her back and lifted her arms to him.

"Why must you yield to me so sweetly?" he asked as he lay down and pulled the blanket to her waist. He came over her naked breasts, and the feel of her so soft and giving beneath him made him shiver. "Ah, Philippa," he said, and kissed her. It was a gentle kiss until he felt her respond to him, and then he lightly probed with his tongue until she parted her lips and he slipped his tongue in her mouth. He felt her start of surprise and said into her mouth, "Touch your tongue to mine."

She did, shyly, as if she were afraid of what

would happen. Then she gasped with the wonder of it and threw her arms—both of them—around his back. He laughed at that, both amazed and pleased to his male soul at her yielding reaction. He taught her how to kiss and how to enjoy all the small movements he made with his tongue. He rubbed his chest over her breasts, and her response was beyond what he'd expected. She was panting and arching up against him, her hands fluttering over him.

"The feel of you," Philippa said, rubbing herself against his hairy chest. "I love the feel of you," and he felt her trying to open her legs for him. He fitted himself there, his sex against her belly, then raised himself and said, "Touch me, Philippa. I can't bear it anymore. Touch me."

She reached between their bodies and instantly clasped her fingers about him. "Oh," she said, and her fingers grew still. "I hadn't thought . . . 'tis wondrous how you feel . . . your strength." And she began to caress him, to stroke him, to learn him, and then she closed both hands about him and fondled him, and soon he couldn't bear it. He pulled back up onto his knees between her widespread thighs and looked down at her. Her sleek long legs were beautifully shaped and white and soft, and he wanted them around his flanks and wanted to come inside her, and he said only, "Now, Philippa, now."

There was in her expression only sweetness and anticipation, and it seeped slowly through his brain that he had become infinitely more sober than when he entered the room.

"Pleasure," he repeated slowly as he paused before guiding himself into her. "Pleasure." He stopped, drew a deep shuddering breath, and frowned down at her. "You're my wife." He eased down then between her legs, and his lips were on her stomach, his hands stroking her, his tongue wet and hot against her flesh. He was moving lower and lower, and Philippa, so surprised that she hadn't the chance to be shocked by what he was doing, yelled when his mouth closed over her.

He raised his head, staring at her in consternation. "Pleasure," he said. " 'Tis for your pleasure."

"Oh."

"Be quiet, wench. This is good."

And so it was, but it was also more, much more. When his mouth took her this time, she lurched upward but didn't yell. She felt the sensation of his mouth into the very depths of her, sensations she'd never before even guessed could exist. She whimpered, her fist in her mouth. His hands slipped beneath her buttocks, and he lifted her, his tongue wild on her and inside her, delving and probing, and she cried out, unable to keep still any longer. And it went on and on, gaining in urgency until she gave herself to it.

Dienwald felt the stiffening of her legs, the convulsions that tightened her muscles, and in those moments his mind was as clear as a cloudless summer day, and he saw her, really saw her, and felt her even as she stared at him, her eyes wide and wild, filled with surprise and passion, and she cried out and arched upward, giving herself to him fully. It was a woman's pleasure swamping her, and he was giving it to her and felt himself sharing it, deeply, and it dazed him. He wanted to shy away from it, to escape it, but he couldn't because he was held firm and close, a part of her, even though he had never known it could be so. Nothing had prepared him for this joining. When she quieted, he raced back, taut and wild and fierce, lifted her hips even higher— but again he looked down at her, and slowed himself. He came into her very slowly, for she was small. It was almost too much for him. She was wet from the pleasure he'd brought her, and the feel of her, the feel of himself inside her, made him shudder and moan until he couldn't bear it and he drove into her, coming over her then, even as he felt her womb. And he exploded then and groaned loudly, heaving into her as his seed filled her.

He didn't want to think, didn't want to feel anymore. It was all too new and too urgent. His head was spinning and he felt ripped apart, for she would see his soul and know that she'd taken him, all of him, and so he escaped her and slept.

Philippa stared at her husband's face beside hers on the pillow. He was breathing slowly and deeply, his fingers splayed over her breast, one muscled leg covering hers. She raised her hand and stroked his hair. He'd promised pleasure, but this had exceeded pleasure. Pleasure was a new gown whose color suited one perfectly. What he'd made her feel . . . It could make one mad, it *was* madness. And she wanted it every day of her life.

Light streamed onto Philippa's face and she opened her eyes and smiled even before she saw her husband's face. Dienwald was on his side, balanced over her, and he was looking very serious and intent. He appeared to be playing with her hair.

"What are you doing?"

"Counting the different shades in your hair. Here is a strand as dark a brown as my own, and next to it is one so pale I can scarce see it against my arm."

"My father once frowned at me and told me my hair wasn't golden."

"He's right. It isn't. It's far more interesting. Here's a strand that's an ash color. So far, I've counted ten different colors. Why did your father want you to have golden hair?"

"I don't know. I just remember that he was shaking his head about it. I was hurt, but then he didn't say anything more. Indeed, he seemed to forget about it."

He went on as if she hadn't spoken, "And the hair covering your mound—"

Instinctively Philippa closed her legs, and he laughed. "Nay, you're my wife now. I'll look my fill and you'll not gainsay me." He laid his open palm over her, cupping her. "You feel warm beneath my hand."

He closed his eyes as he spoke, and Philippa felt a surge of something much stronger than mere warmth beneath his palm. It was desire, and it felt powerful and compelling. Unconsciously she lifted her hips against his hand.

He opened his eyes and looked into hers. "I thought you'd be a greedy wench," he said, a good deal of male satisfaction in his voice, and leaned down to kiss her. She felt his long finger glide over her, slip between her thighs, and enter her slowly. She gasped, and he took the sound into his mouth and kissed her more deeply. Then his tongue moved into her mouth just as his finger was moving into the depths of her and she lurched up, crying out, so overwhelmed by the feelings his actions brought that she was helpless against them. He pressed her down. "Hush," he said. "Lie quietly and enjoy what I'm doing to you."

"It's too much," she said, and began kissing him urgently, frantically, his chin, his nose, his mouth. He laughed into her mouth but it turned quickly into a groan as her tongue touched his.

In a sudden move he rolled onto his back and brought her over him. He arranged her over him, saying, "Sit up, wife, come astride me." He lifted her, his hands around her waist. "Guide me into you."

Philippa was eager and more than willing, and she brought him into her and felt him slowly ease her down over him. She stared at him, not moving.

He smiled painfully and moved his hands upward to cup her breasts. "Move," he managed to say. "Move as you wish to."

She was uncertain and tentative at first, then realized that she could make him insane with lust, moving quickly, then slowing until he thought he would die from sensations of it. She watched his face and quickly learned how far she could push him before drawing back. Then she drew back her head and thrust her breasts forward, her hands splayed on his chest and when his fingers found her, she yelled and jerked, beyond herself, seeking her climax and when it overwhelmed her it overwhelmed him as well.

"It's too much," she whispered a few moments later. She lay with her cheek on his shoulder, her legs stretched over him, his member still inside her.

Dienwald couldn't have said anything if the Saracens had been attacking St. Erth at that moment.

He was barren of wit. He heard Philippa's breath even into sleep. He'd worn her to a bone and he was pleased. He discounted his own feelings of utter contentment. He cupped her hips in his hands. Aye, his wife was a bountiful wench, her flesh soft and firm, and perchance 'twas a fine thing to have her here, at St. Erth, in his bed, for a very long time.

Windsor Castle
May 1275

"Well, what say you, Roland? Do you wish to wed with my daughter? My sweet Philippa?"

Roland chewed slowly on the honey bread. He didn't want to anger his king by saying frankly that the last thing he wanted in his life was a wife to hang around his neck.

The king frowned. "My man Cedric told me of two wenches who visited your chamber last night. I told him to keep his rattling tongue in his mouth."

"Two wenches," Roland repeated, his eyes widening in surprise. "Nay, sire, 'twas three, but I was too fatigued to do much with the third one. I let her assist."

The king stared at Roland de Tournay, his face darkening. Then he burst into laughter. "You make me a flap-eared ass, Roland. Aye, I will tell Cedric he miscounted your wenches. 'Twill serve the beetle-headed clod right. Now, what will you? Have you decided?"

Roland decided to postpone the inevitable anger that would take the king when he knew himself thwarted. "Why do I not travel to see this daughter, sire? Mayhap she will look at my churl's ugly face and shriek in despair."

"Aye, 'tis possible," the king said, stroking his chin as was his habit. "Very well, Roland, go to Cornwall and give the sweet maid your countenance and tell her to behold it with shrewdness. Tell her you are my trusted man. Nay, tell Lord Henry that."

Roland nodded. He didn't mind going to Cornwall. He needed to see Graelam de Moreton. He also trusted that something would happen to save him the fate of being wedded. He was lucky; his luck would hold without his having to insult the king or his bastard daughter. He doubted not that being a Plantagenet, she was beautiful. Edward sired only beautiful daughters, as had his father before him. But whenever Roland envisioned a beautiful face, it was Joan of Tenesby he saw, and he knew it would remain so until the day he died—the beautiful face of treachery that mirrored his folly.

St. Erth Castle

"Aye, 'tis besotted she is, and it's good." Old Agnes spat out a cherry seed, continuing to Gorkel, who was plaiting strips of leather into a whip, "I doubt t' mistress will be able to walk if t' master doesn't let her out of his bed."

Gorkel blushed and missed his rhythm with the plaiting.

Old Agnes brayed with laughter and wagged a gnarled finger at him. "Oh, aye, a beast like you turning red as a cherry pip! Aye, 'tis a wondrous thing to see. Look not sour, Gorkel, 'tis no pain t' master gives the mistress. Aye, 'tis she who plunders his manhood, I'll vow, and wrings him dry and limp."

She cackled until Gorkel, furious at himself, threw the half-plaited whip aside and strode to the well to drink. And there was the master himself, drinking from the well in the inner bailey.

Gorkel watched him straighten, then stretch profoundly. There was a smile on the master's face, a look of vanity perhaps, but in a man of the master's position, Gorkel forgave it.

"Aye, t' master has t' look of a man wrung out of all his seed," Old Agnes chortled close to Gorkel's ear, coming to a halt behind him.

Dienwald heard the old woman laughing and wondered at the jest. The sun was bright overhead, the air warm, and it was nearing midmorning. He became aware of all his people around him, looking at him from the corners of their eyes, smirking—one fellow, a shepherd, was slapping his hands over his heart and sighing loudly. Dienwald decided to sigh too. Then he saw Philippa in his mind's eye stretched on her back, her white thighs parted, her arms flung over her head. He felt a bolt of lust so great it made him reel. It vexed him to realize this effect she had on him, just thinking of her lying in his bed, naked and soft and warm. He cursed, turned on his heel, and rushed back up the solar stairs.

He heard laughter from behind him, but didn't slow. When he flung open the bedchamber door, it was to see his wife standing in the copper tub, naked.

Philippa, startled, brought the linen cloth over her breasts and covered her woman's mound with her hand. Her husband stood in the middle of the room and stared at her.

"You're too plentiful for such a small square of cloth, wench."

When she just stood there returning his stare, Dienwald strode to her, pulled the cloth from her fingers, leaned down, and took her nipple in his mouth. At her gasp, he straightened again and washed the cloth over her tautened nipple. "I think of you and my manhood is cock-sore for your attention. Now, stand still and I will finish your bath for you." He began to whistle as if he hadn't a care, bending over now, the cloth gliding down her belly and between her legs. "Wider, wench, part your legs for me." She opened her legs, her hands on his shoulders to balance herself. She threw her head back when she felt the cloth pressing against her, then his hands, slick with soap, stroking her buttocks. His whistling stopped. He was breathing heavily, and suddenly he was cupping water in his hands and pouring it over her, rinsing away the soap.

"Dienwald," she said, her fists pounding on his shoulders, "you make me frantic."

He looked at her. "Aye, wench? Is that true? This?" And his middle finger slipped inside her.

She looked at his mouth and he felt his blood churn and his member harden. She kissed him, moving against him, shuddering when his finger eased out of her, then plunged in deeply again.

"You're mine," he said into her mouth, and she moaned, kissing him frantically, biting him, her fingers digging into his back. His finger left her and he shoved his clothes aside, freeing his member. He looked at her and said, "I want you to come to me now. Clasp your legs around my flanks."

She stared at him, not understanding, but he just shook his head and lifted her. Her legs went around him and then she felt his fingers on her, stroking and caressing her and parting her, and her breath caught sharply in her throat as he slid upward into her.

She gasped and wrapped her legs more tightly around him. Then he carried her to the bed and eased her down, not leaving her, driving furiously into her until she was crying out, nearly bucking him off her in her frenzy. When his climax overcame him, he yelled, his head thrown back, so deep inside her that he no longer thought of her as separate from him, as a vessel for his pleasure, as a wife to bear his children. She was his and a part of him and he accepted it and fell atop her, kissing her as she cried softly into his mouth.

Late that afternoon, as Dienwald was sitting in his chair drinking a flagon of ale, he looked up to see Northbert run into the great hall, shouting at the top of his lungs. "Someone comes, master!"

Dienwald rose immediately. "That peasant whoreson Sir Walter?"

"Nay, 'tis Lord Henry de Beauchamp. He has

a dozen men, master," Northbert added. "All armed."

Dienwald straightened his clothes, mentally girded his loins, and went to greet his father-in-law. It hadn't taken Lord Henry long to reply to his message.

20

Dienwald watched two stout men-at-arms assist Lord Henry de Beauchamp from his powerful Arabian destrier. He was a portly man, not tall, but strongly built even in his late years.

He was huffing about, wheezing and cursing, and Dienwald soon realized it was with rage, not the result of his exertions. No sooner had Lord Henry seen him than he yelled to the four corners of St. Erth, "You lie, you filthy whoreson! You must lie! You cannot have wedded my daughter! 'Tis a lie!"

For a father who had planned to give his daughter to William de Bridgport without a dowry, Lord Henry seemed unaccountably incensed. Dienwald motioned him into the great hall. "It is not much more private, but the entire population of St. Erth will be spared your rage." He preceded him, saying nothing more. He could hear Lord Henry's furious breathing close to his back, and wondered if he should give Philippa's father such a good target for a dagger.

He motioned Lord Henry to his own chair, but his father-in-law wasn't having any niceties. He stood there facing his son-in-law, his hands on his hips. "Tell me you lied!"

" 'Twould be a lie to tell you that I lied. I wedded Philippa two days past."

Lord Henry actually spat in his fury. "I will have the ceremony proclaimed invalid! I will have it annulled! She had not her father's permission, 'tis a disgrace! Aye, 'twill be annulled quickly!"

"It is very possible that Philippa even now is carrying my babe. There will be no annulment."

Lord Henry's face, already red, now became purple. "Where is she? Where is that insolent, ungrateful—"

"Father! What do you here? I don't understand—why are you angry?" Philippa broke off. So Dienwald had written to her father telling him of their marriage, probably the very day of their wedding, to bring him here so quickly, and he had come and he wasn't pleased. But what matter was it to him? Why should he care?

Philippa walked quickly to her father and made to embrace him. To her surprise, he took several steps back, as if he couldn't bear the sight of her, much less her touch. "You spiteful little wretch! You wedded this . . . this scoundrel?"

Philippa grew very still. She made no more moves toward her father. She saw Dienwald looking at Lord Henry, his expression ironic, and said simply, "I love him and I have wedded him. He is my husband, my lord, and I'll not allow you to insult him."

" 'Tis no insult," Dienwald said with a sudden grin. "I *am* a scoundrel."

Lord Henry turned on Dienwald. "You make jests about your foul deeds! You ravished her, didn't you? You forced her into your bed and then to a priest!"

"Nay, but you will doubtless believe what you wish to believe. However, if you believe any man could ravish Philippa and not sport a year's worth of bruises and broken limbs for it, you are wide of your mark."

"And you, you female viper, what know you of love? You who have been protected all your life from curs of this sort? How long have you known this poor and ragged cur? Days, only days! And you say you love him! Ha! He seduced you, and being a witless fool, you let him!"

"I do love him," Philippa repeated quietly. She laid her hand on her father's arm when he would have erupted further. "Listen to me, sir. He did not ravish me. He is chivalrous. He is kind and good. He saved me from Walter, and I love him. 'Twas *he* who finally consented to marry *me*."

Lord Henry shook off her hand as if it were something abhorrent. He stared hard at her. "You little harlot," he said slowly. "Just look at you, your hair wild down your back like a peasant girl's, your feet bare! I can even smell him on you. You little whore!" He pulled back his arm and struck her a blow hard across the cheek with the palm of his hand. The blow was unexpected, and Philippa went careening backward. She cried out as her hip struck a chair and she went sprawling onto the reed-strewn floor.

Dienwald was on his knees beside her, his face

white with rage. "Are you all right?" He grabbed
her arm and shook it. "Philippa, answer me!"

"Aye, I'm all right. I wasn't expecting a blow.
It surprised me." She felt Dienwald's long fingers
stroke over the bright red mark on her cheek. She
watched him rise and stride to her father. Lord
Henry's men stood still as statues, staring at their
master and at their master's daughter and husband. They would, Philippa knew, protect Lord
Henry with their lives, but they were uncertain
now, afraid to move. It was a family matter and
thus more dangerous than fighting a band of Irish
thieves.

Dienwald stopped six inches from Lord Henry's
nose. "You will listen to me, old man, and listen
well. I sent you a message telling you of my marriage to your daughter as a courtesy. I didn't particularly wish to, but I deemed it proper to inform
you. You didn't want her; you held her in no
esteem; you planned to give her no dowry. You
were going to wed her to de Bridgport! Now you
have no more say in her life. Philippa is now
mine. What is mine I protect. Because you happen to share her blood, I will not kill you, but be
warned. My dagger is sharp and my rage grows
stronger by the moment. You touch her again in
anger and I will tear your worthless heart from
your fat body. Heed me, old man, for I mean my
words."

Lord Henry doubted not that this man meant
what he'd said. He took a step back and dashed
his fingers through his grizzled hair. He looked
toward Philippa, standing now, her hand pressed
against her side. She was very still, her face pale
with shock. He'd never struck her in her life. "I
am sorry to have clouted you, Philippa, but you

have sorely tried me. You ran away, leaving me to believe you dead or murdered or—"

"You know I ran away because I heard you tell Ivo that I was going to be wedded to William de Bridgport. I knew it must be the truth, because my mother was there as well. What would you expect me to do? Roll my eyes in thankfulness and joy and go willingly to that filthy old man?"

Lord Henry collapsed onto a bench, all bluster gone from him. He looked toward Dienwald—his treacherous son-in-law—and managed a bit more anger. "You stole my wool! You killed my men!"

"Aye, I did steal your wool. As for the other, acquit me. I am no murderer. 'Twas one of my people who killed your farmers without my knowledge, something that displeased me. The man responsible is dead. There is naught more I can do to avenge your people. As for the wool, this tunic I wear is a result of your daughter's fine skills. She sewed it, and many others for my people."

Philippa drew closer to her father. "Do you know naught of Sir Walter, sir? He kidnapped me and Dienwald's son and took us to Crandall. He wanted to marry me, Father, and I could find no reason for his ardor. I am a stranger to him, and beyond that, he had a mistress who . . . Never mind that. Did you perchance offer him a reward if he found me for you? Is that what made him want me for his wife?"

Lord Henry's eyes gave a brief renewed flash of rage. "That traitorous slug! Aye, I know why he took you, Philippa, and he would have wedded you . . . but why did he not? You are wedded to this man, are you not?"

"Edmund—'tis Dienwald's son—he and I managed to escape Crandall and Walter."

"Ah. Well, no matter now. I offered Walter no reward, at least not in the way you think. I spoke truth to him, and the malignant wretch planned to gain his own ends. Ah, 'tis over for me. It matters not now. One husband is much the same as another, given that both are calamity to me. If you prefer this man to your cousin, so be it. At least this man wedded you without knowing about you. But I am dead, no matter your choice. 'Tis this man, then, this rogue, who will comfort you whilst you pray over your dead father's body. Will you strew sweet ox-lips on my grave, Philippa?"

Philippa wanted to shake him, but she held to her patience. "But, sir, this makes no sense. Why would Walter de Grasse want to marry me? Why?"

Lord Henry shook his head, mumbling, pulling at his hair. "It matters not; nothing matters now. I'm a dead man now, Philippa. There is no hope for me. My head will be severed from my body. I will be lashed until my back is but blood and bones. I will be drawn and quartered and the crows will peck at my guts."

"Crows? Guts? What is he babbling about?" Dienwald asked his bride. "Who would wish to kill him?"

Philippa again approached her father, but she didn't touch him. "What is it, Father? You fear reprisals from de Bridgport? He's an old man full of spleen, but he has no spine. You needn't fear him. My husband won't allow him to harm you."

Lord Henry groaned. He dropped his head in his hands and pulled his hair all the harder. He weaved back and forth on the bench, distraught, and wailed, "I am undone and spent, and my remains will be fodder for the fields. Beauchamp will be stripped from me and mine. Maude will be cast out to die in poverty, probably in a convent somewhere, and you know, Philippa, she hates that sort of thing, despite all her pious ravings. Bernice will not wed, for she will have no dowry, and the saints know that her humors are uncertain. She will become more sour-hearted and wasp-tongued—"

"You weren't going to give me a dowry."

Lord Henry paid no attention. "Dead, all because I tried to discourage that silly young peacock de Vescy. I lost my wits, and my tongue ran into the mire with lies."

"What lies? Tell me, Father. What does Ivo de Vescy have to do with this?"

"He is to wed Bernice. Rather, he was. Now he won't. He'll run back to York and seek an heiress elsewhere."

Philippa looked at Dienwald. She was no longer pale, but she was confused. He nodded at her silent plea for help.

"You make no sense, old man," Dienwald said. "Speak words with meaning!" It was the tone he used with Crooky, and it usually worked. But it didn't this time, not with Lord Henry. He merely shook his head and moaned, rocking more violently back and forth.

Northbert came into the hall and motioned to his master. He was panting from running and his face was alight with excitement and anticipation. "Master! There is another party here at our gates. The man claims to be Robert Burnell, Chancellor of England, here to see you, master, as a personal emissary from the king himself! Master, he has twenty men with him and they carry the king's standard! The Chancellor of England, here! From King Edward!"

Dienwald exploded in Northbert's face, "Chancellor, indeed! By St. Paul's blessed fingers, your brain becomes as flat as your ugly nose! More likely 'tis Lord Henry's precious nephew, Sir Walter, come to carp to his uncle."

Lord Henry was staring in horror at Northbert. His face had gone gray and his chin sagged to his chest. "It is the chancellor, I know it is. Accept it, Dienwald. 'Tis over now." He clasped his hands in prayer and raised his eyes to the St. Erth rafters. "Receive me into heaven and thy bosom, O Lord. I know it is too soon for my reception. I am not ready to be received, but what can I do? 'Tis not my fault that I spoke stupidly and Philippa was listening. Perhaps some of the blame can lie on her shoulders for creeping about and hearing things not meant for her ears. Must all the blame be mine alone? Nay, 'tis not well done of me. Aye, I will go to my death. I will perish with my dignity intact and will carry no blame for my sweet Philippa, who was always so bright and ready to make me smile. Many times she acted stupidly, but she is but a female, and who am I to correct her? 'Tis done and over, and I am nearly fodder for Maude's musk roses."

"A soldier carries the king's banner!" Edmund shrieked, flying into the hall. He stopped in front of his father's visitor and stared. Lord Henry had raised his head at Edmund's noise, and his face was white with fear. Edmund looked from Philippa to his father, then back to the old man, and said, "Who are you, sir?"

"Eh? Ah, you're the villain's brat. Get thee away from me, boy. I am on my way to die. A sword will sever my gullet, and my tongue will fall limp from my mouth. Aye, a lance will spike through my ribs and . . ." He rose slowly to his feet, shaking his head, mumbling now. Philippa ran to him. "Father, what is the matter? What say you? Do you know the king's chancellor? Why are you so afraid?"

He shook her off. "Boy, take me away. Take me to your stepmother's solar, aye, take me there to wait for my sentence of torture and death. Aye, I'll be thrown into a dungeon, my fingernails drawn out slowly, the hairs snatched from my groin, my eyeballs plucked from their sockets."

Edmund, wide-eyed, said, "Philippa, is this man your sire?"

"Aye, Edmund. Take him to your father's bedchamber. He seems not to be himself. Quickly."

"He pays homage to witlessness," Dienwald said, staring after his father-in-law. "What does this Burnell want, I wonder."

"The king's chancellor . . ." Philippa said, her voice filled with awe and fear. "You haven't done anything terribly atrocious, have you, husband?"

"Do you wonder if the king has discovered my plans to invade France?" Dienwald shook his head and patted her cheek, for he could see she was white with fear. "I shall go greet the fellow," he said. "I bid you to remain here until I discover what he wants. No, go to your father and let him continue his nonsense in your ears. Perhaps he will say something that will make sense to you. I want you kept safe until this matter is clear to me. Heed me in this, Philippa."

She frowned at his back as he strode from the

great hall. He was her lord and master and she loved him beyond question, but for her to hide away whilst he faced an unknown danger alone?

"Come away from here, as the master bids, mistress."

"Gorkel, you shan't tell me what to do!"

"The master told me you would try to come after him. He says your loyalty is dangerous to yourself, for you're but a female with crooked sense. He told me to take you to your steward's room and keep you there until he was certain all was well and safe. He decided he doesn't want you near your father. He believes him mired in folly."

"I won't go! No, Gorkel, don't you dare! No!"

Philippa was an armful for her husband, but for Gorkel she was naught but an insignificant wisp, to be slung over his massive shoulder and carried off. She pounded his back, shrieking at him, but he didn't hesitate. Philippa gave it up for the moment, since there was nothing else for her to do.

In the inner bailey Dienwald waited, his arms crossed negligently over his chest as he watched England's chancellor ride through the portcullis into St. Erth's inner bailey. The man wasn't much of a rider; indeed, he was bouncing up and down like a drunken loon in the saddle. Suddenly the chancellor looked up and saw Dienwald. The man's eyes were intense, and Dienwald felt himself being studied as closely as the archbishop would study a holy relic.

Burnell let his destrier come apace, then turned to an armored soldier beside him and said something that Dienwald couldn't make out. He stiff-

ened, ready to fight, but held his outward calm.
He watched Burnell shake his head at the soldier.

Robert Burnell was tired, his buttocks so sore
he felt as though he were sitting on his backbone,
but seeing St. Erth, seeing this man who was its
lord, he felt a relief so deep that he wanted to fall
from the horse and onto his knees and give his
thanks to the Lord. Dienwald de Fortenberry was
young, strong, healthy, a man of fine parts and
good mien. His castle was in need of repairs and
many of the people he'd seen were ragged, but it
wasn't a place of misery or cruelty. Burnell
straightened in his saddle. His journey was over,
thank the good Lord above. He felt hope rise in
his blood and energy flow anew through his
body. He was pleased. He was happy.

He said to the man standing before him, "You
are Dienwald de Fortenberry, master of St. Erth,
Baron St. Erth?"

"Aye, I am he."

"I am Robert Burnell, Chancellor of England. I
come to you from our mighty and just king,
Edward I. I come in peace to speak with you.
May I be welcomed into your keep?"

Dienwald nodded. The day, begun promisingly
with lust and passion and a bride who seemed to
believe the sun rose upon his head and set with
his decision, had become increasingly mysterious
with an irate and mumbling father-in-law, and
now a messenger from the King of England. He
watched Robert Burnell dismount clumsily from
the mighty destrier, then nodded for the man to
precede him into the great hall.

He was aware that all his men and all his people were hanging back, staring and gossiping,
and he prayed that no one would take anything

amiss. He told Margot in the quietest voice she'd
ever heard from the master to bring ale and bread
and cheese. She stared at him, and Dienwald was
annoyed with himself and with her.

"Where is the mistress?" Margot asked.

Dienwald wanted to cuff her, but he merely
frowned and said, "Do as I bid you and don't
sputter at me. The mistress is reposing and is not
to be disturbed for any reason." He turned back
to Burnell, praying that Margot wouldn't go
searching for Philippa, and cursing the fact that
the servants appeared more eager to serve his
wife than him. If it was so after but two days of
marriage, what would be his position a week from
now?

"I have looked forward to this day, sir," Robert
Burnell said as he eased himself down into the
master's chair. "My cramped bones praise your
generosity."

Dienwald smiled. "Take your rest for so long
as it pleases you."

"You are kind, sir, but my duty is urgent and
cannot be delayed longer."

"I pray the king doesn't want money from his
barons, for I have none and my few men aren't
meant to swell the ranks of his army."

Burnell merely shook his head, forgiving the
presumption of the speaker. "Nay, the king
wishes no coin from you. Indeed, he wishes to
present you with a gift."

Dienwald felt something prickle on the back of
his neck. He was instantly alert and very wary.
A gift from the king? Impossible! An inconsis-
tency, a contradiction. Surely a danger. He cocked
his head to the side in question, already certain
he wasn't going to like what Burnell said.

"Let me peel back the bark and get to the pith, sir. I'm here to offer you a gift to surpass any other gift of your life."

"The king wishes me to assassinate the King of France? The Duke of Burgundy? Has the Pope displeased him?"

Burnell's indulgent smile faltered just a bit at the blatant cynicism. "I see I must speed myself to the point. The king, sir, is blessed with a daughter, not one of his royal daughters, not a princess, but, frankly, sir, a bastard daughter. He wishes to give her to you in marriage. She is nonetheless a Plantagenet, greatly endowed with beauty, and will bring you a dowry worthy of any heiress of England to—"

Dienwald was reeling with surprise at this, but he still managed to remain outwardly calm. He held up his hand. "I must beg you to stop now, Lord Chancellor. You see, I am wedded two days now. You will thank the king, and tell him that as much as I wish I could hang myself for being unable to accept his wondrous offer, I am no longer available to do his bidding. I am already magnificently blessed." He hadn't realized that he would ever be blessing Philippa as his wife with such profound gratitude.

Wed the king's bastard? He wanted to howl aloud. It was too much. Such an offer was enough to make his hair fall out. But he was safe, bless Philippa and her escape from Beauchamp in a wool wagon.

Burnell looked aghast. He looked disbelieving. He looked vexed. "You're wedded! But Lord Graelam assured me that you were not, that you had no interest, that—"

"Lord Graelam de Moreton?"

"Naturally I spoke to men who know you. One cannot give the daughter of the King of England to anyone, sirrah!"

"I am already wedded," Dienwald repeated. He sounded calm, but now he had a target—Graelam—he wanted to spit on his lance. So Graelam would make *him* the sacrifice to the king's bastard daughter, would he! "Will you wish to stay the night, sir? You are most welcome. St. Erth has never boasted such an inspiring and important guest before. And do not beset yourself further, sir. I doubt this will gravely disappoint the king when he is told his first choice of son-in-law is not to be. Indeed, I venture to say that his second choice will doubtless be more to his liking."

Robert Burnell got slowly to his feet. He ran his tongue over his lips. This was a circumstance he hadn't foreseen, an event he hadn't considered as remotely possible. He felt weary and frustrated, bludgeoned by an unkind fate.

Margot made a timely entrance with ale, bread, and cheese. "Please," Dienwald said, and poured ale into a flagon, handing it to Burnell, who drank deeply. He needed it. He needed more ale to make his brain function anew. So much work, and all for naught. It wasn't just or fair. He couldn't begin to imagine the king's reaction. The idea made him shudder. He started to think of a curse, then firmly took himself in hand. He was a man of God, a man to whom devoutness wasn't a simple set of precepts or rules, but a way of life. But neither was he a man to rejoice when providence had done him in. He looked at the man he'd hoped would become the king's son-in-law and asked, "May I inquire the name of our lady wife?"

" 'Tis no secret. She is formerly Philippa de Beauchamp, her father Lord Henry de Beauchamp."

To Dienwald's astonishment, the chancellor's mouth dropped open; his cheeks turned bright red. He dropped the flagon, threw back his head, and gasped with laughter. It was a rusty sound, Dienwald thought, staring at the man, a sound the fellow wasn't used to making. Was the king so grim a taskmaster? What was so keen a jest? What had he said to bring forth this abundance of humor?

Dienwald waited. He had no choice. What in the name of the devil was going on?

Burnell finally wiped his eyes on the cuff of his wide sleeve and sat back down. He ignored the fallen flagon and poured himself more ale, taking Dienwald's flagon. He drank deeply, then looked at his host and gave him a fat, genial smile. He felt ripe and ready for life again. Fate was kind; fate gave justice to God's loyal subjects after all.

"You have saved me a great deal of trouble, Dienwald de Fortenberry. Oh, aye, sir, a great deal of trouble. You have made my life a living testimony to the beneficence of our glorious God."

"I have? I doubt that sincerely. What mean you, sir?"

Burnell hiccuped. He was so delighted, so relieved that God still loved him, still protected him. "I mean, sir, that the Lord has moved shrewdly and quite neatly, mocking us mere men and our stratagems and our little fancies, and all has come to pass as it was intended." And he began to laugh again. He swallowed when he saw that his host was growing testy. "I will tell you,

sir," Burnell said simply, "and I tell you true—
you have wedded the king's daughter. I know not
how it came about, but come about it did, and
all is well now, all is as it should be, praise the
Lord."

"You're mad, sir."

"Nay, Philippa de Beauchamp is the bastard
daughter of the King of England, and somehow
you have come to wed her. Will you tell me how
it chanced to happen?" Burnell smiled a moment,
and added under his breath, "So Lord Henry lied
about her bloody flux. The girl wasn't at Beauchamp. Ah, this tempts me, this ingenious story
he will soon tell me."

Dienwald's brain was a frozen wasteland. His
belly was twisted with cramps. He couldn't feel
his tongue moving in his mouth. He couldn't hear
his own heartbeat in his breast. Philippa, the
king's bastard? Philippa, who didn't have the
golden hair of the Plantagenets but instead a
streaked blond that was uniquely hers? Philippa,
whose vivid blue eyes were as bright as a summer's sky—like the king's, like all the Plantagenets' . . . He shook his head. It was inconceivable,
impossible. She'd leapt from a wool wagon and
into his life, and now she was his wife. She
couldn't be the king's daughter. She couldn't. She
wasn't to be dowered by her father—by Lord
Henry. Oh, God.

"How came it about, you ask? She fled from
her father—from *Lord Henry*—because she heard
him say that he wasn't going to dower her and
was going to wed her to William de Bridgport, a
man of sour nature and repellent character."

Burnell waved an impatient hand. "Of course
Lord Henry wouldn't dower her, 'twas not his

responsibility to do so. The king would. The king, who is in fact her father."

"She ran away, hiding in a wagon of wool bound for St. Ives Fair. She came here quite by accident. We were wedded, as I told you, two days ago."

"God's ways are miraculous to behold," Burnell said in a marveling voice. "I cannot wait to tell Accursi of this. He will not believe it." Burnell then shook his head and gazed at St. Erth's smoke-darkened beams high above, just as Lord Henry had done. Dienwald looked up too, hopeful of inspiration, but there was none, only Burnell saying complacently, "Well, now there need to be no agreements from you, sir. You have taken unto yourself the right wife. All is well. All has transpired according to God's plan."

"Don't you mean the king's plan?"

Burnell simply smiled as if the king and God were close enough so that it didn't matter.

Dienwald opened his mouth and bellowed, "Philippa! Come here. Now!"

She heard him yelling and lowered her brows at Gorkel. She walked past him, head high, into the great hall, and came to a halt, staring from her husband to the man seated in her husband's chair. "Aye?"

"Philippa," Dienwald bellowed, higher and louder, even though she stood not four feet away from him, "this man claims you are the king's bastard daughter, not the daughter of that damned fool Lord Henry. He convinces me, though I fought it. No wonder Lord Henry wouldn't dower you. 'Twas not his duty to do so. He lied about de Bridgport just to keep Ivo de Vescy away from you. Don't you see, you're the king's daughter and thus his responsibility. Damn you for a lying, deceitful wench!"

She continued to stare at him a moment, then transferred her gaze to the other man, who was nodding at her like a wooden puppet. "But this makes no sense. I don't understand. Lord Henry isn't my father?"

Burnell had no chance to reply, for Dienwald howled, "I do have a father-in-law, curse you, wench, but it isn't that fat whining creature in my bedchamber. Nay, him I could have tolerated. Him I could have threatened and intimidated until he did as I wished him to do.

"Nay, my father-in-law has to be the cursed King of England! Did you hear me, Philippa? He is the *King of England.* I, a scoundrel and a rogue, a man happily lacking in wealth and duty and responsibility, have the wretched king for a father-in-law! You have ruined me, wench! You have destroyed me! You are a thorn to be plucked from my flesh. Foul mischance brought you to me, and the devil wove you into my mind and body until I was forced to seduce you!"

Burnell gaped at him. A tirade such as this was unthinkable and completely astonishing. He said in his most reasoned churchman's voice, "But, sir, you will be made an earl, the king has commanded it. You will be a peer of the realm. You will be the Earl of St. Erth, the first of a mighty line to hold power and land and influence in Cornwall. The king will dower your wife handsomely. She is an heiress. You will be able to make repairs to your castle, swell your herds, grow more crops. You will know no want, no lacks. Your lands will prosper and extend themselves. Life will be better. Your people will live

longer. Your priest will save more souls, all of St.
Erth will show bounty and plenty and—"

Dienwald raised his voice to the beams above,
yelling in misery, "I repudiate this wretched
woman! Before God, I won't have the king's
daughter as my wife. I won't be bound to the
damned king or to his damned bastard! I want to
be left alone. I demand to be left to my humble
castle and my crumbling walls! I demand to be
left to my blessedly profligate life and sinful
deeds! Give me ragged serfs and frayed tunics!
Save me from this foul penance! Damnation, my
people don't *want* to live longer. My priest doesn't
want to save more souls!"

He turned on his speechless wife, snarled
something beneath his breath—the only thing
he'd snarled that no one hadn't clearly heard—
and strode from the great hall.

"Your father, our gracious king, bids you good
grace, my lady," said Burnell, for want of anything better. He rose and took her limp hand. Her
face was white and she looked uncomprehending.

He sought words to comfort her, to bring her
understanding, for he imagined it wasn't a daily
occurrence to be told you were the offspring of
the king. "Lady Philippa, 'tis a surprise, I know
it, this news has shaken you about, but all is
known now and all is explained. The king . . .
Naturally, he couldn't have acknowledged you
before—he was wedded to his queen, even though
at the time she was a very young girl. He wanted
no hurt to come to her. But neither did he want
to turn his back on you, for you were his dear
daughter. He gave you for raising to Lord Henry.
It was always his plan to come into your life when
it was time for you to be married."

Philippa looked at him and said the most unlikely thing to him: "Why did the king wish me—a girl—to be taught to read and write?"

Burnell found his mouth open again. Had the girl vague and token wits? "I . . . ah, really, my lady, I'm not at all certain."

"I suppose I had a mother?"

"Aye, my lady. Her name is Constance and she is wedded to a nobleman of her station. She was very young when she birthed you, the king told me. Perhaps someday you will wish to know her."

"I see," Philippa said. At least Lady Maude's dislike of her was now explained. The king's bastard had been foisted upon a woman who hadn't wanted her. It was more to take in than she could manage at the moment, for in truth it was her husband who now filled her thoughts. Her husband and his outrage at what had happened to him.

"My husband doesn't want me," she said, looking away from the chancellor. She saw Old Agnes, Margot, Gorkel, Crooky, and a host of other St. Erth people staring at her, marveling at what she'd suddenly become, chewing it over, and wondering what to do. Would they mock her for being a bastard? Despise her or curtsy to her until their knees locked?

"Your husband is merely confused, my lady. His behavior and his unmeasured words demonstrate that he has no real understanding of what has happened. He must be confusing his new status with that of someone else; he must not comprehend his good fortune."

"My husband," Philippa said patiently, shaking her head at him, "comprehends everything per-

fectly. Understand, sir, he is not like most men."
That is why I love him and no other. "He doesn't
appreciate the sort of power and wealth some
men crave, nay, even covet unto death. He has
never sought it, never desired it. He enjoys his
freedom, and that means to him that he can do
just as he pleases without others interfering in his
life. Now all that has changed because of what I
am. He would never have wedded the king's bastard daughter, sir. Offers of an earldom, offers of
coin, offers of power and influence would have
driven him away, not seduced him. You would
never have convinced him otherwise. You could
not have even threatened him otherwise. But fate
arranged things differently for him, and for me.
He wedded me and now he doesn't want what
I've suddenly become. I don't know what to do."

Philippa turned away from the Chancellor of
England and walked out of the hall.

In the inner bailey she came to an appalled halt.
There was her father running toward Dienwald,
Edmund on his heels, trying to catch the tail of
his tunic. Her erstwhile father was shouting, "My
precious boy! My honorable lord, my savior!"

He caught Dienwald and threw his arms around
his neck and kissed him on each cheek.

Philippa shuddered at the sight.

Crooky came out of the Great Hall, observed
the spectacle, and shouted to the blue sky,

My poor master is now under the king's
  thumb
He wants to weep but his brain's gone numb
He's wed to a princess and will never be free
But he can't do a thing but accept it and be
—the king's proud son-in-law.

Philippa turned on the fool, cuffed him with all her strength, and watched him flail to keep his balance, then roll down the steps of the Great Hall, yelling loudly, "Kilt by a princess! The good king save me!"

21

Dienwald froze to the spot. Lord Henry had grabbed him firmly and was weeping copiously on his neck, kissing his ear, squeezing him so tightly Dienwald feared his ribs would crack, so great was Lord Henry's relief. "You're a fine, honorable lad, my lord. I knew it all the time, but I was just concerned and . . . well . . . Aye, 'tis God who has saved me and given me his blessing! I shall never again question the heavenly course of things, even though the course be a maze of blind turns."

Dienwald suffered Lord Henry for another moment, his mind still confused, when he looked up and saw Philippa cuff Crooky and send the fool flying. He grinned, then felt his face stiffen.

He pushed Lord Henry away. "Get thee gone, my lord! Take your *daughter* with you! I want her

not. Just look at her—she even abuses my
servants!"

"But, my precious boy, my dearest lord, wait!
She's most desirable as a wife, Dienwald, she's
quite comely—"

"Ha! Comely be damned! She's the king's
daughter—that's her claim to comeliness!"

"Nay, not all of it. 'Twas I who raised her, I
through my clerks and priests who taught her all
she knows—and I saw to her lessons and to her
prayers . . ."

"That certainly adds to her value." Dienwald
didn't say another word. He just shook his head
and broke into a run toward the St. Erth stables.
Philippa walked slowly to where her father stood,
looking in incredulous dismay after her retreating
new husband.

"What ails him, Philippa? He's been given the
earth and all its bounty. His father-in-law is the
King of England! Oh, and you *are* comely, doubt
it not, Philippa, truly. It matters not that you
haven't the golden Plantagenet hair." Lord Henry
looked upon his former daughter. "I don't understand him. He howls like a wounded hound and
slinks off to hide. He acts as though he were to
be hunted down and slain."

Philippa merely shook her head. She wasn't
capable of more. Tears clogged her throat, and
she swallowed.

Edmund tugged on her sleeve. "Are you truly
the king's daughter?"

"It appears that I am."

Edmund fell silent, simply peering up at her,
as if to observe some magical change in her.

"What, Edmund, you hate me too?"

"Don't be stupid, Philippa." Edmund stared

after his father. "Father's always boasted that his life was his own, you see. He's told me many times, since I was a very little boy, to be what I chose to be, not what someone else chose for me. He said that life was too rife with chance, too uncertain in measuring out its punishments and rewards, to be what someone else wished. He said he wanted no overlord, no authority to hold sway over him and to keep and hold what was his."

"Aye, I can hear him saying that. It's true, you know. It's what he believes, it's what he is." Philippa turned back to Lord Henry. "I wondered why I was so tall. The king is very tall, I hear. Is he not called Longshanks?"

Lord Henry nodded. "Listen to me, girl. I did my best by you."

"I know it well, and I thank you. It could not have been easy for Lady Maude. She always hated me, but she tried to hide it." At least in the beginning she'd tried.

Lord Henry tried his best to dissuade Philippa from this conclusion, but it was lame going, for Lady Maude had always resented the king's bastard being foisted upon her household. He stopped, unequal to the task.

Philippa looked thoughtful and said, "My hair—'tis not Plantagenet gold, as you just said, but streaked and common."

"Nay, I simply spouted nonsense, that is all. Nothing about you is common. And your eyes, Philippa, they are the blue of the Plantagenets, a striking blue as vivid as an August sky." Philippa rolled her eyes at his effluence. "Aye," Lord Henry continued, rubbing his hands. "Aye, that is bound to please the king mightily when he finally meets you."

To meet the king. Her *father*. It held only mild interest for her now. All babes had to be born of someone. She was a royal indiscretion, nothing more, and that fact was going to ruin her life. "Please excuse me now, sir," she said. "I must decide what to do. If you wish to stay, you will use Edmund's chamber. If the chancellor wishes to stay, then he will sleep—" She broke off, shrugged, and walked away.

"Philippa's not happy," said Edmund to the old man who wasn't Philippa's father. Just imagine, Philippa was the king's get! It frayed the thoughts, such a happening. Did that make the King of England his step-grandfather?

"Your father, young Edmund, will make haste back to reason once he's had a chance to think things through. He's not acting like a man should act, given this heavenly gift."

"You don't know my father," said Edmund. "But Philippa does." Edmund left Lord Henry and walked to Crooky who was still sitting on the ground, rubbing his jaw.

"Aye, I was cuffed by a royal princess," said Crooky, his face alight with reverence and awe. "A real princess of the realm and she wanted to cuff me! Her fist touched me. *Me*, who's naught but a bungling ass and so common I am below common and thus uncommon."

"Nay, Crooky, she's the king's bastard and her fist did more than just touch you. I thought she was going to knock your head from your neck."

"Split you not facts into petty parts, little master. Your stepmother is of royal blood and that makes you . . . hmmmm, what does that make you?"

"Perchance almost as uncommon as you, Crooky." Edmund caught Gorkel's eyes and skipped away.

"The mistress is beset with confusion," Gorkel announced, "and so is the master."

"Aye."

Gorkel ground his teeth and stroked his jaw. "You must speak to the master. You're his flesh. He must heed you."

Edmund agreed this was true, but he knew his father well enough to realize he could say nothing to change his thinking. In any case, there was no opportunity. Dienwald, astride Philbo, was riding out of the inner bailey, alone, a blind look in his eyes. Men called after him, but he didn't respond, just kept riding, looking straight ahead.

In her bedchamber, Philippa sat on the bed and folded her hands in her lap. The situation was too much to absorb, so she simply sat there and let all that had occurred flow over her. Words, only words out of men's mouths, yet they'd changed her life. She didn't particularly care that she was the king's bastard. She didn't particularly care that now the facts of her life had become quite clear to her. She didn't care that Lady Maude had made much of her life a misery. And finally, she didn't care that she now knew why Walter had wished so much to wed her. She could only begin to imagine what prizes he believed would become his upon marrying her.

What she cared about was her husband. She saw his pale face, heard his infuriated words ringing in her ears, blanched anew at his rage over his betrayal. Betrayal in which she had played no part, but he didn't believe that. Or perhaps he did, only his outrage was so great, it simply didn't matter to him who had done what.

If King Edward had been in the bedchamber at this very moment, Philippa would have cuffed him as hard as she'd cuffed Crooky. She would have yelled at him for his damned perfidy—but then she would have crushed him with embraces for selecting Dienwald to be her husband. What was one to do, then?

Life had become as treacherous as Tregollis Swamp. She rose and began to pace. What to do?

Would Dienwald return? Of course he would. He had to, for he had no place else to go and he also had a son he wouldn't desert.

She knew she should give the women instructions; she should speak to Northbert about the lord chancellor's men as well as her fa . . . nay, Lord Henry's men-at-arms. She knew she should find out what Robert Burnell wished to do, and Lord Henry as well, for that matter. Thus, she finally left the bedchamber, duty overcoming loss and fear.

Lord Henry and Robert Burnell were drinking Dienwald's fine ale and chatting amiably. They would stay until the morning, they told her, both of them so ecstatic in drink that she doubted whether Burnell, that devout churchman who never flagged in his labors for his king, could stay upright for much longer. She sought out Margot.

The woman curtsied to her until Philippa thought she would fall on her face.

"You will cease such things, Margot. I am nothing more than I was before. Please, you mustn't . . ." Philippa broke off, stared blindly into space, and burst into tears.

She felt a small hand clasp hers and looked down to see Edmund through her tears.

"Father will come back, Philippa. He must come back. He'll soften, mayhap."

She could only nod. She retired to her bed-chamber, rudely, she knew, but she couldn't bear to be with either Lord Henry or Robert Burnell, her *father's* chancellor.

Dienwald didn't return. Not that night or the following day.

Late the next day following, another man arrived at St. Erth, a man alone, astride a magnificent black barb, and he was searching for Robert Burnell. The chancellor had planned to depart that morning, but another long evening spent swilling ale with Lord Henry had kept him in bed—rather, the former steward's bed—until late that morning. Even now he was pale and of greenish hue.

For an instant Philippa thought it was Dienwald, finally come home, but it wasn't, and she wanted to kill the stranger for her disappointment.

His name was Roland de Tournay. She greeted him, not seeing him, not caring who he was, saying nothing, and merely led him to where Burnell and Lord Henry were sitting before a sluggish fire, trying to ignore their pounding heads.

Burnell leapt to his feet, his aching head forgotten. "De Tournay! What do you here? Is the king all right? Does he need to—"

"I am here on the king's orders," Roland said, waving his hand for Burnell to take his seat again. "I promised him to come speak to you about the heiress—the king's bastard daughter. He wants me to look her over."

Lord Henry bounded to his feet. "De Fortenberry is already the king's son-in-law, sirrah!"

Roland merely lifted a black brow. "The heiress is already dispatched, you say?"

"Aye, to the man the king intended her to have!"

Roland laughed. "A journey crowned with a neat escape for me. So that knave won her, eh?"

Philippa, who'd been listening to this talk, now stepped forward and said, "The king sent you?"

Roland stilled all humor as he looked at the king's daughter. He hadn't known who she was before. But as he looked at her closely now, he realized she had the look of Edward, with her clear blue eyes and her well-sculptured features. She was lovely and she was tall and well-formed, and her hair—ah, it was thick and curling down her back, framing her face. Then, for a brief instant Roland knew a sharp flicker of disappointment that he was too late. But only for an instant. He assumed a bland expression and said, "The king—your esteemed father—simply asked me to see you."

"I am already wedded," Philippa said in a remote voice. "However, it is uncertain whether or not my husband still will claim me for his wife. He left me, you see, when he learned my father is the King of England."

Roland's black brow shot up a good inch.

Lord Henry inserted himself. "You needn't tell this stranger all these things, Philippa. 'Tis none of his affair."

"Why not? The king sent him. Perhaps next he will send William de Bridgport when this man says he doesn't want me. Who knows?" Philippa turned to Robert Burnell and added, her voice hard, "Even if my husband dissolves our union, I don't want this man. Do you hear me? I don't want any other man, ever. Do you understand me, sir?"

"Aye, madam, I understand you well, for you speak clearly and to the point."

By God, Roland thought, staring at the young woman, she was in love with de Fortenberry. How had this come about, and so quickly? There was a mystery here, and he liked unraveling mysteries above all things.

Lord Henry snorted. "It matters not what he understands or doesn't understand. Look you, Roland de Tournay, my daughter was wedded to de Fortenberry before either of them knew who her real sire was. All is over and done with. You can leave with good conscience."

And Lord Henry stared at him as though he'd like to shoot an arrow through his neck. Well, it mattered not. Nor was it such a mystery after all.

"Don't be rude, Fa . . . my lord," Philippa said. "I care not if he remains at St. Erth. There is room, and there is more ale. Why not? Indeed, if he plans to return to London, he can tell the king what has transpired and . . ."

She stopped suddenly and just stared at Roland—not really at him, Roland thought, but through him and beyond him. There was a pain in her fine eyes, a very deep pain that made him flinch. Suddenly she turned and left the hall, simply walked away, saying nothing more.

"Damnable churl," Lord Henry said. "I'd slit his throat if he weren't already her husband."

Roland shook his head. "You mean that her husband left when he discovered she was the king's daughter?"

"Aye, that's the meat of it," Lord Henry said. "I'd like to smash the pea-brained young cockscomb into a dung heap."

Roland smiled at blessed fate. His luck had held him through this brief foray into possible disaster. He could not understand de Fortenberry's actions. Was the man mad? His own motives for not wishing to marry—even the king's bastard daughter— were different; they meant something. Roland decided to stay the night at St. Erth and on the morrow pay his visit to Graelam de Moreton at Wolffeton. The king's bastard daughter was no longer any of his concern. He'd done his duty by his king, and all, for him at least, had resolved itself right and tight. The heiress was already wedded and he had no more part to play.

He remarked upon the political situation with the Scots, the intractability of King Alexander and his minions, and forgot the purpose of his visit. The three men, without the presence of either the master or the mistress of St. Erth, ate their fill and consumed more of the castle's fine ale and kept watch and company until late into the night, talking, arguing, and yelling at each other, all in high good humor.

The master of St. Erth, the soon-to-be Earl of St. Erth, didn't appear. Nor did his discarded wife.

Wolffeton Castle

"Hold him down, Rolfe! Hellfire, grab his other leg, quickly, he nearly sent his foot into my manhood! You, Osbert, keep his arms behind him! Nay, don't break his elbow! Just keep him quiet."

Lord Graelam de Moreton rubbed his hand over his throbbing jaw and watched as two of his men held Dienwald down, another sitting on his legs and a fourth on his chest. Dienwald was panting and yelling and now he was gasping for breath, for Osbert was not a lightweight. His blow had been strong and knocked Graelam off his feet and flat on his back onto the sharp cobblestones of the inner bailey.

Of course, Dienwald had caught him off-guard. Aye, he'd taken Graelam by complete surprise. His so-called friend had ridden through Wolffeton's gates, welcomed by the men because he was a known ally. No one could have guessed that the instant Dienwald dismounted his destrier, he would attack him. Graelam looked down at his red-faced enraged friend. "What ails you, Dienwald? Kassia, don't fret, I'm all right. It's our neighbor here who's gone quite mad. He attacked me like a fevered fiend from hell."

"Let me up, you stinking whoreson, and you'll see how I split you with my sword!"

"Nay, sir," Rolfe said kindly. "Move you not, or I will have to twist your arm."

Kassia stared from Dienwald to her husband. "Ah," she said, "Dienwald has discovered what you did, my lord. He's come to express his disapproval of your interference."

"Aye, loose me, you coward, and I'll debone you, you lame-assed cur!"

Graelam hunkered down beside his friend, his face only inches from Dienwald's. "Listen to me, fool, and listen well. You needn't marry the king's daughter, and you know it well. Both Kassia and I saw Morgan or Mary or whatever her name is and knew it was she you wanted. We decided if you wanted to wed her, you would have her, and the king be damned. There was no reason for us to say anything. We knew you wouldn't bend to any man, be he king or sultan or God. Isn't that the truth?''

Dienwald howled. ''I had already wedded her when Burnell came! She was already my wife!''

''So what is the matter? You're acting half-crazed. Speak sense and I will let you free.''

''Her name isn't Morgan or Mary, damn you! Her name is Philippa de Beauchamp and she is our blessed king's cursed daughter!''

Graelam looked up at his wife. They simply stared at each other, then back at Dienwald. ''Well,'' Graelam said finally, ''this is a most curious turn of events.''

Kassia knelt beside Dienwald and gently laid her hand on his cheek. ''You're obstinate beyond all reason, my friend. You wedded the girl who was intended for you. And she was the girl you wished to wed. All worked out as it was intended to. Everyone is content, or should be. So you're now the king's son-in-law. Does it really matter all that much? You will perhaps have to become more, er, respectable, Dienwald, in your dealings, less eager to strip fat merchants of their goods, possibly a bit more deferential, particularly when you are in the king's presence, but surely it isn't too much to ask. We did it for your own good, you know—''

''Good be damned!'' Dienwald howled, his eyes red. ''Your mangy husband did it because he thought I'd stolen the wine your father sent you! Admit it, you hulking whoreson! You did it to revenge yourself upon me—I know it as I know you and your shifty ways!''

"You won't insult my lord," Kassia said in a tone of voice Dienwald had never heard from her before. It was low and it was mean. It drew him up short, and he said, his voice now sulky and defensive, "Well, 'tis true. He did me in, he did it to spite me."

Kassia smiled down at him. "You reason with your spleen and your bile, not with your wits. Hush now and behave yourself. Release him, Rolfe, he won't act the stupid lout again. At least," she added, giving a meaningful look to Dienwald, "he had better not. Yes, Dienwald, you will now rise and you won't attempt to strike Graelam again. If you even try it, you will have to deal with me."

Dienwald looked at the very delicate, very pregnant lady and grinned reluctantly. "I don't want to have to deal with you, Kassia. Cannot you turn your back for just a moment? I just want to smash your husband into the ground. Just one more blow, just a small one."

"No, you may not even spit at him, so be quiet. Now, come in and I will give you some ale. Where is Philippa? Where is your lovely bride?"

"Doubtless she is singing and dancing and playing a fine tune for the damned Chancellor of England and her fa . . . nay, that idiot Lord Henry de Beauchamp."

"You believe her wallowing in pleasure that you left St. Erth? That is what you did, isn't it, Dienwald? You shouted and bellowed at her and then ran away to sulk?"

Dienwald looked at the gentle, sweet, pure lady at his side, and growled at her husband, "Put your hand over her mouth, Graelam. She grows impertinent. She vexes me as much as the wench does."

Graelam laughed. "She speaks the truth. You've a wife, and truly, Dienwald, it matters not who her family is. You didn't wed her for a family or lack of one, did you? You wedded her because you love her."

"Nay! Cut off your rattling tongue! I wedded her because I took her and she was a damned virgin and I had no choice but to wed her since my son—my demented nine-year-old son—demanded that I do so!"

"You would have wedded her anyway," Kassia said, "Edmund or no Edmund."

"Aye," Dienwald agreed, shaking his head mournfully. "I will beget no bastard off a lady."

"Then why do you act the persecuted victim?" Graelam said. "The heedless brute who cares for no one?"

"Oh, I care for her, but I believed her father to be naught but a fool, and so it bothered me not. But no, her father must needs be the King of England. The *King of England*, Graelam! It is too much. I will not abide it. I will set her aside. She took me in and made a mockery of me. Aye, I will send her to a convent and annul her and she will forget all her besotted feelings for me. She smothered me with her sweet yielding, her soft smiles and her passion. She will hate me and it will be what we both deserve."

Kassia swept a cat off the seat of a chair and motioned Dienwald to it. "You will do nothing of the sort. Sit you down, my friend, and eat. You've eaten naught, have you? . . . I thought not. Here are some fresh bread and honey."

Dienwald ate.

Graelam and Kassia allowed him to vent his rage and sulk and carp and curse luridly, until, upon the third morning after his unexpected arrival at Wolffeton, Roland de Tournay rode into the inner bailey.

When Roland saw Dienwald, he simply stared at him silently for a very long time. The man looked to Roland's sharp eye to be at the very edge. His eyes were hollow and dark-circled for want of sleep, and he had not the look of a man remotely content with himself or with his lot. "Well," Roland said, "I wondered where you'd fled. Your wife is not a happy lady, my soon-to-be lord Earl of St. Erth."

"I don't want to be a damned earl! What did you say? Philippa isn't happy? Is she ill? What's wrong?"

"You yourself said she was besotted with you, Dienwald," Kassia said. "Would you not expect her to be unhappy in your absence?"

Roland marveled aloud at de Fortenberry's outpouring of stupidity. He said patiently, "Your lovely wife happens to care about you, something none understand, but there it is. As you say, she is besotted with you. Thus, in your unexpected absence, she is miserable; all your servants are miserable because she is; your son hangs to her skirts trying to raise her spirits, but it does little good. The chancellor and Lord Henry finally left because life at St. Erth had become so grim and bleak. No one had any spirit for jests, even your fool, Crooky. He simply lay about in the rushes mumbling something about the lapses of God's grace. I could be in the wrong of it, but it would seem to me that you are very stupid, my lord earl."

"I am not a damned earl! I don't recall having required your opinion, de Tournay!"

"Nay, you did not, but I choose to give it to you, freely offered. Your wife is a lovely lady. She doesn't deserve to be treated so meanly."

Dienwald appeared ready to attack Roland, and Graelam quickly intervened. "I expected you sooner, Roland. Dienwald, go lick your wounds elsewhere and look not to bash Roland. He isn't your enemy. And if you spit on him, Kassia won't like it."

Dienwald, still muttering, strode to Wolffeton's training field, there to besport himself with Rolfe and the other men.

As for Roland, he turned to Graelam and smiled. "It has been a very long time, my friend, but I am here at last. This is your wife, Graelam? This beautiful creature who looks like a fairy princess? She calls you, a scarred hairy warrior, husband? Willingly?"

"Aye," Kassia said, and gave her hand to Roland. He touched his fingers to her palm and smiled down at her. "You carry a babe, my lady."

"Your vision is sharper than a falcon's, Roland! Aye, she will give me a beautiful daughter very soon now."

"A son, my lord. 'Tis a son I carry."

Roland looked at the two of them. He had known Graelam de Moreton for many years and called him friend. But he'd known him as a hard man, unyielding and implacable, a valued man to fight at your side, strong and valiant, but no show of tenderness or gentleness in his character to please such a fragile lady as this. But he did please her—that was evident. Roland marveled at it and thought it excellent, but didn't choose to see such changes in himself. No, never. He didn't understand such feelings and had no desire to, none.

Graelam said, "Come, Roland, I assume you have something of import to tell me. Kassia, I wish you to rest now, sweetling. Nay, argue not with me, for rest you will, even if I have to tie you to our bed." He leaned down, his palm gentle against his wife's cheek, and lightly kissed her mouth. "Go, love."

And Roland marveled anew. The two men sat in Wolffeton's great hall, flagons of wine between them.

Roland said without preamble, "I must go to Wales and I mustn't be Roland de Tournay there. You have friends amongst the Marcher Barons. I need you to give me an introduction to one of them. Mayhap I will need to pay a surprise visit."

Graelam said, "You play spy again, Roland? I have no doubt, my friend, that you could dupe God into accepting you as one of his angels. Aye, I have friends there. If you must, you can go to Lord Richard de Avenell. He is the father of Lady Chandra de Vernon. You know her husband, Jerval, do you not?"

Roland nodded. "Aye, I met both of them in Acre."

"It's done, then, Roland. I will have my steward, Blount, write a letter for you to Lord Richard. He will welcome you to his keep. Will you leave for Wales immediately?"

Roland sat back in his chair and crossed his arms over his chest, his eyes sparkling with mischief. "If I may, Graelam, I should like to remain just for a while longer to see what transpires

between Dienwald and his wife and his wife's
father-in-law."

Graelam laughed. "Aye, I too would like to see
Edward's face were he to be told that Dienwald
cursed and fled when he discovered the king was
now related to him! He would surely be speechless for once in his life."

Near St. Erth

Walter de Grasse wanted to spit, and he did,
often. It relieved his bile. He'd argued fiercely
with Britta, who'd clung to him and wept bitter
tears and begged him to stay with her and not go
after Philippa. But he'd dragged himself and his
aching head away.

He would have Philippa, no matter the cost. He
would have her and he would kill Dienwald de
Fortenberry at last. Damned scoundrel! And he
would keep Britta, no matter what either female
wanted.

He'd cursed his men roundly, railing at them
for allowing one lone women with a little boy to
escape Crandall. But it had happened and they
had escaped and now he had to devise another
way of catching her again.

He and six of his most skilled and ruthless men
camped in a scraggly wood not a mile from the
castle of St. Erth. One man kept watch at all
times. It was reported to Walter that the master
of St. Erth himself had ridden off, no one with
him, and as yet he hadn't returned. Walter knew
of the chancellor's visit and of Lord Henry's visit
as well. The fat was now in the fire, and Philippa

as well as Dienwald had been told who she really was.

Why, then, had Dienwald ridden away from his keep alone? It made no sense to Walter.

He saw the chancellor and all his men leave, which was a relief, for Walter had no wish to tangle with the king's soldiers. Then Lord Henry and his men left St. Erth. Walter sat back, chewed on a blackened piece of rabbit, and waited.

Wolffeton Castle

"The wench is what she is, and nothing can change that."

"That is true," Graelam agreed.

"Do you love her, Dienwald?" Kassia asked now, setting her embroidery on her knee, for the babe was big in her belly.

"You women and your silly talk of love! Love is naught but a fabrication that dissolves when you but look closely at it."

"You begin to sound more the fool than your Crooky." Kassia sighed. "You must face up to things, Dienwald. You must go home to your wife and your son. Perhaps, if you are very careful, you could still raid on your western borders. Aye, I think my lord would wish to accompany you. He chafes for adventure now that there is naught but boring peace."

"She's right, Dienwald. There would be no reason for the king to find out. You could be most discreet in your looting and raiding. You would simply have to select your quarry wisely. Aye,

Kassia speaks true. I should like a bit of sport myself, on occasion."

Dienwald brightened. "Philippa likes adventure as well," he said slowly. "I think she would much enjoy raiding."

"It is certainly something for the two of you to speak together about," Kassia said, lowering her head so Dienwald wouldn't see the smile on her lips.

Roland de Tournay, much to both Graelam's and his wife's appalled surprise, said suddenly, "Nay, I don't agree with Graelam. I agree with you, Dienwald. I think you should travel to Canterbury and explain to the archbishop what happened to you. I think he would annul his marriage. After all, the wench wasn't honest about her heritage. She's a bastard when all's said and done. What man would wish to be wedded to a bastard? Aye, rid yourself of her, Dienwald. It matters not if she carries your babe in her belly. Let the king, her father, see to it. You will be happy again and your keep will resume its normal workings. You can return to your mistresses with a free heart and without guilt."

To Graelam's and Kassia's further surprise, Dienwald bounded to his feet and stared at Roland as though he'd suddenly become a toad that had just hopped onto the trestle table and into the pigeon pie.

"Shut your foul mouth, Roland! Philippa knew not that she was a bastard! None of it was her fault, none of it her doing. She is honest and pure and sweet and . . ." He broke off, saw that he'd been trapped in a cage of his own creation, and turned red all the way to his hairline.

"You damnable whoreson, I hope you rot!" he bellowed as he strode with churning step from Wolffeton's great hall, leaving its three remaining occupants to explode with laughter.

22

St. Erth Castle

Philippa stood in the inner bailey, her hands on her hips, facing Dienwald's master-of-arms. "I care not what you say, Eldwin. I won't remain here for another day, nay, not even another hour! Don't you understand? Your master is at Wolffeton—he must be there—licking his imagined wounds and whining to Graelam and his *perfect* little Kassia about what his treacherous wife has done to him."

"And you wish to go to Wolffeton, mistress? If the master is there, you want to berate him in front of Lord Graelam? Rebuke him in front of the men? Mistress, he is your lord and master and your husband. You mustn't do anything that would reflect badly on him. Above all, surely you wouldn't wish to leave St. Erth! Why, 'tis your

379

duty to remain here until the master decides what he will do and—"

Philippa was at the end of her tether. Crooky, who stood beside her, looked knowingly at Eldwin and said, "You are naught but a stringy bit of offal, sirrah! Don't pretend to rise above what you are to tell *her* what she must and mustn't do. She is a princess, Eldwin, so bite your churl's tongue! A princess does what she wishes to do, and if she wishes to fetch the master, well then, all of us will go with her and fetch the master. And the master will be well-fetched, and that's an end to it!"

"Aye, I will go as well," said Edmund, "for he is my father."

"And I!"

"And I!"

Eldwin, routed, looked about at the two score of St. Erth people, who had obviously sided with the mistress. Old Agnes was grinning her toothless grin and flapping her skinny arms at him as if he were a fox in her henhouse. He gave over, but not completely. "But, mistress, all of us can't leave the castle! Old Agnes, you must stay and see to the weaving and sewing! Gorkel, you must keep the villeins at their tasks and see to the keep's safety."

"Aye, and what will ye do, Eldwin of the mighty arm?" Old Agnes said.

"I go with the mistress," Eldwin said, rose to his full height, and stared down at Old Agnes, who promptly moved back a few steps.

Philippa grinned, and Eldwin, pleased that he'd made her smile, and equally pleased that Old Agnes had retreated a bit, felt his chest expand. Perhaps they *should* fetch the master. Perhaps it was the best thing to do. Wasn't there more to his duty than to remain at St. Erth and command and protect the keep?

"Aye, mistress, it will be as our brave Eldwin says," Old Agnes shouted. "I'll keep all these rattling tongues at their tasks! I just hope Prink—the faithless cretin—gives me some difficulties. If Mordrid doesn't smack him down, then I'll have Gorkel flail off his wormy hide."

"Aye," said Gorkel the Hideous, "I'll keep everything and everyone in his place. You aren't to fret yourself, mistress. No one will fall into lazy stupor."

It was too much. Philippa looked from one beloved face to another and felt her smile crack. The past three days had been beyond wretched, and all of them had tried so diligently to make her feel better about her husband's defection. She swallowed her tears, and found herself nodding at Crooky with approval even as he cleared his throat and looked fit to burst with song.

> We go to fetch the master
> We go to bring him home.
> We'll not take a nay from him
> Unless he's torn limb from limb.

Crooky stopped, clapping his hands over his mouth, aghast at the shocking words that had come pouring forth. Philippa stared at him. Everyone stared at him. Then Philippa giggled; several nervous giggles followed. Finally Philippa sobered and turned to Eldwin. "Pick fifteen men and arm them well. We ride to Wolffeton within the hour. As for the rest of you, prepare the keep for your master's return. We will feast as we did the day of our wedding!"

Near St. Erth

Walter was livid. He saw her there, at the head of the men, riding away from St. Erth. Fifteen men—he counted them. Well-armed they were. Too many for him to attempt to capture her, damn their hides.

Where was she going? Perhaps, he thought, smiling, she was leaving her husband. Aye, that was it. She was leaving the perfidious lout.

At last he'd have her. Walter roused his men, mounted his destrier, and waved all of them to follow him. He would follow her all the way to Ireland if need be. He would find her alone at some point along the way. She would have to relieve herself or bathe. Aye, he'd get her.

Between Wolffeton and St. Erth

Dienwald patted Philbo's neck. His destrier was lathering a bit, beginning to blow hard now, but he plowed forward, ever forward, as if guessing they were homeward-bound.

Dienwald would soon have his wench again and he would kiss her and hold her and tell her he forgave all her multitudinous sins, even if she chose not to remember them. He would love her until he was insensate and she as well.

"Ah, Philippa," he said, looking between Philbo's twitching ears. "Soon all will be well again. Even though I'll be an earl, I shan't carp overly.

I will bend my knee to your cursed father when I must, and will show him that I am a man of honor and a man who cares more for his daughter than the world and all its bounty.

"I'll learn to write so that I can extol her beauty in love poems, and recite aloud what I have written to her." Dienwald paused at those outflowing words. Philbo snorted. Dienwald's vow rang foolish, so he quickly shook his head. "Nay, not poetry," he added quickly, "but I will show her how much I desire her and adore her by my actions toward her. I will whisper in her ear of my desire for her and wring her sweet heart with my tender tongue. I will never, ever yell at her in anger again." He smiled at that. Aye, 'twas good, that vow. It was a vow with meat and meaning, and he could hold to it; he was a reasonable man, he was controlled. It wouldn't be difficult.

Aye, he would tease her and love her and bend her gently to his will. He worried not about his own peculiar will, for he was not a tyrant to demand subservience. Nay, his was a beneficient will, a mellow will, a will to which she would submit eagerly, her beautiful eyes filled with pleasure at pleasing him, for she adored him and wanted above all things to delight him.

His brow lowered suddenly, and he added loudly, "I won't promise to become a shorn lamb in the king's damned flock!" He moaned, seeing himself in a royal antechamber, clothed like a mincing buffoon, waiting for the king to grant him audience. It was a hideous vision. It curled his toes and made his heart lurch.

Philbo snorted, and Dienwald ceased his flowing monologue and his dismal imaginings, which, after all, needn't necessarily come to pass. In the distance he saw a tight group of men riding toward him. He counted them, sixteen men in all. What could they want? Where were they going? And then he recognized Philippa's mare and Eldwin's huge black gelding and his son's pony.

What was happening here? Where was Philippa going with his men? There she was, riding right there in the fore, leading them, commanding them. Where was she taking his son? Then he froze in his saddle.

She was leaving him. She'd decided she didn't want him. She'd decided that she was too far above him to belittle herself with him further. She'd left St. Erth—her home—where she belonged. She was going to London, to her father's court, to wear precious jewels and fine clothes and never again worry about being naked and having only a blanket to wear.

His fury mounted and he cursed loudly, raising his voice to the heavens. Aye, and he couldn't begin to imagine all the men who would be at court, wanting her, damn her beautiful face and body, not just because of who her father was, but because of how she—

"Damnation!" he bellowed, and urged Philbo to a furious gallop. He saw Edmund riding close to Philippa, Eldwin on his other side. And there was Northbert, his loyal Northbert, riding just behind her. She was stealing his son from him, and his men were helping her. Rage poured through his body.

"By God," Eldwin said, coming closer to Philippa's side. "That's the master! See, 'tis Philbo he rides! He rides right for us, as if he comes from hell."

"Or he rides toward heaven," Philippa said, smiling.

"Aye," Edmund said from her other side, " 'tis Papa!"

"At last," Philippa said, drawing her mare to a halt. Her eyes sparkled for the first time in three days and her back straightened.

Philippa forgot her anger at her husband at the sight of him galloping toward her. He'd come to terms with matters and realized that he wanted her, only her, and she was his wife, no matter who her sire was. How fast he was riding! She felt warmth pouring through her, knowing that soon he would be kissing her and holding her, not caring that his men were watching, that his son would be tugging at his tunic for his own hug. He would probably pull her in front of him on Philbo so he could fondle her all the way back to St. Erth. Philippa closed her eyes a moment and let the sweet feelings flow through her. He would love her and there would be naught but smiles and laughter between them again. No more arguments, no more boiling tempers, no more shouting down the keep.

She opened her eyes, hearing his pounding destrier, and now she could see his face, and she urged her mare forward, wanting to reach him, wanting to lean into his arms when he drew close.

Dienwald jerked up on Philbo's reins, and the powerful destrier reared on his hind legs, snorting loudly.

"Philippa!"

"Aye, husband. I am here, as is your son, as you can see, and your men with us. We were coming to—"

He allowed Philbo to come only a few feet closer to his men and his wife. He needed some distance from her. He'd stoked the fire and now he was ready to blaze. "You damnable bitch! How dare you steal my son! How dare you steal yourself! Aye, I know where you're going, you malignant female—'tis to your father's court you were traveling with my treacherous men, to bask in the king's favor and gleam riches from him. Perfidious wench! Get thee out of my sight! I don't want you, I never wanted you, and I will whip you if you leave not this very instant, this second that follows the end of my words! Hear me, wench?"

"Papa . . ."

"You'll soon be safe from her, Edmund. We'll return to St. Erth and all will be restored to the way it was before she blighted us with her presence. You were right, Edmund: she was a witch, a curse from the devil, rising out of the wool wagon like a creature from Hades, criticizing you, scorching all of us with her tongue with the first words from her mouth. You won't have to suffer her further, none of us will. You, Eldwin, Galen, Northbert! all of you, leave her side. Ride away from her. She's naught but the most treacherous of beings!" He paused, breathing hard.

"Master," Galen said quickly in the moment of respite, though he was awed by his master's flawed fluency. He waved his hand to gain Dienwald's attention, for the master was staring straight at the mistress, blind with anger. The master was confused; he didn't understand. Galen looked toward the mistress, but she was simply staring back at the master, white-faced and still. "What you think isn't what is true, master. You mustn't believe those absurd words you spout—"

"We return to St. Erth at once!" Dienwald roared. "Get thee gone, wench. No more will you torment me with your lies and tempt me with your sweet body."

Philippa hadn't said a word. She'd stared at him, at his mouth, as if she could actually see the venomous words flowing out. He truly thought she was leaving him, taking his son with her to London, to her father's court? She felt a hollowness inside, an emptiness that at the same time overflowed with pain and fury. She stared at him as he yelled and bellowed and insulted her. It was all over now. So much for her silly dreams of his love.

He was exhorting his men now, calling them faithless hounds and churlish knaves. Then he stopped and stared at them, and his men were silent beneath his volley of fury. A spasm of pain crossed his face. They'd all betrayed him. They'd gone over to her side. He felt blinding grief and anger. Without a thought, he galloped through them. He would return to St. Erth. They could do as they pleased; if they chose to follow her, then they could, curse them. His men fell back from him, scattering, their destriers whinnying in surprise. He heard Galen shouting, Northbert bellowing something he didn't understand or care to. He wanted only to get away from her and the misery she'd brought him. He whipped Philbo into a mad gallop away from her, away from his men, straight through them, back to St. Erth. Away from his son, who'd also chosen the damnable wench.

" 'Tis over now," Philippa said. Her lips felt numb, her brain emptied of feeling and thought. She felt utter and complete defeat. Nothing mattered now. It was better so. Then suddenly she felt the blood pounding through her, felt the heat of fury roil and churn within her, felt such black rage at his stupidity that she couldn't bear it. How dare he, the disbelieving fool!

"No!" Philippa yelled after him. She whipped her mare about and raced after her husband. She yelled back over her shoulder, "Eldwin, remain here! None of you do anything! I'll be back soon! Edmund, don't worry. Your father but needs a sound thrashing!"

Dienwald's men, their ranks already split by the master's wild ride, let her go through as well. She rode straight after her husband, her eyes narrowed on his back, her hands fisted over the mare's reins. She saw Dienwald twist in his saddle at the sound of her mare closing on him, saw the surprise on his face, the brief uncertainty, the renewal of rage.

Philbo was tired and the mare was fresh. Just as her mare came beside Philbo, Philippa, not for the last time in her life, thought with her feet. Without hesitation, she jumped from the mare's back straight at her husband, her arms flying around his back. He stared at her in that wild instant, then knew what was going to happen. He lurched around in the saddle, clutched her against his chest even as both of them hurtled from Philbo's back to the ground. Dienwald twisted and landed first, managing to spare Philippa the brunt of the fall. His arms tightened, and he grunted, the breath momentarily knocked out of him.

The road was narrow and curved, alongside it the terrain sloped sharply downward. They rolled over and over, locked together, down the grassy incline, coming finally to a stop in the middle of a patch of eglantine and violets.

Dienwald lay on his back, Philippa atop him. They were both breathing hard. Dienwald wondered if his body was intact or strewn in bits amongst the eglantine. Then Philippa reared back, looking down at him. She, he saw, was just fine. He felt her belly against him and his sex responded instantly, and he knew, at least, that this part of him had survived the fall, and further, would never be immune from her. Her thick glorious hair had come loose of its ribbon and was a riot of wild curls around her face. Her eyes sparkled with fierceness and he found himself waiting eagerly for her outpouring of rage.

"You stupid lout," she shouted three inches from his face. "I should break both your arms and your head! You ignorant clod! Aye, I'll break you into small pieces!"

"You already have," he said. "Ridiculous woman, I tried to protect you, take the brunt of the fall, but your weight flying at me was enough to crush my spleen and pulverize my liver. When we smashed to the ground, my breath died, as did all feeling in my chest."

" 'Tis the loss of your brains that should concern you," Philippa said, and began to pound him. "You had few to begin with, rattling around in that fat head of yours, and now you have none, my lord husband."

Dienwald grabbed her flailing fists—not an easy task—and finally managed to roll her beneath him. He jerked her arms over her head, clasped her wrists together, and came up to straddle her so she couldn't rear up and kick him.

"Now," he said, looking down at her, his chest heaving. "Now."

"Now what, you buffoon?"

He felt words stick in his throat. Something was decidedly wrong here. She seemed unaware of his mastery over her, whereas he was aware of nothing but the maddening effect she had on him.

"I suppose you've been licking your false wounds, with your perfect little Kassia giving you her sweet, tender succor. Is that it, you wretched ass? Have you spent the past three days bemoaning your hideous fate? Cursing me and all the saints for the misery that has befallen you? And did your perfect little Kassia agree with you and cry with you as you smote your feckless brow? Answer me!"

"Not really," he said, and frowned.

She jerked, trying to free her hands, but he only tightened his grip. He wanted to kiss her and thrust inside her and throttle her all at the same time. Instead, he said in his most commanding voice, "I am your master, wench. Only I, no one else. You came to me and seduced me and I wedded you and that is that. Now, hold still and keep your tongue quiet, for I must think."

"Think! Ha!"

"Where were you going with my men and my son? You were escaping me, 'twas plain to see. You were going to London, weren't you? You were taking my son and going to your cursed father. Tell me the truth!"

She sneered at him and tried to kick him, but he held her securely and all she gained was the pressure of his sex, hard and demanding, against her. It drove her mad and enraged her at the same time. "Aye," she shouted so loudly she hurt his ears, "aye, we were all going to London! To my father—to cover myself with jewels and cavort and frolic and dance with all the fine courtiers."

"That's all you can think about? Gallants and jewels? And what would Edmund have done whilst you were cavorting and frolicking and flirting with these frivolous clothheads?"

That stumped her, for her brain had fallen into wayward paths. He was astride her, his legs tight against her sides, and he was panting, so close she could nearly feel the texture of his mouth on her. She wanted desperately to hit him and then kiss him until he was breathless and so hungry for her that he forget everything.

"Don't look at me like that, Philippa. It will do you no good. I won't give in to you. It won't spare you my wrath. Don't deny it—you're trying to seduce me again. No, you've been disloyal to me, you've—"

She suddenly heaved upward with all her strength, taking him off-guard. He fell sideways, not releasing her wrists, and they were lying there with naught but thick clumps of purple violets between them, face-to-face, their noses nearly pressed together. He couldn't help himself. He kissed her, then lurched back as if stung by a hornet.

"Dienwald . . ." she whispered, and hurled herself toward him, trying to kiss him back.

"Nay, I shan't let you debauch me again, wench. Stay away from me." Blood pounded in her head and with a furious cry she pulled free of his hands and smashed down on him, rolling him again onto his back. She was lying atop him once more, and then she was kissing him, even

as he tried to duck away. She gripped his hair
and yanked hard, holding his head between her
hands, and she kissed him again and again, licking his chin, nipping at his nose, rubbing her
cheek against his ear. He felt her belly hard
against his sex and knew it was nearly the finish.
The finish for him. He didn't understand her. She
was yielding and taking both at the same time,
and it astonished him and pleased him. He stilled
his body, letting her have her way with him.

"Wench," he said finally when she'd momentarily left his mouth. "Wench, listen to me."

Eyes vague, heart pounding, Philippa heard his
soft voice and raised her head to look down at
him.

"You're my husband, you peevish fool," she
said, and kissed him again. "You're mine. I
would never leave you, never, no matter how
great my anger at you and your crazy thinking.
Do you understand me?" And she pounded his
head against the violets. "Do you? I was coming
to fetch you, to bring you home to me, where
you belong. Do you understand?"

"Stop it for but a moment! By the saints, my
head! You're breaking my head! There, stop! Aye,
I understand you. But now you heed me. You're
my wife and you won't ever leave me again, do
you understand me? You will remain at St. Erth
or wherever it is I wish you to remain. You won't
ever go haring off to London to see your father
without me. I won't have it, do you hear me?"

"Me leave you?" That made her stop her kisses
and clear her brain just a bit. "You left me! For
three days I didn't know where you were or what
you were doing. Then I realized you would go to

your beloved perfect little Kassia, so I was coming after you, your men and your son with me!"

In her indignation, she tugged at his hair all the harder and pounded his head several more times against the ground. He groaned loudly, and she stopped. "Your head is crushing the violets. How dare you think those awful things about me? You are impossible and I can't imagine why I love you more than I love—" She broke off, staring down at him, knowing that she'd left herself open to him, open to his scorn, his baiting, his insults.

He suddenly smiled, a beautiful crooked smile that made her want to kiss him until he couldn't think. "Were you really coming after me, to fetch me home?"

"Of course! I wasn't going to London. You honestly believe I would steal your son, leave my home? Command your men to attend me? Ah, Dienwald, you deserve this!" She reared back, her arm raised, yet at the last moment her fist stilled in midair. She stared down at him and saw the gleam of challenge in his eyes, the twist of a smile on his mouth. She cursed him softly, then leaned down and kissed him thoroughly. He parted his lips and let her tongue enter his mouth. It was wonderful. She was wonderful and she was his.

"Aye," he said into her warm mouth, "I deserve all of you, wench."

She felt his hands stroke down her back and pulled her flat against him. His fingers were parting her legs, pressing inward through her gown, to touch her. "Dienwald," she said against his mouth.

He jerked up her gown and his fingers were now caressing the bare skin of her inner thighs, working slowly upward, until they found her woman's flesh and then he paused, his fingers quiet now, not moving, merely feeling her warmth and softness. He sighed deeply. "I've missed you."

"Nay, 'tis my body you've missed," she whispered between urgent kisses. "Any female would suit you, 'tis just that you are a lusty cockscomb and a man who is randy all his waking hours. I have heard of all your other women, I even know all their cursed names for Edmund recited them."

"You would surely make me the most miserable of men were I to take another woman to my bed. Do you know that I dream of coming inside you, deep and deeper still, and all the while you're telling me how it makes you feel when I push into you—"

She kissed him again, wild for him now, unheeding of their surroundings. Dienwald was very nearly removed in spirit as well until he heard Eldwin's soft voice, "Master."

Dienwald wanted nothing more than to let Philippa debauch him right here, in the nest of violets and eglantine, the soft warm air swirling about them. He cocked open an eye even as he pulled down her gown.

"What want you, Eldwin? There is an army bearing down on you and you must know where to flee?"

"No, master, 'tis worse."

"What in the name of St. Andrew could possible be worse?"

"It will rain soon, master—a heavy rain, Northbert says, a deluge that could fill this ditch in which you lie. Northbert reads well the clouds and the other signs, you know that."

Dienwald looked up. It was true, the soft warm

air swirling about them was also dark and heavy
and gray. But it didn't matter, not one whit.
"Excellent, my thanks. You and the men take
Edmund back to St. Erth. The wench—my wife
and I will return shortly. Go now. Wait not
another minute. Hurry. Be gone."

Eldwin wasn't blind to what he'd interrupted.
He turned on his heel and hurried back to the
waiting men. Soon Dienwald heard pounding
hooves going away from them.

"Now, wench."

"Now what?"

"Now I shall have my way with you in the
midst of the violets and the eglantine."

When the first rain drop landed on Philippa's
forehead, she was glad for it for she felt fevered
and so urgent she felt ready to burst. Dienwald
brought her closer to his mouth and caressed her
until she screamed, arching her back, wild with
wanting and with the mounting feelings that
filled her. Overflowing now. And when he left
her, she lurched upward and pressed him back
and he fell, laughing and moaning, for she was
kissing his throat, his chest, her hands splayed
over him, and soon she was crouched between
his legs and her mouth was on his belly, her hair
flowing over him, and she was caressing him with
her mouth and her hands. When she took him into
her mouth, tentatively, wonderingly, he thought
he would spill his seed then so urgent did he feel,
but it was as if she guessed, and left him, easing
him gently with her fingers, before caressing him
again until he cried out with it and pulled her off
him. Then he was covering her, and his manhood
was thrusting into her, deep and hard, and so
sweet that she cried with the wonder of it. And

when he spilled his seed within her, he tasted her tears on her lips.

Dienwald said as he kissed the raindrops away, "I love you, Philippa, and I will never cease loving you and wanting you. We are joined, you and I, and it is for always. Never, ever, will I speak to you in anger again. You are mine forever."

And she said only, "Yes."

He was heavy on her, but she didn't care. She wrapped her arms about his back and hugged him all the more tightly. The rain thickened and it was only then they realized that they were lying in the open, sheets of rain pouring down on them, in the gray light. And then Dienwald saw there was something else beside the rain.

There was Walter de Grasse standing at the top of the incline, staring down at them, his face twisted with rage.

23

Dienwald slowly eased away from Philippa and pulled her gown down her legs, pretending not to see Walter.

"Love . . ." she said, her voice soft and drowsy despite the rain battering down on her. "Love, don't leave me."

"Philippa," he said as he straightened his clothes, "come, you must awaken now."

Sir Walter's voice cracked through the silence. "Are you certain you are through plowing her belly, you whoreson? If the little slut wants more, I shall take her and give her pleasure she's never known with you."

Walter! Philippa sat up quickly, staring at her cousin, who still stood at the top of the incline, his hands on his hips, rain long since soaked through his clothes. He'd *watched* them. She felt at once sick to her stomach and blindly furious. She scrambled to her feet.

Dienwald took one of her hands in his and squeezed it. When he spoke, his tone was almost impersonal. "What do you want, de Grasse?"

"I want what is mine. I want her, despite what you've done to her."

Dienwald squeezed her hand tightly now, and said in the same detached way, "You can't have her, de Grasse. She was never yours to have, save in your fantasies. She's mine. As you have observed, she is completely mine."

"Nay, you bastard! She'll wed me! She'll have no choice, for I'll hold you to ensure her compliance!"

Dienwald stared at him. "Too late, de Grasse, you are far too late. Philippa is already wedded to me with her father's—the king's—blessing."

"You lie!"

"Why should I?"

That drew Walter up for a moment. He eyed his enemy of so many years that he'd lost count. De Fortenberry had been an enemy before Walter had even seen his face, his very name a litany of vengeance. So long ago Dienwald's father had beaten Walter's, but it hadn't been fair, it hadn't been unprejudiced. No, his father had been cheated, cheated of everything, his only son disinherited. "I should have killed you when I had you at Wolffeton. I broke your ribs, but it wasn't enough, though I enjoyed it. I should have tortured you until I tired of hearing your screams, and then I should have sent my sword into your belly. Ah, but no, I waited, like a fool I waited for Graelam to return, certain that he would mete out justice, that he would right the wrongs done unto my father and unto me. I was a fool then, I admit it. I didn't think that Lord Graelam's wife, that little bitch, Kassia—your lover—would dare rescue you. But she did, curse her. Hellfire, I should have killed her for saving you!"

"But you didn't," Dienwald said, bringing Philippa against his side. "And Graelam, not knowing the depths of your twisted hatred, made you castellan of Crandall. But you couldn't be satisfied with your overlord's trust. No, you couldn't dismiss your hatred and forget your imagined ills. You had to kill my people and burn their huts and their crops and put the sword to their animals. You went too far, de Grasse. Graelam knows what you did. He will not allow it to continue. He himself will kill you. I won't have to bother."

"Kill me? You? As for Graelam, you have no proof, de Fortenberry, of any burning or killing. Not a shred of proof do you have. Graelam would never act without proof. I know him well. He thinks he judges character like a god, when he is but a fool. And when he finds you dead, there will still be no proof, and he won't act against me."

"Then you stole Philippa and my son. You will die, Walter, and your enmity will die with you."

"Stole! Ha! I rescued my cousin! Your miserable brat just happened to be with her. I didn't harm him, the little vermin. Skewer not the truth for your own ends."

"Since there is no longer a rescue to be made, since Philippa is my wife with the king's blessing, then you intend now to take your leave of us? You intend to forget your plaints and return to Crandall?"

Even as he spoke, Dienwald saw Walter's men, in view now, yet blurred in the downpour. The shower was lessening a bit but they were still vague and gray. They looked miserable; they looked uncertain.

Philippa said, "Walter, I am wedded to Dienwald. I am his wife. Both Lord Henry and Robert Burnell, the king's chancellor, will attest to it. It is true. Leave us be."

Walter ground his teeth. He felt maddened with failure, his loss surrounding him, gashing into him, twisting him and taunting him. He'd not gained what was his by birthright. He'd gained nothing, less than nothing. Life hadn't meted out justice to him. There would be no retribution unless he gained it for himself. And now he'd stood watching his enemy enjoy the girl intended for him. He raised his face to the skies and howled his fury.

It was a grim sound, terrifying and haunting. Philippa clutched Dienwald against her side, turning her face inward to his chest. It was a howl of pain and defeat and ruin; a cry of loss of faith, loss of self.

Then Walter was silent; all his men were silent, though several were crossing themselves. The silence dragged on. It was frightening and eerie. The rain pounded down and the curving piece of ground upon which Dienwald and Philippa stood began to fill with water. The violets sagged beneath the weight of the rain.

Then Walter, without warning, drew his sword and leapt down the incline, his full weight landing against Dienwald's chest, battering him backward. Philippa was thrown to the side, splashing onto her knees into the water. She scrambled to her feet, flailing about to gain purchase in the swirling torrent.

Walter's sword was drawn, and in a smooth arc aimed toward Dienwald's chest. Dienwald had naught but a knife and he held it in his right hand, then tossed it to his left, back and forth, taunting Walter.

He said softly, "Well, you sodden fool? Come, let's see if you understand the uses for your sword! Or will you just stand there?"

Walter gave a roar of sheer rage and rushed toward Dienwald, his sword straight out in front of him. Dienwald sidestepped him easily, but his foot slipped on the slick grass and he twisted about, falling on his back.

Philippa picked up a rock and threw it with all her strength at Walter. It hit him square in the chest. He looked at her, surprise writ on his face. "Philippa? Why do you that? I am come to save you. You mustn't pretend you don't want to come with me, wed with me, there is no more need. I will kill him and then you will come with me."

Walter turned, but Dienwald was on his feet again, feinting to the right, away from Walter's sword thrust.

On and on it went, and Philippa knew Dienwald must fail eventually. His knife was no contest against Walter's sword. Suddenly there came shouts from the road above.

The men paid no heed.

Philippa paid no heed either. She had grasped another stone and was waiting for the chance to strike Walter with it, but the men were close, too close, and she feared hitting Dienwald instead.

"Philippa! Stand clear!"

She whirled about and looked upward. It was

Graelam de Moreton and he was standing on the road above them. Beside him stood the man Roland de Tournay. She watched through the now gentle fall of rain. Roland drew a narrow dagger from his belt, its shaft silver and bright even in the gray light, aimed it, and released it. It slit through the air so quickly, Philippa didn't see it. She heard a suddenly gurgling sound, then turned to see the dagger embedded deep in Walter's chest. He dropped the sword and clutched at the dagger's ivory handle. He pulled it out and stared at the crimson blade. Then he looked upward at Roland de Tournay.

He looked confused and said, "Do I know you? Why do you kill me?"

He said nothing more, merely looked once again at Philippa, gave a tiny shake of his head, and collapsed onto his face in the water.

Dienwald stood panting over him. He frowned down at Walter's lifeless body. " 'Twas a good throw." Then he looked up at Roland. "I was very nearly the victor. You acted too quickly."

"Next time I'll let your wife hit your adversary with rocks," Roland shouted.

"By all the saints above," Graelam shouted, "enough! Come up now and let us ride to St. Erth. Dienwald, thank Roland for saving your hide. But hurry, for I am so sodden my tongue molds in my mouth!"

Within minutes Philippa was huddled in the circle of her husband's arms atop Philbo. One of Graelam's men was leading her mare. Walter's men hadn't fought, for Lord Graelam de Moreton was, after all, Sir Walter's overlord, and thus they, his men-at-arms, also owed allegiance to Lord Graelam.

Dienwald looked at Graelam. "How came you by so unexpectedly? I was praying, but 'twas not for your company in particular."

"We came by design," Graelam said. "Roland wanted to see the final act of the play he'd helped to write."

"What does he mean?" Philippa asked, twisting about to face her husband.

"Hush, wench. 'Tis not important. Roland is loose-tongued, but he does throw a dagger well."

"But—"

"Hush," he repeated, then said, "Will you continue to welcome me as sweetly as did gentle, perfect Kassia?"

She stiffened, as he'd expected, her thoughts turned, and he grinned over her head.

They were shivering, their teeth chattering, when they finally rode into St. Erth's inner bailey. Once in the great hall, they were overwhelmed with cheers and shouts and blessed warmth and trestle tables covered with mounds of food. All of St. Erth's people were gathered in the huge chamber, and it was noisy and hot and the smells of food mingled with the smells of sweat and wet wool and it was wonderful.

"Welcome," Philippa said, her wet face radiant as she turned to her guests. "We're home!"

She sneezed suddenly, and Dienwald swooped down upon her and picked her up in his arms. He pretended to stagger under her weight, saying, "My poor back, wench! I'm nearly beyond my abilities, with you so weighty with wet wool."

Graelam and Roland watched Dienwald carry her from the great hall, grinning at the wild cheering from all St. Erth's people. "The king's son-in-law is a fine man," Graelam said.

"Aye, and no longer a fool," Roland said. He fell silent, frowning. "I do find it passing odd, though."

"What do you find odd?"

"That Philippa, a girl of remarkable taste and refinement, preferred him to me. I am incredulous. 'Tis not normal in my experience. Why, the harem I kept in Acre, Graelam—you wouldn't believe the appetites of my women! And it was my duty, naturally, to satisfy appetites each night. And they never complained that I shirked my duty to them. But Philippa gives me not a look."

Graelam merely laughed, grabbed a hunk of well-roasted rabbit, and waved it in Roland's face. "You braying ass! Lying dog! Harem? I believe you not, not for an instant. What harem? How came you by a harem? How many women? You satisfied more than one woman each night?"

Crooky chortled and waved his hands toward all the food. "A feast, my lords. A feast worthy of a king or a king's daughter and her friends!" And he jumped upon Dienwald's chair and burst into song.

A wedding feast lies here untasted
The lord and lady care not it's wasted.
They're frolic and gambol without a yawn
They'll play through the night 'til the dawn.

In their bedchamber, warm and dry beneath three blankets, the master and mistress of St. Erth lay together listening to the rain and enjoying each other's kisses. They heard a sudden shout of loud laughter and guffawing from below in the great hall, and wondered at it, but not for long, for Philippa nuzzled Dienwald's throat, saying, "Have you restocked your seed?"

"What?" Dienwald said, and pulled back to look at his wife's laughing mouth.

" 'Tis what Old Agnes said, that I would fetch you home and keep you in my bed until you begged me to let you sleep and restock your seed."

"Aye, all is in readiness for you, greedy wench. I ask for nothing more in this sweet life than to be debauched by you each night."

"A promise easily made and more than easily kept."

Epilogue

Dienwald quickly closed the door to the opulent chamber, locked it, drew a deep breath, then let it out slowly as he sagged against the door, his eyes closed.

"My lord husband, you did well. My father thinks you nearly as wonderful as do I."

Dienwald opened his eyes at that. "He does, does he? Ha! I'll wager you he still thinks Roland de Tournay would have made the better husband and the better son-in-law. And I have to call Roland, that damned brute, friend! It passes all bounds, Philippa."

She wanted to laugh, but managed to keep her mouth from quivering, her eyes slightly lowered. "Roland is just a common fellow, husband, of little account to my life and of no account at all to my heart. And since my father no longer has any say in the matter, it's not important. What did you think of Queen Eleanor?"

"A beautiful lady," Dienwald said somewhat absently, then frowned, moaned, and closed his eyes again. "The king looked at me and knew, Philippa—he knew I'd raided that merchant's goods near Penrith."

Philippa laughed. "Aye, he knew. He was amused, he told me so, but he also hinted to me that I should scold you just a bit—'never be a testy nag, my daughter,' he said—and somehow keep you from plundering about the countryside. I truly believe he said nothing to you because he doesn't want to break your spirit."

"He doesn't want to break my spirit! I don't suppose you told him that you were with me, riding at my side, dressed like a lad, laughing at how easily we sidetracked that merchant who'd cheated us?"

Philippa straightened her shoulders and looked down her nose at him. "Naturally not. I am part Plantagenet, thus part of the very highest nobility. Besides, do you think me an utter fool?"

"Next time we will take greater care," Dienwald said. He pushed away from the door and walked to the middle of their chamber and stopped. The room was dazzling in the elegance of its furnishings, and the overwhelming luxury of it stifled him. The bed was hung with rich velvet draperies, their thick crimson folds held with golden rope and ties. The velvet was so thick, so voluminous, one could suffocate if the hangings were drawn at night.

"The ceremony was moving, Dienwald, and you looked as royal as my father and his family."

Dienwald grunted. He looked down at his flamboyant crimson tunic, belted with a wide leather affair studded with gems. A ceremonial sword was strapped to his waist. He looked well enough, he supposed, but one couldn't scratch in such clothing, one couldn't really stretch. One couldn't grab one's wife and caress her and fondle her and fling her onto the bed and wrestle with her, tearing off clothing and laughing together and tumbling about.

" 'Dienwald de Fortenberry, Earl of St. Erth.' Or perhaps I prefer 'Lord St. Erth.' Ah, that has a sound of proud consequence and arrogant privilege. It fits you well, my lord earl. And Edmund will grow nicely into that appellation, for already he scowls like you do when displeased, and orders me about as if I were his wench."

Dienwald was silent. He sat down in an ornately carved high-backed chair, stretched out his legs, and looked morosely into the fireplace.

Philippa, her humor fled, knelt in front of him and gazed up at his distracted face. "What troubles you, husband? Do you wish now that you weren't tied to me?"

He stretched out his hand and lightly touched his fingers to her hair. It was arranged artfully, with many pins and ribbons and fastenings, and he feared to dislodge such perfection. He dropped his hand.

Philippa snorted and flung away the pins and ribbons, shaking her head until her hair hung free, framing her smiling face.

"There, now do what you will. As you always do when we are home."

Dienwald sat back, his fingers absently sliding through strands of her hair, his eyes still melancholy, as he gazed at the orange flames in the fireplace.

"I'm no longer just me," he said at last.

"True," Philippa agreed, leaning her cheek against his knee. "I'm part of you now, as is the child I carry."

His fingers stilled abruptly and his dulled expression vanished in a flash. "The *what*?"

"The child I now carry. Our babe."

"You didn't tell me." She heard the beginnings of outrage in his voice and smiled.

"Why didn't you tell me? I am the father, after all!" He was ready for an argument, a banging loud fight, but she didn't plan to give him what he wished just yet.

In a voice as calm as a moonless night she said, "I wanted to wait until after you'd met my father and dealt with your honors and position. Now that you've survived all your new privileges and awards and tributes, all the banquets and fawning courtiers, we can return to Cornwall, to our real life. Tomorrow we leave London, and we'll look back on this and know it was but a fragment of something not really part of us, Dienwald, something like a dream that scarce touches us."

"Save that I'm now a peer of the realm and have my coffers filled with royal coin. Royal coin I never sought."

"Aye, I know," she said, gently rubbing her palm on his thigh. And, she thought, grinning, you're spoiling for a fight. You can't bear that I'm being so quiet, so reasonable. Not just yet, my husband.

His fingers tightened in her hair. "Aye, none

of this I wanted. I have been made to feel guilt over a bit of honest thievery, and that from a man who'd cheated me! I won't have it, wench! And now you deign to tell me you are with child! *You* decide it is time that *I* know of *my* babe. You have deceived me, and I shall make you very sorry that you did."

"Just what will you do?"

She was teasing him! He stared down at her laughing face, saw the dimples deepening in her cheeks, and wanted to throttle her. "I will think of something, and don't you doubt it."

Her voice was as demure as a virgin's. "Something worthy of an earl? Worthy of Lord St. Erth, that scoundrel and knave?"

He sought for words but couldn't find a single one, so instead he leaned down, grasped her face between his palms, and kissed her hard.

He pulled away and saw the darkening of her eyes, the sheen of passion building, the soft yielding to him. It was always so, and it always made him feel boundless satisfaction and immense male pleasure. He smiled and kissed her again. His hands left her face and stroked downward until they held her breasts. When she moaned softly, coming up on her knees to get closer to him, to come between his legs, he pulled back and grinned evilly down at her. "There, I have my revenge and it's worthy of any man in the realm who's worth his salt. I started to debauch you, and when you were reach to beg me for it, I stopped."

Philippa stared at him silently for a very long time. He fidgeted, but she didn't move, didn't speak. Then, as he looked at her, two tears seeped from her eyes and trailed down her cheeks. She didn't make a sound. Tears continued to gather and fall.

"Philippa, don't cry. I . . ."

He gathered her against him, wanting to pet her and fondle her and make her forget her tears. When he leaned forward to draw her up, she suddenly jerked back and smashed her fists against his chest. He lurched sideways, and the chair tipped and fell, sending them both flailing to the floor. But he didn't release his wife. They lay in front of the fire, facing each other, and she was grinning at him.

"You give over, husband?"

"I'll give you anything you want, wench."

"Will you love me here, on this soft Flanders carpet, in front of the fire?"

"Aye, I'll make you moan with pleasure before I'm done with you."

"Proceed, husband. I await your pleasure."

He laughed and drew her to him. She was his wife, this king's daughter, and he would wear his earl's laurels as would his sons and his sons' sons after them. And he would repair St. Erth and it would become a renowned and mighty castle, a bastion to defend the king's honor, a protector of those in his domain, in all Cornwall. And his wife would birth him a daughter who would likely marry the small son delivered earlier that summer at Wolffeton.

He knew himself unworthy. He prayed he would become more worthy as time passed.

He prayed also that worthiness had nothing to do with an occasional raid, an occasional theft, an occasional assault on some knave, who would, after all, deserve the fate that would befall him.

Philippa's hands stroked his face, and he kissed

her neck. "I love you," he said, nipping at her earlobe. "As do my son and all the people at St. Erth."

"You don't mind that Edmund chooses to call me Mama?"

"Nay, why should I? 'Witch' and 'Cursed Maypole' don't go well with your new dignities. Now, enough of this nonsense that has nothing to do with what I want to do to your body."

"And what is that?"

"If you will close your lips against your silly female words, I will show you."

SECRET
Song

To my parents, Charles and Elizabeth Coulter,
who passed along what talent genes I can lay
claim to. All my love and thanks.

PROLOGUE

Near Grainsworth Abbey
March 1275

DARIA wished the heavy clouds overhead would free the snow. She wanted the misery of freezing snow blowing into her face, stinging her eyes, mixing with the burning tears.

But as the afternoon lengthened, the weather simply grew colder, the wind more vicious, twisting and ripping through the few naked-branched oak trees that lined the narrow road, but it didn't snow.

She hunched down in her miniver-lined cloak and closed her eyes. Her mare, Henrietta, plodded onward, her head bowed, keeping rhythm with the destrier's pace ahead of her. Every few minutes, Drake, Lord Damon's master-at-arms, would swivel about to see that she still rode docilely behind him, that she hadn't somehow fled without him noticing, that she was keeping herself silent and submissive and obedient. Drake wasn't a bad man, or cruel, but he was her uncle's minion, and he always carried out his master's orders without hesitation or question. Also, she knew, it would never occur to him to question his master's right to dispose of his niece in any way that suited him. She was naught but a female and thus all decisions were made for her and around her.

She had no choices. She knew now that she'd never had a choice. She simply hadn't realized it so starkly before. Before, Daria, the child, had had to obey only occasional commands from her uncle, nothing of the magnitude that would make her want to crawl away and die. After all, what could a man want with a child? But now she was seventeen, more than old enough to be weighed and judged and a value set on her. She was no longer a child and her uncle had seen it and acted on it. A girl went from her father—or in this case, her uncle—to her husband. From one man to another. Chattel of one man to be chattel of another. No choice, no argument. It was as the man dictated, as the man ordered. She felt tears again, and hated them, for crying was useless. Crying meant that there was hope, and there wasn't any of that to be had.

Daria dashed her palm over her eyes, and when she opened them again she saw in her mind's eye her uncle Damon, as clear to her as the armored back of Drake, who rode directly in front of her. She saw him in his bedchamber and she heard his voice, deep and clear and indifferent, his words of a month ago still as fresh as if he'd spoken them but moments before. No, she thought now, he hadn't been indifferent, not at all. It had been an act. He'd been looking forward to this—to humiliating her and then telling her what he'd planned for her. No, her uncle was never indifferent in his cruelty. He relished it.

He'd been sitting up in his fur-covered bed, Cora, one of the castle serving wenches, naked beside him. Upon Daria's entrance into Lord Damon's bedchamber, Cora had giggled and slithered down beside him, pulling the white rabbit furs over her naked shoulders. He appeared not to care that the furs left his own chest bare. He appeared not to care that he was naked and in his bed with his mistress in front of his niece. Of course he'd planned it. There was no doubt in her mind. Daria had said nothing, merely waited for him to tell her why he'd sent for her. He in turn was silent for many moments, negligently stroking his right hand over Cora's shoulder.

Daria had closed her eyes, knowing he did this for her benefit, to show her yet again that a female was naught but what a man wanted her to be.

Daria had felt the familiar feelings of hate, revulsion, and helplessness surge through her. She loathed her uncle and he knew it, and she guessed it amused him, this silent hatred of hers. This *meaningless* silent hatred of hers. What did he want? For her to scream at him, to cry, to cower in humiliation and embarrassment? She stood perfectly still. She'd learned patience with him. She'd learned to wait silent as a rock, giving him no encouragement.

She didn't move. Her expression didn't change.

Suddenly he seemed to tire of his game. He pulled the furs higher over Cora and told her to be still and turn her back to him. "I tire of your sheep's face," he added, his eyes all the while on his silent niece.

"You sent for me," Daria said finally, holding her voice as calm and emotionless as she was trying to hold her body.

"Aye, I did. You're more than full grown, Daria. You turned seventeen two months ago. My silly little Cora here—already quite a woman—is only fifteen. You should have a babe suckling at your breast by now, as do most females. Aye, I've held you here overlong. But I had to wait, you see, wait for just the offer I wished." He smiled then, showing all his very white teeth. "At least next month you will finally have a husband to plow that little belly of yours. And he'll do it enthusiastically, I doubt it not."

She paled and stepped back. She couldn't help it.

He laughed. "Doesn't the thought of a husband please you, niece? Or do you fear and dislike all men? Don't you wish to escape me and become mistress in your own keep?"

She stared at him, mute.

"Answer me, you silly girl!"

"Aye."

"Good. It will be done. When you leave me, Daria, tell your mother I wish to see her. Cora has but whetted my appetite."

Daria didn't move this time, and after a moment, Damon merely shrugged, as if tiring of baiting her. Daria knew he forced her mother, her gentle, sweet mother—his dead half-brother's wife—and had taken her since the accidental death of his half-brother, James of Fortescue, in a tourney in London some four years before. But her mother, Lady Katherine, had never said a word to Daria, never complained, never cried. She was told she was to go to the lord and she went without comment, without objection, to Damon, and later emerged, still silent, her eyes cast down, her mouth sometimes swollen and bruised-looking. But Daria knew; all the servants spoke of it and she'd overheard them. This was the first time he had spoken openly of it before to her. But he wanted her to know, she guessed, but she wouldn't do what he wanted, she wouldn't plead with him, she wouldn't beg him to spare her mother. She said instead, "Who is to be my husband?"

"So you do have some interest, do you? You will doubtless be happy about my choice for you." He paused and she saw the malicious gleam in his pale blue eyes. She knew she wouldn't like it and so did he. She waited, silent and still and cold, wishing now she'd kept her mouth shut and hadn't asked. She didn't want to know, not yet. But Damon said, his voice relishing his words, "Why, it is Ralph of Colchester, eldest son of the Earl of Colchester. They visited Reymerstone, don't you remember? Last November. Ralph told me he is most pleased with you, as is his father."

"Not Ralph of Colchester! No! You would not, he is

loathsome! He raped Anna again and again and he got her with child and—"

Damon roared with laughter. She'd finally reacted and he was pleased with himself. "Aye, I know it," he said, still laughing, shaking the big bed with his mirth. "I made him a wager, you see. I told him that his father and I wanted him to get you with child immediately, and to see if he was capable, I gave him Anna, who was ready to be bred in any case. He impregnated her quickly. I was pleased and relieved, as was his father."

Daria just looked at him, stunned and repelled, but not really surprised. She heard herself ask, "What did you offer as your wager with him?"

Damon laughed again. "So there is still a portion of defiance in you? Well, no matter now. I wagered your mother's gold necklace. The one my half-brother gave her upon their marriage." He watched her face closely.

She gave him no more satisfaction. She'd given him more than enough. She said instead, shrugging, "It is of very little value."

She looked at him, and for an instant, just a brief moment, she thought she saw some resemblance to her father in him. But she wasn't certain. She couldn't remember her father clearly anymore, even though it had been only four years since his death. But her father had been gone so often, for long stretches of time, and he hadn't particularly noticed her even on his rare visits to Fortescue Hall, for she was naught but a girl, a female whose only worth lay in a marriage advantageous to him. Still, surely he hadn't been as vile as his elder half-brother, surely.

And now it was Damon, his half-brother, who would gain the advantages of her marriage.

"What did you offer Ralph and his father? All my inheritance?"

"Why, certainly, most of it, but I dislike your impertinent tongue. Hold it quiet or I will have your mother brought here and she will tell you the value of obedience to me. Aye, Colchester will have most of your immense dowry and I will have the Colchester land that will extend my boundaries all the way to the North Sea. It is precisely what I wanted, what I've waited for so patiently. Actually, I will tell you why I allowed you to become so aged. The boy, Ralph, was mightily ill last year and I didn't know if he would survive; his father was concerned that even if he did survive, he wouldn't still have potent seed. But I was content to wait. He did survive, as did his seed, and aye, little Daria, I have got what I wanted, all of it."

" 'Tis my money, my inheritance! All that my father owned, he gave to me. You take everything, and 'twas not yours to take!"

His face darkened and he threw back the furs. He came to his feet, standing naked by his bed. Cora stared at him as he strode to Daria. For a moment Daria believed he would strike her, but he didn't. He'd never struck her. It wasn't his way. He just smiled at her now, but she knew that it was rage burning bright in his eyes, not amusement.

"Go now," he said at last. "Even you have managed to offend me, which is surprising. Your mother will prepare for your trip to Colchester. You will have wagons full of household items, as every bride should. You are the Reymerstone heiress; thus I have been more than generous with you. I would not wish to make a niggardly impression or leave any person in doubt of my affection for you, for I want no questions. You will leave in three weeks. I will come in time for your wedding, of course. And if you are obedient, I just might bring your mother with me. Well, why don't you say something? No? Leave me, then!"

She stared at him a moment, not at his body—for the very hardness of him, all that pale blond hair that covered him, frightened her—but at his hated face. Then she turned and walked from the chamber.

All she saw, all she could comprehend, was that Ralph of Colchester was to be her husband.

Her mother had held her, petted her whilst she cried, but she'd told her that any marriage—even to Ralph of Colchester—was better than remaining here. She must face it and behave as a lady ought, with dignity and acceptance. With a smooth, serene countenance.

And that was that. But Daria had despised the twenty-year-old Ralph of Colchester with his weak chin and his bowed thin legs and his leering expressions. And she'd seen what he'd done to Anna, fourteen-year-old Anna, naught but a child herself really, big-breasted, and pretty and stupid. She hadn't deserved to be raped repeatedly, but she had been, for the entire week's visit. Twice a day Ralph had raped her. And the men had laughed and clapped the miserable youth on his shoulder and told him his rod was sure and true.

Finally, Daria thought, bringing herself back to the present, raising her face skyward. Snowflakes were falling now, each one falling more quickly than the last, blanketing Drake, his men, and all the wagons in pure white. As the flakes struck her face, she felt the numbing cold of them pierce more and more deeply into her. Henrietta stumbled and snorted and Daria patted her neck. She wondered if Ralph would allow her to ride once they were wedded. She wondered if he would rape her twice a day as he had Anna.

Drake turned, shouting back to her that they would shortly arrive at the Cistercian Abbey of Grainsworth, where they would pass the night.

They were soon forced to form a single-file column, for the road narrowed dramatically, bounded on both sides by huge rocks and tumbled boulders, stark and bold.

When the attack came, it was all the more terrifying because Drake and his dozen men couldn't see their enemy; nor could they defend themselves, held apart in their long line, their horses screaming and lunging in terror. They fell, one by one, struck by the arrows shot from behind the rocks. Some of the men were wearing armor, but it didn't matter, they were rained with arrows and eventually an arrow found its mark in the man's neck or in his face. Other men wore padded jerkins, and they were killed more quickly. But none of them had a chance against an enemy hidden behind rocks and shooting through a thick veil of white snow.

Oddly enough, after the first shock of the attack, Daria wasn't afraid. She knew deep inside her that she wouldn't die. Not today, not by an arrow shot through her chest. When only Daria and her maid, Ena, remained, when all the screams died away and the white air was cleansed of arrows and men's cries, did their attackers emerge, unscathed. They were shouting and laughing at the ease of their victory. Daria saw their leader immediately, a huge man, and he was laughing the loudest as he directed his men to loot the dead, collect the horses, and see to the wagons.

He took off his helmet. He had the reddest hair she'd ever seen.

1

Reymerstone Castle, Essex, England
Near the North Sea
Early May 1275

ROLAND DE TOURNAY found the seat of the Earl of
Reymerstone easily enough. The castle dominated the
rock-strewn promontory that jutted out like a tongue
into the Thirgby River that flowed nearly a mile into
the North Sea. The castle was in the Norman style,
built by the present earl's great-grandfather, and was
more stark and weathered than comfortable, still more
of a fortification and a garrison than a residence. Yet
the present earl had lined the pockets of many merchants to add comfort to the austere gray stone castle,
luxuries such as thick tapestries to blanket the stone
walls and keep out the damp from the North Sea,
Flanders carpets in bright scarlets and royal blues,
beautiful embroidered cushions for the three chairs,
each made by an artisan of great skill. The dozen
trestle tables and their long benches in the great hall,
however, had not changed in three generations, and
past living of all the common men and women who
had shared their meals on the gnarled old tables still
showed clearly, all the scuffs, all the knife-carved ini-
tials, all the old grease.

The great hall of Reymerstone was impressive, Roland decided as he waited for the emergence of the

15

Earl of Reymerstone, Damon Le Mark. Roland knew he was being studied by several serving wenches and sent them a wink that caused giggles and pert smiles. He saw a female hurrying toward him, this one a lady, possibly the mistress of Reymerstone. She was in her thirties, brown-eyed, hair a dull red and of slight stature. She'd once been very pretty. Now she looked faded and tired, her shoulders slightly bowed. She looked beaten down. Her expression, however, when she looked at him, suddenly changed and she looked furtively around her, then approached him quickly, her step light and quick as a girl's.

"You are Roland de Tournay, sir?" she asked in a low voice that was soft and cultured.

"Aye, my lady. I come at the invitation of the Earl of Reymerstone, your husband."

"He will be here shortly. He is otherwise occupied just now." What did that mean? Roland wondered. The woman continued, "I am Lady Katherine of Fortescue, the current earl's sister-in-law. His half-brother was my husband."

"Your husband was James of Fortescue? I had heard he'd fallen by accident in a tourney, just before he was to leave with Edward for the Holy Land. My sympathies, my lady."

She again nodded her bowed head. Roland frowned. Couldn't she look at him, eye-to-eye? Could she possibly be frightened of him?

"Do you know why Lord Reymerstone asked me to come here?"

Her head came up then and he saw the strain in her fine eyes. And there was something else—fear, perhaps, which brought him fully alert.

"It concerns my daughter," she said quickly, glancing behind her. She grabbed his sleeve. "You must find my child and bring her back safely, you must! Ah, here he comes. I daren't remain. I will leave you now, sir."

She glided silently away, gone into the gaggle of serving wenches before the earl had seen her.

Roland had a moment to study the Earl of Reymerstone as he strode toward him. He was a tall man, in his late thirties, lean of build, a full head of white-blond hair, his eyes the palest of blues. His stubborn chin was beardless, his expression was obstinate. He didn't look to be an easy man. He looked to be a man who got his own way, by any means necessary. Roland had survived many of his adult years by correctly summing up a man's character. He'd seldom been wrong in the past five years. Indeed, his only huge mistake had been in his dealings with a woman. A lady, so very young, so very fair, and he a young man of very tender years. He shook off the memory of Joan of Tenesby.

The earl gave Roland a brief nod and Roland knew he'd been weighed in those short minutes as well. "You have come in good time, thank the saints, de Tournay. Come and sit with me. We have much to discuss."

Roland accepted a cup of ale and waited for his host to come to the point.

"I will pay you well," Damon Le Mark said, and raised his own cup for a toast. Roland sent him a bland look and asked, "Whom do I have to kill?"

The earl laughed. "I do not seek to hire an assassin. Any enemy I have I will slay myself. I hire a man who's known for his ingenuity, his ability with languages, and his skill at changing his appearance to suit any situation in which he finds himself. Is it not true that you were accepted in the company of Barbars himself in the Holy Land? That you passed yourself off as a Saracen for two years? That you masqueraded as a Muslim with such finesse even the most devout didn't know you for what you were?"

"You are well-informed." Roland wasn't about to deny the earl's recital. He wasn't vain; nor was he foolishly modest. For the most part, it was true. Odd how the very attributes Roland held to be in his favor sounded vile on the earl's lips. He waited, more interested now. The earl's need must be great. The task must be beyond his own abilities, and it irked him.

Damon Le Mark knew he must suffer the arrogance and impertinence of the young man seated in front of him, a young man who, in addition to his reputation for boldness and cunning, was passing handsome, his lean face well sculpted, his black hair thick and gleaming, his dark eyes bright with intelligence. But he was swarthy as a savage Irishman, and didn't look to be a man of particular wealth or refinement. Damon Le Mark also reminded himself that this man was of no inborn worth at all despite his birth and his heritage. He held no title and, more important, no land. He was a man who made his way by playacting and deceit, and yet he, a man his superior in every way, must be gracious, and he must offer him a great deal of money. It was galling.

"I'm always well-informed," the earl said. "It took my couriers a good deal of time to locate you."

"I received your message in Rouen. I was passing the winter there very pleasantly."

"So I hear." He'd been told by his own man that de Tournay had been living with a very pretty young widow in Rouen.

"Her name was Marie," Roland said easily, and sipped at his ale. It was warm and dark and very smooth. "But do not mistake me. I was ready to come home, very nearly. As soon as the weather grew warmer."

"To earn money by guile?"

"Yes, if need be, though I believe that wit is more to the point than guile. Would you not agree?"

The earl knew he'd been insulting when he shouldn't have. He retrenched, shrugging. "Ah, it's those other things that must interest me, de Tournay, for I wish you not to do them just yet. The reason I asked you here is vital. It concerns my beloved niece, Daria. I will be brief. She was kidnapped on her journey to Colchester, where she was to wed Ralph of Colchester. All twelve of the men in her train were butchered in an ambush. All the wagons carrying her wedding goods were stolen. I want you to rescue her and I will pay you very well."

"Has a ransom been demanded?"

The earl's eyes narrowed and he bared his teeth. "Oh, aye, the damnable impertinent whoreson! I would that you would kill him as well, but I suppose that the rescue of my dearest niece must take precedence."

"Who stole her?"

"Edmond of Clare."

"The Marcher Baron? How very odd." Roland fell silent. It was more than odd. The Marcher Barons, their power and existence granted to them by the great Duke William himself nearly two hundred years before, had little reason to stray from their strongholds unless it was to press west to garner more Welsh land and butcher more Welsh outlaws. It was their responsibility to contain the Welsh, and this they did with endless vigor and impressive continuity. They were in effect little kings, holding immense power in their own feudal kingdoms. It galled King Edward no end, this power outside himself, and Roland knew he planned to curtail their immense influence by defeating the Welsh once and for all by building royal castles all along the northern coast of the country. "I'll push the malignant little lordlings until they're on bended knee to me, pleading with me to leave them something!"

he'd said once, pounding a table with his fist and sending it in splinters to the floor. Roland continued after a moment, "Edmond of Clare's stronghold is between Chepstow and Trefynwy, bordering the southeast corner of Wales. Why would he come across the width of England to kidnap your niece?"

The earl kept a stubborn silence. The impertinence of the knave, asking him these questions. He was furious but he contained himself. He couldn't anger de Tournay, for the man wasn't his to command. De Tournay could leave. Still, he refused to tell him the truth of the matter. He laid the matter on another's shoulders, saying finally, "Clare despises the Earl of Colchester. He wanted revenge so he stole my niece. He wants nearly all her dowry as ransom or he will rape her until she is with child before he returns her to me."

"What did Colchester do to Clare to merit such a chilling revenge?"

Damon Le Mark's face paled and his hand shook. He wanted to thrash de Tournay for his infernal curiosity. He smiled and Roland felt the chill of that smile to his bones. This was not a man to guard your back. Damon shrugged. "I understand Colchester accidentally killed Clare's brother some five years ago. I know none of the actual facts of the incident, and it was Colchester's decision not to tell me more. Now, will you rescue my niece?"

This was doubtless a lie, but Roland let it go. Probably closer to the mark was that the Earl of Reymerstone had killed Edmond of Clare's brother. "When was she stolen?"

"On March the third."

A black eyebrow shot upward. "You wait a long time to reply to Clare's demands."

"I did not wait here doing nothing until my men had found you in that silly Frenchwoman's bed!"

"On the contrary," Roland said with no heat, "Marie wasn't at all silly. What did you do?"

"I made two attempts, and both failed, or rather the men I sent to bring her back to me were fools and blundered. I discovered that my second attempt failed but two days ago. Clare returned one of my men alive with a new message and a new demand."

Roland waited, knowing he wasn't going to like hearing what Clare wanted now.

"The whoreson now wants to wed my niece. He still wants her dowry as well, of course. If I don't send my own priest to him carrying all her dowry with him by the last day of May, he says he will rape her, then give her to his soldiers for their sport. Then, if she still lives, he will have her used until she is with child. Then he will throw her in a ditch."

"I wonder why he wishes to marry her," Roland said, stroking his chin.

"He wishes to humiliate me further!"

"Your niece—is she beautiful as well as rich? Would her face and physical gifts charm him as does her dowry?"

And in that instant, Roland saw quite clearly just what the earl thought of his niece. Living in Reymerstone with this man for master could not have been pleasant. Roland wondered where the mother stood in all this mess.

"She is well-enough-looking, I suppose," Damon said finally, shrugging. "She is but a female, nothing more. Her tongue is impertinent upon occasion, but nothing a strong man can't control. She must continually be reminded that obedience and submission are what are expected of her. As I said, she needs a strong man."

And you saw yourself nicely in that role. "I met her mother. I imagine she was once quite lovely. Does the daughter have her coloring?"

The earl merely shrugged. "No, the girl has dark hair, filled with autumn colors, and her eyes are the oddest green. Pure but dark. Her features resemble her mother's but they are less coarse, more finely drawn."

"I find it fascinating that Clare demands you send your own priest. Do you know why?"

"Clare is a religious zealot. He is a man controlled and dominated by his fanaticism. If he requests I send a priest, it is because he believes a priest will not cheat him of the dowry money, that the priest will fairly wed him to my niece. He does not seem to realize that priests are as venal a company as any. Will you try to rescue her before the whoreson ravishes her? Before the last day of May?"

"You don't believe he's raped her already?"

"No." This was said grudgingly but firmly. Interesting, Roland thought as he said, "Why not? After all, what does a man's religious beliefs have to do with his lust?"

"Edmond of Clare keeps his word, at least that is his reputation. But if you haven't rescued her by the end of May, he will do exactly as he says he will, whether he wishes to or not. I know him well enough, and 'tis true."

Roland held off giving the earl his answer that evening, even though he knew he would go to Tyberton and he knew exactly how he would present himself. The coin he would earn for this rescue would give him sufficient funds to purchase Sir Thomas's small keep, Thispen-Ladock, and the surrounding rich grazing lands in Cornwall. And that was what he wanted. He would no longer be beholden to any man for his survival. When this was over, when the wretched niece was returned to her uncle, Roland would use his wits to further himself, not be at the behest of another. He wanted to remain in England; he wanted to be master of his castle and his own lands, and once he rescued this girl from Edmond of Clare, he would have his wish. It mattered not that Damon Le Mark had lied to him throughout; it mattered nót that it was more than likely he, Damon Le Mark, and not the fat Earl of Colchester, who had killed Clare's brother.

That night Roland was given one of the serving wenches to warm his bed and his blood. She was clean and sweet-smelling and he took her three times during the long night, for he was hungry for a woman after being absent for several weeks from Marie's enthusiastic ardor, and he gave her pleasure as well and wished he could remember her name the following morning to thank her.

He said to the earl as he mounted his destrier, a stark black Arab named Cantor, "As I told you, I will rescue your niece and I will do it long before the deadline Clare has set. You, however, must swear to me that you will try no more schemes on your own. They might endanger me and my plans."

The earl frowned and pulled on his ear, a lifelong habit that had left one earlobe a bit longer than the other, but finally agreed. Roland wondered if his word meant anything. He doubted that it did in the normal course of events. However, a good deal of coin was now in Roland's possession, half of the payment he was to receive. Perhaps that would keep Le Mark out of the game.

"Nor will you send a priest or your niece's dowry. There will be no need."

The earl's pale eyes gleamed. "You have great confidence, de Tournay."

"I will rescue her. Count out the rest of my coin, my lord, for I shall surely return to claim it."

Roland prepared to whip Cantor about, when the earl called after him, "De Tournay! If the girl is not a

virgin, I don't wish to have her back. You can kill her
if you wish to. It matters not to me."

Slowly Roland stilled his destrier and dismounted to
stand facing the earl. He was sickened but not over-
surprised. "I don't understand you. What matter if the
girl is ravished? Her dowry remains the same size,
does it not? Her dowry doesn't constrict even if her
maidenhead is gone."

"All changes if she is not chaste."

"For that matter, how do I know if she's been
ravished? How would you know?"

"I would examine her myself." The earl paused,
then said, fury lacing his voice, "That damned fool
Colchester says he won't have her for his son if she
isn't pure. His foul mother gave his father the pox and
killed him because of the men she took to her bed.
He's terrified that if Daria is ravished, she'll kill his
precious son with disease as well."

Roland was seeing the earl thrusting his fingers into
the girl's body to feel if her maidenhead were still
intact. To humiliate another thus was incomprehensible to him, particularly a girl who had no recourse but
to accept the shame of it.

"Colchester isn't the only unwedded man in the
kingdom," Roland said mildly. "Wed her to another.
She's an heiress, I gather. Most men aren't so absolute
in their requirements for a wife, I doubt."

"She is to wed Colchester, none other. It is the only
match I will accept."

And then, finally, Roland understood. The Earl of
Reymerstone had made an agreement with the Earl of
Colchester, and what he would gain in the marriage
mattered more to him than the dowry. Roland wondered what the bargain was that the two men had
struck.

"If she's a virgin when I rescue her, she will be a
virgin when she arrives here."

"Excellent. If she isn't, then I will kill her and you as well, de Tournay, and I will keep her dowry for myself, since there is nothing else for me."

Roland believed he would most certainly try. He nodded curtly and remounted Cantor. He was on his way to London now, to see the king; then he would ride to Cornwall. He needed to see Graelam de Moreton; then he wanted to visit Thispen-Ladock, just to look at the stone walls and the green hills, just to stroll through the inner bailey and speak to all the people, and know that what he was doing would make this possible for him. He had the time, and in the next two weeks he would make all his plans. He would travel northward from Cornwall to the southeast corner of Wales to Tyberton Castle, domain of the Clares since Duke William's conquest of England. He knew now how he would present himself to Edmond of Clare. He smiled, seeing himself in this new role. He also admitted, his smile widening, that he had a bit of studying to do before he arrived at Tyberton Castle.

Tyberton Castle, on the River Wye *May 1275*

Ena lightly slapped the folds of Daria's silk gown into a more pleasing shape. "There, 'tis lovely ye are now. But the man will find ye lovely as well, the good Lord above knows that. Ye'll take care, won't ye, little mistress?"

"Aye," Daria said. Ena's warnings, admonitions, and portents were daily fare and their impact had dimmed with repetition. Edmond of Clare was surely bent on ravishment, and today would be the day. But he didn't ravish her, and the days went by. Slowly, so very slowly. She wished to heaven that Ena wouldn't call her "little mistress." It was what he called her, and she hated it. She'd been here since the twelfth of March, nearly two

months now, and she wanted to scream with the boredom, the fear, with the awful tension that would never
leave her. She was a prisoner and she didn't know
what her captor wanted of her. At the beginning,
she'd spoken from her terror, not measuring the possible consequences of her words. She asked him, fear
making her voice harsh, "If you ransom me, will you
let me go? Is it just my dowry you want? Why don't
you say something? Why don't you tell me?"

Edmond of Clare had slapped her, not really all that
hard, but hard enough so that she'd felt the pain of it
throughout her body and she'd reeled with the force of
it, nearly falling to her knees. He watched the pain
take her for a few moments, then said easily, this
matter of her impertinence duly handled, "You will do
as I tell you and you will ask me no more questions.
Now, little mistress, would you like to eat some delicious stewed lamb?"

He baffled her. She feared him, yet he hadn't struck
her since that first time. Of course she'd tried to give
him no provocation. She saw violence in him, leashed
in her presence, but she could feel it, just as she'd
always felt it in her Uncle Damon. She saw his control
tested once when a servant had spilled some thickly
sauced meat on his arm. She saw the vein jump in his
throat, saw his clenched fists, but his voice issued forth
mild, and his reproof was gentle. Then why, she'd
wondered, had the servant looked like he was shortly
to die and was wonderfully surprised when he hadn't?

She still didn't know anything. If he was ransoming
her, as she had to assume that he was, she didn't know
what he'd demanded; she didn't know if her uncle had
responded. She didn't know anything, and it was infu-
riating and frustrating. And then she would think: all
he did was slap me. And she decided she would ask
him again. She wouldn't demand, she would ask softly,

something she should have learned to do with her uncle. Ah, but it galled her to be the supplicant.

Ena stepped back and folded her arms over her scrawny chest. "Ye've grown, a good inch taller ye are, and look at yer ankles, poking out over yer feet, and that gown of yers pulls across yer breasts. Ye must have new gowns, at least cloth so ye can sew yerself something that will fit ye. Ask the earl to fetch ye some nice woolen cloth—"

"That's quite enough, Ena. I won't demand cloth for new gowns. I care not if my ankles offend you—it matters not to me."

"Ah, if only we could leave here and ye could wed with Ralph of Colchester as ye were supposed to."

Daria shivered at that gruesome thought. "I would rather become a nun."

These sarcastically spoken impious words brought a loud groan from Ena and a quick crossing over her chest. "Ralph of Colchester was to be yer husband! If he was weak, he would still have been yer husband, and that makes all the difference. He's no savage marauder who should have been a priest, a crazy man who holds ye prisoner and makes ye pray in his damp chapel until yer knees are cramped and bruised red!"

"I wonder," Daria mused aloud, ignoring her maid, "I do wonder if Ralph of Colchester will still wish to marry me. 'Tis a matter of the size of my dowry, I think, not the question of my virtue or my captor's virtue. That and how much his father needs my coin. 'Tis an interesting question, though. Mayhap I'll ask the earl."

That brought a louder shriek from Ena, and Daria lightly patted her arm. "Nay, I jest. Don't carry on so." She turned and walked to the narrow window, only a narrow arrow slit actually, with a skin hanging above it to be lowered when the weather was foul. For the past three days the sun had shone down warm and bright.

But Daria shivered. She stared down into the inner bailey of Tyberton Castle. It was a huge fortress, its denizens numbering into the hundreds, and there were people and animals and filth everywhere. The only time there was quiet was on Sundays. The earl held services and all were required to attend for the endless hours. Until a week ago.

Edmond of Clare was devoutly religious. He spent the hours from five in the morning until seven on his knees in the cold Tyberton chapel. Then his priest held a private Mass for him and only for him, for which all the castle folk were grateful. The earl had been on a rampage for the past four days, for his priest had left Tyberton during a storm one night and no one knew why.

Daria knew why, as, she suspected, did most of the inhabitants of Tyberton, though they would never say so. The priest had no calling for such sacrifice as Clare demanded. He was fat and lazy and all the services had finally ground him down. He'd hated the cold dark chapel, hated the endless hours of absolving the Earl of Clare. Daria had heard him mumble about it, complaining bitterly that he would die of frozen lungs before the winter was out.

Well, now the chapel was empty. There was no mumbled illiterate Latin service to suffer through, no chilled bones from the damp cold air blowing through the thick gray stones from the River Wye. No more suffering for the nose, for the priest had smelled as foul as the refuse pile at the back of the castle. The fellow was gone. All were relieved except the earl.

Daria had found it odd, though, that the earl, such a fanatic in matters of the soul, didn't speak a bit of Latin. The priest had slurred his words, creating them from the sounds he knew the earl would accept, for he himself couldn't pronounce half of them properly and the earl seemed not to notice.

Daria spoke and read Latin, as did her mother, who'd been her teacher. She'd said nothing to the earl about it.

She turned at the knock on her small chamber door. It was one of the earl's men, a thin-faced youth named Clyde who had the habit of looking at Daria as if she were a Christmas feast and he a man begging to stuff himself. She simply stared at him, not moving.

"The earl wishes to see ye," he said, and as he spoke, his eyes traveled down her body, stopping only when they reached the pointed toes of her leather slippers.

She merely nodded, still not moving, waiting for Clyde to leave, which he finally did, his expression sour. Once she'd moved to do his bidding, only to feel his hands on her as she passed him.

"Ye be careful, young mistress," Ena hissed in her ear. "Ye stay out of his reach. Pray until yer tongue falls out, but keep away from him."

"Please," Daria said, shook off Ena's hand, and left the chamber. She lifted her skirts as she stepped carefully down the deeply cut stone steps that wound downward into the great hall of Tyberton. There were only three men in the hall and one of them was Edmond of Clare. He was speaking in a low voice to his master-at-arms, a Scotsman named MacLeod. Daria watched Edmond make a point with his hands, and shivered, remembering when his right hand, palm open, had struck her cheek. He was a big man, with the fierce red hair of his Scottish mother and the dark Celtic eyes of his father. His complexion was white as a dead man's. He usually spoke softly, which made it all the more unsettling when he suddenly exploded in a rage. He was a giant of a man, his chest the width of a tree trunk, the lower part of his pale white face covered with a curling red beard. He was handsome in a savage sort of way, Daria would give him that, but she'd heard that his wife, dead for only six months now, her infant son with her, had lived in fear of him. She was inclined to believe it.

She didn't move, but rather waited until he noticed her, which he did. "Come hither," he called. "I have gained us a new priest. His name is Father Corinthian and he will say Mass for us tomorrow. He is a Benedictine."

Daria walked forward, noticing the priest in his cheap wool cowl for the first time. "Father," she said.

"My child," said Father Corinthian. He pulled back the hood from his monk's cowl and took her hand. Daria felt a shock that drove the color from her face. She wanted to pull her hand away, but she didn't. She looked into the priest's dark eyes and she knew him.

She knew him to the very depths of her, and it was as terrifying as it was unexpected, this amazing and overwhelming knowledge, and she was consumed with dark feelings that she couldn't comprehend and that made her reel with their force. Here was something that was fearful yet real, and it was overpowering. For the first time in her life, Daria fainted, collapsing in a heap to the rush-strewn floor.

2

DARIA awoke with Ena crouched over her, her face parchment white, her lips trembling with fear and prayers.

"I'm all right," Daria said, and then turned her face away. But she wasn't all right; something had happened that she didn't understand. It was frightening. No, nothing was all right.

"But, little mistress, what happened? The earl just carried you here. He said naught. Did he speak harshly to you or strike you in front of that new priest? Did you speak sharply to him? Did he—?"

"Please, Ena, take your leave. The earl did nothing to me. I wish to rest. Leave me now."

The old woman sniffed and retreated to the far corner of the chamber. Daria stared toward the narrow window. A shaft of bright sunlight knifed through, illuminating dust motes in its wake. What had happened to her in the great hall was inexplicable. The priest, that beautiful young man who was a Benedictine, a young man who was dedicated to God . . . and she'd somehow known him, recognized him, felt his very being deep inside of her. How could that be? It made no sense.

It had happened but once before in her seventeen years, this prescience, this foreknowledge, this tide of feeling that had been the curse of her grandmother, a bent old woman who'd died howling curses at her son and daughters. A crazy old woman with wild stringy

31

hair and mad eyes, eyes the same color green as were hers.

When Daria was twelve her mother had told her that her father would be coming home to them shortly to visit with them until he left for the Holy Land. He was currently in London, fighting in a tourney. It was in that instant Daria saw her father, handsome and awesomely forbidding in his gleaming silver armor, astride his destrier, and he was charging, his visor down, lance at the ready. She saw him as clearly as she saw her mother who stood in front of her, staring and silent. She saw his lance buffeted to the side, saw him lifted off his destrier's back and flung into the dirt. She saw the other man's destrier rear back in fright and come crashing down on her father's head. She heard the crunching of the metal, the smashing of bone, and she screamed with the sight of it, the sound of it, the dark feel of it in her mind, the bloody horror of it. And she'd told her mother what she'd seen, but her mother had somehow known she was seeing something, and she was already as pale as the wimple that hid her beautiful auburn hair. "No," her mother had whispered; then she'd left Daria, nearly running, and Daria had known her mother was afraid of her in that moment.

And the word had reached them five days later. Her father's body followed three days after that, and he was buried on the family hillock, his body never again seen by his wife because the destrier had smashed his skull under his hooves.

Now it had happened again. Only this time it wasn't death and terror and pain that wouldn't cease. This time it was a strange shock of recognition, a *knowing* of another person she'd never seen before. She didn't understand what it meant or how to account for it or explain it. Was this poor young priest to die? She didn't think so, but she simply didn't know. But she'd looked at him and felt something deep within her move, open, and then he'd taken her hand as any priest might, and the touch of him had pierced into her, leaving her naked and raw, confused feelings flooding through her.

And like a lackwit, she'd fainted. She'd fainted in front of the earl, and she'd known even as she'd felt herself falling that she was still gaping at the young priest.

There came a knock on the chamber door. Daria turned to see Ena speed to the door and open it slightly to peer out. She heard Edmond of Clare's voice. He pushed Ena out of his way, nearly knocking the old woman to the floor, and strode into the room.

"You're awake," he said, looking down at her from his great height. "What happened to you? Are you sickening with something?"

She shook her head, fearing in that moment what might come out of her mouth if she spoke.

"Then what?"

Should she tell him that her grandmother had died mad, died cursed as a witch, and that mayhap she was a witch too? Tell him that the priest who'd shriven her grandmother had been pale and stammering with fear in the presence of that mad old woman? "I am sorry to upset you. I just suddenly felt faint. The Benedictine priest . . . he is to remain here at Tyberton?"

"Aye. I wanted you to meet him, but you fell at our feet, and the poor young fellow was naturally concerned. You frightened him, and now I must wonder if you did it apurpose, to beg his help, mayhap? To beg his assistance to help you escape me?"

"No."

"I did not really think so. You haven't the guile, Daria, to gain your ends through perfidy."

She stared at him, wondering how he could come to believe she was so transparent. She prayed a moment would come when she would best him with her perfidy.

"He appears a pious and learned young man," Edmond of Clare continued after a moment. "The Benedictines spawn dedicated priests, from what I hear. He will remain here in my service."

"What is his name?"

"He said the name given him at the Benedictine abbey was Father Corinthian. He will hold a Mass for us on the morrow morning. You and I will attend, no one else. My soul is needful of cleansing. As for yours, your sheltered youth sustains you, but still God's word will not come amiss to your ears."

Daria didn't want to see the young priest again, and yet at the same time she wanted to see him, touch him, just once more, just to see if the first time had been a vague aberration, an accident brought about by her fear and frustration at her captivity.

He was a priest, this man who wasn't a man. He was God's man, God's weapon, God's gift to man. "I will come to the chapel," she said, and Edmond of Clare stared down at her silently for another long moment, lightly touched his fingers to her hair. "So soft you are," he said, then left her.

She lay there frozen. There was no meanness in his look or his light touch, but a certain tenderness, and it terrified her. It wasn't lust, yet there was lust in it, and something else far more harmful as well. She closed her eyes. Her heart pounded loudly.

That evening at the late meal, she came slowly into the great hall, glad for its loudness, its sheer number of people, for their very presence was a sort of protection for her. She saw Edmond already seated in his great chair, the new priest seated at his left. The chair to his right—her chair—was empty. Her step lagged. She couldn't take her eyes off the priest. She saw in the rich light of the flambeaux that his dark hair shone clean and silky. He was dressed simply, but unlike other priests she'd known, both he and his clothing were clean. Even in the loose tunic, she could tell that he was lean and well-formed; his didn't seem to be the body of a man who partook only of spiritual exercise. He looked fit and active, a man who could just as easily take his place as a knight and a warrior. But his face held her and she couldn't take her eyes off him as she walked slowly through the throngs of people to the dais. His features were finely hewn, from his arched black brows to the cleft in his chin. He was nearly dark as an Arab, his eyes nearly black as his hair. As he spoke, he used his hands, eloquent narrow hands, to make a point. His expression was intelligent, and more than that, it was clever. He was a priest, surely, but he was a handsome man, and to look upon him gave one pleasure. Suddenly he looked up and saw her, and his face stilled.

To her utter stupefaction, she felt that same shock of recognition explode inside her. She felt bare and exposed, yet she realized in that moment that he didn't see what was there for him to see and understand and take. Aye, take. She saw him stare at her, and he cocked his head to one side in silent question. He had felt nothing; he must believe her mad.

She quickly lowered her eyes and made her way quietly to her chair.

Edmond of Clare nodded at her, saw that her trencher was filled, then turned his attention back to the priest. He didn't appear to have noticed anything amiss.

Roland chewed for a long while on the stewed piece of beef. He needed to give himself time to regain his wits. He saw Daria seat herself on Clare's right, saw her lower her eyes to her trencher.

He heard Clare ask him a question, and he responded. He'd escaped from Clare's company as soon as he could this afternoon after the girl had fallen into a faint at his feet. He'd seen the utter bewilderment in her eyes when she'd turned to look at him, the obvious shock she felt upon seeing him, touching his hand. It was passing strange, and he was inclined to think the girl bereft of wits. It was as if she'd known him, as if she recognized him, but that wasn't possible. He'd never seen her before in his life. And he would have remembered.

She was passing fair. He'd found her pleasant to look at, surely, nothing more or less. Her features were clear and delicately drawn, satisfying the taste of most men, and yet she wasn't beautiful in the purity and perfection of her features. There was strength in her face, a natural vitality that was now dimmed from her captivity. Her dark hair was as her uncle had described it—filled with the rich deep colors of autumn —but even her hair appeared dulled. Her eyes were a pure green that seemed to lighten or darken with her changing mood. This afternoon they'd been as dark as the turbulent Irish Sea in the dawn. Now they were light and soft. She was reed slender, slight of build, but her chin was held high, showing her dignity, her training as a lady. But there was strength and courage in her, he knew it. There was a hollowness in her cheeks, a drawn look about her, again a sign of her captivity.

Perhaps he could even understand why Edmond of Clare wanted to take her as his wife. Perhaps the man had seen the promise in her, the grit. Even as he thought it, Roland shook his head. No, the earl saw a young girl in splendid health who would produce him a string of fine sons. If he were lucky, she wouldn't die in childbed as had his first two wives. Then Roland saw again in his mind's eye her insensible shock upon seeing him. Perhaps it was an attack of bile on her part and not a lack of wit. He prayed it was so. He'd even questioned himself as to his role; had she perhaps seen through him? Seen him as a fraud and a liar? Not believed him a priest for the barest second?

Edmond of Clare put further questions to him, and he replied easily and fluently, for he'd studied his role for the past two weeks, bending on it with all his concentration. He couldn't afford to make mistakes. His life hung in the balance, as did hers. He rather liked the name Father Corinthian; it had a very Eastern sound to it that pleased the aesthetic part of him. But this wretched girl . . . whatever had been wrong with her this afternoon? He would get her out of here soon and he'd get her home even sooner.

He shivered and took another bite of the overly salted stewed beef. He had to find out if she was still a virgin. He thought that she was. From what he knew already of Edmond of Clare, the man, whatever else he was, appeared to understand honor. The girl didn't look in the least abused.

What she did look was bewildered. She didn't face him once during the long meal. Roland determined he would discover the cause of her stupefaction as soon as possible. He passed his evening discussing theological questions with Edmond of Clare. What seemed to prey on the earl's mind was the issue of man's loyalty to another man versus his loyalty to God. Roland quickly discovered that the earl wasn't a stupid man. He also quickly learned that the earl spent the bulk of his time immersing his mind in religious matters, and thus knew more about Church dogma than did Roland. If Roland hadn't been so facile of tongue, he would have found himself several times in grave difficulties.

At one point the earl leaned back in his chair and stroked his thick fingers through his equally thick red beard. "You met the young lady, Daria," he said at last. "I intend to wed her the last day of this month."

"Ah," Roland said, smiling. "That brings up an interesting question, does it not? A man's loyalty to a woman, namely his wife."

"Absurd," said Edmond of Clare, shrugging. "Women are of little worth, save as vessels for a man's seed, and my first two wives failed even at that. They both died, taking their infants with them. You would think they could have left the babes alive, but they didn't, curse their selfishness. But Daria, the girl looks healthy and fit to bear me sons."

Roland felt astonishment at the earl's words. He'd heard men vow before their peers that women were naught but chattel, but to say a woman was selfish because her babe died with her? It passed all bounds. "Who is she?" he asked, taking a sip of wine from his flagon. "She already seems the mistress, since she is obviously a lady."

The earl answered readily, without hesitation, "The niece of a man I have wanted to kill for five years. But with her as my wife, he will be safe from me, curse his rotted soul. It is the compromise I am willing to make. She also brings me a great dowry. I suppose I must forget my revenge upon the uncle with the niece as my wife. Unless, of course, I can get my hands on him with no one knowing of it." The earl fell silent, his expression brooding, as if he weren't completely pleased with the bargain he had made. He said suddenly, "Is it your belief, Father, that if a man fully intends to marry a woman, it is still a sin for him to bed the woman before they are joined in God's eyes?"

Roland felt no astonishment at this question. He felt a surge of raw anger, and oddly enough, a bit of amusement. Edmond of Clare was a man who hated to give in to lust, and if he did, he wanted it condoned and excused by God. But if he did take Daria before Roland could get her away from Tyberton . . . Roland wasn't stupid or naive, and he knew that Damon Le Mark, once he knew for a certainty she was no longer a virgin, would kill her just as he'd said he would. He wanted her back only because of Colchester and what the marriage would bring him, the coveted lands to extend his own acres. And it was only the lands that drew him more than the great dowry. But Colchester wouldn't have her marry his son if her maidenhead had been rent, and thus Damon Le Mark would have to content himself with her money. To get it, he would have to rid himself of his niece.

Roland brought his wits to bear on the earl's question. He said with all the firmness a priest should have at his command, and prayed it was enough, "A man's lust is a matter that should not concern his wife or the lady who will soon be his wife. If he must needs slake his lust, he should do it on another female, one of lesser account."

Edmond of Clare muttered something under his breath but presented no arguments. The interminable evening finally ended in his saying prayers over the assembled men and women of Tyberton. He wanted to impress the Benedictine priest. He fancied he did it well. He noticed that most of the people remaining in the hall appreciated his efforts toward their spiritual salvation. Only a few of the louts fidgeted and leaned from one side to the other. He would see them punished.

Roland bade the girl, Daria, good night, and watched her leave the hall. He prayed he'd saved the girl's maidenhead for another day with his priestly edict. He slept that night in a small niche off the solar, warm enough, but he would wager that in the dead of winter a man's bones would be chilled to the marrow pressed against the cold damp stones, even wrapped in a dozen blankets.

It was six o'clock in the morning and Roland was clean and cowled and vigorously awake. Latin hummed on his tongue. Since he was a small boy, Roland had always preferred the early mornings. His mind was sharper, his wits more acute, his body supple and

strong and ready for action. He made his way quickly
to the damp and depressing chapel.

The Tyberton chapel was long and narrow, with
several wooden carved saints decorating the nave, each
rivaling the other in varying stages of gruesome mar-
tyrdom. It was damp and cold in the chapel and Roland could feel the early-morning fog from the River
Wye waft through the thick gray stones. He thought
again of his goal: the keep and the lands he was purchasing in Cornwall. The keep itself was small, but it
was finely built and was safe and snug and warm,
situated nearer the southern coast rather than the savage and barren northern coast. It would be his once
he'd returned the girl safely to her uncle and collected
the other half of his fee. By all the saints, he wished
this were over and he was there, tilling his own fields,
repairing his own walls, filling his own granaries.

He waited impatiently for the earl and Daria to
arrive, the Mass filtering through his mind. He knew
much of it by heart now, not that it mattered over-
much. Edmond of Clare spoke no Latin, just parroted
the responses; he'd made sure of that when he'd questioned the earl's former priest, a fat lout who was
delighted to take the coin offered to escape Tyberton
and its fanatic owner. As for the rest of the castle
denizens, they could scarce speak the King's English,
from what Roland had heard.

The girl, Daria, came first into the chapel. She was
dressed warmly, a thick wool cloak covering her gown.
It was apparent that she'd been in this chapel many
times before. Her head was covered by a soft white
wimple. Her eyes were downcast. She was either very
religious or she was purposefully avoiding looking at
him. He stared hard at her until she finally looked up.
He saw uncertainty writ clear on her face, blank surprise in her eyes as she looked at him. And there it
was again, that odd way she stared at him. He started

to speak, but Edmond of Clare strode in at that moment. He offered Daria his arm and escorted her to the first bench facing the nave and the priest.

"Father," Edmond said, his voice low and sonorous and infinitely respectful.

Roland nodded benignly. "Be seated, my children, and we will praise the Lord's bounty and laud his beneficence on the Feast of Devotion." He crossed himself and regarded his two supplicants with bland favor. Once they were seated, he began, his voice fluent and low:

> Nos autem gloriari oportet in cruce Domini nostri Jesu Christi: in quo est salus, vita, et resurrectio nostra: per quem salvati, et liberati sumus.

Daria felt the pure sweet tones of the Latin fill her. He spoke beautifully, his voice low and soothing. It was obvious to her that he was learned, unlike many priests, who were illiterate, for he understood what he was saying and gave feeling to the sentiments. As he spoke, she translated his words in her mind.

". . . But it behooves us to glory in the cross of our Lord Jesus Christ: in whom is our salvation, life, and resurrection: by whom we are saved and delivered . . ."

> Alleluia, alleluia. Deus misereatur nostri, et benedicat nobis: illuminet vultum suum super nos, et misereatur nostri. Gloria Patri.

It was beautiful, the words and his voice, and she couldn't take her eyes from his face, his beautiful face that wasn't a man's face, not really, but the face of God at this moment, his speech God's speech, the near-hypnotic movement of his hands binding her and making the earl beside her draw in his breath with the moving beauty of it ". . . Alleluia, alleluia. May God have mercy on us and bless us: may he cause the light of his countenance to shine upon us, and may he have mercy on us. Glory to the Father."

Hoc enim sentite in vobis, quod et in Christo Jesu: Qui cum in forma Dei esset, non rapinam arbitratus est esse se aequalem Deo: sed seme- tipsum . . .

The words continued to flow from his mouth through her mind: ". . . Let this mind be in you, which was also in Christ Jesus: who, being in the form of God, thought it not robbery to be equal with God: but emptied himself . . ."

Father Corinthian paused, oddly, then resumed, his voice lower, his pace quickened.

Neque auribus neque oculie satis consto . . .

Daria's head whipped up and she stared at him. His look was limpid, his hands raised, even as he repeated yet again:

Neque auribus neque oculie satis consto . . .

No, it wasn't possible, yet she hadn't mistaken his words. Her lips parted and she stared at him, even as he said again, in Latin, "I am losing my eyesight and getting deaf."

Hostis in cervicibus alicuinus est . . .

She whispered the words in English, "The foe is at our heels."

Nihil tibi a me postulanti recusabo . . . Optate mihi contingunt . . . Quid de me fiet? . . . Naves ex porta solvunt . . . Nostri circiter centum ceciderunt . . . Dulce lignanum, dulces clavos, dulcia ferens pondera: quae sola fuisti digna sustinere regem caelorum, et Domininum. Alleluia.

"I will refuse you nothing . . . My wishes are being fulfilled . . . What will become of me? . . . The ships sail from the harbor . . . About a hundred of our men fell . . . Sweet wood, sweet nails, bearing a sweet weight: which alone wert worthy to bear the king of heaven and the Lord. Alleluia.''

Daria's expression was one of astonishment and amazement. She quickly realized that the earl, his head raised in proud arrogance before his God, his eyes closed in exaltation, hadn't realized that his new priest, his learned and erudite Benedictine, had been having a fine time mixing the Mass with a layman's Latin. But he hadn't done it in the manner of the last priest. No, this man was educated, and he had the ability to juggle and to substitute, but . . .

The remainder of the Mass went quickly, and the priest seemed to have gathered his memory together, for he made no more references to foes or cut-off heads.

He blessed the earl and Daria, saying, his arms raised, "Dominus vobiscum," and the earl replied by rote to the priest's exhortation of the Lord be with you with "Et cum spiritu tuo."

Father Corinthian looked at Daria expectantly, and she said softly, "Capilli horrent."

Roland nearly lost his ale and bread and his bland expression, so taken aback was he. There was no expression on her face as she repeated, not the expected "Et cum spiritu tuo" but again "Capilli horrent."

His hair stands on end.

The little twit knew Latin! By all the saints, she was mocking him, she could give him away! He looked appalled, as well he might; then he caught himself as he heard her say clearly, "Bene id tibi vertat."

He bowed his head, her words buzzing with the Latin Mass in his mind. *I wish you all success in the matter.*

Roland stepped back and raised his hands. "Deo gratias." He smiled at the earl, who looked as if God himself had just conferred honors upon him.

"Thank you, Father, thank you. My soul rejoices that you are here." The earl rubbed his large hands together. "Aye, I feared whilst there was no man of God in my castle, feared for my own soul and the souls of my people."

He turned to Daria and said, his tone disapproving, "You said something I did not recognize as a response. What was it?"

She didn't pale; she didn't change expression. She said, "It was nonsense. I couldn't remember what to repeat, and thus conjured up the sounds. I am sorry, my lord, Father, it was disrespectful of me."

The earl's face grew even more stiff with disapproval. " 'Tis blasphemous to do such a thing. I shall have the good Father Corinthian teach you the proper responses, and you will learn them now. It is shameful not to know them, Daria."

She bowed her head submissively.

"Yes, my lord."

"Your uncle was remiss in his responsibilities toward you. You will spend the next hour with Father Corinthian."

"Yes, my lord."

The earl nodded once again to Roland and took his leave. They were alone in the dank chapel.

"Who are you?"

"That is quick and to the point," Roland remarked, his eyes on the closed chapel door. "Let me make certain no one is about outside."

"It wouldn't matter if there were a dozen men listening at the door. This wretched chapel is sound as a crypt, the door nearly as thick as the stone of the walls."

Nonetheless Roland strode to the door, opened it, and slowly closed it again. He turned to face her.

"Who are you?" she repeated.

"You speak Latin."

"Yes, I speak Latin. 'Twas something you didn't expect."

"No I didn't. You didn't give me away to the earl. May I assume that you still wish to escape him?"

She nodded and asked again, "Who are you?"

"I am sent by your uncle to rescue you. As you know now, I am no Benedictine priest."

She gave him a dazzling, perfectly wicked smile that rocked him back on his heels. He thought he'd made a perfectly adequate priest, damn her impertinence. He was frowning, but she forestalled him. "But you are an educated man, unlike the previous priest, who could barely string together sounds that resembled Latin. The earl, of course, didn't know any better. Did you get rid of him?"

"Yes, 'twas quite easy, for he was miserable here at Tyberton, and most willing to accept a bit of coin for his absconding. You recognized me, then, yesterday when you fainted? You knew I was no priest from just looking at me? That is why you turned so pale and collapsed?"

She shook her head and looked embarrassed. "I don't know why . . . that is, I didn't know you then, and yet I did know you, perhaps even better than I know myself." That sounded like utter drivel, she thought. She ground to a painful halt and looked up at him for his reaction. Again, that shock of knowledge, that feeling that he was there, deep inside her, part of her, and she took a step back. She wasn't making sense and he would think her utterly mad.

"What is it? Do I frighten you?"

"Yes," she said. "I don't understand this."

Roland chose for the moment to ignore her mysterious words. Indeed he didn't understand any of what she'd said and didn't have time at present to seek enlightenment. "As I said, I am here to rescue you."

"I don't wish to marry Ralph of Colchester. He is lewd and weak and without character."

Roland frowned at her. "That is something that has nothing to do with me. Your uncle is paying me to bring you back, and that is what I shall do. What happens to you then is up to your uncle. He is your guardian. It is his decision. No female should have the power to decide who her husband will be. It would lead the world into chaos."

"This world you men have ruled since the beginning of time stews continuously in chaos. What more harm or disaster could women bring to bear?"

"You speak from ignorance. Mayhap your uncle isn't wise or compassionate, but it is the way of things. It's natural that you submit."

Daria sighed. He was naught but a man, like all the other men who had come into her life. Men ruled and women obeyed. It was a pity and it brought her pain, which she promptly dismissed. This man whom she knew, this man who didn't know her, also didn't care what happened to her. Why should he? This absurd recognition was all on her side, these bewildering feelings had naught to do with him. It came to her then that once he'd gotten her free of Edmond of Clare, she could then escape from him. He cared not, after all, what became of her.

"You have not yet told me your name."

"You may call me Roland."

"Ah, like Charlemagne's fearsomely brave Roland. When do we leave, sir?"

3

ROLAND rocked back on his heels at that. "Just like that? You believe me? You will go with me? You require no more proof?"

Daria shook her head, smiling at him, that dazzling, innocent, yet strangely knowing smile. "Of course I believe you. I am pleased you aren't a priest."

"Why?"

She wanted to tell him that she was delighted that he was a just a man, a man of the world, and not a man of God, but she didn't. He would truly believe her mad. She shook her head again, saying, "My mother, did you see her? Is she all right? You went to Reymerstone Castle?"

"Yes, and your mother appeared well. You have something of the look of her, not her coloring, but something of her expression. If I recall aright, your father was dark as a Neapolitan."

"You knew my father?"

"As a young man in King Edward's company, aye, I knew him, as did most of the young knights. Sir James was brave and trustworthy. It is a pity he died so inopportunely. Edward missed him sorely in the Holy Land."

The chapel door suddenly opened and the earl reappeared. "Well, girl? Tell me the correct response."

Daria didn't change expression. She repeated swiftly, her eyes lowered meekly, "Et cum spiritu tuo."

The earl nodded. "Well said. I am pleased with you.

I have never agreed that women had not the ability to learn, and you have proved me correct. Do you agree with your brothers, Father?"

Roland looked benignly upon Daria as he would upon a dog who had just performed a trick well. He smiled to himself as he said in a pontifical voice, "Women can learn to mouth words—in any language—if they are allowed sufficient time for repetition. 'Tis doubtful she gleans the true meaning, but God is understanding and forgiving of his most feeble creation."

The earl nodded and Daria ground her teeth.

"You will come with me now, Daria," the earl continued. "A tinker is here and I wish you to select a piece of finery you wish to have. You will become my wife at the end of the month, and thus I wish to show you my favor."

She stared at him dumbfounded, and Roland waited, tense and anxious, but she said nothing, merely nodded and followed the earl docilely from the chapel. Only when they were alone did she touch the earl's sleeve to gain his attention. She looked up at him, her expression puzzled, and said, unable to keep her surprise to herself, "This is why you kidnapped me, my lord? You wished to wed me?"

The incredulity in her voice was understandable, as was her question, though it bordered on impertinence. He decided to deal gently with her this time. "Nay, little one, I took you in revenge against your uncle, who is a man I detest above most men. At first I demanded your dowry as a ransom. Then, your graceful presence has made my heart quicken in my breast, and I changed my demand to him. He will send me his own priest and your dowry by the end of May and we will be wedded. Then he will be safe from my vengeance." He frowned even as the words came out of his mouth. "Mayhap not. Mayhap I shall change my mind, for Damon Le Mark is a poisonous snake to be crushed."

"What did you tell him you would do if he refused your demand? Did you threaten to murder me?"

The earl reacted swiftly, for this was beyond what in his mind was permissible for a woman, particularly for a woman who would be his wife. He struck her with his open palm on her cheek and she reeled backward, her shoulder striking the doorway, sending pain jolting through her body.

"Keep your pert tongue in your mouth, Daria! I will tell you what you need to know, and it will be enough for you. No more of your insolence—it displeases me, as it must displease our Lord."

It was odd this rage she felt. It wasn't the same she felt toward her uncle. This rage burned hot within her, but she also saw Edmond of Clare as apart from the awful anger he'd brought her. Her uncle was purposely cruel. Worse, he pleased himself with cruelty and the suffering of others, whereas Edmond of Clare simply saw her—a female—as a being to be constantly corrected and admonished, for her benefit, not because it gave him demented pleasure. He believed devoutly in God, at least in a God that suited his own convictions and expectations, and saw it as his duty to teach her the proper way of behaving. Her rage simmered and she sought to control it.

Roland held himself back in the shadows. It required all his control to do so. He'd heard her question of Clare and seen him strike her.

He didn't particularly wish to, but he found that he admired her in that moment. He saw the grit in her that would grow stronger as she gained years, if only she would be given the least encouragement and opportunity. She didn't cry. She didn't speak. She merely straightened her clothing and stood there stolid and silently proud, waiting for the earl to tell her his bid-

ding. Roland wondered how many times he'd struck
her during her captivity, to show her a woman's place.
He must get her away from here, quickly. Not only
was the earl growing perilously close to ravishing her,
he just might injure her badly in a fit of rage.

During the remainder of the day, Roland examined
the castle and found the escape route he would use.
He learned that Daria had her maid with her, but he
knew the older woman would hold them back and
they wouldn't have a good chance of escaping if they
took her with them. The old woman would have to
stay here. If Daria protested, he would simply . . .
What would he do? Strike her, as did Edmond of
Clare? He shook his head on that thought.

That evening the earl again monopolized him so
that he had no opportunity of speaking privately with
Daria. She no longer looked at him as if he were some
sort of specter to be gawked at, or a man she'd seen
before, perhaps in another place or in another time.
Still, though, she tended to avoid his eyes, and it
bothered him because he didn't understand her.

"There is a debate that fascinates me," the earl
began as he moved a chess piece on the board between them.

Roland moved his king's pawn forward in answer
and waited. He'd learned the value of patience, the
value of allowing the other man to speak first.

"Do women have souls? What do the Benedictines
offer as their belief?"

"It is a matter of some debate, as you know. Even
the Benedictine order finds itself in contention on the
matter." Roland moved out his king's knight in reply
to the earl's pawn move.

"True, true, but surely you, as a Benedictine, believe that women should be chastised for disobedience, for ill temper, for sloth or impiety?"

"Certainly, but 'tis a husband who applies the proper chastisement."

The earl drew back, his thick red brows knitting. "She is nearly my wife. She is young and thus malleable, but still, because she carries the perversity of her gender, and the blood of a man whose heart rots with sin—I speak of her uncle, of course—she grows more impertinent as the days pass. She needs a man's correction. I wish only to provide her proper guidance now."

"She is not yet your wife."

"Does it matter, if she has not a soul, what she is? Wife, harlot, maid?"

Roland's fingers tightened around his queen's bishop. He slowly moved the piece to the knight-five square. "It is my belief that women are creatures of God just as are men. They are made as we are—they possess arms, legs, a heart, a liver. They are the weaker, true, in body and mayhap in spirit as well. But they do have worth. They birth children and protect them with their lives, and thus their claim to God's grace is as great as is a man's. After all, my lord earl, we are unable to procreate ourselves; we are unable to suckle our children. 'Twas God who bestowed upon them these gifts, and it is these gifts that speak to our continuity and thus our immortality."

"You beset me with vain sophistry, Father, and address not my concern. Surely women are vessels, and they have breasts that carry milk, and wombs that hold babes, but are they more? I do not see their birthing us as God's gift to them, for they often die doing it. It also wastes a man's time. The two wives I have held as my own knew not honor or loyalty or fierceness of spirit. They were weak both of body and of mind. I never saw them as more than the means to continue myself."

Roland remembered Joan of Tenesby. He saw her

clearly in that moment and could swear, right now, that her fierceness of spirit had exceeded any man's he'd ever known. She'd destroyed those around her with an arrogance and ruthlessness that staggered him with numbing awareness even now, nearly six years later.

"But you lust after the young Daria, do you not? You bought her finery from the tinker because you wished to please her, to flatter her vanity. But it was your vanity that enjoyed your purchases."

"You twist words, Father. This talk of vanity is an absurdity. As for my lust for the girl, well, God wills it so. If we were not driven to take what the female holds, we would not continue; thus it is our lust that is the true gift from God. God gives them to us and it is our right to use them when they are able. Indeed, it is our responsibility to beget our children in their wombs."

Roland smiled and said easily, even as he moved his king's bishop, "Nay, my lord earl, 'tis you who are gifted with facile argument. You would make a good bishop." Roland suddenly realized that to move his bishop would irrevocably cripple the earl's position on the chessboard. He quickly retracted it.

"Leave it," the earl said, not seeing the danger from the move. Roland replaced the piece and sat back in his chair.

But the earl wasn't interested in the game, but in expressing his own views. He tugged on his ear, cleared his throat, saying finally, "There is another matter, Father. Something that has bothered my spirit for many weeks now. Daria is young, as I said, but I find her occasionally frivolous, impious, exhibiting a woman's vanity. I can break her of these habits. But I now find that I doubt her virtue. You see, I know her uncle well, and he is a vile lecher. And I wonder again and again: Is she still a maiden? Or did her uncle give her to Ralph of Colchester when he visited Reymerstone Castle?"

Roland was shaking his head even before he said quickly, "Nay, her uncle would have protected her, not offered her to Colchester. Doubt it not."

The earl shook his head, unconvinced, not wanting to be convinced, Roland realized in a flash of insight. "I have little trust for women. They seduce men with their beauty and their modest manners, which are really practiced and sly. Perhaps that is how she gained Colchester's favors. I must know before I wed her, I must know, and I will know."

"You must believe me, my lord. The girl is a maid. Her uncle would never have allowed Colchester to have her. She would have lost her worth, her good name, more, the good name of her family. It matters not that he is a vile lecher. He isn't stupid, is he?"

The Earl of Clare only shrugged. He didn't want to acknowledge the truth of his priest's words, Roland realized. Roland looked grim as he said, "Then what you want, my lord, is for the Church to bless your forcing of her before you take her to wive. You want the Church to bless this mad scheme of yours. Truly, my lord earl, I cannot condone that. There is another solution, another way to have your question answered. You will allow me to ask her. I can see through falsehood, my lord. It is a gift I have. I will know if she lies or not. I will tell you true."

"And you will believe, Father, the words that flow from her mouth, or will you examine her for the truth of her vow?"

Roland very nearly rocked back in his chair with surprise and distaste. The earl seemed as vile as did Damon Le Mark. Did the earl really expect a man of God to examine a woman to discover if she still possessed a maidenhead? He managed to say steadily enough, his eyes meeting the earl's straightly, "I will know, when she tells me, whether she speaks the truth."

Roland waited, his fingers so tense they whitened on his black queen. Finally the earl nodded.

"You will speak to her, then. Do it now, Father. I must know."

But the earl did not wish Roland to leave him to his task until they had finished their game of chess. Roland wanted to trounce the earl but he guessed it would not hold him in good stead. Thus, he blundered deliberately, setting his queen in the path of the earl's white knight. It was over quickly.

"You play well, Father, but not as well as I. I will continue to give you instruction."

Roland drew on priestly reserves that must contain, he thought, a goodly supply of humility and deceit. He nodded gravely. " 'Twill be an honor to be so instructed."

His meekness pleased the earl, and he added, "And I will think on your words, Father."

Roland yet again inclined his head. Ten minutes later he was lightly knocking on Daria's bedchamber door.

It was opened by the maid, Ena.

"Is your mistress within?"

The old woman nodded. "He's sent you to her, Father?"

"Aye. I will speak with her. Alone."

The maid looked quickly back at Daria, then left the bedchamber.

Daria was on her feet and hurrying toward him. "What has happened? Do we leave now? What do—?"

"Hush," he said, and took her hands in his, squeezing them. "The earl sends me here to speak with you. He wishes me to ensure that you are still a virgin."

She blinked at him.

It was answer enough, and he smiled down at her. "I know, think no more about it. The earl has unusual views regarding God's interest in his—the earl's—lust. Come, we must speak, and quickly, for I doubt not that he will soon come to see the result of my question."

He was still holding her hands and she felt his vitality flow through into her and it made her tremble with anticipation. He seemed to sense something, and released her hands. He took a step back, saying quickly, "I distrust the earl. He desires you mightily. Indeed he has spoken to me of taking you before you are wedded. I have tried to dissuade him, but I don't know if God's wishes will take precedence over his lust for you, for as I said, he regards his wishes as one and the same as God's. We are leaving Tyberton tonight. Listen to me, for we haven't much time."

Roland spoke low and quick, but he wasn't quick enough, for the door burst open and the earl strode into the bedchamber. He looked from his priest to Daria. They stood apart, and it seemed to him that Father Corinthian was speaking earnestly to her. It seemed innocent enough, but he asked, his voice filled with suspicion, "Well, Father? Is she still a maid?"

"She is a maid," Roland said.

"That is what she tells you."

"No man has touched me!"

"You are a woman and are born with lies trembling on your tongue. I wish to believe you, Father, but I find myself beset with doubts. When you left me, I heard one of my men telling another that all the castle wenches wish to bed you. I will admit that I saw you not as a man before but solely as a priest. Perhaps I yield to false tidings, and if I do, God will surely punish me for it, yet I see you now as a man alone with her."

Roland quickly assumed his most pious pose. "Believe me, I do not see your betrothed as a woman. I see her only as one of God's creatures, nothing more."

Roland spoke calmly, yet his heart pounded in his breast. He realized that the earl wasn't entirely sane.

Edmond of Clare drew a deep steadying breath. He'd behaved badly, he knew it. He'd let his jealousy of his Benedictine priest overcome his Christian sense. He would whip the man who'd spoken irreverently of the priest. But he found himself looking again at Daria. Her cheeks were very pale, her eyes dilated. He realized that it mattered not what she'd said to the priest or what the priest believed. He had made up his mind and he knew God approved his actions.

"I would examine her now," Edmond said, advancing on her. "You will remain to testify that I do not ravish her, Father. And if she isn't a virgin, you will also so testify so that I can then do as I will to with her, for it matters not what a whore wishes."

Roland cleared his throat and his voice rang stern and hard. "I forbid it, my son."

The earl stared at him as if he'd lost his wits. "I am lord here, Father Corinthian, and no other man, even be he a man of God, has the right to gainsay me, for my word is law. Do you understand me? Come, you will be my witness."

But Daria wasn't to submit without a struggle. She grabbed up her skirts and ran from the earl. He caught her quickly, his heavy arm around her waist, and he lifted her, carrying her to the narrow cot, and threw her down upon her back, knocking the breath out of her.

"Damn you, girl, hold still!" He lifted his hand to strike her into submission, saw the priest standing rigid with disapproval near to him, and slowly lowered his hand. He leaned down, his face close to hers. "Do as I tell you or I will beat you when the priest is gone."

He'd spoken softly, so that only she heard him. She

felt his spittle on her throat. He was both enraged and determined.

"Please, my lord," she said, "please don't shame me. I am a maid. What have I done to deserve your distrust? Please do not shame me."

The earl paid no attention. He was as determined as he was excited, his groin twisting with painful need. He wanted to touch her, thrust his finger inside her, feel her soft woman's flesh. He felt sweat break out on his forehead, sweat from his growing lust. Daria felt one of his large hands on her belly, his fingers splayed outward, holding her flat, and his other hand was pulling at her wool skirt, yanking it up, ripping it in his haste, and she felt the chill air on her thighs. She cried out and began to struggle, frantically trying to jerk away from him. His large hand clamped about her knee and squeezed. She cried out against the sudden pain.

"Make no more struggles! Lie still and I will be through quickly."

But she couldn't make herself lie there like a helpless creature, motionless and obedient to his will, whilst he humiliated her, and looked at her and touched her. Not with Roland standing so close, looking wild and furious and nearly savage with rage. Then she realized if she continued to fight him, Roland would attack him and most likely all would be lost. And Roland would die.

To acquiesce to this, the humiliation of it threatened to choke her, but she forced herself to still, closing her eyes against the knowledge of what he was going to do to her. It cost her dearly, but she held herself perfectly rigid, enduring because she had to endure. The earl looked up at her, then grunted, pleased with her surrender.

And Roland understood. He hated watching this, hated the earl's hand touching her. He saw his large hand press her legs wide apart, saw his finger disappear between her thighs, and knew he was touching her. He shook with the compulsion to kill him, yet he knew, as did Daria, that they would have little or no chance to escape, not if he gave in to his fury and killed the earl now. He forced himself to stand there stiff and tense and mute, watching, and it was the hardest thing he had ever done in his life. The earl's face was flushed dark with lust and his breathing was loud in the chamber.

Daria whimpered when one of the earl's thick fingers thrust inside her. As he probed deeper into her, she cried out with the pain of his roughness. He frowned at her and continued deeper, widening her, preparing her for his sex, for he had every intention of taking her soon, regardless. But he knew she was a maid, aye, he knew, but he'd wanted to touch her, to feel her soft flesh.

Finally he withdrew his finger from her body, and his hand from beneath her skirts. He jerked her gown down over her legs. "She is a maid," he said, and he looked down into her face as he spoke.

"Open your eyes, damn you! I will take you to wive and you will be loyal and obedient to me, your lord and your husband. Do you understand me, Daria? Even though you are flesh of your uncle's lewd flesh, it matters not, for you will forget his loathsome nature and bind yourself to me and become what I demand."

The earl rose and looked down at her again. "Rise and straighten yourself. Father, you are my witness that she is still a virgin. Now that it is proved, let us leave her alone."

Roland nodded and his eyes dropped. He very nearly leapt on the earl in that moment, for he saw that his sex bulged against the cloth of his tunic, thick and hard.

He didn't look at Daria, for he couldn't bear to see

on her pale face the misery he knew she felt. He
forced himself to nod again, and motioned the earl to
go ahead of him out of the bedchamber. He knew
deep down that the earl would return to ravish her. If
the Benedictine priest, Father Corinthian, had not
been here bearing witness, the earl would have continued what he was doing. He would have ravished her.
But he would return. He would return tonight; Roland
knew it. He knew he must get her away from Tyberton
first or he would have failed.

Still his rage made him tremble, and he was relieved
that the earl didn't turn to address some question to
him or he might still have wrapped his hands around
Edmond of Clare's neck and wrung the life out of him.

Daria scrambled up from the bed and raced to the
door. She forced herself to crack the door open and
look out. The earl and Roland were gone. She retreated again, closing the door. There was no key to
keep him out. She didn't yet know of Roland's plan
for their escape, only that he would come for her. She
began to pace, feeling so shamed, so humiliated at
what he'd done to her that she couldn't bear being
within herself, being at one with her body. She wasn't
aware that tears were streaming down her face until
Ena slipped into the chamber and gasped at the sight
of her.

"He's ravished you! And that miserable priest with
him! I knew he wasn't a priest, too pretty he is, too
lean and hungry! Aye, both of them—"

Daria, maddened beyond control, turned on the old
woman in a fury and yelled, "Shut your stupid mouth,
you miserable old crone! I will hear no more of your
filth!"

It was shock that made Ena obey her mistress. Never
had the girl spoken thus to her, and she could but
stare at her.

"Leave me! I don't wish to see your hag's face until the morning. Go!"

The old woman scuttled out. Alone once again, Daria stared at the closed door. She felt only a bit of guilt, for Ena had become more and more unstable during their months of captivity. Once she was gone, if she managed to escape, the old woman would be safe enough here. She knew the earl wouldn't waste his time killing her.

She paced until her leg cramped. She sat down on her bed and began rubbing her calf. What to do? Wait for Roland to appear? She simply didn't know. She supposed she had no choice but to remain here until he came for her. Or, she thought, rising quickly, she could try to escape herself. The door wasn't locked. Perhaps she could slip by the guards; perhaps she could race through the inner bailey and no one would attempt to stop her; perhaps . . . It was ridiculous and she knew it.

She'd nurtured such ridiculous plans frequently during her confinement. There was no escape for her; she knew it. Then, she wondered, how could Roland get her out of here? He'd said tonight. But how? She saw no way, no glimmer of a chance.

She was crying again, feeling again the earl's callused fingers digging into her flesh, touching her, pushing against her until his finger entered her, probed inside her, and the pain mixed with the humiliation of it caused her to cry out, covering her face in her hands. And Roland had watched.

It was too much. Something inside her gave way and she suddenly felt outside herself; she felt as outside and as gray as the falling dusk, and filled with numb purpose. She rose and walked slowly toward the narrow window. She measured its width with her hands. She climbed up on a stool and tried to stick her head through the opening. It was too small even for her head. She pushed harder, bruising her temples. Staggering pain coursed through her head. She scrambled off the stool, her hands pressed against her temples, and she stared down at it and then at the window and was horrified. She'd wanted to leap through it; she'd wanted to kill herself. She drew a breath and forced herself to suck in air slowly and deeply. She'd lost her reason. Slowly she lay down on her narrow bed. She closed her eyes. She would remain calm. She would wait; she had no choice. The pain in her head subsided.

She didn't know how many hours passed, if hours indeed did slip by. Perhaps it was a succession of minutes that crept by her, so very slowly, until she wanted to scream. The chamber grew dark with the night; soon the one lone candle gutted.

There was but a quarter-moon to glimmer in the night sky, and its light cast no shadows into the chamber. It was dark and silent. She heard the door open softly. She heard a man's step, a man's steady breathing.

"I cannot wait longer for you," he said, coming to a halt beside her cot. "I am here to become your husband. I have prayed long in the chapel. God approves my actions. You will take me and accept me and obey me."

4

SHE'D KNOWN he would come, and strangely enough, she wasn't paralyzed by fear. She listened to him speak, and some part of her marveled at his ability to bring God to his side, be the matter one of piety or lust. She listened but heard no sound of a key turning in the lock. She knew there was a key, for he'd locked her in the first several weeks of her captivity.

Then he hadn't bothered this time, for he'd seen no reason to. She heard his heavy breathing, heard his footfall as he approached the bed. She heard him trip over the single stool and curse; then he called out, "Have you no candle? I wish to see you. Where is the candle?"

Very slowly, very deliberately, Daria rolled to her side to the far side of the cot. She eased off the side and came onto her hands and knees on the hard stone floor. Could he see her somehow? Hear her heart pounding?

"Daria?" His own breathing was deep and harsh, and she knew he was feeling for her on the bed. She crawled slowly, silently, toward the door.

He yelled her name, knowing now that she wasn't lying there on the bed waiting for him. He roared, wheeling about, and he again tripped over the stool. He kicked it from his path and in the next instant he threw the door open. Dim light from the single flambeau in the corridor wall cast shadows into the chamber. And he saw her, kneeling, her arms over her chest, staring up at him, pale and still.

The earl wondered if he should beat her now for her attempt to escape him; then he thought better of it. Perhaps if he struck her he would hurt her and she would not give him her full attention when he took her. No, he wanted all her attention, he wanted her to look at him when he thrust into her, drove through her maiden's barrier. His heart pounded and his loins grew swollen and heavy.

"Get up," he said, not moving. He was standing there, his arms crossed over his chest, his legs spread, blocking her, he knew, and there was nothing she could do save obey him. But she couldn't.

She didn't move.

"Obey me, now, or you will feel the chastisement of my hand."

Daria believed him. Slowly she got to her feet. She stood there silent and waiting. He smiled at her and held out his hand. "Come, Daria. Be not afraid of me, sweetling. You will be my wife, after all. I offer you this honor willingly and with all my heart and with our Lord's blessing. I will visit pain upon you tonight, but you will open to me willingly and you will accept my seed into your womb. Perhaps you will know some pleasure, but I trust it will not be overabundant. I do not want you to forget yourself like some women do. They are not good women; they are unworthy. My first wife was a whore, abandoned in her cries and demands, but you . . . you will be just what I want."

His words had held her in thrall, and when he moved so quickly and grabbed her arm, she finally shrieked, "No! Get away from me, I don't want this!"

Surprisingly, his hold on her arm gentled. "Fear not, Daria. You are blessed amongst women. God and man will it so. It will be my duty to take you as often as I am able, and you will come to wish for me, surely, in your sweet way, and to ask me prettily to take you. Women are to bend to their husbands; it is in your nature to do so."

64   *Catherine Coulter*

He stopped a moment and gave her a look filled
with such certainty that she wondered for an instant if
she were not somehow amiss in her view of him and
the world itself and not accepting something that was
truly an honor bestowed upon her. Then she laughed.
She'd thought to jump out of that window if only she'd
fit through it. She no longer cared. She leaned back
her head and spit at him, full in the face.

In the next moment he jerked her to the bed and
threw her upon her face. His hand at the small of her
back held her still. The chamber door stood open, but
he didn't care. He wanted to see her and he wasted no
more time. She was his and he would do just as he
pleased. He would honor her in marriage and take her
now because he couldn't bear to wait longer. He'd
already waited too long, been too careful in his delib-
erations regarding her. He ripped up her gown, baring
her to her waist. He stood then and looked down at
her sprawled legs, the rounded buttocks, the narrow
waist. His loins ached and prodded. His breath hitched.
He wiped her spittle from his face. He spread his open
hands over her buttocks, kneading and caressing, and
he marveled at the softness and the whiteness of a
woman's flesh.

She made a sound deep in her throat and tried to
roll away from him. It was nothing, this woman's
token resistance of hers. He merely wrapped his hands
around her waist and flipped her onto her back. He
pulled up her gown and again forced himself to slow,
to study this wondrous gift that he had brought to
himself. He stared at the mound of dark hair that
covered her woman's flesh. He touched her and felt
her flinch. He lifted his hand and said, "Now. Open
your legs, Daria. I wish to see you."

Instead, she lifted her legs, rolled up on her shoulders, and struck him in the chest with her feet. He
grunted with pain and surprise and tumbled backward.

But he caught her, easily, so easily, and she knew she would weaken soon and there could be but one conclusion.

She was screaming at him, kicking when there was naught but air to kick, for he was standing now beside the bed, watching her flailing, holding his hands over his chest, trying to regain his breath. And he was still staring down at her. Then he laughed, a low satisfied laugh. He was amused by her foolish efforts. Even as he unfastened the knot on his chausses he laughed. As he freed his manhood, he stopped laughing and looked at her. He saw her eyes lower, saw that she was staring at him, and was pleased, for he was hard and erect, his sex thrusting out from his groin. He was a good size, many women had told him so, and he wanted some healthy fear from her, at least that first time.

He came down on top of her, pinning her thrashing legs beneath his weight. She felt his sex between her legs, shoving upward, and she closed her eyes against the awful pain she knew would come when he managed to shove himself inside her. She struck his shoulders with her fists, scratched and pounded at his muscled arms. It did her no good at all. Her arm jerked back for yet another blow, this one to his head, when her hand brushed against the brass candle holder atop the small table beside the cot. A fierce joy went through her. She clutched its rough base, raised it as high as she could, and brought it down on his head.

The earl had reared back, his member held in his own hand to guide himself into her, and the blow struck the side of his head. The pain was searing and it rattled him. He fell sideways, still pinning her beneath him. She heard him groan, then fall silent. She struck him again and felt a slight shudder go through him. Then she dropped the candlestick. She tried to push him off her. She heaved and prodded, but she couldn't move him. He was deadweight on her.

She felt tears sting her eyes. She was so close to escape and she was still trapped by him. It wasn't fair, it wasn't . . .

"What in God's name have you done?"

At the sound of Roland's low voice, her tears dried, though she still wanted to cry, but in relief. "Please, hurry, get him off me!"

Roland quickly pushed the earl off her and let him roll onto the floor. He saw that her gown was shoved up to her waist and that her legs were parted and bare. He didn't want to ask, but he did. "Are you all right? Did he . . . did he hurt you?" His own voice flattened, for he'd been late, mayhap too late to help her. The earl had been over her and she'd been naked and . . . When she shook her head violently, he felt such relief his belly cramped.

She was very pale and shaking. He still looked at her, wondering what to say, wondering if he should stick his dagger into the earl's heart, for it was what he wanted to do. He'd prayed he wasn't too late as he'd rushed up the narrow stone stairwell, prayed more devoutly than a Benedictine priest would have done.

He shook his head. He, her rescuer, hadn't done a bloody thing. She'd saved herself.

"Quickly, Daria, rip up your gown. We will bind him and gag him. Hurry, we don't have much time."

She didn't hesitate. She ripped off wide pieces of the precious dark blue wool, watching Roland from the corner of her eye as he bound the earl tightly.

Once the gag was in his mouth, Roland rolled him unceremoniously under the narrow bed.

"Now," he said, rising, "nearly done. You must change now, quickly."

Daria stared at the boy's clothes he thrust into her hands. Then she smiled.

"Hasten, we haven't much time." He lightly touched his fingertips to her cheek. "I know things are moving quickly, but you will be safe now. We will speak later."

He turned his back to her and stationed himself at the open chamber door. He wanted to close the door but knew she needed some light to dress herself in the unfamiliar clothing. He heard her breathing, her clumsy movements. He kept his eyes on the steep circular stairwell just across from the bedchamber. He'd drugged the supper ale in its wooden kegs, but still he couldn't be certain that all the earl's men had drunk enough to knock them out. To his enormous chagrin, the earl hadn't touched any drink. He'd been too intent on getting to Daria. He hadn't wanted to risk impotence with her. Roland listened. It was quiet as a tomb, ominously quiet to his ears.

"Are you dressed yet?"

"Aye," she said, appearing suddenly at his side. Roland turned to look at her. The boy's clothes disguised the woman's curves of her body but she still looked very much a female. Quickly he sat her down on the bed and braided her hair. He tied it with a bit of cloth from her shredded gown, then thrust the boy's cap over her head, bringing it nearly to her eyebrows. He removed a wrapped cloth from his tunic and she saw that it contained mud.

He smeared the mud over her eyebrows to make them black slashes across her brow, then daubed more mud on her face. He grinned. "Wondrous filthy you are now, my lad."

He grabbed her hand and pulled her up. "Listen to me carefully, Daria. You will not open your mouth. You will keep your head down and stay close behind me. When I tell you to do something, you will do it quickly and silently."

It was then she saw that he was still in his priest's garb.

"I'm ready and I will do just as you say."

He patted her filthy cheek, nodding. He'd never in his life rescued a female and he wasn't certain what she would do, or how she would respond. Mayhap faint at a critical moment, mayhap shriek. But Daria appeared to have herself well in control, at least for the moment. He looked once again at the steep shadowed stairwell, then motioned for her to follow him.

When they reached the bottom steps, Daria stared around the great hall. Scores of people were snoring, filling the hall with a low rumbling sound, the ones who sat at the trestle tables slumped forward, their heads beside their trenchers.

"Will they die? Did you poison them?"

He shook his head. "I but drugged their ale. They sleep like innocent babes. They'll awaken on the morrow with aching heads but nothing more. Hush, now."

There were some who were awake, but their eyes were vague and they gave only cursory glances at the priest and the dirty boy with him. One man even called out, his words slurred, "Father, bless me for I have drunk too much and all I see are vipers and they rollick and twist around me. They are evil, Father."

"Bless you, my son, but you deserve every viper that strikes at you. At least you are still awake, whilst your friends have succumbed."

The man looked puzzled, then quietly he fell forward, knocking himself out with the blow, and Daria wondered if he'd cracked his head.

But outside there were many who were fully alert. Roland slowed his pace. He nodded and spoke to the men who crossed his path, seemingly at his ease, taking his time. He saw several of the women look at him with eager invitation and he made his expression austere.

"Where do you go tonight, Father?"

It was the head stableman and he was looking curiously at the filthy boy who was trailing after the priest.

Roland said easily, "You see this little cockscomb here? I am taking this fiend of a boy back to his father for the thrashing he deserves. He wanted to become a knight! He is part Welsh, a bastard shucked off one of Chepstow's masters, and he can't speak clearly enough for even God to understand him. Can you imagine such a thing as the earl accepting this young fool? Well, the boy will go back to his own father and get a good flogging."

The stableman laughed. "Serves him right, the young savage," he said, and stepped back into the stable. Roland followed him quickly, motioning for Daria to stay still. She did, but she didn't want to. She heard only a soft thudding sound from within the stable. She froze, wondering if Roland needed help, but then he appeared again, and he was smiling at her. "Another man resting soundly. Stay here and keep watch."

Soon he reappeared and he was leading a horse. It wasn't much of a horse, certainly not one of the fighting men's mighty destriers. Roland swung easily onto the horse's bare back and gave her his hand. "Come, we must hurry."

She stared in wonder at the back of his head. Did he think to simply ride through the mighty gates of Tyberton Castle? He did. There were a half-dozen guards patrolling, but it was to the porter that Roland spoke.

"Blessed even', good Arthur. I take this scruffy simpleton back to his father at Chepstow, on the earl's order. Would you open the gate for me?"

And to Daria's astonishment, Arthur chuckled, spit on the dry earth, and said, "Aye, by the looks of him, Father, he'll not survive a sound thrashing, the skinny little offal. What'd he do? Piss in the earl's wine?" And he cackled at his own wit.

"He wanted to free the earl's prisoner, the girl, Daria, so she would feel pity for him and let him seduce her. The earl wanted to begin his wedding night soon, so I am his deputy with this foolish boy. I take him because I feared the earl might kill him in his haste to bed the girl and for the boy's impure thoughts."

Arthur laughed and nodded. "Aye, be gone wi' ye, Father. I'll wait for ye to return. Be certain to call loudly when ye near the castle so none of the earl's soldiers lets fly an arrow through yer heart."

"Thank you, my friend. I will hurry. See that the master is not disturbed this night!"

And Arthur cackled anew as he opened the gates. "A pretty little piece she is," he said, his words nearly incomprehensible through his chuckling. "Aye, pretty and tender as a young chick. The earl will fair enjoy himself riding her!" The last sound Daria heard from Tyberton Castle was the laughter of Arthur, the porter. They rode through the portcullis into the outer bailey and out the great oak gates. Several men nodded, but none said anything or moved to stop them. It was that easy. Daria pressed her cheek against Roland's back. "I begin to believe you a magician, Roland. Everything passed so simply. I have thought and thought these past two months and believed I would never escape him."

"I'm very good," Roland said, grinning over his shoulder at her. "I learned long ago that the best ruses were ones that stuck as close as possible to the truth. Well, mayhap I did enjoy myself a bit with the truth this time. I will say we were very lucky. However, once the earl frees himself and sobers up all his men from their drugged ale, he will be after us. We must not tarry."

"I do not wish to tarry," she said, and clasped her arms around his waist. "But this animal, Roland, he looks to have the speed of and strength of a snail."

"Be patient. My own destrier awaits us nearby."

"Will you take me back to my uncle?"

"Not yet. It wouldn't be the wisest course. First we will beset the earl with confusion."

He dug his heels into the horse's sides and the beast broke into a thumping trot.

They rode for only about an hour, northeast, into Wales. Finally Roland pulled the horse off the narrow dusty road heavily bordered with hedgerows and yew bushes and drew up before a small hut of daub and wattle surrounded with sagging, very old outbuildings. A man emerged quickly and strode toward them. Roland smiled at Daria and said, "We will mount my horse now." He helped her down and told her to wait.

Roland walked with the man behind the hut, soon to reappear leading a magnificent animal, lean and strong, black as midnight, and proud-looking as a king.

Daria saw money change hands. The man grinned and said, "Aye, aye, *lle pum buwch, lle pum buwch.*"

Roland gave him a friendly buffet on his shoulder and turned to toss Daria onto his destrier's broad back. The horse merely shifted, not moving, accepting her weight with no fuss. Roland mounted, then said to the man, "Do not forget it is to the southwest you will ride. You will wear my monk's robe and ride this mount at least two hours. Then leave the horse and the robe where our good earl will find them."

The man nodded, spit on the ground beside him, and gave a small salute to Roland.

Daria stared at the man who had come to Tyberton to rescue her. How could she have ever believed him a priest? The other women at the castle had felt he was a man, a man of this earth, a man of the flesh, but she hadn't. He was now wearing a tunic of rough rust-colored wool, belted at his waist with a wide leather strap upon which hung his sword and a dagger. He looked dangerous and he looked intensely alive. She pressed her cheek against his back and accepted the newness of him into her.

As they rode from the hut, she asked, "What did he say? Something over and over again when you gave him money."

"You have a good ear. He said that now he has a place of four cows. In other words, he can now support four cows with the money I gave him for his aid."

To Roland's astonishment, she repeated quite clearly, *"Lle pum buwch."*

"You have learned some Welsh, then, during your two months at Tyberton?"

He felt her shake her head against his shoulder. "No, the earl hates the Welsh. He forbade any of their language to be spoken at Tyberton. If ever he heard anything that sounded foreign, he had the speaker flogged. Besides, he kept me isolated." With those words, she fell silent.

It had been drizzling lightly before. Now it stopped and the sky was hung with dark clouds promising more rain before midnight. Always it rained in Wales, always. Roland tightened the straps of the two bags over his horse's back.

Some minutes later, he realized that Daria was asleep. She was limp against his back and he felt her sliding sideways. He quickly caught her sliding hands and brought them together, holding them over his waist with one of his. He looked around him at the cloud-hung sky and the towering, twisted sessile oaks that seemed to close in on them. The air was pungent with the smell of the sea and the smell of damp moss. It would begin to rain again soon. He sighed, hoping it would stay dry until they drew nearer to Trefynwy. Then they would turn east and travel through the Black Mountains, unforgiving hostile peaks and naked ridges, where they would be safe from anyone trying to find them. He said aloud to himself, to Daria, even though she slept, "I am pleased with you." He meant it. She trusted him so much that she was actually able to sleep whilst fleeing. It was remarkable.

He grinned, raising his face to the cool night breeze. His destrier, Cantor, snorted, and Roland slowed him. They still had a distance to go before Roland would be content to halt and rest for a while. It was doubtful that the earl would discover their trail very soon, if at all. Roland had purposefully planned to travel northward through Wales, knowing the earl wouldn't seriously consider searching in the country he so despised. An Englishman would decide that only a madman would escape willingly into Wales.

Roland laughed softly, pleased with his strategies, for there was something very important the earl didn't know, and wouldn't find out.

He remained pleased until the thunder began to rumble overhead. Wales, the land of endless rain, he thought, staring up at the dark clouds overhead. He had wanted to reach Abergavenny by morning, but now he knew he couldn't. A raindrop slid off his forehead. He cursed quietly, tightened his hold on Daria's wrists, for she'd slipped to the side, and knew he had to find them shelter until it stopped raining.

He knew he was lucky in the terrain in which they now traveled. There were thick forests, which provided not only cover from anyone trying to find them but also some protection from the rain that was now coming down more quickly and more furiously. He knew also of caves in the area. If he wasn't mistaken, there was one of moderate size near to Usk, off the road, just to the west of them. He knew Daria was awake now, he felt her shiver against his back. He dug in one of his leather bags and pulled out a leather jerkin. "Here, we'll hold this over our heads. It will be some protection."

"I have heard that it rains here more than anywhere else on the earth," she said.

"That's very likely," he said, wondering where she'd gotten her information. "Certainly more than in the

Holy Land." The leather jerkin over their heads, Roland continued, to distract both of them from the sodden cold rain, "You will be my deaf-mute little brother whilst we are in Wales."

"Do you speak the Welsh tongue, Roland?"

"Aye, I do. It is one of my talents, this ability to learn languages easily and quickly."

"Then teach me, for I do not like to keep silent all the time."

He almost laughed, for the Welsh language was the most difficult he had learned, more difficult even than Arabic. It was on the tip of his tongue to tell her she wasn't able when he said instead, "What was it that farmer said?"

"*Lle pum buwch.* Now I will have a place for four cows."

Roland had never before met another person who had his talent for languages. He still wasn't convinced at her ability, even though the Latin she'd spoken was fluent and smooth.

"Just teach me enough so that I do not have to be deaf or mute."

Well, why not? he thought. For the next hour he taught her simple phrases, and he had to admit to being wrong. She was perhaps even more adept than he was at picking up the essence of a language, at finding patterns that no one else ever realized were there. By the time he found a suitable cave, one that was empty of mountain lions and bears, they were both sodden from the rain and Daria spoke limited but very Welsh-sounding words and phrases.

"We will wait here until it stops raining—*if* it stops raining. This cursed country does pour rain down all the time."

"Aye, but the smells, Roland," she said, sucking in air deeply. "The salt of the sea, the moss from the very rocks themselves, the heather and bracken. It is such a very *living* smell."

That was true, but he said nothing. He settled Cantor, then turned to look down at his charge. She was very wet and shivering with the cold. He pulled out his last clean leather jerkin from one of his bags. "Put it on."

She stepped away from him into the blackness of the cave and he immediately stopped her. "Nay, stay close, Daria. There still could be creatures there, and I do not want them to eat you or for you to lose yourself in the mountain. I am told some of the caves twist and curve back deep into the mountainside. To get lost would mean death."

She was back quickly, the jerkin hanging loosely around her. "Let us sit and eat some bread the farmer provided us."

Whilst they ate, he taught her the names of various foods and animals. She fell asleep even as she repeated *dafad,* or sheep.

He leaned back against the rocky wall of the cave and gathered her against him. His horse whinnied softly and the soft caw of the rooks filled the silence. He could even hear a woodpecker rapping on a tree somewhere near, and a waterfall loud and violent, slashing through a beech forest close by. She was right about the smells. Even in the dark cave, the smell of turf, bracken, water, and wind filled his nostrils. It was a wild smell, a savage smell, but one that fed and stimulated the senses.

He smiled as he fell asleep holding the girl who would be able to speak Welsh as well as a native if only she had enough time to learn.

It stopped raining near dawn and the sky was a soft rich pink in those brief magical minutes. He started to awaken Daria, when she said quite clearly in English, "I know you, know you deep inside me. It's passing strange and it makes me afraid, but for all that, it makes me feel wonderful."

He shook her awake. He didn't know what she was talking about, and something told him he didn't want to know.

They ate bread and cheese and drank the rest of the warm ale. Daria seemed not to remember her dream, that, or she didn't wish to speak of it. Dry and warm, they left their cave soon thereafter.

They rode through glades and thickets, through small twisted and lichened oaks, by boulders covered with moss. They passed naked rocks that looked wet even though the sun shone down strongly.

Roland continued to teach her Welsh. He felt a brief stab of jealousy at her talent, then grinned at his own vanity. It was good, this talent of hers; he didn't particularly relish having to shield a deaf-mute boy who was really a girl. Now at least she could say something when they met the Welsh, which they would surely do eventually.

And they met the Welsh sooner than Roland would have wished.

5

"AFON," ROLAND SAID, pointing, "river." Then, *"Aber* —river mouth."

Daria dutifully repeated the words. She tapped Roland on the shoulder. *"Allt,"* she said, nodding to their left. "Wooded hillside."

He swiveled about in the saddle and grinned at her. "You are very good," he said.

"Must I still be deaf and mute?"

"For the time being I think it the wisest course to follow. Be patient, Daria." He started to add that she would be home soon, but he knew her thoughts on that and so kept quiet. He wished he personally knew if Ralph of Colchester was a good man, a man of honor. Deep inside, though, Roland imagined that Ralph of Colchester could very likely be a troll and a monster and still Daria's uncle would wed her to him because he wanted to add to his own land holdings. It wouldn't matter to him if the man had wedded a dozen women and killed all of them.

He pulled up Cantor and let his destrier blow and drink from the cold river water. "Would you like to walk about a bit?"

She smiled gratefully and slid off Cantor's back. "Smell the air, Roland. And look at the sunlight on those maple leaves, 'tis magic, all those hues and shades."

She wrapped her arms around herself and twirled about in the small open meadow. *"Glyn,"* she called

77

out, *"fflur!"* She pointed to some sweet-smelling honey-suckle. " 'Tis for fidelity, you know, and the ivy yon, 'tis for permanence."

He grinned at her like a besotted idiot, realized it, and turned away.

"Ah, I wish we could stay here forever!"

"Just wait for an hour or so—until it rains again. When you're wet and cold and thoroughly miserable, you'll change your mind quickly enough."

She waved away his words. "The gorse over there, it protects us against demons, or mayhap from the unending rain, if we wish it hard enough."

He didn't want to wish for anything right now except for the rest of his money. Then his wish for his own land, his own keep in the midst of the beautiful green hills in Cornwall, would come true. He watched her flit from a low yew bush to a lone birch, repeating the names in Welsh. So learning came easily to her. It meant nothing to him, not a thing. So she was bright and laughing. It meant nothing more than her ease of learning. His eyes were on her lips, then fell to her breasts and her hips. Nothing, he thought, turning quickly to pat Cantor's neck. It meant nothing. His destrier turned his head, his mouth wet, and nuzzled his master's hand. Roland said to his horse as he wiped his hand on his chausses, "You are the loyal one, the one who's always known what I wanted, what I needed. You I trust with my life, no one else, particularly not a female. Not even a female who is pretty and bright and sweet."

"You speak to your horse, sirrah?"

She was laughing, a dirty-faced urchin in boy's clothes, a limp woolen cap pulled low on her forehead. The dirt he'd rubbed on her face was long gone, replaced by new dirt, streaked and black, more authentic dirt, all of it Welsh. Even her smooth white hands were filthy. She didn't look at all like a boy to him.

"Aye, it's passing smart he is, and he tells me 'tis nearly time for lunch."

Daria eyed the saddlebags hopefully.

"I'm sorry, but there's nothing left. I must do some hunting."

She looked back from whence they'd come, and slowly, regretfully, she shook her head. "Nay, I'm not all that hungry, Roland, truly. Can we not ride until late afternoon? Then can you hunt? I've wasted time here and I shouldn't have. I'm sorry."

"He's not after us, Daria. There was no one to betray us. Even if the farmer did tell the earl about us, he still didn't know where we were heading."

Still she shuddered even as she shook her head. "He'd know, somehow he'd find out. I just have this feeling." She added quickly, seeing him frown, "He's very smart."

Roland continued his frown, disliking himself even as the words came from his mouth. "So you admired him. Did you not wish to leave him, then? Did you wish to wed with him?"

Her head snapped up. "You are speaking like a fool, Roland!" And then, to her appalled surprise, she burst into tears. Roland stared at her.

The tension, he supposed, was finally too much for her. She'd finally succumbed, but still he was surprised. Until this moment, she'd shown unusual fortitude and grit. To fall into a woman's tears now—when the danger was past—seemed somehow very unlike her.

"Why am I a fool?"

She shook her head, swiped the back of her hand across her eyes, and turned away from him. "Nay, not a fool, just speaking like one." She dashed her hand across her eyes and sniffled loudly. "I'm sorry. Has Cantor drunk his fill?"

He gave her a long look, then said, "Aye." He gave her his hand and pulled her up behind him.

They were riding near to the River Usk and wood-clad hills rose up on either side of them, hills covered with thickets of beech and sessile oaks. Firs towered behind them, thin and high, and many narrow streams snaked through the land, most shallow and a pale stagnant brown under the bright sunlight. But even with the warm sun shining down, there was still the feel, the scent, the sound of water in the air—the streams burbling, distant waterfalls crashing and thudding over wet rocks, unseen water deep beneath the ground booming and gurgling. Daria shuddered. "It's overpowering," she said, and clasped her arms more tightly around Roland's back.

"Be thankful it isn't yet raining," he said. "Why am I a fool, Daria? Nay, *speak* like a fool."

He felt her tense up and knew to his toes that he shouldn't push her for an answer, but he was perverse, he knew it, had known it for most of his years. "Why?" he repeated.

"The earl is a frightening man. I don't believe him mad, not yet at least, but he is a strange sort of fanatic, and his moods shift dangerously. I would have rather wedded Ralph of Colchester's father or his grandfather than him."

"Ah."

He felt her arms tighten about his waist. "Roland, please don't take me back to my uncle. He doesn't worship God, even in a perverted fashion to suit himself. He worships only himself and sees himself as all-powerful, and he's more frightening than anyone because when he chooses to be cruel, his cruelty comes from deep within him, and it is pleasurable to him and so very cold."

"Then I should say you would be pleased to wed

and leave Reymerstone and your uncle's malignant influence."

Again she stiffened, and he disliked himself for being hard, but he was being paid by the uncle to deliver the niece back to him, and with the money he would receive, he would buy his keep in Cornwall and he would live there and it would be his and never again would he bow to another's wishes unless it was his wish to do so. Daria said nothing more. That perverse part of him wished she would.

It was nearing midafternoon when she broke the silence. "I must stop for a moment. Please."

He nodded and pulled Cantor up. He dismounted, then held out his arms for her. She ignored him and slid down the destrier's left side.

"By God, get out of the way, quickly!"

Cantor jerked upward, whirling about to face the human who'd encroached, and he slashed out with his front hooves.

"Move, Daria!"

She fell backward over an outcropping stone and toppled into the grass onto her back.

Roland soothed his horse and looped his reins around a stubby yew branch.

He walked to her and stood over her, hands on hips for a moment, before he offered her his hand. "Don't ever do something so stupid again. You knew better, Daria."

She nodded, ignored his hand, and got slowly to her feet.

"You did it because you were angry with me. Kindly remember that you must be alive and well when you arrive at Reymerstone."

"Aye, that's true enough! If I die, then you will get no coin from my uncle, will you?"

He just looked at her for a long moment, then slowly nodded. "That's true. So take care of yourself."

"I am going into the trees," she said, so frustrated and angry with him and with their situation that she wanted to spit. He watched her walk slowly, limping a bit, into the rich humid-looking foliage. The smell of pine and damp moss was strong. He watched her until she disappeared, and he took stock of their position. Brownish hill-ridges protruded above the woods in the distance, and even in this small glade he could hear the rush of waterfalls gushing over slick naked rocks through the forest to the west. He saw a small herd of wild ponies on a far hillside, silhouetted against a thicket of pine trees, their long manes tangled and unkempt. They were aware of him and stood quietly watching. He walked slowly to a small twisted and lichened oak and leaned against it. Beside the oak stood several boulders fuzzed with moss, left in this unlikely spot long ago, as if tossed there by ancient storms or even more ancient gods. He whistled a song Dienwald de Fortenberry's fool, Crooky, had sung, smiling even as he added the silly words.

> Give up! Give in!
> Sweet Lord, 'tis no sin.
> Kiss her sweet mouth
> And make her sigh
> Give her pleasure, oh my, oh my.
>
> Give up! Give in!
> Sweet Lord, 'tis you who win.
> Kiss her throat and make her lie
> Upon your bed, oh my, oh my.

Surely it was an absurd song, but he sang it again, smiling more widely as he pictured Dienwald and his bride, Philippa, snug in his arms. Crooky had continued with various body parts, rolling his eyes and miming lewdly until Dienwald had kicked him soundly.

Roland heard a scream and stopped singing.

Tyberton Castle

The Earl of Clare leaned back against the cold stone wall, crossing his massive arms over his chest. The farmer was nearly dead, damn his perfidious soul to hell. He'd told his man to go easy, to hold up on the whip, but the blood lust had enthralled him and now the Welsh bastard was hanging limply from the iron manacles, his ribs heaving, his face gray, his eyes fading even as the earl looked at him dispassionately.

"Well, do you wish to continue with this torture or do you want to die quickly? Tell me the truth. Tell me where you got that horse and you'll not suffer more."

The farmer raised his eyes to the earl's implacable face, and he thought: *All I wanted was enough money to have four cows.* But it wasn't to be. He wanted to die. His body was so broken he couldn't have healed anyway, even if the torture stopped now. And the pain was too much, far too much. He said, his English broken and halting, "The man and the boy rode into Wales, 'tis all I know. His was a powerful black destrier, a warrior's mount, strong and enduring. I know not the man's name. He paid me to ride the horse in the opposite direction and leave it for you to find, but I didn't." He said sorrowfully to himself, "No, I was stupid and wanted to keep the horse, and thus I die for my stupidity."

That was true, the earl thought. "Come, man, think! Surely he gave you a name. Come, and you'll die quickly, even the instant after you speak!"

"Roland," the farmer said after another strike of the thong. " 'Twas Roland!"

Edmond, Earl of Clare, stared at the man a moment longer, then nodded to his henchman. He pulled a dagger from his belt and slid it cleanly into the farmer's heart. The man slumped, his head falling on his chest, the manacles rattling as he went limp.

Who, Edmond wondered as he strode back into Tyberton's great hall, was Roland? A man hired by Damon, no doubt, to bring the girl back to him. Well, he wouldn't make it, that damned fake priest to whom he'd given his spiritual trust. But not all his trust. Deep inside he'd known the man was a fraud. He was too handsome, his body too well-honed for a man of exclusively divine concerns. He should have guessed it immediately when the castle women had wanted him so blatantly. And he'd gotten her away so very easily, the damned whoreson.

Edmond called MacLeod, his master-at-arms. He slapped his thick leather gauntlets against his thigh as he spoke. "Prepare a dozen men. We ride into Wales to fetch back the little mistress and the erstwhile priest. He stole her, took her against her will. We will rescue her. Bring enough provisions for several weeks. We ride hard."

MacLeod said nothing. It wasn't his business to disagree or question the lord or even think twice about his commands. The little mistress had left Tyberton willingly enough, everyone knew that, but they would find her, kill the sham priest, and bring her back to the earl's bed. They left Tyberton within the hour, the Earl of Clare at their head.

In Wales

Roland pulled both his sword and his dagger as he ran headlong toward the pine thicket. He heard a soft gurgling sound and felt his blood freeze. Had someone killed her?

He slowed, hearing low-pitched voices—two men— and they had Daria. They spoke quietly, but he made out their words, the soft Welsh clear to him.

". . . to Llanrwst, quickly!"

"But the man, what to do with the man?"

"We'll be gone before he misses her. Leave him, leave him. Go quiet now. Quiet!"

Roland slipped between the pines until he reached a small clearing where a narrow stream sliced through the sodden grass. One man, tall and built like a mountain, had slung Daria over his shoulder. The other man, short and ragged as the Welsh ponies Roland had seen, was following close behind, glancing furtively over his shoulder every few moments.

Suddenly rain began to fall, slow drizzling rain that was gray and silent. One of the men cursed softly.

Roland followed as quietly as he could, but his boots squished in the wet grass. The rain thickened, coming down in dense sheets, blotting out the trees and the hills and adding to the sounds of a rushing waterfall not far distant. There were forlorn caws from rooks and kingfishers. This damned land—one minute the sun was shining brightly and now there was near-darkness and it was but midafternoon. Roland swiped rain from his eyes and crept after the men.

They made their way slowly but steadily to a small cave cut through boulders into the hillside. Roland drew back, watching them enter. He saw a lantern lit and a dull light issue forth. He drew closer, until he could hear the men speaking.

". . . damnable rain . . . *glaw, glaw* . . . always rain."

"Will ye take her, Myrddin? Now?"

"Nay, the girl's wet and nearly dead. Leave her there in a corner and cover her."

So they'd discovered she wasn't a boy. Not much of a discovery, since her disguise wouldn't have fooled Roland for an instant. These men either, evidently. Had they struck her hard? Roland didn't want to admit it, but his first thought was for her, not for the money he would lose if he didn't bring her back to her uncle alive and a virgin.

No, he said to himself. She was goods to be delivered, nothing more. She was a bundle to haul around and return safely to her uncle.

He pulled back and gave himself up to thought. It was still early; the men would have to split up for hunting. The huge man—his name was Myrddin, if Roland had heard the other man aright—didn't look like he would want to miss his supper. Roland was content to wait under an overhang of slick rock, sheltered from the endless gray rain.

It wasn't long before Myrddin emerged from the cave, cursed the rain in a way he'd good-naturedly curse a friend he saw nearly every day, then set off at a trot, his bow and arrow under his right arm. Slowly Roland made his way forward until he stood just outside the cave. He leaned forward until he could see the other man, the short one with the bowed legs. He was kneeling over Daria, staring at her. He slowly lifted the filthy blanket and continued to stare.

Roland suddenly saw the Earl of Clare in his mind's eye, saw his hand disappear beneath Daria's shift, knowing that he would penetrate her with his finger, and as Roland looked on now as another man was gaping at her, his hand moving closer to her breast, Roland couldn't stand it. He leaned nearly double and crossed the entrance into the cave as silently as a bat flying at midnight. The man didn't hear him. The fire the men had set was burning sluggishly, throwing off choking smoke, and Roland inhaled it and coughed.

The man whirled about, and Roland leapt on him. He was of greater size and strength, luckily, and his fingers closed in a death grip about the man's throat. He gurgled and his face darkened and his eyes bulged and still Roland squeezed, his rage overcoming his sense, until he heard Daria whisper, "Nay, Roland, do not kill him. Nay."

He was breathing harshly and released his hold from the man's throat. He rolled off him. "Are you all right?"

Daria took stock of herself and nodded. "Aye. They came upon me when I was preparing to return to you. The large one struck his fist against my head." She shook her head gently as she spoke. "Aye, I'll live, but we must leave here before he returns."

But Roland shook his head. He wanted to kill the man.

And Daria saw what he wanted and said quickly, "I'm frightened."

"You're safe with me. This lout planned to rape you and then hold you for his mountainous friend's pleasure. He's an outcast, a bandit, and I'll not let him live, not take the chance that he'll follow us and try to take you again."

She saw his logic, hated it, but kept still. "Go near to the entrance of the cave and keep watch for me. Don't turn around, do you understand me?" She obeyed him. He joined her quickly enough. Together they watched the fire in tense silence; then Roland rose and went outside. He said over his shoulder, "Stay still, and don't look back at that scum."

He waited outside under the overhang until his legs began to cramp. He shook himself, slapped his hands over his arms, cursed the endless cold rain, and continued to wait.

He heard a man's soft tread. Myrddin was mumbling to himself, and it was obvious he wasn't pleased. His Welsh was rough, yet still it was soft and lulling. "No game, nothing but rain, always rain, always rain." He repeated his words over and over and Roland wondered if he was a lackwit.

He waited, his dagger ready.

Myrddin paused, sniffed the air, then bellowed, a terrifying sound that made Roland start, thus giving away his presence.

"Bastard! Whoreson!" Myrddin was on him, swinging his heavy bow at his head. The man was enormous, stronger than Roland, but less skilled with weapons. But it didn't seem to matter in the slogging rain. Roland slipped and fell heavily, then rolled quickly, hearing the dull thud of the bow come down on a rock too near where his head had been. Myrddin slipped, but he didn't fall; he leaned sideways against an oak, pushed himself upright again, and this time he held a knife in his right hand.

He should have left with Daria, Roland thought wildly, after he'd slit the other man's throat. He'd been arrogant, much too sure of himself, and now, if he died, so would she, but not as cleanly or as quickly. Damn him for a fool.

The man was backing him against the glistening wet boulders, tossing the knife from his right hand to his left and back again. He was grinning.

Roland watched his eyes, and the instant he saw him ready to throw the knife, he hurled himself sideways. He heard the hiss of the blade through the rain and then the dull thud as it struck a rock and bounced off. Myrddin yelled in fury and jumped at Roland, leaping at the last instant to come down hard on his back.

His hands were around Roland's throat and he was squeezing. Roland felt an instant of stark panic, then forced himself to think. Slowly, even as he began to feel light-headed, he eased his knife upward. But he knew it was too late, knew it . . . knew it . . . Oh, God, he didn't want to die, not now . . .

Suddenly, through rain-blurred eyes, he saw Daria standing over Myrddin. He watched, disbelieving, as she brought a heavy rock down on his head. Myrddin lurched back, looked up at her, then seemed to sigh as he fell sideways into a patch of stagnant water.

Daria was on her knees beside him. "Roland, are you all right? Oh, your throat! Can you speak?"

"I'm all right," he said, his voice a harsh croak. "I'm all right." Slowly he rubbed his fingers to his throat and shook his head back and forth. That had been too close, far too close, and he owed his life to a woman. A woman he fully planned to dispose of as he would a horse or household furnishings. He looked up at her face, white and washed clean of dirt by the thick sheets of rain. "Thank you," he said. "Let's leave this place."

They were riding in the heart of the Black Mountains, into the valley of the Afon Honddu.

" 'Tis naught but solitude," Daria said, her voice hushed and awed at the stark desolation.

Roland merely nodded, so tired he could scarce think. "Wait until you see Llanthony Abbey. It was founded over one hundred and fifty years ago by the lord of Hereford, but the monks had no desire for such stark isolation or, as they said it, to 'sing to the wolves,' and thus migrated to Gloucester. In any case, there are still some stouthearted monks who brave this bleak wilderness. They'll take us in and we'll sleep dry and warm this night."

That sounded like a wonderful idea to Daria.

The prior met them outside the small church, and upon hearing that the gentleman and his young brother needed shelter, offered them a small room. The architecture was as austere and stark as the wilderness in which the building sat. Cold and unadorned, all of it, and Daria shivered in Roland's wake as the prior led them to the small meeting chamber where the remaining twenty-one monks took their meals. None were present, for it was late and the monks were at their prayers. Roland was relieved; even monks who hadn't been near other people for a very long time could, perchance, still see Daria as a female, and that would raise questions he didn't wish to deal with.

A small hooded monk brought them a thin soup and some black bread and left them alone. He was Brother Marcus, the prior said, but the man made no sign that he'd heard. The prior, having no more interest in them, also took his leave. The food tasted like ambrosia to Daria. She said nothing, merely ate everything offered to her. When she'd finished, she looked up to see Roland looking at her. His hand was poised in the air on the way up to his mouth.

"What's wrong? Have I done something to offend you?"

She spoke softly, in English, so no one could hear. Roland merely shook his head and continued eating his own meal.

"A bed," she said, "a real bed."

"Actually it will likely be a rough cot made of straw. But it will be dry."

And it was. They had one candle, given to them by the same Brother Marcus. Roland closed the door to the small chamber with a sigh of relief. It held only a narrow cot with two blankets. Roland walked to it and poked it with his fist. "It is straw and looks damnably uncomfortable. But here are blankets, so we won't freeze."

"We?"

"Aye," he said absently as he tugged off his boots. "Ah," he said suddenly, looking up at her. "You're offended that you must sleep by my side? I don't understand you. You've slept by my side for the past two nights."

She said nothing. In truth, she thought it wonderful to sleep beside him in a bed. Quite different from their sleeping blankets in the forest and in a cave. "I don't mind, Roland, truly."

"Don't be a fool, Daria. I'm so tired it wouldn't matter if you were the most beautiful female in all of Wales and I the randiest of men. You don't mind, you say? Well, you should. You are a lady and a maid. 'Tis modest and right of you to protest. But it matters not. Come, get under the blankets. We leave early on the morrow."

She grinned at his perversity and slipped under the blankets, wearing only her shift, thankfully dry. When he eased in beside her and sniffed out the candle, she lay stiffly beside him, not moving. The straw poked and prodded at her, and she shifted to find a more comfortable position. After several minutes of this, Roland said, "Come here, Daria, and lie against me. I'm cold, so you will warm me."

She eased over, coming against his side. She laid her head on his shoulder and gingerly placed her hand on his chest. This, she decided, was something she could become easily accustomed to, this having Roland beside her, holding her against him. She sighed and nestled closer. His arm tightened around her back.

Roland frowned into the darkness. He appreciated her trust, but she didn't have to flaunt it. Did she believe him impervious? "You aren't my little brother," he said, "so cease your wiggling about."

"No, 'tis certainly true," she said, and burrowed closer.

"Daria, I'm not made of stone. Damnation, cease your wiggling."

She grinned into the darkness. "But I'm cold, Roland."

He fell asleep before she did, but he awoke quickly enough when she began thrashing about. He shook his head, shaking away his own dreams. He gently rubbed her back, then lightly slapped her cheeks. "Wake up, come now, 'tis no time for a nightmare."

She awoke with a start and lurched up, gasping. "Oh!"

"You're quite all right. Hush, now."

"It was awful, those men and that huge one, Myrddin. He touched me and—" She ground to a painful halt.

"You're safe now," he said again, his words slow and deep. "No one will hurt you." His right hand was methodically rubbing her back. "I'll keep you safe."

It was dark, the middle of the night, and she gave voice to her bitterness. "You speak to me as though I were your child, Roland, but I am not. Of course you will keep me safe. You must have me alive, mustn't you? Otherwise my uncle will give you no coin."

"Quite true."

"I'm an heiress. I'll give you coin not to take me back."

"Don't be a fool, Daria. You have no access to your fortune. 'Tis well under your uncle's thumb. Accept what is, what must be, and do what a female must do—that is, accede to your guardian's dicta. You must be returned alive and a virgin." The moment he said that, he clamped down on his tongue. Damned imprudent mouth! Mayhap she would be too embarrassed to question him; mayhap she wouldn't have noticed what he'd said; mayhap . . .

She was fast as a snake. "What do you mean, a virgin? What does that have to do with anything?"

"Naught. I misspoke. Sleep now."

"What, Roland? Do you mean my uncle cares about my maidenhood? As much as did the Earl of Clare?"

"Go to sleep!"

She slammed her fist into his belly and he grunted. He grabbed her wrists and twisted onto his side, facing her. He couldn't see her face, but he could feel her warm breath against his cheek. "I said to go to sleep, Daria. You will not question me further."

"But you must tell me—"

"You don't obey well, do you?"

"Tell me," she said, her nose touching his. He remained silent. She continued slowly, "You mean my uncle stipulated I must be a virgin or he wouldn't want me back?"

"Don't be a fool. Be quiet!"

"If I'm not a maid, what did he say he would do?"

"All right, aye, 'tis the truth. He wants you returned a virgin. Are you satisfied now? Know, Daria, that you will be returned as much a maid as when you emerged from your mother's womb."

She digested his words, making no response. Because he didn't know her well, Roland felt relief at her quiescence. He rolled onto his back again, bringing her against his side. "Sleep now, Daria."

"All right, Roland," she said, and her mind was racing with ideas. What would her uncle Damon do if she weren't returned a virgin?

6

ROLAND pressed a gold coin in the prior's hand upon their leaving the following morning. The old man clutched the coin, stared at Roland in surprise, then speeded them on their way with a comprehensive holy blessing.

It wasn't raining and Daria breathed in deeply. "It smells so green and alive," she said.

"*Bore da,*" Roland said.

She butted her chin against his shoulder. "What?"

" 'Tis 'good morning.' Repeat it." And she did. Their lesson continued until Roland drew Cantor to a halt beside a burbling stream. They were high in the Wye Valley and the air was cool, the sky the lightest of blues.

"We'll be at Rhayader soon. They have a market, I'm told, and we'll buy some food."

"Am I still your brother?"

Roland merely nodded. "Keep your head down. You still don't look much like a little cockscomb to me." Just as she was beginning to smile at what she believed a scarce compliment, he added, "I don't feel like fighting any more men who decide you're female enough for them to enjoy."

Rhayader was a sleepy little town that looked more English than Welsh to Daria. There were many sheep about and few people. The market was sparse, most of the goods having been sold much earlier in the day. Roland purchased bread and cheese and some apples.

They weren't approached or regarded warily. They were ignored for the most part. "We're outsiders," Roland told her. "It matters not that we're Welsh. We're not from here and that makes all the difference." She listened to him speak Welsh, marveling at how easily the words came to him, how he rolled the difficult sounds on his tongue, and looking, Daria thought, quite pleased with himself.

They ate their noonday meal on the banks of the Rhaidr Gyw, the Falls of the Wye, Roland translated for her, amidst waving wild grass and heather. It was beautiful and soft-smelling and the roar of the fierce rapids filled the silence. "This is a land more rare than the rarest jewel," Roland said as he chewed on his apple. "When it isn't raining, you want to stare, for the colors are more than just colors—look at the green of the Wye Valley, Daria, it looks soft and velvet it is so vivid."

"Where are we going, Roland?"

"We're traveling first to Wrexham, then to Lord Richard de Avenell's stronghold, Croyland. Lord Richard de Avenell is a Marcher Baron and Croyland lies just beyond the Welsh border, on the road to Chester."

She nodded. "How long will we remain there?"

"Not long," and that was all he would say. He saw that she would question him, and said quickly, "*Menyw*," and touched his fingertip to her chin.

She repeated the word for "woman," then asked, "What is the word for 'wife'?"

Roland looked at her for a long moment, then shrugged. "*Gwrang.*"

She repeated it several times. One never knew. Besides, it made him distinctly nervous and thus she repeated it again for good measure.

Roland fell silent then. He remained abstracted throughout the remainder of the day. They stayed the night under the overhang of a shallow cave. It wasn't raining and thus was pleasant.

"What ails you, Roland?" she asked him the following morning.

"Naught," he said shortly. "Tomorrow afternoon we will arrive in Wrexham."

They rode over a mountain that was topped with an ancient fort so old Daria thought it had probably been built before time began. They rode through wooded valleys and saw three waterfalls. It was magnificent, and Daria was enthusiastic until Roland's silence wore her down. They looked back on the Black Mountains, stark and forbidding even beneath a vibrant sun.

Daria was enjoying herself. This was a freedom she'd never known.

It was evident that Roland was not enjoying himself.

"Tell me of your family, Roland."

"I have a brother who is the Earl of Blackheath. He doesn't like me, has never approved of me. It matters not; you won't have to meet him. I have more uncles and aunts and cousins than I can even remember. Our stock is hardy and our men and women prolific." He fell silent again.

"Why don't you like me?"

He twisted about in his saddle and looked at her. "Why should I not like you?"

"You won't speak to me."

He merely shrugged and click-clicked Cantor into a trot.

"And when you do deign to speak to me, your words are sharp."

"I'm weighing matters," he said, and she had to be content with that.

That night Roland stopped before dark, saying merely, "Cantor is blown. We must rest him."

But it was Roland who fell asleep even as the moon was beginning its rise into the clear Welsh heavens. Daria lay beside him, propped up on her elbow. His breathing was slow and deep. He didn't snore. She looked down at his face as he slept. He looked very young, she thought, all the worries smoothed from his face, and slowly, tentatively, she touched her fingers to his cheek, down along the line of his jaw to his square chin. There was black stubble and she smiled and wondered if the hair on his body was as dark as that on his head. She continued looking at him. It gave her a good deal of pleasure. His brows were naturally arched and black as sin. She wanted to smooth the black hair from his forehead, but hesitated. She didn't want him to awaken and spout angry words at her. She even enjoyed the shape of his ears.

She finally fell asleep snuggling against Roland's back. He wasn't awake to tell her nay.

She awoke with a start, jerking upright. The dream was vivid in her mind and it was alien. She remembered her feelings of knowledge, of deep and complete recognition, when she'd first seen Roland. Now she'd seen the dream he was dreaming. But how was that possible? She shook her head even as she silently questioned herself. She didn't understand how it could be so. She wasn't in his dream, nay, she was merely an observer, yet she seemed to know what he thought. The question was why Roland was presenting himself to her in these ways. She now thought she knew the answer, but she also knew she wouldn't say anything to him. He would believe her mad, or simply foolish, or both.

The following morning, the sky was overcast and both Daria and Roland knew that the rain would begin soon. There was nothing either of them could do about it save bear it.

She said suddenly, hoping to catch him off his guard, "I heard stories from my father, stories about the Holy Land. He said he'd been told it was all heat and white sand and miserable fleas and poverty and children who were so hungry their bellies were bloated.

He said the men were dark and bearded and wore white robes and turbans on their heads. He said the women were kept away from other men, held inside buildings with other women. Do you know anything of this, Roland?"

Roland's hands tightened on Cantor's reins. He'd dreamed of the Holy Land the previous night; he'd dreamed about a meeting he'd attended with Barbars himself and his chieftains, and they'd been in a royal tent set up within sight of Acre. But Daria couldn't know that. This was merely happenstance.

He said only, "What your father told you is true. Hush now, I must think."

Daria practiced her Welsh, forming sentences and repeating phrases he'd taught her the past days. *"Rydw i wedi blino,"* she said three times, until he turned to ask, "Is that just practice or are you really tired?"

"Nag ydw," she said, grinning, and firmly shook her head to match her words.

They entered a small church in Wrexham late that afternoon to get out of the rain. Even the building's warm-colored sandstone looked cold and dismal in the gray rain. They walked beneath the narrow Norman nave arcades, toward the cloisters. There were few people in the church. It was damp and cheerless, no candles lit against the gloom. "It's dark as a well," Daria said aloud, trying to huddle farther into her cloak.

Roland said nothing. His head ached abominably; his throat felt scratchy; every muscle in his body throbbed and cramped. It pained him to breathe and to walk. Even his eyes hurt to focus. The illness had begun nearly two days before, but he'd ignored it, knowing he couldn't be ill, not now, not when he was responsible for Daria. But he was. It took all his resolution not to shudder and shiver beside her.

"Stop," he said finally, unable to take another step.

He leaned against a stone arch. He closed his eyes, knowing that she was looking closely at him, knowing that at any moment she would guess the truth.

But he didn't have time for her to tell him so. He felt blackness tug at him. He fought it, but his fight was futile. He felt himself sliding down against the arch.

The Earl of Clare wondered if Roland had killed the two men, and decided he had. One lay rotting, his head in still green water; the other was curled up in death inside a close-by cave.

"Aye, he killed them, our pretty priest," he said. "But why? Did they attack him?" He paused and paled. Had the men raped Daria? And Roland had killed them because they had? No, he wouldn't accept that. No, he would assume that he'd killed them before they'd had a chance to do anything and left them here. He said aloud to MacLeod, "I wonder where our priest took Daria after he killed these louts? Why did they come into this filthy country? Has he friends here?"

MacLeod didn't know a single answer to the earl's spate of questions. What's more, he was beginning not to care. Like the other men, he was wet and miserable and cold and wanted nothing more than to return to Tyberton, to the stifling warm great hall with its fires filling the huge chamber with smoke, and drink warm spiced ale and fill his hands with soft woman's flesh.

"Do we bury them?" one of the men asked MacLeod.

He shook his head. "They're savages. Let them continue to rot in peace."

Daria knew he was ill, had known for the past day and a half, only she hadn't wanted to believe it and had made excuses to herself for his persistent silence. She'd asked him once that morning if he felt all

right, and he had snapped at her, vicious and mean
as a stray dog. And now he'd fallen unconscious
from his illness. She dropped to her knees beside
him. His forehead was hot; he was caught in the fever.
His body shuddered even in his unconscious state. She
looked about for help. She'd never felt more frightened in her life.

"Roland," she whispered, nearly frantic. "Roland,
please, can you hear me?"

He was silent.

She was terrified, but not for herself. She was terrified for him, but of course he wouldn't care. It didn't
matter now what he thought of her. He needed her.

When the black-robed Augustinian priest saw them,
he hurried forward.

"Father," she whispered, "you must help me."

She realized she'd spoken partly in English, partly
in Welsh.

He looked at her oddly and she quickly said, "He is
Welsh and I am his wife and but half-Welsh. Do you
understand English?"

He nodded. "Aye, for I lived many years in Hereford. What do you here?"

She looked him straight in his sharp, pale eyes. "My
husband was taking me to his family in Chester when
he fell ill. 'Tis all the rain and our hard pace. What am
I to do?"

It was then she realized the priest had seen her as a
boy, and she cursed herself silently. She'd forgotten
and thought only to protect Roland, thinking a wife,
in a priest's eyes, must have more favor than a woman
not a man's wife. She said quickly, "I am dressed this
way for protection. We were set on by outlaws and
barely managed to get away. 'Twas my husband who
got me these clothes."

"A reasonable thing to do. I am Father Murdough,
and who are you and your husband?"

"His name is Alan; he is a freeholder, Father. Our farm is near to Leominster. Please help us."

He had no choice, for he was a man of God and he couldn't leave a man to die in his church. "Stay here. I will fetch my sexton to help us."

It seemed a decade had flowed by with Daria huddled over Roland, before her now-husband, still unconscious, was carried up three flights of stairs over the sexton's huge shoulder and laid upon a narrow bed in a small chamber beneath the eaves of Father Murdough's modest home beside the church.

"Have you coin, child?"

"Aye," Daria said. "In my husband's cloak. Will the sexton see to my husband's horse?"

The priest nodded absently. He'd seen that horse. It was a powerful destrier; unusual that a freeholder would own such an animal. Highly unusual. He wondered who this man really was. As for the woman, he doubted if she carried even a whiff of Welsh blood in her veins. He was glad she hadn't told him her name. He didn't want to know.

But that didn't matter now. Only the young man mattered. Father Murdough became brisk. "I will fetch a leech. The fever must be bled out of him if he is to survive. I will have my servant, Romila, bring blankets and water."

Daria, now frantic for Roland, managed to nod. Left alone with him, she saw that his clothes were damp and knew he must be made dry and warm. She would have to strip his clothes off, something she doubted he would approve of. She was unknotting his chausses when an old woman, tall and thin and proud-looking, her head topped with masses of white hair, entered, carrying blankets and a ewer of water. She had a lovely wide smile and full mouth of teeth. "Here, now," she said in low slurring Welsh, "wait a minute and I'll help ye!"

Together the women stripped off Roland's damp clothes. When he was naked, sprawled on his back, the old woman took a thorough survey. "A fine man he is, aye, fine indeed, all lean and bone and muscle. No fat on this fine lad. Aye, and look at that rod of his! It must make ye as happy as a turtledove."

"You spoke English," Daria said blankly.

"Aye, the father told me to. Me, I come from Chester, and my husband is one of these savages. Aye, but he's a savage that keeps my old bones warm during the long winter nights. Aye, he's mine, he is."

As she spoke, Daria looked down at Roland, at his rod that must make her happy. It lay flaccid against the thick black hair of his groin. He was magnificent and she wished with all her heart that he could keep her warm during long winter nights for the rest of her life.

They quickly covered him, and the old woman said nothing about the reddened cheeks of the young man's wife. "He is so very hot," Daria said, her palm stroking Roland's face. "Please, he will be all right, will he not?"

Romila looked at the girl and nodded without hesitation. "Aye, he'll be well again, and like most men, he'll likely growl and complain until ye'll want to smash in his head, ye'll be so angry with him."

"I hope so," Daria said, and sat beside him. She smoothed the blankets at his throat. She couldn't seem to keep her hands still and they stroked his arms, his face, his hair.

When the leech arrived, a shrunken old man with wise eyes and clean hands, Daria felt hope.

She'd found a hoard of coins wrapped in a tunic in one of Roland's bags. When she paid the leech, he looked at her, clearly startled. "Who are ye, then?" he asked in deep slow Welsh.

"I am Gwen, sir, and I'm his wife."

The old man harrumphed loudly.

"Please, sir, will my husband live?"

"Ye ask me that? I have but one answer and I'll tell ye it on the morrow. Pray for yer husband, lass, and I'll be back in the morning."

It wasn't until the old man had left that Daria realized he'd begun by speaking Welsh to her and had then switched to English. She wasn't, she realized, much of a mummer, if even an old leech could see through her.

She returned to Roland's bedside. She looked at his still face. He was so familiar to her and she knew now that there was some sort of strange bond between them, a bond that he didn't feel, only she. She thought again of the men in their white robes that she'd seen in his dream. She'd been there observing, but she'd also been with him, felt what he'd felt, even understood the strange tongue they'd spoken. And she remembered that one of the dark-faced men had pulled him aside and said softly to him, "I know who you are and I will bring you down—when it pleases me—infidel dog!"

And Roland had thought in those moments: Well, damn, I will have to slit his miserable throat. Daria wondered if he had, and then she didn't wonder at all. He had; she knew it, knew it as well as she now knew him.

She laid her cheek against his heart and slept. He didn't stir until she woke him for some nourishing broth Romila brought early that evening. He ate because she forced him to. He turned his face away, but the spoon followed and he had no choice. When Daria was satisfied, she bathed his face and chest with a damp cool cloth.

The fever rose steadily and her fear kept apace. Near to midnight she offered her life in exchange for his, but she knew that such a request wouldn't find much merit in God's eyes. She was only a woman, her uncle Damon had once told her. What would God care what a silly woman wanted?

She wet more cloths and wiped him again and again. The heat from his body was intense; her fear grew and her prayers became more frequent and more impassioned. At exactly midnight, he opened his eyes and stared up at her.

"Roland? Oh, thank God, you're awake!"

He said nothing, merely looked at her. Then suddenly his expression was furious and he yelled, "Joan, you damned bitch! Get out of my sight before I wrap my fingers around your throat!"

He grabbed her wrist and twisted it hard. She cried out and pushed at him.

But he was strong, and now he was twisting and panting and muttering at her, "Aye, I loved you, I gave you my heart, I offered you everything that I was and would become. But you betrayed me and now you return to taunt me. Bitch, damned perfidious bitch!"

He released her wrist suddenly and slapped her, hard. She reeled back, falling to the floor. "Roland," she gasped, coming quickly onto her knees, "nay, don't move! Nay!"

He was lurching upward, flinging back the blankets. He rose, weaving until he gained his balance, and she stared up at him, terrified and amazed and joyous at the sight of him.

Then, just as suddenly as it had started, his spurt of energy was spent and he fell backward onto the bed. She managed to ease him onto his back again and covered him. An hour slowly passed. He sighed and opened his eyes again. Without warning, he reached up his hand and grabbed a thick tress of hair. "Joan, 'tis you. You won't have my soul again."

She leaned over him because his hold on her hair was painful, and clasped his shoulders. "Nay, Roland, nay, 'tis I!"

He was mumbling now, words she didn't understand, words in that strange guttural language he'd spoken in the dream. The language of the Muslims and the Arabs. Then he said to her, his voice deep and soft, "Forgive me, Lila, of course it's you. You could never be like Joan. Come to me now. I want your breasts in my hands and your hands on my belly. Yes, Lila, bring me your soft body."

Daria sucked in her breath, stunned and fascinated, but she didn't move. Roland raised his hand and now he gently stroked her breasts. "You are still clothed. What is this? Do you not desire me? Why are you still wearing clothes?"

He raised his other hand and caressed both breasts, weighing them in his palms, his thumbs moving slowly over her nipples. She stared down at him, at the intent expression on his face, at the gleam of pleasure in his dark eyes.

"Remove your silk jacket now. I want to feel you."

He believed her to be a woman he'd known in the Holy Land, a woman whose name was Lila. She didn't care, not now. She touched his hands, caressed them as his fingers caressed her breasts, and she could feel the urgency of his need, feel the desire that came from the depths of him.

And she knew then that nothing was more important in her life than this man. She knew that he would be the center of her life, knew that he would be with her until she died. Or, she thought with a pained moment of truth, it was what she wanted to believe. Still, with no hesitation Daria calmly unlaced the boy's tunic she wore. Roland wanted her breasts bare; she would give him whatever he wanted. She pulled the tunic over her head and tossed it to the floor. Thankfully, the chamber was very warm from the fire in the crude fireplace. She saw him smile, and he was looking at her breasts, at their motion as she moved back beside him.

"Come closer. Lean into my hands. Ah, yes, that is what I want. You feel like silk and . . . What is this? You want me, Lila? So quickly? Your nipples are tight, for me?"

She leaned over him, her breasts filling his hands, and whispered, "Aye, Roland, for you. I would be whatever you wished. Just tell me what to do."

His fingers stroked her and she moaned, then gasped, from her surprise. Never had a man touched her thus. She felt stranger still as he continued to explore her, and she knew that she was on the threshold of something wonderful, something she would like very much. She wasn't ignorant of what men did to women, for she had lived in her uncle's house for five long years. She knew very well what happened between men and women, her uncle had seen to that. He enjoyed flaunting his women in front of her. And she'd seen him naked, his rod standing out from his body, but she'd always felt only revulsion, deep, soul-searing revulsion. But not with Roland, never with Roland.

"Lila, bring your breasts to my face. I wish to suckle."

She stared down at him. This was something she knew nothing about. Suckle her? She couldn't imagine a man suckling a woman as if he were a babe. But it didn't matter. She lowered her body and felt his fingers again stroking her breasts, gently tugging at her nipples, and then his mouth was on her flesh and she drew in her breath with the wondrous feelings that were building deep inside her body. She closed her eyes, feeling his warm mouth, his wet tongue, and gloried in the sensations that were growing more intense low in her belly.

"Roland," she whispered, and her hands were on his bare shoulders, sliding beneath the blankets to his chest.

"So sweet," he said, his breath hot and urgent on her. His hands came around her and stroked down her back to her waist, then up again, his fingers tangling into her hair, pulling the braids free. "Lila, you still wear clothes." He sounded surprised and faintly displeased. "I want you naked and over me."

"I'm not Lila," she said even as she pulled off the boy's pants and hose and unfastened the chausses.

When she was naked, she slid down the blankets. She looked at his man's body, taut and hard and shadowed. She smiled and covered him with her body. At the feel of him beneath her, she felt something pass from him to her, something strong and gentle and demanding, something so powerful that for a moment it frightened her. Then she accepted it completely. But he must feel only his own building desire. He sighed at the feel of her body pressing against his. He slid his hands over her back until he was cupping her buttocks.

His breathing became quite suddenly fast and raw. "Bring me inside you, Lila."

He wanted her to bring his rod into her body? She lifted herself and gazed down the length of him. His member was swelled and hard and he moaned deeply, his hips jerking when she lightly touched her fingers to his hot flesh.

And again she felt this urgency in him, this overpowering need, and her fingers tightened around him. He was bucking now, moaning hoarsely. "Now, Lila. By Allah, my need is great. Wait no longer."

Still, Daria wasn't certain what to do. He was very large, surely too large to come inside her. She leaned down and kissed his hard belly. He flinched and moaned. She kissed him again, her mouth lower this time. When her lips touched his sex, his body heaved wildly, and then, suddenly, she saw a glorious naked woman with hair black as a night of sin who was straddling him and holding him between her hands and guiding him upward into her.

Daria cried out with the vividness of what she saw.

She felt dizzy and frightened about the step she was taking, a step that was irrevocable. She was on her knees over him, staring down at him, and then she touched herself, felt the wetness of her flesh and knew it was to ease his way into her. She took him between her hands, ready, but he forestalled her. His fingers were on her belly, stroking her, kneading her, then lower until they sifted through the hair covering her woman's mound. She lurched straight up when his fingers delved through the slick flesh to find her, and she cried out.

"Ah," he said, and he sounded profoundly pleased with himself. "You are always ready for me, aren't you? Always ready to take me. I'm pleased. Shall I give you pleasure now? Before I come into you? Before you ride me wildly?"

"Nay, come into me now." She feared this pleasure he spoke so confidently about, feared what it would do to her. She held herself stiffly above him, feeling his fingers begin a rhythm on her flesh even as his other hand was pressing against her belly, and then he stopped.

"All right, I'll take you now, you're wet and ready for me." Daria no longer saw this Lila, this other woman he believed her to be, this other woman who was no longer in his life. She was in the past; she didn't matter.

What mattered was now.

She closed her eyes a moment. He spoke again, and this time it was in that strange tongue, but more strangely still, she understood what he wanted and she felt no hesitation.

7

DARIA knew if she did what he asked, she would no longer be a maid. She refused to consider the consequences more than she had already done. She raised herself above him again and took his man's rod in her hand. Slowly, so very slowly she pressed him against her, and felt him come easily inside her because she was slick and wet. He strained against her fingers. She eased down just a bit and took more of him. He was moaning, his hands were tightening on her hips, his fingers digging into her flesh. She felt herself stretch for him, felt the tension building in him, powerful and vigorous, and in herself as well, and knew the moment before he thrust upward that the pain was coming and she wouldn't like it. He grasped her hips hard and jerked her down on him even as he bucked his hips upward. The pain was a sharp burning stab that made her cry out, but nothing more, and then he was deep inside her, touching her womb, and it was something she couldn't have imagined. His urgency seemed to lessen and he began to move gently and slowly, nearly pulling out of her, then coming in deeply once more. His chest heaved with effort and sweat covered his brow, matting his hair, and he was murmuring over and over, "Nay, don't move, Lila, don't move! It's been so long, far too long . . . don't move!"

She held still, knowing everything was beyond her now, knowing whatever would come, she had done it to herself. She had set into motion her own future and she was the only one responsible. But she hadn't imagined his touching her like this, his body coming into hers, so deeply, so completely, possessing her so thoroughly. The pulsing, intense feelings of before had faded, lost in the pain of her ripped maidenhead, and they didn't return. But it didn't matter. Only he mattered. He was moaning now, harsh raw sounds from deep in his throat, and then he lifted her nearly off him. He held her above him, his rod barely inside her body, and stared up at her and smiled, and brought her down hard and fast, and she shuddered with the shock of it as she took him completely yet again. He clutched her to him then and jerked wildly.

"Roland," she said, and he looked at her, his eyes clear and bright and dark; then he closed his eyes, hiding the pain his control was costing him. "You aren't like yourself. I'm stretching you, I can feel it, and it's bringing me madness, this smallness. And I ripped you. How can that be? You aren't a maid. How can you still be so narrow? How can I hurt you? Have you found some cream that brings you a maid's tightness again? Or do you cry out with passion? Is that it, Lila, is it passion?"

" 'Tis passion, Roland. It could be naught else but passion with you."

He smiled again, a smile so sweet that she felt as if a fist were clutching around her heart. She hurt, deep inside, but it didn't matter. He wanted her and she would do anything for him. She rode him hard, for that was what his hands directed her to do, and as he jerked and moaned, his fingers wildly kneading her buttocks and belly, she said again, "I'm Daria. Please know me, at least for a moment, know 'tis me."

He suddenly froze and she felt him lurch upward, felt his seed spurt deep inside her. He was heaving, his breath fast and raw, and still she rode him until he whispered, "Enough, Lila. By Allah, you're good, so good. You've worn me down to my bones. I don't think I'll take Cena now. No, she must wait, even though she is hungry, I know, always hungry. You've reduced me to ashes and it was so good, so very, very good."

She stared down at him. He was deep inside her body and he was talking of two women in his bed. She slowly eased off him and saw his seed and her virgin's blood on her thighs and on his man's rod. She quickly pulled the blankets over him again and bathed herself with the cool water. She felt soreness deep inside her.

She returned to him and slipped beneath the covers to hold him to her.

It was during the night that she made up her mind not to say anything to him about what had passed between them. He hadn't known her. He'd believed her to be another woman, a mistress he'd known in a foreign land. It was then she rose and pulled down the blankets. She quickly bathed the blood and seed from his member. She held him gently, marveling at his differentness, at the beauty of him. She raised her eyes to his still face. "I love you, Roland. I will always love you and I will always belong to you and to no one else." She wished she knew the words in Welsh. She wished he could hear her, and she wished that he had smiled at her and known her as Daria.

She would be safe from his questions, if he chanced to remember what had happened, which she strongly doubted. If he did, he would believe it a dream, nothing more. She felt, oddly, content. He was the man destined for her and she'd given herself to him. That, she reminded herself, or she was as mad as her grandmother and seeing things because they were what she wanted to see. Or he was the man she'd been destined to have only for this night and then he would leave her, and all her precious knowledge of him, her deep *knowing*, had all been a lie, a sham. No, she wouldn't accept that.

Someday, perhaps, he would realize that he was tied to her. Perhaps someday he could care for her as she did for him.

She laid her palm on his forehead.

He was cool to the touch. The fever had broken.

So had her maidenhead.

Roland opened his eyes and stared around the small dismal chamber. He had no idea where he was. His head pounded but his stomach wasn't twisting and churning, nor was there the dreadful bone-aching pain that had dragged at his body and reduced him to the strength of an ant. He'd enjoyed excellent health his entire life, and the illness frightened him. It meant he wasn't in control; it meant he had to depend upon others. And he was vulnerable to anyone who took it into his head to do him in. He raised his hand and realized with something of a shock that he was still very weak. He turned his head ever so slightly at the sound of breathing. There was Daria, sitting on a lone chair, sewing a tunic—one of his tunics. She was still dressed as a boy, but her hair was loose and tumbling over her shoulders and down her back. Very beautiful hair, he thought inconsequentially. He'd forgotten how lovely her hair was, with all its dark rich colors. Her brows were as dark and finely arched above those green eyes of hers. Then he noticed that she was pale, very pale.

He felt his throat tighten, and said, "Daria, may I have some water?"

Her head jerked up and she smiled at him, a dazzling smile that would have brought an answering smile to his mouth if he'd had the strength. She bounded up from her chair and her abrupt movement made him wince.

He sipped at the cup of water as she held his head, so gently, as if he were naught but a babe. Again he felt fear, fear that he was helpless and out of control. She, a female, was succoring him, seeing to his needs, nurturing him. It wasn't to be borne, yet he didn't seem to have a choice for the moment. He sipped at the water. She seemed content to allow him all the time he wanted. He breathed in her scent, turned his face slightly so that his cheek was against her breast. She was soft, too soft, and that frightened him as well. He tried to pull away from her.

"Nay, Roland," she said, her breath sweet and warm on his face as she lightly stroked his cheek. "You're not ready to do battle in a tourney just yet."

"What do you know of my strength?"

To his chagrin, she smiled sweetly at him. "Romila told me you would be testy. She says that all strong men hate illness, hate being dependent on others."

That bit of philosophy drew him up. Damn her for being in the right of it. He realized he also hated being like everyone else, hated acting as he was expected to. "No, I don't mind it at all. Your breasts are soft against my face and—"

Water dripped down his chin. He tried for a cocky smile but couldn't manage it. For an instant he saw her expression change into one of wariness and something akin to fear. No, how could that be possible?

"Where are we? How long have I been ill?"

Her smile returned. She said nothing until she'd gently wiped his chin and given him more water to drink. Still, she held him, and he felt the soft thud of her heartbeat against his face. He wanted to stay there, warm in her arms, for a very long time.

"We're in Wrexham, in a small chamber in the priest's house. We've been here for nearly three days now. When you collapsed in the cathedral, Father Murdough helped us."

Roland chewed that over. "The priest then knows you are no boy."

"Aye. I told him you were my husband and that you were taking me to meet your family in Leominster. You're Welsh and a freeholder and I'm but half-Welsh, thus my lacks in the language."

Roland groaned.

"I told him that I was dressed as a boy because you believed it wise for my protection."

"I don't suppose the man of God agreed?"

She chuckled and he found himself smiling slightly in response. "He said aught about it, actually. He's a very accepting sort of priest. I am expecting the leech anytime now. He's not a fool and he has aided you. Do you really feel better, Roland?"

"Aye." He turned his head so he could see her face. "You're pale. Have you remained here, beside me, shut up in this dreary little chamber?"

"Had I not stayed with you, 'tis likely you would have tried to take over the cooking chores and bathe yourself and mend your own tunic."

He gave her an absent smile, then said, "We'll leave on the morrow, at dawn."

She was perfectly still for a moment. "No, we shan't. We won't leave until you have your strength back."

"You dare to tell me our plans?"

Her arms were around his shoulders and she hugged him slightly. "You sound churlish, Roland. Aye, you will do what is wise and not what is stupid. If I have to tie you down, you will remain here until the leech says you are well enough to travel without falling off Cantor's back."

"I don't suppose you've remembered the Earl of Clare and his desire for your fair person?"

"I've not forgotten," she said, and that was all.

His eyes hurt and he said irritably, "Dim the damned lights. I can scarce see."

"All right."

"You're being too agreeable. I distrust that. A female who agrees with a man is having sport with him. Have you spent all my coins?"

She lightly passed her palm over his forehead and through his hair, tousling it, then smoothing it again, paying no heed to his sharp words.

"You aren't my mother, damn you, wench!"

"That," she said, gently pressing him onto his back and straightening over him, "is very true."

He gave a heartfelt sigh. "You are my penance. I wonder if the coin your uncle will pay me will suffice for my days in your tyrant's company."

"Be not sour-natured, Roland, it will do you no good. Now, if—"

He interrupted her. "I must relieve myself."

Daria nodded briskly. "I will fetch the chamber pot and assist you."

Roland looked at her with astonished loathing. "I don't need any help, only some privacy." When she didn't move, he gave her an evil look, threw back the blankets, and sat up. But he couldn't rise; he hadn't the strength. And he'd wanted to. He wanted to intimidate her with his size, mayhap frighten her with his bulging manhood. By all the saints, at present he couldn't intimidate a dwarf. He looked down at himself and knew that even his sex had betrayed him. His member wouldn't intimidate the shiest of maidens, and Daria had proved herself not at all shy. That in itself made him want to howl with humiliation.

Daria didn't draw back. She knew his body as well as she knew her own, for she'd cared for him completely for the past three days. She crossed her arms over her breasts and stared at him. "Will you rise now? Will I have the pleasure of seeing you collapse again? I doubt I have the strength to pick you up, so you will lie on the floor, naked as the day you came into the world, until I have fetched Romila. Two women would then haul you back into bed and see to your needs. Romila, I might add, much delights in examining your body, and she's frank in her assessments. Now, Roland, what say you to that?"

"I say you're a wasp and 'twas foul mischance that brought me to you."

She saw that he was trembling from weakness or perchance from a lingering chill, and forgot her show of mastery. "Roland, don't be foolishly proud. Let me help you. I would let you help me if I needed it."

He was damned if he did and damned ever more if he didn't. He nodded. It was torture, every moment of it. Once he'd finished, he was tucked by her gentle hands back into the cot without a word being spoken. He closed his eyes. He considered slipping out whilst she slept and escaping her. He cursed her uncle's coin. He didn't want it, not if it meant that he had to relieve himself in front of her. She had turned her back, but it mattered not. 'Twas the same thing, and she'd known what he was doing. Indeed, before he'd regained his wits, he doubted not that she'd seen to it even then.

He was embarrassed beyond what he could tolerate, and there was naught, at the present, he could do about it. In the normal course of events, he didn't imagine that he would care in the least if she watched him doing anything at all; but he was helpless and weak, a pitiful specimen, and that made all the difference; that made it intolerable.

Daria watched him from beneath her lids. She was pretending to sew the rip in his tunic, but her eyes and her attention were focused on him. She wasn't certain she understood the depths of his feelings, but she accepted his anger, his sourness. She could only imagine what she would feel like if she were ill and had to relieve herself with his help.

When the leech arrived, she was profoundly thankful. He eyed Roland, spoke in soft Welsh to him, and seemed pleased. At one point, he gestured toward her, but Daria didn't understand his words or Roland's reply. She doubted her husband would be complimenting her.

And as Roland and the leech spoke, she felt free to look at him, and felt such a surge of relief that he was improved that she wanted to shout. When at last the leech turned to her, she was smiling despite her supposed husband's foul humor.

"Yer husband does well," the old man said. "He tells me he will leave on the morrow, and I told him if he does, he'll die and leave ye alone to the tender mercies of lawless bastards. He is now considering things." He paused, giving her a significant look, and Daria quickly paid him. "Nay, worry not, lass, he's not a stupid man." He gave her a small salute and took himself off.

"You give him *my* money, do you?"

"Since I have none of my own, there's no choice."

"So, you found where I'd hidden my coins and now you make free with them?"

"Perhaps I should have pleaded poverty and the priest could have dumped both of us in a ditch. As for the leech, of course I pay him. To put up with your vile temper, he deserves all the coins I give him. Of course, since he's a man and not a simpleminded female, you accorded him more courtesy and attention!"

"You should have told me."

"You're right. I should have somehow roused you and asked humbly for your permission to use the coins. Such a pity I also am paying for the stabling and care of your destrier. Should I tell the priest to throw Cantor into a ditch, perhaps let him run loose until you are ready for him again?"

"You become a shrew, Daria."

"You are merely evil-tempered because you cannot

bear the fact that you, my stalwart rescuer, are all too human. You aren't a god, Roland. You're only a man."

"So you have noticed that, have you?"

She gave him a smile that, had he but realized it, would have shown him just how much she did know. "Aye," she said. "Be patient, my l . . . have patience."

"How can I? The damned earl will come, and then what will you do? Tell him to be patient until I am well enough to protect you?"

She shook her head and spoke without thought. "I should protect you."

He snorted and lost some of his newly acquired healthy color. "No, say nothing more! Bring me food. I must get my strength back."

Daria considered starving him. He was ungrateful and a tyrant and seething all because he himself became ill. As if it were her fault. She sighed. Men were difficult creatures. "Very well. Please rest whilst I'm gone. I will return shortly with food for you." She marveled that she'd sounded so calm. She snapped the chamber door closed with a bit more force than was necessary and walked with a bit more pressure than was fitting for a priest's abode.

Romila took one look at her face and cackled. "Aye, yer pretty husband makes ye furious, eh?"

"Aye, I'd like to strangle him."

"He's a man, child, nothing more, nothing less. Feed him; he'll chirp in harmony again once his belly's full."

If Roland didn't chirp, he at least seemed to regain his calm after he'd eaten Romila's stewed beef and coarse brown bread covered with sweet butter.

"We leave on the morrow," he said, not bothering to look at her. He was calm and sure of himself and of her.

"No."

"In the afternoon."

"No."

"Daria, you will do as I tell you. I am not your husband but I am the man in charge of you, the man responsible for you and, thus you—"

"No. We won't leave until you are well, completely fit, and not before. I have hidden your clothes, Roland. If you behave as a half-wit, you will go naked as one. You cannot force me, nor can you threaten me. I won't let you go until your body is well again."

He cursed long and luridly, but Daria only smiled. He'd lost and he knew it. His foul language was just a man's adornment for his frustration. After he'd cursed himself out of words and into a near-stupor, he fell asleep and she moved to sit beside him. She lightly touched her fingers to his face, and leaning close, whispered, "You have no memory of two nights past, do you? I have wondered what I would do and say if you had. Would I have denied it and claimed it naught but a fevered dream? Or a fancy, mayhap? But it hurts nonetheless, Roland, very much. Now I find I'm disappointed that you don't have any memory of ridding me of my maidenhead.

"I do know, Roland, if you force me back to my uncle and he forces me to wed Ralph of Colchester, I would at least have had one night of love." She paused a moment, aware of tears pooling in her eyes. "Damn you, Roland. You are the most stubborn, the most obtuse of men. Mayhap I will simply inform my uncle that I am no longer a virgin and you are the man responsible. Then would I be safe from Ralph of Colchester?

"But at what cost? Would my uncle kill you? Kill me for my inheritance? Knowing Uncle Damon, I doubt he would have any scruples about doing away with both of us, but—"

"You carry on like a raucous kingfisher. What are

you talking about? I try to sleep to regain my strength, but you babble on and on, numbing my ears."

She very slowly moved her fingers from his face. What had he heard? She tried to remember all of her soliloquy, but couldn't. A silly argument with herself, but it appeared he'd just heard meaningless sounds.

" 'Tis naught, Roland. Forgive me for disturbing you. Sleep."

He grumbled some more, but she didn't understand his complaints, which was probably just as well.

He slept soundly until late that night. After she'd fed him again and seen to his needs, which still caused him to curse and his expression to become taut with humiliation, she slipped into bed beside him, careful not to disturb him. But during the dark of the night, he found her and drew her against him. If was as if he knew her and accepted her and recognized also on a deep level that she was his and he would act as he pleased. His hands were on her hips; then she felt his fingers pushing between her thighs, skimming over her flesh to find her. She squirmed as his fingers probed, his middle finger easing high up inside her and his other fingers gently rubbing her swelled flesh. She turned her face into his shoulder, moaning through her clenched teeth, as her body shuddered with the intense feelings.

Then suddenly his breathing slowed and he fell back into a deep sleep, sprawled on his back, his fingers cupped over her hip. The frantic feelings slowly faded, and again she wondered where such feelings would lead.

She eased her hand down over him and discovered that his rod was full and heavy, but he hadn't moved to come into her. He hadn't had the strength, nor had he really awakened. What he'd done, he'd done simply because she was there beside him, a female whose flesh was eager for him. Had he realized it was her,

Daria, he was holding and stroking, he would have probably fallen off the bed in his haste to get away from her. But he'd slept through his assault.

She didn't understand this sex business, particularly from the man's view. Touching her intimately, then stopping, never coming to consciousness. She awoke first the following morning and eased out of bed. She stared down at him and wanted to shout at the wondrous feelings that surged through her when she simply looked at him. "I love you, Roland," she whispered, then repeated in Welsh, *"Rwy'n dy garu di."* Romila had chuckled when Daria had asked her the words in Welsh the previous day, but had obligingly told her. Daria dressed hurriedly and left the chamber.

She wanted to visit his destrier and see that his care was proper. On the northern side of Wrexham cathedral, down a long narrow street, stood a public livery, a long low building built solidly of straw and dung and covered with a slate roof. Cantor was in the third stall and the toothless brawny individual who showed him to her babbled on about the amount of oats the horse was eating and how the beast had bitten him but good.

Daria finally paid him extra coins, and he beamed, scratching his armpit vigorously.

" 'Tis a fine bit of horseflesh," he said, speaking loudly and slowly to her in his own tongue. "Aye, 'tis true, and ye say yer husband be a freeholder?"

So much suspicion, she thought, nodding. She hadn't had time to think of a better lie, and this one wasn't serving her all that well. There was nothing for it but to stick to her story.

"Aye," the liveryman continued, " 'twere another couple of men in here earlier, and they asked me about this beauty. I told 'em yer husband were that, a freeholder."

Daria felt her guts twist painfully. She knew who the men were, she *knew*.

"They were *saeson*, the slimy louts."

Of course they were English; they were the Earl of Clare's men; she had no doubt of it. What she didn't know was what she should do about it. She scratched her own armpit, saying indifferently, "I wonder if they'll come back. Think you they want to buy the horse?"

The stableman sought his way through her clumsy Welsh, and nodded. "They're coming back," he said, and Daria knew everything had changed. Thank God the stableman didn't know their names or where they were staying. But the Earl of Clare would find out quickly enough. She ran her tongue over her dry mouth. Oh, God, what to do?

"Oh, aye," the stableman suddenly said. "There they be, yon!"

She turned to see two of the earl's men some thirty paces up the narrow street, speaking to a vegetable vendor. She recognized MacLeod, his master-at-arms. He was making descriptive movements with his hands as he spoke. Both men looked tired and impatient.

"I think I will take the horse for a gallop," Daria said.

"*Ond—*"

She waved away his objection and quickly saddled Cantor. The destrier, impatient and bored, neighed loudly, flinging his head up, and it required all her strength to get the bit between his teeth and the reins over his head. "I will return soon," she said to the stableman, and click-clicked Cantor from the stableyard. "I ride toward Leominster," she said, and prayed with all her might that he would repeat that to the earl's men.

As Cantor snorted and danced sideways through the crowded narrow streets of Wrexham, Daria stuffed her hair under her woolen cap. Did she look once again like a boy? She prayed so. She had no idea where she was going. She knew only that she had to lead them away from Roland.

She had coin and she had a strong horse. She wasn't stupid and she could speak some Welsh. Aye, she thought, grimacing. Any robbers who caught her, she could tell them that she loved them. She would ride, she decided in that moment, to the castle called Croyland, to Lord Richard de Avenell. Surely he would assist her.

And what of Roland?

She closed her eyes over that thought. If the Earl of Clare found him, he would kill him. She had to lead him away; far away and quickly. Once they cleared the town, she gave Cantor his head. She knew from the position of the sun that they were riding northeast, toward Croyland, toward the English border.

What would Roland think when he realized she was gone?

8

IT WAS RAINING, a cold fine spray that soaked Daria within minutes. She looked up at the angry gray sky and just shook her head at the endless misery of it.

She'd been riding for three hours now and hadn't seen a single man or woman in the past two. There were sheep, of course, sheep everywhere, and dark forests of sessile oak, thick twisted trees that looked wet to the touch even when it wasn't raining. The road she'd taken had become a rough path with yew bushes crowding on either side, many times their spiked leaves brushing against Cantor's flanks, making him prance sideways. She tried to keep him calm, his pace steady. His strength was great, his endurance greater.

She saw a flock of geese in a muddy field to her right and two badgers in a hedgerow beside her. No sign of the earl or his men. She prayed they were behind her, but far, far behind her.

The rain came down harder, in thick drenching sheets, and she huddled in wretched acceptance over Cantor's slick neck. She wondered if magically, once she gained England, the rain would cease. She couldn't be far from Chester, no, not very far now. And what of Roland? She shook her head. She couldn't worry about him now; worrying about herself had to be paramount.

Suddenly a hare sprang from a thicket in front of Cantor. The destrier reared back onto his hind legs, whinnying in surprise and anger, and Daria lost her hold and fell on her side into a puddle of water. She felt her bones jar with the impact, and for a moment she merely lay there, not wanting to move.

Cantor snorted over her, his mighty head lowered, mirroring her own misery. She tried to smile at being caught off-guard. But she couldn't find even a remnant of a smile. She scrambled slowly to her feet and leaned against Cantor's heaving side. He nudged at her and she pressed closer to him. She felt the vibrations against the soles of her leather shoes. Horses, and they were coming swiftly toward her. Soon they would come into view. It had to be the earl and his men.

She swung up onto Cantor's back and kicked his sides with the wet toes of her shoes. He bounded forward, only to stumble again. She was thrown sideways but kept on his back by wrapping his mane around her left wrist.

He was lame. She sat on his back, knowing it was over, yet unable to accept it. His head was lowered and he was blowing hard. There was no escape for her now.

She clearly heard the sounds of the horses' hooves now. Nearer and nearer, and there was naught she could do. Save wait. *What if they'd found Roland?*

She felt her mind bending and straining, and cursed herself with words she'd heard from Roland. What was she to do? And then she knew. After all, she hadn't the choice to play the fool; too much depended on her now.

She slid off Cantor's back and turned toward the oncoming horses. Even as she recognized the earl's big black Arab, she held herself ready, not moving, aware only that something deep inside her was flinching away from him, from who he was, and what he wanted from her.

I can't bear it if he touches me. I can't bear it. I'll

shriek and kick and die if he touches me . . . if he touches me.

She raised her head and felt the cold shards of rain strike her face. Sharp and stinging and cold, and she welcomed it.

The Earl of Clare raised his gauntleted hand. He stared at the rain-soaked boy who stood beside Roland's huge destrier. His hand clamped over his sword. Where was that damned bastard? In hiding amongst the yew bushes? Leaving Daria, dressed foolishly like a lad, to fend for herself?

He waved his men to a halt. He saw Daria give a start as she recognized him. He watched with growing bewilderment as her expression changed from fear to joy and relief. She was running toward him, not away.

He felt uncertainty as he dismounted from his destrier. He stood still and stiff, watching her race toward him. She was speaking, yelling to him, as she ran. Then she threw herself against him, her arms going around his back.

His hands fisted, yet he made no move against her. He was mired in confusion. She was babbling now, something about how he'd saved her! Saved her!

The earl clasped her upper arms in his hands and pushed her away from him. He shook her.

"What do you here?"

Those weren't the words he'd intended to speak. He'd wanted to strike her, fling her to the muddy road, and strike her again for her perfidy. But he did nothing, merely stood there, saying again, "What do you here?"

She was stuttering, with cold, with fear, with relief . . . He didn't know; he didn't move, just listened as the words poured from her mouth.

"I escaped him, I stole his horse, but the wretched animal is lame and I thought you were he and you would catch me again and I was so frightened . . . so frightened."

The Earl of Clare felt the eyes of his tired men go from him to the shivering girl in front of him. Surely they were listening, but he could tell nothing of their opinions from their weary faces.

He realized suddenly that he didn't care what any of them thought.

"You say you escaped from Roland?"

"Roland? Is that the cur's name?" She shivered and flung herself against his chest again, pressing her cheek against the wet dank wool of his overtunic. "He is no priest, my lord. Please, don't let him catch me again! He told me his name was Charles, but I knew it wasn't."

"You struck me! You, Daria, not that whoreson."

She raised her face and gave him a look that was unholy in its innocence. And, curse her, her voice was high and wavering, like a frightened girl's. "You were trying to ravish me and I wasn't your wife. What was I to do? I was taught to hold my virtue dear until I was wedded. I had no choice but to protect myself or I would have been cursed by God. Then that man— Roland—he came in and forced me to go with him. He's held me close to him, but finally he got drunk in Wrexham and I escaped him and took his horse."

"I only wanted you a bit before the priest married us!"

Her look was austere and severe. There was no more frightened girl in her aspect now. "A female has only her virtue to attest to her character," she said, speaking low, her voice sure and calm and guileless. "I had to fight you until I could fight no more. I would have been cursed by God had I simply given over to you. Surely you understand that, my lord, you must. A man of honor can't ravish an innocent maid, else he will lose all hope for forgiveness from the maid and from God. 'Tis what I was taught; 'tis what I believe. I couldn't allow you to shame me, and thus I did what I had to save myself."

The earl felt the impotent drag of uncertainty. He hated this not knowing, this no longer being confident and convinced of his actions. He'd raged and cursed and pushed his men until they were all so weary they could scarcely sit their horses. And here she was, blaming him! The bedraggled slip of a female was blaming him!

"Where is Roland?"

"I don't know. Somewhere in Wrexham, at least he was early this morning. He was in a sodden, drunken sleep when I escaped him, but he must know by now that I stole his horse. I found out what he intended to do with me. My uncle hired him, you know, offered him a great deal of coin to bring me back. Then my uncle would have me wedded to Ralph of Colchester." She shrugged. "I pray he won't try to find me, but I'm afraid, my lord, afraid that he will come after me again." She looked up at him, pathetic hope in her eyes. "Do you believe he will give up? Perhaps go back to England?"

"Mayhap," the earl said, but he was thinking: But not without his destrier. He looked up at the rain-bloated clouds, felt the endless trickles of rain snake down his back. He cursed. "Clyde," he shouted to one of his men. "We are close to the cave we came upon yesterday. We will spend the night there or at least shelter ourselves until this cursed rain stops."

The men moved quickly from the pitted muddy path. The earl turned back to the shivering girl still standing in front of him. "You're wet." He pulled a dry tunic from a saddlebag and wrapped it around her. "Keep this close about you. I don't wish you to die of a fever."

"His destrier is lame."

"One of my men will lead him." The earl wasn't about to abandon that horse.

The cave Clyde led them to was high-ceilinged and deep enough for the horses to be hobbled at the rear. Daria was settled near the fire, and slowly, teeth chattering every moment, she felt herself dry. She prayed that she'd fooled the earl. She prayed even more intensely that Roland was mending and that he would simply forget her and leave Wales and be safe. He still had enough coin to buy another horse, not one like Cantor, but still, he could buy his way to safety.

She realized that she would probably never see him again. So much for her knowledge of him. All her wondrous feelings, they'd been false, a lie, a dream woven of unreal cloth. She lowered her head to her hands and felt sobs ripping through her. She had no hold on him, none at all, even a hold of honor, for he didn't know that he'd taken hers.

What she'd said to the Earl of Clare wasn't true. Roland would leave Wales and he'd forget her and he'd forget about the money he would have had from her uncle. He wasn't stupid; he would know that the earl had taken her again. The Earl of Clare would bed her and discover she wasn't a virgin and kill her. For then he would know that Roland had bedded her. She couldn't begin to imagine his fury, for he would believe himself cheated and betrayed, though it had been he who had stolen her in the first place.

No, he'd decided that God had blessed him and approved what he'd planned for her. When the earl and God made a bargain, it was madness to try to break it.

She tried to choke back the sobs, but they broke through. She felt a man's large hand on her shoulder, but she couldn't stop her wailing.

"Hush," the man said, and she recognized Mac-

Leod's voice, the earl's master-at-arms. "Ye'll make yerself ill. With this gut-soaking rain, 'tis not difficult."

"I'm so afraid."

"Aye, ye've reason to be, but the earl seems bestruck wit' the sight of ye again. He'll not kill ye, at least not yet. Find ye cheer, lass—we're out of that filthy rain, and that's something to shout to the heavens about, eh?"

"Will he go back to Wrexham to find that man?"

"How do ye know we were in Wrexham?"

Oh God, I forgot, and my stupidity will finish me off. "I don't know, I just guessed you'd come from there. Where did you come from if not from Wrexham?"

MacLeod stared at her pale face, the red eyes, the damp masses of hair streaming down either side of her thin face. Such a pathetic little scrap. It seemed to him that the earl should view her as a daughter, not as a possible wife. He couldn't imagine taking the little wench to bed. She was too wretched, too woebegone, and in the baggy boy's clothes, she looked scarce a decent meal for a hardy man like the Earl of Clare.

"We came from Wrexham," he said, looking away from her into the fire. "We've ridden hard to find ye and that whoreson that took ye from Tyberton."

"Oh," she said, and wrapped her arms around her legs and eased closer to the fire.

"Where is the earl?"

MacLeod shrugged. "Speaking to the men. Here, eat yer dinner. We bought the food at the market in Wrexham. 'Tis right that you eat afore ye lose yer boy's breeches."

MacLeod meant nothing by his words, but Daria saw the earl over her, pinning her down with his weight, hurting her, and she paled.

"Ye're thin, lass," he explained patiently. "Ye must eat something afore yer breeches fall to yer knees."

Daria smiled at him and chewed on the bread he handed her. "Thank you. *Diolch.*"

"So you learned some of this heathen tongue," the earl said as he eased down beside her. "I don't wish to hear it again." He picked up a thick slice of black bread and took a healthy bite. She watched him chew. "All right," she said. He didn't respond. He was staring at her and she knew that he was wondering about her, wondering if he should believe her. Finally, after he'd taken a goodly drink of ale, he said, "This man, Roland. I doubt he'll be witless enough to come after you again, Daria. However, he will come after his destrier. This time he won't find things so much to his liking. I will be ready for him."

"But how could he know that I found you? How could—?"

"The man is one of Satan's tools. Also, he isn't a fool. Who else would take you? He must guess that I would come after you. He'll know that I have you again. He'll know that I'm too strong for him, but still he will come. He'll want his destrier and thus he will come to Tyberton. And I will kill the whoreson there on my own lands, with God's blessing."

His horse but not me. The earl was certain she had not near the value of Cantor in Roland's eyes. Probably in his eyes as well. She wanted to laugh. If she was worth so much less than a horse, why couldn't she simply offer to give the earl Cantor, and be allowed to leave in peace?

She didn't know what to say, so she kept silent. The earl nodded, as if pleased. "You will take off your wet clothes. I don't wish you to become ill."

She turned to face him. Words stuck in her throat. She was frightened and just as angry that this man had such power over her, but she also knew that he wanted her docile and meek. She cleared her throat. She would gain her ends through subservient guile. "I beg you not to ravish me."

"It matters not. I will take you if I wish to."

"Please, my lord." She thought frantically, schemes tumbling wildly in her brain, for only a show of complete compliance seemed to touch him. "It will be as you wish, my lord. But it is . . . I have begun my monthly flow."

Her face was red with fear, not humiliation, but the Earl of Clare chose to believe that she was overcome with a maiden's embarrassment.

It pleased him, this sweet reticence, this guileless deference to him and his wishes. And her gentle confession, telling him of her woman's functions, the final proof of her purpose, gratified him. He felt all-powerful. He raised a hand and lightly patted her cheek. It required all her control not to flinch away from him. "You are still a virgin? That man didn't ravish you, did he?"

She shook her head and kept her gaze steady. He was searching out the lie, but she wouldn't let him see it in her eyes.

"Then I will wed you once we return to Tyberton. I won't distress you again, Daria, with my man's needs. Perhaps you were right to fight me so completely. Perhaps God willed your escape from me so that I would know his thoughts in this matter. Perhaps it is God's will that you not give yourself to me until you are my wife. I make my vow before God. You will remain a virgin until our wedding night. Then I will take you and you will be willing and sweet."

She thought she'd die with the relief of it. He saw it and frowned. "It isn't proper that you shouldn't want me in your bed. Accustom yourself, Daria, for I shall take you as surely as I will kill this Roland, and you will bear me a son before the coming winter wanes."

Pleased with the conclusion he'd wrought with his

utterance, the earl turned and grunted something to
MacLeod. Soon Daria was holding dry clothes and a
blanket. The earl waved her to a darkened corner of
the cave. As she changed into the dry clothing, she
prayed that this time he would keep his word, that she
would be safe from him. She prayed she had God on
her side this time and that God would speak loudly to
the earl.

It rained for a day and a half, sheets of wet cold
rain. Daria wished she could simply succumb to Roland's complaint and die. The earl carried her in front
of him, just as Roland had done. One of his men led
Cantor. The horse no longer limped. The rain stopped
for half a day, then began again, a cold muzzling
drizzle. Upon their return to Tyberton, she almost felt
relief. The rain stopped and the sun shone down,
drying them. It was uncanny.

The day after their return, it was hot. Daria blessed
the sweat that stood out on her brow. It felt wonderful.

And she kept her vigil for Roland.

He was well, he had to be. He was stubborn, obdu-
rate, and he didn't give up. Aye, he would come to
Tyberton—for his horse. But perhaps he could be
convinced to take her with him again.

When she learned there was still no priest at
Tyberton, she wanted to cry to the heavens in joy. She
was safe from the earl until he had one fetched to
marry them, safe, that is, if he would keep to his
word.

Aye, safe. But for how long? Daria turned with a
sigh from the narrow window as her maid, Ena, said,
"Aye, he were in a fury, he were. Cursing and bellowing like the divil hisself, he was, and his men were
sniggering behind their hands, laughing at how ye,
naught but a bit of a female, had done him in." And
Ena cackled as loudly as Romila. "Aye, they laughed

at how he let his lust overcome his piety. But he left quick after ye. He tortured that farmer who'd held the pretty priest's horse for him. Then I heard the earl had a knife stuck atween the farmer's ribs, once he knew what was what. Aye, they left him in the dungeon to rot."

The man who'd wanted only a place of four cows— *lle pum buwch.*

Daria swallowed the bile that had risen in her throat. There was a knock on the door and then it opened, admitting one of the serving women.

It was her dinner on a covered tray. She was indeed to be kept a prisoner. The woman said nothing, merely stared hard at her for a moment, then dipped a curtsy.

Daria waved Ena toward the food. "I'm not hungry," she said, and turned away toward the window again.

The following morning the earl and a dozen of his men left to seek out a band of outlaws that had attacked the small English village of Newchurch, struck whilst the Earl of Clare had been traveling through Wales to find her. She was free, for a while at least. He'd also given orders that she was to be kept locked in her chamber. The earl had patted her cheek before he'd mounted his powerful destrier, but she'd seen the hunger in his eyes and flinched away from it. "Soon," he'd said, "soon now, and I'll have a priest here," and left.

It was midsummer, the ground baked dry from the sun, the sky clear of clouds, a startling bright blue.

And there was a priest now, the earl had told her the previous evening, a priest he'd found in Bristol after he'd searched long and hard, and he would arrive at Tyberton within a sennight. And he would marry her and then he would rape her and then kill her.

She wrapped her arms around her stomach. At least

she hadn't been treated like a prisoner for the past week. The earl had returned flushed with victory over the outlaws. He'd hanged them, all those Welshmen who had still been breathing, that is.

It appeared the earl had given up his conviction that Roland would come for Cantor. She overheard him speaking of Roland to MacLeod and his voice was filled with contempt. "Aye, the pretty whoreson has judged even his destrier to be beyond his abilities to retrieve. He knows I'd kill him slowly and he knows I'd catch him. Back to England he's gone—Daria was right about that."

MacLeod had simply said, "But still . . ."

She knew the earl didn't completely trust her, but there was nothing more she could do to convince him. Indeed she wondered if she should even care. She'd begun to believe herself that Roland had returned to England. And if he hadn't, was he then dead? Was he near to Tyberton even now? No, probably not. Still, she remained meek and soft-spoken in the earl's presence, silent and cold when she was alone. She couldn't be certain that her once-trusted companion, Ena, wouldn't now betray her to the earl.

A single tear coursed swiftly down her cheek. She tasted the salt on her lips but didn't wipe her face. She didn't have the energy. She realized she was thirsty, but there was no water in the small carafe near her narrow bed. Slowly she made her way from her small chamber down the steep winding stone steps into the great hall. There were men lounging about playing draughts or trading jests. Women worked, scrubbing the trestle tables, scattering fresh rushes. No one paid her any heed. She didn't see the earl. She walked outside into the inner bailey.

It was the middle of the day, the time when, if possible, most of the people escaped to find some shade from the overpowering sun.

She walked to the cistern, standing there for a very long time, feeling the hot sun sink through her cold flesh, but there was no warmth deep inside her, only empty cold.

"What do you here?"

She heard the earl's distrust and forced a smile to her lips as she turned to face him. "I wanted a cup of fresh water from the well. It is hot and dry today."

He appeared to accept her words, and strode to the well. He fetched her a cup of water, watching her sip at it.

He said then, his voice filled with frustration and anger, "I have just gotten word that the king rides to Tyberton. He has been at Chepstow, thundering at the Earl of Hereford, I doubt not, and now he intends to come to me."

Daria didn't understand his mood. "But 'tis the king," she exclaimed. "That is an honor and a privilege to have him visit you, a sign of royal pleasure."

He snorted. "There is slight pleasure on either side. Longshanks holds little power here, and it irks him, for he wishes to grind all under his royal heel. He comes to pry and to spy and to threaten. Were I strong enough, would all the Marcher Barons but stand together, we'd send him back to that Sodom city he dwells in, that cesspit London. Let him breed with his whore, and keep away from here. We keep peace and hold the barbarians at bay.

"Aye, the king comes to seek out my strength. I know he would sell his miserable soul to the devil himself if he could wrest power from me, from all of us who keep England safe from the Welsh savages. He has no power here, ha!—no power west of the River Wye—and it isn't just for him to come!"

Whilst he was haranguing, it occurred to Daria that perhaps, just perhaps, the king could help her. Could she find him alone and plead with him for her release?

Would he possibly believe her if she managed to see him? If he didn't aid her, would the earl then kill her? And what matter if he did? He would anyway, once he realized she wasn't a virgin.

She discovered that she was wringing her hands. What was she to do? "Drink your water," the earl said as he handed her another wooden cup.

The King of England sat back in his royal chair and looked at his dedicated secretary, Robert Burnell. The tent protected them from the hot noonday sun, and the king was basking in a good mood. He'd intimidated Hereford, the damned disloyal lout, and now he would arrive at Tyberton and make certain the Earl of Clare knew which way to step around his king. Burnell excused himself to seek some relief outside for a few minutes. His fingers were cramped from writing out the royal exhortations and he needed to stretch his muscles as well. When he returned, there was a strange look on his face, but his king didn't notice. He cleared his throat.

"Sire, there is a maimed old beggar outside who requests to speak with you. He claims to have information of vital importance." The king slewed about in his chair and pinned his secretary with a look that was so astonished that Burnell cleared his throat yet again. "Er, he appears harmless, sire."

Just as suddenly, Edward laughed. He'd just finished a fine meal and felt expansive from the two goblets of sweet wine he'd drunk. He watched Burnell fidget. Odd for a man of few nerves to fidget. "A maimed beggar, you say, Robbie? An old maimed beggar who begs to plead for a royal coin as opposed to a simple soldier's coin? A beggar who offers to share his begging with you if he gains coin from me? Speak you, Robbie, you seem deaf and mute and bereft of your wits as well."

The king was toying with him, Burnell thought, swept with relief for the absence of the royal temper. Edward was smiling, that wolfish charming smile of his that made everyone in his service grovel willingly. He stepped closer. " 'Tis not just a simple beggar, sire."

"I assumed this beggar you sponsor was fit for the king's time and presence. He is no common beggar, in short, but a beggar of royal persuasions, a beggar fit for . . ." Edward broke off, unable to find more glowing wit. "Bring me the fellow, Robbie! And I pray you have guessed aright, for if you haven't, I will cover you with the contents of your own ink pot."

Burnell had no intention of coming back into the king's presence. He left the royal tent. A miserable ancient relic shuffled in. By all the saints, the king thought, the old wretch stank more than a wet sheep and he looked ready to fall over and die, so appalling and pathetic was he. He gave a soft cackle and essayed a deep bow before the king. He sprang back up with no cracking of aged bones or joints.

"I understand it is a royal coin you wish," the king said, frowning mightily toward the beggar.

The old man cackled. "Nay, generous sire, 'tis a woman to warm my bed I wish, a woman wondrous fair with bounteous bosom and—"

The king stared at the old man, his cleverness momentarily extinguished.

"—aye, and a bounty of buttocks, mayhap. A woman as soft of flesh as a rabbit's belly and deep as a well for my mighty rod."

The king burst into laughter. "Shall I offer you first a woman to bathe you? You smell of slime and muck. Who are you, beggar? Not a common sort of vermin, I warrant, not from your polished impertinent speech. Come, I grow impatient with your antics."

"You are always impatient, sire. Your poor Robbie awaits just without, chewing his fingernails to their knuckles. 'Tis true, even a good tale is wasted on you, as is an excellent performance. I have heard it said that London's most wondrous mummers burst into tears at your inattention. Why—"

"Who are you, you miserable impertinent lout?" the royal personage roared as he rose to his full height. To his consternation, the beggar didn't quiver in fear, nor did he retreat even a frightened step. He gave him a filthy black grin and looked cockier than ever.

Then, just as suddenly, the beggar straightened and pulled off bits and pieces of his face. The king sucked in his breath, words failing him, at the hideous process.

Roland stood before him, tall, lean, proud of bearing, rubbing the back of his hand over his teeth. His teeth shone white and his hand shone black. The king shook his head. "I believe it not, and I know how well you can disguise yourself. My God, Roland, I have missed your impertinent insolent self!"

He embraced him. "By St. Andrew's knees, you must bathe," he said, and quickly stepped back.

"Aye, 'tis sheep dung and a few other disgusting things I found on my way here. I will keep my distance from your hallowed presence. I must ask you a favor, and then I will bathe. Have you time to attend to my plea, sire?"

"Robbie vowed you were a beggar worthy to plead before the royal presence. Still, Roland, if I said I didn't?"

"Why, then I should have to tell you of my adventures in Paris, where the ladies performed solemn rites and ceremonies upon my poor man's body with great enthusiasm and imagination. Ah, sire, these are bold and bawdy tales that will make you lick your royal lips."

"I wish to have both your plea and a full and complete accounting of your adventures."

Roland grinned at his king. "You are the answer to

a poor needy beggar's prayers. I hadn't a notion of what to do, and you, like my chivalrous knight, come to my rescue, at least I hope that you will consider championing me."

"You make no sense, Roland. Sit, man!" he continued in a royal bellow. "Robbie, cease your fearful mutterings and come back in here. I need you to protect me from this rapacious beggar!"

"But my stench, sire—"

"It matters not. Just keep three feet between us and I shall survive your odor."

9

DARIA STOOD AT HER POST at the narrow window that gave onto the inner bailey. She knew such fear she could scarce bear it. The priest had arrived just an hour before, and the earl, impatient to have her sanctified in God's eyes, and in his bed, announced that their wedding ceremony would take place this very evening.

It was difficult to remain submissive, but she tried, asking in her softest voice, "But what of the king's visit, my lord? Don't you expect him to arrive shortly?"

"I pray the Almighty that his royal majesty takes his blessed time. He can arrive on the morrow. I will allow him to do that."

She kept her eyes lowered, and her brain squirreled with one idea after the other, each of them useless. The earl continued after a moment, "I have kept my vow, Daria. Forget not that I could have taken you at any time, but I held to my oath. I proved to you that I was to be trusted. I have shown you mine honor. You will have no more cause now to bend against me."

He had kept his oath; she'd give him that. She prayed for the king to arrive right now. She looked into the distance but saw no sign of anyone, just impenetrable forests and rolling hills.

The earl frowned down at her. "I wish you to gown yourself as befits the bride of the Earl of Clare. Do you understand me, Daria? I wish you to smile and show everyone that you come to me with a willing and submissive heart."

She nodded. He stared at her intently for a moment longer, then grabbed her, hauling her against him. He cupped her chin with his hand and pushed up her face. She closed her eyes, forcing herself not to struggle even when his mouth closed over hers. She felt his tongue, wet and probing, and wanted to gag. He released her and said, "I will wed you even though your dowry hasn't yet come from your loathsome uncle. But no matter his damned perfidy. I intend to petition the king for what should be mine and what will be mine, for once you are wedded to me, once I have taken you, even the king can't deny me your dowry, for I have right on my side." With those words, he actually rubbed his hands together, saying in triumph, "There's naught Damon Le Mark can do, for I will have the king with me. And he will yowl and whine and it will do him no good at all. Aye, at last I have won, and I like the feeling." He turned on his heel and left her. Daria stared after him, wondering at his mind.

She shook her head to clear it of the feel of him. Suddenly, from one instant to the next, she felt a sharpening of something inside her, an awareness, a renewed remembrance of something utterly vital to her, something . . . She looked down into the inner bailey, not really seeing anything or anyone specific, but still the feeling was there, that strange feeling, that knowledge that she'd known before. She wondered if her mind had finally snapped.

Then she saw him. A bent old man, with a head of scraggly thick white hair, shuffling in his rags toward the castle well. He was dragging his lame right leg. Stark joy welled up in her and she willed him to look up, whispering his name over and over as she stared hard at him. He did. She saw naught but a wrinkled old face until he smiled and she saw a mouth filled with rotted black teeth.

It couldn't be Roland, but she knew that it was. She waved frantically to him.

But he turned away from her with not a single sign to her, and continued his slow shuffling gait to the well.

His own mother wouldn't know him, she thought, and smiled. He'd come. He'd come for her . . . or for his destrier, perhaps both if she were lucky and Roland cared for her or cared equally for her uncle's money.

How could she speak to the ragged old beggar? Why had Arthur, the porter, allowed him to come into the castle? What ruse had he in mind this time? Her mind tumbled with questions, but mostly she just wanted to see him closely to ensure that he was completely well again. Ah, Roland, she thought, her step light and vigorous for the first time since the earl had brought her back to Tyberton nearly two months before.

When she reached the well, the old man was gone. Vanished. She stared about her, feeling despair weigh down upon her. Had she imagined him? Daria drew a deep breath and turned on her heel. She looked at her toes raise small clouds of dust. She didn't care if her new gown was as filthy as the ragged old man's clothing. She didn't care about anything except finding him.

Roland stood in the shade of one of the barracks and watched her return slowly to the great hall, her step lagging. She'd recognized him instantly. It was impossible, yet she'd known him, and from a distance. It confused and confounded him, that recognition of hers—he couldn't comprehend or accept it. His heart pounded. She'd known him. For God's sake, how? His survival depended on his disguise, yet he hadn't fooled her for an instant.

He moved toward the cooking outbuilding, wanting to keep her in sight. One of the scullions came around the corner and Roland bent lower and scratched his armpit and mumbled to himself, turning a bit on his lame leg, and showing a wince of pain.

She'd known him. But how? The scullion gave him a look of scorn and pity combined, shrugged, then turned his back to relieve himself.

How was it possible? Would she give him away? Not likely, he thought. She was being forced to wed the Earl of Clare, this according to Otis, one of the stable lads. How Otis knew, Roland didn't question; everyone always knew everything in a keep's confines. He'd listened the entire day, and no one had paid any attention to an old beggar. De Clare had kept her locked in her tower chamber for many weeks whilst he'd gone off on one of his raids. Roland cursed at that. If only he could have returned here more quickly, if only he . . . It was too late now for recriminations. She was to be wedded to Clare this very evening. Roland closed his eyes a moment. The king wasn't due to arrive at Tyberton until the morrow. But tomorrow would be too late for all of them.

Clare would have wedded her, bedded her, and even the king himself wouldn't pull her away from a man whose wife she'd become, a wife whose maidenhead had been breached. And, Roland imagined, Clare had finally figured out that once wedded to Daria, he could get his hands on her huge dowry. He wondered if the earl had already taken her. Of course he had. There was no reason why he would not. There had been no priest here to gainsay him.

Roland cursed. They'd been so very close to escaping him before. If only he hadn't become ill . . . the genesis and the revelation of all their problems. Now she was no longer a maid and it was his fault. The situation called for a change of plan. He was adaptable and quick to revise. It had saved his life before. Now perhaps it would save Daria as well.

* * *

Ena's mind was murky, but she knew she was pleased about this, pleased that her little mistress would shortly be wedding the mighty Earl of Clare. She was too thin, but still she looked beautiful in the pale pink silk gown with its darker pink overtunic. Its long sleeves full at her wrists, its waist belted with a golden chain of fine links. Aye, she looked tasty and worthy of becoming the chatelaine of Tyberton. Aye, Ena was very pleased.

Daria's hair was long and loose, denoting a young girl coming to her marriage a virgin. There was a strange smile on Daria's face when Ena had insisted on this old custom, but she'd said nothing. She would have preferred to braid her hair tightly around her head. What would the earl have thought of that? she wondered.

"Ye're excited," Ena said, seeing the glitter in her young charge's eyes. "Aye, ye're ready to settle down now and forget yer pretty young priest. He left ye, and if it weren't fer the earl, ye'd be dead or worse by now. Nay, tell me no lies. I always guessed ye tried to escape, not the pap the earl spread about, curdling the cream even as he spoke the words. But things are the way they should be. Ye're a little lady and ye don't deserve a poor priest, no matter how pretty he was. Ralph of Colchester isn't here, so ye'll have the earl. Aye, all is well again."

Daria lowered her eyes. The old woman saw a lot even though she was becoming more and more vague. She didn't necessarily see the right things, at least in this instance, but still, she didn't want Ena announcing to the earl that the little mistress was all eager and impatient and . . . The earl might well believe she'd released him from his oath and ravish her before the ceremony. Daria gave a restless gesture as Ena plaited in a final white daisy into her hair.

" 'Tis enough." Where was Roland? She felt the now-familiar fear that it was indeed only his destrier he'd come for. She was no longer important to him. He would no longer risk rescuing her. The coin wasn't enough. He'd realized the earl was right. He would have no chance in any case. But how would the old beggar steal his destrier?

"Yer veil, little mistress!"

Veil! Daria stared at the thick gold circlet with its flowing gauzy veil. It would be hot. On the other hand, it would blur her vision. She wouldn't be able to see the earl clearly; she could imagine and dream that . . .

"Give it to me."

There was a knock on the chamber door. Before Daria could say anything, the door cracked open and two women entered, an older woman Daria didn't recognize and a very young one that she did. They entered furtively and quickly, the older woman closing the door behind her.

"What is this? What is it you wish?" The words were scarce out of Daria's mouth when she felt his presence, and she jerked up, staring at the two.

"Well," the older woman said, her eyes lowered, "I come to tell ye, little mistress, that the earl's a loud lout, telling all he's ready to tumble ye the instant the priest pronounces ye his bride."

"I'm ready," Daria said, excitement filling her. By all the saints, was she ready! "Shall we take Ena with us?"

The older woman shook her head. She looked toward Ena and said, "I need yer help, old witch."

"Who are ye calling an old witch!" Ena shrieked. "Here, now! What do ye want?"

Daria watched Roland put his arm about Ena, pull her close, and then lightly smack his fist into her jaw. Ena crumpled to the floor. "Tie her up quickly, Daria. As you probably know, she's defected to the earl's camp. We can't afford to take any chances."

The other woman was young Tilda, daughter of the castle blacksmith, all of fourteen years old and so beautiful that men stopped whatever they chanced to be doing to stare as she passed. She was a bit larger than Daria, her hair a bit lighter, but with the wedding finery, the veil . . .

"She wishes it," Roland said shortly before Daria could question him. "Quickly, out of those clothes whilst I tie up the old woman."

Within minutes Daria was arranging the veil over Tilda's lovely face. The young girl was shaking with excitement, but Daria was worried. Cora was of peasant stock. What would the earl do to her when he discovered the deception?

"Daria, quickly, put on your boy's clothes. And braid all that damnable hair of yours."

"Ah, Roland, you are such a fussy mother."

He grinned at her. "Didn't I fool you for the veriest instant?"

She shook her head. "Not even when you smiled up at me as a miserable old beggar with rotted black teeth."

And he remembered that first time he saw her, that astonishment in her eyes as she'd stared at him, a priest, that *knowledge*, and he frowned. And she'd fainted, as if seeing him had affected her in some way that he couldn't understand. But his disguises were foolproof. But then again, Daria wasn't a fool. He shook himself, tied up the old woman, and shoved her under the bed. Then he stood guard at the door until Daria emerged and touched his arm. "I'm ready."

He turned and saw that she was smiling up at him, complete trust in her eyes, that and complete . . . There was something different about her, something . . .

"Tilda, leave that veil on until you're commanded by the earl to remove it. Do you understand?"

The girl nodded. She was happy! "Thank you, Tilda."

Daria gave her a quick hug, turned, and took Roland's hand.

"Keep your head down and don't say anything."

"This sounds very familiar, Roland."

"I'm your damned mother, silly twit."

All the castle servants and retainers were outside the keep, for the day was hot and dry and the Earl of Clare had provided kegs of ale and more food than most of the people saw for a year. There was much merriment and shouting and wild jests. She didn't see the earl.

"Aye," Roland said to a soldier who offered him a goblet of ale and asked him what he was about. "Just look ye at the little fiend. Trying to peep at the earl's bride, he was. I'll strip off his hide, the little impertinence!"

And on and on his charade progressed, as Roland, confident as the pope himself, made his way through the throngs of people, initiating conversation with some, and thus making Daria's heart jump into her throat, and insulting the soldiers with friendly motherly taunts.

They made it to the gates. Arthur, the porter, was grinning widely, showing the wide space between his two front teeth. He was holding a mug of ale in his beefy hand and he waved them through without a look, without a question.

Daria pulled on his woman's sleeve. "Your horse! Cantor!"

Roland turned at that and gave her a ferocious frown. "Hush!"

Once they were without the castle walls, Roland took her hand and pulled her into a brisk walk.

"Thank you," she said.

"A mother is supposed to protect her son. Keep your tongue behind your teeth."

"But, Roland, you've left Cantor."

"Not for very long."

"Oh. The earl said you'd surely come for your destrier, but not—"

"But not for you?"

"That's what I thought as well until I saw you yesterday, and then I prayed that perhaps you would also take me."

"You forget, Daria, there is much coin awaiting me at Reymerstone. If I allowed the earl to wed you, I wouldn't gain a penny."

She felt a stab of pain so intense it nearly choked her. "I am still only a valuable bundle to you, to be delivered and then forgotten."

"You also left me to rot in the charge of that vicious leech and that officious woman Romila. At least you didn't steal all my coin or I would have had to pay Romila with my poor man's body. Old enough to be my mother, and she wanted me to bed her! I had to beg her for my clothes."

"I don't believe you! Romila told me how to deal with you and . . . I tried to save you! And I did!"

"You will weave your tales later, once we are far from Tyberton. Cease your chatter now and walk. I've a horse in that copse."

"Where are we going?"

"Why, to see the King and Queen of England, of course."

Edward and Eleanor stared at the older woman who was chewing on a stick, her sagging breasts thrust forward in her slovenly gown, her dirty hand firmly around the young boy's arm.

"Well, here he is, sire! All full of himself and crowing like a peacock once I told him the king wanted to see him."

Edward just shook his head and started to laugh. The queen looked at him oddly and said, "I don't understand, my lord, is this—?"

"Aye, 'tis our Roland, an old shrew, with her son."

"Your highness," Roland said in his deep voice, and bowed to the queen. "And this is Daria, daughter of James of Fortescue, and niece of Damon Le Mark, Earl of Reymerstone. This is my second rescue of the lady and, I profoundly pray, the final one. The Earl of Clare desires her mightily."

Daria was overwhelmed. She started to speak but discovered that she had only a stutter. She gave an awkward curtsy in her boy's clothes.

"Your father was a fine man, Daria," the king said warmly. "We miss him sorely. As for you, I salute your disguise, Roland. Most resourceful. I shouldn't want you in my bed, however."

"I don't know," Eleanor said thoughtfully. " 'Tis a fine woman she appears to me, such experience of men she shows in her eyes, my lord husband. Save for that dark stubble on her jaws, I vow I'd confide in her on the instant."

Roland grinned at the queen, whose sweetness of expression rivaled her beauty and whose belly, he saw, was swelled yet again with another babe. "I thank you both for taking us in. I should like to resume my manhood and, your highness, if young Daria here could resume her gowns and ribbons?"

"Certainly," the queen said, and lightly clapped her hands together. "Come, child."

It was later in the afternoon when Daria saw Roland again. He was in men's clothes again and looked so beautiful she wanted to run to him and fling him to the ground. She wanted to kiss him and stroke him and tell him how much she loved him. He was speaking, however, to several of the king's soldiers, and she contented herself for the moment just looking at him. When one of the soldiers took himself off, she approached him and lightly touched her fingertip to his sleeve. He turned to look down at her and froze. Her look was intimate; there was no other way to describe it. And tender and . . . loving.

He took a backward step.

"Are you all right?"

"Aye," she said happily. "Do you think the earl has wedded Tilda yet? You don't think he'll harm her, do you?"

Roland shook his head. "I do think he'll bed her, though, and make her his mistress. She's a beautiful girl."

"You aren't objective; you are, after all, her mother. Are you well now, Roland? I was so worried about you and I didn't know what to do when the stableman told me of the men asking about Cantor."

"So that's what happened," he said. "I didn't know, couldn't understand, why you'd left so suddenly and with no word to anyone. I tried to search for you but managed only to get down the stairs and collapse again."

Her fingers tightened on his arm, caressing him now, and he frowned. "Daria, what is the matter with you?"

She realized what she was doing and in the same instant realized that he had no idea why she was doing it. She looked at him hungrily, then quickly released his arm and turned away from him. "Naught is wrong. What will happen now? How do you know the king and queen? They seem to be your friends. I heard someone say that we were traveling to Tyberton tomorrow. How can that be true? The earl will—"

He gently touched his fingertips to her mouth. "Trust me," he said. "All will be well and I will have my destrier back. And you will soon be on your way back to Reymerstone."

Her expression became stony, but he ignored it, turning away from her.

That evening, Queen Eleanor, having correctly judged

Daria's feelings by simply asking her how she felt about Roland de Tournay, imputed similar feelings to Roland, for, after all, the girl was wealthy, quite lovely, and . . . The queen smiled, saying to Roland as she sipped at her sweet Aquitaine wine, "Do you wish to be wedded before you arrive at Tyberton, just to ensure that the earl won't scream down our royal ears?"

Roland dropped the braised rib to his trencher. He looked first to Daria, saw that she was staring open-mouthed at the queen, and said quickly, "Your highness, I plan to return Daria to her uncle. It was a mission I accepted. I vowed I would return her to him a maid and otherwise unharmed. There is no question of marriage between us. I fear you have misunderstood the situation."

Eleanor cocked her head to one side in question as she turned to the king. Edward looked grave. " 'Tis you I don't understand, Roland. You are my friend and you are a man of honor. 'Tis true you accepted the mission to rescue Daria, but all of that has changed now. *You* changed it when you . . . well, never mind that now. You must realize that you can no longer return Daria to anyone, not now. You have a responsibility toward her. She is a lady, Roland, *your* lady."

Roland felt mired in confusion. He opened his mouth, but a servant appeared to fill the royal flagons with more sweet wine. Roland curbed his questions until the young man bowed his way out of the royal tent.

"I don't know what is happening here," Roland said, staring directly at Daria now. "She is my responsibility. I readily acknowledge it and accept that she will continue to be so until I return her to her uncle."

Daria was in her turn staring from the king to the queen and back again. They wanted Roland to wed her? All because she had confided in the queen that she loved him? Love had naught to do with anything.

Even she knew that, not when it involved a dowry the size of hers.

But they fully expected Roland to wed her. Why?

She cleared her throat, saying before the king, whose complexion had reddened, could interrupt, "Nay, your highness, 'tis not for me to beg Roland to become my husband. 'Tis true I am passing fond of him, but that has naught to do with anything. Pray do not make him feel sorry because I told you of my feelings for him. He's not responsible for my feelings. He will do as he pleases; as for me, I will try to dissuade him from returning me to my uncle. Perchance I shall have to smash his head and escape him." As an attempt at wit, it failed utterly.

"But, my dear child," the queen began, only to stop when the king said coldly, "Roland, you cannot be lost to all honor, surely you must realize—" He paused as the queen lightly closed her fingers over his. She whispered something to him. His eyes narrowed, then sparkled.

Eleanor looked at Daria. She said in a very gentle voice, "Did you not tell him, my dear?"

Roland jumped to his feet. "This goes beyond all bounds! Tell me what, by all the saints?"

"Quiet, Roland," the king said.

Daria wanted to jump up and yell as loudly as Roland. What was happening here? "I don't understand, your highness. If you mean have I told him that I care for him, nay, I haven't. He wouldn't want to hear such words from me."

"Damnation, Daria! What are you mumbling about? What do you mean, I wouldn't care?"

The king leaned over and buffeted Roland's shoulder. "You're a virile warrior, as potent in bed as you are on the battlefield, Roland, and now you'll have yourself a wife. Don't struggle further against your fate. 'Tis about time, I think. The queen and I will act as godparents, and you—"

"Virile? What is this, what are you—?" His voice fell off abruptly and he stared at Daria. Her face was washed of color now, her eyes wide, her pupils dilated, her hands tight fists in her lap. "Tell me," he said. "Tell me now or I will haul you outside and beat you senseless."

"Roland!"

"She will tell me what is happening here!" But he knew, indeed he knew what she would say, and it sickened him to his very soul.

"She is with child," the queen said.

Roland couldn't comprehend her words even though he knew they were the words she would speak. With child! "By all the saints, *whose* child?"

Daria only shook her head, but the queen knew no reticence. Her voice was sharp. "Yours, naturally, Roland!"

"Mine? But that isn't possible. I never—" Again he stopped. All became clear to him. The earl had had two months to ravish her, and doubtless he had whenever he'd wished to. God, the girl was pregnant with the Earl of Clare's babe! He felt a wrenching pain in his gut. He felt a spurt of hatred so strong for the man he nearly choked on it. And Daria hadn't told him, hadn't even hinted at it, damn her! He wanted to strike her; he wanted to yell and strike himself. Instead, he drew a deep breath and said to the king, "If you would forgive us for a moment, sire, I would like to speak to Daria in private. As you and the queen have guessed, I hadn't realized any of this. She hadn't told me a thing. Daria, come outside."

She obeyed him instantly, her head down, pale as death, the queen thought, watching the couple leave the tent, as if she were going to her execution.

The king stared after the man he'd known for six years, the man who'd worked for him tirelessly in the Holy Land, risking his life with every breath he took, with every word he spoke in Arabic, the man he trusted with his life.

He turned to his wife. "There is some sort of problem here, Eleanor?"

The queen looked as confused as her spouse. "I didn't mention her pregnancy to her, Edward; the child isn't a wife, after all, and I had no wish to embarrass her. I assumed she knew she was with child, assumed that Roland was her lover. She conceived the child about two months ago, I'd say. It's very odd. She didn't know she was with child. Evidently she'd known no illness, no vomiting."

"Not so very odd," the king said. He leaned over and kissed his wife. He laid his hand on her swelled belly. "Do you not remember our first babe, Eleanor? 'Twas one of your women who suggested to you that you might be with child. You didn't know, hadn't guessed."

"You're right, dear lord. By the saints, whatever will we do? I had no idea both of them were ignorant of the fact."

"They will wed, as is fitting. They are both of the proper rank, they are both young and of good health, and you said the girl cares for him."

"She loves him."

The king waved that consideration away. "Roland will come about. He has no choice and he isn't a cruel man or an unjust one. She is a lady and he will wed her. She is also an heiress, and she will bring him sufficient dowry to buy the land and keep he wishes in Cornwall. A good solution. I've worried about him and his future. In the near future I might even raise him to the rank of his sour-natured brother, the Earl of Blackheath."

The queen was chewing over the more romantic side of the situation. "The girl loves him more than . . . why, I cannot think of a good comparison, my lord, save to say that she loves Roland de Tournay as much as I do you, husband."

"Ah, well, that is sufficient, I should think," the king said, and sat back in his chair with satisfaction.

Outside the tent, Roland saw the several dozen soldiers posted around the royal tent and knew that he must contain his ire. He jerked her along with him, feeling her resistance. At the perimeter of the royal encampment, he paused and turned to her. Words and curses and confusion all whirled about in his mind, but he contented himself with, "Speak, Daria."

"I don't understand how the queen . . . Perhaps she is mistaken, because I haven't felt ill or . . . It must be very complicated—"

"Being with child is the simplest thing in the world! All that's required is that a man plow a woman, nothing more, not a single blessed thing!"

"I didn't know, I tell you! I suppose the queen recognized signs in me that I hadn't noticed. I haven't been very aware of things, Roland. A prisoner isn't, you know."

His hold tightened on her arm and she winced but made no sound. He shook her. "All right, you didn't know you carried a babe. Now you do know. It's true, isn't it? Have you had no monthly flow? Have your breasts swelled?"

She shook her head. He wouldn't stop; she knew him well enough to realize he would keep questioning her, keep pounding at her, until she told him the truth. Ah, the truth. That was the only thing he wouldn't believe. He had no memory of that night. What was she to do?

"Very well. Now, you will not lie to me. It will do neither of us any good. The earl had you, didn't he, took you before I got back to rescue you? Did he rape you when he first caught up with you? I thought that he would take you, for there was no priest to try to hold him back from going to your bed. It is his babe you carry. Why didn't you tell me he'd ravished you? Why? You know I still would have rescued you if you'd wished it."

"The earl didn't force me," she said, her voice low and dull.

He cursed and stomped away from her. He yelled at her over his shoulder, "Damn you, Daria! A female is born with lies writhing in her mouth, just waiting for a gullible male to come within her orbit. More fool I! By all the saints, I will take you back to the Earl of Clare this very night! You said he didn't force you. Therefore you were willing. No wonder you left me in Wrexham. You couldn't before, but then I was too ill to know what you were about." He smote his forehead with his palm. "Will I never cease being a fool?"

"Evidently not."

He turned on her then, fury radiating from him. "There was no need for you to escape with me this second time, at least none that I can think of. He must have plowed your belly until you were well used to it. Unless you wanted me to punish him? I cannot fathom your mind, curse you! Tell me why you escaped with me. Why?"

10

"THE EARL didn't ravish me, nor did I give myself to him willingly. He made a vow that he wouldn't touch me until we were wedded, and he kept it. I believe he was quite proud of himself that he didn't break his oath. 'Tis not his child that grows in me."

Roland could but stare at her. He'd believed her guileless, candid, faultless as a child. But she wasn't a child. She was a woman and she was with child. Whose could it be? He'd been with her constantly, save when he'd been ill in Wrexham. If the earl had forced her, why didn't she admit it? Did she think he would blame her for that whoreson's violence? When he'd come to rescue her that second time, he'd fought the knowledge that the earl had raped her, for it had made no sense to him that he wouldn't have. But she was claiming that he hadn't taken her. He shook his head.

"Then who plowed your belly?"

She looked at him straightly. The time for deception was long over, as was the time for protecting him from the knowledge of what he'd done. He wanted the truth; very well, then, he would have it. "You did."

She winced as he laughed, even though she wasn't surprised at his reaction. He marveled aloud, "Such a lie as that can never work, Daria. A man knows when he takes a woman. It isn't something that passes unheeded like a belch. When is this babe of yours to arrive?"

"Since I know the precise day the babe was conceived, I can figure it out quickly enough."

158

"And just when was this precise day?"

"In Wrexham, over two months ago."

He'd been so very ill there; he hadn't protected her. "Were you ravished there? You went out alone and a man attacked you? You can admit it to me, Daria. I won't blame you, I swear it. Come, tell me. Were you ravished there?"

"No. You didn't ravish me."

"You tempt me to beat you, Daria. I order you to cease spinning your tales."

"When you were sick, you became delirious and you were dreaming of a woman—no, women—whom you'd bedded in the Holy Land. I . . . well, I cared for you and I decided that I wanted you to be the man who would make me a woman."

He could only stare at her. "You're telling me that I took you—a virgin—and have no memory of it?"

"You believed I was Lila."

He drew back, stunned to his toes. "Lila," he repeated quietly. "She would have been naught more than a fevered dream. I couldn't have made it into something remotely real; I couldn't have taken you in her place, not unknowingly. It's absurd. I couldn't ever mistake you for her in any circumstance. You aren't a thing like her."

"No," she said sadly, turning from him, "you appeared to care for her mightily. And there was Cena too."

"Cena," he repeated, feeling like a parrot. Roland shook his head. This was lunacy, all of it, her lunacy, and she was trying to draw him into it. "Listen to me, Daria, and listen well. I don't remember any of this, and I'm not lying. I can't believe that a lady—a virgin— would allow me to breach her maidenhead without marriage . . . nay, you claim you even assisted me to take you?

"And just how many times did I—a man fevered

and ill and tossing about out of his skull and evidently
as randy as a goat—just how many times did I take
you, Daria?"

"Just once."

"Ah, I see. And as a result of plowing your virgin's
little belly, you are now with child."

"Yes." Daria was beginning to wonder if she could
still believe herself. He'd demolished her quite thoroughly.

"And you expect me to believe this? Truly? Why
are you doing this to me? What have I ever done to
you to deserve such treatment? Why are you lying to
me? Ah, I doubt not I was so fevered that I dreamed
myself in other places with other people and that I
may have spoken of people in my past, Lila and Cena
included."

She looked at him. She was weary. She supposed it
was the babe she carried that was pulling on her. She
had nothing more to say, no proof to give him, no
other arguments to present. He thought she was going
to speak again, and slashed his hand through the air.

"No, Daria, no more. I'm tired of your lies. And
now you've managed to seduce the king and queen
with your charming innocence, though you and I both
know it is all false. God, how could I be such a fool?
Again and again it would appear, only this time you
make me appear the villain, a liar without conscience."

"I'm only telling you the truth." He looked at her as
if he hated her, and Daria felt such pain that she
couldn't bear it. She'd known he wouldn't believe her,
but still the reality of his feelings made her raw. She
turned on her heel and broke into a run. She cared not
where she ran, only that she get away from this man
who hated her and despised her for a liar.

"Damn you, I'm not through!"

But Daria didn't slow even at his furious shout. She
felt a stitch in her side but didn't stop. When his

fingers closed about her arm, she cried out and turned on him, her fists pounding his chest. "Let me go! What care you where I go? Or what I do?"

"I don't," he said, his voice calm now. "Well, that's not precisely true. I do care. However, I told you once, I believe, that your uncle didn't want you back if you were no longer a virgin. And it's very easy to determine that, as you must remember."

She closed her eyes over the memory of the earl thrusting his finger inside her, pressing against her maidenhead. She shivered with the memory of it, the humiliation of it made more awful because Roland had been there, watching.

"I fancy your uncle would kill you were you to return to him now, for he would want your inheritance if he couldn't have the land from Ralph of Colchester. You're naught but an encumbrance to him now, Daria, nothing more. But you know that, don't you? Thus the reason for all your tales? You're simply trying to save yourself."

"And what am I to you?" She regretted the words the moment they were out of her mouth. Her face blanched.

He gave her a brutal look. "A mission to be accomplished, a possession to be returned to its rightful owner. Once valuable chattel, Daria, but now you are worthless."

"Stop it!" She slapped her hands against her ears to shut out his cruel words.

He clasped her wrists, pulling them away. "Tell me the truth, Daria." He shook her. "I'll help you, I swear it, but you must tell me the truth."

"I did tell you the truth! You were fevered. At first you thought I was a woman named Joan. You yelled at me and accused me of betraying you. I tried to reason with you, but it was no use. Then you spoke that strange language and you called me Lila and you wanted her to cover you, to allow you to come into her body. I didn't know what you meant, but you showed me. You wanted to suckle her breasts and you scolded me for still wearing clothes when you wanted me naked."

"And so," he said, his eyes hard and disbelieving, his voice filled with sarcasm, "you hurried to rip off your clothes, ready to do whatever I asked of you. There was a Joan—'tis likely I would speak of the bitch if I was out of my head. But nothing else, Daria. An innocent young girl wouldn't allow a man to command her to sacrifice her maidenhead."

"And you spoke of Cena but said you were too fatigued for her. She would have to wait."

He tensed, resisting. But no, he could have spoken of both women. A fevered man could speak of any ghost or memory. A fevered man wasn't, however, strong enough to force a virgin to give over to him.

"I have told you the truth, Roland. That I did it was perhaps foolish, but I lo . . . I wanted you to be the first, I wanted to know you"—*to have your hands on me, feel you kissing me, holding me . . . I wanted the memory*—"if I was to be forced to wed with Ralph of Colchester, I wanted just the one time for myself, for there would be nothing more that I could have." There, now he had the truth, all of it. She watched the anger pale his eyes and tighten his expression.

He shook his head. It was foolishness and lies, all of it. "No. I cannot accept it. Why would you give yourself to me knowing that I believed you to be another woman? That I was speaking her name, seeing her, feeling her when I came into *your* body—knowing I believed it to be her when I kissed you and caressed you? It is absurd. No woman I have ever been with would do such a thing. And I have known many women, Daria. A woman would sooner stick a knife in the man's ribs and curse him to hell."

"Perhaps it is absurd. Perhaps I am absurd. I don't know. I haven't much experience with men and their ways, or ladies either, for that matter." She looked at him and her eyes were as sad as her voice as she said softly, "All I know is myself and what I feel." She drew a deep breath and blurted it out. *"Rydw i'n dy garu di,* Roland."

He stared down at her for a very long time. Finally he said, his voice emotionless, "Lying bitch." He turned from her and strode away, yelling over his shoulder, "Leave if you wish. I shan't stop you. By all the saints, I care not if I never gaze upon your face again. Return to your uncle, or, if you're afraid to, then return to the Earl of Clare. Perhaps he'll still want you if he hasn't plowed Tilda silly by now and finds he's forgotten all about you and your dowry and his hatred of your uncle."

He forced himself to keep walking. He forced himself not to turn back to her. She couldn't love him, damn her lying heart! She couldn't. It made no sense. *No more sense than her recognizing him instantly, no matter his disguise.* Who had told her the words in Welsh? He shook his head. He didn't care.

He knew he must return to the king and queen, explain somehow. Convince them of the truth without their believing Daria to be a conniving whore. . . . He cursed. What to do?

"The Earl of Reymerstone would kill me, and I wouldn't blame him. Worse, he would kill her as well, and he would do it without hesitation, without mercy."

Edward merely shrugged. "It isn't as if you were a peasant, Roland. Your family is as old as his, and—"

Roland interrupted his king. "You don't understand, sire. The man wanted Daria to wed Ralph of Colchester, and only him, because in return he would gain the lands he wants to add to his own."

"And then the Earl of Clare abducted her?"

Roland nodded.

"The story is complicated, is it not? Like one of your tales, Roland, with many twists and unexpected turns. Only this tale, well, it is up to you—regardless of all your protestations—to find a satisfactory ending."

"You refuse to believe that I am not the father of this child? Have you ever known me to lie to you?"

The king looked troubled. "No, I haven't. The queen is convinced that the girl is telling the truth. Listen, Roland. 'Tis possible that you took her believing her another, is it not?"

"Not that I can imagine. Can you imagine it yourself, sire?"

"No."

"She also claims that she is with child after but one plowing. One time and she becomes pregnant? I cannot credit that either."

At that the king smiled even as he shifted restlessly in his chair. "I can, Roland. It happens frequently. I can attest to that."

Roland fell silent. The king fell equally silent. He detested tangles like this. He wanted to face down the Earl of Clare and strip him of his power; he wanted to strip all the Marcher Barons of every drop of power they possessed; he, the King of England, wanted the power in Wales and he wanted to build castles to assert his power and bring the damned Welsh to their knees before him, their king . . . and here he was instead trying to solve a problem that had no apparent solution. None that was satisfying. Unless . . . "There is a way out of this perhaps. We can keep the girl with us until she is delivered of the babe. If the babe resembles you, then you can wed her. If it resembles the Earl of Clare—does he not have hair red as scarlet? —then it is proved."

"And what if the babe looks like no other? Or looks like its mother?"

The king cursed softly. "What do you think, Robbie?"

Robert Burnell, silent to this point, looked decidedly uncomfortable. "Do you wish an opinion likely to conform to the Church?"

Roland snorted.

"Go ahead, Robbie."

"The Church would hold that the woman, regardless of her rank or supposed innocence, was the one culpable. It would be her fault and none other's. She would bear the censure and the condemnation and—"

"Hold! 'Tis enough, damn you."

"She would be viewed as a harlot, a deceiver, a stain on her family's honor—"

"Be quiet, I tell you!"

"But, Roland," the king said reasonably, "you claim it cannot be your babe. Thus, she lies. To protect whom? Robbie, what do you think Stephen Langton would have recommended?"

"He would have doubtless ruled that she be deprived of her dowry, and shunned and reviled by her family and all those who'd believed in her virtue."

Roland looked appalled. "If that were true, then she would die, the babe with her."

Robert Burnell shrugged. "Aye, very likely."

"I suppose the Church would also say that was proper—two dead—but the man responsible free and absolved!"

"The man is but weak of the flesh," Burnell said. "The woman is the evil one who plots to exploit the man's weakness."

"Such a testament to the mercy of God and his infinite fairness. It sickens me."

Roland rose swiftly to his feet and paced the vast interior of the royal tent. He cursed fluently in four languages.

"Very well," Edward said, watching Roland closely. His friend wasn't indifferent to the girl. He saw the likely result in that moment. Aloud he said, "I see two options. The first, she is returned to her uncle, and the second, she is returned to the Earl of Clare. Are there others?"

Roland said on a sigh, "Her uncle will kill her if she's returned to him. If by chance the child she carries isn't the Earl of Clare's seed, why, then he would kill her too."

"As I inquired of you two," the king said patiently, "are there any other possibilities?"

There was dead silence. Roland could hear a soldier laughing from a goodly distance outside the royal tent. He could hear his own heart beating a slow steady rhythm. Then he laughed.

He turned, and the king knew in that moment that Roland had accepted the inevitable. But still, what if she carried another's child? He couldn't simply force his friend into a corner.

"Very well. I am the other option. I will wed her."

"But I have yet to see the Earl of Clare," Edward said, raising his hand. "Be reasonable, Roland. I can determine if he is the father and whether he will or will not abuse her. I am said to be a good judge of men. Well, let me judge this Earl of Clare. Perhaps he will want her, and if it is his babe she carries, then—"

"She claims to despise the earl. Even you wouldn't wish to hand her over to a man she hates. Nor is he a gentle man. He would abuse her endlessly, believe it, and once you were gone, who would there be to stop him?"

"But if she deserves his abuse, if she is lying for some reason unbeknownst to us, then his treatment of her will—"

"I will wed her," Roland repeated, and he looked defeated and very weary.

The king looked pleased, but he turned his head in time so that Roland did not remark upon it. Roland did care for the girl, regardless of the paternity of the babe she carried. She could bring him a goodly dowry; the King of England would see to it. The world was filled with bastards. Even his precious daughter, Philippa, was a bastard. It mattered not, not when there were money, land, and prestige involved. He would pray the child would be a female. Thus Roland wouldn't have to pass his worldly possessions down to another man's son.

"Aye," Roland said more to himself than to anyone else, "it is likely that the earl did rape her and she is too ashamed to admit to it." But why me? *Because she loves you, that's why. She believed she had no other choice.*

The king said nothing. He wasn't stupid. He nodded to Robert Burnell. "Send Eric to her majesty and inform her that we are to have a wedding right now, or as soon as Daria can be prepared."

Roland looked a moment as if he would protest; but he held his peace, resuming his pacing the tent. The king drank the remainder of the sweet Aquitaine wine. "The wine comes from Graelam de Moreton's father-in-law," he said to break the tense silence. "It is excellent. You will shortly be neighbors. And you will keep an eye on my dear daughter, Philippa, and that scoundrel husband of hers. Aye, de Fortenberry is a scoundrel, but the girl wanted him, wouldn't hear of anything else, as you well know. Wedded him, and that was that."

Roland was drawn from self-pity for a moment. "She didn't know of you when she wedded him, sire."

"More's the pity. Someone should have known. She looks like me, all that beautiful Plantagenet hair and those eyes of hers. Aye, someone should have known."

"De Fortenberry won't shame you."

"I will keep the royal eye on him nonetheless," the king said, and sat back in silence now to watch Roland continue his pacing.

His pacing stopped suddenly when the queen unexpectedly came into the tent. She looked worried.

The king rose quickly and went to her. They spoke softly together.

He frowned, then sighed, saying, as he turned to Roland, "Daria refuses to marry you."

"*What?*"

Eleanor said, "She refuses because you believe her a liar and naught more than chattel or a possession to be returned to her uncle for money. She claims she would rather go to a convent."

"I hadn't thought of that as a possibility," Edward said in a thoughtful voice. "Perhaps that is the best, perhaps—"

"It isn't the best! A convent would drain her of all spirit." He saw her suddenly in that small valley in Wales, breathing in the clear air, her arms wrapped around her, so happy in her freedom that he'd smiled as she'd danced. "No, she isn't fashioned for the religious existence. It is absurd. She is being willful. Damn her for an ungrateful wench!"

"But, Roland—"

"I shall thrash her, now! Have the priest readied. I will fetch her. Is she in your tent, your highness?"

"Aye, Roland, she is there," Eleanor said, and said not another word. When the king would have spoken, she clutched his arm.

"Damned female!" Roland muttered as he strode from the royal presence without permission. "She besets me with her ingratitude, her pricks, and her thanklessness! Aye, I'll beat her!"

"All will be well now," the queen said, and smiled up at her husband.

Daria was alone in the queen's tent. She was sitting on a thick Flanders carpet, staring fixedly at the swirling red-and-purple patterns. Her arms were wrapped around her stomach. She knew she should rise, should prepare herself to leave. Would the king allow her to enter a convent? Would her uncle allow her to remain there? She'd heard that convents demanded huge amounts of money—indeed, dowries, because she would be the bride of God—to take a lady of her class. What if her uncle refused? She shook her head; she simply didn't know. Anything would be preferable to the Earl of Clare or Ralph of Colchester. Besides, she didn't want to die, and the earl would surely murder her once he discovered she no longer possessed a maiden-head. She thought of Roland and lowered her head. She felt tears well up and blinked them back. She swallowed. No, what had happened, she'd done, and it was she who would carry the responsibility.

When he strode into the tent, she raised her head to face him, her expression not changing. She'd expected him to come; after all, hadn't he made a grand sacri-fice? Wouldn't he now be angry to have it flung back in his face? But only for a little while. Then at least he would remember her fondly, for she'd released him from a gesture he'd hated to make in the first place. She couldn't make him pay for his generosity. She would have no honor if she did.

"Hello, Roland. What do you want?"

He didn't like her emotionless voice or the dullness in her eyes, nor did he like the fact that she was sitting cross-legged on the floor, her hair spilling down her back and over her shoulders.

He drew a deep steadying breath. He said quite calmly, "I want to know why you told the queen such nonsense."

She raised a brow at that but made no move to rise. She simply looked at him until he dropped to his haunches beside her. "Why, Daria?" He was three inches from her face. He didn't touch her.

"I am profoundly religious, Roland. No, you wouldn't believe that, would you? Very well, the truth. There is naught else but a convent. I wish to live. You said yourself that this would happen if you returned me to my uncle. He would kill me to have my inheritance. I know for a fact that the Earl of Clare, were he forced to wed me, would beat me and my unborn child to death, for he would know it wasn't his. It is not so hard to understand, is it? I don't particularly wish to die. I'm quite young, you know."

"I'm offering you another way. I won't kill you, nor will I beat you."

The pain threatened to choke her.

"You will marry me, Daria. Now, at once."

She shook her head. "Nay, I can't do that either."

"You believe I am lying? You believe I would beat you? Abuse you?"

"No."

"I shan't murder you, even if I do manage to gain your immense inheritance."

"I know."

"Then . . ." He growled in fury. "This is your grand gesture, isn't it? Free the poor man because he cares nothing for you? But first, bring him to his knees, make him grovel and plead, make him offer to do exactly what it is you wanted all the while. Then you scorn him? You are more perverse than that damned bitch Joan of Tenesby! I won't tolerate it, Daria, not for another instant!"

She had the damnable gall to simply sit there and shake her head.

For one of the few times in his life, Roland knew such anger that he nearly choked on it. "By the saints, I will thrash you, Daria!"

He hauled her to her feet and flung himself onto the queen's chair. He dragged her over his thighs and brought his right palm down hard on her buttocks. She froze, then reared up frantically. She made no sound, but she struggled furiously. She was strong, he thought, as he brought his hand down again. He admired a silent fighter.

"Not even the smallest sound from you, eh? You're a stubborn wench. Should I pull up your gown and let you feel the heat of my palm on your bare flesh?" Before she could speak, if she would have spoken, Roland had bared her to the waist, ripping her gown and her shift. But he didn't strike her again. His hand remained raised in the air. He stared down at her buttocks, white and smooth and rounded, her long white legs, sleekly muscled. He swallowed. He moaned, then cursed. He shoved her off his legs and rose. He stood over her, panting, his hands on his hips. "Damn you, Daria. I would have remembered if I'd taken you, remembered your lovely buttocks at the very least. Now, prepare yourself, you stupid wench. You will wed me, and it will be tonight, before I change my mind, before I realize that you have shoved my honor down my throat. If you continue to refuse, I will beat you until you howl for mercy. No one will prevent me—don't think that anyone will!"

He said nothing more, merely strode to the tent opening. He turned and pointed his finger at her. "I mean it, Daria. You will wed me, and not another word out of your shrew's mouth."

11

THE BENEDICTINE PRIEST Young Ansel, as he was affectionately called, exercised unflagging loyalty first to Robert Burnell and then to King Edward. He performed the marriage ceremony with as much dignity as his twenty-three years allotted him. His voice shook only a little when he spoke the soft Latin phrases. He thought the bride lovely and modest, and though she looked at him once, and that when he mispronounced a Latin word in his nervousness. A coincidence, he thought, swallowing. As for the groom, Young Ansel found him somewhat forbidding. For all his presence, he seemed absent from the proceedings.

Roland de Tournay was unwilling, Young Ansel finally realized, and wondered at it. He couldn't ask, of course; it would be considered an impertinence. Even though he was the king's second priest, Burnell had advised him never to take liberties. The royal temper had yet to consider him a friend.

Young Ansel looked at the bride more closely as he blessed the couple, and thought that perchance she was ill, so pale was she. He glanced over at Roland de Tournay, wondering if he saw how pale and still she was. But the knight was looking beyond Young Ansel's left shoulder, his face expressionless, his eyes cold. As he'd thought before, the groom seemed absent. He also looked miserable.

There were congratulations, exuberant and bawdy, because the king wished it so and his servants and soldiers willingly obeyed him. He wanted everything to appear as normal as possible. He wanted no talk about Roland, no talk about Daria. Even Robert Burnell managed to exclaim in modest enthusiasm several times. The queen hugged the bride and spoke softly to her. Young Ansel wondered what she said.

Eleanor was worried. As she gently held Daria, she said softly, "Do you feel ill, child?"

Daria shook her head against the queen's shoulder. She couldn't stand close to the queen because of her swollen belly. I will become like this, she thought blankly, and for a moment stared down at her own thin body. She'd known no illness from the babe as yet. How could there be a living being in her belly? So small? She wished her mother were here holding her. Perhaps her mother could make sense of it.

"You're afraid, then. Afraid of your new life, perhaps even of your new husband?"

"Aye."

"My sweet lord speaks so highly of Roland, has always done so. He's a man of honor and loyalty and he never treats his vows lightly. You're also an heiress and thus will bring much advantage to your husband. 'Tis important, you know. Have no fear, Daria."

"No."

The queen frowned over Daria's head at her husband. He was still loudly extolling Roland's good fortune, alternately buffeting Roland's shoulder as he gave him thorough advice and telling him he would soon be so rich he could well afford to assist his king. Edward raised his eyes at that moment and met his wife's gaze. He quieted, then said to Roland, "It is done. You are now a husband and soon you will be a father."

"It is amazing."

"It is done," Edward repeated. "All of us will go to Tyberton on the morrow. I wish the Earl of Clare to

see you and know that Daria is yours now and that he
has no claim on her. I wish him to know that you have
my favor.''

Roland wished that as well. He nodded. He wondered how the earl would react. He wanted in odd
moments for the man to become violent. He wanted
to fight, to bash in his head, to relieve his frustration.

"I have had a tent prepared for you, my friend. You
and your bride will spend the night there. I see the
queen has released Daria. Come, we will dine now
and drink to your health and your future.''

There was nothing for it, Roland thought. He wanted
to yell at the king that the last thing he wanted to do
was spend the night with the girl who was with child
and who was also his wife. He even managed to smile
at Daria as he helped her into the chair beside his at
the quickly erected banquet table. They were outside
under the bright stars and the full moon. Torches lined
the perimeter of the royal encampment. There were
one hundred people milling about, eating their fill,
turning at odd times to salute the bride and groom.
All the food, Roland learned, came from the larders
at Chepstow. He wondered if the Earl of Hereford
would starve come winter. It appeared the king had
stripped the castle granary bare. Perhaps in the misty
future the king would visit him in Cornwall and delve
with a free hand into his granary.

"Eat something, Daria.''

She wanted to tell him that she would vomit if she
did, but she said nothing, merely picked up a chunk of
soft white bread and chewed it. When he turned away
from her, she spit it onto the ground.

"You will be silent tomorrow.''

"What do you mean?''

"I mean that we go to see the Earl of Clare. You
will be silent and not flit and flutter about on me. I
want neither your advice nor your protection, if that is
what you're about now.''

"I don't think I've ever fluttered about on you, Roland. As for my protection, 'tis true, I succeeded that one time."

He shrugged with masculine indifference. "Perhaps, perhaps not. Nor have you ever been silent. I wonder if the earl has guessed that you carry his child. I would imagine that his rage would know no bounds. Therefore, you must keep silent and let me deal with him."

"I don't carry the earl's child. Therefore he could have no rage, save the rage that he's been made to look the fool and he's lost all my dowry."

He just looked at her, thin-lipped, then tipped back his goblet and drank deeply of the red Aquitaine wine.

" 'Tis true, Roland. You must be careful, for I don't believe him entirely sane. Seeing you, the embodiment of his undoing, might make him act foolishly."

He made an elaborate pretense of turning to speak to Burnell. Inside, his stomach churned with anger at her. By all the saints, she'd gained what she wanted, so why did she continue to play the abused innocent? She infuriated him. He drank another goblet of wine. But he couldn't become drunk.

"You're very fertile if you indeed became with child with but one plowing."

"I am or you are."

He stiffened but his smile remained firmly in place. Did he really expect her to change her tune now?

"Then I'd best take my fill of you whilst you carry the babe. I'll be tired of you by the time the child is born and that will be just as well. I don't wish to have a dozen babes hanging on to me within as many years."

She wanted to yell at him; she wanted to howl at the glorious full moon. She did neither. She lowered her head and played with the bread on her trencher. He was trying on purpose to hurt her. She wouldn't let him see that he was succeeding.

"You have been so very kind to me, your majesty,"

Daria said later to the Queen of England. "I thank you, truly."

"Fret not, child. I will see you again. You and Roland will come to London, or perhaps my lord and I will visit Cornwall. Now, my dear, allow my ladies to prepare you for the night."

With those prosaic words, and not a bit of well-meant advice, the Queen of England left her to the ministrations of two ladies-in-waiting. The ladies weren't so reticent as their mistress. They'd drunk their share of wine and were thus giggling and giving Daria advice on making a man shudder madly with lust.

Roland paused outside the tent and listened to the women's laughter coming from within. And then he eard Daria's voice, puzzled and low, "Truly, Claudia, how do I do that? Just tell him to stick it into my mouth? Would I not choke? Would I not hurt him with my teeth?"

"Silly girl! Daria, you must stroke your hands over his body and follow your hands with your tongue and mouth. 'Tis a wonderful sound."

Roland's eyes widened. So the queen's ladies were as bawdy as any others. So they were educating Daria. Then his smile turned to a frown when she said, "Perhaps Roland won't like me to do that because I wouldn't do it well. Perhaps he would want another, more skilled and—"

"Daria, hush now. The only way for you to become skilled is to practice. Ask your husband if he minds that you practice on him. Then watch him lick his lips and watch his eyes grow large with anticipation."

Roland didn't hear what his wife said to that. His *wife*. It was almost more than a man of few years but vast experience could take in. He hadn't wanted a wife, not yet, not until his keep in Cornwall was in proper condition and he'd become . . . bored. He shook himself. Bored! He wouldn't ever become bored, and how could his mind assume that taking a wife was the cure for boredom anyway?

He pulled back the tent flap and chuckled at the drunken grins he received from the two women. Their thoughts were clearly writ on their faces, and his sex responded. He quickly turned to Daria. She simply stood where she was, staring at him. With new eyes, he thought. Was she seeing herself take his rod into her mouth?

Claudia poked her elbow into Daria's ribs. "Practice, my dear, practice!"

"Good night, Daria, and enjoy what God and the king have given you! The saints and women know there aren't many men as potent and well-formed as this one. Aye, he's a lovely lad, he is."

The two women eyed Roland through wistful drunk eyes, Claudia brushing her breasts against his arm as she went past him.

Daria stared, feeling no particular anger at the woman. They'd dipped freely into the wine, and Roland *was* a beautiful man. She supposed it made Claudia forget herself. Roland was standing there saying nothing, merely looking at her.

"Will you take their advice?"

Her face turned instantly red. "You . . . you heard what they told me to do?"

"Aye, I heard. 'Twas excellent advice."

She straightened her back and looked him squarely in the eye. "Then I will do it. But you must tell me what to do, Roland. I have no wish to offend you or perhaps hurt you."

"This is a very strange conversation," he said as he began stripping off his outer tunic. He tossed the wide leather belt onto the fur-covered floor. "The queen's ladies were most eager to teach you what to do to me."

"They seem to understand men," she said, frozen to

the spot, watching as Roland matter-of-factly removed his tunic. There were three candles lit in the tent, in a brass holder sitting atop a small sandalwood table. There was a low cot covered with animal furs. There was nothing else in the tent. When Roland was bare to his waist, the candlelight casting darkening shadows over his body, Daria found herself staring openly at him. He was lean and firm, dark hair covering hisc hest. When she'd seen him in Wrexham he'd been ill and lying on his back. He'd been beautiful, she'd thought that very clearly, but she hadn't recognized the sheer strength of him, the tautness of his arms, the fluid motion of the muscles in his back and shoulders, the ridges of muscle over his belly. She swallowed, for now he was stripping off his chausses. He stopped then and looked at her. "Why do you stand there? Get off your clothes and into the bed."

She didn't move. As an order from a loving bridegroom, it lacked even a dollop of warmth.

He raised a dark eyebrow. "Since you carry a babe, I can assume that you have seen a naked man. I am no different from any of my fellows, Daria." He rose straight and tall and naked, and the look he gave her was mocking. She didn't want to look at him but she couldn't help it. Her eyes fell immediately to his groin. His man's rod lay flaccid in the bush of thick black hair.

But she knew he would grow large, very large, and he would want to thrust himself inside her body. She swallowed and turned her back to him.

She heard him chuckle. " 'Tis best to begin your caressing of me whilst I'm still in this state. Now, get off your clothes."

"All right." Quickly she doused the three candles, throwing the tent into gloom. The torches from without cast dim shadows into the interior, but at least he couldn't see her clearly. She was embarrassed. Before, he hadn't known *her*, hadn't really touched *her*, hadn't really taken *her*. But now he was well; now he was virile and eager; now he was her husband and would look at her.

"What are you doing?" She whirled about, consternation writ plain on her face.

"I'm merely lighting one candle. I don't wish to fumble in the darkness. Get off your clothes, Daria. I wish to see your breasts and your belly. I have paid dearly for the privilege. I will not tell you again."

With those emotionless words, he climbed into the narrow cot and pulled a fur to his waist. He crossed his arms behind his head and looked at her. Her hands stilled, then fell to her sides. She couldn't bring herself to remove her clothes in front of him; she didn't want to respond to his indifferent command. She was afraid; she knew he didn't want her, she knew that he would take her tonight simply because she was here, she belonged to him, and she could have been any woman to ease him.

Yet this man was her husband, and she must make the best of it. She tried again to untie the ribbons on her overtunic, but her fingers were clumsy and cold. Finally she loosened it enough to pull it over her head. Her gown was loose-fitting, but again she couldn't manage to unlace the strings that crisscrossed over her breasts.

Her husband simply lay there looking at her, his eyes hooded, just looking, as if he didn't really care, as if he simply wanted her to obey whatever order he gave her because he was the master and she wasn't, and because he was angry at her and wanted to punish her.

Suddenly it was simply too much. She looked at her shaking fingers, looked at him and saw that his expression was as cold as the waters of the North Sea, and whispered, "Nay, I cannot." She saw him jerk upright, and slowly, very slowly, she eased down to her knees. She felt tears sting her eyes; felt despair wash over her. She covered her face with her hands. And she cried silently.

Roland drew back as if he'd been struck. There was his bride, in a heap on the floor, crying! Damn her! Aloud he said furiously, "You have what you want, you cursed wench! And for whatever reason you wanted *me* as your husband, not the Earl of Clare, not God in a precious convent! Well, now you have me. Cease your damnable wailing. It but enrages me. A woman's tears mean naught; they're a sham. I won't stand it. Stop it now, Daria!"

She got a grip on herself. She was being foolish, and crying, indulging herself, her mother had told her, was something a girl shouldn't do with a man she loved because it wasn't honorable or honest. As if Roland would care. "Yes," she said, wiping her eyes with the back of her hand, "I'll stop crying. I'm sorry, Roland."

She rose slowly to her feet. He watched silently as she regained her control. She hiccuped even as she stripped off her gown. When she stood in the soft candlelight wearing only her thigh-length linen shift, he could see the faint outline of her nipples, the outline of dark hair at her groin. He wanted to see all of her. After all, he'd paid dearly for the right. "Remove the shift."

Her fingers went to the narrow straps on her shoulders, then stopped. "I cannot."

"Why can't you? You're certainly not a maid, so why this excessive modesty? Do you prefer that I strip the shift off you?"

"Nay. 'Tis the only one I have. I must be careful with it."

"Take it off, Daria. You are vexing me with your disobedience, and if you'll remember, you promised before God to obey me."

She felt humiliated. She searched for a shred of pride and managed to find enough so that she could stare straight ahead, not at him, and quickly pull off the shift. *Pretend you're alone; pretend he doesn't exist, that he doesn't lie there, watching you, seeing you.* And she didn't look at him, simply stared beyond him, feeling the soft linen shift pooling at her feet. She removed herself from the naked girl standing there for his examination, a man who was her husband, a man who disliked her heartily and believed her a liar and a female with no honor.

Roland stared at her, unable to help himself. He'd had no idea she was so very nicely shaped. Her breasts were high and full and as white as her belly, her nipples a pale pink. She was too thin. Her ribs were visible, and her breasts appeared almost too heavy for her slight torso, but he didn't mind that. He did wonder how she could be carrying a babe in that flat stomach of hers. He imagined she would begin to fill out soon enough. Her legs were long and sleekly muscled. He liked that. He remembered many of the women whose beds he'd shared whose bodies were white and soft, too soft. Daria was firm, and even in her thinness, she looked strong and able. He pictured her legs tightening around his flanks and felt his muscles tighten and his sex swell. He wanted her, but then again, he told himself silently, he would want any decent-looking female who was standing before him naked.

"Come here," he said. "Let me examine more closely what I have bought with my future."

"You forget that my money purchases a much nicer future than you expected."

"Aye, you do indeed improve my lot with your vast array of coin, but I pay with myself, Daria, and I keep paying until I die. I told you to come here. I am weary to my bones of your lies and protests, and I know I must take you at least once this night, even though I don't particularly wish to. It is my duty and I won't shirk it."

"You could pretend that I'm Lila again."

He sucked in his breath, rage and frustration pounding through him. "I told you once that you are nothing like her, more's the pity. If you don't come here, you will regret it."

Still she stood there in the center of the tent, naked and white and stiff as a lance. "Will you strike me as my uncle did? As the Earl of Clare did?"

His guts twisted at her words. It was rage at her now needless pretenses, nothing more. He rose from the bed and strode to her. He suddenly saw the fear in her eyes, and something else . . . She jerked back.

He clasped her upper arms tightly and pulled her against him. At the feel of her body against him, he felt a leaping of nearly painful need, felt his sex jutting against her belly. "Yes," he said as he grabbed a handful of her hair and pulled her face close to his, "yes, I will pretend you're Lila. Even if that fails, even if I recognize you, my wife, it still shouldn't be too difficult for me. I haven't had a woman for a long time, and even you will do." He kissed her closed lips, and he was hard and demanding. He was the master and he would prove it to her.

"I'm not Lila."

He released her, her quiet words flowing warmly into his mouth and into his soul, helpless words, despairing words.

He stepped back and looked at her face. She was not the girl he'd believed her to be. He pressed his open palm to her flat belly. "A babe is within, yet you are so small." His fingers kneaded her. "You say it is my babe, but I know that isn't true. You are a mystery to me, Daria. I remember the girl I rescued from the earl, the girl who traveled with me through Wales, the girl whose gift for languages rivals my own, the girl who was brave and fearless when those outlaws took her.

"And then there is the other Daria, the girl who has lies forming in her mind even as she thinks, and she, I fear, is the girl I married. Who are you, nay, what are you, and why have you done this to me?"

She closed her eyes against the pain. "I didn't wish it to be this way, I swear it to you, Roland. When you were ill, when you believed I was Lila, it was my decision to come to you, to give myself to you. I swore then to myself that you would never know, that I would never tell you, for I wanted no guilt from you, no pity. I even bathed my blood and your seed from you so that you wouldn't wonder. I was stupid, for it didn't occur to me that I could become pregnant. It never occurred to me that such a thing was possible."

He pushed her away from him. "Come to sleep when it pleases you to do so."

He doused the candle, and as she stood there naked and shivering in the middle of the tent, she heard him burrow beneath the furs on the low bed, and she said, "You have so quickly forgotten your duty?"

He cursed her then, his voice low, his words crude. He rose and she felt his fingers close over her arm. He dragged her to the bed and threw her down upon her back.

"Well, wife, evidently you desire my body. Or will any man's body do? No matter, since I have no choice, it will have to be my man's body you endure. But it's all you will have of me. And know, Daria, that a man can plow any woman, it matters not to him. To see a woman's parted legs, that's all that is necessary for a man. That's all you will be to me—an encumbrance, a duty, a body to take until I tire and grow bored."

He came down over her then, his body pressing hers into the furs, and he kissed her hard, forcing her mouth to open, and when her lips parted, he thrust his tongue inside and she felt his anger, tasted it, and her body froze. He reared over her and laughed. "You regret your desire now, sweet wife? Well, 'tis a pity, for it's too late, for you are now mine legally and in the eyes of God. Open your legs and do it quickly, for I wish to be done with it. I look forward to losing myself in sleep and mayhap I will be lucky and dream about Lila and Cena, two women who were honest in their need for me, and hadn't a traitorous thought in their heads."

"Roland, please, don't do this. Please, don't hurt me, don't—" Her voice broke off on a gasp when he grasped her thighs and pulled them apart. "Let me see if you are ready for me. I have no wish to rend your woman's flesh, 'twill but make you hurt to walk and to ride, and thus prove an inconvenience to me." His fingers were probing at her, delving inside her, exploring, and she tried to pull away from him, to free herself from him, but his hand came down flat on her belly, holding her still and silent even as his finger slid inside her, stretching her, working her. She felt her flesh become damp and soft because her body recognized him and wanted him even though she wanted to weep with the pain of what he was doing to her.

"By all the saints," he said, his finger pressing more deeply into her. "You're small, but your body is hungry. I shan't force you. No, you shan't scream of ravishment to me, ever. I have never forced a woman in my life, and besides, with you, it would be impossible. You're eager as any wench, probably more so than the two ladies who advised you."

She tried to reach him just once more. "Please, Roland, don't do this to me, not in anger, not—"

But he was paying her no heed and she knew he was apart from her. He was between her thighs, spreading them wider still, bending her knees and lifting her hips with his hands, bringing her upward. "No pleasure for you, wife, save what you can gain for yourself. Actually, little enough for me. My duty . . . 'tis naught but my damned man's duty." And without warning, without another word, his fingers pried her open, and he thrust himself into her in one powerful stroke.

She yelled at the shock of him and the burning of her flesh as he plunged deep, spreading her for himself, and then she was crying, but she stuffed her fist into her mouth, waiting helplessly, waiting silently, for him to finish with her. He'd been right, there was no pleasure for her. She wondered dully in those moments if there was such pleasure to be had for a woman ever.

He was breathing hard, plunging repeatedly into her, pulling out, then thrusting deep again. Again and again, until she heard him suck in his breath as if he'd been struck. Then he was hammering into her, deep, then shallow in short strokes, his hands frantically kneading her hips as he brought her higher for his penetration. Then he moaned, and she felt his seed come into her body. That was familiar to her, that deep joining that had eased her virgin's pain, for he'd belonged to her then, completely, and she'd possessed him.

She sobbed, unable to keep the sound to herself, not from any pain in her body, but from the pain in the very depths of her. For even in his man's possession of her, she was alone, deep within herself, as was he.

He was gasping for breath over her, his chest heaving from his exertion. He was still deep inside her and she could feel his member moving and shifting. There was still no pain, for his seed eased her and his member wasn't as swelled now. No, he hadn't ravished her body, but he had ravished her spirit.

"There," he said once he'd regained his breath,

"I've done my man's duty by you, wife." He pulled out of her quickly, eagerly, and her body flinched in reply.

"What, Daria, no passionate little moans from you? No thanks for my taking you as you wished? Do you mean to tell me that you were unable to give yourself a woman's pleasure? You surprise me. Your body was more than willing to take me in and pull my seed from me. You're a stubborn girl, but no matter. I will sleep now. Do not disturb me further this night."

He climbed off her and fell upon his back. She felt him pull the furs up. Slowly, very slowly, she straightened her legs. Her muscles protested. She felt his seed seeping slowly from her body, but she was too uncaring of it, of him, of herself, to pay much heed.

She lay there quietly. She heard his breathing even into sleep. She realized that she should have never told him the truth. She'd placed the responsibility on his shoulders just as she'd sworn to herself that she wouldn't do. But it was his babe she carried. How could he believe her if he had no memory of it? Well, it was over now. She listened to his deep slow breathing and knew that she still loved him but that now it wasn't enough, this love of hers, not nearly enough. Mayhap it would never have been enough, in any circumstance. He hated her and there was no reason for him to cease doing so.

Unless the babe looked like him. Unless somehow he remembered that night in Wrexham. It was her only hope, a slim one she knew, for she herself looked nothing like her own mother or like her father. But there was nothing else for her.

12

THERE WAS COMPLETE SILENCE in the great hall of Tyberton Castle. The Earl of Clare stood tight-mouthed, fury blotching his face, turning it as startling a red as his hair. He stared at the man who'd stolen Daria from him. The man who had made a fool of him twice. Hell and the devil, what was the damned knave doing with the king?

The earl said in a loud voice, "I see you have returned this man to me, sire. He's a thief and I will hang him this very day."

"Not as yet, my lord," Edward said pleasantly. "Not as yet. Come, have ale fetched. My queen is weary, as are her ladies." He added his famous Plantagenet smile, which had no discernible effect at all on the Earl of Clare. "I have a great thirst as well."

It was then that the earl saw Daria. He started toward her, then pulled himself upright. He held his peace. There were too many present to overhear him. He would wait.

After the queen, her ladies, and Daria were seated comfortably, the earl approached the king. To his chagrin, the whoreson Roland remained at the king's side, drinking from his flagon as if he had not a care in this world. He looked young and fit and strong—a warrior—not a pretty priest covered with a frayed cowl. How had the man gotten Daria away from him again? What kind of disguise had he used?

"I would beg to speak with you, sire. 'Tis important and regards this man here."

187

"Ah, yes," Edward said, his voice deep with amusement that the earl didn't hear, "I believe you wish to accuse this man of something?"

So the king wished the knave to remain. So be it. He drew himself up and contempt dripped from his voice. "Aye, he's a thief, sire, and he stole *her!*" He pointed a finger toward the queen's group of ladies. "Did he tell you that he pretended to be a Benedictine priest? That he, a savage and a heathen, even pretended to say a *Mass* for me? Not only did he rob me, sire, he blasphemed God's name and profaned the Church."

The king, diverted, turned to Roland. "Did you really play the priest?"

"Aye."

"Did you do it well?"

"For the most part. Only Daria knew that I misspoke some of my Latin Mass. The earl here understands naught but what he speaks. I could have recited Latin declensions and it would have made him feel holy just the same. Nay, 'twas Daria who understood immediately I was a fraud."

"Daria! You call her Daria! 'Tis absurd! A female cannot understand God's word! You lie to me and to your king. I understood all your mistakes, but I am a good man, a tolerant man, and I merely believed you nervous in front of me, and I chose not to humiliate you. Aye, I willingly forgave your lapses. Sire, give him over to me and I will deal with him quickly and fairly." He panted himself to a halt, then, unable to help himself, yelled, "I demand that you turn the man over to me, sire!"

"Hold, my lord," Edward said. He shifted in his chair—the earl's own ornate carved chair—and continued mildly, "Listen well, for I grow bored with your plaints and your commands to your king. This man is Roland de Tournay. He is my man, sent by me and none other to rescue that girl, Daria, from your imprisonment. Her uncle, the Earl of Reymerstone, pleaded for my help and I gave it. I told Roland to use whatever means necessary to accomplish his mission. Of course I didn't wish any blood to be shed, and he accomplished that as well."

Roland said not a word. He simply gazed at the king in admiration. He'd never believed the king so quick of wit before. He'd rather looked forward to this confrontation, but he'd assumed that the king would allow him to handle the earl, to do whatever he had to do, short of murdering the man.

He saw that the king was much enjoying his playacting. Roland, for the first time in their acquaintance of many years, remained silent. As for the Earl of Clare, he could not now make further demands, not after the king's explanation. Roland felt resentment at the king's interference, and some amusement, for the earl's hatred and immense frustration was very nearly a tangible thing, and there was naught the man could do, save silently choke on it.

Edward had no intention of allowing the two men to fight, for Roland would kill the earl, of that he had little doubt. He was younger, he was stronger, and he was smarter. And besides, he himself still needed the Earl of Clare, rot the man's miserable hide, needed him to fend off the Welsh outlaws, until he could build his castles and assume control himself. Then the Earl of Clare could drown in a Welsh swamp with the king's blessing. He discounted his friendship with Roland de Tournay; it couldn't be a consideration in the royal decision. No, the king didn't want Clare dead now. Moreover, he'd gained advantage with Roland, for that talented fellow wouldn't be able to refuse his king anything, not after this. Why, he would even have Roland's fine destrier returned to him. He thought about the look on the earl's face were he to tell him

that it was his, the king's, destrier, and he had merely
loaned it to Roland. The earl would surely swallow his
tongue in his rage.

The king smiled at the earl, a gracious smile. He
didn't believe in pressing a man's face in offal unless it
was necessary. A king could afford to be beneficent in
victory; it was also in his noble character, unless, of
course, he wished it otherwise. "So you see, my lord,
Roland accomplished his mission. If he offended your
religious feelings, I will reprimand him soundly. Further, it seems he became enamored with Daria and
she with him. After he rescued her again—the second
time, he played the bent old hag, did you know that?
No, well, that time, he brought her to me. They were
wedded last night, my lord, by mine own priest. He is,
in fact, a Benedictine priest, I can attest to it."

For a long moment the earl simply stared, not at
any person, but inward, and there he saw bleakness
and rage. He couldn't accept it. He looked toward
Daria, who stood next to the queen. This man, this
Roland de Tournay, had wedded her and bedded her.
"They left me with a peasant girl, garbed her as Daria
for her wedding with me. If she hadn't giggled, I
should have married the little slut!"

"She was most toothsome, my lord," Roland said.
"I handpicked her myself."

The king grinned, then harrumphed and said, his
voice serious, "This peasant girl, my lord, what have
you done with her? Not harmed her, I trust."

The Earl of Clare turned a dull red, for certainly
he'd bedded her, taken her with little delay; even as
his servants and soldiers feasted, he'd taken her to his
chamber and plowed her small belly. He'd hurt her,
but not badly. What had she expected to happen to
her once her lord had discovered the ruse? Any other
man would have had her beaten to death. But it didn't
matter. It wasn't at all the point. The earl shook

himself much in the manner of a wet mongrel and bellowed, "Daria! Come here, immediately!"

Daria felt the queen's hand lightly squeeze her fingers to hold her quiet. The queen raised her head and smiled at the king. Both the queen and Daria wished they'd heard what had been said, but they hadn't.

"Aye," the king called, "let Daria come here. Let her tell the earl that she is wedded to Roland de Tournay, by her own will, with no royal coercion."

Daria rose slowly. She felt as if she were in a strange dream, filled with loud voices from people who weren't really there, weren't actually real. She walked across the cold stone floor of Tyberton's great hall, seeing the people who'd served her, who'd watched her, seeing some of them smirking now at their lord and his predicament, others gazing with hatred upon her. The queen had assured her earlier that the king wouldn't allow the two men to fight. She hadn't believed her before, but now she did. Further, no matter what Roland believed, no matter what he thought of her, she was his wife. She must not shame him. She stiffened her back and thrust up her chin. She didn't look at her husband.

She walked directly to the Earl of Clare. "Yes, my lord?" she asked pleasantly. "You wished to speak to me?"

The earl stared down at her a moment. He wanted to strike her and pull her against him. She was pale, but even so, she didn't appear to have any fear of him. He'd strike her first, he thought, not hard, just with enough force to recall her to her duty to him; then he'd take her and hold her. He could feel the softness of her body, the narrowness of her when he'd penetrated her with his finger to find her maidenhead. She had no maidenhead now. She'd wedded Roland de Tournay. Blood pounded hard and fast in his head and in his groin. He said in a harsh voice, "You have truly wedded him? Willingly?"

"Aye. I am his wife."

"By all the saints! You lied to me when I caught up to you finally? You hadn't escaped him in Wrexham? You were not trying to find me?"

"That's correct, my lord. He'd fallen ill and would have been unable to fight you if you'd found us. I learned that you had arrived in Wrexham and had discovered Roland's destrier at the local stable. I had to save him from you, for I knew you would kill him with no hesitation. I took his destrier and led you away from him."

Roland didn't move. He didn't change expressions. He felt something move deep inside him, a feeling like the one he'd experienced the previous evening when his release had overtaken him. He'd wanted briefly to hold her tightly against him, caress her, and kiss her, and forget all else. But he'd managed to keep his mouth shut. He'd managed this time not to give a woman power over him. He'd managed to hold himself apart from the still and silent woman lying beneath him. He'd held steady; she'd already betrayed him once. She wouldn't betray him again.

Even if she wasn't lying about saving him, well, then, it still didn't matter. She'd lied about the other. There was no other explanation for it, the Earl of Clare had raped her the moment he'd recaptured her. And Roland felt the familiar rage with that knowledge. She had saved him; he accepted it as being plausible, though he'd never before known a woman with such initiative.

The Earl of Clare howled. "I offered you everything! Damn you, girl, you could have been a countess, not a simple knight's lady, doomed to poverty—"

"Oh, I shan't be poor, my lord," Daria said, interrupting him with great pleasure. "Don't you forget how you desired my dowry as much as my fair hand? My dowry and revenge against my uncle? Well, all is now Roland's."

Reason deserted him. The earl's fist struck her hard against her jaw. Daria staggered backward with the force of his blow, falling to the stone floor. Roland leapt upon the earl, his fist in his throat, his other fist striking low and hard in his belly. The earl yelled and stumbled backward, his balance lost. Roland didn't pause. He jumped at him, hurling him to his back with his fist hard in his chest. The earl's sword crashed loudly against the stone. Roland stood over him and hissed, "You strike someone with not a tenth of your strength. Well, I am her husband and I will protect her from such vermin as you." He kicked the earl hard in the ribs, then dropped to his knees, grabbed the earl by his tunic, jerked up his head, and pounded his face twice with his fist. He let his head drop back with a loud ugly thud.

"Enough, Roland," the king called. "Have some ale. That sort of work makes a man thirsty."

But Roland didn't heed the king. He saw the queen's ladies surrounding Daria, helping her to her feet, brushing off her gown. He strode to them and they fell away from her. He didn't touch her for a moment, just stood there before her, looking down at her.

"Look up at me, Daria."

She obeyed him. He clasped her upper arms in his hands.

The earl—the damnable sod—had struck her hard. Roland lightly touched her jaw. "You will look a witch come evening," he said. "But your eye won't blacken. Does it pain you much?"

She shook her head, but he knew it must hurt her. It pleased him, this unexpected stoicism of hers.

"Hold still." As gently as he could, he touched his fingertips to her jaw, probing, making certain it wasn't broken. She didn't move, didn't flinch once.

He saw that she was now looking beyond him to the still-fallen Earl of Clare. "Did you kill him?"

"Of course not. Do you believe me a madman?"

"I have never seen a man fight another as do you."

Roland grinned and rubbed the bruised knuckles of his left hand against his right palm.

"Aye, Roland," the king called out. "How come you to destroy another man with such strange motions?"

"A Muslim fellow in Acre taught me. He said that Christians and their notions of honorable fighting left him and his brothers roaring with laughter. They said English knights with their heavy, clumsy horses and their armor that baked them alive under the sun made them shake their heads with wonder. They could not understand how we could be so stupid. They weren't of course in Barbars' army. They were outlaws and street thieves."

The king, fortunately for all those present, chose to be amused. "Street thieves!" They heard a moan and the king nodded to several of the earl's retainers who had been standing frozen in place, not knowing what to do. They rushed to their master's side and assisted him.

"I cracked two of his ribs, made him impotent for a week, and severely bruised his throat, rendering speech difficult and painful for him, for three days, I'd say. Nothing that won't heal with time. Perhaps I should have made him permanently impotent. But the fellow doesn't have an heir. I found myself in sympathy with him at the last instant."

Daria looked from him to the king and back again. She saw her husband's dark eyes were sparkling with pleasure. He'd enjoyed hitting the Earl of Clare, pounding him to the stone floor. She touched her fingertips to her jaw. The pain flashed through her head and she closed her eyes a moment to gain control. To her surprise, she felt his arms go around her. He lifted her high in his arms. "My lady needs to rest," Roland announced to the assembled group. "Sire, if it pleases you, I will remove her to her former chamber, the small room where the earl held her prisoner for so many months. I doubt not that the earl will insist upon his king and queen having his own chamber. Pain tends to bring a greater measure of reason to a man."

Roland carried her up the winding narrow stairs to the upper level. The old woman Ena was crouched at the top of the stairs. When she saw Roland carrying her mistress, she stretched out a skinny arm and pointed a bony finger at him and howled, "Ye've hurt her!"

"Nay, old witch, your precious earl struck her. She will rest now, and your presence isn't necessary."

Daria said not a word. She wrapped her arms more tightly around Roland's neck. "He moved so quickly I didn't have time to avoid his fist."

"I know. I was so surprised at his stupidity that I, too, stared for a good second before I had sense enough to attack him." He eased her onto the narrow bed and straightened, looking down at her. He said awkwardly, "I'm sorry he struck you, Daria. I wasn't much of a protector."

She said nothing, merely nodded. Her head hurt and her jaw pulsed with pain.

"What you said to him—was it true? Did you truly lead him away from me?"

She heard the disbelief in his voice. She turned her head away from him. "Aye, it's true. I lied to him and pretended that I'd escaped you. I made him believe that I rejoiced at his finding me. He didn't see through it."

"Then he brought you back here and forced you, raped you. He got you with child then, didn't he?"

"No. He didn't touch me. I convinced him that we would both rot in hell if he forced me without marriage first. I told him he would ruin mine own honor if he took me without marriage first. I begged and pleaded. I prayed he would not be able to find a priest, and so he didn't, until that same day you came for me again. I was also fortunate that he left me for much of that time to search for Welsh outlaws."

"I see," Roland said, his voice emotionless. He strode across the small room to the window slit. He stood there gazing down into the inner bailey. This is where Daria had stood, helpless and a prisoner, for so many days. He turned suddenly and said, "Why don't you have sickness from the babe? I have heard it common in women to be ill." He shrugged. "To vomit, to feel weak. Are your breasts not sore?"

"I am tired more of the time, but nothing more."

"Your breasts are not sore? Did I hurt you last night?"

She couldn't bear it, this insistence of his, this distrust. "Leave me alone, Roland. You didn't hurt me last night, not physically. You merely made me feel defiled and helpless, worth less than nothing." There, she'd said what she felt. She watched him pale, but only for a moment. His eyes narrowed on her face and he said, his voice even, too even, "You are certain you are with child?"

So he wondered now if even that was a lie. A lie to trap him into marriage? She marveled at his mind, and said calmly enough, "I wasn't, but the queen was. When I doubted her, she laughed and told me she had considerable experience in matters of knowing when babes were in a woman's belly. Should you like to question her, Roland?"

"Sarcasm doesn't suit you, Daria."

"Your endless distrust doesn't suit me!"

His brows lowered and his dark eyes, so full of sparkling pleasure such a short time before, were now cold as a moonless night. "Remain here. I must return to the king." He strode to the door, then said over his shoulder, "It isn't true that you have no value at all. Do you so quickly forget all the wealth you bring me?" He left her then without another word, another look.

Daria had no idea of the time. Since it was the midsummer, it would remain light until very late in the evening. She was bored, but she didn't want to go to the great hall. Her jaw still throbbed, but not as much now. She stood by the open window slit, a spot where she'd spent so many hours, and stared down into the inner bailey. There weren't as many people about. It must be later than she'd thought. Her stomach growled and she crossed her arms over her belly. It was then, sudden as a streak of lightning, that her belly cramped, nausea flooded her, and she dashed to the chamber pot and vomited up what little food she'd eaten that day. She was heaving, her jaw aching ferociously after her exertion, kneeling on the floor over the pot, when the chamber door opened. She hadn't the energy to turn about, but she knew it was Roland. She heard him suck in his breath, heard him quicken his step to her. She felt his large hand on her shoulder.

She still didn't raise her head. Another wave of sickness hit her and she jerked and shuddered with dry heaves, since there was no more food in her belly. She felt weak and stupid and so listless that she didn't care at that moment if he was repelled at her illness. She remained still, bent over the chamber pot, breathing heavily, sweat trickling down her back and between her breasts.

"Come," he said, and slipped his hands beneath her armpits and raised her to her feet. She hadn't the strength to support herself and sagged. He half-dragged her to the bed and laid her down. She closed her eyes. She didn't want to see him, didn't want him to see her, not like this, not green and shaky and weak as a feeble old woman.

She felt a wet cloth on her face. Then he said, "Here, drink this. 'Tis naught but cool water."

She didn't want it, but she allowed him to raise her head and put the goblet to her lips. She sipped at the water, then felt her stomach twist. She gasped and jerked off the bed, back to the chamber pot.

Roland watched her, feeling more helpless than he had in his life. He watched her vomit up the water, then watched her body convulse and heave. He was out of his element in this; he turned and left her.

Daria didn't care, not about her husband's quick defection, not about anything, save the fierce knotting and unknotting in her belly. She finally slipped onto her side, her face against the cold stone floor. She didn't care about that either. It felt good, this coolness. She lay there, trapped in her weak body, content that she wasn't heaving into the pot. She wanted nothing more. Slowly, after some minutes, she lightly brought her hand to her belly. "My child," she said softly, feeling at once ridiculous and strangely content, "you have finally announced your presence to me. I but wish that you hadn't done it with such vigor."

The queen herself appeared, Roland behind her. "Ah, my poor child," Eleanor said, rueful sympathy in her voice.

"Place her on the bed, Roland. She will be better presently."

Daria didn't resist, nor did she acknowledge the queen's presence. She simply didn't care. She didn't look at her husband when he lifted her, cursing softly at the coldness of her body. "Move aside now and let her sip at this."

"Please, nothing," Daria said, her hand swatting weakly at the flagon the queen held, but the queen would have none of it.

" 'Twill settle your belly, my dear. Trust me. Did I not tell you that my experience in these matters is vast? Drink, now. That's it. Slowly, just small sips. Very good. That's enough now. Just lie back and close your eyes."

The queen smiled at Roland. She was pleased with his reaction to his wife's illness. He'd come running into the great hall, interrupting the king, but not caring, so afraid was he for Daria. "Worry not, Roland. She will be fine. It is important that she eat lightly and very often. She has gone too long without eating, I suspect. This drink I gave her, I will give you the ingredients. When she is ill again, you will prepare this for her."

Roland sounded appalled. "She will be ill that violently again?"

"She is with child, Roland. 'Tis common, unfortunately, but it will pass soon. Another month or so and she will feel much better."

Daria nearly groaned aloud. Another month! She wanted to turn her face to the wall and sleep through that month.

"Now, my dear," the queen continued, "one of my ladies is bringing you some food. You must always eat slowly, and just a little. I will leave you now with your husband. He is as pale as you are, he was so frightened for you."

Roland looked as if he would protest that description, but he wisely kept his mouth shut. He had been afraid, it was true. He thanked the queen, accepted food from Damaris, and returned to his wife. She looked small and weak, lying there on her back, her arms limp at her sides, her eyes closed. Her thick braided hair looked damp with sweat, dull and heavy.

"Daria," he said. "Come, sit up and I will give you some food. Just a little, but you will do as the queen says."

"Please go away, Roland. Please. I don't want to eat, ever again, as long as I live."

"You must. If you don't, the babe will starve."

That was true, and she sighed. "All right, leave the food and you go away."

"Why? I've seen men vomit until they turned as white as a woman's belly. It is no reason for you to feel embarrassed, Daria. Come now and eat. I must return shortly to the king. He demands to be foremost in all his people's thoughts. He'll forgive me this lapse, but only this time."

She obeyed because she knew him well enough to realize that once Roland made up his mind to do something, he wouldn't bend or change it. She wanted to feed herself, but gave that up. She felt too weak.

He sat beside her, feeding her small chunks of white bread, dipping some of them into the meat gravy. And he spoke to distract her. "My destrier has grown fat and lazy, but I don't despair. Once we are in Cornwall I will work him until he is lean again." He wiped a trickle of gravy off her chin with his finger. He paused, then said, a touch of resentment in his voice, "The king has meddled again. He fears that your uncle will roast my body over live coals if I go to Reymerstone to announce my marriage to you and demand your dowry. Thus, the king will send Burnell and a dozen of his men to do the dirty work for me."

She felt such relief at this news she wanted to shout to the rafters with it. She knew Roland wouldn't like that, so said instead, "You wanted to see my uncle?" She looked both appalled and surprised. "You looked forward to confronting him?" She couldn't imagine anyone actually wishing to be in her uncle's presence. His sarcasm, his cruelty, his viciousness. She shuddered unconsciously.

"He won't hurt you again, so cease trembling when you speak of him. Aye, I wanted to see his face and dare him to gainsay me." Roland gave a heartfelt sigh. "A pity, but what can I do? Edward must interfere, curse him. He enjoys playing the great mediator. In any case, you and I and several of the king's men will travel to Cornwall whilst poor Burnell travels east to

Reymerstone. I have spoken to each of the men, and they wish to join my service. They have families in Cornwall, wish to return there, and the king, since he is wallowing in his peacemaking, won't be offended."

Daria felt much better. The food settled in her stomach and she felt her strength returning. She finally looked at Roland. "Cornwall? You have family there? Your brother? We go to them?"

He shook his head. "Nay, my brother and all the family are near to York, in the northeast." He paused a moment and looked past her, seeing something she couldn't see, something that pleased him, something he wanted very much. "It's a beautiful old keep called Thispen-Ladock, owned by a man named Sir Thomas Ladock. It's not all that large and impressive, but Sir Thomas has no son or grandson. He has promised to sell it to me.

"The area around the keep is scarcely peopled. I want to build and charter a town and bring tradesmen there and farmers and blacksmiths." He broke off suddenly and closed his mouth. "I speak too freely." And too passionately, he added to himself.

"We will leave on the morrow."

"As you will," she said.

He rose. "I must return to the king to see what other pleasures he's planned for me. How sets your stomach?"

"I'm fine now."

He stood there frowning down at her. "Will you be able to travel?"

Was there another choice? she wondered. Would he leave her here? Drop her in a ditch somewhere? "Aye, I'll be fine."

He looked at her a moment longer, feeling uncertain, feeling guilt that she would have to travel, feeling resentment that he would have to go slowly so she wouldn't become too ill.

He said from the doorway, "Sleep now. I won't bother you tonight. I will go to argue with the king once again, but I don't think he will change his mind. He is the most stubborn man in all of England. He insists that someone will try to slit my throat unless I go directly to Cornwall, and he doesn't want that to happen until after I have sired my first—" His voice disappeared in a low curse. He was silent as death, and so was she. "We will leave early, if it pleases you."

She wondered, once he'd gone, what he would have done if she'd told him it didn't please her at all. So the king believed her a liar as well. It didn't particularly surprise her. He was a man, after all. Her stomach twisted suddenly and she tensed. Then her muscles eased again. She fell asleep still clothed and dreamed of her mother, abused by her uncle. What was she to do about her mother?

13

THE MORNING AIR was thick with fog. Daria, bundled to her chin in one of her winter cloaks, waited silently for Roland to finish speaking to the king.

She'd already said good-bye to the queen, kissing Eleanor's hand as she curtsied deeply and thanking her with great sincerity for her care and advice. The queen had even prepared a large vial of the herb drink should she become ill again.

"You will be patient with Roland," the queen had said, hugging her, wishing she could spare her pain but knowing that she couldn't. She would pray that the babe closely resembled Roland; there was naught else she could do. "He is a proud man, loyal, and sound in judgment save, it appears, in the matters of the heart. I heard it said that once, many years before, he gave his heart to a girl who betrayed him. I know no more than that. My lord told me that, saying that Roland had been miserably unhappy at the time, and had confided only that much. It must have soured him, my lord said." She looked smug as she said that, pleased that her husband, King of England though he be, was faithful to her and only to her. Daria nearly burst out that the girl had been Joan of Tenesby, but she held her tongue. Roland wouldn't thank her to tell his secrets.

The queen added, "When you arrive in Cornwall I hope you will visit St. Erth Castle. It is where my husband's daughter lives with her husband, Dienwald

203

de Fortenberry. Philippa is a sweet but spirited child and plants gray hairs in her husband's head. It will be your husband's decision, of course, to select where you will reside until he has managed to purchase this keep of his."

"He just told me of Thispen-Ladock last evening."

The queen said comfortably, "Worry not that he is closemouthed. He isn't in the habit of confiding in others. Roland will come to tell you many things before long. I am pleased the earl did not resist returning the clothing and household goods that you were carrying to Colchester when he abducted you. You and your Roland will be finely prepared once you move into your new keep."

Daria glanced back now, seeing that the pack mules disappeared into the fog, so thick it was. She did bring Roland many things for his new keep. She didn't bring him only herself. No, indeed, she brought him more coin than he needed, and rich furnishings, for at the time he was planning for her to wed with Colchester, her uncle's pride had been at stake. She remembered Roland's sour look at the sight of all the goods half an hour before. She'd wanted to slap him when he said, "I feel like a greedy merchant, traveling about with all my wares. Mayhap I can sell some of this to Graelam."

"The goods are mine," she'd said instead, so furious she was pale with it. "Don't you dare speak of selling what is mine. Some of the materials were stitched by my own mother."

He had looked up at her then, astride her mare, and he'd smiled and said, "Nay, sweet wife, you have nothing now. Did you not understand? All you have is a claim to my name and protection, and were I you, Daria, I would believe that both had a very hollow ring. All this rubbish, well, I shall do exactly as I please with it." He'd turned away from her then to speak to the men.

At least her belly was calm this morning, for she'd drunk some sweet goat's milk and eaten a piece of soft white bread. For that she was thankful. She allowed herself to know some excitement. After all, regardless of what Roland said or did, she was beginning a new life, one she hadn't known would exist such a short time before.

"Are you ready, Daria?"

She gave him a temperate smile. "Thank you for getting Henrietta for me," she said, patting her mare's neck as she spoke. She realized then that Roland wasn't looking at her, rather he was testing and pulling at the straps on her saddle. He looked up at her now as he also stroked her mare's neck, his fingers touching hers. "Your Henrietta is as fat as Cantor. No matter, both of them will be strong and lean within the week. You will tell me if you feel ill."

"Yes."

He lightly touched his hand to her thigh, nodded, and strode to the head of their small cavalcade. Daria turned and waved toward the keep. The queen, in her endless kindness, was very likely still gazing at her from one of the castle windows. She waved even as they rode from the inner bailey of Tyberton. At the last moment, she turned again, and her eyes met the Earl of Clare's. There was no expression on his face; but his eyes—she flinched at the fury she saw in them. She shook off the bolt of panic she felt. After all, he had nothing more to do with her life. He couldn't harm her now. He couldn't strike her ever again. And, after all, if he hadn't abducted her, hadn't brought her to Tyberton, well then, she would never have met Roland. The vagaries of fate were something to think about.

The fog burned off within three hours and the day grew warm. Much to the men's surprise, Roland called a halt. He gave them no explanation, merely rode to where Daria sat her mare and pulled his destrier in beside her. He said nothing, just looked at her.

"Would you like to rest for a few minutes? Relieve yourself?"

She nodded.

"Which? Or both?"

She gave him a look and simply nodded again. He laughed, dismounted his horse, and clasped her about her waist, lifting her from her mare's back. "Are you certain you don't miss the old woman? I could send one of my men back to Tyberton for her if you wish it."

"Nay, she frightens me now. She is no longer steady in her thinking. The earl won't harm her."

"Very well. There will likely be a willing wench to assist you once we reach Thispen-Ladock. Tell me when you are ready to leave again." He turned away to leave her in privacy.

Daria remembered the old woman's mumblings of the previous evening when she'd slipped into the bed-chamber. She didn't cease shaking her head, back and forth, back and forth, as if she had no control over her own movement. "He's not an earl," Ena had said in her sour old voice, plucking up her skirts and shaking her head again. "He's a rogue, not to be trusted, at least not with you, little mistress."

"That's nonsense and I'll be pleased to hear no more from you!" The old woman merely scowled at her and took herself out of the bedchamber. Daria sighed. Just moments later, Ena had slipped back into the chamber and called out, her voice even more sour and shrill, "Not even an earl, and yet ye wedded him! Shame on ye, little mistress! Ye jest wanted a pretty face. Now, the Earl of Clare—he was a fine man . . . a bit rough, but it is as a man should be, not all kind and soft like yer pretty priest . . ."

Daria shut out the memory of Ena's words. She turned and walked back to the horses. She wanted to sit beneath a tree and lean back and close her eyes, but she knew that Roland was likely pacing in his wish to be gone. She stretched, lightly touched her fingers to her flat belly. "I'm ready, Roland," she called out.

But it was Salin, a seasoned warrior of some thirty-odd years, who came to lift her back onto Henrietta's back. His face was intelligent and ugly, his hair thick and dark brown, curling around his large ears. He looked fierce and mean, but his voice was gentle.

"If you wish to stop again, mistress, you have but to call out to me."

"Thank you, Salin."

As she rode behind her husband, their pace slow and steady, Daria thought back to what Ena said once Daria had convinced the old woman to tell her what had happened to Tilda after she and Roland had left her in Daria's place.

" 'Twas a pity," the old woman said. "Aye, a rare pity, and the earl struck her hard, not on her face, for even he thought her beautiful, but he smashed his fist in her chest and cracked a rib, I think, by the screeches from the little slut. He knew it wasn't you, oh aye, right away he knew, and he struck her. The priest—a little worm with no guts—he said naught, merely stood there wringing his dirty hands. The earl then pulled the girl from the great hall and dragged her to his bedchamber. He plowed her good. Her cries were loud, and then there was nothing." Ena had spit then, a habit Daria hadn't noticed before. "She deserved it, of course, the little harlot. You should never have left, little mistress. The earl wouldn't have struck you."

Daria felt bile rise in her throat. She'd been so unthinking, so selfish, and all the while that poor girl was lying somewhere within the castle walls in pain.

"Aye, then the earl told her—leastwise that's what I heard one of his men saying—if she pleased him, he'd keep her, but only if she kept her cries behind her teeth. One of the women bandaged her ribs for her. I hid and he forgot about me," Ena added, her voice filled with her own cunning.

Daria felt the shift in the air. The hot summer breeze had cooled considerably, and black clouds were gathering overhead. It would rain, just as it had in Wales. She realized she viewed the coming rain with little dread, so used to the wet Wales days and nights she'd become during that short week with Roland. But the endless rain had made Roland ill. Her brow furrowed with worry for him.

"What bothers you, Daria?"

She smiled at him, unable not to even though his voice was temperate at best. "It will rain, and I was remembering Wales." Her frown reappeared. "I was remembering that you sickened in all that rain."

"It wasn't the rain that sickened me."

She cocked her head to one side in question.

"I gave you my last tunic and thus wore a damp one for three days. The wet sank into my chest."

"You shouldn't have given me the tunic."

"Probably not, but I did. How do you feel?"

"I'm fine."

He rode beside her, silent now. But she felt the tension building up in him. She waited for his attack, knowing it was coming. Finally he said, "Why did you become ill so suddenly? You said you'd felt nothing before, no sickness of any kind, nothing at all. I don't understand how it could strike you with no warning, and then only after you learned you carried a babe."

"I wondered that as well. The queen said it was probably because I'd been so worried, so drawn into myself with other matters. Once I knew about the babe, once I'd accepted it and recognized its presence, then my body acted as it should."

He only nodded. It would be foolish of him to begin an argument about what the queen herself had said. "There's a Cistercian abbey about three miles ahead. We will beg shelter there for the night."

The abbey was as old as the gnarled oaks that circled its perimeter. Jagged shards of stone were falling from the walls to lie on the fallow ground, unheeded and dangerous to the unwary. When a brother appeared at the front gate, Roland dismounted and spoke to him. Within minutes another came and motioned Daria to follow him. She looked at Roland, but he only nodded to her. The brother led her to a separate building well apart from the main abbey. It was gray and forbidding, low-roofed, its stone walls jagged and crumbling. They walked through a narrow damp corridor with a rough earthen floor to a small cold cell-chamber. It was more than dismal, it was miserably cold, and Daria found she couldn't stop shivering. The dinner brought to her by another cowled brother, who said nothing at all to her, consisted of a thin broth and hard black bread.

She looked at the broth with its layer of grease congealed on the top, felt her stomach churn, and turned away to sit on the edge of the cot. The straw in the thin mattress was molded and damp and poked upward. She moved, but there was little relief.

Daria was hungry and cold and thoroughly miserable. Did God want women to be treated so poorly? Was that why they were shunted to dismal cells like these and hidden away? Were women to be punished for some reason she hadn't been taught?

She fell to shivering again, only to look up and see the congealed soup in front of her. Her stomach pitched, for she imagined herself sipping at that disgusting soup, and to her dismay, she heaved up the lunch she'd eaten earlier in the afternoon, barely reaching the cracked earthen pot in time. Her knees throbbed with pain, for she'd skidded on the hard dirt floor in her rush to get to the pot. She remained on her knees, her arms wrapped around her stomach, trying to breathe shallow breaths, to think of other things, to distract herself. In her mind's eye, she saw the farmer who'd helped her and Roland and she saw him horribly mutilated from the torture the Earl of Clare had inflicted on him. The cramps returned with a vengeance, and she retched and retched, her body shuddering with the effort, and she was trembling with weakness.

"Where is the vial the queen gave you?"

Daria didn't look up. She didn't know why he'd come. She wished he hadn't. She wanted to be alone and she wanted to die, by herself. She wanted no onlookers. She started to answer, but another spasm took her and she was beyond speech and thought for many moments.

Roland felt real fear in those moments, watching her shudder and heave with sickness, more fear than he'd felt the previous evening when she'd been ill. He said to Salin, who stood behind him, "Bring some water and clean cloths. Aye, and some decent food, some hot broth." He snorted at the soup on the tray. "If I had to eat that disgusting swill, I would vomit my guts up too. If the brothers say anything amiss, break their necks."

She felt his hands on her shoulders then and she tried to straighten, to show that she had some pride left, but all she could do was hang her head and tremble and shake, weak as an autumn leaf.

"Come," he said, and efficiently lifted her into his arms. Rather than laying her onto the narrow cot, he sat on the cot and held her on his lap. "This damned bed is harder than a moss-scraped rock in Wales."

Then he paused a moment, feeling the chill of the room.

Roland frowned. She couldn't remain here; she would sicken. The abbot had assured him that his wife would be fine, the lying whoreson. What to do? The abbey had such strict rules about females. Did they believe that the sight of a woman would make all the brothers swell with lust?

He felt Daria twist in his arms with another cramp. He held her more loosely, rocking her, telling her it would be all right, soon she would feel better. She quieted and he drew her more closely to his chest. She was shivering violently, and he cursed softly.

"I'll fetch you the queen's medicine now." He laid her on the cot and rose over her. She looked so pale it frightened him. And thin. He supposed he'd be thin too if he vomited all he ate. He shook his head and set himself to looking through her packets. He'd just given her some of the herb medicine when Salin returned.

Daria saw the look on the older man's face. His eyes were filled with pity. She hated it. She turned away, facing the wall.

"You will lie still for a few minutes, Daria, then eat. I don't want the broth to cool. Salin, I wish to speak to you outside."

"One of the brothers told me the chamber's a punishment cell," Salin said matter-of-factly when they were alone. "It's used only when one of the brothers commits a sin. He's whipped, then forced to remain in one of these chambers for several hours, never for an entire night. He would probably have to murder someone to be forced to do that. And as you now know, the chamber is also used for females who have the misfortune of needing to stop here for the night. Your lady will become truly ill if she remains in there."

"Punishment cell," Roland repeated blankly.

"Aye, I asked one of the brothers when you left. He said your wife would sicken but good if you left her here."

"It's raining," Roland said.

"Aye."

"It's their abbey and we can't break their rules, no matter how miserable they are. However, since I can't take her back to the main building, then I shall have to remain here. Fetch me all the extra blankets you can find. And, Salin, say nothing to our hosts."

The older man merely nodded and took his leave. Roland returned to his wife, who still lay on her side facing the grim rough stone wall, her legs drawn up. She hadn't vomited for a while, a good sign, he hoped.

"Now some broth, Daria."

Her only reply was a groan, but he didn't hear it. When she didn't move, he drew her up in his arms and fed her the broth very slowly, watching her expression.

She finally opened her eyes and looked at him, wonder in hers. "I feel just fine now. It is so very odd, this illness. I want to die and then I want to conquer a new land."

"No fights for you this night. I will remain here with you. If it weren't raining, I would stay outside these dismal ruins, but as it is, we must be glad for the shelter."

He continued to feed her and was relieved when the color began to return to her cheeks.

When Salin returned, his arms piled high with blankets, Daria began to smile. Then she giggled, for only his fierce dark eyes showed over the blankets, and Roland, so surprised at the unexpected sound, grinned at her.

He said to Salin, "See that all the men settle in, and don't let any of them do anything to annoy the brothers. If any of the brothers are bothersome, ignore them. The saints know we wouldn't want any of the monks punished and sent here to share the cell with us."

Roland doused the single candle not many moments later. He lay on his side on the miserably uncomfortable cot and drew Daria against him, feeling her press her bottom against his belly. He bore most of the weight of the blankets. Without thinking, he lightly kissed Daria's ear. "Sleep well," he said, and pulled her even more tightly back against his chest and into the curve of his body.

Daria whispered, "Do you ever snore, Roland? Not just soft sounds, but snorting and blowing like a sickening horse?"

"I don't know. You will tell me."

"You should have to sleep in the same room with Ena. It is a torture in itself. She was once married, you know, many years ago. My mother told me that her husband left her because of the noises she made. He said it wasn't worth having the woman's body if he had to suffer along with it the sounds made by a pig and a horse."

Roland hugged her and she pushed her bottom more firmly against his belly. "Don't do that," he said, his voice sharp with sudden pain. "Don't."

She felt his swelled sex and held herself perfectly still. She didn't want him to humiliate her as he had on their wedding night. The memory of it brought back the pain of his anger, the pain of the shame he'd made her feel. She shook her head even as the thoughts twisted through her mind. She would forget that night. He'd been frustrated and angry and taken it out on her. He'd been kind to her since then. On the heels of those thoughts, Daria wondered if women always sought to excuse men when they behaved like ravening beasts.

Roland woke her immediately the following morning at dawn. The rain had stopped during the night but the sun was hidden behind thick gray clouds.

He was on the point of rolling off the cot, taking Daria with him, when he remembered her condition, and said quickly, "Don't move. Just lie there for a few minutes." He came up on his elbow and looked down at her face in the dim morning light. "What does your belly think this morning?"

"I don't know yet."

"I must go now, but you lie here until Salin brings you some warm milk to drink and some bread."

He eased off the cot, then rose to stand there. She grabbed his sleeve and he turned back to look down at her.

"Thank you, Roland. You are very kind."

His voice was stiff as his back after a night on the sorry cot. "You are my wife. I don't wish you to be excessively uncomfortable."

"Even though you believe it is another man's babe I carry?"

"Sound not bitter, Daria, you have no reason. Rest now, I will see you in a while."

Her stomach remained calm throughout the day. Roland drew their company to a halt every couple of hours, as if he knew almost to the minute when she needed to relieve herself or stretch her back and walk about.

That evening the sky was clear and Roland decided to bypass another abbey whose grim silhouette against the evening sky made even Salin grimace.

"We will camp in that copse of maple trees," he said, and it was done.

He didn't hold her that night, for it was warm and only a mild breeze sifted through the maple leaves overhead. Daria missed him, but she said nothing.

Two days later they mounted a rise, and in the distance Daria saw a beautiful Norman castle, its crenellated towers rising proud and strong above the thick stone walls.

"This is Graelam de Moreton's castle, Wolffeton. We will remain here until I have made our keep ready. His lady's name is Kassia."

"The queen thought you would bring me to St. Erth."

He merely shook his head. "You will doubtless meet Dienwald and Philippa, but we will stay here for a time."

Daria looked around her. She loved Cornwall; it was savage and bleak and desolate, and it awakened all her senses, the stiff breeze from the sea ruffling her hair, its scent clean and salty. It wasn't a lonely place despite the barren desolation. It warmed her, this region, and she knew it as home.

"Is your keep far from here, Roland?"

"Nay, not far." He watched her breathe in deeply. "You don't mind the ruggedness of this place?"

"Oh, no, not at all, truly."

"Good, since it will be your home."

And she was pleased about that. He saw that she was pleased and wondered at the pleasure and anger it made him feel, both at the same time.

Unfortunately, she was doomed to meet the lord and lady of Wolffeton with her eyes closed and her belly heaving, for no sooner had Roland helped her down from Henrietta's back in the inner bailey of Wolffeton than she was vilely ill. She heard a man's deep voice and a woman's higher one, filled with concern and gentleness. She turned her face into Roland's shoulder and heard him whisper, "Don't be embarrassed. Kassia will see to your comfort."

Not ten minutes later, Daria was alone in a spacious chamber filled with bright light from three window slits, its stone floor covered with a supple wool rug

from Flanders. The bed upon which she lay was so soft
she sighed with delight, able to ignore her churning
belly for a few moments.

She heard the woman say to her, "If you are ill
again, the chamber pot is right here. Roland tells me
you have some potion from the queen herself. Your
husband is fetching it for you."

The woman said nothing more until Daria, her stomach eased, opened her eyes and managed to smile.

"My name is Kassia and I'm pleased that Roland
has wedded and that you will remain with us for a
while. And you are with child! How very fortunate
you are. My own babe is but a month old. His name is
Harry and he looks just like his dark-visaged warrior
of a father. It's not fair, but of course Graelam merely
grins in that superior way of his and says he is the
stronger and thus his son must resemble him in all
ways."

"It is good that he looks like his father," Daria said.
"The child is lucky as well. His father will acknowledge him."

Kassia de Moreton, lady of Wolffeton, thought this
a rather odd thing to say. She cocked her head to one
side in silent question. The young woman lying on her
back, her face as pale as the white wimple that covered Kassia's hair, said nothing more. Her lips had
become thin and Kassia worried that she would be ill
again.

But Daria wasn't ill; her thoughts were bleak. She
wanted to cry, but that solved naught. She could see
her mother weeping silently, her hands covering her
face, weeping that meant nothing to anyone, and certainly never changed anything.

"Would you like some warm ale, Daria?"

She forced a smile to her lips. "Aye, and I thank
you."

"Please, call me Kassia."

Downstairs in Wolffeton's great hall, Kassia de Moreton said to her husband, "What do you make of all this, my lord?"

"Of Roland and his new wife? Why, I should like to see her when her face isn't green and when she isn't shuddering with illness."

"She is with child."

"Aye, Roland told me. Odd, the way he said it. Not the way a man should, I don't think."

"You mean, my lord, he didn't begin to strut about like a smug cock with his announcement?"

But Graelam didn't return her humor with his own. He shook his head, looking thoughtful. "Something is amiss. Do you mind keeping the girl here whilst Roland travels to his keep—rather the keep he will soon own?"

"Not at all."

Later in the afternoon, Daria, embarrassed at her illness, emerged from the chamber feeling as wonderful as she had when Roland had become her husband. She was walking down the winding stone stairs when she met him coming up. She stood on the step above him.

He said nothing for a few moments, studying her face.

"I'm fine," she said quickly. "I'm sorry. This illness, it annoys me."

He still remained silent. Then he stepped up onto the step with her, pressing her against the stone wall. He felt the length of her legs, her soft belly, her breasts flattening against his chest. He raised his hand and absently began caressing the line of her jaw.

Daria began to tremble. She couldn't help it. She closed her eyes and leaned into him, wishing he would close his arms around her, wishing he would kiss her and tell her that he'd missed her and wanted her. "Roland," she said.

Roland said nothing.

He continued to stroke her jaw with his callused fingertip. When she unconsciously leaned her face against his hand, he withdrew, turned, and left her. He called over his shoulder, "If you are well enough, there is food for you in the great hall."

The main meal of the day at Wolffeton Castle was served in the late afternoon. The sun still shone outside, for it was deep summer. The hall was filled with laughter and jesting and howls of outraged humor.

Daria sat beside her husband, picking at her food. The herring was delicious, she knew it, but she was afraid to eat because she didn't want to become ill again, at least not today.

She heard Lord Graelam speaking to Roland about the king and his grandiose plans for castle-building in Wales. "So he is now visiting all the Marcher Barons. Eating them down to bare granaries and assessing their strength. Edward has always employed sound strategies."

Kassia turned to her new guest. "Try eating some of this soft bread soaked in the milk."

"I feel wonderful, truly, it's just that I wish to continue feeling this way. I don't like Roland to see me when . . . well, he is very kind about it, but . . ." Her voice dropped into nothing.

"But nothing," Kassia said briskly. "Now, tell me of your adventures. I overheard just a bit, and wish to know everything."

The evening passed pleasantly. Daria had begun to relax and to smile again. When Kassia excused herself to feed her babe, Harry, Roland turned to his wife and said, "Are you fatigued? Would you like to retire now?"

She nodded, feeling weariness tug at her.

Roland looked down at his empty trencher and said, "I will come to you tonight, since you are well. Prepare yourself for me. You belong to me, and if you aren't ill, then I wish to treat you as a man does his wife."

She hated the coldness of this, hated the man he became when he remembered himself her husband.

"What do you mean that I am *to prepare myself?* Do you wish me to stand naked in the middle of the chamber when you enter? Do you wish me to lie on my back with my legs parted? What is it you wish, Roland?"

He sucked in his breath, surprised at her attack. He wouldn't allow her sarcasm at his expense. "I wish you to cease your insolence, Daria. What I meant was simply that you know I intend to take you tonight, so be prepared for it."

"Will you treat me as you did on our wedding night or will you be gentle and tender and call me by another woman's name?"

"There was no other night save our wedding night, damn you! Lie no more, Daria, it annoys me!"

"Then you won't be gentle. You will take me without speaking a kind word to me. You will treat me like a slut who deserves naught else but your contempt."

He leaned close to her, for her voice had risen. "Speak softly, wife. I have no wish for our host to wonder why you become the shrew."

She rose, not waiting for him or one of the servants to assist her. She hissed down at him, "I won't *prepare* myself, Roland, as you so sweetly say it. I don't want you to come to me; I don't want you to treat me like a convenient body to be used by you. Sleep you with one of the castle wenches, I care not!"

She swept from the dais, leaving her husband to stare after her, half of him wanting to thrash her, the other half wanting to rip off her clothing and caress her and kiss her until she screamed for him to come into her.

Under his breath he said, "Damned unreasonable wench."

"I believe I have told you before, Roland, that women are the very devil."

Roland looked at the fierce warrior who sat on his right side and grinned reluctantly. "Your lady is sweet and guileless and tender as a ripe peach. You cannot mean her."

"No, but I did, at one time. 'Twas not too long ago. I misjudged her severely. I hurt her repeatedly. Now I would sever mine own arm before I would see her sprain her little finger."

Roland had nothing to say to that. He merely raised an incredulous brow.

"Your wife is upset—nay, she is but a bride. You are wedded less than a week. She isn't at all uncomely, Roland, and I assume that you found her much to your liking, since she is with child. So—"

"I don't wish to speak of the babe or of her."

"Ah, you simply wish to bend her to your will?"

" 'Tis a beginning. I begin to believe her well-broken, then she flings her sarcasm at my head. I like it not."

"The problem, Roland, is that a man's will seems to shift and change with the passing minutes and hours, particularly if the lady resides in his mind or in his spirit."

"I simply desire her, that is all. She resides nowhere, certainly not within any part of me. Any female would do just as well. Any female would probably do better, since Daria is so ignorant, she must be instructed to . . . well . . ."

To Roland's relief, Graelam de Moreton held his peace. Indeed, he turned to speak to his steward, a craggy-faced man named Blount.

Roland drank another flagon of ale in splendid silence, left to himself by his host. He chewed over his own feelings of ill use at the hands of a female who should be babbling her gratitude to him, who should be fully aware that she would be lying dead in a ditch if it weren't for his generosity. By all the saints, he'd tended her with compassion whenever she'd been ill. And here was Graelam quoting pithy words that were likely from some minstrel's lay. At last he bade his lord and lady a good night and strode from the great hall, his destination his wife's bed.

There would be no sarcasm from her mouth when he covered her.

14

DARIA SAT on a narrow chair close to one of the window slits. The night was clear, a half-moon glowing through an occasional cloud. A breeze cooled her brow. There was a lone dog in the inner bailey below. He occasionally raised his head and barked when a soldier strode by on his way to the Wolffeton barracks. Time passed.

Daria knew he would come to her eventually, so she wasn't startled when the chamber door opened and then quietly closed. Nor did she move.

She didn't wait for him to command her, but said only, not turning to face him, "I mean it, Roland. You will not shame me again." She was pleased her voice sounded firm in the silent chamber. She desperately wanted to look at him, to see if the expression on his face had gentled. His words told her of his expression as he said calmly, "I will do just as I please with you, Daria. You are my wife, my chattel, my possession. And what I please to do with you now is plow your belly."

She was glad that she wasn't facing him. She felt the night breeze flutter through the tendrils of hair on her forehead, felt the softness of the night on her face. "I remember the first time—I loved you so very much, you see, and there was nothing on this earth I wouldn't have done for you. I was terrified that you would die, terrified that you would be gone from me when I'd just found you. I wanted you, all of you, and that

222

night I knew that you would teach me what it was like to be joined to the man I loved, and I was happy. When you were fevered and wanted me—"

"Nay, I have never wanted you," he said, and was thankful she hadn't turned, for she would see the lie in his eyes.

"Very well, you wanted that woman Lila. You didn't hurt me overly, even in your urgency, and I remember those feelings that were building deep inside me, low in my belly, I think, but then when you came into me, there was pain and the feelings left me." Now she turned to face him, her head cocked to one side in question.

"Were those feelings real, Roland? This woman's pleasure you speak about, is it real? I have wondered."

"When you take a lover, perhaps you will learn the answer."

She continued as if he hadn't spoken. "Then, just as you were about to spill your seed inside me, you stared up at me and your hands tightened about my waist, and in that instant I thought you recognized me, knew *me,* knew that you were joined to *me,* not that woman Lila."

Daria shrugged and turned back to the window slit. "Perhaps I was wrong; perhaps I wanted so much for you to whisper my name, to moan that you loved me. Perhaps you will never remember that instant in time when you were with me, when we were together, when you belonged to me—"

He laughed, a low, mocking laugh. "Remember a moment of time that is naught but an elaborate fancy of yours? A fabric you have woven of unreal cloth? If I remember aright, you say that you bathed my sex and groin afterward, that you—my embarrassed little virgin—wiped me free of your blood and my man's seed."

"That's right. There was no embarrassment. I'd cared

for you because you were ill, and I loved you. Aye, I bathed you because I didn't want you to wonder and perhaps guess what had happened between us, and feel guilt and obligation for me. As I told you, it was my decision to give myself to you, and thus the responsibility was mine. But then it all went awry. For that, Roland, I am truly sorry. But the child, *our* child . . . I just wanted—"

He sliced his hand through the air. "Enough of your prattle, Daria. The saints know you've gotten exactly what you wanted, though I cannot see that I am such a prize to any woman. So you have me and my name; your child will have my name. And if it is a male child you birth, why, then, I will have my honor shoved down my throat to the day I die."

"Roland, would you have still not wanted to marry me if I had not been with child?"

He stared at her, for a moment nonplussed. He held himself silent over the words that wanted to pour out of his mouth. He said then, quietly, "If the king had still insisted that I marry you, then yes, I would have."

"And you would have been kinder to me when you took me?"

"Enough of this! I will hear no more of your ridiculous surmises, Daria. I will tell you that now—this instant—I want nothing more than to sink into your soft woman's flesh. Remove your clothing and lie on the bed. Be fast about it, I have not had a woman in a long time."

"You had me not very long ago."

"That duty hardly counted. It was a simple rutting, a coupling to be endured, little more. Perhaps I shall take my time this night and plow you until I am sated on your skinny body."

"No."

He walked to her then and very gently clasped her upper arms in his hands. He turned her around until she was facing him. His breath was warm on her face. His voice was as cold as his eyes as he said, "Never will you refuse me. Never."

"I'm refusing you now, Roland. I must. I cannot allow you to grind me beneath your heel, I cannot allow you to treat me like I'm worth naught but an afterthought."

"I'm the one ground down, Daria. There is a proverb my father used to throw into the breach at odd moments: and that is, a man must begin as he means to go on. You will not gainsay me; you will not willfully disobey me in anything. I won't tolerate that. I have paid too dear to allow it. I will force you, Daria, if you continue to refuse me."

She didn't move. Then, suddenly, she jerked free of him and dashed to the chamber door. She heard the chair crash to the floor, heard him trip over it. She was through the door in an instant, his flung-out arm missing her shoulder by inches.

"Where will you go?" he yelled after her. "You stupid girl, where will you go?"

He heard her dashing footsteps on the winding stone stairs. He heard a loud cry and a thud. His heart heaved to his throat, and he dashed to the top of the steps just outside the bedchamber door. He took them two at a time, nearly falling himself in his haste. Around the curve of the stairs, he saw Salin, consternation writ on his ugly face, bending down to where Daria lay slumped against the stair wall.

"What happened?"

"She flew into me," Salin said. "Then she bounced back and struck her head against the stone." He waited for Roland to rush to his wife, but he didn't come any nearer. He waited another few moments, then leaned down and picked her up. She was conscious now but her eyes were vague on his face.

"You're all right, little mistress," he said. "You just

knocked the breath from yourself and lightly coshed your head." Salin didn't wait for a word from his master. He carried Daria into the chamber and laid her gently on the bed.

"Shall I fetch Lord Graelam's leech?"

"Nay. I shall see to her." Roland waited until Salin saw himself out, and then turned to close and lock the chamber door.

He returned to his dazed wife, methodically felt her arms and legs, then just as methodically began to remove her clothes. She gave him no fight now.

"I struck my head. It hurts dreadfully."

"I heard the crack, but there is naught but a small bruise forming. You're too stubborn to be sorely hurt by a knock on your head. If it hurts you, well, then, you deserve it, I should say."

"Will you force me now, Roland?"

He stilled, frowning down at her. "I don't want you; I should have to think of other women in splendid detail if I wished to regain my desire. As for stiffening my rod, I don't think it possible, at least not with you."

Still he continued to pull off her clothing. When she lay on her back, naked, he rose and simply stared down at her. He studied her, stroking his fingertips over his jaw, his expression one of indifference. "You're so very flat. 'Tis hard to believe a babe lies in that skinny belly of yours. Mayhap the father was a dwarf."

She lurched up, grabbed the half-filled carafe from the table beside the bed, and flung it at him. It struck his chest, splashing a wide arc of water up onto his face.

But it cost her dearly, and she turned away, her eyes closed against the pain in her head. She cared not at the moment whether he would seek retribution or not. All had gone wrong. She heard him suck in his breath; then there was nothing. Finally she heard his footsteps going toward the chamber door. He said as he unlocked and opened the door, "I am leaving on the morrow. You will remain here with Lord Graelam and Lady Kassia. They will take care of you."

She sat up quickly, her heart pounding as fiercely as her head. He would leave her! "I would go with you, Roland. Please, take me with you, don't leave me here, it's not right. I'm your wife! You go to purchase your keep, do you not? I shan't be a problem for you. I won't be ill, I swear it. Surely you will need me, surely—"

"Need you? I need no sickly female to slow me down. You can't control when you vomit."

He didn't look at her again, merely walked from the chamber. She heard him say through the partially closed door, "Cover yourself. The sight of your breasts does nothing in particular for me, but one never knows. Some of Lord Graelam's men might be less fastidious than I."

Daria slowly pulled the covers over herself. Her head pounded from the blow she'd managed to give herself. At least it had kept him away from her, kept him from using her as a man would use a vessel from which to drink and slake his thirst.

He was leaving. Without her. She wondered if he would ever return for her.

She felt nausea, hot and urgent, well up in her. Her head forgotten, she leapt from the bed, making the chamber pot just in time.

Daria was awake when Roland left the following morning at dawn. She'd been awake for countless hours. She stood wrapped in her bedrobe, watching from one of the window slits as he mounted Cantor, spoke further to Lord Graelam, then finally motioned his men through the raised portcullis. As if she willed it to be, at the last moment he turned to look up. She waved to him frantically, wanting to call after him, wanting to beg him to take her with him . . . He turned back again, his expression never having changed at the sight of her.

Daria didn't leave her post at the window. He was going to his keep and purchase it with her dowry. Well, at least her father's vast wealth was bringing a measure of pleasure to someone other than her cursed uncle Damon.

She stood there a very long time. She was still standing there even as the inner bailey of Wolffeton began to fill with people at their work. There were so many people, so many animals everywhere, cows and dogs and pigs. But it wasn't at all like Tyberton or her uncle's castle, Reymerstone. She realized it was because the people were boisterous, loud. They were shouting at the top of their lungs and arguing and abusing each other. And they were laughing. Aye, that was it. The folk weren't doing their work with sullen faces and slumped shoulders and empty eyes. They were insulting each other in great good humor. Daria continued to watch. She wondered at the differences.

Then she saw Lady Kassia de Moreton, her likely unwilling hostess, emerge from the great hall. She was wearing an old gown and a white wool cloth over her head. She looked for all the world like another of the serving wenches. Behind her was an older man with a besotted grin on his face. He was carrying two trays piled high with sweet-smelling pastries, honey and almond, Daria thought, sniffing, her mouth suddenly watering. To her astonishment, Lady Kassia paused, gazed around the noisy den, then whistled as loud as any soldier. Within moments she and the older man were surrounded by the castle folk and their hands were swarming over the warm pastries on the trays.

Daria wished she could whistle like that. She could

let it loose in Roland's ear when he next annoyed her. Daria smiled. It felt odd to smile, she realized, and forced herself to smile even more widely. She would very much like one of those warm pastries.

If her hostess was unwilling, Daria saw no sign of it. At the sight of her, Kassia smiled, waved her hand for her to come to her, then jerked off her white kerchief with the next movement of her hand. She looked like a small graceful dervish, her skirts twirling, her wide sleeves flying away from her wrists.

"Come, Daria, I've saved one of Cook's pastries for you. Yes, sit there and eat. Truly, you must break your fast, 'twill keep your stomach settled. Oh, my dear, you look tired. Did you not rest well? Your lord left very early this morning. You miss him, I suspect. Well, Roland is a handsome lout. When you've eaten, I will present my Harry to you and you must promise me to proclaim him the most beautiful babe in Christendom. He looks like his hulking father, which I insist isn't at all fair, but alas, no one heeds me. Ah, but I told you that already, didn't I? My lord is always telling me to slow down in my speech for I repeat myself."

Daria had no chance to reply to this outpouring, for Kassia had swept away from her, humming beneath her breath, speaking to the serving wenches, laughing, calling for more food for their guest.

By the afternoon Daria wanted to weep with sheer loneliness. How she could be lonely in a castle filled with people who were nothing but kind to her, she couldn't have said, but she was nevertheless. She spent time with Harry, duly complimenting him to his proud mother. He was a beautiful baby, and when she held him, she felt tears sting her eyes. Her babe—Roland's babe—would never know a father's pride. He would know only indifferent kindness at best and coldness at the worst. Roland would never be physically cruel.

She knew that, though she didn't know how she knew it. He had certainly changed toward her.

She turned from her post on the eastern ramparts of Wolffeton Castle. There, in front of her, stood the lord of Wolffeton himself, Graelam de Moreton. She felt a shock of fear at his size, for he was a large man, a warrior of great skill she'd heard Roland say, and his expression wasn't naturally one of gentleness. He looked forbidding and ruthless. She thought of him with the slight gentle Kassia and wondered at it.

"You must be careful," were Graelam's first words to her. "Forgive me for startling you, Daria, but you must take care. You carry a babe, and the walkway here isn't all that wide."

He'd come to the ramparts to caution her to take care? She nodded solemnly. "Thank you, my lord."

Graelam turned to look out toward the sea. "Roland won't be gone long, not more than a sennight, I doubt. Then he will return and carry you back to his keep with him."

Only if he were forced to, she thought, but said only, "Where is this keep, my lord?"

His dark brow raised in surprise at her ignorance, but his voice was calm enough as he said, "Not more than fifteen miles to the northeast of Wolffeton. It's a tidy keep, not sprawling and dominating like Wolffeton with its sheer size, but still it is a home that will see the de Tournay line through many years. Roland is disappointed that it isn't closer to the sea, for he likes the smell of the salt and the feel of the sea winds on his face. The man whose family has held it for many years is old now and tired and has no male heirs. He was great friends with Roland's father and he wishes Roland to have the keep."

"I know it is called Thispen-Ladock and owned by Sir Thomas Ladock."

"Aye, combining the names of the two major fami-

lies who have owned it since the time of William—and
it is between the small villages of Killivose and Ennis.
The largest village is Perranporth on the northern
coast. Didn't Roland tell you of the keep and its
location?"

She merely shook her head, and Graelam continued
after a thoughtful moment. "There is little chance of
invasion, thus there is little need for vast fortifications.
There is little more than peace now, endless peace
that drives a man distracted."

She laughed at his mournful tone and he stared at
her, then grinned. "Mayhap I should move my family
to the Welsh borders. The spirit of fighting always
resides there."

"But only until King Edward manages to clip the
wings of all the Marcher Barons, and he's determined
to do it. Aye, he wants to begin his castle building as
soon as possible. I fear we are to be cursed with
naught but peace in the future."

"Despite Edward's plans, I don't agree. Englishmen
and Frenchmen love nothing more than a violent dispute, and if there isn't a likely one in the offing, they
will invent it and then they will rally about to bash
heads. Don't forget the Scots or the Irish. They'd as
soon cleave an Englishman's chest as speak to him.
Now, allow me to assist you off this precarious perch.
My Kassia sent me up here to be the knight to your
damsel."

My Kassia.

That sounded very nice; it also sounded incongruous
coming from a man who could with a single sword
cleave a man and his horse in two. *My Kassia.*

To Daria's utter dismay, she burst into tears. She
covered her face with her hands, so humiliated she
couldn't bear it, yet the tears kept coming and she was
gasping for breath as she tried to still them. She felt
him then, standing before her for a moment, blocking

out the warm sun; then his arms went around her and he drew her to him. His arms were gentle and his hand was even more gentle as he pressed her head to his shoulder.

" 'Tis the babe that upsets you so unexpectedly. You mustn't be ashamed, Daria, 'twill pass, you will see. My sweet Kassia suffered bouts of very strange feelings, some of them making me want to weep, others making me hold my sides with laughter."

" 'Tis not the babe!"

"Oh?"

" 'Tis Roland, my husband—the man who scorns me, the man who feels nothing but contempt for me, the man who wedded me because the king commanded it!"

Graelam had not a word to say to that. He wished devoutly that he was on the ground at this moment and his wife was magically in his place. He felt awash with protective feelings that he had no business feeling. He could still think of nothing to say to her. Her sobs had quieted but her shoulders still quivered.

"I'm sorry," he heard himself say. "Everything will be better soon." By all the saints, his thinking continued, 'twas a stupid, loutish thing to say, meaningless all in all. When he was nearing despair, she sniffed, trying to gain control of herself.

"No, 'tis I who am the sorry one," she said, wiping her eyes with her fisted hands as would a child. But she wasn't a child; she was a woman grown, who was married and carried a babe in her womb.

"Come," he said, inspiration returned. "Let us go to the great hall. Kassia will give you a goblet of milk. Aye, that will make you feel better."

When Kassia saw her husband's anguished look, she immediately set aside her task of the moment and shooed him willingly away. She escorted Daria to her chamber, scolding her all the way. "Now, you will tell me what is the matter with you. I will fix it if I can, even though my husband is always exhorting me to keep my tongue still and away from others' problems. Come, speak to me, Daria."

But Daria couldn't get the words out. Pride and misery stuck them in her throat. She remembered her unmeasured outburst to Lord Graelam and wished she could sink into the stone floor. She simply shook her head. " 'Tis but the babe," she said, "nothing more, just the babe," and Kassia knew with those few words that there would be no more forthcoming.

"Very well. You need to rest now. I will visit you later with some sweet white bread and some ale, or if you feel well enough, you can come to the great hall. We will see."

Daria, alone again, retreated to her bed and dutifully lay down. She lay there unmoving for a very long time. She was, after all, quite used to being by herself. Odd, though, how all the hours she'd spent alone hadn't taught her patience and serenity. When Daria finally rose, it was evening, and Kassia came for her with a smile. Daria managed one in return and followed her hostess to the great hall.

It was during the long night that followed that Daria came to a decision. Early the following morning, she approached Lord Graelam.

"My lord, I wish a favor from you. I ask that you lend me several of your men."

This was a surprise. Graelam looked closely at the girl standing in front of him, stiff and straight-backed. She was thin, pale, and looked resolute as a mule. "You wish to go somewhere?"

"Aye. I wish to go to my husband's keep. My place is with him, not here with you, a charge on your good nature. He will accept me; he must, for he is my husband. May I please borrow some men?"

What man could deny her such a request? But he

shook his head; he'd promised Roland to keep his wife
safe. Sending her off with some of his men, even
though the area was secure to the best of his knowledge, wasn't what Roland would expect of him. "I'm
sorry, but I cannot. You must remain here at Wolffeton
until Roland returns for you."

If Roland returns, she thought, and turned away.
His refusal was nothing more than she'd expected. He
was a man of honor—and a man's honor only extended to another man, never to a woman.

She kept a smile on her face throughout the morning. Early in the afternoon she approached Kassia. "I
wish to exercise my mare, Henrietta. Should I take a
groom with me?"

It was the perfect approach and she caught Kassia
off-guard. For a dreadful moment Daria feared that
Kassia, rallying quickly, would insist upon accompanying her, but just as the request was about to issue forth
from her mouth, a nurse came into the great hall with
a squalling Harry in her arms.

Daria, two young grooms in attendance, rode from
Wolffeton within the hour. She was careful that Lord
Graelam was well-occupied on Wolffeton's vast train-
ing field and thus didn't see her leave.

The afternoon was hot, with the sun beating down
overhead, but Daria didn't mind. She told her two
grooms that she wished to ride northward along the
rugged coast. Because they didn't know what was in
her mind, they willingly agreed.

Daria stared at the stunted trees that grew close to
the sea. The continuous sharp pounding gale winds
bent them nearly double. They would veer eastward
soon, she reckoned, near Perranporth. One of the
grooms had obligingly told her of the location of her
husband's keep, Thispen-Ladock. They had answered
her guile and questions with prompt smiles and answers. She had fifteen miles to ride. She wasn't certain

how long a time that would take, but she would do it. Her immediate problem was how to rid herself of Graelam de Moreton's two men now that she knew where to ride.

Two hours had passed when Daria, wanting to gnaw on her fingernails, finally called for a halt at the sight of the oak trees. A forest of them, thick and impenetrable. It was her best chance at losing her protectors, and she intended to take it now. She lowered her eyes, resurrecting a modest blush as she told them she had to take her ease for a few minutes in the copse of twisted oak trees.

They looked at each other but said nothing. They could not very well accompany her whilst she relieved herself. Daria thanked them sweetly, then dismounted Henrietta. She looked over her shoulder as she entered the forest, to see the men walking their horses, speaking intently to each other. She smiled. They'd believed her.

She walked Henrietta a good fifty feet into the thick forest, then quietly mounted again. She would be well gone before they realized she'd escaped them.

They, after all, had no idea that she even wanted to rid herself of them. She nudged Henrietta's fat sides and the mare quickened her pace, following the narrow trail through the forest.

Daria heard shouts, but they were far, far behind her. She saw the thinning of the oaks and knew that soon they would be through the forest, and Henrietta, if she hadn't grown too fat and lazy, would easily outdistance the grooms, even if they decided to try to follow her.

She rode another hour, finally slowing her mare's pace when she became winded. The salt air was harsh and wonderful against her face and the smells of the moss and the trees and the sea itself reminded her of Wales.

She saw a rough wooden sign to her left that was printed crudely: PERRANPORTH. She'd made good time. She decided to skirt the fishing village, just in case someone should try to stop her. She was a female alone, and she knew well enough what could happen to her.

She was hungry but ignored it.

She cut eastward away from the sea when the sun began to drift down in the distant west. She saw no one. It was as if she were the only one inhabiting this place. At first it comforted her, made her feel safe, but as time passed, she began to worry.

When she saw the smoke rising in the distance, she felt equal amounts of fear and hope. She slowed Henrietta to a walk, letting her pick her way over the rough, jagged-edged rocks. Finally she dismounted, tied her mare to a lone yew bush, and crept closer. It was a camp. She saw several women and about half a dozen men. The women were preparing the evening meal; the men were lounging about on the ground, some of them whittling, others sitting cross-legged, laughing with their comrades, others speaking to the women, their suggestions lewd in the extreme. Daria wondered if they were Gypsies. She'd never seen any, but it seemed possible. Then a large, well-garbed man came into her line of vision. He was fat and jolly-looking, his bald head shinning even in the twilight.

He spoke to one of the men, slapped one of the women on her bottom, then reached his hand around and slid his fingers down her tunic. The woman squealed and laughed and rubbed her bottom against him.

Daria drew back.

She would continue on around their camp. She wanted to take no chance that they would try to hurt her or hold her for ransom. She'd spent many months a prisoner and had no intention of spending another moment as one.

She got quietly to her feet and turned to walk back to Henrietta, when the mare, seeing her mistress, raised her head and whinnied loudly.

"Shush! Do be quiet, Henrietta!" Daria ran to her mare and scrambled onto her back.

She wasn't fast enough. She heard shouts and calls and running boots. A man's hands grabbed her ankles and yanked her back down to the ground, catching her around the waist before she fell.

Daria fought. She fought without thinking, without hesitating. She fought as she remembered Roland fighting, with her elbow in the man's throat, her knee in his groin, twisting frantically to keep the man from getting a firm hold on her. The man bellowed with pain and rage as her fingers dug into his shoulder. Another man joined him and her arms were grabbed and pinned to her body.

15

DARIA WAS PANTING, still wildly jerking and pulling, but the two men had a firm hold on her now. One of them whom she'd managed to gouge in the throat had raised his fist, blood in his eyes, when another man's voice shouted, "Hold, Alan! Don't strike her!"

"She nearly knocked my throat through my neck, the bitch! How could a little wench know how to do that?"

"Don't hit her," the man said again. It was the fat well-garbed man and he was walking as quickly as his bulk would allow toward them.

Daria quieted, trying to calm her heaving breath. She felt the roiling nausea in her belly, but managed to keep down her bile.

"Well, 'tis indeed a charming little pigeon," the fat man said, coming to a halt in front of Daria. "Pretty she is, and young, very young. Who are you, little pigeon?"

Should she tell him? Would she endanger Roland? What to do? He no longer looked quite so jolly as she'd initially thought when she first saw him.

"No words? I don't think you're a mute, are you?"

She shook her head, then said, "I'm afraid. Your men are hurting my arms."

"True, but you nearly brought my poor Alan low. A man doesn't like to have a woman do such things to him. It humiliates him to the point of violence. Release her, lads, but keep your eyes sharp."

Alan cursed and gave her arm a vicious twist before releasing her.

"Who are you?" the fat man asked again.

"My name is Daria."

"A lovely name, a very nice name withal, but by all the saints, it tells me little. Who is your family?"

"The Earl of Reymerstone is my uncle."

"She's naught but a vain little slut. She made up that name! She's a bitch and a liar!"

"Alan, please, my boy, calm yourself. If she's a liar, then I will return her to your fond embrace. As for her also being a slut and a bitch—well, I don't know if a woman's talents could grant her all that. Just because you haven't heard the name doesn't mean it can't exist. Where does your family live, my girl? Why are you here wandering about all alone? Ah, look at this very fine palfrey. Only fine oats and wheat in her fat belly, not sour swamp grass, I'll wager. You're not an impoverished little pigeon, are you?"

She knew the man could see the lies in her eyes but she couldn't hide her expressions or change them. Finally she blurted out, "I am the guest of Lord Graelam de Moreton! At least I was until early this afternoon."

"Another lie, Master Giles! The little bitch seeks to continue her deceit. I have heard that de Moreton is much pleased with his wife. He wouldn't have a little slut staying there under her nose."

The fat man, Master Giles, didn't chide Alan this time or tell him to be quiet. His eyes narrowed on her face and slowly, very slowly, he raised his arm. His hand was plump and white, too white for a man's hand, Daria thought, vaguely repelled. His fingertips with their longish nails lightly stroked over her throat. She flinched, wanting desperately to jerk away, but she held herself still, trying to remain outwardly calm at least. Suddenly, without any warning, the fat fingers dug with surprising strength back into her neck. The scream that gurgled at the back of her throat was choked down as the awful pain swept through her.

"The truth, little pigeon, or I will rip out your voice from your neck."

He was close to her, and she felt his breath, hot and sweet, on her face. She heard Alan laugh, heard a woman suck in her breath. She felt nausea in the pit of her belly, growing stronger, more insistent, rising, and she couldn't do anything about it this time. "Please . . ." His fingers eased off and she jerked back her head, grabbing her throat, gasping through the burning pain for air.

Then she twisted away, fell hard upon her knees, and vomited.

The fat man looked down at her and his voice was cold with disgust. "When she's finished throwing up her guts, bring her to the camp. I have many more questions for her. Mayhap we have a prize here, a quite valuable prize. And you, Alan, leave her alone; I want none of her pretty flesh bruised, none of her bones twisted. I have a feeling that we're all going to be pleased with her unexpected arrival."

Daria felt a tap on her shoulder. She could picture those fat white fingers and she shuddered, her stomach still roiling wildly.

"If you can hear me, girl, know that I will have answers from you, true answers, else it won't be a pleasant future for you."

At the moment, Daria couldn't even imagine a future, much less a pleasant one. Her belly cramped and twisted. She remained on her knees, her head down, waiting for the nausea to leave her.

"Hurry up," Alan said, and he kicked her thigh.

"Don't bruise me, you wretched animal, you heard your fat master."

"Ha! More bile in your mouth, eh?" Suddenly he

grabbed her elbow and jerked her to her feet. It was pride and nothing else that kept Daria upright.

She would have walked beside him, but he wanted to humiliate her and thus hurried his step, dragging her. She lurched like a drunken sot, trying desperately to keep her balance.

Alan released her when they reached the camp.

"Ah, little pigeon, do sit down." She looked up to see the fat Master Giles sitting on a finely carved chair, chewing on a tremendously large piece of fowl. He looked absurd, sitting there in the midst of a forest, in front of a fire, his ragged men and women around him.

"Who are you?"

"I? Why, I am Master Giles Fountenont, no reason to hide that. I am well-known in these parts—call me a princely fellow, a merchant, a man of a vast array of talents and resources, a man of ample parts as you see, and these are my people, loyal to their bones, all of them. Aren't you, sweetling?" He grasped a passing woman by her arm and pulled her onto his lap. She laughed and turned inward so that he would feed her a bit of the meat. Daria watched her rip off the meat with strong crooked teeth. "Off with you now, and bring this little wench something to eat. I don't want her to starve before I decide what's to be done with her. Aye, she's emptied her belly in fear. We must fill it again."

The woman slid off his fat legs and went to the cook pot that sat amid the fire embers. Master Giles said, "Aye, little pigeon. I am on my way to Truro to my own splendid lodgings there. This"—he waved about the forest—"all this is but a pleasant respite for me."

One of his men grunted and spit out a bone.

The woman brought Daria a thick piece of bread piled high with honey and a goblet of ale. Daria accepted it gratefully. After she'd drunk deeply, Master

Giles said, "Now, the truth, else Alan here will shred your nice gown and acquaint himself with your doubt-less lovely body."

Daria didn't want Alan near her. The truth, then; there was no choice. She raised her chin unconsciously as she spoke. "I am wedded to Roland de Tournay. He left me at Wolffeton whilst he journeyed to his new keep. I missed him and wanted to join him. That's all. I would appreciate your help, Master Giles. My husband's keep is called Thispen-Ladock."

If Master Giles was at all surprised at this revela-tion, he didn't show it. "Ah, so he buys Sir Thomas Ladock's land. Well, well, a nice little keep with more stinking sheep than people to tend them. I have heard of your husband as well, a brave knight, I've heard it said, and popular with our king. Aye, this is an inter-esting tale you tell, little pigeon."

" 'Tis no tale, 'tis the truth."

Master Giles didn't doubt it for an instant. It was simply that he wasn't certain what to do about it. Truth be told, he was nearly bowled out of his chair at who she was. "Tell me, why did you leave de Moreton? And all alone? 'Tis not very clever of you."

Daria swallowed another piece of honeyed bread, giving herself time to think. But there was still no choice. Master Giles wasn't stupid. "My husband had ordered me to remain at Wolffeton, but I missed him sorely. I had to leave without Lord Graelam knowing it."

Master Giles heaved his bulk from his chair. He clapped his hands, and one of the women rushed for-ward. She handed him a wet cloth. He wiped his hands and face on it and tossed it back to her. Like a king he was, a king in a ragged kingdom. If Daria hadn't been so afraid, she would have laughed aloud at his pretensions.

"I will think about what to do with you, little pigeon." He walked away from her, saying over his shoulder, "Roland de Tournay. Aye, this is a problem that requires much thought."

One of the women handed Daria a blanket and told her to stay close to the fire.

But she wasn't to be left in peace. Alan came toward her sometime later, and in his hand he carried a long skinny rope. He dropped down beside her, and when she tried to draw back, he closed his fingers over her shoulder and squeezed.

"Onto your belly, you little bitch."

He didn't give her time to obey him, but roughly pulled her onto her stomach. He grabbed her hands and pulled them behind her. She felt the rope wrapping about her wrists, once then twice. Then he pulled the rope tight and she moaned aloud at the pain.

"There's no reason to torture her, Alan," a woman's voice said. "You're just angry because she hurt you. What would you have had her do—laugh and welcome you with a jest when you tried to capture her?"

Alan made a coarse remark and pulled the rope tighter.

He rose then, and she felt him looking down at her. Finally he left her alone.

Daria didn't move for a long time. Finally she rolled to her side, facing the dying fire. He hadn't covered her and it was becoming chilly. There was no sound now, no movement from the other men and women.

She fell asleep for mere minutes at a time, from exhaustion and from a numbing fear that was fast draining the spirit out of her. Her arms were numb, her position uncomfortable. Since there was nothing for her to do, she knew she had to make the best of it. She stared into the now-smoking embers. She listened to an owl and the answering whinny of a horse. She hoped Henrietta was all right, hoped they'd fed her mare. She hoped the babe was all right. She felt tears sting her eyes and swallowed. She'd meant only to join Roland; she hadn't meant to get herself into trouble. But she had, and now she was a prisoner again. All this tumult that had happened in the last six months of her life made her realize that the first seventeen years of her life had been rigidly uneventful, the days mundane and utterly predictable in their sameness despite the small cruelties of her uncle. She'd always been fed, provided with nice clothes to wear, learned her lessons in peace, and been bored withal. The boredom she'd known during her captivity with the Earl of Clare had always been underlain with fear. Now she'd brought fear down on her head again, all because she'd dashed heedlessly from safety and into the waiting arms of fat Master Giles, who was a villain, and strutted himself about like a royal prince.

She thought of Alan, ragged as the others, only more vicious, and shuddered. She thought of Master Giles and his white fat hands, and his oily voice, and the shudder turned into violent shaking.

The night was dark. Only a quarter-moon shone down from overhead. There was little wind, but still the leaves on the surrounding oak trees rippled and swayed, making her start with fear at the soft rustling noise.

She was awake in the deepest hour of the night, just before dawn, for her bound arms were numb no longer. The pain was excruciating. She felt sorry for herself and wanted to weep. If she could have, she would have willingly kicked herself for being such a fool. She'd left the safety of Wolffeton, and for what? For a foolish girl's dream, a fantasy that had nothing to do with reality. Reality was being the prisoner of a spiteful man named Alan and a fat horrid man named Master Giles. She tried to breathe deeply and slowly, tried to turn her thoughts away from the pain in her arms. In the next instant a man's hand covered her mouth and his warm breath was near her ear. "Don't move. I'm here to save you. Don't make a sound or any sudden movements. Do you understand?"

Daria nodded. The hand raised from her mouth, and slowly, she turned over to look up into the shadowed face of a man bent over her who was a perfect stranger. He shook his head and she saw the sharp silver sheen of a knife. He looked as ruthless and hard as any man to her. Would he kill her? She felt the blade sink into the ropes around her wrists. She was free. She wanted to raise her arms but she found she couldn't. She stared up at him and he saw the pain and helplessness in her eyes.

The man merely shook his head at her again, grasped her around the waist, and lifted her. He walked silent as a shadow, carrying her over his shoulder. He stepped over one of Master Giles's sleeping men and the fellow never stirred.

He strode deep into the forest, then finally stopped and eased her to her feet, propping her up against an oak tree. "There," he said, and patted her cheek. "Work the feeling back into your hands and arms. Stay here and keep quiet. I have a meeting with Master Giles and it won't take very long." He started suddenly, then turned, his voice angry. "Philippa, no, damn you! Stay here with her, do you hear me? I demand that you obey me! By all the saints, I shouldn't have allowed you to come. I'm naught but a stupid whoreson and you're a meddlesome wench. I should have known that you—"

Daria heard a woman's low laugh interrupt the man's harangue; then suddenly she felt her legs simply fold beneath her. She heard the man say something, his voice sharp, but somehow distant from her; then she heard no more.

How much time had passed? Daria wondered. She

didn't open her eyes; she was afraid to. She wasn't on the ground, she knew that. She was lying atop furs, and a warm blanket covered her. All that had happened trickled slowly into her mind. Still she didn't move. There was a lighted flambeau thrust into the ground near her, not really needed now, for the forest was filled with the soft gray lights of morning.

"You're awake."

It was the man who'd saved her. Slowly she opened her eyes. He was sitting beside her. He was younger than she'd first believed, but his face—it was hard and ruthless, his eyes cold. Like Roland's face when he'd come to believe her a liar. Had she fallen into the clutches of another scoundrel?

"Aye," she said, and was surprised that there was obvious fear in her voice. She was swamped with fear and cold. "Will you hurt me?"

His eyes warmed with surprise at her words. He tucked another blanket over her, saying in a soothing voice, "Just lie still. You've been through quite an ordeal. I've had dealings with Master Giles before, and he's a knave and an outlaw for all his pretty speeches and dainty manners. Did he deluge you with pretty speeches? Aye, I can see that he did—there's distaste in your eyes. Now, when you're ready, tell me who you are and how the fat old toad caught you."

He smiled then and it changed his face.

"You really won't hurt me?" He shook his head, saw that she was still frightened, and said easily, "Very well, let me begin. My name is Dienwald de Fortenberry and I suppose I am also something of a rogue, but no, I wouldn't hurt you. I saw you there, saw that villain Alan hurt you, but I couldn't get you free just then. I had to wait until they all slept. It took hours before the guards gave it up. No, I won't hurt you."

"I am Daria de Tournay, wife to Roland de Tournay."

Daria wasn't certain what she expected, but the

man's eyes widened and he stared at her, silent for fully two minutes. Then he laughed deeply. "It is passing odd," he said at last. "Roland—your husband. That defies reason. Yea, passing odd, and it's delightful."

"You know my husband?"

"Aye, he saved my life not long ago. It was a magnificent bit of work—he threw a knife and it sliced cleanly through the fellow's heart. Needless to say I call him friend. So Roland has returned to Cornwall . . . aye, 'tis passing odd. Why aren't you with him?"

And so Daria told him her pitiful tale, not sparing herself, acknowledging her thoughtlessness. ". . . And so Graelam didn't know I'd left. I guess his two men will tell him. He won't be pleased; my husband won't be pleased either."

"Ah," Dienwald said. "Here is my wench of a wife. Philippa, come meet the girl who is wed to Roland."

There was laughter in his voice and Daria wondered at it.

Philippa de Fortenberry was a tall graceful girl of about Daria's age. She was wearing a wool cap and boy's clothing. Her face was intelligent, full of life, and her eyes the most beautiful blue Daria had ever seen. They were her father's eyes. She was meeting the king's daughter. "The queen told me all about you and the king called you his sweet Philippa. It's a pleasure to meet you. I only wish it could be somewhere else."

"Aye," Dienwald said after a moment, "that's true enough. My wench here is the king's daughter, blast her eyes, but since there's naught I can do about it, I shall just have to extol her endless virtues, at least when her father is within hearing. You're wondering how your husband sits in all this, I imagine. Well, Roland had been instructed by the king to come to Cornwall and marry Philippa. Unfortunately for the king and fortunately for Roland, she'd already wedded me. Which leaves two unfortunates, but I am too noble to repine openly. Of course I would have relinquished my claim to her large hand, but she convinced me that if I did so, she would lie down in a ditch and die.''

Philippa de Fortenberry laughed, hissed something in her husband's ear, and punched his arm. "Ignore his braying, Daria. Like most men, he is naught but an ass, a wonderful rogue ass, but nonetheless . . . I am only relieved that we chanced upon you. All is well now.''

"Why are you here? You're female, just like me, and yet you're dressed like a boy and you're with him. I don't understand.''

" 'Tis all right. Dienwald doesn't understand either. You see, my dear, my husband needs me desperately. I tell him what stratagems to employ, how to proceed with his rescues, and how to execute a revenge. I am pleased that he performed according to my instructions. Aye, that foul cretin Master Giles has been served his comeuppance.''

"What did you do to him? And all the others? There were two women and at least six men. And that horrible Alan.''

Dienwald said, "Only one of them died, and the others, well, Daria, I vow they are at this moment more cold than embarrassed. Can you imagine fat Master Giles seated on his princely chair, naked as a toad?''

"You took their clothes?''

Philippa and her husband were grinning like happy fools, nodding together. "Aye, and bound them tightly.''

"That's wonderful! Oh, how I should love to walk up to Master Giles and laugh at him!''

"Perhaps we'd best not this time,'' Dienwald said. "Actually, if you're feeling all right now, we should catch up to your brave husband.''

"You know," Philippa de Fortenberry said, her voice provocative as she swept her thick lashes over those brilliant eyes of hers, "I wonder now that I didn't accept Roland. Ah, such a noble creature, a man of such virile parts, such—"

Dienwald de Fortenberry rose in a swift movement, turned on his wife, and, wrapping his hands around her hips, lifted her high and tromped away with her.

Daria stared after him, disbelieving and sorely confused. These people were beyond strange. Well, she'd met the king's daughter and she was lovely, her blue eyes so bright and vivid and full of mischief and light.

She heard a yowl, part laughter, part fury. Several minutes passed before Dienwald reappeared. He was wiping his hands on his thighs. But he was now all business. "We must leave soon. As I said, we have nothing to fear from Master Giles and his oafs, at least for a while. But why tempt the capricious fates? I wish to deliver you safely to Roland. Where is he?"

" 'Tis not far, I don't think. He went to purchase lands and a keep called Thispen-Ladock."

"Ah, 'tis not far at all. Are you well enough to travel now?" Dienwald helped her to rise. "I do wonder what Graelam will say. I wish I could but see his face now, at this precise moment."

"Do you know everyone, sir?"

"Call me Dienwald. Actually, if you speak to my wife, she'll suggest other useful names to you. As for Graelam, it is his wife who knew me before her fierce husband did. So many tales lie in this head. And now you've added another. Also, we're a small society here in this part of Cornwall, so it isn't passing strange that we're all known to each other. What is passing strange is that we are all friends." He laughed at that.

"I am delighted that something lies in that head of yours," said Philippa, walking up to them. "Let me help you," she added, offering Daria her hand. She looked startled when Daria jerked away from her and rushed away, only to fall against a tree and vomit.

"Goodness, what did you say to her, wench?"

"Nothing, my lord husband. Oh dear, if she is ill—"

"We will travel slowly. There is no need to rush about now. Master Giles is taken care of." He rubbed his hands together and smiled a very evil smile.

Daria accepted the goblet of water from Philippa and washed out her mouth.

"I am with child," she said. "I'm not ill. The sickness comes and goes, and I hate it."

"I must say that Roland wasted no time in his duties," remarked Dienwald. "How long have you been wedded?"

"Not long," said Daria, and allowed Philippa to wipe a damp cloth over her face. "Thank you. That is wonderful. I'm all right now, truly. It's morning and the babe has but told me that he is ready to begin the day. Can we leave now to find my husband?"

She saw Philippa and her husband exchange glances; then Dienwald turned to her. "Aye, let us go now."

"My mare, Henrietta, Master Giles took her."

"I have all of Master Giles's horses. It is sufficient repayment, I think, for his thievery."

"Don't forget all his clothes," added Philippa, sniggering behind her hand.

There were a dozen men in their troop, all of them in high spirits. Daria heard them saying:

". . . Did you see the expression on his fat face when the master told him to remove his tunic?"

". . . Did you see the woman's face when he did?"

". . . I thought she'd faint when he wore naught but his fat white skin."

". . . Aye, that little rod of his shriveled even more!"

". . . Master Giles won't cheat our master again, that's certain!"

On and on it went, and when Daria chanced to see
Dienwald's face, she saw that he looked insufferably
pleased with himself. The heavily clouded skies cleared
and she saw her new host and hostess quite clearly
now.

Philippa had pulled off her wool cap, and her hair,
thick and lustrous and curly, of a dark honey color,
tumbled down her back. She was laughing, riding close
to her husband, and Daria saw that their hands were
clasped between their horses. It hurt her to watch
them. She remembered Wales, remembered those hours
with Roland when he'd cared for her, laughed with
her, complimented her when she repeated the Welsh
words and phrases correctly . . .

Dienwald turned in his saddle and said, "We aren't
far from Thispen-Ladock. Another hour. Do you feel
all right, Daria?"

No, she wanted to shout at him. She couldn't begin
to imagine what Roland would say when she arrived.
She closed her eyes a moment, then squared her shoulders. "Aye, I'm fine," she called back, but Dienwald
wasn't fooled for an instant.

"This is all passing strange," he said in a quiet voice
to his wife. "Roland seduced her, got her with child,
and married her? Why did he leave her at Wolffeton?"

"For that matter," Philippa said thoughtfully, "why
did she leave to come to him? Is she simple? Surely
she would realize the danger."

"Just as you did when you ran away from Beauchamp?"

One of her more colorful adventures that had turned
out marvelously well. Philippa lowered her brow and
giggled.

Dienwald squeezed her fingers and sighed deeply.
"I feel for poor fat Master Giles. I dread to think what
would have happened to the poor old bastard had you
landed in his domain rather than mine."

Daria heard the two of them arguing, insulting each other, and laughing. She wished it didn't hurt. She turned her head and looked toward the vast expanse of rolling green hills and clumps of thick maple and oak forests. There were sheep everywhere, and wheat crops, the waving stalks turning the horizon gold. There were no more barren cliffs or naked rocks and bent trees. The land became more gentle with each passing mile. Daria was tired, she admitted it, but she wasn't about to ask her host to stop for her.

The girl, Philippa, wouldn't ask. She'd keep going until her husband dropped in his tracks first, even if it killed her.

Roland came to the fore of the keep's ramparts at the shout from one of his men.

"A cavalcade comes, master. I know not who it is."

Sir Thomas Ladock, old in heart if not in years, looked toward the oncoming riders, his dark eyes full of intelligence. "Why, I think it is Dienwald de Fortenberry. Do you not see his banner, Roland?"

"Dienwald!"

"Aye, I met the boy some years ago. His banner is distinctive—the eagle and the lion with the clashing swords between them. His father was a wild man— eager to fight, eager to love, and eager to laugh. Is Dienwald like his sire, Roland?"

Roland smiled. "Aye, he is."

"There is a woman—no, there are two women— riding with about a dozen men, I'd say," Salin called out.

Roland stared hard then, for he felt something strange stirring within him. It was an odd feeling; it had come from nowhere that he could fathom. It was simply there, and he waited for the feelings to become something tangible he could grasp. And as the cavalcade drew close, he saw his wife riding her mare on

Dienwald's left. And there was Philippa on Dienwald's right, dressed in boy's clothes, her beautiful hair wild and free.

Roland said in the most measured voice he could manage, "It appears, Thomas, that you are shortly to meet my wife."

"Your wife," Sir Thomas repeated, staring toward the group of riders. "What is she doing with Dienwald?"

"I shudder to know the answer to that."

Salin smiled. "She missed you, my lord. And she came to you."

"Don't think she is so sweet and guileless, Salin. All women carry the scourge of Satan in them."

Sir Thomas, more astute in human nature than he cared to be, turned and looked long at the young man he wished had been his own son.

"Life is vastly unexpected," he said. "Let's descend, my boy, so that we may greet our guests."

16

SIR THOMAS was fully aware that Roland was angry. His entire body had seemed to tighten, to become rigid, as Dienwald de Fortenberry's party had come closer. As the minutes passed, Thomas realized, oddly enough, that the young man's anger was directed at the slight girl astride the beautiful palfrey. His wife, he'd said. But why was he so displeased to see her? They'd not long been wedded. He remembered, so many years before, how he'd not let Constance out of his sight or bed for nearly three months. Something was decidedly wrong here. He looked at the young man, saw that he was closed as tightly as a clam, and said nothing.

Roland made no move toward his wife when the small cavalcade came to a halt in the inner bailey. It was Salin who lifted Daria from her palfrey's back. Roland introduced his guests to Sir Thomas, passing over his wife as if she weren't there. Roland continued to ignore his wife even after Thomas took her hand in his and bade her welcome to Thispen-Ladock. Dienwald's men were directed by Salin to the dilapidated barracks. Thomas led his guests into the great hall of Thispen-Ladock.

"You surprise me, Dienwald," Roland was saying to de Fortenberry, his voice sounding mildly defensive. "You are leagues from St. Erth. What do you here? Come you to spy on me?"

"Now, that's sport I hadn't considered. Nay, Roland, Philippa and I were out a-hunting fat two-legged prey and we found him in due course, along with your sweet wife."

"I see," Roland said, and turned to Thomas. He didn't see a thing and he was so furious that he couldn't bring himself to speak. His wife, his sweet, guileless wife, had convinced Dienwald and Philippa to bring her here to him. Ale was brought. Servants served it. No one said much of anything. Philippa looked from Daria to Roland, and she frowned. Daria sat silent, her head down, her hands clasped in her lap. This was her future home, she was thinking, and she was appalled. Her distress at Roland's obvious cold welcome was momentarily forgotten as she stared around her.

The great hall was damp and cold and its overhead wooden beams so blackened from years of smoke that it was impossible to see the roof. The trestle tables were battered and carved and laden with grease and bits of dried food. There were no lavers, no sweet-smelling rushes on the stone floor, no tapestries on the stone walls to contain the chill. It smelled old and rancid. She shivered.

"Are you cold?"

She looked up at her emotionless husband's voice and shook her head. She offered him a tentative smile, which he did not return. Roland, instead, turned to Dienwald. "Tell me about this fat prey of yours."

Philippa de Fortenberry laughed. " 'Tis a fine tale, Roland."

"Hush, wench, you'll ruin the humor of it if you rattle on. A tussle with Master Giles, Roland, a fat rogue I doubt you've met as yet. The fellow was near St. Erth one fine day when Philippa and I were away from the keep. We believe he probably waited until he saw us leave. He offered goods to Old Agnes and Crooky, and his oily tongue won them quickly to his way of thinking. In short, when Philippa and I re-

turned some two days later, we owned supposedly fine
bolts of cloth and the price paid had been wondrous
low."

Philippa laughed again and said, "When we un-
folded the cloth, we found that it was filled with moths
and they'd already chewed it to bits. You should have
heard Crooky, Roland, he broke into a song that
burned even my ears! It seems that this cloth wasn't
the same cloth Master Giles showed to Old Agnes, the
cloth she had so very carefully examined. This was his
special cloth, for replacement after his sale. Crooky
then noticed that castle goods were missing, such as a
gift from the queen—a beautiful wrought gold laver—
and several necklaces from the king. Oddly enough,
even Gorkel the Hideous believed oily Master Giles.
He was overwrought to learn of his thievery. We ordered him to remain at St. Erth, else Master Giles
might have found his flesh flayed from his fat body."

Who, Daria wondered, was Gorkel the Hideous?
He sounded a monster, with such a name, but Philippa
was laughing.

"So you and Dienwald rode after him," Sir Thomas
said, much enjoying himself. He was sitting forward,
his goblet of ale balanced on his knee.

"Aye," Dienwald said in a mournful voice, "but the
wench here continued to call a halt every few hours,
so it took us many days to catch up to Master Giles."

"I'm not a wench! I'm your wife!"

"Why?" Daria asked. "Why did you keep stopping?"

Dienwald gave her a wicked smile. "My wench
here—my wench/wife—wished to ravish my poor man's
body." He shrugged. "What could I do? To refuse her
makes her cross and peevish—you may be certain that
I've tried it. My men were most understanding of her
needs and of my surrender. Indeed, once when I refused her for the third time, they begged me to give in
to her. Ah, and so I did."

Philippa poked him in the ribs. "You will come to a very bad end, Dienwald."

"I already have, wench. I already have. Brought to my knees by a female giant who could have been used to make two quite proper-size wenches."

"I shall write my illustrious father and tell him that you show me no respect at all, that you wound me and mock me without respite—"

Roland interrupted. "The king, Philippa, is currently visiting the Marcher Barons. We left him at Tyberton, the stronghold of the Earl of Clare. You must hold your complaints against your rogue of a husband until the fall, when he and the queen will return to London again."

"Wound you, Philippa?" her husband inquired, his brows drawn together, his expression perplexed. "I thought it was many weeks now since it was a question of wounding, you being such a hearty wench, and—"

Philippa shrieked at him and clapped her hand over his mouth. "Forgive him, sir," she said to Sir Thomas, "his wagging tongue dances a fine dance at my expense and at your embarrassment."

Daria was smiling, she couldn't help herself, until she realized that Roland was looking at her. Her smile froze.

"So continue with your tale, Dienwald," Roland said pleasantly. "Finally you found Master Giles."

"Aye, in the Penrith oak forest not far from here. He had six men, one of them in particular a vicious lout, and two women. He'd just caught Daria and didn't know what to do with his prize. She was coming to see her husband, Roland, something that Philippa would do as well. Females! They have no sense, no means to weigh what they should or shouldn't do. They act because their feelings dictate they should, and we must come to the rescue."

Philippa wanted to continue with the jest, but she

could feel the awful tension between Roland and Daria. She didn't know why there was such tension between them, but she wanted, oddly enough, to protect Daria.

Dienwald was also well aware of the strain between these two. "That vicious knave—Alan was his name— well, he was brutalizing your wife here—"

"You mean he raped her?"

Well, Dienwald thought, pleased with the gratifying violent reaction from Roland. He raised his hand. "Oh, no, I mean that he enjoyed causing her pain. Fat Master Giles chided him—part of their game, I suppose —and finally she was allowed to sleep, although Alan bound her wrists much too tightly. It was near to dawn that I slipped into their camp and brought her out."

"And then my dearest husband enjoyed himself, Roland. He stripped all Master Giles's people down to their skin and Master Giles as well. He left them there, bound, and we took their horses and their clothes and the cloth we had supposedly bought. Master Giles was bound naked to his throne!"

"A decent-enough punishment, I suppose," Thomas said. "Are you feeling all right now, my dear?" he asked, his eyes on Daria. "A very frightening time for you."

"I'm fine, truly, sir."

"She wasn't earlier," Dienwald said. "She vomited until I believed she would fall over, so weak she was."

To his surprise, Roland's mobile features stiffened and he said, "Her vomiting is due to the babe she carries."

"So she said," Dienwald remarked. "You are to be congratulated for your swiftness, Roland."

"I call it wonderful potency," Philippa said with a mocking voice. "Virility, aye, that's it."

"Yea," Roland said, his eyes on his wife, "I am of a swiftness that defies my own logic."

Sir Thomas cleared his throat. He was vastly uncomfortable with all the eddies of tension that swirled around them. "You are all my guests. Had you come a sennight from now, you would be Roland's guests. Before you arrived, he and I were talking about the renaming of Thispen-Ladock."

"I'm not certain, sir—"

"Be quiet, Roland. You will begin your own dynasty, not continue mine. My family had their due of years. 'Tis now your turn. And that includes a name for your ancestral home." He turned to Daria. "Now that your wife is here, we can secure her opinion."

"I suppose Graelam and Kassia don't know that you ran away from Wolffeton?"

She shook her head. "Not when I did it. They must know now."

Roland felt full to bursting with bile. He said abruptly, "Excuse me, Thomas, Dienwald, but I would speak with my wife. Daria, come with me now. Philippa, I believe there is some bread and cheese. Tell a servant to fetch some."

Daria knew she had no choice, even though now she wanted nothing more than to remain in this dank gloomy great hall and sip at warm ale. She'd been through so much to get to him, and now that she was here, now that he was standing impatiently in front of her, she didn't want to move.

He took her arm and led her to the narrow winding stairs on the east side of the hall. The stairs were very steep and very narrow, more deeply and irregularly placed than any she'd ever before seen. Roland preceded her. There were three chambers along the bleak corridor, and he led her into the second. "This is where I sleep now; when the keep belongs to me—in seven days' time, as Thomas said—then I will remove myself to Thomas' chamber."

"And where will Sir Thomas go?"

"He will leave his keep and journey to Dover. His

daughter lives near Corfe Castle with her husband and many children. Thomas has no male heirs, thus the sale to me of Thispen-Ladock. But he needs coin for his daughter and her family, for his son-in-law is ill. When the king's men arrive from their meeting with your uncle, I will have enough coin to pay him.''

"Will there be enough coin after you pay Sir Thomas for reparations on the keep here? It is in horrible condition.''

It was true; he'd thought the same thing in much more explicit words, but her condemnation but added fuel to his smoldering fire.

"This is your home now, madam. I suggest you change your notions of what is horrible and what isn't. As to the remainder of the funds, why, you will have no say in how I wish to dispose of them. None at all. Now, you will tell me why you so foolishly left Wolffeton. You will make me understand why you scorned Kassia and Graelam and traveled by yourself. You will tell me why your stupidity passes all bounds known to man.''

"I very nearly made it here safely.'' She shrugged, looking toward the narrow window slit that had a rough animal hide nailed over it. "I was merely unlucky to chance upon Master Giles's camp.''

"Ha! I should say you were luckier than God's own angels to be rescued by Dienwald. The world is filled with the Master Giles sort. Do you have any idea, can you begin to guess, what could have happened to you?''

She looked down at her hands, for it hurt to look into his cold, furious face, a face she'd recognized from the first moment she'd seen him so long ago, it seemed. "I was a prisoner for many months, Roland. I had a very good idea of what could have happened.''

"Still, it made no difference to you. Why did you do it, Daria? Why?''

She was twisting her hands together, she knew it, but couldn't still their frantic motion. Slowly she raised her head and said simply, "You're my husband. I wanted to be with you. I couldn't bear to be left in another's care, not really belonging, an unwanted guest."

The ring of truth was unmistakable and he flinched at it. "Damn you," he said, his voice low and deep, filled with frustration. "I can't very well take the time to return you to Wolffeton, not now." He strode away from her, pacing. He turned suddenly. "I suppose when you're not vomiting, you can be of some use here. The saints know the servants don't do a blessed thing, and what they do accomplish needs to be redone."

She said nothing to that, and it enraged him that she would sit there like a stone, taking his fury without returning any of it. "You're naught but a stupid sheep. You will remain here in this chamber until I send for you. Do you understand me?"

"Yea, I understand you."

He wanted her to rest for a while, but he realized that he'd made it sound an order. But he didn't correct himself. It would be wise of her to simply learn to obey him.

But why? she wondered as she watched him stride from the chamber. Why did he want her to stay here alone? Was he ashamed of her? Roland left the chamber without looking back at her. She tried to call up the Roland who'd been a Benedictine priest, the Roland who'd been her friend and her rescuer. But all there was now was the Roland who hated her and believed her a liar. She walked the confines of the chamber for the third time, then threw back her head. Was she to be a prisoner again? She left the room and made her way carefully down the stairs. As she neared the last curve, she heard Roland's voice. He was speak-

ing quietly, but his words seared through her as if he'd
shouted them at the top of his lungs.

"That one night—well, Gwyn, no more. My wife is
here now."

"She's skinny and ye don't care for her," Daria
heard a soft, very feminine voice say. "I saw how ye
didn't want to look at her, how ye ignored her. I'll
keep ye warm, master, and make ye happy. She'll not
mind, that one—"

"That is perchance true, but the answer remains the
same. Speak no more about it, Gwyn. See to dinner
preparations now. We have guests, and I don't wish
them to think this is a pigsty and the food they're
served nothing more than swill."

The girl said something else, but Daria couldn't
understand her words. The girl's name was Gwyn and
Roland had taken her to his bed. He'd seen her naked
and he'd kissed her and thrust himself into her body.
She felt a pain so sharp, so deep, that she couldn't
bear it. Slowly, holding her belly, Daria slipped down
to sit on the cold stone step. A soft keening sound
came from her throat.

It was that sound that Roland heard. He frowned,
then strode up the stairs, coming to an abrupt halt.
There sat his wife, leaning against the cold stone wall,
her arms wrapped around her, her eyes closed tightly.

She'd overheard him speaking to Gwyn.

"So now, my faithless wife, you would add eaves-
dropping to your other talents."

She paid him no heed. He called her faithless? Another low keening sound came from her throat and her
arms tightened around herself.

"It isn't well done of you, Daria. You disobey me
yet again and leave the chamber when I commanded
you to remain there. Well, now you know that I took
the offered favors of another female. You also heard
that I dismissed her because you are here now and I

won't shame you. Just look at you! Sitting there like a rigid statue, bleating like a sheep—"

She flew at him, so quickly that he had no time to find another word, no time to move from her path, no time to see her fist flying toward him. Her fist struck him hard on the jaw and he lost his balance, crashing backward against the stone wall, stumbling on the lower stone step. She struck him again, yelling at him, "Bastard! Whoreson bastard! I'm not a bleating sheep! I'll not let you judge me so poorly again!" This time she struck him with her fist low in the belly, and he jerked forward even as he went crashing down the remaining few steps to sprawl on the stone floor of the great hall.

She was on him in an instant, coming down onto her knees, striking his chest with her fists, yelling at him even louder. "I hate you! Unfaithful knave! Unspeakable cur! God, I hate you!"

Roland had knocked himself silly. It took him several moments to clear his head sufficiently to realize what was happening. Unlike Daria, he saw that the hall was filled with a score of people, Thomas and Dienwald included, and they were struck to silence by what they saw. They were watching his wife flail at him. They heard her screaming at him. Then he felt her hands go around his throat, and she was squeezing as hard as she could, her body trembling with the effort, silent now, so beyond rational thought that her eyes were blank and faraway.

Then she erupted again, even as she raised his head only to bang it down again to the stone floor, "You share what is mine and mine alone with another woman! You break faith with me, you break your vows! Then you call me a faithless wife! You call me a stupid sheep for saying naught about it! Well, no more, Roland. I'll kill you, I swear it, I'll kill you if ever you even touch another woman!"

No longer was she a stupid sheep, that was true. No longer was she a bleating sheep. He felt her fingers digging into his throat but she didn't have the strength to choke him, though her desire was great. He forgot about their audience. He slowly brought up his arms and grasped her wrists. He pulled them away from his throat.

She was trembling, shaking, but she was still screeching at him like a fishwife. "No more, Roland! I'll kill you, I'll kick you in the groin! I'll—"

He jerked her off him; then as gently as he could, he lowered her onto her back. He was over her in an instant, kneeing her legs apart, coming down to lie on top of her.

It was then Daria heard male laughter followed by more male laughter, and that was followed by lewd remarks, and then there was a woman laughing. It was then she saw all the people looking at them. It was then that she realized what had happened, and she looked up into her husband's face, her own as white as her belly.

"Will you hurt me now?"

"Hurt you? What do you think you've been doing to me? My head isn't a ripe melon, even though you seek to crack it open! Nay, even though you are a vicious killer, I shan't throttle you as you were trying to do to me. Now, wife, I think you've humiliated both of us quite enough. You've given a fine exhibition to everyone. I'm going to pull you up now, and if you dare attack me again, it will go badly for you. Do you understand me?"

"Aye, I understand."

He released her, and hauled her to her feet. In the next instant she drove her knee into his groin. Roland jerked upright, stared at her in stunned, horrified silence, then felt the waves of nausea flooding through him, felt the debilitating pain begin to grind him down.

He grabbed his belly and sank to his knees, his body heaving.

The male laughter stopped. The lewd jests stopped. Daria, aware now of what she'd done, raised her head and saw that everyone was silent, staring at her, their expressions appalled and disbelieving. She was beyond thought now, beyond anything in her experience that could break through and guide her, and thus picked up her long skirts and ran from the great hall.

She heard Philippa shouting out her name, but she didn't slow. She ran and ran, stumbling once on uneven cobblestones, ran beneath the raised portcullis, through the narrow high tunnel that connected the inner bailey to the outer bailey, ran until she was at the open front gates of the outer bailey, and still she ran, holding her side and the ripping pain that was roiling through her. She was outside the keep now, and there were many people, but none tried to stop her. They paused in their duties and stared after her and called to her, but none made a move after her.

She ran until her legs collapsed beneath her, and then she fell on a soft grass-covered incline and rolled over and over until she reached the curved bottom of the ditch, and she lay there, not moving, not able to move in any case. She gasped for breath, afraid to move now because she was aware of the babe in her womb and she felt terrified that she'd harmed it with her mad dash from the keep, and her fall. She lay there until her breathing calmed. She lay there feeling the warm sun soak through her clothes, warming her flesh. She lay there knowing that when she did move there would be consequences that she didn't want to face. She quite simply wanted to die.

But she didn't die.

When Roland saw her lying there on her side, her cheek pressed against the soft green grass, her eyes closed, he thought she was dead. Fear raced through him and he skirted the steepest part of the incline until he could run to her without falling or skidding.

He dropped to his knees beside her, but he was afraid to touch her, afraid that she was hurt in some way he couldn't see.

"Daria."

She didn't want to open her eyes, but she did. Slowly she raised herself until she was on her knees in front of him.

"You're all right?"

She looked at him straightly, unaware of the grass stains covering one side of her face, unaware that her hair was filled with grass and twigs and was hanging loose down her back and over her shoulders, unaware that her gown was ripped and one sleeve hung down to her elbow.

And she said, "I hope you're no good to Gwyn anymore. I hope you're no good to any woman anymore."

Roland sucked in his breath, all his fear for her dissolved at her words.

She was gasping out the words, her eyes dilated, unheeding of him or what he could do to her. "I hope you return to the Holy Land and that you find Lila and Cena and tell them that you're no longer a man and that—"

He didn't strike her. He clapped his open hand over her mouth, shutting off her spate of words.

"Enough, damn you." He pulled her against him and his face was close to hers, his breath hot on her flesh. "Now, madam wife, I am taking you back. You have caused quite a commotion. You have caused me no end of trouble, what with your violent attack on me and your irritating dash from the keep. You left Philippa telling me that your violence was caused by the babe, that you weren't thinking clearly because of it . . . by the saints, she was trying to protect you, even after you tried to bring me down."

"I did bring you down. You fell on your knees and I was the one who made you do it."

"Daria, I do recommend that you close your mouth and keep it closed. I would beat you, doubt it not, but I would do it carefully so that your child isn't harmed. Indeed, I would be more careful than you . . . tumbling down this incline like a half-wit. You defy logic, wench, you surely do. Now, will you come along with me willingly or do I beat you here?"

She wondered if he truly would strike her. If he did, would she cry and plead with him to stop? Would she grovel and whimper at his feet? She wouldn't. She would die before granting him such pleasure. "When you beat me, will you use your hand or a whip?"

Roland couldn't believe her words. Nor could he believe the entire situation. Well, she'd finally shown spirit, more than he'd ever wished to see, more than his aching groin would ever have wanted. As to his emotionlessly spoken threats, it rocked him to his core that such things had come from his mouth. Never in his life had he struck a woman; he believed men who hurt women to be despicable, animals, of no account at all. But here he was telling her that he would beat her, and she'd accepted it, accepted it even though she should know he wasn't that kind of man, for she'd traveled through Wales with him, known him to prefer laughter to scowls, good dirty fighting to torture and cruelty. "I don't use whips, even on recalcitrant animals."

She dusted off her gown and straightened her back. She didn't speak again, nor did she look at him. She got to her feet and started walking back toward the keep. She felt her muscles begin to tighten and knew she would be painfully sore before too many more hours passed. Perhaps more than her muscles would be sore. Perhaps, if he beat her . . .

She noticed sheep now, so many of them that the air was filled with their scent. The trees that covered the gentle hillocks were green and thick and straight. The land was beautiful and soft, not harsh and savage and barren like the northern shore.

"How far inland are we here?"

Roland gaped at her. Was she simple, with this abrupt change of tone and subject? "About twelve miles."

"I miss the smell of the sea."

"So do I. Keep walking."

"Will you humiliate me in front of Dienwald and Philippa?"

"You attacked me in front of them. Why shouldn't I do the same to you?"

"Why did you take that girl to your bed?"

Roland shrugged. It was difficult to give an outward show of indifference, but he managed it. He shrugged again for good measure. "She is pretty, clean, and enthusiastic. I was in need of a woman, and she had many talents. She was available and willing."

"I see. So a wife is just another vessel for you to use. Every woman—every *comely* woman—is to be available, as is your wife. I don't like it, Roland, but I see now that there is naught I can do about it."

"You overheard me tell Gwyn that I wouldn't come to her again, that I wouldn't because my wife had come."

"I see. So it is in your man's code of honor not to disport with other females when your wife is present. I am gratified, sir, by this show of chastity and male honor. However, I care not now what you do. Take all the wenches that appeal to you, I care not. It keeps you from me, and I thank the saints for that. You've done naught but hurt me—"

" 'Twas just once, damn you! Our wedding night. 'Tis true, I wasn't as gentle as I could have been, but—"

"Nay, 'twas twice. Our wedding night and that first time, in Wrexham."

He cursed, long and fluently and loudly. Her words pushed him beyond sanity, beyond reason, and he was a man, astute and logical and not at all mean-spirited. Until he got near her, his wife, his damned lying wife.

"I should send you back to Wolffeton, but I doubt Graelam would want the keeping of you now. By God, he'd have to have you watched just as the Earl of Clare did. Nay, I shan't ask that of him. I wonder. Perhaps after several weeks, would you try to convince him that the babe you carry in your womb is his?"

He caught her wrist before she could strike him. He hauled her close and said very softly, not two inches from her nose, "Do not strike me again, Daria. I give you fair warning. Never again."

17

To the surprise of all the visitors present, the evening meal was delicious. The herring was baked to perfection, tender as snowflakes melting in the mouth, the slabs of beef spicy with herbs Daria couldn't identify. Whoever was the cook here deserved to be praised. The myriad rush torches that lined the stone walls cast vague shadows and softened the harshness of the great hall, and in this gentle light the lacks weren't all that noticeable. Indeed, Daria thought as she was savoring a particularly fine bite of stewed potatoes and turnips, it was warm and cozy. She swallowed blissfully, then grinned when she chanced to see Sir Thomas smiling at her.

"You are surprised at the quality of my food." He shook his head. "At my age, food is one of the few pleasures left. The cook is an individual I would send my men to protect. Aye, I wonder what your husband would say if I asked to take my cook with me when I leave."

"I think I should hunt the fellow down, Sir Thomas, and offer him the world to remain."

"Where did you find this god of a cook, Sir Thomas?" Dienwald called out over a mouthful of sweet almond bread dripping with dark amber honey. "Can I steal him away with me under the cover of darkness? Or perhaps steal him under cover of my large and beautiful wife?"

Daria laughed, as did everyone else. She hadn't

270

believed earlier that she would ever want to eat again or even smile again, and here she was eating her head off and laughing until her ribs ached.

Tomorrow, she knew, Dienwald and Philippa would return to St. Erth, and she would be alone with her husband. She smiled at Sir Thomas. Perchance he'd choose to remain longer. At least he would be here until the king's men arrived with her dowry.

"Actually," Sir Thomas said, lifting a delicate herring fillet for all to see, "my wondrous cook is a bent old crone who tells me that her great-great-great-grandmother cooked for the Conqueror himself. Supposedly it was Mathilda herself who gave instructions to that long-ago Alice. You needn't worry that I'll steal her or that Dienwald will whisk her away. I believe all her magic lies here at Thispen-Ladock."

"I'm devoutly thankful for that," Daria said.

Roland was chewing thoughtfully on a piece of braised mutton. It was so tender that his mouth watered even as he chewed. "I don't know how you remain so thin, Sir Thomas. A man could become a stoat quickly enough."

"A young man newly wed, Roland? Fie on you! You will be far too busy, far too occupied with your new bride, to gain flesh on your belly."

"Aye, 'tis true," Dienwald called out. He stood suddenly and pulled up his tunic, baring his belly and his chest. "Look and feel pity for me, Roland. I was once possessed of a magnificent manly body, just weeks ago, in fact. But now my ribs stick out like barrel staves, my belly sinks into my back like a riverbed in a drought, and all because of the demands placed on me by my new wife. She works me harder than the meanest of our serfs work our oxen. This marvelous food keeps me alive, Sir Thomas, to toil at least another day in her demanding service. Then once again I shall have to avoid strong winds. And—"

Suddenly, without warning, Philippa de Fortenberry jumped to her feet, grabbed her husband's neck by his tunic, and stuffed a large handful of green peas into his open mouth. He sputtered and choked, spitting the peas in every direction. He turned on his wife, blood in his eye, and yelled, "My strength after this meal is awesome, Philippa. I can even reduce you, an oversize female with the strength of a female water buffalo, to begging within seconds."

Daria shook her head, she was laughing so hard. The two of them never seemed to tire of baiting each other.

"Begging for what, Dienwald?" Sir Thomas asked.

"Why, begging me to pleasure her, naturally."

Philippa squeaked, scooped up another handful of peas, but her husband was quicker. He reached down, grabbed her by the waist, and threw her over his arm. He kissed her then, hard and long, in front of the entire company. When he finally released her, she was laughing and pummeling at his chest. Only Daria saw the desire in her eyes, the flush on her cheeks, the softness of her open mouth as she looked into her husband's face.

Daria turned away, unable to bear their unity. She wondered if perhaps Philippa had known that Dienwald was meant for her and only for her, when she first saw him. The men were cheering and shouting out jests and trying to catch the serving wenches who were near to them, and they were successful most of the time because the women were laughing just as hard as the men and wanted to be caught and wooed so humorously.

Roland remarked to her, "There was a time when all wasn't a rainbow sky between them. But I remember that the anger that flared was all on Dienwald's side. As I recall, he was furious that she dared to have the king for a father."

Daria's head whipped up and she stared at him. "That makes no sense."

"When you come to know Dienwald, you will understand. Now, Daria, I have promised a game of chess to Sir Thomas. There is no reason for you to begin your duties as mistress of this keep until the morrow."

He was dismissing her, and she rose stiffly, both from hurt at his careless rejection, and from her sore muscles, and bade her good-nights.

Sir Thomas watched her walk slowly and gracefully from the great hall. Then he noticed she was limping slightly and he frowned.

"She fell," Roland said shortly, his eyes also following his wife's progress.

"Aye, so I heard from one of the women."

Roland cocked a black eyebrow.

"I heard she was running like a terrified little hen from the fox."

Roland said nothing.

"Did the fox catch the hen?"

"No, the hen brought herself low with no help from the fox. I see that Dienwald and Philippa are unaware of us, Sir Thomas, and likely to remain so. I venture to say they will shortly retire abovestairs. Shall we go to the chessboard?"

Daria was awake when Roland came into the chamber, quietly closing the door behind him, but she held herself very still. She didn't want to argue with him, didn't want to hear his cold emotionless orders, or, perhaps worse, his silent indifference, his contempt. She could see him clearly from the silver stream of the moonlight through the window slit; he was disrobing and she couldn't keep herself from watching him if she'd been ordered to. His movements were beautiful, supple and lithe, and as he turned or bent down, moonlight glittering off his back, his arms, the long shadowed line of his leg, she felt his grace touch her deeply.

She didn't move. She thought she heard him sigh, but wasn't certain. The bed gave under his weight. He settled on his side, his back to her. Within moments she heard him breathing deeply and evenly. Still she didn't move. She awoke during the night to the sound of rising winds. A storm would probably blow in from the sea before morning. But it was cold now, and would become colder soon. Slowly Daria curled up against her husband's back. His legs were drawn up and she fitted herself against him, snuggling closer, feeling the warmth of him, and settled her cheek against his back. She lightly laid her arm over his side onto his chest. His breathing didn't change.

She kissed his back and pressed closer. His flesh was smooth and firm and the muscle beneath solid. He was naked. She was wearing a shift, but it had ridden up and her legs were bare against his. In the dark, in the deep silence of the night, she could pretend that he loved her, pretend that he was once again the Roland who'd come to her as a priest, who'd saved her from those two bandits in Wales. Not that other Roland who was her husband.

She kissed his back again, savoring the feel of his flesh, the scent of him, the taste of him. She wished she could tear off her shift and be naked against him, but she couldn't. She couldn't imagine what his reaction would be. He would leap from the bed, cursing her, or perhaps he would take her, as a man could a woman, and he would hurt her.

She closed her eyes against that pain. This moment of time was hers and she intended that it be what she wanted it to be. She would deal with tomorrow when it came. She fell asleep unaware that his hand clasped hers now.

Roland was fully aware of softness and warm breath against his back. He awoke alert, his eyes wide in the dull light of dawn. It wasn't yet raining, but the winds

were high. Daria was pressed against his back. He felt
the smoothness of her bare legs against his. He closed
his eyes a moment, savoring the feel of her. He held
her hand against his chest, his fingers lightly caressing
hers. He supposed he'd held her hand all night, but he
hadn't awakened before. He'd accepted her closeness,
something that was odd, for he was a light sleeper,
having learned through the years that a man drawn
deep into sleep was very likely a dead man soon enough.
But she'd lulled him.

He was hard as a stone. He wanted to laugh at
himself, at his randy body. Instead, he grimaced even
as he very slowly turned to face her, drawing her close
against him. Her shift rode higher; he felt her thighs
against his. Felt her warm breath against his throat,
her long hair tangled over his shoulder and chest. Her
legs moved, twisting until his covered hers. He closed
his arms around her back, drawing her closer to him.

His sex was near to bursting. He could simply ease
her onto her back, come over her, and slide deep
inside her, all within the space of a moment. The
thought nearly sent him over the edge. But no, she
wouldn't be ready to accept him. She'd be tight and
cold and he would hurt her as he'd done the night of
their wedding. No, he would control himself. He would
make her ready; he would have her moaning for him
before he sank his rod deep inside her. He would give
her a woman's pleasure, he would make her tremble
with the power of it, he would make her whimper as
the spasms gained control of her, and he would control her and her body, and when she accepted him
through her pleasure, then and only then would he
take her. And she would accept him willingly because
she would have no choice, for he would have con-
quered her body.

His touch light as a moth's wing, Roland's fingers
stroked over her back, smoothing the shift over her

buttocks, his fingers curving inward, and he realized
he hated the shift, hated anything between his fingers
and her flesh. He shoved the stout linen upward,
pausing only when she moaned against his throat, then
burrowed more closely against him. His fingers splayed
over her naked buttocks. In that moment, he was
certain his seed would burst from his body. He couldn't
believe he was so sorely tried at the mere touch of her
flesh. He closed his eyes against the rampant wild
sensations until he regained some semblance of control. He wanted to touch her, ease his fingers inside
her and feel the tightness of her, the damp that his
caressing would bring to her.

His fingers closed between her thighs, and to his
surprise, her thighs opened and she was pressing back
against his fingers, her back arching slightly, pressing
her breasts more firmly against his chest. Was she
awake? Did she know what she was doing? But then
she sighed softly, and her buttocks were soft and relaxed again, and her breath was deep and even once
more. He wondered at the dreams that were coming
into her mind now, and he smiled, a nearly painful
smile as he gently eased his middle finger inside her.
He sucked in his breath, holding his finger still with a
will he didn't know he possessed. The feel of her—it
was something he couldn't have imagined, and yet
he'd known many women, felt their bodies and caressed them with his fingers and his mouth, knowing
them as well as it was possible to know a woman, but
this was beyond his experience, beyond anything he'd
ever felt, and it frightened him. Suddenly he shoved
his finger upward, deep inside her, and he felt her
muscles clenching around him, tightening and squeezing, and a harsh moan came from his mouth.

"Daria," he whispered, and he was kissing her temple, her cheek, nudging back her head with his other
hand, kissing her lips, her throat. And his finger moved

deep inside her, widening her for him, feeling the heat of her and wanting his member where his finger was, and his belly was cramping and hurting, his sex heavy and aching with his need. She was ready for him now, soft and moist, and all he had to do was ease her onto her back and draw her thighs apart . . .

But still he held back, even though he couldn't stop kissing her. He eased his finger very nearly out of her, then pushed and probed, sliding in deeply again, and she groaned, her body stiffening, then shuddering slightly. He wanted to shout with the pleasure of it. Then he touched her woman's flesh and found it hot and swelled. He couldn't wait further. He eased her onto her back and came over her, still kissing her face, and then he reared over her, coming up to his knees.

"Daria, wake up!"

Even as she focused on him over her, he pulled her shift up, baring her breasts.

Just as suddenly, he was covering her, and he was kissing her breasts, kneading them gently, sucking at last on her nipple, and she wanted to scream with the sensation of it. The dream had been making her wild, but the reality of Roland and his fingers and his mouth knew no comparison. She wanted him, no dream of him, no soft illusion of him.

But he couldn't wait, simply couldn't, and he slid down her body, parting her legs wide, and his mouth was on her as she wailed, a high, thin sound, and he smiled even as he felt himself near to bursting. She was tightening all over; he felt it, felt her thighs tensing around his shoulders, felt her fingers clutch his hair, heard the tearing moans from her throat. He raised his head just a bit, his breath hot on her swelled flesh, and he commanded her, "Daria, let go now. Let go and come to me."

She didn't understand his words, but her body did. Her flesh heaved with the knowledge, she opened the

very depths of herself to him, fully and eagerly, and in
the giving she found a pleasure that neared pain, so
intense it was, so powerful and demanding, so urgent.

She screamed, but his hand was covering her mouth,
and it freed her to cry out again and again, and her
body bucked and heaved and she felt damp with sweat
and loose and apart from herself, but it didn't matter,
nothing outside them mattered, and it just went on
and on. He raised his head and she wanted to weep
with her body's disappointment, but only for an instant, for his hands were sliding beneath her hips,
lifting her to him, and in the next instant his member
was thrusting deep, filling her. She cried out again,
her hips rising to pull him deeper, and the shocks of
pleasure renewed and pulsed through her and her
fingers dug into his arms, and she was lurching up to
kiss him, and he met her then, even as he came into
her, only to nearly withdraw again, and when he emptied himself into her, he covered her mouth with his
and she took his moans and knew the dream could
never rival the man.

He fell on top of her, his member still deep inside
her. Almost as soon as she felt the wonderful weight
of him, he pulled back and she wanted to protest, but
he was mumbling, "I don't wish to hurt your babe,"
and then he brought her with him onto her side and he
was still inside her, only not so deep now, and she felt
his words sear through her mind. *Your* babe. She
wanted to weep with the pain of it, but her body was
languid and soft and his body was against hers and he
was gently rubbing his hands up and down her back,
over her side, lightly touching her belly, then moving
quickly away, to her breasts, weighing them and caressing them lightly, as if he'd guessed at their new
tenderness.

"You liked that," he said, nibbling her earlobe.
"You liked that very much."

"You're inside me, Roland. That is wondrous . . . you're a part of me."

"Aye, and I always will be. Every night I'll come deep inside you and you'll cry out to me to bring you more, and I won't disappoint you, Daria. Never again will you accuse me of misusing you. You now understand a woman's pleasure. I'll not let you forget it, not let you think another man can give you what I can. You screamed when I brought you to your release, and you screamed again when I came inside you. I liked that very much. Your breasts are as soft as the flesh between your white thighs. The way you feel . . ." His voice hitched and he fell silent.

She was exhausted from the force of this pleasure, and he seemed to know it. "Sleep now, dearling. Sleep."

And she did, knowing that he held her tight, knowing that in this she had pleased him, yet knowing too that in the end, nothing had changed between them. Except perhaps . . . aye, now perchance he would come to her with gentleness as he had tonight and there would be no more distrust and anger. He would come to her with pleasure for both of them.

When she awoke some hours later, she was alone. There was a basin of water and she quickly bathed and dressed and made her way down into the great hall. It was still fairly early and Dienwald and Philippa were seated at one of the trestle tables, eating and talking to Roland and Sir Thomas.

Dienwald looked up and saw Daria staring fixedly at her husband, her face flushed, her lips slightly parted. His grin was wicked as a devil's as he said loudly to his wife, "Would you observe that expression, wench . . . nay, not your own, Daria's. Now, I would say that she was well-pleasured last night. Is it true, Roland? Did you gladden your wife?"

"I cannot control him, Daria, forgive me. But I can

offer him food so that he can keep up his strength and his mouth closed. Here, husband, chew on this wonderful honeyed pastry."

Just as suddenly, the odor of the sweet pastry sent her stomach roiling wildly and she gasped in distress and flew from the hall.

When she returned, Roland handed her a goblet of fresh milk. "Drink this slowly and then eat some of this bread. Alice told me it was just for you, made with special herbs that came from her great-great-great-grandmother, and it would make the babe happy as a little stoat."

Daria said nothing. She was embarrassed. The bread did settle her belly, and as she chewed slowly, she listened to her husband say, "I would certainly enjoy you extending your stay, Dienwald. I would put you to work. The eastern wall needs more men and labor than I have at present."

"You mistake the matter, Roland. I am a lazy lout, of no account at all. 'Tis my sweet wife here who is the worker. She pines to work. She languishes when she is not about some task. And she rides me constantly now to make repairs on St. Erth. She wears me down. Alas, Roland, I must return her to her home. I fear I cannot leave her to direct your reparations, for my son, Edmund, is more and more on her mind."

"Aye, the officious little tadpole," Philippa said fondly. She turned to Daria. "Once you've settled in and Roland grows bored with his domestication, then you must come to St. Erth and see this hornet husband of mine in his nest. It's a pleasing nest and he carps not overly."

"My uncle has no friends," Daria remarked later to Roland as they watched Dienwald, Philippa, and all their men ride from the keep. "No neighbor wants to see him even from a distance. He was always fighting, arguing, trying to steal their lands, debauch their daughters and wives, and I used to wonder when one of them would sneak into Reymerstone and slay all of us in our beds."

"The king's uncle, now dead, God bless his soul, bound men together here in Cornwall with his smooth wit and his unspoken power. Aye, if any of the lords hereabouts wanted to wage war on his neighbor, he would regret it, for the Duke of Cornwall acted swiftly. Dienwald was the only renegade, and he was only an occasional renegade. The duke chose to be amused by him. And once Dienwald was wedded to the king's daughter, his fate was sealed. How do you feel, Daria?"

"Fine. Thank you for the milk and bread."

"Actually," he said, frowning into the distance, not looking at her, "I meant from last night. Was I too rough with you? I have heard it said that a woman's breasts grow very tender. I did not mean to give you pain, if indeed I did."

She shook her head quickly, and Roland, not hearing her speak, slewed his head around to look down at her. Her face was flushed.

His expression hardened. "You won't now pretend that you were forced or abused, will you?"

"If you won't pretend that, then I shan't either."

"Nay, I shan't pretend pain when there was naught but pleasure. You gave me great pleasure, I admit it."

He'd looked away from her again and she joined him in searching the horizon for nothing in particular.

"You are sweet," he said abruptly. "Your taste pleased me. If I think of tasting you, I grow hard and randy as one of our goats."

That was a surprise. "But it is only morning!"

"Look yon, Daria, to the southeast, at the base of that small hillock. There is a field of summer flowers there, thick as a woven mat, and warm and sweet. I would take you there and strip you naked. I would caress you and let you caress me and watch the sweat dew your soft flesh as the passion builds in you, and when you are twisting beneath me, I would taste you again and then press you down in the bed of fragrant flowers and sink into you."

He saw the pulse pounding in her throat, the heated color on her cheeks, the wild anticipation in her eyes. He smiled, pleased. There was no reason to argue with her, to constantly make her pale and draw back, no, there had been too much of that. He was wedded to her and that was an end to it. He would simply make the best of it; to discover that she was filled with passion would bring unexpected satisfaction to his future days and nights. *And what of the child? If it is a boy, he will be your heir and you will have to swallow your bile and your honor. . . .*

Roland shook his head. There was naught he could do to influence the sex of the child. Nothing. He wouldn't fret about it. He'd never really fretted in his life, yet he'd done more of it in the past weeks than he had imagined possible. It solved naught, this fretting, and it made him nervous and irritable. "Come," he said, his voice curt, "I'll introduce you to the keep servants. You are the mistress now and they must accustom themselves to the fact. It has been many years since a lady was in residence here. Sir Thomas tells me most of the keep servants are well-meaning, but they've grown lazy." He paused a moment. "I trust you have the training to oversee the work?"

"Aye, my mother did not neglect my household duties."

"But she found opportunity to teach you to read and to write. Very unusual, I should say. Did you know that Philippa is St. Erth's steward?"

"I have not been taught those duties. But if someone will but show me, then—"

"Nay, there is no need. You will meet my steward

shortly. If he is a cheat, well, then, I will flail his buttocks and throw him into a ditch."

Daria grinned at that, then said, her voice diffident, "My mother, Roland. I worry about her. My uncle abused her, and since I was there she had no choice but to obey his wishes in all things."

"Think no more about it," he said, finality in his voice. Daria bit her lip, keeping her ire down.

Alice, the many-times-removed offspring of the Great Alice, had pain in her joints. Daria stood a moment in the cooking outbuilding, watching the old woman stir a stew with a long wooden spoon. It pained her, but Daria didn't know her well enough as yet to suggest a possible remedy. She praised her cooking, which was easy since her words were true, and settled back to hear advice on her pregnancy.

The advice journeyed through time back to the Great Alice herself, whence all knowledge began, Daria realized. She was close to nodding off when Alice, remembering her pastries, yelled, "By all the saints! Go ye, little mistress, and lie ye down. I'll send one of those lazy wenches with something fer ye to eat."

She slept away the afternoon. When she awoke, Roland was seated on the bed beside her. His look was intent and by far too serious for her peace of mind. Had he been there long? Just looking at her? What was he thinking?

"Hello," she said, and stretched. "Oh, dear, is it late? Have I slept long?"

"Long enough. How do you feel?"

She consulted her stomach and smiled. "Fine. Alice's bread boasts better results than the queen's herbs. Shall I rise now and see to your evening meal?"

"Nay, 'tis still early. You will remain here with me for a while. I've been watching you, Daria. I'm glad you're awake. I want to take you now."

The chamber was filled with sunlight, the high winds of the previous night had mellowed into a gentle breeze fit for a hot summer day. He wanted her now? When he'd spoken of the field of flowers, she'd felt the beauty of what he'd said, but not the embarrassment of it. "But it's very bright, Roland. There is a lot of light."

"I know. I want to part your white thighs and look at my wife. Now, let me assist you with your gown."

Her hair was loose and tumbled from her rest. He wrapped a thick tress around his wrist, slowly but inexorably drawing her face closer to his. "Look up at me, Daria."

She did, and he watched, fascinated, as her tongue lightly touched her lower lip. "You don't even realize that you make me want you, do you? Just looking at your pink tongue, and I'm harder than a stone." He laughed suddenly, released her hair, and began to undo the lace fastening down the front of her gown.

18

EVEN AS HE PULLED and tugged at her clothes, his movements becoming more jerky, more clumsy as his need grew, Daria was thinking: And what of Gwyn? Am I simply to forget that he broke faith with me? And if I bedded with another man, what would he say? Would he even care? She shook her head at the unfairness of it, then felt the warm summer air on her bare flesh and looked up at him.

He was staring at her breasts.

"Am I as nice as Gwyn? Do I please you as much?"

Roland had forgotten Gwyn. He'd used her unthinkingly and he'd been left feeling he'd been very wrong, that he'd broken faith with his own honor. And, truth be told, he'd had no thought for Gwyn, for his wife had filled his mind even as he'd found his release. It was no excuse, he knew that, accepted it. Her unexpected words caught him off-guard and dug at his guilt, and made him angry at himself for feeling guilt. He was thinking her breasts more beautiful than any woman's he'd yet seen. His fingers itched to stroke the soft underflesh, to move gently over her nipples until they tautened, to make her shudder and moan with the feelings from it. He felt as though she'd doused him with freezing water.

"Not really," he said, and drew back, now looking at her face. "Gwyn's breasts are much fuller, her nipples a darker plum color and soft as velvet. Her breasts quivered, as if apart from her, when I caressed them, and they filled my open hands to overflowing."

She was unable to keep the pain his words brought her from showing on her face, but she had asked him. What had she expected? That he would tell her she was the most exquisite creature imaginable and that Gwyn was nothing? She tried to cover herself then, but he grabbed her wrists and pulled them down.

"Enough of this damned nonsense. Listen to me, Daria. You're my wife. I choose to look at you. Don't throw the other in my face again. It happened; it's over with. Now, wife, I don't want you ever to cover yourself in front of me unless I tell you it is all right."

"Will this other happen again, Roland? And again?"

He shook his head again, saying nothing.

Her breasts were heaving and she saw that he was staring at them again, still holding her wrists in front of her. Her gown was bunched at her waist. Suddenly he pushed her onto her back and came down beside her. He lowered his head and brushed his cheek against the underside of her breast, back and forth, slowly moving upward until his tongue touched her nipple and she felt a shock of such intense excitement plunge through her that she gasped aloud with the strength of it. And she felt humiliated because she'd gasped. His tongue played over her flesh and the feelings built, becoming more insistent, more urgent, making her thighs quiver.

"Please, Roland."

She didn't know if she was begging him to stop or begging him to continue caressing her with his mouth. She felt his fingers stroking her other breast, lifting it, and then his warm mouth closed over her other nipple and she lurched up. He laughed softly, his breath hot on her even hotter flesh, and she wanted to tell him to leave her, to go take his whore, that she didn't believe him, but what came from her mouth was a soft, pleading cry.

His splayed fingers slipped beneath her bunched gown and rested on her belly. He raised his head and looked into her face. "On your back, your belly is still flat. I can believe there isn't a babe in your womb."

She thought she saw a shaft of pain in his dark eyes, but he lowered his head again quickly to her breast and suckled her until she was shaking, her fingers digging into his upper arms, her head thrashing back and forth, her hips lifting and falling, wanting, wanting . . .

His fingers eased through the curls over her woman's mound and found her, and once again he raised his head to look down into her dazed eyes.

"Do you like that, Daria? My fingers on you? Do you know how you feel to me?"

His voice followed the cadence of his fingers: deep, caressing, rhythmic. She opened her mouth and a low moan emerged. He leaned down and kissed her, and his tongue eased into her mouth and she burst into her climax at that instant. She cried out and he took her cries deep within himself, reveling in the wild thrashing of her hips as his fingers kept to their rhythm. So much passion in her, he thought, dazed and triumphant with the evidence of it. He was hurting now, his body trembling with the force of his lust. He left her, unable to wait longer, and she was lying there, her legs sprawled, the gown in a tangle about her hips, her breasts heaving, and her eyes were bewildered and lost. Lost until he came over her, lifted her legs, and drove into her.

He thrust his tongue into her open mouth as his sex plunged more deeply inside her.

He felt the rippling pleasure as her fingers now dug into his back, and his pleasure built and built as she lurched and bucked frantically beneath him. He cried out into her mouth, his breath warm, his member so deep he touched her womb, and he found release so profound, so overwhelming, that it touched the deepest part of him.

He kept kissing her even though his body felt drugged with exhaustion. He needed to kiss her, craved to kiss her; he craved the taste and texture of her mouth. And she drew him to her, and he wasn't in any mood to fight it now. And he continued to kiss her, nibbling at her lower lip, touching his tongue to hers, feeling her delight when she initiated the touching.

Finally, sated, his body still sealed to hers, he knew he must regain control, control of himself, control of her. He raised his head and said, "There will be no more talk about Gwyn. There will be no more talk about any women before Gwyn. Why should I seek out another woman when I have you? And you, Daria, are so passionate that I wonder how you remained a virgin for as long as you did. Of course, I really don't know about your virginity, do I?"

Shock made her reel, but she recovered herself quickly. "You were there when the Earl of Clare made me lie on my back, when he made me hold still, and he thrust his finger into me. You were there and you know I was a virgin, yet you wish to wound me. I hate you, Roland."

"I'm inside you, and you're wet and hot around me. Don't be a fool, Daria. There is no part of you, save your woman's perverse vanity, that could possibly hate me."

"Then I hate this need you seem to have to hurt me. I hate your cruelty, Roland. I don't understand why you do it."

He pulled out of her and rose, straightening his clothes with abrupt clumsy movements, for his body was sluggish and slow from the intensity of his release.

He was, truth be told, angry at himself. The words had come unbidden from his mouth; her damned virginity—of course he'd stood there whilst the Earl of Clare had . . . He shook his head. He couldn't bear to think of that. *When she thinks about it, what does she feel?* More fretting, and now he'd shoved her away from him yet again. He didn't particularly understand why he'd baited her either. But it didn't matter. It put him back in control, firmly away from her. He smiled, but it wasn't a pleasant smile. At least he'd gained pleasure from her before he'd pushed her away, and pushed himself away as well. As to what it felt like to kiss her, he refused to be touched by it. "I thank you for the diversion. You wrung me out and it is a good feeling. Now, I think it wise for you to go to the hall and oversee the servants. I wouldn't want them to forget you are their mistress."

She lay there, her body still pulsing slightly with lazy shocks of pleasure. She watched him stride quickly to the door. He turned and said over his shoulder, "You are mistress here. See to your duties."

"Are you one of my duties?"

"Aye, and you've done well by me last night and today. Very well indeed. I shan't complain at your lack of skill. It will come. A wench with your enthusiasm will learn rapidly. And I am a good teacher. Aye, Daria, I am your first responsibility and you will see to me whenever I wish it." And he left her, and she thought she heard him whistling before the door closed behind him.

She was such a fool, she thought wearily as she rose from the bed, to think that he could possibly have changed with her arrival. She should have remained at Wolffeton. But to do what? To sit about doing nothing at all while Kassia went humming about her duties? Whilst Kassia laughed and teased her husband and nibbled his ear when she didn't believe anyone saw? No, staying there would have destroyed her.

Daria grinned then. By coming here she'd learned what passion was all about, and she quite liked it, even if Roland must needs ruin it after he was through with her. She more than quite liked it. Roland wasn't the only one to feel as though his body was shattering, flying out of control, yet demanding more and more until it was all chaos and sensation and nothing else mattered. He used her and she would use him. It was even. She wouldn't think of anything else. She would care for her babe when it was born, shower her love on her son or daughter. And she would use her husband and ignore his foul words.

It was true about passion, she thought again, her eyes closing as a vague tremor of feeling passed through her. It was beyond any experience that she could have imagined. If Roland thought of her as only a convenient receptacle for his lust, why, then, she would view him as a convenient . . . What? She wasn't certain how to divide up a man. She touched her fingertips to her lips. She could still feel him, feel his hunger, his urgency, and then his simple enjoyment of kissing her. He'd acted like a starving man. Ah, she loved to kiss him as well. Well, then, she was fortunate that she enjoyed his kisses. She didn't need anything else from him.

She felt his seed on her thighs, rose slowly from the bed and bathed herself, but the scent of him lingered and the scent of her as well, and she wanted to weep because there was no part of her, even her perverse vanity, that hated him.

What was she to do?

It was obvious to her now what she had to do. If any niggling feelings for her husband crept unasked into her mind, she would simply take him to her bed until the feelings disappeared and she was glutted with passion.

She went down into the great hall. Soon she would take things into hand. But not now, not whilst Sir Thomas was here. She quite liked him, she didn't wish to hurt him or make him feel an outsider. The servants seemed to respond to her nicely, she realized with some relief by the time the evening meal had been justly consumed. She suspected that Old Alice, the resident autocrat, had dictated that she was the mistress and thus to be obeyed, bless her. Even Gwyn smiled at her, and did her bidding with satisfying speed.

There was no one to hold her in dislike save her husband.

Two weeks later, on the first Monday in August, the king's soldiers, led by Robert Burnell, arrived with Daria's dowry from the Earl of Reymerstone.

They also arrived with something else.

Burnell was weary to his bones, worried that the king was suffering from his absence, and relieved that the Earl of Reymerstone hadn't tried to murder him, though he'd seen the burning hate in the man's pale eyes, and known that it had been close for a time. Burnell didn't know if God had interceded on his behalf, but it made him feel blessed to believe it was so. The Earl of Reymerstone had allowed them to leave with a dozen mules, all laden with more goods that would have been Daria's had she married Ralph of Colchester. If Burnell hadn't insisted upon reading the marriage contract the earl had signed with Colchester, he never would have known about all the other goods. And that had made the earl all the more furious. Thank the good Lord he hadn't tried to murder them on their journey to Cornwall.

Daria looked from Robert Burnell's tired face toward the mules. There were coin, plate, jewels—she knew that there had been more that her uncle would have brought to her wedding. But so much more? Daria was stunned at the number of laden mules that came into the inner bailey, one after another.

So much, and now it belonged to Roland.

It was then that she saw her mother. Daria let out a yell and darted between people and animals and piles of refuse and deep gouges between cobblestones toward the woman who was bent over her palfrey.

"Mother! You're here! Oh, my!"

Roland turned quickly away from Burnell. "What the devil goes on . . . what is this, sir?"

The two men watched as Salin strode to the woman, and gently as he would handle a babe, lifted her from the mare's back. Roland saw his wife enfold the slighter woman, saw tears streaming down her face, saw her shoulders heaving as she kissed and hugged her mother.

"I had to bring Lady Fortescue, Roland," Burnell said, turning away from mother and daughter. "The earl—I saw him strike her viciously and repeatedly before I stopped him. It was after I'd made the demands, and he realized there was naught he could do—at least I prayed he wouldn't lose his head and murder me. He was yelling at her that he'd show her what he'd do to her bitch of a daughter when he got his hands on her. I knew he would kill her if I did not bring her away with me. She is still weak—several ribs are bruised, I think—and her wrist is hurt, but bound securely. She's a nice lady, Roland, soft-spoken and gentle."

Roland remembered the woman when he'd first gone to see the Earl of Reymerstone; he remembered the weariness in her eyes, the acceptance of things when there was no hope to change them. He felt a surge of guilt so powerful he shook with it. He should have instructed Burnell to bring Daria's mother away with him, but he hadn't thought of it. He'd been too locked into himself and his sense of abuse by the daughter's hand. He'd been nothing but a selfish lout.

"I'm glad you saved her." He nodded to Burnell and strode to Lady Fortescue.

"My lady," he said, and watched her try to straighten at his greeting, watched her try to offer him a curtsy.

"Nay, don't! Daria, your mother isn't feeling well. Take her to your solar. She must rest."

Daria saw her mother's bruised body a few minutes later in the solar when she helped her onto a narrow bed. She closed her eyes a moment, wishing more than anything that her uncle was present and that she had a knife. She would kill him. And she would enjoy it. She sent word to Alice, and a sweet-smelling warm potion of wine and herbs quickly arrived. Daria stayed with her mother until she slept. She smoothed back the vibrant red hair, still untouched by gray, saw the lines smooth from her mother's face. She lowered her head in her hands and wept. She should have demanded that Roland fetch her mother. But she hadn't. She'd been to consumed with herself, with the babe, with Roland's distrust of her. She'd been selfish, unforgivably selfish. After a long time Daria rose, straightened her gown, and called to Gwyn, who was cleaning in Sir Thomas's bedchamber. She asked her to remain with her mother.

"She's a beautiful lady," Gwyn whispered. "I'll see that she's all right."

Why should she have ever hated Gwyn? Daria wondered blankly as she walked down the winding stone steps.

Daria felt a bystander in the transaction between Burnell and her husband. She stood quietly in the great hall, watching the men bring in trunk after trunk. Sir Thomas, Robert Burnell, and her husband opened each trunk, commented on the goods, smiling sometimes, drinking ale. Then there came the leather coin pouches, and she watched as Roland solemnly passed the counted-out coins to Sir Thomas. The men embraced each other. Still she didn't move.

She heard Roland tell the men to take two of the trunks to his bedchamber. It was her bedchamber as well, but in important matters such as this, it was the man's. She'd learned that well enough during the past two weeks. The time had passed quickly, for there was so much newness at Thispen-Ladock, so many places to visit, so many new people to meet. Nor, Daria thought, as she saw to it that Burnell and the king's men were served quantities of ale and sweet buns from Alice's huge ovens, had she taken the reins in hand as yet. Actually, the reins had simply seemed to drift slowly yet surely there, and one day she was the mistress and all asked her for direction and orders. Roland had said nothing, nor had Sir Thomas. She seated herself finally, still saying naught. Her goods, her coin . . . but it was as if she wasn't even there.

" 'Tis incredible," Burnell said, sat back in his chair, and sighed deeply. His eyes remained closed as he bit into another sweet bun filled with raisins and almonds and nutmeg.

"Keep your thoughts away from my cook," Roland said, then laughed. "You will not seduce her from me even though you are a man of God."

"But the king, Roland, his belly would mellow from such wondrous food and—"

"He would become fat as a stoat, belch in foreign dignitaries' faces, sire no more children off the queen because he would be constantly eating, and she would be repelled, aye, Burnell, and he would die one day from gluttony, and England couldn't afford that loss, sir. And it would be your fault, all for lusting after my cook."

"Perhaps," Daria said, sitting forward, her eyes sparkling now, for the man who had spoken so humorously was the Roland she had met and known in Wales. "But what is a certainty, sir, is that Alice has no choice but to remain here. You see, she is tied to this place by bonds that go deeper than the spirit, all her skills derive from this earth and none other, and she told me that she must remain here else she would lose all her knowledge and abilities."

"Ah," said Burnell, and frowned deeply.

Roland shot his wife a surprised look and she returned it limpidly.

"You are blessed with a golden tongue, wife," he said to her some moments later when Sir Thomas turned to speak to Burnell. "Poor Burnell!"

"Perhaps my lie was a bit more effective, but yours was by far more humorous, Roland. I'd forgotten how you could make me laugh."

"There isn't much to laugh about now, is there?"

"I suppose not, and I miss laughter. I miss it more than I minded the endless rain in Wales."

He gently clasped her face between his hands. He tilted up her chin and kissed her mouth. He continued kissing her, light, soft kisses that made her flesh warm. After a moment he released her, and to her surprise, he asked, "How is your mother?"

"Alice made a potion for her. She is sleeping soundly at present, and Gwyn is with her. She will fetch me when Mother awakens."

Roland picked up his goblet and began to examine the texture of the carvings on its surface. "I'm sorry about your mother, Daria."

She said even as she shook her head, "Nay, 'tis I who am at fault. I wasn't thinking clearly. I should have realized that my uncle was capable of—"

"Your mother is a beautiful woman. You look like her, you know, save that your hair isn't so strong and pure a red."

"True. I always thought I'd been diluted, though of course she would tell me that it was I who purified her." Daria pictured her mother's bruised body and suddenly, without warning, she burst into tears.

Roland saw the men turn to stare aghast at his wife. Conversation began to die. He waved a hand, then turned to her and said quietly, "I know you are hurt, hurt that you think you failed her, but you didn't. 'Twas I who failed her. Hush, now, Daria, else Burnell will tell the king that I abused you in front of everyone and with no provocation, and he will annul our marriage and take all your dowry from me. Sir Thomas will kick me out from my new home and I'll be cursed to wander the world again. Let me tell you that wandering grows tedious and I want no more of it."

His words were amusing and his voice was light and teasing, so she was able to ignore the truth of his words, and sniffed, wiping her eyes with the back of her hand.

"I'm sorry. I don't know why I did that."

"The babe," he said, not looking at her.

Daria hugged her arms around her belly. There was a slight roundness now and her waist was thickening. She wondered when he would look at her and be repelled.

"I haven't enjoyed you since this morning and my body is sorely deprived."

They were in their bedchamber. Daria closed her eyes, accepting more kisses, returning them with growing enthusiasm. When he caressed her and came into her body, he was kind and gentle and loving. If afterward he withdrew and became cold, well, it seemed it was her price to pay. She found she couldn't become cold as well as he did, so she said nothing, merely tried to pretend sleep as quickly as possible. Slowly, even as he continued kissing her, his hands still cupping her face, her hands lowered, stroking over his belly, lower, until her fingers closed about his swelling member. He moaned, his body jerking at her touch. Then he shoved against her fingers, and he was larger now, nearly too large for her hand, and she held him between her hands, lightly stroking him, gliding downward to touch the rest of him, and he was breathing hard and low and his kisses were deeper and more demanding and she continued to caress him until he jerked back from her, his chest heaving. She'd only touched him like this some three days before and she was more than pleased with her discovery. He'd said nothing about it, but his reaction when she touched him and caressed him with her hand was more than gratifying. She remembered the queen's ladies and their advice and knew that soon she would touch him with her mouth. She wondered how he would react to that.

He stared down at her now but his eyes closed suddenly as she squeezed both her hands around his member. He said her name softly, then, without warning, lifted her onto her back on a narrow table, knocking off the basin to the stone floor. It cracked, but he didn't notice. Her jerked her hair free, threading his fingers through it until it hung down off the edge of the table, thick and tangled. He pulled her forward until her hips were at the edge of the table, her legs dangling. "Don't move, Daria."

She couldn't have moved in any case, for if she did, she would probably crash like the basin had to the stone floor. Her gown was tangled about her legs. She couldn't see him, but she could hear his breathing, and it was harsh and raw. Then he was over her, and he was lifting her legs and settling them over his shoulders, jerking away her gown, lifting her hips with his hands. He pulled her slightly forward, cradling her buttocks in his hands, and slid deeply into her. She cried out and he stopped.

"Do I hurt you?"

She shook her head.

He withdrew only when he knew if he didn't he would lose himself completely. He pulled out of her, his chest heaving, sweat filming his body. She felt his fingers on her, stroking over her inner thighs, moving closer, closer still, until he was touching her, caressing her, and then she felt his finger go deeply into her and she lifted her hips, nearly sobbing aloud with the wonder of it.

Then he lowered her legs and pushed her back on the table. He widened her thighs and brought his mouth down to her. He tried to hold her still, but he couldn't. She was wild and frantic, bucking against him, and he quickly lifted her and tossed her onto the narrow bed. When she wailed, her body going into frantic spasms, he came quickly into her again, and felt her legs close around his flanks, drawing him deeper and deeper still.

"Daria," he said, and let his release overtake him.

For many minutes neither of them moved.

"It is a good thing that Burnell brought the rest of my clothes. You are violent with my gowns, Roland."

He grunted, his mind still so blurred from the pleasure that he couldn't think.

As he came back to himself, Roland recognized that he was changing, and it frightened him. He was coming to need her, his wife, and seek her out. Not any deep part of him, not the spiritual part of him, but his body recognized her as its mate and his body's need seemed to grow stronger and more demanding. And it wasn't simply because she gave herself so sweetly to him—no, it was more, and more still, and it fretted him. It was as if this particular girl was meant to be his.

He withdrew his sex and his spirit from her. Then he withdrew his presence.

It was relatively simple to keep his distance from her, for Burnell wished to rest for several days and it was Roland's duty to show him the countryside and tell him his plans for Thispen-Ladock. As it was Daria's duty to provide for Burnell's pleasure, she was also occupied. And with her mother. He knew she spent many hours with Lady Fortescue. It wasn't until the last evening of Robert Burnell's stay that Lady Fortescue came into the great hall for the evening meal. She was lovely, he saw, her red hair warm and vibrant, her eyes bright and soft. Roland greeted her warmly. Sir Thomas insisted that she sit beside him.

At the close of the meal, which made everyone sigh with gluttonous pleasure, Roland rose from his chair, his goblet of ale raised high. He said to Sir Thomas, "You have provided me with my home and the home for my sons and my sons' sons. I thank you, Sir Thomas. You have given me land and a home that will remain in my spirit until the day I die. You have told me, Sir Thomas, that I must make Thispen-Ladock mine completely, that I must select a new name that will reflect what I am and my line. It was difficult to find such a name until I realized at last that I was a wanderer, and a lover of many lands. I saw the world, and I would bring the essence of what I saw here, to Cornwall, here to this keep, and all will come to know it as Chantry Hall. Chantry is the name of a man I knew in the Holy Land. He saved my life and he taught me that freedom of the spirit was the most precious of God's gifts to man. My thanks to you, Sir Thomas, and to you, Robert Burnell."

"Hear! Hear!"

Daria stared at him, emptiness filling her even as her goblet overflowed with wine poured by an excited servant. The speech he'd just made was wonderful and fluent and moving. She hadn't known about it. She hadn't know about any of it.

She turned slightly and saw that her mother was looking at her, and she quickly lowered her eyes, raised her goblet, and sipped at the wine.

I am nothing more to him than one of the mules who brought his riches to him. She very slowly rose from her chair and walked from the great hall.

Only one remarked her leaving.

19

"IT WILL RAIN SOON. Do you miss Wales and the end-less rain that soaked you to your soul?"

Daria didn't look back at him. She stood on the northern ramparts, wishing she could see the sea from its vantage point, but there was naught but the soft moonlight over the green rolling hills. It was warm this evening, the air heavy from the rain that would fall before midnight.

"Aye, I miss Wales," she said.

"Why did you leave the hall? I had thought it a good time to celebrate. I had thought Burnell would enjoy his final night if I filled it with laughter and jests and Alice's incredible array of food."

"Worry not, Roland. He is enjoying himself, as is everyone else."

"Why did you leave?"

She shrugged. "It didn't matter if I was there or not, Roland. All this"—she turned then, spreading out her arms—"all this is yours. It has nothing to do with me. I hope you enjoy it, Roland, for to your mind, you've accepted dishonor and lies to gain it. I hope every sheep gives you delight, every shaft of wheat endless bliss."

"Your wishes for my joy warm me, Daria, but they seem a trifle incomplete. You don't wish me mindless pleasure from all the cows that graze the eastern acres?"

She thought her eyes would cross with fury, but she held on to herself, turning away from him, leaning on the stone ramparts. She swallowed, still saying nothing.

301

"Did you drink too much wine?"

She shook her head.

"Then you aren't ill?"

She was silent.

"You haven't vomited for nearly a week now. If you are feeling ill now, it isn't right. Speak to me."

She wondered how he knew that, but didn't say anything. She sighed deeply and turned once again to face her husband. "I'm not ill. I think I will go for a walk now. I bid you good night, Roland."

"What you will do, Daria, is return with me to the great hall and see to your guests."

"They are not my guests, Roland. They are *yours;* they are here at *your* keep; they are here at *your* pleasure; they are enjoying *your* bounty, not mine. I have naught to do with anything. Don't lie to me about them being my guests. I am nothing here and they are nothing to me."

"It is a pity you removed yourself before I could finish my toast."

She looked at him warily, not willing to trust him an inch. "What do you mean?"

He flicked a piece of lint from the sleeve of his tunic. Her eyes followed the movement and she was looking at his long fingers when he said, "Without you—and your magnificent dowry, that is—I wouldn't be able to make needed repairs on the keep. Without you I wouldn't be able to increase my herds, hire more soldiers, bring in more peasants, and see to luxuries within the keep. Because of you, Daria, I am able to bring my home to its former glory now rather than in the misty future."

It *was* his home, just as all she had brought him through the marriage was his as well. She shoved him out of her way. Because she caught him off-guard, she was able to slip past him. She raced along the narrow rampart walkway to the wide ladder that rose from the inner bailey.

He watched her climb down the ladder. She moved carefully, even in her anger, to protect the babe in her womb. He watched her dash across the inner bailey, gracefully avoiding refuse and puddles of water and two sleeping goats. He turned back and took her place at the rampart wall. He leaned his elbows on the rough stone. The night winds rose and the air thickened. He wondered, suddenly, without warning, what his father would think of him right at this moment. He saw his father's face after Roland had finally told him of Joan of Tenesby's treachery. He could still hear his deep soft voice as he said to his second son, "Listen, Roland, and listen well. You were played the fool, boy, but it didn't kill you. It hurt your heart and your pride, nothing more. It won't last, these sorrowing feelings. In the future, when you hear of the man who weds Joan of Tenesby, you will feel pity for the poor fellow, for he had not your luck. Nay, he will have gone blindly to his fate. You will tread more carefully now, and when it comes your time to wed, you will know what to seek and what to avoid in a wife. Honesty, Roland, honesty is a rare commodity in any human, man or woman. When you find honesty, then you will be the winner."

Honesty, Roland thought. *Honesty*. Rare indeed, and he hadn't found it.

He turned away from the ramparts wall. No, he hadn't found honesty and he was himself becoming more dishonest with each passing day.

Just that morning, as the soft pearl lights of dawn had filled their small bedchamber, he had pulled Daria against him, then rolled on top of her. He'd felt the small roundness of her belly and it had driven him mad. He'd taken her quickly and left her. And he'd wondered if this child she carried would look like the Earl of Clare.

*   *   *

Katherine of Fortescue felt wonderful. She was sitting in the small apple and pear orchard at the rear of the keep. It was a warm day with a thick hot sun, but the dense branches of the apple tree shaded her well enough. She set another perfect stitch in the gown she was sewing for her daughter. She surprised herself by humming, something she hadn't done in so long she'd thought she had forgotten, but she hadn't. She hummed louder, charmed by the sound and by her nearly delirious sense of freedom, then burst into song. The gown dropped unheeded to her lap. Her voice was thin but true and she sang until she heard Sir Thomas chuckle behind her.

She turned to smile at him. "Do you come to silence the hideous noise, Sir Thomas?"

"Nay, I come to smile and feel my old bones warm."

"Old bones! You speak foolishness, sir! Why, you are still a young man."

"If it pleases you to say so, I shan't cavil." He seated himself beside her on the narrow stone bench. It had belonged to his grandmother. So many years had passed, so many events had shaped what he'd become now . . .

"I'm glad you haven't yet taken your leave," Katherine said, looking at Sir Thomas straightly.

"Roland has asked me to stay." He shrugged then, adding, "I cannot, in any case. Your sweet daughter . . ." His voice trailed off. "Nay, ask me not, Katherine, for I know not what trouble lies between them. I act as the block of wood between the two of them, a comfortable block, stolid and silent, and both of them look to that block for ease and safe conversation. Think you I should take my leave?"

She shook her head and set another perfect stitch.

"You are a woman of good judgment," he said, plucking a long piece of grass and wrapping it around his callused fingers. "You don't meddle. You treat your son-in-law with respect and kindness. You don't frown your displeasure at him when you see your daughter's pale face. You don't try to tell your daughter what she does wrong and try to correct her."

Katherine grinned at him. "I am lazy, sir! Why should I work when Daria wishes to assume all the responsibility?"

"You lie, my lady. It is your wisdom that holds you silent, that and your love for your daughter."

"Like you, Sir Thomas, I shan't cavil if you wish to pay me compliments."

Sir Thomas said abruptly. "Are you healed?"

Her fingers stilled and she was silent for many moments.

"I'm sorry to distress you. It is just that I would kill the Earl of Reymerstone were he here. Indeed, I wonder if I shouldn't pay the bastard a visit when I leave here and show him the contempt I feel for his worthless soul."

Her hand shot out and closed over his clenched ones. "Damon Le Mark is a paltry creature, Sir Thomas. He knows no honor, no loyalty, and his treachery has rotted his soul. Ah, he knows pleasure because another's suffering gives it to him. Let him die in his own misery. And he will die as he deserves to, I know it."

"But he would have killed you had not Burnell brought you here!"

"I don't think so. He'd beaten me worse than that several times before."

Sir Thomas drew back, pain and shock contorting his features. "I must tell Roland. I must, for it is his right to avenge you."

"If you tell such a thing to Roland or to my daughter, I will call you a liar. Leave go, Sir Thomas. Another lady lived that meager life at Reymerstone. A new one, reborn if you will, sits here with you, humming and singing wildly as a berserk sparrow. This

lady is happy and content and deems herself the lucki-
est of women. Sit here quietly for a moment and I will
fetch you a flagon of ale. Should you like that, sir?"

Sir Thomas watched her walk gracefully toward the
cooking outbuilding. He admired her. He thought her
exquisite.

A week later Daria straightened from speaking to
the dairymaid at the sound of horsemen arriving at the
keep. She wiped her hands on her gown and walked
quickly toward the inner bailey. It was Graelam de
Moreton and three of his men. He looked like a pagan
warrior, ruthless and overpowering in his black-and-
silver mail, astride his huge destrier, and she felt an
automatic frisson of fear. And then he smiled and
shouted, "Roland! Bring your worthless hide over here
so that I may tell you what Dienwald and Philippa
have said about you!"

Roland was striding to him, yelling out insults in
fine good humor, and clapped his shoulder after he'd
dismounted his destrier. The two men embraced, then
stepped apart, Lord Graelam saying to his man, "Rolfe,
see to Demon. Where is your wife, Roland?"

"I am here, my lord."

She offered Graelam a deep curtsy.

Graelam stared at her silently for several moments.
"My Kassia and I worried about you, Daria. What you
did was foolish. My belly curdled with fear when the
two grooms returned, red-faced, without you."

"I'm sorry, my lord. 'Twas thoughtless of me."

Graelam strode to her and very gently raised her
chin in the palm of his gloved hand. He studied her
face, not seeming to care that her husband stood not
six feet from them, that the inner bailey was filled with
chattering men and women and scampering children.

Roland said from behind them, his voice sounding
his irritation, "I sent you a message immediately,
Graelam, that my wife was safe and with me."

Graelam turned then to Roland. He smiled even as he shrugged. "Kassia worries, Roland. She wanted me to come. She wanted me to ensure that Daria was comfortable in her new home and that the babe was settling in nicely as well. Thus you see me here awaiting your hospitality."

"Oh, dear! Please, my lord, come into the hall. My mother is here with us now and I wish you to meet her. Do you also know Sir Thomas?"

Roland found himself grinning reluctantly after his wife, who, after babbling like a cawing rook, picked up her skirts and dashed much too quickly, he thought, suddenly worried, across the crooked cobblestones and up the wide stone steps into the great hall.

"You've disconcerted my wife, Graelam. I believe it the unlikely combination of your fierce face and your gentle manner. How do your own lady and your squalling babe?"

"She is well, as is my son. I should apologize to you, Roland, but it never occurred to me that Daria was so unhappy at Wolffeton."

Roland was uncomfortable. He shrugged. "Have Rolfe bring your men inside the hall. By now Daria has provided enough ale to quench the thirst of every man within our walls."

Roland turned and strode toward the hall. Graelam de Moreton followed more slowly behind him, thinking about what the devil he should do. His wife's words were still clear in his mind. "I'm worried, Graelam. There is strife between them, but there is caring as well, at least on Daria's side. Please discover what is wrong and fix it."

He shook his head. Kassia cherished this peculiar notion that he could fix anything, be it a war between two neighbors or squabbles between a man and his wife. There was trouble between Roland and Daria, no doubt about that. Graelam sighed. He preferred trying to fix the differences between two countries. He foresaw several days of watching Daria and Roland and trying to come up with some sort of solution that would please his wife, whatever the hell that could possibly be.

Daria sat alone in the solar, slowly and carefully grinding herbs just sprung up from her garden. It was a hot day and a line of sweat snaked down between her breasts. The sweet smell of rosemary filled her nostrils. She fanned herself with her hand and wished she could move closer to the window. But she couldn't. She'd spread the various herbs in small separate piles on the table in front of her, and any breeze or sudden disturbance would send the herbs wafting away in the hot air.

Her mother was likely with Sir Thomas. That was proving to be an interesting development, she thought as she transferred three pinches of rosemary to the fragrant dill. Days before, Sir Thomas had borrowed a dozen of Roland's men and they'd carried money to Sir Thomas's daughter and her family. At Roland's insistence, Sir Thomas had agreed to return to Chantry Hall. He was nothing loath, she thought, seeing her very lovely mother in her mind's eye, smiling up into Sir Thomas's weathered face. The man was besotted with her.

Daria added exactly three pinches of coarsely ground foxglove to a small batch of finely crushed poppy flowers. She had very little and must hoard her supply. She wondered how Roland was faring with the dour old farmer who held demesne lands at the northern boundaries of Chantry Hall. Roland had taken four men and ridden from the keep early that morning and should return soon now. She looked toward the window slit. The sun was settling downward. Yes, he should be returning soon now. . . . Just to see him, she thought, just to look at him whilst he spoke, to hear him laugh. I'm naught but a fool, she told herself, knowing that it was true and knowing too that there was nothing she could do about it.

He hadn't touched her for a week now, not since he'd placed his hand on her belly and felt the slight bulge there. She paused in her work, remembering how he'd been frantic to leave her after he'd taken her. He was so distant from her now that he might as well be back in Wales. She shook her head, and wiped the film of perspiration from her forehead with the back of her hand. She wouldn't think of him now. There were other things to fill her mind and her time.

She began to sing softly as she added just a dollop of basil to a concoction to ease stomach cramps. The afternoon grew hotter and her fingers slowed in their tasks. Suddenly, without warning, Daria froze where she sat, her fingers still, her eyes staring straight ahead. A huge door opened, right in front of her, and she saw herself passing through it into a field of dazzling white. The white was thick like fog, yet pure and dry, and it surrounded her yet didn't seem to really touch her. And there, as she stood silent and quiet, she saw Graelam. He was working on the eastern wall, dislodging old stone, lifting a mighty slab, turning to heave it away from him, then moving back to grasp another. Men were talking and looking at him as they in turn lifted the stones he'd heaved to them and in turn passed them to others. There was so much stone to be removed so that the wall could be rebuilt. She watched as he yelled something to one of the men, breaking his rhythm as he did so, his back turned to the wall. Suddenly there was a loud rumbling sound and the wall collapsed. Huge slabs toppled downward. She saw Graelam whip about, saw the stones strike his shoulders and chest, battering him to his knees. The stones rained down thick and hard, and covered him.

The men surrounding him were yelling frantically, trying to escape danger from the avalanche of stone. Thick dust from the crumbling stone swirled about, filling the air with thick gray debris. And then there was awful silence. Just as suddenly, the white disappeared and she was back in her chair, her left hand still held out in front of her. Daria jumped to her feet, upending all the herbal portions, and dashed from the solar. She didn't doubt what she saw. It was the same sort of vision she'd had when she saw her father die so many years before.

She saw her mother speaking with one of the wenches in the inner bailey and screamed to her to follow. She raced to the eastern wall, and as she neared, she heard men shouting and yelling.

She ran until she reached the exact spot where Graelam had fallen. Men were hurling rocks aside, on their knees, digging frantically. She shoved several of the men aside and heaved the stones off him. Several smaller stones tumbled against her, striking her hard, but she ignored them, ignored the brief stabs of pain. She knew exactly where his face was and she knew she must clear it so he could breathe. She heard the men arguing, and someone tried to pull her away, but she turned and saw him draw back at the look on her face. She worked until she thought her arms would crumble as had the stone wall. She saw him. Finally his chest and head were clear. He lay on his side, his arms over his head to protect himself. He was perfectly still.

"No!" She screamed the word, and she heard herself as a child screaming the same word over and over after she'd seen her father fall and the horse crush his skull.

"Graelam!" She fell to her knees beside him. The men, speechless and afraid, moved aside for her, making a circle around her. She grabbed Graelam's arm and heaved him over and onto his back.

"He's dead!" one of the men muttered. "Dead. There's naught ye can do, mistress."

"He's not dead," Daria said, and she slapped his face, hard, again and again. "You won't die! Graelam, damn you! No! You won't die, not like my father. I won't let you! No!" Still he didn't move, and she felt fury flood through her. She'd seen what had happened, yet she was to be impotent again. She wouldn't accept it. She pounded his chest with her fists, screaming at him, berating him not to die, not to leave his family, not like this. And she struck him again and again. She was trembling with fatigue and fear, yet her rage wouldn't let her stop. She pounded her fists again and again on his chest.

Then, suddenly, Graelam's chest heaved, and heaved again. Then he groaned, the most beautiful sound Daria had ever heard in her life.

She yelled with the relief of it. She'd won. He hadn't died. The vision hadn't shown her something beyond her control. It hadn't been a prediction, it had been a warning. She shook his massive shoulders, then grasped his face between her hands and stroked his brow, his jaw, his head. No damage as far as she could tell. Then he opened his eyes and looked up at her.

He frowned, his eyes narrowing in pain.

"Graelam," she said very quietly, her face close to his, "you're alive. My father died and there was naught I could do about it. But you lived. You lived, my lord!" She held him, her cheek pressed against his throat, speaking words, nonsense really, her voice becoming more slurred by the moment.

"What the devil is happening here!"

The men stumbled back to allow Roland through. He stopped cold at the sight of his wife on her knees holding Graelam and speaking to him in a singsong voice.

"Daria, what happened? Graelam, what—?"

She turned then and smiled up at him, tears glistening on her dust-streaked cheeks. "He'll live, Roland.
It happened just like my father, but Graelam lived. It
was a warning, not a prediction." She rose then, and
said very calmly, "Please help Lord Graelam to the
keep. His ribs are likely badly bruised. Be careful.
Roland, I shall have Alice prepare a brew for him to
ease his pain."

Without another word, she walked away from him,
walked past her mother, her steps brisk and her head
thrown back.

His questions would wait. Roland directed his men
to lift Graelam. The men grunted and heaved in their
burden. "Go easy," Roland said, and helped in the
task. Once Graelam was lying on his bed, bared to the
waist, Roland saw indeed that his ribs were bruised
badly. He felt them, then nodded. "Daria is right.
You will be fine, but sore as Satan for a good week.
What happened, Graelam?"

"I was working on your damned wall, Roland. It
collapsed suddenly, without warning, and the stone
buried me. That's all." But it wasn't all, Graelam was
thinking. Something very strange had occurred. It was
as if he himself had quit being, but of course he
hadn't. He'd been buried under the rubble . . . he
remembered quite clearly the pain of the striking stones
as they'd hit him; then he'd suddenly been separate
from the pain, outside of it somehow, and he'd seemed
to be surrounded by a very clear whiteness that was
blinding yet somehow completely clear . . . nothing
more, just . . . white, thick and impenetrable, yet
clear. And then he'd heard Daria screaming at him,
screaming that he wouldn't die, not like her father had
died, that she wouldn't let him. And then he'd come
back into the rawness of his body, even felt the pain of
her fists hammering over and over again against his
chest. And the white had receded, moving slowly away

from him, then whooshing out of his sight in an instant
of time, and he was awake and filled with life and pain
and she was above him, babbling nonsense at him and
stroking his face with her hands.

"What happened to Daria's father?"

Roland stared down at his friend.

"No, I'm not out of my head. What happened to
him?"

"He died. In a tourney, some three years ago."

"I see." But he didn't, not really. He said very
quietly, "Your wife saved my life, Roland."

"She pulled stones off you, that's true. But not all
that many. The men hauled off the bulk of them."

"Nay, 'twas more . . . much more. The stones, they
had already hurt me . . ." Graelam fell silent. He said
nothing more until Daria entered, carrying a goblet in
her hand. Her mother followed her, strips of cloth
over her arms.

Daria paid no heed to her husband. She sat beside
Graelam, smiled down at him, and said, "Drink this,
my lord. It will take away the pain and make you sleep
for a while. My mother will bind your ribs. Have you
pain anywhere else?"

Graelam shook his head, his eyes never leaving her
face. He drank the bittersweet brew. His head soon
lolled on the pillow, but before he closed his eyes he
said, "Thank you, Daria. Thank you for my life."

"What did he mean, Daria?"

She raised her head and looked at her husband. "I
couldn't let him die. I couldn't let the vision end like it
had with my father. I just couldn't. I have failed too
many times in my life. I couldn't fail in this."

She stood then and straightened her gown. She left
the chamber then, saying nothing more.

Roland said to Katherine, "Your daughter is behaving strangely. What is she talking about? I don't
understand."

Katherine shook her head, motioning Roland to help her. Between them they managed to bind Graelam's ribs with strip after strip of stout white cloth.

Whilst Roland stripped off the remainder of Graelam's clothing and brought a light cover to his waist, Katherine walked to the small window slit and looked out.

"Stay a moment, Roland," Katherine said once he'd finished.

"I should go see to Daria."

"In a moment. Did she tell you about her father?"

"Only that he had died in a tourney in London just before Edward left for the Holy Land."

"There was something else. She saw her father die."

Roland stared at her. "I beg your pardon, my lady?"

"Daria saw him die, three days before word reached us that he'd been killed accidentally in that tourney in London."

"You mean she had some sort of vision?"

"Aye, I suppose that is as good a word as any. In any case, it happened."

Roland was thinking of her telling him that she'd known him the moment she'd first seen him. She'd recognized him deep within her. He shrugged, irritated, for it was the kind of thing a man couldn't touch, couldn't look at and say it was real or wasn't real. He didn't like this sort of talk. It was nonsense. Anything that smacked of visions belonged to prophets in mountain caves, not to young females.

"I realize it's difficult for you to accept, Roland. Just imagine what it is like for Daria. Evidently she saw Graelam being crushed by the stone wall. But somehow she brought him back."

"He was never dead! He was simply unconscious . . . and only for a few moments, nothing more."

"Perhaps," Katherine said. She gave him a sad smile. "Don't hurt her with this, Roland."

His head snapped up. He said, his voice quite cold and quite distant, "I'm not a monster."

He left her then, saying over his shoulder as he paused at the chamber door, "I will send Rolfe to attend his master. You must rest, Katherine."

Roland found Daria in the orchard. She was seated on what was now called Lady Katherine's bench. She was staring down at her hands, clasped in her lap.

He sat beside her, saying nothing.

"Lord Graelam is all right?"

"Aye, he will survive. He's sleeping now."

"Will you send a message to Kassia?"

"I probably should before Graelam regains his wits. He detests illness or weakness. But his wife should be told, just in case something goes wrong, just in case he is hurt internally and—"

"No, he isn't hurt internally."

Roland looked at her then, his eyes narrowed. "You have no way of being certain of that, Daria. No way at all. Why do you say it with such assurance?"

"I just know," she said, her voice now as distant as his.

"How do you know?"

"It matters not. I have much to do now, Roland. If you need me for naught else, then—"

He quickly grasped her wrist and pulled her back down. "I won't accuse you of being a witch, if you're afraid of that. My men just might be thinking that, though. You're not stupid, Daria. You know there might be talk. I want you to tell me exactly what you did so that I may combat it."

"I shoved the men aside and pulled off the stones myself. You see, I knew exactly what stones to shove aside to clear his head and his chest. Then I saw that he was motionless, that he wasn't breathing, and I was no longer just afraid. I was furious, so enraged that I couldn't control it. It is an odd reaction for me, but it happened. I was so angry that I struck his chest with my fists, again and again, and screamed at him like a shrew. That is likely what your men will gossip about. They will say that I lost all reason. But Graelam breathed again and he moaned and then he opened his eyes."

"He was merely unconscious."

"Yes, he was merely unconscious."

He looked at her profile, his mouth thinning. "You weren't there when the wall collapsed on him."

"No, I was in the solar mixing herbs."

"How did you know what had happened?"

"I saw it happen."

Roland was silent for many moments. He was aware of bees swarming about the apple tree behind him. He heard sparrows flapping their wings in the still hot air. The heavy smell of grass filled his nostrils. This should be a peaceful spot, but it wasn't. There were mysteries here, and things he didn't understand, and there was pain as well, and he knew he was the cause of it. He didn't know what to do. He didn't begin to know what to think about this. He rose and looked down at his wife.

"I must send a message to Kassia. Doubtless she will arrive shortly to see to her lord."

Daria merely nodded.

It was deep in the middle of the night. A storm was blowing in. Just as lightning streaked across the sky, Daria awoke, pain convulsing her belly, a cry erupting from her mouth.

20

DARIA had never imagined such pain. It welled up in her, overpowering her, capturing all of her within it, and she couldn't stop it, couldn't control it. The pain shrieked in her belly, twisting and coiling, until the screams were pouring out of her mouth. She wrapped her arms around herself, drawing her knees up, but nothing helped. Then, suddenly, just as the pain had started, it stopped.

Roland lurched upright at her first cry. He'd just come into their bedchamber a short time before and was on the edge of sleep. "Daria!" He clasped her arms and tried to bring her about to face him, but her pain was keeping her apart from him, apart from understanding, apart from even the knowledge of him and his presence. So he held her until she quieted. She lay on her back, staring up at him, panting heavily.

"It's gone," she said, her voice low and harsh. "It was horrible but now it's gone."

"What pain? Where did you hurt?"

"My belly. Cramps, awful twisting cramps and—" Her eyes flew to his face. "Oh, no!"

Roland quickly lit several candles. He turned back to see her standing beside the bed, staring down at herself. He felt himself grow cold at the sight. Blood blotched red on her white shift, blood streaked down her legs, puddling at the floor between her feet.

She looked up at him, her eyes blank. "I don't understand." Another cramp seized her, and she fell to her knees with the force of it.

She was losing the child. She was bowed on her knees, crying out, jagged, tearing cries. He lifted her high in his arms and felt the vivid agony of her body as she twisted and heaved against his hold. He laid her onto her back, watching her immediately roll to her side, her legs drawn up, her arms around her belly.

"Hold on!" he shouted at her, then ran from the bedchamber, grabbing his bedrobe as he went.

He met Katherine in the narrow corridor. Her face was pale in the dim light.

"What's wrong, Roland?"

"It's the babe, she's losing the babe!"

Katherine ran past him. She stood over her daughter, wishing she could take the pain from her, magically take it into herself, but she couldn't, of course. She pushed sweat-soaked hair from her daughter's forehead, speaking to her softly. " 'Twill soon be over, Daria. Soon now. Don't frighten your husband so, daughter. But look at him, his face is as pale as the dawn light and your pain becomes his. Come, Daria, give him your hands and he will help you."

Roland moved automatically to do as Katherine bade. He was grateful for any instruction, for he felt so damnably helpless. He grasped his wife's fingers, then eased his hold so that she could grip his hands instead. She saw him, at last. "Roland, please make it stop!" She was gone from him for many moments, locked into the pain of her body.

Daria felt a mighty twisting that wound tighter and tighter, against all reason, crushing her within it, and she prayed in that instant for oblivion, for that thick whiteness she'd seen that afternoon. But she felt everything; nothing faded, nothing lost its sharpness. She felt the flood of liquid down her legs, and she knew then that she was losing the babe, losing her babe, Roland's babe. The wet was sticky and warm and she screamed at the ending of her child's life. She screamed for herself and her own loss and she screamed for the loss of the unborn child. She was aware that someone's hands were on her body, warm water and cloths were touching her gently, and Roland was holding her face against his chest and she could feel the sharp loud rhythm of his heart and he was speaking to her, yet she didn't understand his words. Slowly, as the screams that clogged her mind and her throat finally pulled away from her, releasing her back into herself, she made out his words, soft but insistent, pulling at her, lulling her.

"Hush, Daria, hush now. You're all right. Everything is all right now. Hush." And he was rocking her, kissing her sweaty forehead, and for a moment in time she was comforted and allowed herself to heed his words and his gentleness, and gave herself over to him.

She heard her mother's voice. "I can see no damage done, Roland. Now I must get the bleeding slowed. Just remain as you are. Hold her and soothe her. Keep her as quiet as you can. Try to . . . comfort her."

He did, kissing his wife's temple, speaking to her endlessly of the farmer he'd visited and the man's four daughters who'd wanted to come back to Chantry Hall with him and serve his beautiful wife. Aye, they'd all heard of her, of her kindness, of her gentleness. He talked and talked, of nothing and everything, yet none of it was important and he knew it, but it didn't matter. Daria was quiet. He watched Katherine bathe the blood from her daughter, watched her make a thick pad of white cotton cloths and press it against her. He saw the crimson cloths on the floor beside the bed.

It was over.

Daria felt the smooth edge of a cup pressed against

her closed lips. She opened her mouth at Roland's command and drank deep. She lolled back against her husband's arm, aware that the potion she'd drunk was drugged, aware now that Roland was stripping off her bloodied chemise and bathing the sweat from her body. She felt the soft cool material of her bedrobe as he wrapped it around her. When she was on her back, she opened her eyes to see her mother and Roland standing beside her. But they weren't looking at her, but at each other, and Katherine was saying quietly, "It isn't uncommon at all, Roland. She will heal and there will be other children for you. Also the vigorous activity this afternoon—she lost the child, but she did save Graelam. A choice God doubtless approved, Roland. It was no one's fault."

Roland was silent.

"It's for the best, Roland," Katherine said, unable to bear the empty pain of his silence. She really meant nothing by her words, just feeling so helpless that she said anything to ease him, for it hurt her to see him so shattered and withdrawn into himself. She wished he would say something, anything. But he remained silent. And she said again, " 'Tis for the best, Roland."

Daria felt darkness clouding her vision, closing over her mind, but she fought it. She laughed, a raw ugly sound. "Oh, Mother," she gasped, the words pouring out unbidden, "you're so very right. It is for the best. Roland's best. This child is dead and Roland is silent because he knows he must wait until he can yell his relief to the world—he is a man of some wisdom. He doesn't wish to shock you or any of our people, Mother, with his rejoicing." And she laughed and laughed until the tears streamed down her face and she was choking on them, and then suddenly she felt his hand strike her cheek and the laughter and tears died and she succumbed to the tug of the poppy juice. She saw her husband's face, drawn and white; then she saw nothing.

Roland stared down at his wife's pale face. Bloodless, he thought blankly, his eyes going toward the soaked cloths. So much blood. "You're certain she will be all right, Katherine? She's so pale . . ."

"She's lost a goodly amount of blood, but withal, she's strong and fit. She'll come through this, Roland. She'll regain her strength and come back to you."

He continued to look at his wife's face, continued to listen to her breathing, continued to feel her damning words sear through him.

"What did she mean—that you would yell your relief?"

Roland looked up at Katherine of Fortescue. Slowly he shook his head. "She meant nothing," he said.

Katherine was tired, worried to her very soul, and thus she spoke harshly, without thought. "She meant something, all right. I'm not blind, Roland. There is strife between the two of you. My daughter is bitterly unhappy and you, well . . . you seem so distant with her, so removed from her. Damn you, what did she mean? What have you done to her?"

And Roland said simply, giving it up because he was so unutterably weary, "The king and queen know of it, but no one else. The child she carried wasn't mine."

Katherine drew back, so surprised that she dropped some of the bloodied cloths. "Not your child? That makes no sense at all! No, that couldn't be—"

"I don't know whose child it was. More than likely it was the Earl of Clare's, or perhaps another's, a man I never knew of. No, it wasn't her fault, I would swear to that. Daria is good and true. She would never betray me. She was raped." He paused, raising Daria's limp hand and pressing his mouth to her wrist.

Katherine continued to stare at him. He moved restlessly, saying more to himself than to her, "But you see, she insisted the child was mine. She refused to back down, even though all pointed to fabrication. I have assured her repeatedly of my protection, promised that I would think no less of her, and begged her to tell me who had taken her against her will, but she kept insisting that the child was mine, that she'd given me her virginity one night when I was ill, out of my head with fever. I don't understand her, but now it is over and there will be no more dissension between us."

Katherine wished desperately she hadn't pushed him. What he'd told her—it was something she would never have imagined. She guessed he would regret speaking the truth to her, feel anger at her for goading him, so she said nothing more. She felt exhaustion creeping into her very bones; she looked down at her daughter and knew she would sleep for many hours now, healing sleep. She nodded to Roland and left the bedchamber. When she opened the door, she saw Sir Thomas standing there. She wasn't surprised to see him. She smiled and said, "I would very much like to rest now, sir."

"I will assist you to your room, Katherine," Sir Thomas said, and gave her his arm.

Roland eased onto his back, and clasped his wife's wrist. He felt the pulse, strong and steady beneath his finger. She would live. He felt relief so profound that he shook with it.

No, he wouldn't be shouting his relief. He wouldn't be shouting at all. He wished he'd kept his mouth shut, but it was too late now.

Graelam de Moreton sat up in his bed, his wife standing over him, her hands on her hips. They looked to be in the midst of a colorful argument.

"If there are wagers to be made on the outcome of this conflict, my groats are on Kassia."

"Get out, you lout! And take me with you!"

"Nay, Roland," Kassia called out, laughter in her

voice, "stay. Graelam becomes more and more un-
manageable, but perchance you can convince him that
he will be rendered impotent if he doesn't allow himself enough time to heal. I have told him that is what
happens to men who don't obey their wives' common-
sense instructions."

"That's her latest dire prediction," Graelam said. "I
refuse to believe it. You don't, do you?"

Roland kept his expression steady. "I can see why
she would be concerned," he said at last. "After all,
you have always told me that your rod is a woman's
bliss. Were something to happen to it, why, then,
what would she do?"

Kassia gasped. "Roland, did he say that, truly?"

"Of course I didn't say any such thing!"

" 'Twas something like that, if I recall aright. Nay,
you're right, Graelam. You told me that a man's rod
was a measure of a warrior and that, therefore, you
were as great as Charlemagne himself."

Graelam threw a carafe of water at Roland, then
fell back against the pillows at the pain it brought him.
He cursed fluently and with all the frustration in his
soul.

He felt his wife's soft hands on his chest, lightly
stroking him, and the pain, incredibly, eased. He opened
his eyes and looked up at her. "You think you are well
in control, don't you, wife?"

She leaned down and kissed him. "Aye."

"He does better, Kassia?"

She gave her husband a long look, then raised her
head. "He mends, Roland. I cannot, however, continue losing at draughts with him. He isn't altogether
witless and must soon guess that I am allowing him to
win."

Graelam smiled at that. "I improve, Roland. 'Tis just
that I am so damnably bored! It's been two days
now!"

"Lady Katherine tells me that you should be well enough to be out of your bed on the morrow."

"And Daria? When will she be up and about again?"

Roland shrugged, and bent to retrieve the wooden carafe from the floor.

"It's because of me that she lost the babe. I am sorry for it, Roland."

"Lady Katherine said it was God's will that you be saved. If that is the truth of it, then so be it. There is no blame here, Graelam. Rest now, and obey your wife. Daria does well enough. Kassia, when you wish to be relieved of this giant's company, you will send me word. Now, Rolfe awaits outside to see you, Graelam. Some matter of little importance, I imagine, but he doesn't wish you to feel impotent."

Roland left Graelam's chamber, his destination the stables. He wanted to clear his mind, to leave all the pain and hurt behind him for just a few hours.

Not that Daria had said anything to him.

She'd said nothing. She'd slept throughout that day, awakening in the early evening to drink some beef broth prepared especially for her by Alice. Roland wanted to see her, hold her, perhaps, assure himself that she was all right, but when he had entered the room, it was as if she wasn't there. A pale copy of her lay in the bed, but Daria, *his* Daria, was gone. As was the babe. She'd looked at him, then turned away. He'd slept that night in the great hall, wrapped in a blanket, one of the castle dogs at his feet.

It was nearly dark in the bedchamber, yet she made no move to light a candle. The air was cooling finally after the intense heat of the day, and Daria pulled a light blanket over her. It brought her no pain to do so. She felt no pain at all, just a soreness and the damnable weakness.

Her mother came into the room quietly, her stride

light and graceful even though she carried a tray doubtless filled with an assortment of marvelous foods from
Alice. Daria closed her eyes, but it was too late.

"Nay, love, pretend not with me. You must eat."

Daria felt the soft sting of candlelight against her
eyelids. She didn't want to be awake, she didn't want
to be *here*. She said aloud, her voice still raw and
hoarse, "I wish I had died, Mother. It would have
solved every problem."

"It would have solved your problem and only yours.
You wouldn't be feeling a thing. But everyone else's?"
At least she'd spoken, at last, Katherine thought, even
though what she said made her mother's heart wither.
She continued, speaking her mind. "You will bear
your pain just as everyone around you bears his own.
But that isn't the point, is it, Daria?"

"The point is that I have no more excuse to remain
here, in *his* castle, eating *his* food, sleeping in *his*
bed."

"It isn't a matter of excuses."

Roland's voice came from the doorway. Katherine
whirled about, wondering how much he'd heard. As
for Daria, she turned her face away, closing her eyes.
Katherine watched him as he strode into the room. He
looked tired, she thought. He said to her even as he
looked only at his wife, "I will see that she eats,
Katherine. Sir Thomas grows restive in your absence.
I would appreciate your being our hostess until Daria
is well again."

Katherine looked down at her daughter, then back
at her son-in-law. She wanted to beg him to go gently,
but his face was now closed, his eyes cold, as if he
guessed she would press him again. She said nothing.
Roland waited until the door closed after her; then he
moved to stand beside the bed.

"You will eat your dinner."

Daria said nothing, nor did she move.

"You're not dead, Daria, so there are still problems abounding, and you must help to solve them, and that means that you must get out of that bed. I can't regain your strength for you. You must do it for yourself. Now, eat, or I will force the food down your throat. I won't tell you again."

When she didn't respond to him, he leaned down and clasped her under her arms and pulled her up. He smoothed the pillows behind her and straightened the covers. "Have I dislodged the cloths?"

"No."

"Do you have any pain?"

"No."

"Good. I will place the tray here and you will eat. I won't leave you alone until you have done so."

She turned to face him. For the past two days he'd kept his distance from her. Now it seemed that he was changing his tactics. His voice was cold, his face set. His dark eyes, so beautiful and deep, regarded her with no emotion at all. He looked tired, and she wondered what he'd done during the day.

Why was he bothering? Why was he playing the worried husband? It made no sense to her. He would likely gain an annulment, despite her pregnancy, since he would claim it had been another man's seed that had grown in her.

She said aloud now, "Why are you doing this? What do you want? I will give you an annulment, though I doubt anything I would say would have any bearing on it."

A black eyebrow shot up. "Eat some of these stewed carrots and beans."

Daria ate several bites of the stewed vegetables. They were delicious and she realized she was starving. Her mouth began to water. She took a bite of mutton, marinated in some sort of incredible dill sauce, and roasted until the meat was falling from the bone. She nearly moaned aloud at the wondrous taste of it.

She continued to eat. Roland merely watched her, saying nothing. He was so relieved, he could think of nothing to say in any case. She was still so very pale that it scared the devil out of him. He'd allowed her two days; nothing had changed. She'd fallen even more deeply into depression. She was retreating even further from him. He would allow her no more time, in the hopes she would regain her spirit. He would take over now.

"I vow eating Alice's cooking is preferable to dying," he said at last as she chewed on a hunk of soft white bread.

She continued to chew, looking straight ahead.

He wouldn't continue to let her ignore him. "Dying is the coward's way as well. It wouldn't solve any problems at all. You would just be buried with some of them, yet the feel of them would still exist and eat at others who still lived."

She looked at him then, her expression as closed as his own. "I care not about your problems, Roland. They are yours and thus you are responsible for them. I would that you leave me alone. I would that you would seek an annulment."

"It appears obvious to me that you will gain neither of your wishes. Don't tell me you wish to contemplate visiting a convent again?"

Daria closed her eyes and leaned her head back against the pillows. She wanted to shudder at the thought of a convent. Her belly was full, but she felt so tired, weary to the depths of her, and now he was baiting her.

"Please go."

"No. I've left you alone for two days. No longer. Now I will carry you to Graelam's bedchamber. He wishes to see you. His guilt is palpable and you must assuage it."

"*His guilt.* That is utterly absurd. It was my decision

to try to save him, not his. If there is guilt to bear, it is mine and no one else's."

"That's what I told him, but he refuses to accept my word. Do you need to relieve yourself?"

She shook her head at that.

"Good. Let me take the tray, then." He paused, looking down at her. Katherine had braided her hair, but it was lank and lifeless. There were purple smudges under her eyes, but it was her eyes themselves that frightened him. They looked vague and lost. He shook himself. It made no sense. She would come around. He would make her come around. At least there was some color in her face now from the meal she'd eaten.

"I don't wish to see him."

"I don't care what you wish," he said. She didn't fight him, merely held herself stiffly until she didn't have any more strength, then laid her head on his shoulder as he carried her to Graelam's bedchamber.

Roland kicked the door open with his foot and called out, "I have brought you a treat, Graelam. What say you, Kassia? Shall I place my wife in bed with your husband? Perhaps we could begin a row of invalids. I would go find others. What do you think?"

"I think they're both too weak to shame us, Roland," Kassia said, and smoothed a place beside Graelam. "Place her here if you wish it." But Roland shook his head, saying, "Nay, I believe I shall continue to hold her. She's warm and soft. Bring that chair closer, Kassia."

Roland settled into the chair, his wife held close against his chest.

"Now, Graelam, as you see, my wife is mending. Unlike you, she is pliable and docile. I told her to eat, and she ate. She lies gentle and uncomplaining in my arms."

"Whilst you, husband," Kassia continued, sitting beside her husband, "carp and complain and make me want to throw that chair at your stubborn head."

Graelam stared at the pale-faced girl held in her husband's lap. With Kassia and Roland here, he would never come to know what was in her mind. Soon, he thought. On the morrow he would visit her. He said now, his voice gentle, "I'm glad you ate your dinner."

Daria nodded. She felt Roland's arms around her, holding her as if he cared about her. She felt his warmth, the hardness of his man's body, and wanted to weep. She felt pain so harsh it filled her and broke her completely, and she turned her face inward against his throat.

Roland felt her tears, felt the tremors in her body, yet she made no sound, just that awful racking of her body. He looked at Graelam and Kassia, their expressions appalled and concerned. "I will see you again," he said to Graelam, and carried his wife back to their bedchamber. He didn't release her, merely eased down on the bed, still holding her closely against him. "Are you cold?"

She didn't reply, just continued to cry without making a sound. It tore at him, this silent pain of hers. He spoke to her then, quietly, his voice pitched soft and deep. "If I could change what happened, I would, Daria. Doubt it not. I do not rejoice that you lost the babe, for I could have lost you as well. I want you to mend, to smile again, to come back to me. Please, don't weep."

"When you last took me, you felt the babe and hated me and you hated him."

Her voice was a whisper, and wet with hurt. He closed his eyes, remembering clearly that morning, remembering clearly how he'd felt when he'd touched the slight mound in her belly. He'd left her without a word. How had she felt?

"It isn't true that you don't rejoice."

"Daria, listen to me. I'm your husband. I have told you before and I will tell you again. I would protect you now with my life. Then I would have protected you with my life. It seems that ever since that first time I saw you, I was ready to protect you. I don't know why you won't name the father. Perhaps it is because you fear I would be killed by him, for I know you care for me. But it's no longer important. You are important, you and I and our life together."

She stopped crying then. These tears were for the child, his child, and for her, and for the emptiness in her heart. Slowly, for she was so very weak, she lifted herself to look at him. "I will say this just once more, Roland, then never again. The babe I carried was yours, conceived that night in Wrexham. If you cannot bring yourself to believe in me, to believe that I would never lie to you, ever, then I wish you to seek an annulment. I don't wish to remain here."

"Daria—"

"No, make no more protestations. I had prayed the babe would come in its time and it would look like its father—like you, Roland—that it would be a son and he would be dark like you, his eyes so black they looked like a moonless night, that when he smiled, it would be your smile you would see smiling back at you. It was a hope that I held deep within me, praying that it would be so, praying that then you would realize that I hadn't lied to you. But God decided otherwise. Now there is nothing for you save my word to you." She broke off on a gasp.

"What's wrong?"

"The bleeding . . . oh, God!"

Roland quickly eased her onto her back. He jerked open her bedrobe and saw that the cloths had become dislodged and there was blood on her thighs. "Hold still," he said.

After he'd bathed her and replaced the cloths, he straightened over her. "Are you warm enough?"

She nodded, turning her face again from him.

"Salin told me today that he'd heard of a band of about ten men a day or so away from here, camping in the open. They weren't recognized."

She remained silent, locked away from him.

"From the description he got from a tinker, though, it sounds like your esteemed uncle. A tall blond-haired man with pale flesh and a destrier more powerful than any he'd seen before. I wonder if your uncle would be stupid enough to try to enter the keep and kill me. He's a fool if he believes he can accomplish it."

"My uncle would never attack you in the open. He is treacherous and he will find a way, doubt it not. He will seek to take something precious from you, and then he will use it as leverage against you. Perhaps jewels, perhaps coin."

"You are all that is precious to me and I vow he'll never come near you again."

He heard her draw in her breath.

He smiled down at her. "Would you like to play draughts with me now? Like Kassia, I could cheat so that you would win."

21

GRAELAM DE MORETON waited patiently until Lady Katherine disappeared down the stairs, then walked down the narrow corridor, carefully and as slowly as an old man, his ribs pulling and aching. He slipped into the bedchamber, quietly closing the door after him.

Daria was lying on her back, her eyes closed, a thin cover drawn to her chest. He walked to the bed and stared down at her. Her dark hair was loose on the pillow. Beautiful hair, he thought, darker than Kassia's, yet mixed with the same vivid autumn colors. She was still too pale, her bones too prominent. As if sensing him, her eyes opened and her breath choked in her throat before she recognized him in the dim light.

"Lord Graelam! You startled me." She struggled up to her elbows. "Should you be out of your bed, my lord? Shall I call Kassia for you? Your ribs, surely they aren't healed sufficiently as yet. Shall—"

He smiled at her and gently pressed her back down. Her bones felt so very fragile under his hands. He sat beside her and lifted her hand, holding it between his two large ones. "I would speak to you," he said.

He saw her withdraw from him in that instant, her expression now carefully blank, her eyes wary, an invisible wall now firmly set between them.

"Nay, don't retreat, it's a coward's way and I know you aren't a coward, Daria. A coward wouldn't have

332

thrown aside my men to get to me and heaved at those damned rocks until she was numb with the pain of it."

"Sometimes there's nothing left."

He snorted at that and said something so lurid she blinked, staring at him. He grinned at her and nodded. "Aye, my men told me what you did. Indeed they seem to talk of little else save your bravery. They were amazed, and yea, somewhat frightened, for you seemed possessed to them. Yet you saved me, and for that I think they will forgive you almost anything." He grinned. "My men are loyal."

"As is your wife."

"Very true. She would try to slit an enemy's throat were I threatened. She hasn't the physical strength, but her spirit is above boundless."

Daria said nothing more, and Graelam looked away from her, toward the window slit. "I know the truth."

"Nay!"

"There is humiliation in that one small word, Daria," he said, looking back at her. "No, your husband didn't confide in me, though I wish he had. Actually, I listened to your mother speaking to Roland. They didn't know I was there. She was upset and was pressing him, but he withdrew from her just as you have from me. This is a puzzle, this strange tale of yours, but not unsolvable. I'm surprised you would give up. I'm disappointed in you. It isn't the act of the woman who saved my wretched life."

"He won't believe me. Should I continue to protest my innocence until he retreats completely from me?"

"So, it's a matter of him not remembering that night. I wonder how to stimulate his memory."

"Nay, 'tis a matter of him refusing to believe me. I'm his wife and I love him, I always have, ever since the moment I first saw him disguised as a priest when he came to Tyberton to rescue me."

Graelam laughed, much to Daria's surprise. "Nay,

don't look at me like I'm a monster with no feelings. It's just that early in my marriage to Kassia, there was a matter of discord between us. I didn't believe her innocence in a certain matter. And then, finally, it simply was no longer important, for I had come to love her. The truth came out later, but it didn't matter by then."

"There is a difference here. Roland doesn't love me and I doubt he ever will. The king forced him to wed me. Nay, more's the truth, his own honor forced him, for he did care about me; he felt sorry for me. He also wanted my dowry. And now there is no way I can prove the truth of my claim. You see, I swore to myself that Roland would never know. I didn't want him to feel guilty that he'd taken my virginity. I didn't want him to feel responsible for me, for all of it had been my idea. Then I was with child and everything changed. I was sorry for it, but there was naught I could do. And now there is no reason for him to trust me, to believe anything I say. There is no reason for him to ever care for me again."

"Why do you harp on that? Are you a shrew? Are you bitter-tongued and harsh? You haven't an answer, I see. Let me ask you this, Daria. Who does Roland believe to be the man who raped you?"

"Most likely the Earl of Clare. But if he didn't rape me, why then, Roland just accepts that another man must have, a man he doesn't know about, a man who must have attacked me in Wrexham whilst Roland was ill in his bed."

"So if I were to bring this Earl of Clare here and he denied having raped you, Roland still wouldn't be convinced?"

She shook her head.

Graelam stood slowly, for his every move brought pain from his bruised ribs. "You saw that wall collapse on me. You saw your father die. What is this with Roland?"

"It is just that when I saw him, I knew him. Deep inside, I knew him, recognized him as being part of me. I know it seems strange, mayhap even close to madness, but it is true."

"I doubt it not. I will leave you now, Daria. Please remember that a coward's way isn't your way. Do not disappoint me; do not disappoint yourself. I am in your debt. I always pay my debts, but I must consider all this very carefully. Aye, very carefully indeed."

He left her and she was again alone. And she pondered his words.

"Have you heard aught else?" Roland asked.

Salin shook his head. "He's gone to ground, the filthy whoreson. I don't like it, nor do I like the stories I've heard about the Earl of Reymerstone. I would take some men and search him out. I would like to split him."

It was Roland's turn to shake his head, and he did. "Nay, Salin, not yet. When it is time for the hunt, I will lead the pack. But I cannot leave yet, not until . . ." His voice trailed off.

"Until your lady heals," Salin finished for him. "Gwyn told me she smiled this morning. 'Twas a matter of a new overtunic sewn for her by Lady Katherine."

Roland wished he'd seen that smile. Over a week had passed since she'd miscarried the babe. She seemed well again, though she was too thin and there were the dark smudges beneath her eyes. Yes, he wished he could have seen her smile. Either he or Graelam played chess with her in the evenings. Kassia refused to play against Daria, saying that women were too smart to go against each other. Roland wondered at Graelam's attitude toward Daria. He teased her and mocked her skills at chess and laughed at her until Daria began telling him he was a lout and a bore. Graelam only teased her more. And since two nights ago, Roland had begun sleeping in his own bed again. But he'd made no move to touch his wife.

The previous evening he'd seen her looking at him and he'd returned her look before she had time to glance away. The pain in her eyes had smitten him deep. He'd wanted to say something to her, but she'd withdrawn immediately and he wasn't ready to scale that wall as yet, for, in truth, he didn't know what to say. His life had become a damnable tangled mess and he loathed it, yet he felt powerless to change it.

Both Salin and Roland looked up to see Lord Graelam de Moreton striding toward them across the inner bailey. He looked strong, fit, and fearsome in his black-and-silver mail. For a man who'd very nearly met his maker not too many days before, his appearance now bespoke something of a miracle. His men gazed upon him with looks approaching awe.

He was slapping his gloves against his thigh. He looked thoughtful and mildly worried.

"I believe you are healed, Graelam. Shall I buffet your ribs or shake your hand?"

Graelam grinned at Roland. "You will now have peace and perchance some success at chess, my friend, for I am leaving you. It is time I returned my wife to Wolffeton."

An odd way to say it, Roland thought. "And what do you then, Graelam?"

"Why, I'll rot in my own castle, what else?"

"I don't know," Roland said, frowning at him. "I don't know."

Graelam pulled on his gauntlets. "Mayhap I'll go a-raiding and steal some of Dienwald's sheep. He is a joy to behold when he's bulging with fury. Ah, and does Philippa ever make him bulge! Ah, my errant wife. Kassia! Come, dearling, and bid your good-byes to your kind host. Then you can bedevil me all the way back to Wolffeton."

Daria watched Graelam and Kassia and their soldiers ride from the keep. She wasn't particularly surprised when Lord Graelam suddenly turned in his saddle and looked for a long moment back at the castle. It seemed as if he was searching her out. She wondered at him. So fearsome a warrior, yet so kind to her. She would hate being his enemy, for she knew he would show no quarter. She felt suddenly unsteady and eased into a chair. The damnable weakness. It wouldn't leave her. Kassia had told her what to expect, at least what had happened to her after Harry's birth. Then she'd kissed her cheek, saying as she gripped her hands, "You saved my husband. For that I am in your debt for all time. I always pay my debts. Don't give up, Daria." Skirts swirling, Kassia had left her.

Chantry Hall was filled with people, shouting and laughing and buffeting each other, the children arguing and shrieking, and still Daria felt utterly alone even in the chaotic hall. She couldn't bear the furtive pitying looks, and thus remained alone in Roland's bedchamber much of the time. Daria rose now and pulled her new overtunic over her gown. It was a pale blue wool and very soft to the touch. She would show her husband her new finery. Perhaps he would smile.

He was speaking to Salin in the inner bailey, and both men looked ready to ride out. She paused on the bottom stone step of the great hall, the early-morning sunlight blazing down on her face, warming her. Roland looked up. He stared at her, unmoving. He said nothing. He raised his hand in a small salute, then turned on his heel and strode toward the stables, Salin at his side.

Ah, yes, he remained kind to her when he chanced to be with her. Nothing more.

But then again, she didn't expect much more than

that. She didn't see him at all during the days, for he worked beside his men to repair the eastern castle wall, the one that had collapsed on Graelam. It was nearly completed now. Time passed, and with the passing days, her strength returned. As for the interior of the keep, Daria worked diligently to see it cleaned, the trestle tables scrubbed, the lord and lady's chairs polished to a high sheen. And then, one morning she was able to see the thick oak beams crisscrossing high above the great hall. So many years of smoke had blackened them and it had taken hours of sweating and cursing to scrub them clean. She smiled, pleased with herself. Roland's keep was becoming almost pleasant. The reeds on the floor were sweet-smelling, the jakes had been thoroughly limed, and only a strong wind blowing in a westerly direction brought any noxious odors to the nose.

Now she needed to see the outbuildings whitewashed, needed to purchase goods and a few new furnishings for the great hall and its antechambers. The goods that had made up her dowry had added warmth, the two brass lavers gleaming, they were so highly polished, the chair cushions thick and soft, and the two tapestries sewn by her grandmother, on the far wall, giving color and protection from the damp. But she had to wait to purchase any further goods, for it required Roland's approval. She spent her afternoons sorting through herbs, mixing those potions she knew, sewing companionably with her mother, and giving instructions for the castle servants through Gwyn, the girl Roland had slept with, the girl who was friendly and quite nice, the girl Daria couldn't help but like.

She wore her new overtunic again, loosely sewn with wide sleeves, over one of her old gowns her mother had altered for her. She was too thin, but food still made her feel faintly ill. She girded the braided gold belt more firmly around her waist, pulling in the material. She brushed her hair and left it loose, thick and lustrous from washing, nearly to her waist.

Roland entered the bedchamber and came to an abrupt halt. She became still under his scrutiny.

"You're lovely."

"Thank you."

"I must see to some jewelry for you, Daria. Something delicate, perhaps emeralds to match your eyes."

She stared at him, wondering what was in his mind, wondering why he was speaking thus to her.

"I should prefer purchasing a few more goods for your castle, Roland."

"Oh?"

"Perhaps several more carpets, some cushions for your chair here in the bedchamber, mayhap even a tapestry for the wall here, for the damp is very bad, Sir Thomas told me, during the winter months."

Roland appeared thoughtful for several minutes, then said, quite unexpectedly, "Did you know that Philippa is the steward for St. Erth?"

"Aye, you told me that once."

"Should you mind detailing our needs and balancing them against the coin we have remaining from your dowry and from my cache? Next year I suspect we will have excess wool to sell and that will make us more self-sufficient. Graelam and I spoke of which markets were best and which merchants in this area didn't try to steal your destrier from beneath you during the bargaining."

"You aren't jesting? I wouldn't have thought a man would approve such an activity for a woman."

Roland shrugged.

"I should very much like to do these things, Roland."

"When you have completed your entering, discuss it with me. Then we will decide what is to be done first."

She could but stare at him before the words blurted out. "Why are you being like this?"

"Like what?"

"Kind to me . . . as if you cared what—"

He cut her off, for he simply couldn't bear to hear the rest of her words. "There is work to be done and you are capable of doing it. Don't you believe yourself able to accomplish it?"

Her chin went up. "I am quite capable."

He smiled at her then, his dark eyes warm and approving, and Daria would willingly have cut even Lord Graelam's throat had he threatened her husband.

It was the second day of September. The air was crisp and cool. An early-autumn day it was, with a clear sky overhead and a bright sun that made the different colors of the countryside all the more vivid. Daria breathed in deeply. She came out of the great hall at the sound of shouting and stood on her tiptoes to see what was happening. There was her husband, stripped to the waist, breathing heavily, sweat glistening off him. He was circling another man, a huge lout who looked quite able to rip her husband into pieces. The men-at-arms had formed a large, loose circle around them and they were yelling and shouting. Daria froze when the other man suddenly lunged. Why were the men just standing there? Why weren't they helping Roland? She watched in mute horror as the man grabbed Roland around his waist and lifted him. She saw his massive arms bulge, the muscles flexing, and she knew he was strong enough to squeeze the life from her husband. Why, she wondered frantically, had she seen the wall collapse on Graelam and not seen her own husband about to meet his death? Why weren't his men doing anything?

She acted without thought, terror for Roland gripping her, making her frantic. She grabbed her skirts, pulling them above her knees, and dashed down the deep stone steps into the inner bailey. She was scream-

ing as she ran. She reached the loose circle of men and
began to curse them, pushing and shoving them aside
until she was within the circle. She raised her fist at
them, screaming, "Why aren't you doing something?
You miserable cowards! You filthy whoresons! You
will stand by and let him be crushed to death?" Several of the men who had heard her looked as if they'd
turned into stone, staring at her, not moving a finger.
Furious, she ignored them. She was so close to Roland
and the huge man that she could hear their breathing,
hear their lurid curses. Somehow Roland had gotten
free, but just as she nearly yelled her relief, the huge
lout lunged again, screaming a terrible curse, and Daria,
all thought frozen within her, jumped on his back just
as he grabbed for Roland.

She clutched him around his thick neck, yelling,
pummeling the top of his head with her fist. "No!
Don't you dare touch him! I'll kill you!" She managed
to wrap her legs around him and she tried to choke the
life from him, jerking his head back and crushing
inward with her forearms. She squeezed her legs around
him as he'd done to Roland with his arms, but it was
nothing to him. She screamed and yelled and punched
him, beyond thought, so furious and frightened that
for many minutes she didn't realize that the man was
standing perfectly still, not even trying to dislodge her
from his back, and that there wasn't a whisper of a
voice anywhere near them.

"Daria!"

Through the haze of fear, she heard her name. She
shook her head, pounding the man's head as hard as
she could.

"Daria! By all the saints, stop it!"

She looked up then and saw Roland standing beside
her. She realized then that the man whose back she
was clinging to like a demented fool was standing very

quietly, not moving even a finger, just letting her strike him.

"Come, that's quite enough." Roland was holding out his arms to her.

"But I don't wish him to hurt you and . . ." She sent her fist into the side of the man's head one more time.

"By all the saints, stop it! Rollo has few enough brains without you pounding the rest out of his head! Cease your attack! Come!"

She released her hold on the man's neck and dropped her legs from his waist. She flung out her arms and Roland caught her and lifted her down to stand on the cobblestones.

But she was still gripped in her unreasoning fear. But Roland seemed to be all right. She was crying now, not realizing it, her hands running over his face, down to his shoulders, touching him, probing at his flesh, assuring herself that he wasn't hurt. "I was so afraid . . . I thought he was killing you, he is so large and—"

It was the complete and utter silence that made her slow. Not a whisper of a sound. Her voice dropped off and she became as still as everyone around her. Slowly she turned to look at the man. He was still standing quietly, just looking back at her, a curious blend of confusion and amazement writ on his ugly face. And all their people were now in a loose circle around her and Roland, staring at her and whispering behind their hands.

She raised her face. "Roland? He didn't hurt you? You're all right, truly? I don't understand."

Something was very wrong. She saw the myriad of emotions cross his expressive face. There was anger, oh, she could feel waves of anger flowing from him, but then it was gone, swept away by something else . . . something . . . He was laughing. He threw back his head and roared with laughter. Soon the entire inner bailey was filled with people who were howling with laughter, holding their sides, screaming with laughter. She stood there, not understanding. The huge man was now laughing as well, deep gritty laughter.

They were all laughing at her.

What had she done?

She realized at that moment that her gown was ripped under her left arm. Sweat was streaking down her face . . . nay, not just sweat, but tears of rage and fear at the man who'd been attacking Roland. One of her leather slippers lay on the ground near her. Her hair had come loose from its bound coil and was hanging over her shoulder. The laughter swelled, overwhelming her. She felt apart from all of them; she felt ridiculous; she felt a complete fool.

She cried out, a small broken cry, and grabbed her skirts yet again, and began running toward the narrow tunnel that connected the inner bailey to the outer bailey. The portcullis was raised and no one blocked her way.

"Daria! Wait!"

Roland's laughter died as quickly as it had sprung up. He looked at Rollo, the hulking fellow he'd been wrestling with.

"Thank you for not hurting her," he said. "All of you—back to your chores."

The laughter quieted a bit, but the men and women watched the master dash after his wife.

Salin said to Rollo, "Mayhap 'tis the best wrestling match I've ever seen. Mayhap it will bring an excellent result."

Rollo banged the side of his head with the heel of his hand, as if to clear it. He said with genuine surprise, "She jumped on my back and pounded my head. She tried to break my neck with those skinny little arms of hers."

"Aye, you'll have a bit of a black eye for your labors, but your neck's thicker than an oak tree. No danger she'd twist that part of you off."

Rollo shook his head, staring after Daria. "I could have killed her, yet she attacked me."

"Aye," Salin said. "He's her husband."

"A female attacking me," Rollo said, shaking his head. "I will leave now and return to my farm. Tell the master I will return whenever he wishes to continue our match. When I tell my wife of the little mistress attacking me, she will laugh until her eyes cross."

Roland gave up yelling after his wife. He would catch up with her soon enough. And he did, just outside the castle walls, just at the top of a slight hillock covered with thick green grass. He grabbed her arm, but she jerked free of him, and he stumbled at the same time and lost his balance and the two of them went tumbling over the side of the embankment down the grassy slope. They'd done this same tumble before, he thought blankly even as he fell. Roland tried to protect her, but it wasn't possible. They came to a halt at the bottom, Roland on his back and Daria on her side.

She lay there gasping for breath, quite unhurt, at least in body. She was so humiliated that she regained her breath more quickly than she probably would have, and lurched to her feet. She saw Roland lying there, looking up at her, a huge grin on his face. She cried out and scrambled back up the slope, only to feel his hand around her ankle. He pulled, very gently, and she fell backward against his chest. He was still laughing. At her. She saw red and turned on him, crying out, smashing her fists into his chest.

"Stop it! You bastard, stop laughing at me!"

Roland stopped quickly enough. He pulled her against

him, flattening her arms to her sides to protect himself, and held her still. "Hush," he said. "Hush."

"I'm not the one laughing! I hate you!"

"No you don't. Don't lie, it doesn't become you." And he chuckled, and in between chuckles, he leaned down and lightly nipped at her bare throat. Her gown was now ripped nearly to her waist, and then he felt the hot smooth flesh of her shoulder against his mouth, he felt a surge of desire so strong he shook with it. No, he didn't want to laugh now. By all the saints, it had been so long, so very long.

He didn't think, just acted. He grasped the straps of her chemise and ripped them apart. He pulled the soft worn cotton to her waist, baring her breasts. She wasn't moving now.

"You're so damned beautiful."

He didn't touch her, just stared down at her heaving breasts. She gulped and tried to pull away from him, but he held her still, her arms still pinned to her sides.

"Are you well?" he said, and his voice was harsh and deep. "Inside, are you healed?"

But he didn't wait for her to answer. He couldn't. He leaned down and kissed her, hard, his hands cupping her face between his palms, holding her still for him. At the touch of his mouth against hers, Daria felt a great relief begin to fill her, but it changed and became something else, something urgent and frantic and wild.

"Part your lips. Yes, that's right. Touch my tongue, Daria. Ah . . . so sweet, so very sweet you are. Do you like my hands on your breasts?"

He was lightly stroking his fingertips over her breasts, lifting them in his palms, not yet touching her nipples, just stroking her lightly, as if to learn her. Then his hand dipped down to stroke over her ribs, then he was jerking away her gown, ripping it without hesitation,

and finally it fell, pooling about her feet. He yanked at
the chemise and then she was standing naked, sup-
ported by his arm, his hand stroking over her breasts,
his mouth and tongue against hers.

She turned to him then, wanting more, wanting all
of him now. When she pressed herself against him, his
hands became frenzied on her back, sweeping downward to cup her buttocks. He lifted her, fitting her
against himself, and she felt his urgency, felt the hardness of him, and he was so hot, so intensely alive, and
he wanted her. A bolt of sheer lust went through her
and she moaned against his mouth.

He set her away from him but her hands were on his
clothes, pulling at the fastenings, and both of them
were clumsily trying to strip him, but it took much
more time than they'd thought it would.

But then, despite her help, Roland was naked and
standing before her, and she hurled herself at him,
pressing hard against him, flinging her arms around his
neck, and she raised her face for a kiss and he gave
her all his need and desire. Then he lifted her. "Wrap
your legs around my waist, quickly. I'm going to come
upward into you, Daria, deeply into you . . ." And
she felt him fitting her legs around his flanks, felt his
fingertips between her thighs, stroking upward until he
found her. He parted her swelled woman's flesh with
his fingers and she gasped and lurched, wanting to
help him but not knowing how to. And he was breathing so harshly, and she was too, that neither of them
heard the shouting. Then he was easing inside her,
pushing upward, slowly, just a bit at a time, his body
trembling at the control he tried to exert, and she was
gasping at the feel of him, wanting more, yet it was
tight and so sweet, the feel of him inside her . . .

"Roland! Daria!"

He shoved his full length into her, driving upward,
kissing her breasts as she arched her back at the feel of

him. "By all the saints," he gasped, and eased her down upon her back against the sweet-smelling grass. And he began to ride her hard and deep.

"Roland! Daria!"

He froze over her, a look of astonished chagrin coming over his features. "Oh, no," he said, and his voice was filled with pain. "By all the saints, I don't believe it." He began to curse.

She stared up at him, not understanding, until she heard their names shouted a third time.

He pulled out of her, his chest heaving, his member swelled and hard and wet from her. He looked for a moment utterly bewildered and uncertain of what he should do. Then he shook himself into action.

"Quickly, dearling, quickly. It's Sir Thomas and he draws very close." Roland saw that she was still held in thrall by her passion, and he ignored his own nakedness to help her dress again in her ripped clothes. "Hold them together. That's it. Are you all right now?"

She was holding the bodice of her gown together over her breasts and she was just looking up at him.

"Are you all right?"

She shook her head, no words in her mind, not a single one.

He smiled, a painful smile, and touched his fingertips to her mouth. "I know, dearling. This night there won't be any interruptions. By all the saints, you're lovely."

When Sir Thomas and Lady Katherine appeared at the top of the slope, it was to see Roland clumsily pulling on his clothes and Daria, standing there like a half-wit, watching him.

"I think," Sir Thomas said to Lady Katherine, "that our presence is more than a nuisance."

"You don't think he'll hurt her, do you?"

Sir Thomas smiled down at her. "Hurt her? I'll

warrant he was making her wild with pleasure until we came along and ruined it all."

Katherine jerked just a bit at his words, and said slowly, "I don't think that's possible."

"So it was like that with you, was it? A pity. If you'll allow me, I will show you that a man can please you. Come, let's leave them. I daresay Roland won't particularly wish to converse with either of us at the moment. Actually, he is probably beyond putting two words together."

22

ROLAND couldn't clear his mind. He couldn't seem to focus on anything outside himself, outside her. His body was in control, or out of control, he thought blankly, his senses filled with her, her sweet wild scent, the tangled masses of hair tumbling down her back, her ripped gown showing patches of smooth white flesh. He grabbed her hand and pulled her around. He didn't care that they were in plain sight of the castle. He simply didn't think about it. He looked down at her mouth, soft and slightly parted, and moaned.

"Daria." He kissed her, pulling her up tightly against him, bringing her to her tiptoes. When she responded to him, arching upward, he trembled with the force of his need. He lifted her in his arms and strode toward a small copse of oak trees just to the east.

She wasn't pliant in his arms. She was as frantic and wild as he was. She kissed his chin, his mouth, his nose, wet, soft kisses that sent him into a near-frenzy. He felt her warm tongue on his ear, her sweet breath on his cheek. He started running. She wrapped her arms around his neck, choking him in her fervor to get closer to him.

Her ripped clothes became quickly shredded. He eased her down on her torn gown and found he couldn't wait. He came over her, parting her legs, bending her knees, and he nuzzled her white belly, kissing her, nipping light kisses, his hands stroking up and down the backs of her thighs, widening her legs, drawing nearer and nearer, and she was lifting her hips, wanting him there, closer . . .

When his mouth touched her, she cried out and lurched up, so astonished at what he was doing and how his actions made her feel that she was beyond words. "Hush, darling," he said, his breath hot on her flesh, or perhaps she was the one who was hot, for her need was beyond what she could have imagined, the roiling sensations were pushing her, making her twist and arch her back, making her legs tremble uncontrollably. It was beyond anything she could understand, and when he pressed his palm against her belly to hold her still, she lay there staring up at the sunlight that filtered through the oak leaves like silver spears. It was so beautiful, she thought, so very beautiful. But it wasn't the glistening sunlight that filled her senses, it was his mouth on her woman's flesh, and she wanted more and more. . . . Her breasts were heaving and her hands kneading his shoulders, pulling his head closer to her, and suddenly she spun out of herself, crying out again and again. Roland held her thighs, feeling the rippling spasms, the tightening of the sleek muscles. At each wrenching cry, he felt himself grow and swell, both his spirit and his member, for he reveled in her pleasure, the pleasure he was giving her. His groin was throbbing, painfully full with his need, but her release was more important, this wild pleasure of hers that went on and on and drew him into her, sending both of them beyond all thought. He gentled his mouth on her, drawing softly and slowly now, feeling her legs relax, feeling her entire body loosen, and he came up between her legs and said, "Daria, open your eyes. Look at me. I want you to see me coming into you."

He came into her powerfully, his entire body shuddering, not slowing in his pace, and he wrapped his arms around her thighs, lifting her and sending himself deeper inside her. His rhythm was hard and fast and deep, and he felt so frenzied, so out of control, he thought he would die of it. Suddenly he came out of her, the sensations too much, driving him too quickly. He lurched back and gently eased her legs off his shoulders. He pulled her upright to her knees, facing him. "I want to kiss you whilst I take you," he said, and pulled her legs around him and eased her down on his member. He closed his eyes at the feel of her. He kissed her, his tongue deep in her mouth just as his sex was deep in her belly. So deep inside her he was, she thought, and he was hers, in this precious moment he was hers and he was part of her, and there was nothing but him, and she was filled with him, and she was crying with the wonder of it.

He buried his face against her neck as he gained his release, trembling, then tensing incredibly, moaning against her throat, and she felt the wet of him deep within her and she held him as tightly as she could.

Roland lazily kissed her throat until his heart had slowed its furious pounding. Gently he eased her back onto the ground, covering her, his member still deep inside her. He lay over her, balancing himself on his elbows, looking down into her face. Her eyes were more green now than before, and he wondered how this could be so; green and vague and soft, and he saw himself reflected in her eyes and wondered if he filled her mind as he filled her belly. He prayed so, for she filled him. Her hair was tangled with stray twigs and bits of grass and small clods of dirt. Her cheeks were flushed and her lips warm and swelled. "You're beautiful," he said, and it was true. He kissed her mouth, remembering now when he'd first kissed her, he hadn't wanted to stop. Just to kiss her . . . and the instant she responded to him, he felt his member swelling again and he wanted her once more.

Very slowly he slid deep inside her, then withdrew

almost completely, smiling when she lifted her hips to bring him back into her again.

"Can I give you pleasure again?"

"I don't know," she whispered, and pulled his head down. To kiss him. She loved his mouth, the texture of his flesh, the scent of him, as much as he craved her. Her body moved with his, unbidden, and when he quickened his thrusts, she dug her fingers into his back and moaned.

"I like the sound of that," he said, and eased his hand between them. To his besotted surprise, the moment his fingertips touched her, she grew frenzied, crying out, twisting beneath him, bucking upward, nearly throwing him off her in her passion. And she was crying out, quaking with the nearly painful feelings that held her, and he doubted there was a more beautiful sight in the world.

She shouted out his name in the moment of her release, and in that same instant he spewed his seed deep inside her, unable to wait, unable to do anything except to surrender to this joining, this incredible mating with her, with his wife.

It was many minutes before he could raise himself on his elbows. His muscles felt fluid. "I think you've killed me, wife."

To his pleasure, she flushed, and he laughed. He dipped his head down and kissed her mouth. How he loved to kiss her. It was many minutes before he raised his head again.

"I like to see you blush. It pleases me, but know, Daria, that a wife is expected to lose her head over her husband. 'Tis a requirement of marriage, I understand, this display of abandoned passion. Now, it appears you've twice lost your head, and that, wife . . . well, that makes me feel like a conquering warrior."

"What about your head?"

" 'Twasn't my head I lost, dearling. 'Twas all my seed."

She ducked her face into his chest and she breathed in deeply. He smelled of sweat and of the sweet earth and of her as well.

"What is this? Embarrassment from the most wanton of my women?"

"Women! I am your only woman, Roland."

"Aye, the females hereabout aren't all that comely, so perhaps I shall have to rely on you for my pleasure." He kissed her again, marveling as he did so how she drew him, charmed him with her mouth, her taste, and how he'd forgotten that during the past months, how he'd kept himself apart from her, not wanting to think of her, not wanting her to touch him in any way. He frowned as memories razed through his mind, memories he didn't want now.

She poked him in the ribs, bringing him back to her. "Nay, don't move, Roland!"

He sighed. "I'm sorry, sweetling, but you've depleted me, stripped me of my manliness, plundered my seed. I must rest for a while and garner my strength. Then you can have your way with me again."

"All right," she said, and snuggled against him. After a moment she raised her head and gave him a siren's smile, her green eyes so wicked he was again utterly charmed with her, this wife of his. "Will you need much time?"

He groaned loudly; then, because her mouth was there, just inches from his, he kissed her.

They were silent for some moments; then Roland said, his voice as neutral as a fool's smile, "Rollo is a huge fellow, a rock of a man, and stronger than an ox. Also, he is slow of foot and of reaction. That is what evens the contest."

"I don't wish to speak of that. I made a fool of myself."

She could feel him smiling. His entire body seemed to warm with his humor. "True, but had he been a knave, why, then, you would have saved me. Rather than being a fool, you would have been a heroine."

"I'm a fool and I can't go back. And look at me—my clothes are in tatters. Everyone will know what you have done to me!"

"Mayhap they'll think I beat you instead."

"But your clothes are in nearly as sorry a state. Nay, they'll know what we've done."

"That is a problem—the condition of our clothes. I will set my mind to finding a solution."

In the next moment, he was snoring loudly.

"Roland! Cease your noxious noises! You're pretending!"

He kissed her ear, nuzzling at her throat until she raised her head and gave him her mouth.

"It's odd, you know. I've always thought kissing a woman was pleasurable, but nothing more, really. But you, Daria, your mouth drives me mad with lust. Aye, I'll kiss you until God removes me from this miserable earth."

And as he kissed her, she lightly laid her hand on his hip. He jerked and kissed her harder. "And what will you do if I touch you here, Roland?" Her hand dipped to his flat hard belly. She could feel his muscles tensing, feel the crisp groin hair beneath her fingers and his smooth hot flesh. "And here?" she whispered into his mouth as her fingers lightly closed around his member.

Roland had not believed it possible, but at the touch of her warm fingers closing around him, he swelled until he was pressing against her palm, pushing, thrusting against her fingers.

"This is what I'll do," he said, and fell onto his

back, bringing her over him. "Ride me, Daria. Take me."

She gave him that siren's smile again, her eyes crinkling with laughter and newly considered passion, and he shook with that smile and that look in her eyes, and he lifted his hips as she settled herself over him. When she took him and guided him upward into her, he closed his eyes and gave himself over to feelings he would never forget.

When she neared her release, he pushed her, and she went wild, bringing him with her.

"I shall surely die now," he said between gritted teeth, but he was still heaving upward, still clasping her hips in his hands, still touching her womb, and the stark intimacy of that touch held him captive for many moments. He was stunned at this mating. It should have been slow and tender, but it had been as frenzied as the first time.

"Killed by a greedy wife who wrings me out and tosses me away."

"I'm not tossing you anywhere," Daria said, stretching out over him. She nuzzled her face against his chest. "I can't even move, so how could I have the strength to heave you away?"

He was thoughtful for a moment. "This is very strange," he said at last. "Never in my life have I taken a woman so many times in so short a length of time."

She raised her head and frowned at him. "But I thought that perhaps we could—"

He slapped her buttocks. "You're lying and you just don't do it well."

"No, I'm teasing you, Roland. You enjoy me. I like that."

She looked so pleased with herself that he was obliged to chuckle. "Aye, I enjoy you. Now, however, we must see to ourselves, somehow, before Salin sends out a party to search for us."

"Must I try to stand up?"

"Aye, and so must I."

"My legs are wobbly and I can't feel any bones."

His felt just as unsteady, but he only smiled as he helped her up. They stood facing each other, dirty as urchins, smiling, smelling of sweat and sex and grass. He cupped her breasts in his hands, and she, smiling a slightly crazed smile, cupped his member between her hands and felt the heat of him warm her to her heart.

He sighed and stepped back. "There's no hope for it," he said, glancing about at their strewn torn clothes.

No one said anything when the master and mistress came into the inner bailey looking like they'd been attacked and rolled in the dirt.

Roland had stroked his fingers through her tangled hair, but it had done little good. Daria was very aware that a multitude of eyes were staring at them and knowing what had happened. And if they didn't know immediately, her downcast eyes and the bright flush on her cheeks gave them away. Roland, curse him, was smiling like a fool.

She quickened her step and looked at her toes. Her other slipper had somehow disappeared. Roland chuckled beside her, then leaned down to whisper in her ear, "Such energy, wife. I thought I'd drained you of every ounce, but no, here you are ready to race me to our bedchamber."

"I'm a woman, Roland. I have great endurance."

"And I'm a man and filled with vigor."

He leaned down, cupping the back of her neck in his hand, and kissed her, in front of all their people, in front of the children, in front of all the dogs and cats and goats, and because kissing him was more wonderful than nearly anything else she could imagine, Daria kissed him back, pressing upward against him.

She dimly heard a raucous cheer and flushed from her hairline to her dirty toes.

He continued to kiss her until he was satisfied with his result. Then he raised his head and gave her the most insolent grin imaginable. And he said softly, smiling down at her flushed face, "You're mine, all mine. Never forget that, ever. Have water fetched for us. I shall join you in our bedchamber very shortly."

"I would say that things have improved between your daughter and Roland."

Katherine turned smiling eyes to Sir Thomas. "Aye, it would appear so. She looks so . . . at ease with herself."

"She has the look of a woman well and truly pleasured, Katherine. Her eyes appear even greener. Were her father's eyes that startling color?"

"Nay, her grandmother had eyes as green as spring grass. She shares nothing at all with her father."

"You should be proud of her. She's a lovely girl. If she continues to be so well-pleased with her husband, I doubt not that another babe will soon grow in her belly."

Oddly enough, Roland shared that thought nearly at the same time. He was watching Daria chew on a braised meat bone with great thoroughness. Her teeth were white, her tongue pink, her concentration profound. He wanted her again; he wanted her to kiss and fondle his member with such absorption as she was giving that damned meat bone.

It was perplexing, this effect she had on him, and as mystifying as it was belated. He'd kept his distance from her, both mentally and physically, since their marriage. Until today. Until she'd run out of the great hall screeching at the top of her lungs and jumped on

Rollo's back, uncaring about herself, wanting only to save her husband. A woman who didn't love a man wouldn't do that. Even as he'd felt anger, then amusement, in the depths of him, he'd felt valued, he'd felt incredibly cherished. And now everything had shifted, changing even before he'd had time to question it, and, he suspected, this damned change was irrevocable. He'd never before considered himself a man to be a slave to his phallus, as were some men he'd known. Even when he'd been in the Holy Land and played the indulgent owner of six women, each of whom was eager to do nothing but please him, he hadn't been controlled by lust. And yet here was his wife, too thin, but with flesh softer than a summer rain, her cheeks rosy from the sweet wine she'd been drinking, and he wanted to jerk the meat bone out of her hand and pull up her gown and take her here, right now, this very instant. He was hard and swelled, and he was vastly relieved that the full-cut tunic covered him. He shifted painfully in his chair.

If he continued to want her, she would soon be again with child. His child this time. He sat back, listening to all the voices that filled the great hall, blending together in a low rumble, the individual words indecipherable. It was pleasant, all this noise, and it gave him peace, strangely enough. He looked over at Lady Katherine and Sir Thomas. Thomas was smitten, no doubt about that, besotted to the roots of his grizzled hair. He wondered about Katherine. Perhaps they would wed. If that happened, he hoped they would remain at Chantry Hall. The idea of having a large family surrounding him was satisfying. It made him feel needed; it made him feel like he belonged. Finally there was a place for him and he would fill it with those he cared about and those who cared about him.

Roland took a slow drink of his wine. He replied to

a question from one of his men. As he spoke, he heard Daria's clear laughter. It warmed him more than the sweet wine. Then, quite suddenly and unbidden, he remembered walking beside her into the cathedral in Wrexham to get out of the endless Welsh rain. He was sicker than the devil's dog, aye, he remembered that. He'd felt weak, and his throat was raw and his head pounded and he'd wanted to puke. He remembered desperately trying to keep control of himself, but he couldn't. He remembered clearly when his mind blanked away and he was sliding to the floor. He remembered nothing else. But he should remember more, and he didn't understand why he couldn't. He frowned as he emptied his flagon.

Why couldn't he remember anything else? Two days were missing from his life. Two days until he'd come to himself to see Daria standing over him, and he remembered the feelings of humiliation when he'd had to relieve himself but was too weak to see to it without her help. But even much of that time was blurred and indistinct in his mind. He saw an older woman standing over him, smiling and giving him an evil potion to drink. Her name was Romila and she hadn't told him Daria was gone, disappeared, until he'd threatened to go search for her. What had he done in those two days? Had he possibly taken his wife's virginity during one of those two nights?

Graelam de Moreton felt good, for at least ten more seconds. He felt very good during those seconds, for under guard on the eastern side of his camp was the Earl of Reymerstone. Then he heard a woman's voice and he started to his feet, dropping the wooden goblet of ale, when he recognized that the voice belonged to Kassia. And then she was striding up to him as if she were conqueror of the damned world, dressed like a boy in tunic and hose, a feathered cap over her hair, and she was laughing. When she got five feet away from him, she let out a whooping yell and hurled herself at him.

He caught her, holding her tightly to him. She was laughing and babbling, her words tumbling to and fro, saying things about paying her debt to Daria, and here he was doing the same thing, and they'd more than paid back their obligation, and wasn't it wonderful.

Graelam shook his head, set his wife away from him, and tried to look fearsome. It wasn't difficult, for he was stripped down to a loincloth, preparing to bathe his sweating, dirty face and body. He was large and hard, and when he wished to, his expression could be as frightening as the devil's.

"Oh," Kassia said, looking at him from his toes to his mouth. "Oh," she said again, and she smiled up at him brilliantly. "You're nearly naked, Graelam."

He clasped her waist between his hands and lifted her. When her nose was right in front of his nose, he said, "You are here in my camp, a wild and lonely place that lies twenty miles from Wolffeton, a place you shouldn't be, and you are garbed like a silly boy in clothes you shouldn't be wearing, and you are grinning like a half-witted wench. I heard your wild babbling but understood it not. Now, madam, you will tell me what the hell you're doing here and why—"

She laughed, leaning forward to kiss him. "I will tell you everything, my dear lord, if you will but let my feet touch the ground again. I should love some ale. This tracking makes one vastly thirsty."

"Kassia!"

She danced away from him, and he watched her, shaking his head, knowing she would tell him everything in her own good time. He commenced with his bathing. When he felt her take the wet cloth from his hand, he smiled, and gave a contented moan as she scrubbed his back.

He was naked now and they were alone in his tent and she was standing between his legs, her fingers massaging his scalp.

"I was worried about you, Graelam."

" 'Twas naught to worry even little Harry. The Earl of Reymerstone wasn't expecting me, needless to say. I took him and his men with no bloodshed. He lies yon in a tent with Rolfe and three of my soldiers guarding him. He's a very unhappy man at this moment, and likely confused as to why I, a stranger to him, would take him prisoner."

She leaned down and kissed him. "Let the lout suffer awhile longer."

"And will you tell me what you've done, Kassia?" he asked, all calm inquiry. "Clearly this time."

"Aye, I will tell you, my lord. I have the Earl of Clare with me, and four of his men."

"You what?"

His incredulous reaction warmed her to her fingertips. She grinned hugely. "I owed Daria a debt for saving your life. You were going after the Earl of Reymerstone, but what was I to do? Oh, yes, I overheard Rolfe speaking of it, that's how I found out. There was a shortage of enemies. Then the most wonderful news came to Wolffeton whilst you were gone. The Earl of Clare—that Marcher Baron who'd held her captive for all those months—had come into Cornwall to try to recapture her. Nay, Graelam, don't bellow at me! Please, heed me, my lord, for I have right and reason on my side."

Graelam's face was white and grim. He couldn't believe his ears, couldn't believe what his wife—this cocky little twit—was telling him. "Continue," he said, but he wasn't at all certain he wanted to hear the rest of it.

Kassia, happily, was unaware of her husband's mental upheaval, and continued, "I saw it as a sign from

God, Graelam, surely you must understand that. You were gone and thus I saw it as a divine signal for me to act. It was my opportunity to repay my debt to Daria. None of my men—your men—were hurt. The Earl of Clare lies bound and in some discomfort in the small copse just beyond your camp. The man has the reddest hair, did you know that? The fool had thought to sneak into Chantry Hall, steal Daria away, and disappear like a thief of some brilliance. I told him that I wouldn't allow that. He's equally as unhappy as the Earl of Reymerstone, I daresay."

Graelam stared at his wife, at his delicate, white-skinned, very small wife. "I should beat you," he said, his eyes darkening.

"I pray that you don't, my lord, for I am very weary from my hunting."

He rose, towering above her, his naked body gleaming in the lone candlelight, and pulled on a bedrobe. As he belted it, he heard her say from behind him, "I would prefer you naked, husband. Just to look at you makes me hungry for you, not for a boring meal."

He turned on her, roaring, "You won't make me forget your reckless stupidity, Kassia! Don't try your woman's wile on me!" He paused, eyeing her, then said, "There is some bread and meat left from our supper. I will have one of the men bring it to you. Remain in this tent or it will go badly for you." With those threatening words that didn't make Kassia tremble in the least bit, Graelam strode out of his tent. He quickly found Rolfe, his master-at-arms.

Rolfe grinned at him. "Nay, my lord, don't bite off my tongue. Your lady took him fairly, and your men protected her well. I've bedded him down on the western side of the camp. Both our knaves are well-guarded, my lord."

Graelam could manage nothing more than a grunt. Rolfe chuckled. "I don't lie to you. Your men did guard her well, my lord. Indeed, they much enjoyed themselves, taking the Earl of Clare and hearing your lady crow in triumph. Would you like to sit down and drink a bit of this wine? It's from Lady Kassia's father. It will warm your innards, my lord, and make you smile."

Graelam, knowing there was nothing for it, did as Rolfe suggested. Rolfe asked, "What will ye do with the foul churls, my lord?"

"Ah," Graelam said, and sat back against the trunk of an oak tree. "We have a surfeit of earls, both so black of soul I doubt the sun will rise fully on the morrow. It's amusing. I suppose we could ransom them for a goodly sum, ransom them, that is, if there is anyone who cares whether they live or rot."

"They were both after revenge," Rolfe said, shaking his head at the wickedness.

"I'll take both of them to Roland. Then my debt to Daria is paid."

Rolfe grinned over the rim of his goblet. "Don't forget your lady, my lord. She'll ride beside you, proud as a little peahen, for after all, she did catch the Earl of Clare. She now considers her debt paid as well. Did you know that Clare has the reddest hair I've ever seen on a man?" Rolfe shook his head, continuing when his master remained silent, "And neither knows the other is here. Do they know of each other, I wonder?"

"Indeed they do. They're mortal enemies, from what Roland told me."

"Now, that's interesting. What will Roland de Tournay do with two earls?"

"If he's wise, he'll kill them both. But knowing Roland, I venture to think he'll devise a punishment that will make both of them howl into eternity. He's got a devious mind, Rolfe."

"Like your wife's, my lord?"

Graelam gave him a sour look. "Aye, just like my damned wife's." He rose to his feet and stretched. The smell of the sea was sharp tonight and the wind was rising. Dark clouds scuttled across the sky, covering the three-quarter moon, then leaving it to shine brilliantly. Graelam breathed in deeply, bade Rolfe and his other men good night, and strode back to his tent.

His wife was waiting for him, just as he'd ordered her to, only she was quite naked and lying in his narrow cot.

He heard her giggle even as he stripped off his bedrobe.

23

KASSIA DE MORETON gave her husband a wounded look. "You didn't tell me they knew each other, Graelam."

"Villains usually do," Graelam said.

"I wonder what would happen if we simply left them alone together."

"They'd probably kill each other. Roland told me that there is bone-deep hatred between them. Evidently Damon Le Mark killed Edmond of Clare's brother some years ago. I know not more. Mayhap Roland will tell us what is between them."

The two earls stood separated by the width of Chantry Hall's inner bailey, each surrounded by both Graelam and Roland's men. As for Roland, he and Daria were staring from Graelam to his small wife, who stood by his side, straight and proud and tousled in her boy's clothes. What was left of her braids was still tucked up under her cap.

Roland shook his head, still looking dazed. "I know no more than that, Graelam."

Beside him, Daria said, her voice bewildered, "You mean each of you captured one of them . . . to pay back your debt to *me?*" At Kassia's pleased nod, Daria said, "But there is no debt! If I made you think you were ever indebted to me, I should be hung up by my toes and flayed—"

"Hush, Daria," Graelam said. " 'Tis done. The two men were here in Cornwall, and each was up to no good. They are evil, and they deserve whatever punishment Roland decides to mete out to them. My wife and I, well, we simply eased matters for your husband here. Nothing more.''

Lady Katherine stood behind her daughter, her eyes on Damon Le Mark. Just seeing him again made her tighten inside with fear, made her throat dry and her hands clammy. Daria could feel her mother's rigidity. She turned and said quickly, her voice low and soothing, ''Mother, nay, don't be frightened of him. Damon can't hurt either of us, ever again. He's bound, Mother! Look at him!''

Katherine heard her daughter's voice as if from afar. ''He was coming here to kill you and your husband. Doubt it not, Daria.''

''Of course he was,'' Roland said cheerfully. ''He failed, Katherine. Do as Daria says—look at him. Isn't he now a pathetic specimen? A man like him who's been stripped of all his fine power has nothing much left. Power gave him the illusion of substance. Now he's of no importance at all. Believe me, Katherine, and don't fear him ever again.''

Daria was staring at her husband with wonder. She saw her mother draw a very deep breath, and the dreadful gray pallor began to leave her cheeks. She saw Sir Thomas gently take her hand into his gnarled one and lightly squeeze it. To her delight, her mother turned and smiled up at Sir Thomas.

Roland nodded. ''Now, come inside, all of you. Aye, Graelam, bring even that ragged boy there with all the hair. I should like to hear why you appear so bewitched with a skinny lad who hasn't even the years to grow a beard yet.''

''The little lad only appears skinny in these absurd garments,'' Graelam said. ''Without them, it's a very different lad. And with the proper encouragement, why, 'tis a lad with much promise.''

''That's quite enough,'' Kassia said. ''Ho, Daria! Come rescue me from this loutish humor.''

But Roland held tightly to Daria's hand. "Come into the hall and tell us how all this comes about."

"Will I hear counsel to tell me to thrash the little one here?" Graelam asked of no one in particular.

"There are better things to do to a wife," Roland said. He clasped Daria's fingers more firmly and pulled her closer. "Of course, that path leads to exhaustion and near-collapse and besottedness."

Graelam looked at them thoughtfully. It took only his departure to bring the two of them together? He'd been the one standing in their path? It was a lowering thought. He saw that Kassia was also remarking this new closeness with the same surprise.

Once they were seated at a trestle table, goblets of wine in their hands brought by a beaming Gwyn, Kassia said simply, "As I said, we are repaying our debt to you, Daria, nothing more. My husband hunted the Earl of Reymerstone, and I, well, I was fortunate enough to learn that the Earl of Clare was in Cornwall as well. Both wanted to take you. As for Roland, I doubt not they had bloody revenge in mind for him."

Roland felt the slight tremor go through her body as she said, "I don't want you to think that way! I don't want a reward, because I did naught more than anyone else would have done!"

Graelam smiled. "Does this mean that you wish us to let the earls go free?"

Daria stared at him, suddenly mute.

"He's got you there, dearling. No, Graelam, and we both thank you, even though we wish you hadn't endangered yourselves."

"The only danger that will come to my wife now is from my hand on her buttocks. Listen, Daria, you saved my life. As for Kassia here, well, she fancied that my life was also worth something to her."

Roland laughed. "Whilst I sit on my arse safely within the walls of my castle, the two of you are out

capturing treacherous rogues and bringing them to
me. For judgment? This will take some thought."

Graelam nodded. Kassia said, shaking her head,
"Nay, Roland, they are here for Daria's judgment. It
is her debt we repay." She turned to smile at her
husband. "We do hope, however, that neither of you
have any more enemies lurking just beyond the hills. I
try to keep my husband safe."

"I do not. Do you, husband?"

Roland looked thoughtful for a very long time before he finally shook his head. "Any more knaves
would be a scruffy lot, unworthy of your exalted attention, Graelam."

"Good," Graelam said. "I've a fancy to rot a bit
within my castles walls for a while."

Kassia leaned forward, pulling off her boy's cap as
she did so. "Can you tell us more about these two
men, Roland?"

"As I told Graelam, Damon Le Mark murdered the
Earl of Clare's brother some years ago. Clare never
forgot and his hatred grew. That was why he kidnapped Daria. It was his revenge. But then he wanted
to take her to wive and he wanted her dowry as well.
As the Earl of Clare himself told me, it would have to
satisfy him."

Daria continued. "Damon knew the real reasons for
my kidnapping, but he didn't tell Roland. He made up
some tale that Roland never believed."

Katherine said very quietly, "No, he wouldn't tell
the truth, even if he had a choice. He didn't even tell
me, and that I don't understand at all, for it would
have tormented me to hell, and thus afforded him
great pleasure."

Everyone turned to Lady Katherine in surprise.
"What do you mean, Mother?"

"I mean that Damon should have told me what had
happened. He would have enjoyed my misery. I simply wonder why he chose not to."

"You knew the Earl of Clare had kidnapped me. You knew he wanted to wed me."

"No, I didn't know that he wanted to wed you. Damon didn't tell me about that." She shook her head. She looked pale and very, very sad. Then she smiled, a bittersweet smile that held a good deal of acceptance. "The truth is sometimes difficult, Daria. But now it is your right to know. It is true that Damon Le Mark did indeed murder Edmond of Clare's brother. His name was David and he was young and innocent, as was I, and we fell in love. It was so many years ago. My parents had promised me to Reymerstone's half-brother, Daria, but I didn't want him. I wanted only David. Of course, what a girl wants makes no difference to anything. I was forced to wed James of Fortescue anyway. But before I became his wife, I went to David. It's probable that David is your real father, my love. The Earl of Clare is thus your uncle. Damon found out about this some time ago, possibly from his half-brother, for my husband never believed you were the product of his seed. Damon caught David some five years ago and murdered him. He sent word to his half-brother of what he had done, and my husband rejoiced. He laughed when he told me. Even though they were but half-brothers, you see, they were very close. They were very much alike in many ways save that James was skilled in arms and fighting. He was seen as honorable and brave. But it was his conceit that he held up for all to see as his honor, and most were fooled by it, including you, my daughter."

There was utter silence in the hall. Sir Thomas coughed.

"If the Earl of Clare had but looked at Daria, he would have seen that her eyes are very nearly identical to his brother David's. But evidently he didn't see any resemblance. His brother never told him about me or about his daughter. David protected both of us, Daria. But of course Damon knew."

"So that's why my father ignored me, why he never kissed me or petted me or told me he loved me."

Katherine nodded. "I'm sorry, Daria. Every time he looked at you, he would then turn to me and his hatred made me shrivel. He never struck you. He never hurt you. I told him if he did I would kill him. Not with a knife, but with poisons. He believed me, for he knew I had the recipe for many of your grandmother's potions. But then he was killed and we were at Damon Le Mark's mercy."

Roland remembered the sad-eyed Katherine when he'd first visited Reymerstone. So Damon had avenged his half-brother by taking his wife to his bed and by murdering her lover. He probably believed it a fitting punishment for her infidelity. It was more punishment than anyone should have to bear. He too found himself wondering why Damon Le Mark hadn't taunted Katherine with the possible marriage between her daughter and her daughter's uncle, the Earl of Clare. Then it occurred to Roland that he hadn't because such knowledge might have gotten back to Colchester, and Damon Le Mark had wanted that marriage more than anything.

Roland turned to his wife. He couldn't bear the anguish here, the years of secret, unspoken pain. He said, his voice light, "What say you, wife? Do you want their ears chopped off? Shall we make them into eunuchs? Do you want me to run them through?"

"Nay," she said, shaking her head. She looked at him then, and she was very pale, her eyes bewildered. "I very nearly married my uncle."

"Yes, but you didn't." *But your uncle raped you, didn't he, and you could have delivered a child born of incest.*

Katherine said, "I didn't realize that the Earl of Clare could possibly think of wedding Daria, it never came into my mind, else I would have gone mad. I'm sorry, child, truly, but I didn't want you to know the truth and perhaps despise me for it and—"

Suddenly Daria laughed, deep, raw laughter that was ugly in its pain. It rang out in the great hall and the anguish of it was more than Roland could bear. He shouted, as he grasped her upper arms and shook her, "Daria, stop it!"

But she couldn't. She covered her mouth with her hand but the laughter still came out, muffled and deep and wrenching. She gasped for breath as she choked out the words. "It is too much, Roland, far too much. Don't any of you understand?" Her laughter was dying now but her voice was sharper, more shrill. "Don't you see? My God, if I hadn't lost that babe, if I had birthed the babe, it still could have looked like the Earl of Clare, for he would have been the babe's uncle!" Laughter spewed out of her mouth. Roland stared at her.

"Aye, 'tis true," she said, her voice now oddly singsong, "and then you would never have believed me, Roland, never. You would have looked at that babe and remarked, 'Aye, look at all that red hair. The Earl of Clare is the babe's father and I am vindicated in my belief that my wife is a liar!'" Daria broke free, whirled about, and looked one last time at her husband. He was still staring at her, his face very pale, his hands now fisted at his sides.

"There's no winning, Roland, at least not for me. It is over and I have lost." She turned to Katherine. "You won't berate yourself again, Mother. Now, if it is truly my judgment, then what I wish is this: I want the two of them put together. I want the two of them to fight it out. Each deserves to fight the other. If the Earl of Clare hadn't been a coward, he wouldn't have kidnapped me, he would have met Damon and challenged him as a man of honor should face another man who is his enemy. As for Damon Le Mark, he is despicable. He should have told Roland the truth about my birth, but he kept silent. He cared not what became of me; he cared not if my uncle bedded me. Perhaps he even thought it would be a fine jest on my mother and on the Earl of Clare, but he wouldn't have said anything, not until it had been done."

Daria looked straight at Roland and laughed. "One more time for my lie, Roland, then never will you hear me protest again. The Earl of Clare didn't bed me, no one save you did. He humiliated me but he didn't bed me. Now, are my wishes to be considered?"

Roland felt mired in the swirling tensions surrounding him. They were also within him and he didn't like it. So the Earl of Clare hadn't raped her. He believed that now. Daria was incapable of fostering such a deception in the face of learning that the Earl of Clare had been of her blood, her damned uncle, by all the saints. It still left him puzzled and beset by confusion. Her laughter and her pain made him raw.

He nodded slowly. "It will be as you wish."

Graelam said then, "And if one kills the other? What would you have done with the one who wins?"

Daria said quite without emotion, "He will go free."

Roland nodded his agreement, but in the next instant he shared a look with Graelam and a silent pact was made.

The afternoon was hot, the early-fall wind harshly dry and chafing.

Daria knew she would never forget the looks on the two men's faces, the fury, the raw hatred. They'd been stripped down to loincloths and given swords, maces, and axes.

She didn't want to watch, but she did, as did her mother. The scores of people surrounding the two men were silent. Daria knew that by now all of Chantry Hall knew what she'd screamed in the great hall.

All of them knew that her two uncles would fight to the death.

Both men were her uncles. It was insane. She looked at her mother, hoping she was all right, but she couldn't tell, for there was no sign, no expression, on Katherine's face.

She heard the sudden ringing of the heavy battle swords. She heard the curses of the two men as they lunged and withdrew from each other. She could feel the poison of their hatred for each other.

It didn't last long, though it seemed an eternity. Damon Le Mark fought bravely, with all the enmity in his soul, but he was no opponent for the Earl of Clare, whose fighting skills were honed daily on the Welsh outlaws. She saw the Earl of Clare lift the sword with both hands, saw the sword descend, and knew that Damon Le Mark was dead. At the last instant, just as Damon Le Mark jerked sideways, then back, the Earl of Clare used the sword as a spear instead, sending it straight ahead. It sliced through Damon Le Mark's chest and came out the back, flinging him onto his side on the ground. He was dead before he rolled to his back.

There was a shock of silence. The Earl of Clare stood over his dead enemy, and he was smiling. She couldn't believe what happened then. She watched her husband, now stripped to his loincloth, step into the circle, a battle sword in his hand. As he lifted it, he grinned and yelled at the Earl of Clare, "Did you know, you filthy whoreson, that Daria is your niece? She is of your flesh, you damned fool! Your brother, David, was her father! Had I not taken her from you, you would have committed the gravest sin in God's eyes! What say you to that, you stupid sod?"

The Earl of Clare calmed his breathing. He looked at the young man before him, knew him for a dangerous warrior, and wanted to kill him. The humiliation

Roland had meted out to him at Tyberton was a raw wound. Roland had thrashed him like a mewling pup, in front of the king, in front of all his men and servants. Well, now he had a sword. He'd killed Reymerstone and now he would kill this impudent bastard. "You lie," he shouted. "I would have surely recognized her if she had been of mine own blood. She is not!"

Graelam started forward, fury writ on his face. "Roland, this is not for you to do!" he yelled. "Damn you, come out of there! It was to be my turn!"

But it was too late. The two men faced each other. The earl, his red hair blazing in the hot afternoon sun, was the larger of the two, a massive man whose power was evident in each movement he made with the heavy sword. He'd but slightly exerted himself to kill the Earl of Reymerstone. He looked at the young man who was dark as a Muslim, and smiled. He knew that after he killed Roland he would himself be killed, but for now he didn't care. He would have his revenge. He roared and lunged, only to have Roland feint to the left. He was left panting, feeling like a fool, his sword slicing through air.

Daria looked at her husband. He was more slightly built, leaner, his body hard and taut, but he was strong and agile and very fast. He'd dropped the battle sword and was now swinging an ax in his right hand. Then he tossed the ax to his left hand and back and forth, taunting the Earl of Clare, until he bellowed like an enraged bull, and charged Roland again. Roland danced lightly to the side and struck suddenly, fiercely, with the ax. It thudded loudly against the earl's sword. Roland looked surprised; then he gave the earl a look of approval before quickly spinning to the left out of the range of the earl's pounding sword.

Daria touched her hand to Graelam's sleeve. "Nay," she said quietly, "he will be all right. He will kill the earl."

"You cannot possibly know—" Graelam's impatient voice dropped off. He stared at Daria.

"He will kill him," she said again, her eyes never leaving her husband. "Nay, I'm not seeing a vision. I saw him fight the Earl of Clare in the presence of the king at Tyberton. He is very skilled, and what he does is unexpected."

"He's an evil fighter," Graelam said after a moment watching Roland. "That's true. Look at that! Aye, Roland fights with his brains."

"He also learned tricks from outlaws in the Holy Land."

The Earl of Clare was bearing down on Roland, trying to corner him, striking again and again, not letting up, forcing him back with the raw power of his strength.

Suddenly Roland tossed the ax aside. Salin slipped a long slender-bladed knife into his hand and Daria heard Graelam heave a heartfelt sigh. " 'Tis over now," he said.

"How do you know that?"

"Just watch."

Roland slipped away from the earl, dodging right; then he turned on the balls of his bare feet, and fast as lightning, reached out and sliced a clean diagonal line through the thick red hair on the earl's chest. The earl looked down blankly at the oozing bloody line that marked his chest and howled with fury. "I'll kill you, you whoreson!"

Roland laughed. "Again, you bastard!" He spun about, his arm extended, and he struck so quickly it was a blur. Now a bloody red X stood out on the earl's chest.

The earl was so beside himself with rage he began to hammer with the mighty sword, wildly slicing it from side to side in a wide swath.

Graelam said quietly, "He's no longer thinking. He

is reacting, nothing more. He doesn't realize that his incredible strength isn't an asset. He doesn't realize he won't touch Roland. Roland has learned that his brain is his best weapon."

Daria watched Roland lightly back away from the earl, not coming to a stop until he was a good fifteen feet from him. The earl was yelling, howling his fury, and he was readying to charge, his sword raised above his head.

Slowly, very slowly, Roland aimed the knife and released it with a smooth flip of his wrist. It sang through the still air and thudded softly into the earl's chest, just at the point where the X crossed.

Edmond of Clare stared down at the quivering pale ivory handle that still vibrated from the strength and speed of Roland's throw.

He looked up then, first at Roland, then toward Daria. "I wanted your dowry, not you," he said. "You're not of my blood, I would have known if you were, for David kept nothing from me. He would have told me. Nay, you're naught but—" He crumpled where he stood.

Roland was covered with sweat and dirt and he had a huge satisfied smile on his face.

"Nay, berate me not, Graelam," he called out with great relish. " 'Tis over now, and he was mine, not yours, not anyone else's." He turned to his wife. "Be ready to leave Chantry Hall at first light tomorrow morning. Pack enough clothing for a month. Speak to Alice and have her prepare ample food supplies for us and seven men." He was still grinning when he turned to Sir Thomas. "Thomas, you will see to Chantry Hall's safety whilst we're gone. And, Katherine, worry not about your daughter."

"No," Katherine said slowly. "I don't think I shall now."

"Where are we going, Roland?"

Roland walked to where his wife stood, and he looked down at her, saying nothing for a very long time. Finally he raised his fingers and cupped her chin. "We go to Wales."

"Why?"

He leaned down, saying very quietly, so only she could hear his words, "I took your virginity, yet I have no memory of it. I want that memory back, Daria. I want the knowledge of your eyes upon me when I came into you that first time. I want my awareness of you when I first touched your womb."

They reached Wrexham twelve days later. Incredibly, it had rained only twice. Incredibly, they'd met no outlaws. Incredibly, Roland was whistling when they entered the Wrexham cathedral.

Daria was praying hard. She didn't know what to expect, but praying seemed the best approach.

Romila opened the door at Roland's pounding. She was grumbling about louts bothering until she recognized him. Then she smiled widely, rubbing her hands together as she looked him over from head to toe. "Aye, oh, aye, 'tis the pretty lad whose body and face have provided romantic fodder for all the girls in Wrexham. I've told them of your endowments, my lad, described to them how your flesh feels beneath a woman's hand. Ah, when I told them about the size of your rod . . . Is it you, Daria? Well, well. What do you here? What—"

And on and on she went, and Roland just smiled at her and listened to her babbling. Daria said nothing.

After a time, Roland asked if Romila would take him upstairs to the chamber where he'd been in bed for nearly two weeks.

"Nay, Daria, I wish to go alone," he said to his wife when she would have followed. She nodded, and watched the two of them climb the narrow filthy stairs. She wondered, half-smiling, if Romila would try to seduce him once in the bedchamber.

Salin said from behind her, "Roland is a fair man."

She only nodded and began her prayers again.

Upstairs, Roland stood in the middle of the small airless chamber. He looked at the bed where he'd spent hours he didn't remember at all, and more hours he did remember that he couldn't begin to count. He looked at the chamber pot in the corner and shook his head at those memories. He turned to Romila, cutting off her outpourings of vulgar suggestions. "When I was brought here, I was out of my senses?"

"Aye, ye were, me lad."

He looked toward the window and saw Daria standing there, quiet and still, looking out onto the courtyard below. He looked at the chair. He remembered clearly Daria sitting in that chair, sewing on one of his tunics.

"Yer little wife took good care of ye. Even when ye were a testy lad, she only smiled and shook her head and loved ye. O' course, she did ask my advice now and again, and I told her ye'd be in fine form again soon."

He remembered the spoon touching his mouth, remembered Daria's soft voice telling him to eat, telling him he must regain his strength.

"Aye, oh, aye," Romila said, her voice wistful and teasing at the same time. Then she laughed aloud, raucous and loud. "And I remember more than I should, ye randy goat!"

Roland turned slowly to face her. "What do you mean?"

Romila cackled and looked again down his body. "Aye, a randy goat ye were even when ye were out of yer head with the fever and yelling strange things in savage tongues. I knew ye'd not been married to yer little wife long, but still I couldn't believe that ye had such a dreadful need in yer manhood! Men and their seed—always wanting to spill it, no matter if they're dying."

And Roland said again, his heart pounding slow dull beats, "What do you mean?"

"I mean that yer randy body didn't know ye was frightful sick, oh, no, ye horny pretty lad!" She laughed again and looked at him as if she'd like to throw him on the bed and rip off his clothes.

"You do?" he said.

"Oh, aye, me pretty boy. I come up that night, for yer little wife was so tired and so frantic with worry for ye that I was worried about her, and then I stopped outside the door and heard this moaning and groaning and I heard her cry out, and I opened the door, all afeared that ye was dying, and there ye were, holding her on top of ye, lurching yer rod into her, and she was crying, and then ye moaned deep and took her but good. Aye, ye made her ride ye hard." Romila stopped, smiling fondly at Roland. "I like a man whose rod isn't struck down along with his body. Aye, yer a bonnie lad."

"Thank you," Roland said blankly. He flung his arms around Romila, lifted her high, even though she weighed about the same as he did; then, as he lowered her, he gave her a loud smacking kiss on her mouth.

"Thank you," he said again. As he made his way back down the stairs, he thought: By all the saints, I wish I could remember. Just a moment of it, just an instant. He wondered if perhaps someday he would.

Not that it mattered. Not that what Romila had told him mattered all that much. It struck him then that he wanted to spend the night here, with Daria, in that bed. He wanted her on top of him and he wanted to take her again, here, just as he'd taken her so long ago.

He whistled.

At nearly midnight, a howling storm blew up and the animal hide that covered the window thudded and flapped loudly. On the narrow bed, Roland was sprawled on his back, looking up at his beautiful wife, naked, her hair loose down her back, watching her come down on him, then move as she wished to, then arch her back, bringing him so deep into her that he thought he'd die from the pleasure of it.

He saw nothing but his wife, Daria. As he watched her reach her pleasure, he told her, "I love you, Daria, and you will never doubt me."

She yelled her release, and he grinned, wondering if Romila stood outside the door listening to them, cackling like a witch. Then he moaned, and he forgot all save his enjoyment of his wife.

EPILOGUE

London, England

THAT HOT SEPTEMBER AFTERNOON when two peers of the realm had met in the outer bailey of a little-known castle in Cornwall to fight each other to the death didn't reach the ears of the king until well into October. The tale was, much to the king's displeasure, little embellished by the king's son-in-law, Dienwald de Fortenberry, whose mournful expression showed his disappointment at not having been present at the fight. Not that it mattered to anyone.

Both men were long dead and no one really cared now who had killed whom and how. But the king, in a flash of unpredictability, decided he wanted the details, all of them, and he quickly realized that Dienwald wasn't being completely frank with him. He knew that Roland was involved, as was Graelam de Moreton. He was angered, yet at the same time the king was pleased that the three men felt loyalty to each other. But shouldn't they also trust their king, the lame louts? They should; it was their duty to do so.

He considered threatening Dienwald with torture for lying to him, his dear papa-in-law, for he knew that Dienwald was withholding all the doubtlessly interesting parts of the truth from him. Then he looked at his daughter, Philippa, saw that she was grinning at him and knowing that there wasn't anything he could do. He held to his kingly control, then yelled for wine.

381

The king wasn't angry beyond his second goblet of wine, for after all, he now had two very rich holdings in his royal, always needy hands. Neither earl had left an heir, much to the king's joy—Burnell had quickly found that out—save for a cousin to Reymerstone who was a puling boy and not worthy of either the title or the lands. The king gave guardianship of Tyberton to one of his own trusted knights with the admonition that the moment he ever thought of himself as an arrogant Marcher baron, his king would ensure that his ale was poisoned. He'd thought to reward his son-in-law with Reymerstone, then decided he hadn't yet proved himself sufficiently loyal to his king.

After the first of the year, the king recalled the tale again, and decided he would discover what had happened from the horse's mouth. He sent a messenger to Chantry Hall, insisting that Roland de Tournay and his wife visit London and give the royal ears a full accounting.

Roland sent a return message by the king's soldier:

Sire:
   I beg your indulgence and forgiveness, but Daria and I cannot travel to London to bask in your royal presence for some months yet. She is with child. We would ask that you receive us in the late summer.

"Humph," the king said when Robert Burnell had finished reading the brief letter. Then he looked up, puzzled. "But I thought she was already with child, Robbie. Shouldn't she be birthing it by now? I remember Roland wedded her because she was pregnant. Don't you recall, the queen told us of it?"

"She miscarried the babe, sire, late last summer I believe I was told."

The king wondered for a bitter moment how Burnell seemed to know everything, even insignificant details

such as the miscarrying of a babe by one of his Cornish
baron's wives, but he was too proud to ask. "That is
what I thought," the king said. "I must tell the queen
there's to be another child. She will be gratified. She is
most fond of Daria and Roland, you know."

"Aye, sire, she is."

The king looked suddenly very pleased with himself.
"The child Daria miscarried, it was the Earl of Clare's,
was it not, Robbie? Do you not remember? He'd
forced himself upon her and Roland, despite the fact,
insisted upon wedding her?"

"Aye, sire, your memory is flawless and surpasses
all that is imaginable."

The king smiled his beautiful Plantagenet smile. "Do
you jerk at my royal leg, Robbie?"

"I, sire? Nay, I would never be guilty of something
so ignoble."

The king rubbed his hands together and rose. "Well,
that's that. I have lands I sorely needed and a cartload
of coin for my coffers. My subjects appear to have
sorted things out amongst themselves. You look tired,
Robbie. Why don't you rest a bit this afternoon?"

It sounded a fine suggestion to Robert Burnell, and
he nodded.

The king turned to leave the chamber, then smacked
the palm of his hand against his forehead. "I almost
forgot! Bring your writing materials, Robbie, there's a
delegation from some Scottish fool wishing to beg our
royal favor."

Burnell sighed, then smiled. "Aye, sire. Immediately."

Chantry Hall, Cornwall

ROLAND AND DARIA stood on the northern ramparts of Chantry Hall, looking over the rolling hills dotted with at least one hundred sheep chewing at the sparse winter grasses. It was early January, but the air was crisp rather than cold and the sky blue and clear. It was a Cornwall day that delighted every man and woman living within its boundaries.

"It warms the heart," Roland said, waving an expansive arm toward his sheep.

"It also gives a very peculiar order to the air," said his wife as she drew her thick cloak more closely around her.

Roland hugged her to his side, kissed her temple, then pointed eastward toward the king's departing messenger, Florin, who'd spent the night and imbibed too much ale. "I wonder what Edward will say when he receives my missive."

Daria laughed. "If Florin arrives intact with it! Husband, your reply to your king bordered on the cocky. It was rather in Dienwald's insolent style, I think."

"Ha! Dienwald slinked about when the king taxed him in October about our two dead earls, fumbled all over himself and in general laid claim to being a better fool than Crooky."

"That's what Philippa said, not Dienwald."

"As I recall, he smacked her bottom for that. Do you think the king also wrote to Graelam and Kassia?"

"We will be certain to ask when they are next here." Daria turned and smiled up at her husband.

"Do you feel well, sweeting? Our babe sits content in your womb?" He drew her against him as he spoke, and gently rubbed his palm over her swelling belly.

"Aye, both of us are filled with well-being and both of us are getting quite hungry."

Roland gave her a mournful look. "If you had told me that but a few months ago I would have considered your hunger to be of a more felicitous nature. I would have lifted you over my shoulder and carried you into our western pasture and loved you amongst the eglantine and bluebells. But now I must play the forbearing husband, all patience and long-enduring, whilst my babe gleans all your attention. It is difficult, Daria, for I am young and lusty and filled with lavish excesses and—"

She grabbed his ears and pulled his face down, nipping the tip of his nose, kissing his mouth again and again. "There is no eglantine now, Roland, but there are pine cones in the forest. What say you, husband? Are you all words and plaints or will you give me deeds?"

"And I thought I was the only one suffering from excesses," he said, and lifted her high against him, her feet off the rampart wooden walkway. "No forest bed for you, Daria, but a soft bed where you will be winsome and soft and so dear to me I want to weep with it."

"You become a poet, Roland. I think first I shall have Alice prepare her wonderful mulled wine. 'Tis to dull your randy senses so I may have you energetic yet controlled in your excesses."

He looked at her with such love that Daria forgot her attempts at wit and every other scrap of humor that had come into her brain. He eased her back down and she leaned against him, hugging her arms tightly around his back.

"Life is sweet with you, Roland. Life is all I could wish it to be."

"Even with the smelly sheep and us standing downwind from them?"

"Aye, even that. Come now, my lord husband."

"If our king but knew who the cocky one really was

at Chantry Hall I vow he would knit me with fine words until I died."

"I will tell Philippa. Then we will see."

"I shall tell Dienwald." Roland paused, adding on a wide grin, "I haven't the faintest idea what Dienwald would do."

"Show me what you would do."

"Let us get to it then," Roland said and led her down from the ramparts and into the great hall.

ABOUT THE AUTHOR

Catherine Coulter, bestselling author of the *Magic Trilogy* and the *Night Trilogy*, has also written three contemporary novels, *False Pretenses*, *Impulse*, and *Beyond Eden*. She does her writing in beautiful northern California, where she lives with her husband, Anton, and her cat, Gilly. Catherine enjoys hearing from her readers and answers every letter she receives.